D1047009

SO LONG AS LOVE REMEMBERS

One short sleep past, we wake eternally,
And Death shall be no more; Death, thou shalt die!

JOHN DONNE

SO LONG AS LOVE REMEMBERS

Russell Janney

HERMITAGE HOUSE, NEW YORK
1953

Published simultaneously in Canada by George J. McLeod, Ltd., Toronto, Canada
MANUFACTURED IN THE UNITED STATES OF AMERICA

Library of Congress Catalog Card Number: 53-10613
First Printing, August, 1953

TO RUDOLF FRIML

GENIUS AND FRIEND

CONTENTS

SO LONG AS
LOVE REMEMBERS

Blackstone Studios

In 1925 the sensation of the theatre was the young producer, Russell Janney, with his hit operetta, *The Vagabond King,* of which he was co-author as well as producer. To the present day, *The Vagabond King* has been continuously revived.

In 1946 the sensation of the book world was *The Miracle of the Bells* by Russell Janney, who at the age of sixty-one began to write his first novel. For a period of thirteen months *The Miracle of the Bells* was the nation's number one best-seller.

In 1951 Mr. Janney began to write his second novel, *So Long As Love Remembers.* The sweep of his story, however, carried him far beyond the original length he had planned and the novel was not completed until early in 1953.

Although, after his graduation from Yale in 1906, Mr. Janney set out to be a writer of fiction, the theatre has claimed him for most of his life. He was at first a press agent for famous stars; then he became co-producer with Stuart Walker of Tarkington's *Seventeen;* then he produced his own shows.

Like the hero of *So Long As Love Remembers,* Mr. Janney is extremely fond of cats, and there are always several like the one in the picture above who share his New York apartment.

PROLOGUE

THE CLOISTERS

ALTHOUGH thousands of miles from her homeland, she seems content. For here, as well as there, she gazes out upon a river. The river, there, was a small one, and wound its gentle way through fertile fields, which were tended by peasants. The nearby town was just a village of thatch and rough stone.

Here, the river is very wide and great, with steep, tree-banked cliffs directly opposite; and on her own side, although there is a tree-bearing park, directly behind it are crowded streets and teeming tenements.

The river, there, was called the Loing, and the village La Celle. Here, the river is called the Hudson, and the adjacent human habitations are the northern West Side of the City of New York. The people living nearest her, here, are also—if not peasants—humble folk, who have to work to eat, and to have roofs over their heads and shoes for their children. So I believe she is happier than if she were housed in the great palace on Fifth Avenue, which is named the Metropolitan Museum of Art.

Her home, up on high land above the river, is called the Cloisters.

Although not then dreaming that she was destined to travel to a far and distant land, she was early to be concerned with much travel. For in the Year of Our Lord 1144, she sent an entire company of Knights Templars on the Second Crusade, to the distant Holy Land. Her very birth was not unconcerned with the First Crusade. For her first home was a Knights Templars monastery, founded by one of the great fighting leaders of the cult, Hugh of Vermandois, brother of Philip, King of France.

She is very beautiful and she represents the Virgin holding the Christ Child. She must have been a faithful reproduction in sandstone of the half French, half Polish peasant girl who posed for her making—the peasant girl then a novice, and later to become a nun and a Blessed Saint.

She differs in two ways from other representations of the Virgin and the Child. Her hair, if one looks closely, is parted in the middle; parted tightly; and a thick braid of it is drawn across her head at a slight angle, slanting down so as to hide the left ear. All this beneath the customary Queen of Heaven crown.

One hand is missing. Broken and lost, through the centuries that included the religious persecutions; the destruction and neglect of monasteries; the French Revolution. It would ordinarily be supposed that that hand held a rose, a prayer book, a Sacred Heart: some symbol of peace.

The hand held a sword! A great, two-handed sword that was fully as long as she was tall. She was known then as *the Madonna of the Sword.*

But the hand was lost, and the sword was lost. If she had not journeyed to America, all record of it even would have been lost. For here, in the City of New York, in the present Age of the Atom and Television Shows (I know not which is the most to be dreaded), a young man saw her and loved her.

Perhaps he even saw and loved the girl who had posed for her carved sandstone reproduction.

We shall observe, and judge.

PART ONE

THE NIGHT CLUB

✣ 1 ✣

TIGHTPANTS HALKA played a small, upright piano on a small platform in a honky tonk. He was one of the three "key thumpers" that played there—in rapid relays from eight P.M. to four A.M.—each piano player having a vocalist that was his musical (to use the adjective loosely) partner in the "act." Tightpants and his singer gave eight shows nightly. So did the other two acts.

The piano players were male in sex. Two of the three singers were women.

Tightpants (as did the other key thumpers) also sang in a falsetto tenor voice—but he did not fancy himself in that role. It was just a part of his contract. The management guessed—and guessed rightly—that it would induce laughter. Piano strings, not vocal chords, were Tightpants' instrument.

It should immediately be stated that this honky tonk was not honky tonk in location, or in prices. Only in its cultural grade of entertainment. It was located on three floors of a converted, ancient brownstone tenement on a famous night club street just off upper Times Square, City of New York. First floor, the Harmony Bar. Second floor, the dine-and-dance and entertainment section. Third floor, the offices and storage rooms.

It had several uniformed doormen. Customers arrived in taxis and even limousines. The cheapest drink was a buck and a half, and the cover charge per person was three bucks fifty. You were fortunate if your check added up to less than fifteen dollars.

It was named the Horse and Buggy, and was supposed to reproduce the gay, naive, and unfettered spirit of that bygone motorcarless day.

We forgot to mention that its youthful hat-check girls had the superior arrogance that was a sure indication of first-class night club management.

And "shed not a tear" (we quote from a favorite line of a favorite Horse and Buggy song) for the financial status of these six hardworking "entertainers." While their weekly remuneration was not equal to that of the waiters and the doormen—if tips were counted—it was quite ample for a living wage; and three free drinks and a supper meal were included. Like the waiters, they had a Union and a compulsory minimum wage.

So much for the economic aspects of the Horse and Buggy Night Club, Inc. . . .

Tears—if they are desired—ought better be shed for certain spiritual aspects of these six entertainers. Aspects, we hasten to add, which were not recognized, and did not trouble, the operators of the bistro, or its select, free-spending clientele.

They—the entertainers—were, with the exception of one youthful key thumper, of middle age. No one of them had planned to climax his (or her) career at the Horse and Buggy Night Club, Inc., where they were dressed in the supposed attire of that day.

The men wore loud-checked suits; stiff, upstanding collars; and small, ridiculous derby hats crowned their heads. The two ladies were encased in corsets which promoted a supposedly humorous bulge of hips and breasts; while the occasional lifting of long skirts, disclosing high-button shoes, woolen stockings, and long, lace-bordered "panties," were sure belly laughs.

What an absurd period it must have been! No platform shoes, no strapless, vanishing-neckline evening gowns, no home-permanent hairdo's, no Cadillac convertibles, no atom bombs!

An observing patron, however, might have sensed, now and then, that these entertainers had immortal souls—that while they did not mind the guffaws, they were not exactly thrilled by the spoken word as hurled at them by well-liquored guests who wished to impress table companions by their high order of sophistication and wit. Interruptions and suggestions such as "Ah, change your record!" or "Meet you after the show, grandma!" showed an especially inventive and brilliant mind.

No—some of these entertainers had had dreams—ideals; might still, in spite of the Horse and Buggy, cherish them.

Now this is the saga of Tightpants Halka, youngest of the entertainers—he was barely thirty—and a girl (not a lady of the Horse and Buggy), and a Song; but perhaps a paragraph or two about his fellow artists there will not be boring.

Molly Dorcey, who sang the comedy songs in a throaty contralto, had, as a child, been a member of the vaudeville team known as the Dancing Dorceys. The father, the mother, and another sister. Molly sang as well as danced, and had dreamed of someday breaking into the "legitimate." She had indeed once obtained a small part with Raymond Hitchcock. The show had failed. Her sister died. Her parents grew too old to travel. Anyway, motion pictures completely knocked out vaudeville. She now supported those parents, and lived in the hope that some "picture magnate," or at least a talent scout, would see her and offer her a Hollywood contract.

She was approaching fifty, but, after all—Marie Dressler had gotten such a chance at middle age! Molly's big hit was a song called *I Fell Down and Went Boom!* She had sung it thirty seasons before in the show that failed, and it had remained her feature number through the years. Songs cling to the singers that first made a success of them. Like *Kiss Me Again* to Fritzi Scheff. Or *Every Day Is Ladies Day to Me* to the late Dan Dailey.

Annette Blair sang the ballads. At sixteen, she had been a Ziegfeld Follies girl—and a beautiful one. She had a natural voice as well as a natural figure, and started to take singing lessons. The next year she had a solo song, and the year following played in a Follies sketch with the great comedian W. C. Fields. She seemed on the road to the top. Then she met and fell in love with "Handsome" Dan O'Shea, big-time gambler. They were married. Partly because of his jealousy, and partly because she was soon to have a baby, she left the stage.

"Handsome" Dan didn't look so handsome when, one midnight,

Annette went to the city morgue to identify him. Bullets in the face do not improve one's appearance.

"Handsome" Dan O'Shea had made the occupational error of delaying too long the payment of a sizable wager to a fellow operator at race tracks. Annette was left with a son four years old, a male wardrobe of sixteen suits, fifty custom-made shirts, a hundred and three neckties, and twenty pairs of gentlemen's custom-made shoes—but no money. She brought on her mother from Steubenville, Ohio, to help care for the child, and went back into the theater.

But her luck had run out. Prima donna in Number Three road shows was the best she could get. "The Student Prince," "Desert Song," "Maytime," half a dozen others. All one-nighters, out on the road. Finally she took night club jobs to be with the child.

She had now been doing that for ten years. The "child" was now a sophomore at Harvard. She sent him a seventy-five dollar money order each Saturday out of her hundred dollar weekly salary. She lived for the boy, who planned to be a doctor.

Tommy Fain, the oldest of the piano players, had had his hour of greatness, and lived in its memory. For two years he had been one of the four husbands (the second one) of Eva Duray, the famous "It Girl" of vaudeville. He used that proud fact in his announcement of a number he always played, speaking thusly: "Ladies and Gents—I will now play the late Eva Duray's famous song which I played for her many times at the Palace. She was my beloved wife in those happy days. Need I tell you the name of that song? *Nothing Can Bother Me.*" And he played it with various keyboard flourishes while the aforementioned Molly Dorcey sang the classic words.

Willie (Rubber Face) Newman was the second piano player. He alone was entirely content with his job. His specialty was to "mug it" as he played, while big John Alton, a strident baritone, sang words.

Willie also had a very clever trick of playing with one hand while with the other he banged the piano top up and down at certain rhythmic places in the songs. It was most effective with the Horse and Buggy audiences, who would collaborate (musically speaking) by banging glasses on their tables. John Alton, his companion singer, could even vocally top this din, since he had been the baritone for two seasons with George White's Scandals. That had been *his* hour of glory.

2

So, at long last, and with apologies for the digressions, we come to a still young piano-player known as Tightpants Halka. He was apparently only about thirty years of age.

Although he had been playing there for a full year, very little was really known about "Mr. Tightpants" by either his employers or his fellow hired hands at this night spot. He alone did not (after two of the three free drinks) boast publicly or privately of past glories. He alone did not discuss hopes of future and more exalted employment, though it was rumored that he was writing a symphony —whatever that was. He was a "foreigner," and foreigners had crazy ideas like that.

He reported each evening promptly at 7:30, and punched the card assigned to each employee in the large time-clock placed just inside the entrance door in the basement of the establishment. He then proceeded to the men's dressing-room at the rear of this basement, and changed to his costume for the night's work. He did that work methodically and efficiently, with little to say to fellow artists. He did not play cards with them at intermissions, or mingle with guests at the bar. He returned to the dressing-room, and seemed to be meditating.

Sometimes he would jot down notes on the sheet of blank music paper he always carried in his pocket.

One hint of his past came, through the curiosity—a friendly curiosity—of the *I-Fell-Down-and-Went-Boom* lady, Molly Dorcey. As a part of their costumes, the three piano players wore loud, double-breasted vests, across the front of which stretched heavy, imitation gold chains attached to large closed-faced watches. Taking out these out-dated watches, snapping open the covers, observing the time thereon, was a sure fire laugh. Or winding them with a small key attached to the other end of the gold-colored chain, which ends and keys reposed in the opposite vest pockets.

In fact, Willie (Rubber Face) Newman, that exceedingly comic fellow, had built up this piece of "business" into a real show-stopper.

He would suddenly pause in the very middle of a number, take out the watch, open its face-lid and exclaim, "Ladies and fellow check-paying suckers—no laughter please, this is a solemn moment—it is now the exact hour of eleven-seventeen—" (or whatever hour it then was) "—and I had promised my old friend who gave me this watch, the late Diamond Jim Brady, to always wind it at this hour. What a man! What a pal! He always dropped around to the night spot where I was playing, and would say on leaving, 'Rubber Face—my day would not be complete without you.' A real lover of the arts—that gentleman. And on my twenty-fifth birthday he presented me with this small token of his admiration and affection. 'Wind it each night at the hour of—' (and Rubber Face injected the exact time at that moment) '—and think kindly of me—your friend and admirer.'

"So, ladies and fellow suckers—no laughter please—I must ask you to observe a moment of complete silence, while I perform a rite in memory of the greatest sucker of us all."

Rubber Face then proceeded to wind the time-piece, having concealed in his hand a gadget which emitted a harsh grinding, not unlike the cranking of a Model T Ford, with each turn of his key. The fact that he had never laid eyes on the great Gay-Nineties spender did not trouble him.

It made for a laugh—a surprised and very subtle laugh—as he explained in detail to his fellow entertainers. "You see, they think it's going to be a solemn moment—and it ain't! Get me?" he explained. "The *build up*—that's what makes any laugh great—the build up!"

Now it had been noticed that piano-player Tightpants Halka used his own watch, when he changed into his costume. For he possessed one nearly as large as the "prop" watches, and it had a snap face-cover of gold, and was wound with a small key which one inserted at its back—having snapped open another cover. So there was no objection from the management.

Because of her constant good humor, her optimism, her comradely social nature, her lack of any pretense of being what she had not been, middle-aged Molly Dorcey was the most likely to penetrate the reserve of a man like Tightpants. She alone talked with him often when they were waiting to go on. But the conversations were topical, and divulged nothing in particular regarding this piano-player's past.

Then, one afternoon, she was walking through Madison Square Park—near where she lived—and saw her fellow worker sitting on a bench. He was looking at the inside of the back of his watch.

Molly greeted him effusively; the little man rose politely—his invariable politeness, even around the Horse and Buggy, had been a unique characteristic noticed by all—and invited her to share his park bench. But she noted that he hastily replaced the watch in its proper pocket.

"Do let me see your watch, Tightpants!" she exclaimed. "I've noticed you use it even in the shows. My father has one of those old-fashioned watches. My mother gave it to him when they were married. I believe he'd rather lose me than lose that watch! Ha Ha. I like old-fashioned things myself—I'm afraid I'm just an old-fashioned girl who never grew up!"

Tightpants liked Molly Dorcey. He unsnapped the watch from its chain, and handed it to the woman.

"It belonged to *my* father," he said, "and before that to my grandfather. Friends in Vienna sent it to me when my father died."

It was indeed a beautiful example of a goldsmith's art. Intricate, interlaced designs bordered the thick, bulging covers. On the back cover was a coat of arms.

"What does this stand for?" asked Molly Dorcey. "I don't blame you for wearing it always. It is beautiful."

"That is the coat of arms of the old Emperor Franz Josef," said Tightpants. "My grandfather was in his service. He himself presented it to my grandfather."

"Your grandfather was a diplomat or a general?" asked the now doubly curious Molly.

"My grandfather was the Emperor's coachman," said the little piano player simply. "My father said that my grandfather worshiped Franz Josef."

The singer of comedy songs at the Horse and Buggy was not a little awed. She held in her hand a timepiece that had been in the hands of an Emperor! Even if this grandfather, to whom it had been presented, was just a coachman. "And you never told us this before! You never mentioned it in the shows!" she exclaimed. What *her* accompanist, he who had been briefly married to the great "It Girl" of vaudeville, would have made of such an heirloom! Or Rubber Face, the bosom pal of Diamond Jim Brady! Hallelujah!

"Oh, I don't think anyone but maybe you would be interested," said Tightpants. "And I never liked to bring my personal life into my work."

"May I open it?" asked Molly. "The part you were looking at when I came along?"

"If you wish," said Tightpants. "I will open it for you." He took the watch, pressed a hidden catch and the curved inside sprang into view.

There was a picture of a young girl pasted against the gold. A very lovely young girl. An oval face—delicate chin and nose—wide brow—large eyes. But perhaps the most noticeable feature was the hair—parted tightly in the middle, drawn down tightly to almost conceal the ears; and passing across the top of the head a thick braid that slanted a little lower on one side—it seemed like a sort of coronet—almost a halo.

Molly Dorcey gazed in fascination. "How beautiful—how very beautiful!" she exclaimed. And although the print seemed comparatively new and modern—it showed the shoulders wearing a modern-cut evening gown of some sort of lace—she asked, "A girl back in Vienna?"

"A girl in New York," said Tightpants. "Perhaps she looks, what you might say 'foreign.' Her people were Polish immigrants."

"I was in a show once with a Polish girl," said Molly. "She was the most striking of all the show girls. Some Polish women are very beautiful. Did you—did you love her very much?"

"She was my wife," said Tightpants Halka simply.

"Where—where is she now?" asked Molly Dorcey, and was immediately sorry she had asked. For a look of intense sorrow showed on the man's face. Perhaps the beautiful Polish girl had left this funny looking little piano player—deserted him for someone of more money and consequence. A girl as attractive as that could have had whatever she wished.

"She died three years ago," said the man. "The year before I came to the Horse and Buggy. I believe that she is now in whatever it is that is called Heaven. I believe she was—and is—a Blessed Saint."

Molly Dorcey, whose hit song was *I Fell Down and Went Boom,* felt a mist gathering in her eyes. She dabbed those eyes with the corner of her handkerchief. She pressed the hand of the man beside her.

"I'm sorry. I should not be so inquisitive," she said. And then, "Might I ask you her name?"

"Her name was Olga," said Tightpants Halka.

❖ 3 ❖

THERE WAS ANOTHER INCIDENT involving Molly Dorcey, late of the Dancing Dorceys. Having seen Tightpants in Madison Square Park, she surmised (and rightly) that he lived in that neighborhood—consequently in the same part of Manhattan as she and her elderly parents.

Christmas came, and the Horse and Buggy was closed for the day before and Christmas Eve. Not through any religious scruples, but because it had been found that even in New York, on that day and eve, citizens preferred to be with their families and friends at home.

Molly asked Tightpants to have dinner with her and her people. Some other friends, mostly theater folk, would also be there.

Tightpants at first declined with thanks. "I don't go out very much. I wouldn't be good company," he said.

"Now you just crawl out of your shell and come," insisted the uninhibited Molly. "I'm twenty years older than you are, and I know what will be good for you! You need a mother, that's what you need. My mother and father will like you, and maybe you'll like them. They're much more refined and civilized than I am. Ha Ha. I've told my father about your watch, and he's crazy to see it. What would you be doing on Christmas Eve anyway? Where would you eat your dinner?"

"I'd go out for my dinner—some restaurant—" He got no farther.

"Listen, Mr. Tightpants, I like New York. I love it," interrupted Molly, "except on Christmas Eve. That is, if I'm alone on Christmas Eve. You gotta have friends that day, if on no other day! It always makes me heartsick to look into arm-chair restaurant windows Christmas Eve, and see gents like you eatin' ham and beans all alone! It ain't Christian, and it ain't gonna happen to a nice gentleman like you while I'm around and kickin'. We always have a Christmas tree and plum pudding—had them even when we was out in the sticks playin' Orpheum time. Five shows that day sometimes, but we had our tree in whatever lousy hotel-room we was cooped in. My younger sister was alive then. She would be about your age. Now you just stop makin' excuses and come. We live at 110 Lexington Avenue, corner of Twenty-Eighth Street. Here—I'll write it down. Second floor rear—name's on the bell down stairs. Expect you at seven. Sooner if you want."

So Tightpants, having carefully pressed his extra pair of broadcloth trousers and put out food and milk for his mother cat and the four kittens, donned his best Homburg and proceeded to the Dorcey home.

It was the usual informal gathering and dinner of simple folk that the very wealthy are never privileged to enjoy. The elderly father and mother; half a dozen of their friends; a parish priest who turned out to be from a little church on Second Avenue that Tightpants knew well; their neighbors on the same floor—a young married couple, the husband being a trouble-shooter for the Telephone Company.

The only other person from the Horse and Buggy (except Tightpants) was a short and wide and most pleasant middle-aged man who was the show electrician at the night club. He and his wife, now equally short and wide, though she had once been the slender, premier dancer at Hammerstein's Victoria Theater. The electrician was known around the night club as "Bennie."

It was Bennie who had most cleverly arranged the lights on the Christmas tree which stood in one corner, so that, at the proper moment, it could be made to sparkle and glow like some visitant from Fairyland. This effect was not only because of the tiny colored bulbs in the branches of the tree, but also because of a spot light concealed behind a screen at the opposite corner of the room.

Before this "spot" was a revolving disk of various colors, which disk did revolve because of an electrical attachment started by the pressing of a button. The electric current was also attached to a small music box at the tree's foot, which at the same instant that the lights began to glow, started to play "Silent Night" in a most pleasant, tinkling melody.

The light-effects at the Horse and Buggy were another of its attributes not "honky tonk," and they were due to the skill and artistry of this humble stage-hand. Tightpants had long ago become friendly with this man. Possessing a skill of his own, like a true artist he recognized a superior skill in others.

First, however, came the dinner, with Molly popping in and out of the small kitchen, as she assisted her mother in its preparation—a preparation that had been going on since early morning.

The odors that came from the swinging door of that kitchen were truly glorious—a saliva-inducing mixture of roasting turkey, piquant cranberries, potatoes of the variety known as "yams," and a variety of sauces of secret ingredients that floated out into the small living room.

And while awaiting all this grandeur, there was a large bowl of a fragrant punch, with a rum base, that stood on a small table, and to which the company helped themselves with a large ladle into small, cuplike glasses.

Finally the big table in the middle of the room was cleared of books and papers—collapsible, swinging ends brought up—extra boards inserted in its accordion-like middle section; and so—ample eating room made for all. Molly spread over this triumph of architectural construction a snowy cloth of thick, sparkling linen; gleaming china and silver appeared from a closet; and soon there was a festive board—as they say—that Old King Cole, with all his resources, could not have bettered.

There were not enough chairs of course. A sofa was moved up, and books placed under the cushions, to raise those seated thereon to a proper table level. Two stools were brought from the kitchen. The Telephone Company neighbor went for two more chairs from his apartment. All seated, and the table fully spread, the good priest pronounced a blessing, and the feast commenced.

No multi-millionaire with chefs, butlers, and maids, could have purchased such blessed fellowship, and such lavish beneficence.

But it is of the entertainment that followed the dinner—that followed the plum pudding, and the four, inch-and-a-half thick, well brandied mince pies and the bubbling coffee—to be exact; it is this entertainment that concerns this chronicle.

There was a baby-grand piano in one corner. Molly disclosed a talent hitherto unknown to Tightpants, by sitting at this instrument, and playing the accompaniment to her mother and father doing the great number from their old vaudeville act. It was called *While Walking in the Park One Day,* and continued to specify the time as "In the merry, merry month of May."

The father donned a stiff straw hat, and took up a cane from the hallway. He and the mother locked arms, and proceeded to sing the simple, naive words, while doing a tap dance of ancient vintage. It brought laughter, applause, and a tear or two. The mother secretly wiped her eyes when they had finished.

She and her man had first performed it fifty years before. And they were still together—still able to sing and dance, though in a somewhat less acrobatic fashion, *While Walking in the Park One Day.*

Another guest, a tall, goatee'd, elderly gentleman, who looked and talked like a college professor, and who had been introduced as Mr. Blackman, turned out to be "Blackman the Magnificent." A famous magician, not exactly unknown to music hall audiences twenty years before. He had brought some of his gadgets, and made a half dollar pass through the bottom of a water glass, then somehow got it into the narrow neck of a soda bottle—and more mystifying still—shook it out again, his hand concealing the top of the bottle.

He produced boiled eggs from Tightpants' ears; borrowed five-dollar bills which he apparently burnt completely to ashes in a match flame, then returned the bills unscathed to their owners. Molly thought she held a small, red sponge in her closed hand, and when, at the tap of his wand, she opened that hand, out tumbled at least fifty sponges! Sponges of every color of the rainbow! He performed many other baffling illusions with several packs of playing cards.

And at the last Molly turned to Tightpants and said: "Now play something for us, Mr. Tightpants—at least you've got a better string-box than at the club. Ha Ha! That piano is my mother's pride and joy."

Tightpants went to the instrument, and ran his fingers up and down a scale. It was an excellently toned pianoforte, and in perfect pitch. Molly expected that the Horse and Buggy key thumper would launch into a popular, sentimental number—*In the Shade of the Old Apple Tree—Wait Till the Sun Shines, Nellie*—some one of the numbers he played nightly at the night spot. Instead, he played Claude Debussy's beautiful *Clair de Lune* and then, encouraged by a rapt attention, the frantic *Sunken Cathedral* of the same genius composer.

An almost stunned silence had spread over the small audience. They realized that this was not the hack performance of a hack accompanist. A beauty, a fervor, a tone picture came out of those baby grand strings; a magic that could only be created by a very talented artist. Mr. Tightpants paused, and there was spontaneous applause.

"Please, Mr. Halka, play some more for us," said Molly Dorcey's mother. "This room has seldom heard music like that."

"Yes—yes!" said the father. "Please play some more."

Molly Dorcey was too astonished to speak. Was this the Number Three—because he was the last engaged—key-thumper of the Horse and Buggy?

Finally, since Tightpants was looking at her, as his hostess, for approbation, she managed a "Please, Tightpants, please."

So the little musician went into the Chopin *Scherzo in B Flat Minor, Opus 20,* and followed it by a wild *Mazurka* of the same composer. Then the *Sonata in F Sharp Minor* by Schumann, and the Beethoven *Piano Concerto Number 12, Opus 13.* As they demanded more, he played Beethoven's *Sonata Number 21 in C Sharp Minor,* which is known as the *Waldstein Sonata.* Its three thrilling, contrasting movements filled that small room as only very great music and a very great technical performance could fill it—fill it, and banish all else from a listener's conscious mind.

Still they demanded more, and he gave them the popular *Prelude* of Rachmaninoff, and then the beautiful *Adagio Allegro in F Minor* of Mozart.

The priest asked for "Adeste Fideles" and the little man from the Horse and Buggy made it sound like a Heavenly Choir. At least, so Molly Dorcey's mother exclaimed. Asked by the priest if he knew George Frederick Handel's *Messiah,* Tightpants played several of its inspired movements.

He played steadily for two hours. And even then, his audience wished for more of his playing.

Molly Dorcey, at the Horse and Buggy the next evening, said to her special friend, the head bartender, "Holy cats! How that little guy, Tightpants Halka, can hit the piano keyboard! I had him over to my home last night, and glory be! What he could play—and how! All them old time, dead, foreign composer-guys that they call classics, and played 'em without any sheets of music in front of him. Knew 'em by heart! Say—what the hell is he doing in this joint!"

Molly did not know that she and her friends had been listening to probably the greatest performer of Chopin, of Liszt, of Schumann, of Bach, of Beethoven, of Mozart in America. Maybe even in Europe and America.

Such are the vicissitudes of Fortune and Fate, in a world in which one must eat to live and work.

The party at Molly Dorcey's had doubtless lasted well past midnight, but at a quarter till twelve the priest had excused himself because he had a Midnight Mass at his church. Tightpants also begged to be permitted to depart, and he also went to a Mass.

But it was not to go with the good priest. It was to a Polish Catholic Church on West Forty-first Street.

He had attended the Christmas Eve Masses there (when they were in New York) on happier Christmas Eves, with the girl whose picture was in his watch. The service and the songs were in her language. The songs were especially beautiful—old Polish hymns from the ancient land where most of the worshipers had been born.

The girl had loved those songs. And he always remembered what she had said; could imagine that she was standing beside him then, the lights high up in the vaulted ceiling catching a bit of the thick braid of hair that, exposed by the saucily tilted Russian-style cap she wore in the winter, projected down across her right ear—like a saint's halo, it seemed to him—he could hear her saying again: "Duszka—you'd never mistake this for anything but a Polish church. Look at all the upturned noses! 'Upturned to Heaven, at least for this one night,' my father used to say."

"I think that yours is always upturned to Heaven," he had answered with a smile. "Your blessed little upturned nose!"

He had not expected, however, that it was destined to proceed to that locality so very soon.

✤ 4 ✤

TWO OTHER INCIDENTS in connection with the Horse and Buggy at this period may be of consequence and import to an understanding of this chronicle.

The small upright piano on the small platform in the main room on the second floor would quickly get badly out of tune. This did not seem to worry anyone—customer or entertainer or management—with the exception of the player known as Tightpants.

Ordinary "being thumped" each night, seven nights a week, fifty-two weeks a year, for eight straight hours nightly, would alone account for some variance from strict concert pitch, even in the most sturdily built and most conscientious of instruments. And the supposedly comic machinations of player Willie (Rubber Face) Newman did not exactly help to keep the steel strings at a perfect tonal stretch.

For besides the earlier mentioned banging of the top, this particular performer had another neat and laughable trick of raising his leg, and striking the keyboard with his leather-shod heel as the grand climax of one hilarious number. He was secretly practicing so that he could double the effect by raising *both* legs, and striking both the bass and treble clefs at one and the same time—using *both* heels—while still sitting on the piano bench!

It was going to be difficult, but, true artist that he was, Rubber Face thought it could be accomplished.

So, one afternoon, having slipped a small, eight-inch-long, steel tool in his inner pocket, Tightpants Halka proceeded at the unusually early hour of four P.M. to the West Fifty-first Street bistro where he was employed. He mounted the now silent stairs, and continued upward to the third floor where, at one end of the hallway, was the private office of his employers.

The small, closed door read

THE
HORSE AND BUGGY NIGHT CLUB
INC.

and in smaller letters at one side, and below it, were two names.

Harry Levine
Larry Kennedy

These two gentlemen were the partners owning the night spot. Both were graduates *cum laude* (so to speak) of another festive period of New York history, the Gay Twenties. Both had their restaurant and entertainment training in the life-saving speakeasies, which were the principal products (along with organized gangsterism and a general disrespect for the law) of the noble Prohibition Act.

Mr. Levine, heavy set and heavy jowled, had started adult life as a professional wrestler, then became head bouncer for the famous "Nellie and Bill's" of those days, and had risen rapidly to be its manager. Though a bit shy of what we call a "formal education," a native astuteness had more than made up for this deficiency; and the fact that he had a brother on the Liquor Law Enforcement Squad of the Metropolitan Police had helped no little.

Mr. Kennedy had had a varied career as a small-time pickpocket (but with only one short jail sentence, a fact however that required the present liquor license to be in Mr. Levine's name only); rum runner across the Canadian border; small time theatrical booking agent, in which profession his pickpocket ethics and training came in handy; and now, half owner of a very prosperous and law-abiding night spot.

It was Mr. Kennedy who engaged the "talent" and supervised the dine-and-dance floor and the shows. Mr. Levine's department was finance and the Harmony Bar.

Tightpants knocked timidly on the door.

He would have knocked on any door before entering, a quaint habit doubtless due to his Continental background; but in this case knocking would have been necessary, for the door was securely locked. This, although the two partners were within. They always kept it locked—a hangover from speakeasy operating precautions. The pressing of a button underneath the desk-top of Mr. Levine would release the catch.

And there was another customary ritual before a pressing of the desk button. Two rituals in fact. Any loose currency on the desk was swept into a locked, desk drawer. If any part of the previous night's receipts happened to be there, it might be considerable.

Then one partner would proceed to the door.

Now inserted in the central door-panel, just above the outside insignia, was a small disk of metal. By turning this disk from the *inside,* one could see just who was *outside,* without the person *outside* having a similar, vice versa, *inside* view.

I hope no reader is confused. It was one of the cleverest and most valuable inventions of the age.

When Tightpants knocked that afternoon, both partners were in executive session. A really important conference. Should they have corrected certain building code violations having to do with the electric wiring of the premises, a corrective that would run into the spending of several thousands of dollars; or should they, more frugally, slip a few hundred to the inspector involved?

It took a bit of careful and clear thinking.

Mr. Levine was for economy. Mr. Kennedy thought the rewiring should be done now, while business was booming. There might be a new inspector another year, when receipts might not be so satisfactory.

At the interrupting knock, partner Kennedy, who was pacing the carpet at the time, stopped talking and proceeded to the peep hole.

"It's only piano player Tightpants Halka," he said, turning to Mr. Levine seated behind the desk. "I hope he ain't quittin'. He's the most reliable key thumper we've ever had."

Tightpants had indeed been in their employ an entire year without missing a single night. Or showing up intoxicated. An all-time record for the Horse and Buggy.

"Well, let him in," said partner Levine, and he pressed the open-sesame button beneath his desk top.

Tightpants was admitted. He removed his Homburg, and proceeded respectfully to the front of the flat-top desk. He had previously bowed ceremoniously to his two employers, speaking: "Mr. Kennedy—Mr. Levine."

"Well, Tightpants, what can we do for you?" asked Mr. Kennedy, with a show of geniality. "I hope all goes well in your work."

"I have come to ask a great favor," said Tightpants, "and I hope you will not think me forward or presumptuous in asking it."

Mr. Levine stiffened, and a hard look of battle showed in his small, piglike eyes. "A great favor" from hired hands could mean only one thing.

It meant a touch. A loan. An advance against salary not due for four more days. Once started, they kept it up; if not every week, every alternate week. It messed up the books. Then, when they had drawn a particularly large amount, they quit. Vamoosed. Left town. And the unfortunate Horse and Buggy, Inc. was left holding the bag, for maybe as much as an unearned hundred bucks! He had listened to all the excuses—"a sick wife"—"a child going to the hospital"—"an overdue insurance policy." He started to lay down a protective barrage.

"Tightpants," he said, "Mr. Kennedy and I like to help people. Particularly loyal employees like yourself. But business has not been over good lately. I know; a lot of people comin' in. But poor spenders. There's no money in the food-end any more. Just in the drinks. And lately they've taken to drinkin' beer. All them radio commercials, I think. Them singin' commercials about beer being New York's favorite beverage! Them commercials ought to be abolished! Abolished by law! And look at the entertainment we are giving 'em for free! Absolutely free, except for a ridiculously low three-dollar-fifty cover charge. Fine performers like you and Rubber Face. I was just tellin' Mr. Kennedy, it's awful! Not the show—expenses I mean. And the taxes! State and City and Federal taxes. You have no idea——"

Mr. Levine paused for lack of breath. He had anyway probably said enough about the desperate state of the Horse and Buggy finances.

"Well—" he added, "just what is this favor you wish? As I said, Mr. Kennedy and I like to help people, but I'm very much afraid it is impossible at this time."

Tightpants had stood, hat in hand, listening attentively. From loose talk around the bistro, he knew that the place was supposed to be "coining money." But no hint of this knowledge showed itself on his simple, expressionless, small face. He spoke.

"What I wish does not involve any expense to you, Mr. Levine. And I have already spoken to the electrician, and he will gladly come in and help me on his own time. Put on a light for me, I mean, and stand by. Maybe hold a hand spotlight, now and then, so I can see into the insides."

"My God, what insides?" asked Mr. Levine. This sounded still more alarming than a touch.

"The insides of the pianoforte in the main room," said Tightpants. "I want to put it in better tune, if you don't mind, and will permit me. I have my own wrench that I am quite sure will fit. If I could work on it for an hour or two, it would be a different instrument. And then I would not let it get out of tune again—if I had your permission. A few twists each week would keep it in perfect pitch."

Mr. Levine gazed up at the innocent wrench and the equally innocent little man before his desk. He heaved a sigh of relief. He had been a little fearful when the piano player had reached to his inner coat pocket for the wrench.

An old associate of his had recently requested a cash loan, and to be hidden until he could hop a plane for Mexico; and enforced this request by a revolver carried in an under-the-shoulder holster.

He now turned to Mr. Kennedy in the face of this strangest request ever made to him in his not uneventful career. But he was indeed very greatly relieved. The man did not want an "advance."

Mr. Kennedy swallowed. "Why—why sure," he gasped. "Sure, Tightpants, sure! You can twist it—I mean tune it, if you wish to."

Mr. Kennedy had been as equally dumfounded as had been Mr. Levine by the nature of piano-player Tightpants' "great favor."

"Thank you both very much. You are most kind," said the recipient of this generosity, and, his mission successfully accomplished, he started his usual bows and his usual farewell "Mr. Kennedy—Mr. Le——"

But Mr. Kennedy had now recovered his astute self, and his responsibility for protecting the cultural standards of their establishment arose in his mind.

"Just a moment," he interrupted. "Are you sure you *understand* the tuning of a piano?"

"Quite sure," said Tightpants.

"But—but you are not a professional piano tuner, are you?" asked Mr. Kennedy.

"Not exactly I suppose," said Tightpants apologetically, "but where I came from, one was taught how to keep one's instrument in perfect tonal pitch—" and seeing the look of incredulity on Mr. Kennedy's face, he added, "like—like a violinist tightening his strings and testing them, or a harpist striking chords and twisting the pegs before starting to play. I have had this wrench and used it for many years."

And Tightpants again held up the innocent instrument with which he intended to operate.

That quite plausible, though heretofore unheard of, attitude of a key-thumper toward his piano seemed to settle the matter for artistry-responsible Mr. Kennedy, but Mr. Levine had also recovered his poise, and the matter of finance arose in his sloping and wrinkled brow.

There *must be* some financial catch in an employee wanting to do something without extra pay! And then there was the matter of the Musical Union, a thorn in that gentleman's flesh for some years because of their outrageous and uncompromising "minimum-wage-and-hours" demands.

"Are you sure your Union—" (he nearly said "damn Union") "—will permit you to do this without charge?" he asked suspiciously.

"Quite sure," said Tightpants. "I have done it where I have played before. There is no objection, if I do it on my own time, as they say."

"Ah yes—on your own time," repeated Mr. Levine. Those were pleasant, sweet words—*on your own time*. Words too little used and heard in this selfish, money-grabbing world. "I think—I think however," continued Mr. Levine, "that we had better put it in writing. . . . Miss Friedberg! Miss Friedberg!" and he called loudly toward a closed door at one side. A not ill-formed young lady promptly appeared with a notebook and a poised pencil, and hitching her tight skirt to a proper secretarial level just above the knees, deposited a shapely chassis in the chair beside her employer.

"Take a short letter, Miss Freidberg, and type it immediate . . . Date, of course. Then write—'Horse and Buggy Night Club, Inc., Gentlemen. I——' "

He was about to say "Tightpants Halka," but realized that would not be a strictly legal or business form.

"I have forgotten your initials," he said to the little man still standing before his desk.

"S. J." said Tightpants. "S. J. Halka."

"To be sure," said Mr. Levine. "Ought to know them, as I been seein' it now for a whole year on the salary sheet." This latter statement with an attempt at friendliness. A compliment, not a complaint.

Then, returning to the waiting secretary, he resumed dictation.

"I, S. J. Halka, do hereby agree that any piano tuning I may do on the instrument located on the premises of the Horse and Buggy Night Club, Inc., shall be done on my own time, without a charge of any kind, substance, or nature; and that I will not now, or at any future date thereafter, or hereafter, present a bill for the same to said Corporation, or cause any bill for said aforementioned work to be presented to said Corporation, or to any of its duly elected officers thereof, or to any officers that may or shall be duly elected thereto."

Mr. Levine paused in the composition of this legal masterpiece and addressed Tightpants. "It isn't that I doubt your word, Tightpants.

But in these tax-ridden days, one must be careful. And particularly now. Any unusual and unnecessary expense——"

"I quite understand," said Tightpants without the trace of a smile.

So presently the document was brought in, typed on the stationery of the Horse and Buggy, Inc., at the bottom of which was the advertisement of a well known whiskey, for which advertisement the stationery was paid for by that distiller. Tightpants had meantime been permitted to seat himself in a chair by the window. He came to the desk, signed the agreement.

"Put it in the safe with the other contracts," ordered Mr. Levine to Miss Friedberg.

That lady (and the document) then vanished from Tightpants Halka's life, and from this tale, but not without a seductive backward glance of female eyes, and a slight swishing of well turned female hips in the gentleman key-thumper's direction. Miss Friedberg secretly hoped to someday break into "show business," feeling that she had the proper equipment therefor.

So now Tightpants did repeat, with two slight bows, his "Mr. Levine—Mr. Kennedy," and departed as he had come.

Half an hour later he was seen (and heard) in shirtsleeves, and with a flashlight held by the show electrician, tightening certain hidden bolts and then striking and listening carefully to the sound of the keys of the main-floor pianoforte.

The two partners—on his departure—had stared at each other and simultaneously burst into langhter.

"I'll be damned!" said Mr. Levine. "Wants to tune our piano on his own time! Do you think he's quite right in the head?"

Mr. Kennedy smiled wisely. "When you've been around them musicians as much as I have, Harry, you'll know that they are all a little cuckoo in the noggin," he said. "But this little guy Tightpants is O.K. Best piano player—strictly as a player—we ever had. Hasn't got the one called Rubber Face's technique, but he's awful good on them sobby ballads. Some night listen to his *I Wonder Who's Kissing Her Now* if you want to hear real melody. So let him have his fun tinkering with the string box. He can't make it worse than it is. Guess it did need a bit of tunin'. Hadn't been tuned for over two years. I was goin' to speak to you about it next month. It's upkeep, and we could take the cost off the tax——"

"We take it off anyway," said Mr. Levine decisively, "and that goes to prove what I've always been tellin' you, Larry. Don't take no hasty action about nothing. Now, by not actin' hasty, we got it done for nothing. Free gratis.

"I sort of liked that little guy too. He seemed O. K. to me. Honest like. No honesty in your hired help no more. Honest but a little dumb. Well, you can't be everything. I hope to God we don't have no trouble with his Union over it. If they ever find out someone did somethin' for nothin' around here!"

He had to smile as he brushed that novel thought from his mind. Then, with a frown at the summons-like papers on his desk, "Let's get back to this matter of a damn building code violation. Why the hell should we spend—"

Let us leave these two public spirited citizens to their discussion.

5

THE OTHER INCIDENT occurred about six months later, and was of a somewhat different character.

It was a football night in New York—a Columbia-Yale game—consequently all higher educational night spots were doing nicely. The Horse and Buggy was bursting at the seams. Five deep around the Harmony Bar, and extra tables crowding the main room upstairs.

And co-proprietor Levine was pleased to note—as he had noted on like occasions before—that the higher education led to a higher appreciation of alcoholic beverages. Very little unscholarly beer. Martinis, Manhattans, Old Fashioneds, Stingers, straight Rye-and-Scotch were the order of the evening. Several parties were drinking champagne.

Mr. Levine, his stocky figure encased in a new tuxedo costing a cool hundred and seventy-five dollars, was himself circulating among the patrons, not only as a matter of good fellowship to personally greet known customers, but as an extra bouncer in case of difficulties, he having not entirely forgotten his skill in that fundamental phase of night club operation.

It was a noisy, festive crowd. The heckling (for the most part good natured) of the entertainers was more in evidence than usual. Willie

(Rubber Face) Newman and Molly Dorcey minded it the least, their act being a rowdy one, helped rather than being hindered by jovial interruptions. It fell the hardest on Tightpants and ex-prima donna Annette Blair, their songs being of a more serious and quiet order. *In the Shade of the Old Apple Tree* or Victor Herbert's *Ah Sweet Mystery of Life,* which Annette sang really well, were not enhanced by an obbligato of a chanting of the game score, or shouted tributes to Annette's still excellent figure such as "You for me, baby!" or "Come and sit on Papa's knee."

Tightpants also came in for his share. Musically critical celebrants would exhort him to "Play louder!" or "Don't you know some live stuff? We want *Won't You Come Home, Bill Bailey!"* But having gone through this sort of thing on former gala nights, these two were managing to bear up, and to finish their numbers with outward dignity, if with some inward annoyance.

Poor Annette had no *I Fell Down and Went Boom* song to wow 'em with, and Tightpants had no tidy tricks like hitting the bass and treble clefs with both heels.

At a table just in front of the entertainers' platform was an especially boisterous group. The host was a gentleman from Syracuse, N. Y., who was vice president of the Syracuse Nut and Bolt Company. He had to lead a sober life in that thriving, up-state metropolis, being also a director of a Loan and Trust Company, a Bank, President of a business executives club, and he was on the Board of Managers of a church.

Once a month, however, he made a "business trip" to the big, wicked town at the mouth of the Hudson, on which trip he preferred that his wife did not accompany him, she being a moving spirit in the Daughters of the American Revolution and the Women's Christian Temperance Union.

With some customer friends (who could usually "dig up" a couple of girls) he would spend the several New York evenings cementing new and old accounts with open handed dining and drinking, where the atmosphere could cause him to forget his restricted Syracuse environment.

Life—he felt—owed him this relaxation. The cost of the "parties" went on the Nut and Bolt expense account.

He was a very large, florid gentleman, generally popular in what ready-to-wear haberdashers describe as the "executive group," his only fault being that after the first ten New York Scotch highballs he became a trifle crude and noisy. He had the dubious (though he was secretly proud of it, and would boast of it to less fortunate cronies in Syracuse) distinction of having been barred at certain periods from certain more sedate night spots. But being a free spender (due to the aforementioned "expense account" which he alone had to O. K.) he was generally welcomed.

This was his maiden visit to the Horse and Buggy.

He had attended neither Yale nor Columbia, but after a hearty dinner, preceded by numerous rounds of cocktails, he became a violent and noisy partisan of the Sons of Eli, Yale having happened to win the afternoon's game. So—after hearing them once or twice, he joined lustily in the traditional Yale songs and cheers as voiced periodically by bona-fide Yale graduates, and even introduced himself to several nearby tables apparently occupied by New Haven alumni.

"Didn't have the good fortune to go to your college," he said, "had to work for *my* living from boyhood. But always have been for the bulldog. I'm what you boys would call a self-made man. But if I had been able to go to a university, it would have been to Yale. Good old Yale! R. H. Bankhead's the name. Vice-president of the Syracuse Nut and Bolt Company, Inc. If you're ever in my city, look me up. Anyone can tell you where to find me. R. H. Bankhead. My friends call me 'Good old R. H.' "

During the first show, good old R. H. had been reasonably quiet, being occupied in filling his gullet with the really excellent food provided by the Horse and Buggy. Also in getting acquainted with the three ladies whom his customer guests had "dug up" for this occasion. But by the time the second show had come around, he had settled back over his eighth highball, and felt the need of impressing his companions—and the room at large—with his knowledge of cosmopolitan night life.

Even pianist Rubber Face Newman became a little peeved when his gag about the Farmer's Daughter was ruined by this gentleman's constant interruptions.

Tightpants and Annette Blair fared very badly at his hands with *The Last Rose of Summer* and several Stephen Foster songs. After their last number, and as they were leaving the small stage, he had loudly called—"One moment, please! I have a special request. Waiter!" (and his waiter obediently approached) "Take this ten dollar bill to those two pall-bearers. Tell them it's so they can go the hell home and go to bed. This is a celebration for a mighty victory for good old Yale. Not a funeral. But maybe those two are for Columbia. Columbia graduates! Ha Ha! Anyway, this will pay 'em to keep quiet while *I'm* here."

Tightpants and Annette made their exit, not accepting the generous financial contribution. In fact Miss Blair took the bill, tore it in two pieces, and tossed it on the floor. There was a smattering of applause for this action. The gentleman from Syracuse had overplayed his hand.

Half-owner Levine had been watching. His sympathy was entirely with Miss Blair and Tightpants. Not so much because of the annoyance they had been caused, as because this guest seemed to have about eaten and drunk to his full capacity (as it were), and the check would not be increased by his longer presence. He moved to the table—first motioning a waiter to recover the torn bill, which he deposited in his vest pocket.

The inference was that he would return it to its donor, but this inference was wrong. Pasted together later, it went into the night's gross receipts.

One of the arts of successfully operating a night spot was to accomplish what in some businesses is called the "turnover." Especially on a crowded evening. Guests had to be turned away if too many diners ate, drank, and then lingered (languidly or boisterously) through several shows. It became a dead loss if they stayed on beyond drinking and eating capacity.

Mr. Levine had a stock argument that sometimes worked. He approached the "dead" table, introduced himself, and artfully suggested that after ten P.M. there was an extra city tax on food and liquor. "It was only fair that he warn good customers about this charge, which he personally considered to be an outrage. . . . Political graft, you know."

Usually, especially with noisy out-of-town spenders, it brought about the desired result. The victims asked for their check—having thanked him—and left.

Not so the gentleman from Syracuse.

"Who cares about a damn New York City tax!" he said. "Not *my* organization, the Syracuse Nut and Bolt Company. Glad to help out your bankrupt city! Ha Ha! And tax or no tax, I like your place! Like it except for that completely lousy last 'act.' You ought to can that turn. Can it, and solder down the lid tight! Ha Ha! Tell the waiter to bring another round of drinks! No lemonade! And serve the people at that next table. Old Yale friends of mine! Put it all on my bill!"

"Many of our patrons like those old songs," said Mr. Levine defensively, but somewhat mollified by the new drink order, he let the matter rest. Anyway, he had that torn ten dollar bill safely in his pocket. That entitled the guy to stay a short while longer. Mr. Levine always tried to give value for cash in hand.

And Mr. Levine was just a little weary—not his usual robust, assertive, persuasive self. There had already been two fist fights down in the Harmony Bar. He had had to assist in the ejecting of four customers. One of them had left an unpaid bill, and another given the bartender a personal check on Kansas City, Mo., a piece of paper of doubtful value.

He wanted no more trouble that evening. These college-game nights, although good for business, always meant trouble. The higher education was not all it was cracked up to be. Prize-fight nights were much more orderly. Or a World Series, when a New York or Brooklyn team was in said series.

So Mr. Syracuse stayed on. He ordered still more drinks. He had a secret reason for staying. He wanted to see if "that lousy act" had been fired, as he had ordered. He was accustomed to having his orders obeyed.

Tightpants Halka and Annette Blair had of course not been discharged. But when it came around to their turn again, about eleven P.M., Miss Blair, learning from Mollie Dorcey that her tormentor was still there, decided not to appear. The insulting ten-dollar bill still rankled. She with a son in Harvard! And this stupid "Yale man" —for so she regarded the Nut and Bolt vice-president!

Still, she used discretion. She did not want to lose a steady job. She pretended to be ill.

So, after the Rubber Face-Mollie Dorcey act, Tightpants went out alone. He had had to do this on several occasions. Not long before, a new act that had only been there a week, completely failed to show up. Tightpants had gone out and performed a "solo." He had not of course played Brahms or Handel. He had acquired a popular-number repertory that "got by." That was what he was expected—and expecting—to do at this 11 P.M. emergency.

He made a brief announcement. "Ladies and gentlemen, my singer, the lovely Annette Blair, is ill-disposed. I will do my best to entertain you alone for the next quarter of an hour. I hope I can play some favorite numbers that will meet with your approval."

But on looking down at the table directly before him, as he made this respectful announcement, he perceived the evening's bad boy making a wry face. The gentleman added to the pantomime by holding his nose, and reaching up backward with one hand as if pulling a chain.

It caused loud laughter from his companions of the evening. It did something else to the little fellow who then seated himself on the piano stool.

Tightpants did not go into Jerome Kern's lovely *All the Things You Are* as he usually did. He struck a mighty and thunderous chord—at least as mighty and thunderous as the small, upright piano would allow. And as he did this, he thanked Heaven he had fully retuned the instrument only two days before. And then, he played the glorious, tempestuous *Prelude* of Rachmaninov as few performers, including its genius creator, could have played it.

It held this rabble audience. By this time, anyway, things had become a little quieter. Even Mr. Syracuse had to listen—listen with a frowning, flushed face.

At the end there was applause. Real applause. Great music does have its effect—even on the most savage beasts, as the saying goes.

And so encouraged, Tightpants again spoke. "Thank you, ladies and gentlemen. That—as you know—was the *Prelude in C Sharp Minor* of Sergei Vasilevich Rachmaninov. I will now, with your permission, try to play for you a piece in an entirely different mood—a piece that was a favorite of a very dear friend of mine." And he started the not so well known but very quiet and lovely *D Minor Sonata* of Franz Liszt.

But the Nut and Bolt executive was now fully aroused. Here was this cheap fellow, who probably didn't make more than a hundred dollars a week, and whom he had told to get out, brazenly back, and flaunting himself by some cheap trickery into gaining applause. This applause, moreover, to the man's muddled brain, seemed a personal affront to his musical judgment. He, whose salary was fifty-five thousand a year, plus a bonus on sales, plus an unlimited expense account!

Why, he could buy this piano-thumping beggar, body and soul, for what he, R. H. Bankhead of the Syracuse Nut and Bolt Company, Inc., made in one week! One day!

Patriotism also entered into the matter. The shrimp spoke and looked like an alien. He probably had no right even to be in this country!

Mr. Syracuse had half realized he could not shout down the thunderous music of the great pre-communist Russian, but Herr Liszt's gentle melody could easily be topped. He arose, if a bit unsteadily, from his chair, to give voice to his righteous indignation.

"I told you, you little rat, to go home to bed," he repeated loudly. "I didn't like you then, and I don't like you now—or this cheap, lousy, high-brow tune! Who wrote it anyway? Sounds foreign to me. Well, give him my compliments and tell him he stinks. Here—I'll pay you both off once more—", and he tossed two quarters to the platform. "That's what you are worth. That's what your lousy foreign song is worth——"

The dine-and-dance room of the Horse and Buggy became suddenly silent. Two waiter-bouncers from far corners started to move to the immediate vicinity of this protester's table.

Mr. Levine, just mounting the stairs from the bar, heard a portion of the words, and at the risk of splitting his new tuxedo trousers, quickened his stair-mounting to a two-steps-at-a-time run.

But little S. J. Halka (as his name appeared on the Horse and Buggy salary list) was the first to reach the patriotic, quarter-tossing gentleman from up-state. He had made the distance from his platform in four short steps. And he stood very quietly before the astonished critic of his song and that song's composer, and spoke very quietly. His eyes, however, were flashing, and if one had noticed his hands, particularly his fingers, one would have seen that they were poised like talons. The arms still hung limply at his sides.

"Just what did I understand you to say, sir?" he asked.

Mr. Syracuse repeated, and more loudly even than before, "I said that you were a cheap, foreign rat, playing a cheap, ratty song written by some cheap foreign bastard——"

The gentleman got no further. Tightpants sprang—literally sprang—at his insulter's throat. Around that throat closed the steel, spring-like fingers of a trained pianoforte player—fingers that were as strong as any metal, and far more flexible. The large man gave a gasping cry. One of the party girls screamed. The attack was so unexpected that Mr. Syracuse had no time to even raise his arms in defense. He sank gasping to his chair, the little musician above him and clutching his ample neck in a death grip.

But there was no death.

The bouncer-waiters, the man's male table friends, and finally the husky Mr. Levine (now arrived on the scene) managed to pry those fingers loose. Two waiters seized Tightpants, but the piano player stood perfectly quiet, his arms again relaxed at his side, and made no further hostile move. The absurdity of holding him was quickly realized, and the waiters proceeded to the other party in the argument.

Tightpants' victim lay gasping across his chair—but gasping, not lifeless. There were some dark purple marks about his throat.

Mr. Levine, of long experience in various forms of restaurant mayhem and violence, now took charge. He knew exactly what to do.

First he ordered a bouncer-waiter to stand by the single stairway exit and see that no one left the room. He wanted no excited patron phoning for the police. There was really no need of that precaution, for curiosity kept all diners and drinkers in their places, unless they had risen and pushed forward to better view the fracas. Then he spoke authoritatively to all, his voice topping the excited chatter.

"My friends—it is nothing. Do not be alarmed. Everything is now under control. Just a friendly misunderstanding. Boys will be boys." But looking down at the sputtering vice-president of the Syracuse Nut and Bolt Company, he added, "If there is a doctor present I wish he would step forward."

A young man at a far corner table called out, "I am a doctor, sir," and the diners on that side of the room made way for him. He bent over the gentleman from Syracuse who was now becoming gurglingly audible—"I have been assaulted"—"I might have been murdered!" —"You will find out who I am!"—"That fiend should be arrested!" And he as suddenly lapsed into a drunken stupor.

The doctor loosened the man's tie and collar and made a hasty examination. "He'll be all right," he said. "No ligaments broken. A little sore around the neck for a few days. He's drunk, and probably a good thing; his relaxed condition prevented any real injury. Get him home," this to the table friends, "and bathe his neck with a liniment. Here is my card if you need me later."

Mr. Levine thanked the doctor, told him his dinner and drink check was cancelled, then took the names of the Syracuse gentleman's three male friends. The three ladies preferred not to give theirs, seemed only anxious to make a departure. The fact was, they also were not especially anxious to be interviewed by the police, with whom they all had a passing acquaintance. And one of the men of the party said to Mr. Levine, "Don't worry. And we rely on you to keep this matter quiet. We do not want any trouble or publicity. Especially publicity. Please let us have the check."

After suspicious scrutiny and a questioning of some items, the check was paid, the night club manager noticing that the money was taken from the Nut and Bolt man's side pocket, from which a roll of bills had been several times before in evidence. And Mr. Syracuse, once again conscious and protesting, was helped down the stairs, and out into a reviving night air and a concealing taxi.

Meantime Tightpants stood perfectly still, awaiting the storm he expected to break over his head as soon as proprietor Levine returned. Several patrons pressed forward and attempted to shake his hand.

"He had it coming to him," "We'll leave our names if you need witnesses," were some of the comments.

Mr. Kennedy also now appeared on the scene, having been summoned from the upstairs office, but before he could get into the picture, partner Levine was back. And he was still in command.

"Mr. Kennedy, get the next act onto the platform," he ordered. And to the patrons, "Our entertainment will now continue. Have fun. And although I foresee no further difficulties over this little matter, if anyone who actually heard and seen it will care to leave your names with Mr. Kennedy, I will thank you. . . . We will both thank you," he added, not to leave partner Kennedy out of any broad policy statements.

He then turned to Tightpants Halka.

"You, sir, will kindly follow me upstairs to my office," he commanded.

Tightpants obeyed. He realized that what he had done was entirely wrong, regardless of the provocation, but somehow he was not sorry.

He would be discharged, of course. Well, maybe he could get some other job. He liked the Horse and Buggy engagement, because it seemed permanent; was not dependent on the success or failure of some show, as were the engagements in theater orchestras. It gave him his full day free to work on his new symphony, over which he had been laboring for six months.

But that was that. Everything had to reach an end.

Mr. Levine unlocked the private office door, entered, and motioned Tightpants to enter. He switched on the light. He proceeded to his desk, and seated himself. He looked up at Tightpants, now standing before the desk, with a heavy frown.

"Well?" he said, "Mr. Tightpants, well?"

"I apologize, Mr. Levine, for what has happened. I am sorry. I am not sorry for what I did, but I am sorry for causing you and Mr. Kennedy trouble. If any punishment is handed out, it should be to me. Not you. You have my address. I shall not leave the city. I am sincerely sorry to leave your employ. You and Mr. Kennedy have been most kind to me."

"Wait a minute, pal—not so fast," said a surprisingly friendly Mr. Levine. The frown was still there, but an expression of the mouth belied that frown. "Just what in hell happened? What did he say to you, to make you go off your nut? Did he insult you beyond the usual razzing this kind of a night? You know what we have to expect on nights like these."

"He insulted me, and before me, Miss Blair," said Tightpants, "but that was not why I attacked him. I am used to personal insults. I do not mind them any more."

"Why the hell then did you grab him? Did he pull a gun on you, or raise a hand to strike you?"

"No sir," said Tightpants, "it was neither of those things. It was just what he said. He insulted a friend of mine. Said that his song 'stank'—I believe that was the word he used. It is a very great song, written by a very great and honorable friend."

Mr. Levine now dropped entirely his attitude of sternness. "A friend?" he asked. "You did it because he insulted a friend?"

"Yes sir," said Tightpants. "He insulted Franz Liszt."

Mr. Levine now made a surprising request. "Sit down, Mr. Tightpants," he said, and motioned to a chair.

Tightpants moved around the desk and sat.

"I am considered a tough character," said Mr. Levine. "You have to be tough to get ahead in this night club racket. I came up the tough way. Made a lot of enemies—and a few—a very few real friends. You learn to sort out the friends from the double-crossers. I got where I am today because of friends—real friends. Friend of mine in wholesale liquor lent me the dough to start this joint. He's now on a vacation in Atlanta, State of Georgia—a small matter of income tax—but I've just engaged the best damn mouthpiece—lawyer that is

—in Washington, and we hope to get him back in circulation quick. I don't trust many people no further than I can see; but I've always said: 'Stick by *real* pals—when you're sure they're real.' That's been my motto. You never regret it, no matter what the cash expense. Take Mr. Kennedy and myself—there was a day he could have testified—No matter—he refused to 'sing,' and stuck by me, and I stuck by him."

Mr. Levine paused. The mention of loyal Mr. Kennedy recalled something else to his mind. He leaned toward Tightpants, and continued.

"Last time you were here, I think, we talked about your tuning our piano. And I remember that you said you would do it on your own time."

"Why yes," said Tightpants. "I hope there's been no trouble about that!"

"No trouble at all," said Mr. Levine, "and I was noticin' it just the other day—in the tax deductions, that is—well, you wouldn't understand. Anyhow, we're going to pay you five dollars a week extra for this tuning work from now on, startin' immediate this week——"

"Then—then I am not discharged!" gasped Tightpants.

"Who the hell said anything about you being fired?" said Mr. Levine. "Only—well—please don't get into no more fights with customers. Them fingers of yours seem to be damn strong. What a toehold you could take! What a wrist-lock you could t'row! If you weren't so damn small I'd put them strong fingers of yours to a real use—put you into a real racket—professional wrestling. Big money in it now. I've a pal who stages bouts at St. Nick's . . . No—You're too damn little. Too bad. It's a sweet, sweet racket!"

Tightpants rose. "I—I am very grateful to you, Mr. Levine, and also to Mr. Kennedy," he said.

"O. K.," said Mr. Levine. "Now go back and do your piano act. I think your singing partner will go on, with that big noise from Syracuse gone. Cheap skate too—they squawked about the tax charge on their check, and didn't leave no tip for the waiter."

Tightpants proceeded to the door, and just as he was opening it, Mr. Levine called, "By the way, what did you say was the name of this friend of yours the guy insulted?"

"Liszt—Franz Liszt," said Tightpants, turning.

"Bring him in some night for dinner and to see the show," said

Mr. Levine. "I'd like to shake his hand, and tell him personal what a loyal pal he has in you. Maybe he don't know. Took a chance of losin' your job to stand up for him! That is tops in my book! Professional song-writer, is he?"

"Ye-es. A—professional song writer," said Tightpants. "But I am afraid that I cannot bring him in."

"Why not?" said Mr. Levine.

"Well—he's—he's still back in Europe," said Tightpants.

"Too bad," said Mr. Levine. "When you write him, tell him what you did tonight. And if he comes to this country—they all do, sooner or later—bring him in for dinner. The check for food and drinks and the cover charge will be on the house."

PART TWO

VIENNA

1

TIGHTPANTS HALKA was not our piano player's baptismal name. And it most surely did not refer to the multi-colored plaid trousers he wore while performing at the Horse and Buggy. It referred to trousers that had been made of the finest pin-striped broadcloth by the most expensive tailor of his native Vienna.

The year had been 1928, and it was the year he had come to America. He was then a very young man. He had come to America to make a concert tour with the highly publicized Czech violinist, Viktor Reimalsky. The first concert was to be given in the Hall known as Carnegie, City of New York.

His real (and legal) name was Stanislaus Joseph Halka. He had been so christened and baptized by an Archbishop at a side altar in the great medieval Cathedral of St. Stephen with its five-hundred-year old South Tower, which was, and is, as much of a landmark of Vienna as the Eiffel Tower is of Paris. And the striking Hapsburg eagle was vividly pictured in bright tiles on the slanting, adjacent roof.

Even by the time he came to America, he was entitled to preface his name by the abbreviated Dr., because of his degree at the Meister-Schule of the University. One of the youngest men ever to acquire such a degree. Doctor of Music and Literature.

As the reader has already guessed, he was not then, and still was not, a striking figure. Small and frail, with a head, especially a forehead, that seemed too large for his slight body. Beneath the forehead a round, pleasant face, containing a very small nose, but below it a friendly, full mouth. There was very little chin, and what was there would have been typed "receding." His always carefully combed hair was a straw blond.

It was his teacher of pianoforte in the Vienna Conservatory of Music, Professor Herr Anton Lavar, who had first noticed his eyes, though the now dead mother had doubtless noted their unusual depth and expressiveness long before.

"I have a most talented pupil," he confided to his wife, "a student of the pianoforte who plays with his eyes as well as his hands, and a judicious use of the pedal. That means that he plays with his soul. Today we were working on a newly discovered composition by Liszt, a Piano Concerto marked *Opus Number 2 in C Minor,* and his eyes seemed to change with each change of mood in the scoring. This lad has a future. I predict he will go far."

"I hope that he goes farther than you!" replied Frau Lavar. The estimable lady had a brother who played the "traps" in the orchestra of the Karl Theater, and made double what her husband earned at the University.

"Eyes get you no kronen; that is, unless you are a courtesan!" she added.

It seemed that even in cultured Vienna there were those who evaluated Art by the dollar!

Young Stanislaus Joseph had been chosen to accompany the already known violinist to America largely on the basis of economy. Of course, talent entered into the matter, but the astute Vienna "artists' agent" did not see the necessity of spending too much for a mere accompanist to a great star. Still, the pianoforte player must be top drawer. Stanislaus Joseph had within the year graduated with highest honors at the Meister-Schule. He was especially proficient in his renditions of Bach and Liszt, the specialty of the great violinist.

The offer of five thousand kronen, about twenty-five dollars for each concert, seemed a fabulous sum to the young pianist.

And a fabulous sum to his fellow students, his teachers, and the friendly neighbors in the tenement where he lived with his elderly father.

The boy had been born, and grew up, in a seven-hundred-year-old rookery in the poorest quarter of Vienna. It was one of those ancient houses built around a central inner court—five stories reached down below its sloping, mansard roof, and housing (even in the small rooms directly beneath that roof) a beehive of poor working people.

Some fifty families were crowded there. Fathers, mothers, grandfathers and grandmothers, and dozens of small children. The very poor breed rapidly in every land. Perhaps because they have no other relaxation.

The young Stanislaus Joseph's father, however, was his only "family," and that father worked humbly in a bakery.

The father had not been without ambition. He had planned to own his own bakeshop some day, and make a specialty of *sachertorte,* a chocolate cake at the making of which he was most expert. He also possessed a minor talent of drawing, and had sketched out various signs which would be placed above this shop, like ZUCKERBÄCKER (Sugar-baker), and above it BESITZER—FRANZ JOSEF HALKA. *Besitzer* meant "sole proprietor."

Halka senior had been named, like hundreds of other children, after the great Austrian Emperor. We already know that *his* father had been the Emperor's coachman.

But all these dreams had "come to naught," as they now say in radio literary circles. An addiction to a very potent drink called *schnapps* on pay-day nights, plus the illusion that, while under this influence, he was an expert *schnapsen* player—a café card-game in which the stakes were often high—had prevented his *zuckerbäcker* ambition ever getting beyond the sign-drawing stage.

Finally, past middle age, and suddenly becoming a father, he lived in the hope that this soon motherless boy would learn the trade, and achieve this high, but seemingly mirage-like, ever-vanishing goal.

All went well about this latter ambition. Taken occasionally to the kitchen of the bakeshop where the father worked, the little lad, Stanislaus Joseph, seemed fascinated by the huge, white tile, coke-burning ovens, into which were pushed great wide, long-handled wooden slabs whereon reposed the raw tarts, Napoleons, *golatschen* (a pastry filled with jam), strudel and various other confections that made up the sugar-baker's art, and which, after the proper heat application, came out brown and golden and succulent.

And—most wonderful of all—the boy seemed to take a real joy in being permitted, one memorable day, to take the *dressiersack*—which was a small, liquid-containing canvas bag with a narrow metal cone at its bottom—and actually write in red piping-jelly "Frohliche Ostern" on some of the Easter cakes that were being made. The precision with which he did this, although having to trace each letter separately, for he was hardly old enough to spell so long a word as "Frohliche" (Happy), made the father especially proud and hopeful.

It exhibited for all to see an inheritance of the "drawing" talent of his sire. The sign above the Halka dream bakeshop of the future would be in good parental and traditional taste.

But if Halka senior only knew it, there was one alarming omen, one interest of the little lad, that he should have regarded with dire foreboding. The metal tank supplying heated water for the shop operations had an escape valve, and steam escaping from this valve made a not unpleasant whistling noise, almost—one might say—a musical noise. The lad would stand for minutes before this phenomenon, entranced by the pleasant, rhythmic sound.

But the father's interest in schnapps and the card game of schnapsen (in which he could, with proper vigor, "snap" down the cards, but seldom the winning card) was to lead to the final undoing of these high plans for the boy's future as a bakeshop proprietor.

One pay-day night, *he did win!* His opponent was unable to meet the loss in cash, and schnapsen-player Halka was obliged to accept a small accordion in lieu of a seven-hundred kronen debt.

It was the first musical instrument that had appeared in the humble two-room home. The father had tossed it in disgust into a closet—what help could it be to a potential master-baker? He intended to take it to a pawnshop the next Monday and obtain whatever numismatical equivalent would be given therefor.

But Sunday morning, the then eight-years-old Stanislaus Joseph discovered it. He found that not unlike the bakeshop steam escape valve, it made pleasant noises when compressed and expanded, and these noises could be further varied by pressing small buttons at one end. In fact, he took to it as a caged bird to the sudden discovery of wings.

That night, he slept with it clutched in his arms, and the father did not have the heart the next morning to take it away from the lad, who had never possessed many toys.

In a short week the little boy was producing real music from this accordion, playing real melodies that he had heard at school or in the church, and even trying to imitate the regimental military bands that one daily met on the Vienna streets.

Even then, the father did not realize the full measure of disaster that had befallen him—that the lad's interest in stirring puff-paste and writing on birthday cakes with red and green piping-jelly, not to mention the glorious goal of a Halka bakeshop—had completely passed into limbo. Dead as last year's snows, as Master François Villon wrote it.

So lacking was that father in true perception that he regarded this new manifestation in his son simply as a further evidence of a true artistic temperament, that would assist in the baking of a superior *sachertorte.*

Perhaps, with this creative ability, the lad would even invent some entirely new pastry that would make the name of Halka known throughout all Austria! The father himself was working on a highly secret recipe for a prune trüffle, which recipe, when perfected, he intended passing on to his son and heir.

One Saturday, the day he would sometimes take the lad to the bakery, the boy brought along the small accordion. By this time he had learned some of the old Viennese folk songs, and he sat and played them for the other men in the bakeshop kitchen, which was just back of the retail store with its counter and several small tables for customers who ate their purchases on the premises.

The proprietor, hearing the music, came back into the workroom.

Halka senior thought at first that it was to object to this perhaps interruption of work; but, instead, the proprietor asked the lad to play again and again. And now was about to be disclosed one of Life's grimmest tragedies.

For this proprietor, strangely enough, was not happy in what would have been Heaven for Halka senior, namely, the ownership of a fine and prosperous *conditorei!*

This bakeshop proprietor was a frustrated musician. And he only worked and lived for the Sunday evenings when, with three other equally frustrated friends now in "trade," the four of them met at their several homes to play chamber music together. He himself played the cello.

He asked Halka senior to stay a few minutes that day, when the shop closed.

"What do you intend doing with that fine son of yours?" he inquired.

"Why, sir," said the baker, and he was most agreeably surprised at this interest in his son, "I want him, of course, to finish his regular schooling. I, myself, only went through the fifth grade, for my father had died and I had to help support the family. I want the boy to finish his *volks-schule* and then a year at the *Gymnasium*. That is enough, and not too much education, for an honest working man. And then, by which time he will be fifteen, I have hoped that perhaps you would hire him as an apprentice, so that he can learn the baking trade from the bottom, as I did."

As the employer seemed about to interrupt, he added hastily so as to get in his full sales talk, "Oh, I know that it is most presumptuous of me, but believe me the child is already showing an inclination and talent. He has often asked to be permitted to stir the fülle for the *creme schnitten*. He even really filled some of them one day! And how he can use the *dressiersack!* He wrote the *aufschrift*—the inscription—on several of the large cakes at Easter, and did it even better than I could! I believe, please God, my son will have a great future with the *dressiersack* pourer. A very great future!"

The bakeshop owner smiled. And then he laughed. It was not a laugh of derision. It was a kindly laugh. But little Stanislaus Joseph's father was completely mystified.

"I am telling you the gospel truth," he said earnestly. "He really could write *'Frohliche Ostern'* fully, and in two colors, chocolate and giftgrien! You can ask any of the other bakers——"

The kindly owner put his hand on Halka senior's shoulder. "I'm sorry," he said. "I was not laughing at you, or at your boy's talents. I was laughing at myself. A memory, brought back by your mention of the *dressiersack* and Easter cakes.

"I also had to become a baker because *my* father wished it. He had this shop before me, as you may know. I hated it. I wanted to be something else. One Easter eve I planned to go to a Brahms concert at the Musikvereins-seel. I had the reserved admission ticket in my pocket. At the last moment I had to remain in the shop and write 'Happy Easter' on fifty large cakes, using the *dressiersack*. It was very wicked of me, maybe sacrilegious, but I was so angry I wrote 'To Hell With Easter' on each and every one of them. Then I left them to set and locked the shop. I had been left there alone.

"Some of the cakes were sent out early the next morning, before my father saw them. Some of them got put into our own windows. That was why I laughed when you mentioned the *dressiersack*. But what my father did to me—God rest his soul—was no laughing matter then! I got such a caning that I could not sit down comfortably for a month!" And the shop owner laughed again at his memory.

Halka senior could only stare.

"God in Heaven!" he said, and crossed himself.

"No," said the bakeshop owner, "I'm not going to help make an unwilling *dressiersack* wielder out of that boy of yours. He might, some night, ruin my business, as I almost ruined my poor father's! One *'Zum Teufel Mit Ostern'* on Easter cakes is enough for any one shop!

"That little lad, with your permission, Halka, is going to have the chance I did not have. My wife and I have no children, as you doubtless know. So I can't do it for my own. He is going to have the chance to be what I wanted to be—a musician."

"But—but—" sputtered Franz Josef Halka. Such a proposition stunned him. He did not know whether to be grateful or to flee. Uppermost in his mind was that retribution for his sins of Saturday night schnapps drinking and schnapsen playing had at last caught up with him.

For was not this all the result of bringing home that cursed accordion for a drinking-gambling debt?

"Go home and think it over," said the bakeshop owner. "I believe your son has talent. He played those folk songs with feeling and expression, and I take for granted that he played them entirely by ear, as we say. I know. I am a bit of a musician, though I could not really study till after my father died. I was forty years old then. My instrument is the cello, but I think we will start your lad with the pianoforte. A very fine teacher is a friend of mine. One cannot start too early. I discovered that. It will not interfere with his regular school. I will pay all the expenses of the music lessons."

✣ 2 ✣

FRANZ JOSEF HALKA did not take a tramcar home. He walked. He had to think—a form of exercise that did not get much practice. And he could think better—as many a better man can do—as he walked.

His only son a professional musician. Did he, Franz Josef Halka, know anything about musicians? No. Did he know any? No. The boy's mother, who had died two years after her only child's birth, had liked music. Could sing. She had lived in hopes of their some day having a piano, but that day never came. *Schnapps* and *schnapsen*. He had loved her, in his way. The boy looked and seemed like her, not at all like himself. He was robust and rough. The little lad was frail and gentle like. Would he be doing for the boy what he had not done for the gentle mother, if he accepted this amazing offer from his employer?

He reached the tenement without arriving at a decision, although in reaching it he had passed three churches and said a "Hail Mary" to himself as he passed each one.

He decided that he must consult one of the good parish priests of the neighborhood church.

Confessions were being heard as he entered the shadowy church. Folk were waiting in the pews to take their turns in the confessional booths along the side. Perhaps it would help to have at least a clear soul (if not a clear mind) before resolving such a lifetime matter.

So, first, Halka senior entered a booth and for the thousandth time confessed to an over-indulgence in schnapps and schnapsen playing, those being his only venial sins, along with an occasional oath taking the name of the Savior in vain when the cream puff filling was lumpy. Then he launched into the problem that was driving him out of his senses.

Should he give up all the magnificent dreams of his son's career in the making and selling of fine pastry, and permit him to transfer his youth, his undoubted and already manifest skill in the use of the *dressiersack* and piping jelly to this unknown thing called "music"?

Halka senior knew that his employer was an upright man and a good Catholic, but after all, he did not use this music as a profession. Rather he used it like schnapsen playing—a relaxation. And maybe (like schnapsen) a not entirely praiseworthy relaxation!

So Halka senior hoped, without putting the thought into so many words, that the confessing Father would advise against it on religous grounds.

Baker Halka had a vague idea that professional musicians were, as a class, unreliable—even ungodly. Vagabonds. Beggars. Religiously and economically—outlaws!

There was a strolling gypsy violinist who would appear evenings at his favorite schnapsen-playing café, who, after fiddling various wild-sounding dances, would pass around his much battered, weatherbeaten hat, and was grateful even for a single kronen.

He most certainly did not want *his* only son to grow up into something like that!

But even Heaven was against papa Halka. This particular priest was the one who played the organ and directed the choral singing of the altar boys. He seemed to have no understanding whatever of the glories of *sachertorte* baking. A prune trüffle recipe to revolutionize world trüffle-making left him unmoved. He very strongly advised a musical career, if the opportunity were offered. Even in the church itself there was a need of boys who could grow up to master the pipe organ and the arranging of religious chorals.

The die was cast. The Rubicon crossed. After his school the following Monday, the little lad came to the bakeshop, and the owner himself took the boy to the studio of the pianoforte teacher whom he knew.

✣ 3 ✣

LITTLE STANISLAUS entered into a new and wonderful world. It will be a matter of surprise to the readers of this tale, who had, as young people, hated "practicing" when forced by loving parents to "take piano lessons," that this new world was due to a piano!

The lad had never seen one, or if he had, it had had no meaning except as a piece of furniture in shop windows. At the school was a small, wheezy organ, which must be pumped with the feet. This music teacher possessed a beautiful pearl-inlaid Beckstein concert grand, a heritage from *his* father. And at this first interview he sat and played half a dozen Chopin *Sonatas,* and then one by Beethoven; more, to be sure, for his friend, the music-loving bakeshop owner, than for the prospective pupil.

But this prospective pupil, sitting there and listening, was born anew.

"Music," before this experience, had been the somewhat blatant, unshaded sounds from his small accordion. There was a strong melodic line of course, but that was all. The parish church music had been of the same order, and even when his father had taken him to the great Cathedral of St. Stephen on special fast days, and he had listened to the music of one of the world's finest organs, it had always blazoned out chords and melodies at top pitch.

But here, in this small studio room, with the framed pictures of Brahms and Mozart, and Beethoven and Handel, and Chopin and Haydn and Schumann, on the walls, was a magic box with a row of white and black keys, by the touching of which sounds could be evoked of tenderness or anger, of humility, of pride, of despair and courage. Of both ugliness and beauty.

Not that the little Stanislaus Joseph so analyzed it at that time. He only realized that it was all not the same—yet it all came from the touching of these same black and white keys! And a great, overwhelming desire swept over him to be able to do what this teacher could do, as that teacher sat before that wonder instrument.

"May I—may I try it, sir, please?" he asked with a pathetic eagerness and shyness, fearful that he was too bold, fearful that never again would come such an opportunity!

The great music teacher understood. So did the bakeshop owner. They turned a knob so as to raise the seat of the piano-bench. Then the teacher placed a thick, wide book on top, to bring the small arms parallel with the keyboard.

Stanislaus Joseph Halka was seated for the first time before a pianoforte.

The teacher took his hesitant right hand and placed the fingers on the keyboard. "Like this," he said, and with the thumb on the Middle C, the other four fingers ranged along the D, E, F, and G. "Now press down on one key at a time," he instructed.

The lad had had the practice of pressing the buttons on his small accordion. He pressed the C with his thumb, at first fearfully and hesitatingly. The sound came back—clear and gentle. Encouraged by this wonderful result, he pressed the keys, one at a time, beneath his other fingers, going up the simple scale.

"Now play it back down," said the instructor. "Go back down just as you ran them upward."

The lad did as instructed, with more confidence this time. And then, the small miracle!

He played, with the one hand, a little melody, using only those five notes. It went like this—

C, D, E, C, (a slight pause) F, E, D—(a longer pause)
F, E, D, G, (a slight pause) E, D, E—

It was the turn of the two older men to be startled. The teacher seated himself on the bench by the lad and cried, "Play that again, just as you now did!"

And putting his own skilled hands to the lower part of the keyboard, he played along with the lad; played a variegated accompaniment that made a bit of real melody ring out in the studio. For on the second repetition of the two short phrases, the lad instinctively brought it to a proper end by changing the last three notes to a final, downward progression that was E, D, C!

The teacher leaped up from the piano bench. He lifted small Stanislaus Joseph Halka to the floor. And the dignified musicians on the wall gazed down at a most undignified spectacle. Two middle-aged gentlemen seized each a hand of the lad, and joined their own hands, and went dancing about the room! The teacher and the bakeshop owner were also "wired for sound," as we would now say. They were chanting:

"Do ! Re ! Mi ! Do !—Fa ! Mi ! Re !
Fa ! Mi ! Re ! Sol !—Mi ! Re ! Mi !—"

and so on, to the end of the jingle. Little Stanislaus had to jig with them, not at all understanding this strange behavior of his elders.

"Herrlich!" cried the great teacher, *"A wunderkind!"* as they finished the second round of the room and paused for breath. "At last I have a young pupil in whom I will take an interest. A real interest! You tell me he never touched a pianoforte before! He will touch one many, many times from now on! How many lessons can he take a week?"

And so little Stanislaus Joseph Halka, son of Franz Josef Halka, baker, became a pupil of the great teacher Herr Dr. Gustav Emil Mayerhoff, who, as a very young man, had been a student of the very greatest of all the pianoforte musicians—Abbe Franz Liszt.

Stanislaus Joseph was to go to the studio each day after school for half an hour. And on Saturday mornings at ten A.M. for an entire hour.

✣ 4 ✣

THE LESSONS PROCEEDED as per schedule. They went beyond the schedule.

Sometimes the after-school lessons lasted an hour. Sometimes the Saturday ones lasted two hours. So interested did the great teacher become in the quiet, homely little fellow who literally worshiped a piano.

In a month he was playing rather complicated exercises by the great Austrian master of technique, Czerny.

(Does that name bring back to some readers, as it does to this reporter, heart-breaking hours when one was made to sit on a hard piano stool and "practice," while through the window one could see—and hear—unenslaved, free, American lads playing baseball or football! Or in the winter time, have visions of the bobsled-run down the hill at the end of North Main Street, or hear the alluring, tantalizing groaning of the ice straining against the banks of the frozen river, ice calling to feet that longed to be skate-clad, and glide majestically over that same! But feet that at that moment had to reach to press ugly pedals—and release them—at the end of each measure of this tyrant—this wrecker of childhood happiness—Czerny!)

They didn't have baseball and football—probably not even bobsleds in the Vienna of that period—but young lads did play a form of stick-ball called *fussball,* and another outdoor game named *rauber und wachter*. Our Stanislaus Joseph did not sigh for them.

Those black and white keys of his teacher's pianoforte (not to forget even the pedals) were his recreation as well as his task. He loved those keys and pedals as other lads loved their marbles and their tops.

But this matter of a piano for practice soon became a problem.

His teacher had only one piano, and he had other pupils—many pupils, in fact. The bakeshop owner volunteered to let the boy go to his home on certain days, and use the excellent baby grand installed there. But this home was in quite another section of Vienna from where the lad lived with his father, and necessitated a complicated changing of tram cars to reach.

Also, the lad often longed to practice in the evenings, after he had finished his regular school "home work."

The bakeshop owner once again asked Halka senior to come to the front of the shop after his working day.

✣ 5 ✣

HALKA SENIOR HAD BEEN GOING through a soul-tearing period. To set one's hopes on an only son becoming Vienna's greatest *zuckerbäcker*, and have that dream suddenly and completely wiped out, was something that one did not recover from in an hour. Or a day, or a week, or a month. Not to mention the prune trüffle recipe intended to revolutionize the Austrian pastry art.

That dream was ended, he realized only too well. No longer did the boy take joy in coming to the bakeshop and stirring the great kettle of puff paste. No longer did he want to take up the *dressiersack* and either with glazier or piping jelly write "Happy Birthday" or "Merry Easter" on the large chocolate or vanilla cakes called *sachertorte.*

He did not seem to want to come there at all! Just wanted to pour over books filled with rows of lines covered with black dots on stems; and he would sit before the table in the home as if before a pianoforte, raising and lowering his fingers against that table-top as if he were touching the keys of a piano.

He was still a good lad about the house work. He swept and cleaned the two rooms after his father had gone to work, and before he himself must start for school. He washed the breakfast dishes. Made up the two small beds, which were arranged like bunks. In cold weather he went out for charcoal for the small stove that heated the rooms. He emptied the ashes from this stove and carried them—and other garbage—down to the court where it was put into large cans to be collected by the Municipal Council—or so the collecting wagons said.

But—these tasks finished—he was back to the books of black lines and dots—and trying, rather pathetically, to pretend that the kitchen table was a pianoforte.

Papa Halka realized the need for a real piano, since he must apparently become reconciled to his son being a *musikant*. It was as if one was studying *sachertorte* baking without an oven.

Well—if a *musikant* was what his son was to be, he wanted that son to at least be a good one! Not like the beggar gypsy who played for kronen in the schnapsen-playing café. Or the piano player in another café he sometimes visited, who placed his hat on the top of the instrument, and seemed grateful for any pfennigs customers might condescend to leave therein!

The crying and immediate need was for a real piano in the home.

He had journeyed to the Ringstrasse and priced them in several shops. Even the smallest ones were forty thousand kronen. His entire wages for four months! He had seen one in a pawnshop window in his own *Favoriten* District, but even it was thirty-thousand kronen, and it did not look to be in very good condition.

He had gone even further. Made a sacrifice supreme. For three weeks now he had stopped going to the café for schnapps and schnapsen on pay-day evenings.

The first evening of this self-imposed curtailment of a life habit was one he would never forget. It hadn't been so terrible the first hour. The lad, studying his school books (though he saw no use in geography and mathematics, now that music had entered his young life) had suddenly looked up, realizing that something was amiss in the routine of the home. It was Saturday night, and his father was still there at eight P.M.

"You are perhaps ill, father?" he had asked.

"No, my son, I am quite well. A little tired, but well," and the father had crossed himself.

"But—but this is Saturday," said the lad. "You are not going for coffee to the café, and to meet your friends?"

This "going for coffee" had been the explanation heretofore to the boy, and to the boy's mother before him.

"No—I don't think I will go there any more," papa Halka had replied. Then he sighed heavily and forced a sickly smile.

"But why? Don't you like coffee any more?" asked the lad with a child's persistence.

"I still like coffee," said the father, "but from now on, I will spend Saturday evenings at home—with you, my son."

The lad got up from his books and came to his father's side. "I think I have the kindest father in the world," he said, and kissed the stubbled cheek, "but I will be quite all right alone, if you really wish to go to the café. After the school work, I want to study a new exercise the music master gave me today. If I had a piano to practice it on, I think I would know it by tomorrow."

The little lad did not mean to hurt. He was stating a simple fact. That was all. But he saw the pain in his father's face. He tried to explain.

"I did not mean that you ought to have one. Truly I didn't. I know that they cost thousands of kronen. And I am happy just as it is. I am happy that I can learn to play one, and maybe someday I can earn money by my playing—as my teacher earns money——"

"Hush—hush," said the father. "Listen. I have spent enough kronen in my life at the café to buy three pianos. From now on I save that money. We will have a piano as soon as I can save enough. Your dear mother, rest her soul, always wanted one. I did not understand then. I think perhaps I do now."

"That would be wonderful," said the lad, "only I do not like your missing your coffee Saturday nights at the café. I wish there could be some other way."

"That is the best way," said the father, and returned again to his stupid newspaper.

But after a month, it all seemed of no avail. A whole month of savings amounted to only four thousand kronen. At that rate it would take two years to get enough ahead to do this thing for the boy!

The fourth Saturday was the most difficult. He was by then beginning to realize the apparent hopelessness of it all. He had put the money each week in a tobacco can. That night, when the boy had finally gone to bed, he still sat by the window. People were passing on the street far below. Laughter and chatter came up to him, for it was early Fall and the window was open. He looked at the watch he always carried—the watch we know was later to belong to the boy.

Even selling that watch would not make a piano possible. He had already asked a pawn broker what he could get for it. Not much. "Too old-fashioned. That kind of watch is not sold any more. Worth only the metal it is made of. . . . Now if it were a new, Swiss watch —a stem-winder—" So spoke the pawn broker.

The people passing below were probably going to some favorite café. He could still go also. The hour was not late. And there was that money in the tobacco can.

He got up and took the tobacco can from behind the bread box. He emptied it out and counted the small banknotes. Four thousand, one hundred kronen. Utterly no good for the buying of a piano, but what a good time that amount would give him at the café!

And perhaps he would win at schnapsen. Win a lot! Enough to buy this cursed piano. At least he would not have to quit after the first few rounds. That had been the trouble before. He always had to quit before he could really get started.

And a few sharp drinks of schnapps! He needed that badly. His throat burned for it. He was entitled to it. A man could not live without some pleasure. Some relaxation.

Suddenly he stuffed the sizable wad of money into his pocket. It was mostly in hundred kronen notes. He put on his coat and hat. He looked at the lad sleeping in his upper, berth-like bed. The lad looked like the mother. He hesitated. Then he hardened his heart and tiptoed out of the rooms.

The saved money was in his pocket. His own money earned by hard labor. But he felt like a thief. A thief in his own house! He even tiptoed down the five flights of stairs. No one must hear him leaving with this money.

He hastened, almost ran, through the half-dark streets of the district given to tenements. When he reached the main thoroughfare where the café was situated, he walked. He did not want to attract attention there. That part was well lighted with not only more frequent street lights, but with the lights from the shop windows. The shop-keepers knew that it was the usual pay-day night, and were wide open to get what they could.

He reached the outside of his café. From within came laughter and voices and the sound of raucous music from a big music box—the ancestor of our modern juke box. This one had only three or four tunes which were cut on a brass cylinder which revolved against small metal pins, but it could produce plenty of so-called melody.

Just as he was about to enter, he saw the gypsy violinist coming toward the door. The man was dirty and starved looking, and he doffed his battered hat and held it out as Franz Halka was about to step into the doorway.

A beggar. A cringing, dirty beggar! That was what his little son was coming to. That was what he was saving his money for, to help make that son like this creature. No! He would put an end to it tomorrow. No more silly music lessons for the lad. No more wasting of time over crazy books of black lines and dots with stems.

The bakeshop owner was wrong. The priest was wrong. He—Franz Josef Halka—knew what was best.

And then there came before his eyes the face of the sleeping lad back in the upper berth at the tenement. And the picture of the small figure sitting at the kitchen table, trying to pretend that it was a pianoforte. Raising each finger and pressing it down, as he looked at the thin, paper-bound music-exercise book propped up against a coffee can. And he heard the gentle voice say, "I think I have the kindest father in the world."

The gypsy beggar was still waiting for a handout, and to permit a patron whom he recognized to enter first.

Franz Josef Halka did not enter. And the gypsy was startled beyond his customary "Gracia" to receive a whole hundred-kronen note in the battered hat. And to see the man who gave it to him, turn suddenly and walk very rapidly away.

Franz Josef Halka did not go directly home. He went to the great Cathedral of St. Stephen. The church where he and the sweet mother had taken the little Stanislaus to be baptised. Where he had first had dreams of the bakeshop that should belong to that son.

The massive doors were locked for the night. But a passing police officer saw a tall, strong working-man kneeling on the wide entrance steps. The man knelt there for a few moments, then arose and walked away.

And little Stanislaus Joseph did not know—or did he?—that half an hour later his father, who had come very quietly into the rooms, had reached up and kissed his forehead. He would have his piano if it took five years to save for it! Ten years! It was the little lad's happiness that would count from now on. And Halka senior slept the first untroubled sleep he had slept since the boy had started his music lessons.

It probably would not have all happened so in America, where sentiment is a thing to be concealed—to be ashamed of—and family tradition in work is unknown.

Please to remember this. This man was just a simple Austrian.

6

HEAVEN DOES SOMETIMES help those who try to help themselves. The next day was the one that the bakeshop owner sent for papa Halka.

This summons, however, was received not without some perturbation. Calm now, and fully resolved on his future course, Halka senior hoped to God there was not some change of heart about the boy's lessons! That perhaps he had not been doing well. That the lessons might be at an end.

Well, if that were so, he himself would try to take over. If not a lesson every day, there might be a lesson twice a week. He could go without the new Sunday suit he had planned to buy. He could buy a cheaper grade of meat for the nightly *kaiser-schmarrn*—the imperial stew. Maybe have meat-stew only twice a week.

And it did occur to him also that maybe his own work in the bakeshop was not satisfactory, or at least had not been the past month. He had been nervous and irritable. The mental strain he had been under, and one or two mistakes he had made as a consequence, might have been too much for the owner's patience. Like that first pay-day he had decided not to go to the café.

Reaching this decision that afternoon, after a morning of mental turmoil, he had filled a whole tray of a hundred supposed strawberry Napoleons with a lemon mixture meant for tarts. They had been baked and sent to a very special customer giving a dinner, who had boasted of the strawberry Napoleons she would have as dessert—and behold, they were not filled with strawberry at all, but with a lemon-tart filling—a flavor she detested.

And then the afternoon of the second week's payday, when he had left a small flavoring spoon in the puff paste—though fortunately that error had been discovered by a fellow worker.

He need not have worried about this interview. The owner spoke first

"Halka, I must apologize to you."

"You—apologize to me!" gasped the bakeshop worker. "I want to explain about that terrible mistake of the strawberry Napoleons. It is I who owe apologies. On that day——"

The owner interrupted. "Forget strawberry Napoleons. To hell with them! This is a matter of real importance to us both. It concerns your son. And first, as I said, I apologize for not asking you before to come to the teacher's to hear how he has progressed. It is quite amazing. Already he can play a simplified version of the beautiful *Mazurka Opus 68, Number 3* of Chopin! I could hardly believe my own ears as I listened. Or my eyes as I watched. But there is a vital need to him now. He should have——"

"I know," said papa Halka.

"You know what?" asked the shop owner.

"That he should have a pianoforte at our home, so that he can practice," said Halka.

The music patron who ran a bakery smiled. "I'm glad you agree to that," he said. "For I have been a little worried that you disapproved of the boy's interest in music. I have heard from some of the other men that you were not exactly enthusiastic——"

"I wasn't," said Halka honestly. "But it is different since last night." And he told his employer just what had happened, not sparing the enormity of what he had intended to do.

"Starting today," he continued, "I shall save every penny that I can. Maybe you will let me work over-time and Sundays, so that I can save a little more. It may take a long time, but my son shall have an instrument of his own."

"It is about that, that I have sent for you," said the other man. "My wife and I will buy your son a piano. Probably a small one. The season has not been too good to me. But I can at least manage a spinet. Your home, I take it, is not large, and a spinet style will probably fit it better than a baby grand. In fact, we have already picked one out. I want to arrange for its delivery.

"I will let you off tomorrow afternoon early. You will first come with me to the lad's lesson. Then, with your permission, we will go to your home, Number 10 Quellenstrasse, isn't it? And the spinet will be there as a surprise."

Franz Josef Halka was speechless. He could have fallen on his knees before this benefactor. But he also had an objection.

"I don't know how to thank you, sir," he said, "except to work harder for you in the bakeshop. To never again make a terrible mistake like the one about the lemon Napoleons. But I cannot accept such an offer, unless you permit me to also help. I don't know what a spinet—as you call it—costs. But I want you to take out of my wages each week twelve hundred kronen. Take it out until the cost of the instrument has been returned to you. I am very much ashamed, that, after all you have done about paying for the lessons, I, his own father, cannot buy this needed instrument."

"That is all right," said the owner. "Your wages are not large. I wish they could be more——"

"You pay the highest wages in the district," said Halka. "Everyone knows that."

"Still—they are not for luxuries. You are sure you want me to do this?"

"Very sure," said Halka.

"Very well," said his employer. "But we will settle it this way. I will take out twelve-hundred kronen a week. But only until half the cost is paid. My wife and I will meet the other half. It will then be our joint gift. You are not going to cheat me entirely out of the pleasure of seeing that lad with his own piano, and the feeling that a part of the pleasure is my doing."

It was so arranged. One week later, little Stanislaus Joseph was surprised and pleased to find his father, along with his patron, at the studio of the teacher. The father listened to his son go through his exercises. He gazed about the comfortable studio with its quaint furniture, its framed pictures on the walls.

Maybe all musicians were not café beggars! Maybe his son could some day have such a studio.

Then they all proceeded to the Halka home. They even took a cab, in celebration of a coming event. It was the first time little Stanislaus had ever ridden in a cab. When the bakeshop owner had paid the driver, they climbed the five flights of stairs and entered the Halka living quarters.

In one corner of the larger room stood a little spinet. And its bench before it. Halka had gone home that morning to receive it, after the lad had departed for school.

A happiness of childhood cannot be properly described.

One who has never made a child really happy does not know what it is to live.

Little Stanislaus was made to understand that it was the joint gift of his father and the bakeshop owner. He kissed his father. He stood before the bakeshop owner, not quite knowing what he should do in the presence of such greatness and such kindness.

The bakeshop owner knew. He held the lad close in his arms for a long moment. His life had now not been a useless one.

And the teacher too was not to be left out of this Visitation of the Magi. He took from his inner pocket a small instrument made of shiny steel. It was a wrench.

"This is my part," he said. "I now give you this tuning wrench, Stanislaus Joseph, and I will teach you how to use it. You have a good ear for pitch. Always keep your piano in pitch. Just a turn, now and then, and it will always respond to your playing with loving pride. I've often thought that pianos are human. They have souls. They know when those who use them, love them."

And that was how Stanislaus Joseph Halka, twenty years later, could propose the use of such a wrench on a small piano in a distant land.

There were only two Wise Men, instead of three, at this Visitation. One giving of his money. One of his skill. And a loving father. Maybe there was a mother there also, standing in the shadows, glad in the pleasure of her son.

Instead of a stable and a manger, it was a poor Vienna tenement, five flights up. And the Child was ten years of age. But I believe an Angel or two was hovering overhead.

Did He not say, "In as much as you have done it unto the least of one of these, you have done it unto me——"?

7

THIS IS NOT a case history of Austrian student life. And I fear that the next ten years of Stanislaus Joseph Halka would not be typical of that life, so engrossed was he in the studying of the pianoforte.

Shy and retiring, he did not make many friends. Of girls, no friends at all. He finished his regular schooling in grade schools and the Gymnasium, which would be like going through our so-called high school. Among other things, he did study French and English. This on his music teacher's advice.

"You will, perhaps, sometime play your instrument in these countries," he said. "In London—in Paris. As a young man I had employment for a season in London with an orchestra. It is a help if you know their rather dreadful language. It is not a musical language, but one has to speak it there, even in the musical profession."

The teacher did not even mention New York. New York—America—was too distant a place to enter this old-fashioned maestro's calculations. And America—he had heard—was a land devoted entirely to a thing called "jazz." He devoutly hoped no pupil of his would ever have to be exposed to it!

The boy then moved on to specialize entirely in his music at the University. The bakeshop owner and his teacher obtained a scholarship for him. He studied harmony, composition, the basic uses of other instruments so that he would understand the so-called scoring of these instruments in an orchestra.

But mainly he devoted himself to perfecting his technique as a performer on the pianoforte.

One special day of these school years stood out in his memory, but it had to do with the bakeshop, not the classroom. The lad had reached the age of fourteen. There came an evening that all the workmen of the shop went secretly back to the bakery. The next day was the twenty-fifth anniversary of the proprietor's wedding, and they planned to make and present to him a huge cake.

Stanislaus Joseph went along with his father. And he had his part in the final touches of this cake.

He took the *dressiersack* and with red liquid icing drew across its top the five lines to make music bars. Then against this he wrote some notes in a golden-colored icing—the first few notes of an old Viennese song meaning "May you live long." The German words he wrote beneath the notes were *Hoch soll er leben.*

And as the father watched the lad wield this familiar bakeshop tool, there was again the old pang of what the boy had missed by not becoming a master *zuckerbäcker!* By now he would be an expert on Napoleons, sachertorte, ginger-bread, prune trüffles, apricot tarts. Instead of that, he was still a student on the works of some men whose names were Haydn, Dvořák, Grieg, Bach. Ah well, God's will be done. At least he was not turning out to look like the Gypsy beggar player of the violin!

And then there was one Christmas Eve—or rather the afternoon of that eve. The lad had on that day brought his accordion to the shop. He sat and played some old traditional songs for his father's fellow workers, and they all sang together as they worked *Oh Wie Ist Es Kalt Geworden* and *Schnee Flocken So Weiss Sie Tanzen Am Eis.*

Both songs spoke of winter's cold and snow and ice, but the spirit of that workroom was warm with fellowship; with love and pride in a useful employment; and regard for a kind and considerate employer.

Several lines of Gingerbread Devils, just out of the great oven, were hanging on a cooling board. These were little, brown, man-like figures a foot or so in height, made up of thumb-shaped and round, joined-together, ginger cookies. The legs, for example, were two longish ovals, joined at what would be the knee. The body—a fat, round cookie. The arms, bent akimbo, were made of two more long ovals, and the head a skull-shaped morsel. Nose and mouth were white roasted almonds, and the eyes were sinister black raisins, all these having been pressed into the soft dough before it was baked. Two red sugar horns rose from the heads. And the bodies and arms and legs were well decorated with still more almonds and other nuts and bits of candied fruit.

These most edible "Devils" were supposed to go to "bad" boys on St. Nicholas's Day. But I fear they were a great favorite also with good boys. At Christmas time the Vienna bakeshops had to make hundreds of them.

Young Stanislaus Joseph looked at these hanging, grotesque little figures, and went into a fantastic, gypsy-like melody on his small accordion. The men stopped work, lined up, and did a dance to it. The proprietor came in and even joined in the dance.

"What is it you are playing?" he asked the boy. For the dance melody was strange to him.

"Why—just nothing," the young man said. "It's the melody I think the Ginger Devils would like, if they came to life and danced."

"Let me write it down," said the bakeshop owner. "My friends and I will learn it at our next meeting. It has a pleasant swing."

"You musn't tell my teacher about it," laughed Stanislaus Joseph. "He'd say it was most frivolous."

"One must be frivolous sometimes," said the bakeshop owner. "Do you ever try to write your own melodies?"

"I hope, someday, to write a symphony," said the lad most earnestly. "I hope to thereby merit all you have done for me."

Little did Stanislaus Joseph dream how the writing of *that Symphony* would be identified with music bars in icing across a bakeshop cake!

✣ 8 ✣

THE LAD WAS ALREADY HELPING about the family expenses. And helping as a result of this musical training. He played on Saturday afternoons for a voice teacher—as an accompanist—and earned two thousand kronen each week. For two vacation periods he had been a relief piano player in a small café that specialized in fine music. He now earned enough to pay for his clothes and help his father about the food and rent.

Also, to purchase the new music he was constantly needing for his studies. Phonographs with round, hard-disk records were appearing in the music shops, and he saved the money to buy an inexpensive one. It had a huge horn, and you wound it up to run for each record. But with it he was able to hear the authentic playing of some of the pianoforte masters of that day—Paderewski, Rachmaninov, Wolf-Ferrari, Rubinstein, De Pachmann.

The spinet in the home had long since been paid for—half of it by deductions from the father's weekly wages. And the lad had realized the sacrifice that father had been making. He understood why his parent no longer went to his favorite café on pay-day evenings. He realized that this café and its pleasures was, in only a slightly lesser way to the father, what his music was to him.

The boy considered himself unusually fortunate in that his daily work was also his relaxation, in that his work was also his greatest pleasure.

And in that work he had established a group of friends. A most curious group. He did not usually speak of them as intimates, because he feared that if he did, he would be regarded as perhaps a little queer—maybe even out of his head.

Stanislaus Joseph Halka felt that the great composers, whose music he studied, were his daily companions. For at the University, along with the study of their immortal compositions, he had learned about their mortal lives. For him, these mortal lives continued into the very present.

His Vienna had been *their* home. Even if they had not been born there, as he had been, their great work, the crest of their genius had flowered there. Gluck, Haydn, Mozart, Beethoven, Brahms, Czerny, Schubert, Richard Strauss. And most of them had studied in Vienna, even as he was studying.

So he might seem to be a lonely boy as he walked the ancient streets from his home to his teacher's, or to the Conservatory.

He was not alone.

Some days it was the fiery Beethoven who accompanied him, talking of his anger when the upstart Napoleon had commanded a concert, and how he—Beethoven—had refused to perform because the conqueror of Europe had dared to specify how he—*Beethoven*—should dress for the occasion!

Some days it was the gentle Mozart, speaking of a new opera he would call "The Magic Flute" and how it was so cold in his rooms (there being no money for fuel) that he and his wife had danced an hour that morning to keep warm.

Or Chopin, speaking always of his beloved Poland.

One day Franz Schubert (he had been Vienna-born) discussed the great violinist named Paganini, whom he had heard perform the night before, and regretted this wondrous talent was not devoted to a better instrument—the pianoforte. These Italians! And one day Herr Schubert was very sad, because he had no money to buy music paper, and he wanted to write down a new song running through his head before he forgot the melody.

And Franz Liszt, the glorious, explained to the lad how he believed the pianoforte could be like an entire orchestra—the melodies supported by rich, complicated harmonies.

Indeed, this boy was not alone.

He was too humble and too young to know Franz Lehar, to know Leo Fall, Emmerick Kalman—or any others of the then living great ones. But these old masters, long dead as the world called it, received him and walked with him, and seemed happy to be in his company.

Not so his father. There were no immortal Master *Zuckerbäckers* in Franz Josef Halka's memory directory. No ghost geniuses of prune trüffle fame; no great inventor of *sachertorte* to walk with him and bear him company in hours of loneliness. The good man had never heard of Master bakeshop owner *Ragueneau,* made famous by Rostand in *Cyrano de Bergerac,* or that cook whom Alexander the Great carried even into battle. And he had forgotten all about that childhood immortal (but nameless) culinary expert whose pie was filled with singing blackbirds when "set before the King."

No. He—like most of us—had to depend on living companions. On a drink and a card game to bring comradeship and conversation.

One Saturday, after their supper of *kaiser-schmarrn* and coffee and cheese, which the father had prepared, and as the boy sat at his spinet and practiced a new composition by Rudolf Friml, a young and new Bohemian composer, he glanced up at his father. He suddenly realized that his father was growing old, that there were new lines in the longish, trouble-worn face, that the shoulders were not as straight and firm beneath the rough working shirt.

The older man sat in his large chair by the window. He had read through his *Kronen Zeitung,* his favorite newspaper, which he had brought home with him. Read such matters as had interested him half a dozen times. And now he gazed out of the window with a look of utter loneliness.

He was not unhappy to be in the company of his son, but their conversations were soon exhausted because they had no great mutual interest. Try as he would, the older man could not understand most of the complicated musical exercises that seemed to delight and almost hypnotize the boy. To discuss details of their construction was quite beyond his power of brain and words. And he felt that the lad's questions about the bakeshop day, while sincere in their concern for his personal welfare, were just polite inquiries regarding the prices of hard-flour and the shortage of oranges and lemons which had to be imported from Spain for the making of certain cakes.

There was not a breathless awaiting of answers to these questions, which would denote a proper appreciation of their basic importance.

So, this Saturday pay-day evening (the lad had observed his father putting the wages in the tobacco can now kept behind some of his school books in the small bookcase), he suddenly closed his spinet cover and stood up.

"Father," he said, "change to your other suit. Put on your white shirt. We are going out."

The father forced a smile. "No, I am too tired," he replied. "I may just take a walk around the block—I don't have to change for that—and then I think I will go to bed."

"Please change to your other clothes," said the lad. "It's not for me. It's because I know you will be happier that way, where we are going."

Changing to "his other clothes" at the boy's request had always meant a Symphonic Concert at the Musikvereins-Gebaude, for which the lad was often given free seats at the University. Once or twice it had even meant free gallery seats at the Volks-Oper, or maybe the lad had bought these from money he had himself earned. Both were equally wearing on the older man.

As he had sat and listened, or pretended to listen, he could not help but think how much more pleasant it would be to be sitting in the old café—a glass of schnapps before him; fellow workingmen all around him; a promising deal of cards for schnapsen in his hands!

The clink of glasses, the snap of the cards as they hit the table, the confused talk on all sides, the music box playing loudly and blatantly—*that* was a Symphony Concert to his liking!

But having given it up for the two years of paying for the spinet, he had been afraid to return to it. Money should be saved for other things the lad would need—a larger piano like the one at his teacher's—a studio of his own when that time came—many, many things.

He was a man of pride, and he could not let the bakeshop owner go on eternally paying for the needs of a grown son. It was different when the lad was small. But now——

The boy understood his father's lack of enthusiasm—he had seen him actually fall asleep at the last Brahms concert—but he said, "Just this once more, father—please."

So Franz Josef Halka resignedly changed to his "Sunday" clothes, and father and son together went down the five flights of stairs and out into the street.

But presently the father noticed that they were not proceeding to the Opern-Ring District where the great theaters and concert halls were located. They were only going toward a busy section of the working quarter in which they lived!

The father knew well the route they were taking. He had last taken it, as we know, some years before, with a month of saved-wages in his pocket and a month of turmoil in his mind.

Half a block from a most familiar doorway, the older man tried to stop, but the lad took his arm and urged him on.

"Courage, father," he said. "We must conquer our aversions—our dislikes. And face temptation with bravery."

Did the lad have some idea of walking him past the beloved café (beloved at least in retrospect) on the way to his damn night's Concert? This thought crossed the older man's mind. Did his son now fathom his longing for the old, happy evenings, and was going to prove to him that those evenings were forgotten and no longer a lure? Most unhappy and even unkind trial! But he permitted the boy to lead him on.

Before the door of the bistro they stopped.

"Father," said the lad, "this is where you are going tonight. And every Saturday night from now on." And before the older man could speak, he had reached into his coat pocket and taken out a roll of hundred-kronen notes.

"Here is two thousand kronen," he added quickly. "I earned it last week with my playing as an accompanist, and the copying of some music for one of the University teachers who plays in an orchestra. It's high time I am doing something for you besides just helping a little about rent and food."

"But—but," stammered Halka senior, hardly daring to touch the money.

"No buts about it," said his son, and pressed the small bank notes into his father's hand. "More than a year ago I found out what you did for me. But I couldn't do anything about it till I was earning a little more money. I found out that you had given up your one evening of pleasure so that I could have the spinet. Well, now I have it—have had it these six years. And you are going to have your happy evenings again with your friends. I now go back home to *my* one pleasure—the pianoforte that your sacrifice made possible."

The older man could not think of words. He just clasped the lad tightly in his arms.

"O.K.," said the boy, with the desire of youth to hide his own sentiment. He had picked up the phrase "O.K." from an American student at the University. And as his father proceeded through the door he called, "Father—just one thing. Go easy on the schnapps, but bear down hard on the schnapsen! Good luck! I've always known I had the best father in the whole world. Show them you are also the best schnapsen player in all Vienna!"

So his son knew all, the older man thought, and he was just a little proud of how the lad had disclosed that knowledge. And the boy thought, it was all like a popular song he had played that afternoon for a voice teacher—a song from America that said—"To each—his own."

His father to the schnapsen table. He to the keys of his spinet. To each—his own!

Success at both required patience, learning, skill. And success, in both cases, was a gamble.

9

AT TWENTY-ONE, Stanislaus Joseph Halka graduated from the Conservatory and the Meister-Schule, and because of quite unusual proficiency and talent was voted the degree of Doctor. One of the youngest men ever to attain such an honor.

It came about largely because, after some six years at the head of his classes in music theory, musical form, harmony and counterpoint, he composed a Sonata of several movements for the string quartette, which the Herr Professors found to have a splendidly strict adherence to classical form and style.

It is to be doubted if it would ever be whistled on the streets of Vienna—but it pleased the powers of the Conservatory very much.

The boy's real talent (and love), however, was in playing the pianoforte. His teachers considered him the finest technician over Gluck, Schumann, Haydn, Mozart, Chopin that they had graduated in many years. He had entered several of the pianoforte classes at the age of twelve, that being the very minimum age of entrance. Before that, four years of private lessons with the great teacher who was the bakeshop owner's friend. And he spent all possible moments in improving his technique.

But in a musical center like Vienna there was a host of other excellent musicians, both young and old. Talent and a Doctor's degree were not the only attributes that could push a young man ahead in a highly competitive world.

Even in the arts, an aggressive personality, an ability as a self-salesman were important. Stanislaus Joseph was shy, not especially prepossessing in looks, and he felt that he had still much to learn. This latter unique feeling was an especial handicap.

His old, private teacher, with whom he had always kept in musical contact, understood and sensed all this, and invited the young man to make his professional start right in his already established studio as his assistant.

The boy also now played regularly for several hours in the evenings at one of the better cafés where the Strauss waltzes and grand opera selections were the musical entertainment. And he was often asked to be the special accompanist for concert singers and violin players.

One of the violinists happened to be Viktor Reimalsky, a handsome, fiery young performer who had attained publicity both as a player of his instrument and a participant in several romantic episodes with women of the titled classes. Young Stanislaus Joseph went to Prague to be the accompanist at a special concert. He participated in concerts with this artist in several Austrian cities—Salzburg—Graz—Linz.

His fees were not of much consequence, but he was gaining audience experience. And with his studio and café work in Vienna, he already, at the age of twenty-one, made twice as much as his father, who had labored forty years as a master baker. So, at long last, that father was fully reconciled to the son's choice of a trade.

There seemed no danger of the boy having to put his hat on the top of a piano in a cheap café, and cadge pennies from patronizing drinkers!

Then came the sudden offer to go to faraway America.

An American concert impresario had heard the box-office favorite Reimalsky give the Prague concert (also read his publicity), and with a not especially flattering judgment of his homeland audience taste, decided that the flamboyant personality of this violinist would "pack 'em in." At least he so informed his home office by trans-Atlantic telephone.

It was necessary to carry along an accompanist. Reimalsky recommended the shy, unobtrusive, but technically perfect Stanislaus

Halka. He could be gotten cheap, and would not want billing to distract from his own famous (and somewhat notorious) name.

But there was tumultuous debate as to the advisability of accepting this offer. The bakeshop owner, the lad's patron saint, thought it an excellent move. Especially as the initial concert was to take place in a palace called Carnegie Hall, which he had heard was a very fine building indeed, and an almost certain springboard to success.

The workers in the bakery were all for it when they learned that the young man's wage would be twenty-five American dollars a concert, which in kronen amounted to five thousand of this Austrian money standard—double what most of them could make in an entire week of ten-hour work days!

One of the men had a cousin in this New York, where this Carnegie Palace was located. He worked in a bakery on a street called York Avenue, and could advise the lad as to where to live and places to eat, at which they would have decent cooking in the Viennese, or at least the German, style.

The principal objector was his old teacher. Already prejudiced by his knowledge of the domination of "jazz" in this America, he had lately been receiving each week a magazine published in New York—a magazine to which some wag of a former pupil had entered the teacher's name for a year's subscription. It was headed *THE UP BEAT,* and beneath this title was printed the modest statement *"America's Leading Musical Authority."*

It listed weekly the "Leaders In Sheet Music," "Song Leaders On The Air," "Most Phonograph Records Sold," "On The Hit Parade This Thursday"; and nowhere could the teacher find any mention of Gluck or Bach or Schubert or Haydn! The strange sounding titles of all compositions named seemed to be in a sort of jargon, and there was a baffling familiarity in the printed first names of the composers—most of them seemed to be known as "Buddy" or "Fats" or "Bing" or "Spike" or "Hot Lips"! And the very week the lad received his American offer, the leading article in this *"America's Leading Musical Authority"* was entitled:

BOOGIE WOOGIE SWEEPING THE COUNTRY!
ALL PIANO PLAYERS TURNING
TO NEWEST SENSATION OF SHOW BIZ

Herr Professor (and "Dr.") Gustav Emil Meyerhoff had not the slightest idea what *Boogie Woogie* was, and "Show Biz" was a new term to him, but he did understand the words *piano players,* and this new form of playing with its absurd and to him alarming name, seemed to bode no good to any pianoforte performer of the classics who dared venture there. There must be "light music" of course—in Vienna there were the waltzes by Strauss and Lehar and Leo Fall—but compositions named *The Hepcat's Jamboree* and *Ash Can Serenade,* which headed all *UP BEAT* lists, could certainly not be either in the best of taste or in a proper technical style.

In one section however of the Halka acquaintanceship there was no doubt about whether to accept or reject this American offer. The neighbors of the tenement building in which Halka, father and son, lived. In which indeed the lad had been born.

They had followed the boy's career from accordion to spinet, and on through the University. The young man would still come down to the court yard of the rookery on summer evenings, and on his accordion play the Folk Songs to which the children liked to dance, while the older folk sang.

Once even, on a holiday, the spinet itself had been carried down the five flights by willing hands, and young Stanislaus Joseph had played a whole concert, as it were, of Schumann and a little known French composer named Claude Achille Debussy, and the gypsy melodies of a Czech composer named Antonin Dvořák.

So when news of this American possibility was handed from neighbor to neighbor—"Have you heard?—Franz Halka's son has been invited to give concerts in America!" it seemed that an honor of the first magnitude had come to the whole tenement.

Surely there could be no hesitancy in its acceptance! For America was a land where artists became wealthy and famous in a single week!

And something must be done beyond a mere expression of approval, a mere mention on the stairways and in the court yard, and a calling from window to window.

It was Grete Ebenstein who called the mass meeting in her ground-floor apartment that very evening.

The widow Ebenstein owned the tobacco shop on the corner, also dealing in candies, newspapers, and ten kronen tickets on certain legal (and illegal) lotteries, so she knew all residents of all ages. A hundred or so of these residents managed to crowd into her three-room flat, and she addressed them (somewhat inaccurately) as follows.

"We have all heard of the great honor that has come to the son of our respected neighbor, Franz Josef Halka, living in 5D. The fame of his son, Stanislaus Joseph, whom we have seen grow to manhood amongst us, has spread even to distant America. In one week he leaves with the well-known violinist Reimalsky to show these Americans what genius on the pianoforte can attain. It is not enough that we, who are his family, one might say, simply wish him God speed. 'God speed' butters no parsnips! We must give him a token of our respect and love, not to forget our gratitude for the many times he has given us freely of his genius right here in our court yard. What present shall we jointly purchase to honor him for this long journey?

"Don't nobody suggest anything cheap! This is a time to open our wallets and even dig into the money hidden under the mattresses and in the clothes closets. And will the gentlemen kindly refrain from dropping cigarette ashes on my clean floors."

The suggestions came rapidly. A watch. A ring. A chipdiamond-set pair of cuff links and a tie pin. Mizzi Enzell, who operated a delicatessen, gained applause by announcing that she personally was going to give the young man ten strings of *Wiener Wurstel* so that he would not by any chance go hungry on the long boat trip.

Suppose the journey was taken on a stupid English vessel, with no *Wurstel* at all aboard! She had heard that these anemic British existed mainly on buns and tea! The stomach-minded Mizzi also suggested that Herr Karl Petyrek, who drove a brewery wagon, get his employers to contribute a small keg of good Viennese *Schwechater* beer, so that the lad would not possibly perish of thirst while crossing salt water.

But amid serious and comic banter and debate, no real gift suggestion emerged as ideal.

It was pointed out that the young man did not care for jewelry. What *did* he care for? His sole interest seemed to be centered in his music—his pianoforte playing—and what could one give a pianoforte player short of a new pianoforte!

It remained for a little known, very elderly, tiny man who lived alone with his five cats in a top-floor rear room, to make the brilliant proposal.

His name was Herr Otto Woltner. It *was* known that he was a retired character-actor from the national Burg-Theater, and he existed on a small pension from that state theater.

The children knew Herr Woltner best, for on sunny mornings he would sit in the court yard and tell them fairy stories written (he said) by two men named Grimm and Hans Andersen. He would also act scenes that he said he had played in theaters, not only in Vienna, but in Berlin and London and Paris; but the children liked the fairy tales best.

A man named Shakespeare had written most of the plays, and being an Englishman he was often not a little dull and boring.

Herr Woltner's world was entirely a dream world.

So it was a matter of surprise, when there came a pause in the hubbub over the merits of a watch or an inkwell of solid gold, the main body of which was a lion rampant, while the lid would be the bust and head of Ludwig van Beethoven (Miss Hulda Brabie worked in a sort of department store where such a monstrosity was to be had) and in this pause the retired actor arose from the chair by the kitchen sink where he, because of his age, had been permitted to sit, and raised his hand.

Although small in stature, he was a unique figure in this gathering of somewhat roughly molded working-class folk. His features were of a classic mold, and his white hair was still thick and long and wavy.

His customary dress also had set him apart. In contrast to the loose fitting working blouses and baggy trousers worn by most of the men, he was always seen in a tight-fitting black coat of worsted, the edges of which were taped with a black silk binding; and his trousers were a pinstriped broadcloth, and cut tightly to his slender figure. A flowing artist's black tie completed his sartorial ensemble.

If one observed closely, the coat and trousers were quite a little threadbare, as well they might be, since he had owned and worn them daily for thirty-two years. But he always kept them in perfect repair and properly pressed, the trousers having a sharp crease and the coat lapels fitting neatly against his collar bone.

"My neighbors," he said, in the still rich voice that had carried to many a top-gallery of continental theaters, "I apologize for speaking in this gathering of comparative youth, and about a problem of youth, but I humbly think that here is a matter where my own personal experience will be of moment and value.

"I myself, as a very young man—indeed, my friends, I was young once—had an offer to go to a foreign country to play a role in a theater production. The fine English tragedian, Sir Henry Irving, had seen my performance of the Lord Chamberlain Polonius in the immortal Shakespearean tragedy of *Hamlet, Prince of Denmark.* I should explain to those of you not familiar with that work, that Polonius was an old man, such as I now am, but even as a young actor I had specialized in character roles. Right here in Vienna, in the Burg-Theater, before many of you were born, it was my privilege to create the role of the Second Weaver in that great social tragedy by Gerhart Hauptmann *The Weavers,* and the dramatic critic of *Das Neue Wiener Tagblatt* wrote of my performance, 'Truly a fine artist has arrived.' And in Budapest the next season, of my playing of the role of Captain Adolf in that masterpiece of the master August Strindberg called *The Father,* the *Budapest Times* wrote——"

Here Frau Ebenstein interrupted. Not too rudely, for she respected this elderly, genteel man who stopped at her shop each morning for his packet of economical *Egyptische* cigarettes; but she had hark-ened many times to the old actor's reciting of past glories, and this gathering was not a time for further listening.

A farewell, Godspeed gift must be decided upon for young Stanis-laus Joseph Halka. The time was going to be short. The music student was to sail (so it was reported) in one week from that day.

"Just what is it that you suggest for our gift to young Herr Dr. Halka?" she asked. "And do not please put your lighted *Egyptische* on my sink edge. It will leave a brown burn-stain."

"Yes, yes, of course," said Herr Woltner, quickly retrieving his *Egyptische.* "Of course—the farewell gift. Bear with me, if you will, while I recite a part—only a small part—of a speech I had in Sir Henry Irving's production at his Lyceum Theater, situated just off the London Strand—probably the most famous of all London temples devoted to the thespian art—a building constructed in the classic Greek——"

"But your suggestion about a farewell gift," interposed widow Ebenstein, a little more firmly this time.

Herr Woltner sighed and compromised. The haste of the modern world!

"I will cut the speech to which I refer to the bone," he said, "though to relish its full wisdom and flavor, it should be recited in its noble entirety. I must first, however, tell you it concerns a father's advice to his son, about to go abroad. Indeed, almost the first line is *'The wind sits in the shoulder of your sail.'* But the pertinent lines I refer to are as follows. *'Costly thy habit as thy purse can buy, but not expressed in fancy; rich, not gaudy; for the apparel oft proclaims the man.'* "

Herr Woltner repeated the immortal words, first in English; then in the excellent German translation he had used when playing the role in Berlin and Prague and Vienna.

Frau Ebenstein was of a quick mind. You had to have an alert intellect to sell certain policy and lottery tickets and avoid the police. She was the first to pierce the pungent meaning behind the old actor's barrage of oratory.

"Clothes! It's clothes you mean!" she cried. It was a startlingly simple suggestion, but it had the ring of genius.

"But the lad has clothes!" said Mrs. Grete Hinterhofer, who had been an ardent advocate of the Lion-Beethoven inkstand.

Chairman Ebenstein ignored this comment. She addressed the retired actor. She felt that he had something of epic stature in his mind.

"Proceed," she said. "Proceed with your idea, Herr Woltner, but please get to the point."

"Ah yes—the point—the nub—the backbone—the pith—the core," said the old actor, quoting from one of his dramatic successes, and he would have proceeded to quote further, but he caught the piercing eye of Mrs. Ebenstein. He coughed, and returned to the subject of the discussion.

"The—er—lad *has* clothes, of course. I also had 'clothes' when I first went to England for that memorable engagement. The clothes of a green goose just out of school! And when I appeared at the stage door of the Lyceum—just off the Strand—the door-tender thought me a delivery boy! Even the great Sir Henry looked me up and down and eyed me coldly, as if he must have made a mistake in engaging me. He had interviewed me in my costume, back in the dressing-room of the Royal Theater in Berlin.

"No—our Stanislaus Joseph must enter the Continent of America dressed as the Herr Doctor of Music that he is! We must not permit *him* to be mistaken for a delivery boy. For on a first entrance—if I may be so permitted to say—oft hinges mighty success or direst failure.

"What more fitting, then, but that we, his friends who have nurtured him from childhood, should see that he makes such an entrance fittingly and properly attired? I know whereof I speak. It took me a whole month to gain the respect of my fellow players in London, because of my inadequate wardrobe. *I* had been given a watch as a farewell gift by the well-meaning members of the theater company here in Vienna. I pawned it, in order to seek out the proper tailor and have some proper artist's raiment hastily constructed to my order."

"Do you mean that as a *musikant* he should wear a Band uniform like the red and blue *Bosniaken* of the Military Bands?" asked Herr Hans Hinterhofer, who worked in a slaughterhouse and was always impressed by anything red in color.

The old actor was patient. And he fully realized the climax to which his unique suggestion was climbing. He also knew his tenement neighbors to be simple folk. He therefore explained, and did not make jest of this palpably absurd but sincere inquiry.

"I refer to no uniform," he said gently, "except that it might be said to be the uniform of an artist. A gentleman artist. It is also, to use that word, the uniform of a diplomat, of a statesman, which trades might be considered a lesser form of artistry. I myself humbly but proudly wear such clothes, though my two suits are a little shabby and even repaired in unmentionable places. But they originally came from the hands of the finest tailor in Vienna, and neither age nor weather can destroy their fundamental texture or cut."

Here Herr Hinterhofer, slaughterhouse worker, showed himself to be a true gentleman. He realized how foolish had been his question about the *Bosniaken* whose gaudy costumes were on the order of Turkish Zouaves. He suddenly lifted the little actor in his strong hands and placed him high on the chair by which he stood.

"I am a thick dunce," he cried. "This, of course, is what Herr Woltner meant. And I should have known. The owner of our slaughterhouse so dresses on Sunday, only his coat is called a cutaway, sloping down from the waist into the tails behind, like—like the tails of a fine bull, if that bull had two tails," he added uncertainly, not being able for the moment to find a simile outside his profession.

It was quickly decided by a unanimous and wall-splitting "Ja!" Young Stanislaus Joseph Halka would be presented with two complete civilian suits of clothes—one coat the regular length, the other a cutaway. And an evening suit with two coats—one a tuxedo—one for the so-called white tie outfit. He already had the latter garments—

had been obliged to acquire them for his café and concert accompanist-playing, but it was believed he had bought them secondhand, after first renting them on trial.

That would not do at all for an appearance at the great Palace of Carnegie in New York. Especially as the report had already spread about the tenement that this structure was fronted in bricks of solid gold!

Ex-actor Woltner was appointed to make contact that very evening with the Halkas, and take the young man the next morning to the most famous of Vienna tailors. These three suits were to be rushed through regardless of expense. Widow Ebenstein would advance any necessary money for down payments, and the full cost being established, collection from all tenants would be made at once.

Actor Woltner was also empowered to purchase shirts, collars, ties, a proper hat (a black Homburg was the right thing, he advised) and any other necessities for a "traveling gentleman-artist." The old man visibly grew years younger at the prospect of all this pleasurable responsibility.

"The tailor we will go to is Knize of Karntnerstrasse," he said. "I stop in often to chat with him. His father made all my street clothes. And the son now makes the clothes for Franz Lehar and Leo Fall. And the clothes for all the high civilian officials of the government. Our young gentleman will indeed show America how to dress, as well as how to play the pianoforte."

Miss Hulda Brabie, of the Inner-City Departmental Stores, contributed a final, crowning suggestion. Hulda had been a little miffed at the sudden collapse of her inkwell proposal, which chagrin had not been lessened by a complete ignoring by Actor Woltner of the suggestion that these clothes could be bought ready-made from the men's furnishing department of her store, and probably, due to her connection, at a reduced cost. She arose and asked a most pertinent question.

"When Herr Stanislaus Halka gets all these fine suits—how is he going to carry them to this America? In a *rucksack* over his shoulder? Or does he maybe wear them all at once—one suit outside the other? What about a steamer-trunk and a suitcase or two? Our store is now having a sale of fine luggage——"

Her suggestion was immediately adopted. And Herr Hinterhofer—as an expert on animals, skinned and unskinned—was appointed to inspect these suitcases to be sure they were of the best leather. "There are hides and hides," he said laconically, "and some hides aren't hides at all!"

And it was indeed this kindness and faith and generosity of young Halka's humble neighbors that made for him the final decision to accept the American offer. How could he let such people down?

* * *

A week later he left the Ost-Bahnhof (East Station) by train for Bremerhaven, the German port of departure. The party included the violinist, his manager, his valet, and the American concert impresario. Stanislaus Joseph Halka was the best dressed figure of the lot.

And these finely made clothes, one suit on his person, the others in the complete shiny outfit of new, solid leather luggage, had a psychological effect on the lad.

Heretofore his everyday (and Sunday) garment had been the suits of flannel-like grey material called *Loden,* the cuffs and neck trimmed with dark green bands. The coats buttoned high, with no lapels as we understand them. The buttons of brown antler horn. And his hats (when he wore one)—shapeless, soft-brimmed head coverings, low in crown and with wilting, narrow edges. The usual garb of a University student.

Now his head was crowned with a shapely ten-thousand-kronen Homburg. His suit was a tailor's dream of absolute perfection in texture, in cut, in its form-clinging fit.

Actor Woltner had impressed upon the tailor shop that the honor and prestige of Vienna—indeed of all Europe—were at stake in its making. No prime minister would have been ashamed to wear it. The white, pleated shirt beneath was stiffly starched, as was the standing collar. The tie was of the finest black silk.

Overnight these things changed the lad to a mature manhood.

Most boys reach such a maturity because of a love affair. Preferably a tragic one. This boy's only love was his pianoforte. No woman —in the sense of a love affair—had crossed his path. Yet now—bidding goodbye to his old teacher, to his bakeshop owner patron, to his father—he felt himself no longer a boy.

He had no feeling of grandeur. It was rather a feeling of great humility that he was permitted and had the right to be encased in such garments. He must try (with God's help) to live up to their potential by a clean, unselfish devotion to the art they represented.

It was the feeling a young priest could have at his first Communion —his first Mass in the shining robes of his faith.

Do not smile at this simple, unsophisticated attitude. Remember that, like his father, he was at heart a simple Austrian.

He did not then know that these clothes, in particular the tight, well-fitting trousers, were also to give him a name that would follow him to the very end of his life.

✥10✥

HAD HERR DR. STANISLAUS JOSEPH HALKA been a little more worldly-wise, or a little older, he would have been slightly disturbed by the fact that his train ticket to Bremerhaven entitled him to ride Second Class, and that he was booked in a compartment along with the great violinist's valet.

Had the whole party traveled in this manner, it might have been considered merely a matter of economy; but since Herr Reimalsky and his manager and agent were in a private First Class compartment (the American impresario traveling alone in another), one might safely draw the conclusion that an "accompanist" was considered to be a sort of servant, and not the social or artistic equal of the violin performer.

However, in the excitement of the departure, this was not noticed. The young man's farewell delegations nearly filled the station platform, and it was probably fortunate (or unfortunate) that the carriage of the violinist was at the other far end of the long train. Jealousy might have flared then and there.

Almost the entire Halka tenement population was on hand. Most of the women and children, and some of the men, had dressed in the gay, traditional national costumes of red and black and yellow. The presence of several king-size accordions in this group, not necessarily playing the same compositions at the same time, made certain that the send-off was not a silent one.

There were a number of Stanislaus' former fellow students and several teachers from the University. And of course the bakeshop owner, his old teacher, and his father.

But the gathering was perhaps climaxed by the arrival of the dozen or so fellow workers from his father's bakery, all wearing their spotless white suits and the high, white, flaring balloon-topped, stovepipe hats of the chef's trade the world over. They arrived singing lustily *"Hoch soll er leben!"* They hoisted the young man to their shoulders and marched him around in a small circle, depositing him finally on top of a luggage truck.

There, they pushed a small accordion into his hands—he discovered it was his own—and shouted to him to play his *Gingerbread Devils Dance!* And when he, quite overcome by all this attention, haltingly did so, they locked arms in a line and performed a grotesque dance which they had carefully rehearsed. It was an instant hit with the tenement folk and the students; even the Herr Professors joined the laughter and applause. An encore was demanded and given.

And as a final tribute, the foreman of the shop drew from under his loose fitting jacket a familiar instrument. It was the shop *dressiersack!* And the foreman made a little speech.

"We give our beloved *dressiersack* to the best pianoforte-*dressiersack* wielder in all Austria! If they don't appreciate your music in America, just you show 'em how you can write *Frohliche Ostern* on a *sachertorte* cake!"

So, amid laughter and music, and dancing and cheers, the platform master's shrill whistle sounded, and the trainman's authoritative *"Alle Einsteigen!"* (All Aboard!) rang out. The young man's baggage consisting of a brand new small steamer trunk and two new suitcases (all had been duly inspected and passed by hide-expert Hans Hinterhofer, Graduate of the Municipal Slaughterhouses), had already been wheeled to the proper compartment.

And at the door of that compartment the lad had embraced his old teacher, his patron the bakeshop owner, and his father. If there were moist eyes about evenly distributed among four grown men, it can perhaps be pardoned.

And the bakeshop owner, just before the train pulled out, pressed into the lad's hands a long wallet. The name "Herr Dr. Stanislaus Joseph Halka" was engraved in gold letters along its bottom edge. "Don't open it until you are gone," his patron requested.

The wallet contained a draft on a New York bank for 500 American dollars. Four hundred—so the enclosed note stated—from the owner and his wife. One hundred from the workers in the shop. "With much love and wishes for much good fortune," it read.

So Herr Dr. Stanislaus Joseph Halka did not notice, or if he had noticed would not have much cared, that his carriage was a Second Class one, and that he was parked alongside the Reimalsky valet, who was a nice fellow.

Ten cars ahead, the violinist said to his Viennese manager, "What's all the disgusting noise and hubbub back there along the platform?"

"Some cheap politician going somewhere to make a speech," replied the manager. "A filthy rabble!" And he added, "I hope that fool accompanist is on the train. I gave him his ticket yesterday, and explained to him fully about the trip. I told your valet to look out for him. We change cars at Berlin."

PART THREE

LA MER

1

THE SHIP AT BREMERHAVEN was the great *Europa,* pride of the pre-war German *Norddeutscher Lloyd.* The violinist and his manager were quartered in a suite de luxe on the upper deck. The American impresario had his own suite. Dr. Stanislaus Joseph Halka, with the valet, occupied a small, two-bunk cabin in the Second Class.

But not for long.

The Three Goddesses of Fate—Clotho, Lachesis, and Atropos—whom the Greeks and Romans believed controlled all destinies, perhaps sometimes like to have their little jest. Or maybe Almighty God just sometimes becomes a little annoyed at pomposity and the "merit the unworthy takes"—the *contumely* also mentioned by Master Shakespeare, meaning *insulting rudeness*—and bothers Himself to take a hand, even in a matter of minor moment.

The Three Fates (or Almighty God), in whichever you believe, must use an earthly instrument to carry out their earth plans. In this instance they used Professor Herr Anton Lavar, teacher of the pianoforte at the Vienna Conservatory of Music, the gentleman who had first noted that young Stanislaus Joseph "played with his eyes as well as his hands and a judicious use of the pedal." The gentleman with a wife who had retorted, "Eyes get you no kronen; that is, unless you are a courtesan."

Professor Lavar had had a roommate when *he* was a humble student of music at the Conservatory. That roommate was now, thirty years later, Kommodore Hugo Frederick von Steinburg, commanding officer of the liner *Europa*.

And on the morning of the sailing of that "luxury liner" (we quote the novel phrase from the Imperial Line's travel-office "brochure"), in the mail stacked by his personal steward on his Kommodore's cabin desk, was a letter from Herr Professor Lavar.

The Kommodore did not get to the reading of his mail until his ship was well out into the North Sea. He was on the high bridge with the First Officer, the captain of the guiding tugs, and the harbor pilot, personally sending the signals to the engineers far below decks in the bowels of the mighty floating structure; for in his hands was the departure safety of two thousand passengers and a crew of nine hundred souls.

But when the great vessel was at last free of the bug-like tugs; when the harbor pilot had left by his ladder, down over the side, and puffed back to Bremenhaven in his small launch; Kommodore Hugo Frederick turned over the bridge to his First Officer and proceeded to his cabin quarters.

First he took off his gold braided cap, and his stiff, padded coat (which were immediately taken by his personal steward), and settled in his chair before the small mahogany desk, in the small room which might be considered his "office."

This ship commander's suite had an unusual layout, and some unusual furnishings and decorations.

To begin with, it consisted of three rooms—this office; a large parlor (one might say); and a bed room. There was also a small kitchen, and the usual bath facilities. Even the office room, in which ship's business was conducted, had rich furnishings. And along with its wall-photographs of ships, and other more or less maritime subjects, was a small, framed Master's License—his first command, which had been a small freighter. Beside it—these two were directly behind his desk—was the diploma of his graduation from the Vienna Conservatory of Music.

But it was the adjoining parlor that was utterly unique—unique for a man of the sea lanes. It was the parlor of an art collector and musician.

On its walls were pictured scenes from great Operas. There were fine prints in color of Beethoven and Chopin, and framed autographed photographs of Caruso, Mary Garden, Rachmaninov, Chaliapin, Paderewski, Franz Lehar, Stanislavsky, Otis Skinner, Max Reinhardt, David Belasco. There was a striking van Gogh, a Renoir, and a priceless Whistler. One wall was completely hidden by a tapestry—almost as valuable as any in the Louvre.

The furniture was from an Italian castle, and the wide, high bookcase contained volumes in German, French and English, and they were obviously volumes that were read by their owner—not just decorations in fine bindings. Shakespeare, Anatole France, Guy de Maupassant, Kipling, Ibsen, J. M. Synge, Hauptmann, Victor Hugo, Baudelaire, Francois Villon, Miguel de Cervantes, Mark Twain, O. Henry, Conan Doyle were some of the names on title bindings.

And with all these—two crossed fencing foils with their screened masks; a set of much used American boxing gloves; a signed photograph of Jack Dempsey saying, "I'd sure need to be in training if I climbed into a ring with you, my pal"; and an enlarged photograph of the racehorse Man of War.

But the most unexpected items in this sea-going parlor were two great concert grand pianos, completely filling one end with their long, curved, high polished casings. They were set parallel, the open keyboards facing each other—an indication that they were used for the playing of duets. One was a *Büttner,* and the other a beautiful *Bösendorfer.*

And there was always music on the stands of both instruments—it might be a book of Chopin *Sonatas*—a composition by Rimsky-Korsakoff—a song by Franz Peter Schubert. Sometimes the piano score of the newest operetta.

A man of the sea, a worshiper of Neptune, who also was concerned with the Art of the Muses, the Art of Self-Defence, the breeding of fine horses, a knowledge of literature and painting.

Being seated at his desk in the "office" room (his chair was upholstered in the finest of tooled leather), the Herr Kommodore first crushed the burning end of his cigarette in an ash tray that came from a palace in Venice, then reached in the top drawer and lovingly took out a very old, years-stained meerschaum pipe. On the bridge he smoked the long cigarettes, which were especially made for him by a noted tobacco shop in Bond Street, London, and which he carried in an ample gold case. But the somewhat battered meerschaum pipe was his cabin mistress.

He reached for his tobacco—it was mixed especially to his order in Berlin and was in a jar of Ming china—crushed the fragrant particles into the ample bowl, lit it with a long-stemmed Swan Vesta match, which matches in their long, flat boxes also came from London. And having taken three lung-filling, soul-satisfying puffs, he tackled the sizable pile of letters.

It was his custom to glance at their exteriors before commencing the task of opening them, his clerk-secretary standing by to slit open and remove the contents of the "business" envelopes. Any personal mail—a letter from his country estate manager in Bavaria—from the trainer of his steeplechase stable then running at Longchamps near Paris—other letters in feminine hands from attractive female passengers who had sat at his Captain's Table during former crossings, he opened himself.

But the letters were mostly "business." Communications from the Head Office at Hamburg. An analysis from an Oil Company. A statement from his broker in Berlin. A dozen others of minor importance. Three were obviously from ladies—ladies who had been flattered by his attentions—two he recognized immediately—the handwriting of an American prima donna, and that of the flirtatious wife of an English diplomat stationed at the British Consulate in New York.

He was giving himself the pleasure of trying to guess who the third letter was from—a French marchioness, or a buyer for a great Paris dress maker (both ladies having excellent figures, and both letters postmarked *Paris*) when his glance fell on the next enveloped communication.

The address was in longhand, not typed, but it did not show the orderly, delicate penmanship of a lady. It possessed a quite masculine swing and carelessness. In the upper corner of the envelope was an imprint *Vienna Conservatory of Music.* And above this, in the same handwriting as the address, the abbreviated title *Prof.,* and following it, the initials *A. L.*

The not unpleasurable vision of the two ladies of Paris was instantly blotted out from the Kommodore's mental speculation. Blotted out completely, as a matter of small consequence. For Kommodore Hugo Frederick von Steinburg knew that masculine handwriting well, although he had not seen it for ten years or more. Even if he had not known it, the *Prof. A. L.* in the upper corner would have informed him.

Informed him and given him a warm glow, a softening of the keen eyes, a tingle of pleasurable anticipation that ran over his entire sturdy body.

"Anton! Anton!" he said half aloud, "Dear blessed old Anton!"

Sometimes there is a friendship between two men that transcends all other forms of human relationship. For it is devoid of the jealousy, of the possessive selfishness that is almost surely bound to exist in a relationship between the sexes. More often than not it has started during school days when two lads have shared the same room, the same food, sometimes the same clothes (as far as the then important matter of neckties is concerned) and the same pocket money, when one's allowance from home did not arrive promptly. A pure, unselfish, shining devotion that years cannot dull. That no competition, no personal gain—or loss—can destroy. A friendship of the purest gold.

The friendship between Anton Lavar, son of a humble music teacher, and Hugo von Steinburg, second son of a noble and wealthy house, was such a friendship.

And it had been tested by the most acid of trials. They had both fallen in love with the same young girl.

Anton had won her. Perhaps she had been a little fearful of the constancy of the tall, dashing Hugo, though fascinated by his charm and daring. Perhaps a form of mother love drew her to the smaller, somewhat negative Anton who seemed to worship her. I do not know what motives work to make up a maiden's mind.

At any rate, it was Anton who walked with her to the altar (his necktie being out of Hugo's drawer), while Hugo stood loyally and bravely by as "best man."

And Hugo, much to his noble father's relief, had given up his music career, and gone to sea as a Lieutenant on a ship of the great German line in which his family were heavy stockholders. Turned to his other love—the sea—a love in the blood of his ancestors for untold centuries.

The hurt of losing the girl had soon vanished. There were too many good looking *Fräuleins* in every port! The hurt of giving up his music was solaced by the fact that he did not give it up. He only gave up the violin, in which he had majored at the Conservatory. He kept up his playing (and love) of the pianoforte, on which he was still a skillful amateur.

There was one curious result, however, of his divorce from professional musicianship. He acquired an antipathy for the violin. And for violin players.

So plan the Fates—or Almighty God!

This was the letter that Kommodore Hugo Frederick von Steinburg opened and read—a letter in the same rather large and somewhat careless handwriting (t's not always crossed or i's dotted) as the address on the envelope.

My Dear Old Friend,

You will be surprised to hear from me after all these long years. But you have been often in my thoughts, and Alma and I have followed your career with pride and affection. I know, of course, that you are now the Kommodore of the new liner *Europa,* and I suppose I should vision you in your gold braided cap and uniform, standing on the great high bridge of your mighty ship (its pictures and yours were in all the papers at the launching), looking seaward through binoculars, or issuing stern orders to your officers —maybe orders even to the ocean waves far below! But, my dear old comrade, I do not see you that way at all.

I see you on the *Ringelspiel*—the Carousel they now call it—in the Prater, the day you insisted on standing astride two of the plunging wooden horses, and somehow managed to hold your footing, while the owner almost wept tears of terror that you would be hurt and he be sued for damages! I see you that same day taking the place of the Spieler on the Dwarf-Side-Show platform and shouting his lingo as you clanged his attention-attracting bell —"Come on everybody! See the Father Dwarf! The Mother Dwarf! All the little Kiddie Dwarfs! Me? I am the Kiddie Dwarf who fooled them! Maybe Mama Dwarf had a boy friend!"

Or I see us at the Ringstrasse Cafe—you always had to pay the bill at *that* expensive place—and you always could win the contest as to who could drink the largest stein of beer at one breath! I fear, my friend, that you do not practice such antics on the bridge of the liner *Europa!*

And do you remember the night we went and sang a certain song under the window of the Herr Dr. chemistry professor (a man we both loathed because of his classes—poor worthy, innocent gentleman!). You wrote the words of that song—words not, as I recall, complimentary to either the noble science of chemistry or to its teachers—I composed the so-called music —and we were both suspended for six weeks! Your parents in distant Berlin did not know about the suspension; but mine—in Salzburg! Alas—it came nearly being the end of my student career. The only thing that saved me was that you wrote them and took all the blame, which was not true at all. I hated those terrible chemical formulae and bad smelling test-tubes quite as much as you did!

But enough of our youth. Sometimes it just seems yesterday. Sometimes—

long, long ago. The reason for this letter is that there is booked on this voyage of your *Europa* a young man who graduated only last year from mine and other classes; a young man whose skill at the pianoforte is the most promising I have known in my many years of teaching. He is on his way to America for a concert tour as the accompanist of a violinist (please, dear friend, do not let that prejudice you) for the boy is only twenty-one, and must start at the bottom of the ladder. The violinist, named Viktor Reimalsky, is, in my opinion, second-rate, but he has achieved much popularity and publicity, and perhaps that is what America wants.

The lad is not second-rate. He already has his Doctor's degree. But he is a rather timid soul, not so very attractive in appearance; but seat him at the keyboard of a pianoforte and you forget all else about him. He came from very humble parents, but I well know your great, democratic heart. In Art you will find him a nobleman. If you still have your two pianos—as I know you had on former vessels—permit him to play with you the Mozart *Sonata in D Major*. Or Debussy's *En Blanc et Noir*. Have him play Beethoven's *E Flat Sonata, Op. 31 No. 3,* or parts of Schumann's *Carnival*. Have him play all of it! And almost any other piece of classic worth. For if you still love fine music and fine, sensitive performance (and my heart tells me that you do), you can have eight days of real joy on this voyage. You have of course a ship's orchestra aboard, but I can imagine they are more proficient in modern dance music than the pieces you and I so loved.

The boy's name is Stanislaus Joseph Halka. He is a native of Vienna. He is a Doctor of Music. Do not let his modesty throw you off. He will tell you he is only a beginner. I hope he doesn't talk that way in New York, where I understand self-praise is very important. I love the lad as a fine, unselfish soul and a true artist. He knows nothing of this letter or our friendship. I have kept it as a surprise for him. In fact, I only learned yesterday that he would sail aboard your vessel, and I hope that this letter reaches you in time.

My friend, my dear dear friend, come to see us when you have a vacation. How I long to clasp your hand in mine. And yes—watch you down a huge stein at one breath! I won't make you try the merry-go-round trick, that I promise.

My love,

Anton

P. S. Alma also sends her love. I have always believed that she really cared more for you than for me. But I also believe that you really were the victor. So do not be depressed if you think of her. I love Alma—we will go to the grave hand in hand—but I would not wish any other living man the misfortune of being her husband! Much less you, my dear dear friend.

A.

Kommodore Hugo Frederick von Steinburg looked up at his waiting clerk-secretary. He pushed his mail aside.

"The letters can wait," he said. "There is a passenger aboard by the name of Stanislaus Joseph Halka—*Doctor* Stanislaus Joseph Halka," he corrected. "Find him. Give him my compliments and bring him at once, here, to my cabin."

2

Herr Kommodore von Steinburg did not return to his business mail. He did open a telegram from the Weather Bureau headquarters which informed him of normal conditions of sea and air for the next week ahead. He had also a most competent First Officer who had been his aide for years—was in fact the First Mate on that freighter that was the Kommodore's first command.

He took up again the letter from Professor Anton Lavar. And his mind went back to Vienna—the home of his mother, who had been the daughter of the Count von Hagensteil.

He saw two lads in student *Loden* bent over text books of Harmony and Counterpoint, in a small room of a *Meister-Schule* dormitory. He heard Anton say: "Hugo, do you think that some day we will master all this? And I'll have to ask you for a loan of a hundred kronen. I'll confess to you, I've just met a beautiful girl and I'm taking her tonight to a new operetta called *The Merry Widow* at the *Theater an der Wien.* That is, if you can loan me the ticket money. They say it looks like a success. My allowance hasn't yet arrived."

The Herr Kommodore arose from his desk, moved into his parlor and seated himself at the Bösendorfer concert grand. He placed Anton's letter on the music rack before him. He ran strong fingers (fingers equally strong in the gripping of a fencing foil, or on the reins of a steeple chase jumper, or within the confines of a pair of American boxing gloves) up and down the ivory keys, then plunged suddenly into the middle of a *Rhapsody* written by the god of all pianoforte players—Franz Liszt.

And he again heard Anton's voice—"Too loud—*too loud,* my friend! Go easy on the pedals."

But Hugo Frederick von Steinburg tossed delicate shading to the

North Sea winds. This was not a moment for *pianissimo*. It was a moment of exaltation and great joy!

His clerk-steward was standing in the doorway as he finished. This steward knew better than to interrupt when their Kommodore sat at the Bösendorfer. He held in his hand the typed, alphabetically arranged list of the First Class passengers, which he had obtained from the Purser.

"Your pardon, Herr Kommodore," he said, "but there is no such passenger as Dr. Stanislaus Joseph Halka aboard. Here is the Purser's own final list."

The steward was right. There was a whole page of H's, but nowhere the name of Halka. And no name at all like it, in case there had been a mistake in spelling. The steward spoke again.

"Your pardon, Herr Kommodore, but perhaps this gentleman is traveling in the Second Class, or maybe in the Tourist's Class."

"Impossible," replied the Kommodore. "I have here a letter from an old friend—"

"Permit me to recall to you, Herr Kommodore, that three voyages ago we located the Herr Dr. Engelhart the scientist, whom you wished to meet, in the Tourist Class. He was traveling with some of his pupils——"

Kommodore von Steinburg walked rapidly to his desk in the office room. He took up the ship communication telephone and pressed the button connecting him with the Purser.

"Kommodore von Steinburg speaking," he said. "Look immediately on the Second Class and Tourist Class lists for a passenger by the name of Dr. Stanislaus Joseph Halka. I will hold the wire. It is important."

The answer came quickly. It was the Purser himself who now spoke, not the clerk who had answered the telephone.

"Yes, Herr Kommodore. There is a passenger listed as S. J. Halka. Perhaps that is the person you mean. He has a cabin down in F Deck, Second Class, with another passenger listed as Franz Rodar, who is described as the man servant of Herr Viktor Reimalsky, who occupies the Blue Suite on Deck A, First Class. This cabin companion of Herr Halka is also listed in the First Class with his employer. Under the R's. 'Viktor Reimalsky and man servant.' "

"Hold the wire," said Kommodore von Steinburg. He returned to the Bösendorfer and took up the letter from Professor Anton Lavar.

He checked the name of the violinist in the letter, the violinist "second-rate," as his friend Anton had described him, the violinist for whom Dr. Stanislaus Joseph Halka was the accompanist.

Kommodore von Steinburg's eyes became suddenly very hard. The strong jaw tightened. "The swine—the filthy, cheap swine!" he said as he moved back to his desk telephone.

"Kommodore von Steinburg," he again announced. "Is there a vacancy in any of the First Class cabins?"

"Only the Bismarck Suite on the Promenade Deck just below you," came the reply. "It had been taken by the wealthy American gentleman Herman Frick and Mrs. Frick, but we had a last minute telegram that he was detained in Berlin. I am going to move the American motion picture star, Gloria Alta, and her husband to that suite, as they are unhappy about their small quarters, so their former cabin will be free——"

The Herr Kommodore interrupted. "The Bismarck Suite is already taken. Dr. Stanislaus Joseph Halka of Vienna will occupy it. He will be moved there at once."

"But I have already promised Miss Alta——"

"You will have to tell the lady that you did not know that suite had already been taken over by me," said the Kommodore with emphatic finality. "And be certain that on your *List of Passengers* booklet Dr. Stanislaus Joseph Halka is named, under his full name and title—have you got that? No 'S. J. Halka'——"

The Purser swallowed. He had one more worry—and he did not like to give up the idea of accommodating the beautiful Gloria, and the prospect of a sizable gratuity therefor. He spoke again.

"You know, Herr Kommodore, that Herr Halka is in a hundred and twenty dollar cabin—do you think he can afford the Bismarck Suite? Its price is twenty-four hundred American dollars."

Kommodore Hugo Frederick von Steinburg was rapidly losing his patience. "Herr Purser," he said, "who asked about the price of the suite! Charge it to me. Charge it to the Norddeutscher Lloyd! And make no mistake about that name—the full name and the title of Doctor. By the way, there is a Steinway concert-grand pianoforte in the parlor of that Suite, is there not?"

"Yes, Herr Kommodore. It was put there for Herr Sergei Vasilevich Rachmaninov. I had intended to have it put back in the small music room off the lounge——"

"See that it remains in the Bismarck Suite," said Kommodore von Steinburg—and again—"Make no mistake about that name on the printed lists—*Dr. Stanislaus Joseph Halka.*"

"Yes, Herr Kommodore," said the Purser, and the sharp click of his instrument indicated that his captain had hung up with a bang.

"God!" he said to his assistant. "What's hit the Old Man! He's sure good and sore about something. Glad it hasn't been my fault! Twenty-four hundred American dollars! Well—I guess he has it all right."

Back in the Herr Kommodore's office, that gentleman turned to his clerk. "You heard my conversation," he said. "Go immediately to the Second Class—you know the cabin—and bring Dr. Halka to me. Take my steward with you—move all Dr. Halka's baggage to the Bismarck Suite. The man servant who also occupies that cabin can doubtless help. You and the man servant attend to all that. I will explain to Dr. Halka whom I wish to see at once."

The Kommodore whirled and strode to his Bösendorfer. He seated himself and hit the keys with several thunderous chords. Then he played with great vigor Herr Wagner's *Ride of the Valkyrie,* which immortal scene was pictured in fresco on one of his parlor walls.

"The swine—the filthy, cheap swine!" he repeated. And then, "Of course—a violin player."

I believe that the Three Fates—*and* Almighty God—were having a quiet chuckle on their respective cloud thrones.

There was one more incident of a somewhat humorous character. The Purser felt he had better show the Herr Kommodore the exact spelling of the name of this "Second Class" Halka person (who seemed to be of such importance), and at the same time he could submit the names of the some twelve passengers selected to sit at his dinner table in the Main Dining Saloon. This latter was an honor much sought after.

The Purser arrived as the Valkyrie Maidens were arriving at the great Hall of Wotan in Valhalla. Kommodore von Steinburg slammed down the lid of his pianoforte keyboard and turned.

"Well, what now, Herr Purser?" he asked in no friendly voice.

"Your pardon, Herr Kommodore, but I wish to make sure that I spell the two Christian names of Herr Dr. Halka correctly," the Purser said.

The Kommodore took the proffered typed sheet and inspected it. "Correct," he said. And handed back the paper.

"I also have made up your dinner table list," said the Purser. "I hope it meets with your approval. There are several very distinguished personages aboard. His Excellency Mohammed Abu Bey; the Marchioness Agnes Di Villarey; The Right Honorable The Earl of Worcester and his Countess; the American Ambassador to Berlin and Mrs. Gerard; the American picture star Gloria Alta whom I mentioned before; Miss Margaret Parish the American chain-store heiress; Sir Godfrey Landray the British explorer; Wilfred Hilton the playwright; Herr Viktor Reimalsky the violinist——"

The Herr Kommodore again interrupted. "Eliminate Herr Viktor —No." A grim smile crossed his strong features. "Eliminate some one of the list, but not Herr Reimalsky the violinist. For I wished placed at my right, Herr Dr. Stanislaus Joseph Halka of the Bismarck Suite. Make no mistake about these two. Put Herr Viktor Reimalsky directly across the table. The arrangement of the others I leave to you.

"As you say, I will have most interesting table companions on this voyage."

The Kommodore sat himself at his desk, and took up his "business" mail. Just as he finished with it, his clerk-steward arrived with a mystified (and somewhat frightened) Herr Dr. Stanislaus Joseph Halka.

3

Herr Viktor Reimalsky, violinist "second-rate," had a partial warning of the eight-day period of deflation directly ahead of him. Franz Rodar, his valet, reporting to dress that gentleman for dinner, also reported the amazing circumstance that he had just completed the removal of accompanist S. J. Halka to a grand suite just below the Captain's quarters, apparently on orders from the Captain himself.

He also disclosed the credible fact (credible to the character of S. J. Halka but not so to the mind of Herr Viktor Reimalsky) that the accompanist had strongly insisted that the valet also be moved to share these new quarters.

"I declined with thanks—I hope I know my station," said the humble Franz Rodar.

"I hope you continue to know it," snapped Herr Reimalsky, "and this collar button is not the one for my tuxedo shirts. Will you ever learn, *dummkopf!*"

The violinist was boiling within. And unable to find further fault with Mr. Rodar, he turned on his innocent manager as the basic cause of all calamities. His language to that unhappy gentleman cannot be recorded. "Moreover, with such a beginning, where would they be in this uncivilized America where he had heard all men were considered free and equal? Free and equal, undoubtedly, to insult their betters." The reminder by this manager, that this S. J. Halka had been the violinist's own selection, did not help matters at all. "The manager should not have selected a ship commanded by a nitwit who apparently had some underground connection with lousy accompanists."

A notation regarding valet Franz Rodar.

He also had heard that in America all men were considered "free and equal." It seemed unbelievable, but he had heard it from his sister who had emigrated with her husband to a State named *Kansas* where they now owned a farm near a town named *Wichita*. And that sister only a waitress in a cheap Vienna restaurant!

Mr. Rodar had ascertained that the Reimalsky tour played this *Wichita*. He was holding his peace (and his station) until their arrival there. Then, in a speech which he was privately rehearsing, he intended to inform Herr Viktor Reimalsky of his resignation, to take immediate effect, and of his opinion of the said Viktor Reimalsky.

He was making a list of German and Bohemian adjectives he would use. I regret that these also cannot be recorded.

To return to the *Norddeutscher Lloyd* luxury liner, *Europa*.

The Kommodore and his new friend were a little late arriving at the dinner table. And I fear that on that first afternoon out, the navigation of the ship had been pretty much in the hands of the First Officer.

After a long chat about Vienna and the University, and a lunch in the Kommodore's cabin, the lad sat at one of the concert-grands and played for his host the Chopin *Ballade in F Minor*—the one that starts so sadly and builds to a great, exciting climax. The Kommodore had a *Toccata* by the Russian Prokofieff, which he had had difficulty in performing, and Stanislaus Joseph, after ten minutes of study, played it at sight. And finally, they tried several duets—the lad at the Büttner and the Kommodore at the Bösendorfer. A Mozart *Sonata in D Major;* Debussy's *En Blanc et Noir;* some Latin works entirely new to the lad—the Argentine one called *Guastavino,* a Brazilian one called *Nepomuceno.*

An afternoon to be long remembered.

At four, the Kommodore reluctantly left the pianos and went to the bridge. He suggested that Stanislaus Joseph rest on the couch for a while—or did he wish to also go up to the bridge? The young man —a very thrilled and excited young man by now—chose to go to the bridge.

Stanislaus Joseph understood little of the shiny brass instruments and their clock-like dials, even with the Kommodore's non-technical explanations, but he understood the great power that they controlled, the power that thrust this huge floating hotel through deep waters far below. A power and magic that in its way were not unlike the power and magic of great music.

Both existed in God's universe, waiting to be discovered, to be regimented, to be directed by some frail human mind and hand that would elevate that mind and hand to almost divine omnipotence.

No such power in music? There was an obscure Colonel, one Rouget de Lisle, who reached out, who set down for human minds a Hymn named *March of the Marseillaise*. It had its effect, so I am told, on world destiny. Perhaps even a greater effect than an engine named Diesel.

Presently they moved outside, and stood for a long while on the narrow, open platform of bridge that extended in each direction from the portion that enclosed the instruments of navigation. They were both silent now.

I know not the thoughts of the older man. I think they were still back at student days in Vienna, and if he looked at the lad beside him he saw Anton Lavar, who had not been unlike this boy in figure and face. The Anton so different from himself, but whom he loved as he had loved no other man—or woman.

The young man, high there between the sea and the sky—and it seemed to him that he was nearer to the sky than to the sea—gazed in complete fascination at the distant horizon, where the sky met the sea in a huge circle that undulated slightly with the movement of the waters.

And the lad thought: "God has been good to me, quite beyond my poor talents, my poor deserts. Help me, God, to give something of worth to Your great world; to repay the trust and faith of fellow men; never to falter in the high ideals that in Your mercy You have placed in my heart and mind."

So Youth must dream—if the disillusionment of Age is not to mummify the world.

He was not to forget that stretch of open bridge. He would shortly hear a strange tale that concerned it, and he would, one other day, hear a stranger one.

The tall man of late forties spoke at last.

"Anton," he said, "we must now go to change for dinner. Your baggage has been removed to your new quarters, which are just below mine, on A Deck. My steward will show you. Return to my quarters at six-thirty. You sit at my table in the dining saloon."

Did he realize he had called the lad *Anton?* I do not think so, for he made no correction in his statement.

And that is why I believe the thoughts of Kommodore Hugo Frederick von Steinburg were not on sea and sky, but deep in an ancient Austrian city, far inland.

✣ 4 ✣

IT WAS NOT the fault of Dr. Stanislaus Joseph Halka that he and the Kommodore were late for the first saloon dinner at the Captain's Table.

The young man returned promptly at six-thirty to the Herr Kommodore's quarters. And he sent a fervent mental message of thanks to the kind neighbors back in Vienna who had provided him with a faultlessly made Tuxedo—the garment the Kommodore's steward had advised him to wear. For not being a frequenter of Captain's luxury-liner tables, he was not sure how he should dress.

Valet Franz Rodar could have advised him, but, as we know, that expert on a gentleman's dress was at that moment occupied elsewhere, with the finding of the proper collar button for his employer's exalted shirt.

While the young man was happy and even proud of his well-fitting raiment, he was not enthused about the Bismarck Suite. Curiously enough, he would have been happier back in the two-bunk cabin.

The lavish furnishings, the silks and satins of the bedroom, the heavy, deep rugs, the rose damask drapes of his "parlor," along with the inlaid paneling of its walls, were just a little frightening. After all, he considered himself only a simple working artist, who had as yet done nothing to merit the reward of luxury.

He was not sure that he ever wanted *that* form of reward! His "friends" in artistry, Mozart, Franz Schubert, even Beethoven, had never wanted it—had even scorned it. Could it be that a desire for ostentation and show had been completely omitted from young Stanislaus Joseph's makeup? Omitted along with the high objective of acquiring (no matter in what manner) what was presently to be called a "fast buck"? Omissions *fatale* in a world pretty much given over to a fighting for and the gaining of such prizes. Undoubtedly it would work against his ultimate success. But he was not old enough or experienced enough to realize the vital importance of these matters. Still a simple baker's son. Poor lad!

He was old enough and understanding enough, however, to appreciate the kindly thought and intent of his new friend the great Kommodore, and he did like the Steinway concert grand, though fearful of putting fingers to keys that had responded to the touch of Sergei Vasilevich Rachmaninov. The Kommodore's steward had not failed to tell him of this great former occupant of the Suite.

So he arrived back in the Kommodore's quarters on the minute. But the Herr Kommodore was still dressing, having stopped in the very middle of his toilet (clad only in undergarments and shirt, leaving the personal steward standing and holding the ready dinner trousers) while he strode to the Bösendorfer and went over a passage in the Mozart *Sonata duet* where he realized he had been out of tempo. Then, when the lad had arrived and he was nearly dressed, he had insisted on their once more playing it together (the steward now holding the Kommodore's beribboned dinner jacket, and looking anxiously at the marine clock atop one of the bookcases.)

So, at last, they started for the dining saloon, the Kommodore having at the final moment suggestively put in his pocket the letter from Anton Lavar, along with his gold cigarette case. And as they entered the completely filled saloon (sea-illness not as yet having overtaken any passengers) Kommodore Hugo Frederick von Steinburg placed a strong and friendly gold-braided sleeve across the shoulder of Dr. Stanislaus Joseph Halka.

His other selected guests were in their assigned places. Waiting the arrival of their host for the next eight days. They hastily arose as the Kommodore and Stanislaus Joseph reached their chairs.

One guest, directly opposite, swayed very slightly and gripped the gilded top of his brocaded chair, while his sharp eyes widened, then contracted.

Herr Reimalsky, although forewarned regarding the Bismarck Suite, had not foreseen a seat at the Captain's right for his Second-Class-parked accompanist!

The Purser made the formal introductions, and then proceeded to his own table. Several of the table guests were old friends of the Kommodore. He knew the American Ambassador and Mrs. Gerard from several previous crossings. Sir Godfrey Landry was an old acquaintance. Also Mohammed Abu Bey.

When they were all seated, and the sherry (or cocktails if they were preferred) was set before the guests, the Kommodore proposed a toast.

"I usually drink first to the ladies present," he said, "but tonight I will break the custom, for I have at my right a very special guest. He might be named *Youth*—the Youth that most of us have left too far behind us—at least we males have left it! But all afternoon I have had the privilege and the pleasure of going back again to my own youth in Vienna. Youth and my first love, Music.

"And so I propose a toast to my new friend who already seems like an old friend, since he comes to me straight from my dearest of old friends, Professor Anton Lavar of the University of that city.

"I drink, and I hope you will all drink with me, to Stanislaus Joseph Halka, Doctor of Music from my old University, and to his success in America, where he is presently to give a pianoforte concert in Carnegie Hall. To Dr. Stanislaus Joseph Halka!"

Our young man was deeply touched by this great kindness, but at the same time deeply embarrassed. The faces all around the table were smiling and friendly—all but one face. The face of the gentleman directly opposite him had colored to a reddish purple. That gentleman raised his glass, but simply raised it and barely touched it to grimly hardened lips. There were enthusiastic murmurs of "Speech! Speech!" from the great picture star, the English playwright, the American Ambassador and his wife.

Stanislaus Joseph had never made a "speech" in his life.

"I do not quite know what to say," he commenced haltingly. "I am young—that is the only part of the Herr Kommodore's description of me that is correct. For in music I am still just a student, hoping to some day merit the trust and sacrifice of a great patron back in the Kommodore's Vienna, and the patience and kindness of my teachers, who made my education at the University possible.

"And this concert in New York is not *my* concert. It is the concert of Herr Viktor Reimalsky the violinist, who sits here with us. I am simply privileged to be his pianoforte accompanist. And so, I raise my glass to Herr Viktor Reimalsky—and I hope you will all come to his concert."

Applause—and a second toast was drunk; but Herr Reimalsky noticed that the Kommodore did not drink, and when it was over he spoke again.

"My young friend is far too modest," he said, "though it is a trait quite out of fashion with most musicians. Weather permitting, there will be a ship's concert one of these evenings. I hope to persuade him to play for us. I have heard such playing this afternoon as I had not heard since my friend Sergei Rachmaninov, who by the way occupied the same Bismarck Suite where Dr. Halka is my personal guest, was good enough to delight me with. Perhaps even before the ship-concert evening, Stanislaus Joseph will play for some of us there. Or in my cabin.

"But in my own quarters, I warn you, you will also have to listen to me at the pianoforte! And I have no modesty. None whatsoever!"

Again the good-natured laugh was not joined by violinist Reimalsky. That gentleman began to have a premonition that he was in for the most humiliating meal of his career.

There were quite unpremeditated moments of embarrassment when the British explorer asked Herr Reimalsky if he played the Liszt rapsody called *Räkoczy March* which was his favorite, not realizing that it was the master's most complicated effort of pianistic legerdemain—anathema to a violinist. And on turning to Stanislaus Joseph he was innocently told that it was also a favorite piece of the young man.

Then and there an engagement was made for the next day that Sir Godfrey Landry would come to the Bismarck Suite to hear it performed. "As best I can," Stanislaus Joseph had said. "It is a piece I hope some day to really play."

"I will be there also," said the Kommodore. "I think I can promise you we both have something special to look forward to. I don't think even Herr Liszt will be let down!" And he launched into a discussion of Franz Liszt and the import of his symphonic poems—paving the way for Tschaikovsky and Strauss—a discussion that completely ignored the opinions of the gloomy-faced violinist.

"He was the Jack Dempsey, the Man of War of the composers," the Herr Kommodore explained, turning to His Excellency Mohammed Abu Bey, patron of sports, breeder of fine horses; and the dark-skinned, handsome Arab prince laughed heartily at the comparison. Not so Herr Viktor Reimalsky.

"Really!" he said in French to the lady at his right (the Marchioness Di Villarey), his tone expressing his complete disgust at such vulgarity. But that lady, who had been a tennis champion in her youth, exclaimed "Fine! Wonderful! Now, for the first time, I will understand and love Franz Liszt!"

And the Herr Kommodore had secretly planned a special climax for this first dinner.

After meeting the lad and hearing him play and liking him, he had sent for the expert pastry cook of the great ship's kitchens. He knew this genius to be not only a great cook but a sculptor of no mean ability.

Together they planned (in the Kommodore's office while the lad was in the parlor) a "baked Alaska," which (if any reader is so unfortunate as to never have experienced), is a large confection all ice-cream within, and without—a thick protective layer of baked icing made of the whites of eggs and sugar.

Do not ask me how this magic of a frozen *inside* and a hot *outside* is accomplished! There are still some matters completely beyond my comprehension like differential calculus, radio waves, and baked Alaskas.

The outside shape of this marvel can be whatever one desires, and can achieve—a great circular cake; a ship; a castle; an animal such as a trumpeting elephant or a charging bull; a Christmas tree; a Liberty Bell. After being admired and savored, it is sliced with a great flat silver knife, and the ample portions placed on the waiting china plates.

So, after the roast and the red Burgundy course had been cleared away, the Kommodore's personal steward brought in a large silver platter, held high before him, and, with a low bow in which the Kommodore had carefully rehearsed him, placed the platter and its suprising contents before our Stanislaus Joseph.

It was a beautiful white- and gold-baked Alaska, and was molded to represent outwardly a concert-grand pianoforte! There was even a miniature keyboard of white keys and black—the black ones being a dark chocolate; and on the music rack was a representation in icing of an open music sheet with chocolate music bars across it and chocolate notes up and down the bars.

The "Ah's!" and the "Oh's!" around the table were spontaneous. The Kommodore glowed with pride and pleasure. Stanislaus Joseph was too surprised and thrilled to even speak—surprised and thrilled and happy until he glanced across at the glowering face of Herr Viktor Reimalsky. That gentleman was just a little stunned by this (to him) crowning insult. He finally managed a "Most interesting—most interesting" but there was a hidden menace in his tone.

The boy said at last: "I do not deserve this honor. The confection should have been in the form of a violin."

"It is in the form of the greatest instrument ever devised so that human fingers and human minds could bring celestial music to this unhappy world," spoke the Kommodore with a fiery sincerity. "The instrument of Chopin and Beethoven and Liszt and Rachmaninov! The instrument to which I predict our young friend here will bring glory and honor.

"The violin, which our young friend so generously mentions, is all right in its way—I myself studied it as a green lad for a number of years—but the real music artistry of the world has come from the divine pianoforte. This, with all respect to you, Herr Reimalsky. If you are a real artist, I regret that your talents have not been directed toward the pianoforte. The violin is, properly, just a single instrument in an orchestra assembly. The pianoforte is an orchestra in itself!"

And he spoke with such finality that the subject was dropped. Their host, it seemed, was almost fanatically prejudiced. And as he spoke he had thumped his hand several times against a letter in his jacket breast-pocket.

Only Stanislaus Joseph noticed this and guessed its meaning. Stanislaus Joseph and the Three Fates and Almighty God.

It also seemed almost sacrilege to cut into and devour such a masterpiece as the steaming "pianoforte."

"But the looking at it is only half its magnificence!" cried the Kommodore, his mood of good-humored banter returning. "Wait, my friends, till its flavor touches your palates as well as your nostrils! Then you will really know culinary perfection!" (He addressed his old friend Mohammed Abu Bey): "A veritable glimpse of your Prophet's Paradise to come!" (And to the violinist he said): "I believe, Herr Reimalsky, that it will even make you a convert to the pianoforte!"

Herr Reimalsky only tightened his lips at this pleasantry, but His Excellency Mohammed Abu Bey had a suggestion.

"Such glory should only be disclosed, be sacrificed, by the artist who made it."

The steward was sent to bring the Master Pastry Cook. He came presently, smiling and dressed in the white robes and the great white cap of his holy office. He was grandly introduced by the Kommodore; modestly received the applause and praise of the table guests; and himself expertly carved his souffléd dessert into proper portions for the steward to set before each worshipper.

Only Herr Reimalsky barely tasted his portion. His companion on the other side was the middle aged Miss Margaret Parish, chain-store heiress, world traveller, favorite of several crowned heads of Europe, reportedly one of the richest women in the universe. He turned to her.

"This pastry should make the young genius feel quite at home," he said. "His father worked in a bakeshop, I am told."

But the violinist was to have no better fortune with her than with the French Marchioness.

"How very interesting," replied the American heiress. "My own father started his chain-store empire in Cincinnati, Ohio with a small bakery. I must tell the boy all about it."

It is to be feared that from the point of view of personal prestige, and the impressing and making of new friends, Herr Viktor Reimalsky's first *Europa* dinner was a complete and utter *durchfall,* which might be translated to mean in American slang "a washout." A complete and utter "bust."

✤ 5 ✤

HE HAD NOT NOTICED the photograph when he had first looked about the Kommodore's parlor. For it was a small one, closely framed without a mat, and hung against the wall just over one end of a bookcase.

And there was no personal inscription of regard or friendship written across its surface.

But he stood before it that evening, having again been invited to the Captain's cabin after the dinner hour, and gazed at it with a strange fascination. The Herr Kommodore had left the room for some minutes, being summoned to the instrument room on the bridge just above them.

It was a photograph of a stone statue of the Holy Mother holding on her left arm the Christ Child. The right arm, over which hung the graceful drapery of the Virgin's upper garment, was broken off at the wrist. The missing hand (he thought) had held a Sacred Heart or a small scepter. The right hand of the Infant Jesus was also gone, and these mutilations—the jagged edges showing that they were mutilations—gave a peculiar pathos to the figures.

He could not tell, but would have judged that the statue was slightly smaller than life-size, and probably had looked down from a recess in the inner walls of some ancient church.

Such holy images were set in niches of several of the older churches in his Vienna. Or high above, in the carved frescoes over arched stone-doorways.

Both sculptor and model must have been ideal. So skilled had been its creator that the stone figure was intensely lifelike. It *lived*—even in this photograph. The camera had been set to catch it in a slight profile, and the features of the Virgin were very beautiful. There were the elongated eyes and brows so dear to the medieval artists—on the perfect lips just the trace of a heavenly, archaic smile.

And the noble forehead bore two crowns. One was the small, circular coronet that was the usual head ornament of such representations. Its base was a plain circle, and the top rim of its narrow circumference was carved into numerous sharp, evenly placed points.

The other "crown" was the hair itself of the young Holy Mother. This hair was quite heavy; parted tightly in the middle above the forehead; and a thick braid of it extended tightly down to cover the left ear, and apparently went completely around and over the head just beneath the man-made and doubtless once gilded crown.

The lad thought: "I have never seen a face so utterly lovely. I must ask the Kommodore about this photograph."

But he had no need to ask. As Stanislaus Joseph stood there, completely engrossed in silent admiration, the Kommodore returned.

"I see you have discovered my statue," he said, and came and stood beside the young man. "I call it my statue, but do not jump to a conclusion. I fear I am not religious. I have not attended Mass or been to confession for many years. But perhaps it would please my good mother, who departed this life these many years, if she knew that I often look at that photograph, and as I do so, think of her.

"Perhaps, on that Last Day, I will have two friends to plead for my wicked soul before God's justice bar—my saintly mother and the girl who is that statue. I was thinking about the statue just now, as I stood on the open bridge beneath the stars. Sit down, Stanislaus Joseph, and I will tell you a strange, strange tale."

First the Kommodore shed his snug dinner coat and put on a loose-fitting, deep-pocket jacket that would have been more in keeping within a racetrack paddock than a ship commander's cabin. Then he took up his *meerschaum* and slowly filled its bowl. And he pushed toward the lad his silver desk-box of the special cigarettes.

"I perceive you haven't yet discovered the friendship of a pipe," he observed with a smile, "else you would have produced one by now from a secret pocket. Ah well—you are still very young. You have your youth—I have my pipe," and the Herr Kommodore took a long and pleasurable draft, and blew the blue smoke in a great circle toward the paneled ceiling of the cabin.

Hugo von Steinburg evidently did not think this division of blessings an unfair one.

"And now, to tell you about that statue," the older man continued, "the statue which you can soon see in reality, if you choose, for it is in the New York whose docks we shall reach, God and the Longshoremen's Union willing, within the next eight days.

"That photograph was given to me by a wealthy German-American brewer of the City of Brooklyn, which I believe is really a part of New York.

"It is the photograph of a priceless sculpture he had persuaded the French Government to sell to him from the ample collection in the Paris Louvre, with the understanding that he was presenting it to the New York Metropolitan Museum of Art. He was a great art collector and a great philanthropist. He had gone to America as a poor immigrant boy, I believe, and had prospered. He had already purchased and had given several great paintings and carvings to the Museum.

"He had discovered this particular image in an obscure corner of the French treasure palace in Paris, and, as he said, fallen in love with it. Nothing could escape that gentleman and his checkbook if he set his heart on acquiring it! I understand it was partly his money that financed a famous baseball club of his adopted city, because he felt that this American game was one of the bulwarks of American freedom and free speech. You will hear much of that game and that ball club (as they call it) before you have been there long.

"Do not attempt to give a pianoforte concert on an afternoon when one of their championship games is being played!

"This German gentleman—he preferred to be called 'American gentleman' for he was an American citizen—arrived at Bremerhaven for one of our first sailings.

"I will not forget that arrival. Along with his considerable personal baggage and four German wolf-hounds he was importing, he had a long box which looked exactly like a coffin! He insisted on seeing me personally, presented his credentials, and while giving way to a rule against traveling four huge dogs in his cabin (they were placed in our very excellent Kennels on A Deck Second Class), he seemed adamant in wanting his huge box placed in his quarters.

"That also was against regulations. Staterooms were for passengers and purely personal trunks and grips—not freight!

"He wanted this box in his cabin, not for use, but for safekeeping. He finally explained to me what it contained. He had all the papers regarding it—the bill of sale, the export permits, et cetera. It was then that he gave me that photograph, which he had had taken in the Louvre, before the packing of the statue.

"The coffin-like box of course contained this statue.

"Apart from regulations, I persuaded him to let me have the box placed in our strong room. That room is in Hold Number 2, deep in the ship, and is entirely cased in steel. It is, in fact, a huge safe, not unlike the vaults of a bank.

"It is where we place shipments of gold bullion. Or any other articles of great value. This vessel could get on fire, could sink, but whatever was in that room would still be there. We could only take the responsibility for absolute safety of valuables if they were placed in that Number 2 Hold vault.

"The only keys are kept by me, here, in my cabin safe. Twice each day the ship's Master of Arms comes to me, receives those keys, and accompanied by an armed guard, goes down into the Hold, enters this strongroom and personally checks each tabulated item. The keys are then returned to me till the next inspection.

"I explained to the Master of Arms the priceless value of this long box. Even gold bullion could be replaced, but this art treasure could not.

"Never was any shipment so carefully guarded.

"I made a friend of this elderly German-American gentleman, who died shortly after this voyage, leaving the ball club and his fortune to a son whose ambition was to play the saxophone in his own jazz band—at least so I read. Our mutual interests in the arts and in sports drew us together, though I never could understand the American game of baseball! Ah well—we can't be appreciative of all things, I suppose," and the Kommodore reached out and relit his pipe with a Swan Vesta.

"I think it was about the third day out that the gentleman suggested that he actually show me the statue. 'You have been judging me quite mad,' he said, 'to be so excited over a carved piece of stone. I want you to see for yourself. I don't feel that I am taking back a mere stone image. It is as if this figure were flesh and blood. The unknown sculptor who made it—as near as I can learn back in the Twelfth Century—must have been a true genius.'

"So that late afternoon, for the day's last inspection, I took him to the hold, along with our Master of Arms and the guard.

"The outside casing of this coffin-like box was heavy oak, and had a strongly hinged lid held tight by four separate padlocks. Its owner had the keys to these padlocks—each padlock having its own special key. The lid opened to disclose another casing, this one of heavy bronze. It was in reality an expensive, waterproof, fireproof coffin, and to its two lids had been added heavy locks.

"The owner unlocked only the smaller lid—the lid that in general use would have disclosed the face and shoulders of the deceased person.

"The old gentleman gently removed some cotton protective covering, and I looked down upon a face of wonderful charm. Well—you can see it there in the photograph. Only, my photograph is a reproduction in black and white, while the effigy, as was the practice with such medieval French sculptures, was delicately painted. Somewhat faded of course, but the slightly smiling lips were red, the cheeks tinted, the eyes amazingly lifelike in the deep blue of the pupils, the eyebrows a dark brown.

"And the dark brown hair, with its thick braid beneath the gilded crown, seemed so real that you felt if you touched it, you would not touch painted stone but human locks.

"The beautifully molded neck and shoulders were flesh colored, with the left breast bared, which breast was next the head and body of the Christ Child, held high to be opposite the Virgin's face. The figure's garment was painted a dull red, with raised green jewels around its upper edge.

"I could then understand my passenger's almost infatuation with his prize—and his great concern about its safety.

"'I have viewed many medieval holy statues,' said its then proud possessor, 'but I think this one is the most beautiful in all history. And the Louvre people know very little about it, except that it was found in a bell tower of the ancient church at La Celle, near Moret-sur-Loing in the vicinity of Fontainebleau, and that it came originally from a nearby monastery of Knights Templars, now in ruins. And there seems to be a legend that it was posed for by a young peasant girl who became a Nun and then a Saint. What a ravishingly beautiful child she must have been!'"

The Kommodore rose from his chair, again relit his pipe, and proceeded to the bookcase, taking the framed photograph from its fastening and placed it against his Ming tobacco jar on the small table between himself and the young man.

"Now comes the strange part of it all," continued the Kommodore, "and to this day I cannot believe it really happened. The cotton protection was put back, the bronze lid closed and locked, and the oak box securely fastened. We returned to my cabin; I replaced the keys of the strong-room in my safe; and after several cocktails went to the main saloon for dinner.

"It was one of those gala nights as we used to call them. The orchestra leader and the purser's hostess would arrange them. Those who wished came in fancy costume—either such costumes as they could devise, or they could hire a selection of Pagliaccis, Red Indians, Arabian Sheiks, Swiss Mountaineers; with the ladies as Gypsies, Ballerinas, Peter Pans, Cleopatras.

"Even at the dinner table many were in costume, and almost everyone at least wore a grotesque paper cap. Such organized gaiety never appealed to me, but the passengers seemed to like it, and the proceeds swelled the Seaman's Fund.

"I made my appearance at the ball as brief as possible. Had to judge a dance contest—dancing being a subject I am particularly ignorant about. It was eleven P.M. before I escaped.

"I escaped to the bridge. There was a strong head wind and the sea was running high. Even this great ship was plunging a bit. It was the kind of wind that could and did by morning lash into a sixty-mile-an-hour gale with waves fifty feet high. And as I climbed the outside ladder to reach the open part of the bridge, I was surprised and annoyed to see a figure already there, especially as that figure was a woman, and obviously a passenger.

"Passengers were never allowed on the bridge, except by my invitation. And I would not have allowed anyone there on a windy night. The woman's loose dress blew out in waves—like a flag. It was a sort of drapery—not at all the type of garment usually worn. It occurred to me that it was someone in fancy ball costume—and the open bridge was certainly no place for a lone female at such an hour.

" 'Madam,' I called, even before I reached the top of the ladder-like stairway, 'I must ask you to come down at once. It is not safe for you to be here alone in a rapidly rising wind.'

" 'Monsieur le Capitaine,' she said without turning as I reached her side, and I noted that she was addressing me in the French language, 'I suppose that this is what you call *La Mer*—the sea. I now look upon it for the first time, but I am not afraid, though many strong men had told me of its storms and terrors. But I think I like a river better. Tell me, Monsieur le Capitaine—are there rivers in this America to which we are going—or is it all just a great flood of tossing waters?'

"Still she had not turned. And I had noticed that on her head was a small golden crown—a crown with sharp points set closely together. There had been several female passengers at the fancy ball dressed as Queens—Sheba—France—Somaliland—but they had all been hefty dowagers, and the north wind which blew backward this lady's soft draperies outlined a slender figure of great loveliness. I always had an eye for a good figure. I would, I believe, have long since noted such a figure among my lady passengers!"

Again the Kommodore's *meerschaum* had gone out, and he reached for another Swan Vesta and striking it, slowly applied the ample flame.

"Then only," he continued, "did she turn her face to me, just as I was again going to ask her—order her if necessary—to leave the bridge.

"Her figure had been outlined against the sky by the swaying lights from the crow's nest on the short mast just aft of the bridge, and as she turned, one of those lights caught her face full on. I had looked at the faces of many lovely ladies in my time, but never a face such as hers. It was incomparable, breathtaking—it seemed to glow; and yet there was modesty, almost a holiness about it. And it was then that I noticed the thick braid of hair that swept down tightly, covering the ear that was nearest me.

"And I knew—or thought I knew—where I had seen a face like that before! It was the face of the Virgin's statue in the bronze coffin down in our Number 2 Hold—a face that had haunted me ever since I gazed at it that afternoon. The slightly elongated violet eyes, the noble forehead, the delicately curved nose and mouth and chin—delicate yet strong. Courage was there, and just a touch of sadness. Even the half smile on the lips was a sad one—as the smile of the Mona Lisa often appears to be. I could not shout admonitions in such a presence.

" 'Madam,' I said, 'there are of course many rivers in America—a very great river into the mouth of which we will proceed when we dock in New York.'

" 'I am glad to know that,' she said, 'Oh—very glad. And I hope I shall be able to see this river from my home.'

" 'You have friends, Mademoiselle, in America—you are voyaging there to remain?' I asked.

" 'I think that I shall be dwelling in America for some years,' she said, 'though I have no friends—no acquaintances even—in that land as yet. I believe, however, that I am to meet one there who will become a very great friend. The friend I have been waiting to meet for a very long time. A long, long time.'

"And this beautiful girl sighed as I had heard no human being sigh. The sadness crossed her face like a cloud across the gold of the moon that was high overhead.

" 'But, Mademoiselle, you are very, very young,' I spoke, 'and if I may say so, with your great charm you will soon make many friends. Many young men, I should think—yes, many older ones will desire to know you—did you not just tell me that many strong men had told you of *la Mer*——?'

" 'I nursed them,' she repeated, still in a mood of sadness, 'when they returned broken from the Wars—the slaughter at Odessa—Damascus—was very great—until I too caught a fever—Ah, Monsieur le Capitaine—it is hard to die when one is only twenty-two. One does not then know that it is not Death to be feared. Only Life—only loneliness——'

"The infinite melancholy of her voice—the still consuming sadness of her features greatly moved me. I forgot entirely my mission of ordering her to leave the open bridge.

"I had a rose in my lapel—placed there by our ship's official hostess when I was designated as the judge of the dancing contest of the fancy dress ball. I took this rose from my coat and held it out to the lady in the costume of a Queen.

" 'Permit a much older man to present a rose to the most beautiful girl it has ever been his fortune to look upon,' I said.

"I think it was the most sincere compliment I have ever paid a woman.

"She took my rose. 'If life could grow and blossom like roses!' she said. 'No wars—no hatreds—no cruelty—no illness of mind or body—no loneliness——'

"She as suddenly shook off her somber, philosophic mood. The look of brightness, of courage returned to her features. The mystic, angelic smile became a real smile of human friendliness.

" 'And now I must depart, Monsieur le Capitaine,' she said. 'I know that you have broken the rules of your command to permit me to be standing here. And you have not been harsh with me. You have permitted me to talk with you. For your great kindness I shall pray for you——'

"She paused, gazed at me steadily, then spoke these quite amazing words: '—and I will tell you this for your comfort, for I know *you also* have known loneliness—*there is a Golden Cross in the great Record Scroll opposite your name—the name of a German sub-*

marine commander who saved the lives of the men on an enemy ship he had just torpedoed and sunk, and set those men ashore. A Golden Cross—not an Iron one—Herr Kommodore Hugo Frederick von Steinburg——'

"I was too astonished to speak for a moment. This girl was telling of an incident during the great World War. She could have been but a child then—maybe not even born. And as I did start to speak she had swept past me, and was descending the steep stairway-ladder to the deck below.

" 'But, Mademoiselle,' I cried, 'who are you? How can you know of such things!'

" 'I know, Monsieur le Capitaine,' she said over her shoulder. 'Do not ask me how.'

"From the foot of the ladder she moved into the doorway of the passage that led past my cabin—the cabin where we are now sitting, Stanislaus Joseph, though it was only one room then, and had just a simple spinet in one corner of it. At the end of the passage she passed swiftly down the flight of stairs to the large vestibule below. I could not keep pace with her. The noise and music and laughter of the fancy dress ball was straight ahead of us, coming from the main saloon. She moved quickly into the dancing throng—I tried to follow but lost her. Several festive-minded passengers had seized me, protesting my absence, and that I should join them. When I was free of them, she was completely gone.

"I never saw her again.

"I returned to my quarters. I searched out the photograph of this Madonna—it was then in one of the drawers of my desk. The resemblance was striking—and I also had in mind the vivid picture of the real statue that I had viewed that afternoon. But of course it must have been just a coincidence—an amazing resemblance—some girl maybe traveling second-class or cabin-class—who had been asked to attend the costume dance. I meant to go through the public rooms of these quarters the next morning—to look over the Purser's list for a young French girl traveling alone.

"But words she had said kept coming back to me.

"She had named two battles—*Odessa—Damascus*. I had not thought of it at the time, but come to consider it now, these were not battles —even Near-Eastern battles—of the World War. Still, their names had a dimly familiar ring to my ears. At the University I had specialized in History, as well as in Music. Suddenly it came to me. I went down to the ship's library where there were volumes of the excellent *Encyclopaedia Britannica.* I quickly found the pages. There were the names. *Odessa. Damascus.* Military disasters—victims of which this girl said that she had nursed.

"They were battles of the Crusades. The Second Crusade of the year 1148!

"Then, believe me, I was really excited—disturbed. I rang for my steward and sent him for the Master of Arms. We took the strong-room keys from my safe and proceeded down into Hold Number 2. Inside, we switched on the powerful lights. The coffin-like box was in its place, securely locked. I tested the locks and they were firm. Then something on the floor, near the box, caught my eye.

"It was a rose—such a rose as I had given to the lady on the bridge, half an hour before!

"I turned to the Master of Arms. 'How do you account for the presence of this flower in the strong-room?' I asked sternly.

"The man seemed confused. But not amazed, as I assure you I was at that moment.

" 'Herr Kommodore,' he said, 'I suppose I broke a regulation. But the American gentleman who owns the property has had me place a rose on this box each night. Yes, he paid me to do it, sir. And I would return the rose to him after my inspection the following morning. Only today—I did not leave a rose!

" 'The gentleman sent for me and told me he was going to try to persuade you to let him bring you here today—as he did—and that perhaps I had best not leave a rose today. I had told him it was against strict orders to leave anything in this room—but it seemed a harmless, sentimental gesture. The long box contained a statue, he had told me. I assure you I had examined each flower, to be certain it did not contain an explosive. . . . I do not know how this rose is here tonight! Perhaps I forgot this morning to remove the one given me yesterday—or dropped it as I left. I hope there is nothing wrong with the shipment. I will explain to the gentleman that I can bring no more roses here.' "

Again the Kommodore relit his pipe. He took up the framed photograph of the Louvre statue, and returned it to its place over the bookcase. He turned to the still-seated boy.

"Stanislaus Joseph," he said, "to this day I do not know what to believe. There was no passenger resembling this girl on the ship. I went over the entire list, and inspected all rooms, as they had not been inspected on any voyage before! I even inquired about the possibility of a stowaway in the crew's quarters. I satisfied myself no young girl was being smuggled across.

"I told the German-American about it all. He only laughted. 'You old country Germans are still too imaginative,' he said. 'We Americans are sentimental—yes—but our feet are firmly on the ground. My baseball team is playing in Brooklyn the day we land—if we land on schedule. Let me take you to a game. You ought to know my new manager. There's a realist for you! I predict he will be a success in life. He'll bring you back to earth from your sea fancies.'

"Where is the statue now?" asked Dr. Stanislaus Joseph Halka. "We are only in New York a week or so before our tour, but I would like to see it, if that is possible."

"Quite possible," said the Kommodore. "It's standing in a branch of the Metropolitan Museum called the Cloisters. This building is removed somewhat from the center of the city—a center named Times Square—but you can reach it easily by motor bus or taxicab. I have been there once or twice when we have remained over in New York more than a day.

"If you do go to view it, take a rose with you and place it there for me. A rose for remembrance of the strangest adventure of my life. And the most beautiful girl I have ever gazed upon. But I suppose that was all some sort of a dream. I do not really know. How can I know? Well—come to the pianofortes again. Let us play the first movement of Debussy's *La Mer*. You have told me that you know it. That is why I especially wanted you to come back with me tonight.

"We will play it for the Lady of the Statue—wherever she is—whoever she is."

And that is how Dr. Stanislaus Joseph Halka, pianoforte player, accompanist for the American tour of violinist Viktor Reimalsky, first heard of the Madonna of the Sword—though then she was not known to him or to any other living man by this designation.

In the Kommodore's cabin these two men of widely separated years, but both young with music, played together the first two movements of *La Mer*. The first, *the waves and the shore;* the second, *conversation of winds and waves*. Then the boy bade the Herr Kommodore good-night and returned to his quarters.

Kommodore Hugo Frederick von Steinburg sat for a while and

smoked his *meerschaum*. The cabin seemed very empty when the boy had left. He felt—as he sometimes had felt of late—very utterly alone.

The photographs on the cabin's walls, all with their friendly inscriptions, still seemed something out of a dim past. Many of the personages were now dead. And the ones who were alive—did they ever remember him? He knew too well the short length of shipboard friendships. They ended at the gangplank landings—seldom were resumed unless there was another crossing on his ship. . . . His family in Germany—all dead.

He was the last member of the house of Steinburg. And he would die too, someday, and leave no son to carry on.

And when his hour came—would anyone really care? The beautiful women with whom he had flirted—the strong men he had met in business—in racing—would any of them shed a tear of true sorrow? What was it the Girl of the Statue had said that night on the bridge —*no wars—no hatreds—no cruelty—no illness of mind or body—no loneliness*——

Loneliness. That was the most dreadful of all. The most to be dreaded—if one only knew.

The Kommodore arose and went to his closet. He took from the inner pocket of his dinner jacket the letter from Professor Anton Lavar. He read it over again . . . Anton would care. Dear, blessed old Anton. Anton—of all the hundreds he had met and known.

He seated himself at his desk. He took a sheet of the engraved personal letter paper and started to write.

"My dear, dear Anton," he commenced. "Do not say that I really was the victor. For you have your hearth—your own true wife—you are moving toward the grave (as you say) hand in hand *with someone. With someone*—Anton. I walk alone. Very terribly alone sometimes. I——"

He stopped. This would not do. He must not depress his dearest, his only true friend. In the morning he would write a proper letter. He went to the Bösendorfer. He shook himself and struck the keys with great vigor, as if by so doing he could rid himself of the mood. Then he plunged into the third movement of *La Mer*. The movement *of storm and agony and struggle*.

Like Stanislaus Joseph Halka the Kommodore had Music also. Music to arouse—to calm—to be a companion to whom one could tell the soul's most secret bitterness.

PART FOUR

AMERICA

✣ 1 ✣

I HAVE CAUGHT flashes of it at the *Kino*—the cinema; I have stared at prints in art stores—but I had no idea that the reality could be so wonderful."

Stanislaus Joseph Halka spoke the words very quietly, not being given to hyperbole, as he stood on the bridge of the *Europa* an early morning, seven days later. But his heart was beating just a little faster.

The great liner had crept through the Narrows; saluted, as it were, the majestic Lady who holds high her torch named *Liberty*, and was slowly moving past the sky-reaching clump of towers that is lower New York City.

"It's like—it's like great music!" he added. "For me, the Lady holds up a baton, not a torch; holds it to the world and will presently turn to conduct a Symphony such as that world has never heard before! Those great structures—are like—are like—" but the lad paused in some embarrassment, feeling that his quite unexpected torrent of words were sounding very foolish to the sight-hardened, professional voyager at his side.

But the Herr Kommodore understood. And he did not ask the lad to finish out his simile. He thought he understood without words.

And he understood that Manhattan had again won, at first sight, another convert—as it had before charmed millions from alien lands and drawn them to its bosom of steel and glass and concrete, never to let them go.

He placed a comradely hand on the lad's shoulder. "I've looked at it perhaps a hundred times," he said. "I had another ship before this one that ported at New York. But I always am swept by the same lift of spirit. Great music—great music! And yet—many, many Americans never look at it! The good United States citizens on this boat are now in their cabins busily camouflaging their customs declarations, so as to defraud their excellent democratic government of as much customs duty as possible!

"But look back and down on the Second Class decks. They are lined with us aliens, drinking in those symbols of courage and enterprise and eternal reaching for something higher. If I were a young man again—Ah well, I am not. I envy you, Stanislaus Joseph, that your work has brought you here."

"I think that I am going to like it," said the young man. "I know that I shall!"

"These Americans do not live in the past—as we are inclined to do," continued the Kommodore, "but if you become homesick for the past, you can find it at the end of a short motorbus ride. The Metropolitan Museum of Art, the Frick Museum, the Morgan Collection, and do not forget the Cloisters and to take a rose with you to place before my Statue of the Virgin.

"And go and look at two great, high-vaulted halls that the natives of the town scarcely notice at all, certainly not with any admiration or awe. One is called the Grand Central Station, and the other, located not far from it, the Pennsylvania Station. The Colosseum of Rome will not give you any greater feeling of grandeur. And in both places you can stand on a raised platform and view humanity, as if you were a God looking down from some mountain. In fact, in one of them the curved ceiling is plotted with the stars arranged in their proper constellations.

"This amazing City of New York that can be all things to all men! And they say it also possesses the most corrupt governmental organization in the entire world!"

The Herr Kommodore laughed, indicating that he did not entirely believe this latter statement. And what matter if it were true, if, in spite of it, there had been created this vista of magic towers that was wheeling past on their right!

In his cabin on A Deck, Herr Viktor Reimalsky pulled back the curtains of his porthole window. He saw no magic minarets of a modern Bagdad: expression of man's faith and courage and struggle to attain the heights. No long-stemmed notes of a great Symphony written against the sky itself.

Only ugly crudeness; expressions of commercial greed; high soulless walls attempting by mere size to flatter a race of money-grubbing shopkeepers, who, like one of his table companions, had risen from bakeries or worse, in places with crude names like Cincinnati.

"How horrible," he said, and pulled back the curtain to shut out the unaesthetic sight. "I hope this Carnegie Hall in which I am to play, has some vestige of culture and architectural design."

"It has a large seating capacity on the lower floor, and four balconies," said his practical-minded Vienna manager, who had been in America before. "I have a cable that the advance sale is most encouraging."

"Ah yes, the advance sale," said Herr Reimalsky, and his tone indicated the forbearance and resignation with which a true artist must endure the less sensitive but cash-saturated atmosphere of barbarian countries.

Herr Reimalsky's crossing had not been a happy one. After that first historic dinner at the Kommodore's table, he had made no further appearances thereat. He had sent word by his manager that he was "ill disposed." And he had at other hours "sulked in his tent," as it were.

He had emerged for the ship's concert, his invitation to play at that same being due (had he only known it) to the insistence of our Stanislaus Joseph. And with the young man at the pianoforte, he had performed most credibly a *Sonata* by Cesar Franck, which was one of his standard concert pieces. The applause was sincere and deserved.

But he could not help but note that the greatest applause—it might almost have been called an ovation—came when his humble accompanist and the Herr Kommodore played together Beethoven's *Thirty-two Variations in C Minor,* an extra piano having been moved from a small music room to the main lounge.

"What can you expect," the violinist said sotto voce to his manager, "when that little nobody has wheedled himself into the good graces of the ship's Captain," which was partly true as regards the reason for the tumultuous applause, the Herr Kommodore not being exactly unpopular.

But no "wheedling" had been committed by Dr. Stanislaus Joseph Halka. He had in fact declined to play alone, feeling that it would be an affront to his employer.

So, finally, Stanislaus Joseph, having bade farewell to his friend the Herr Kommodore, walked down the First Class canopy-covered gangplank, and set foot on the American continent. That is, on a projection from the American continent, that same being the long, shed-like dock extending into the Hudson River.

But even the wood flooring of this bare structure felt good to his feet. He could not have explained why—he felt that he had come to his real home. So, indeed, had hundreds of others before him. So had doubtless the Pilgrims as they stepped ashore onto the legendary Rock.

That magnetism—that curious, you might even say, "radiation of gravitation" that is America.

His entrance papers were all in order—the Herr Kommodore and the Immigration Officers who had boarded the ship at Quarantine had seen to that—and he proceeded to a space under the letter H, where his and other baggage of travelers whose names commenced with that letter was being stacked.

And presently, as arranged, the valet Franz Rodar came to the H section (after having seen to the landing of Herr Reimalsky), with his own small personal belongings on a hand-truck, a grinning black porter doing the propulsion.

The happiness of the porter—who had been assigned to Second Class landing stations—was because the estimable Herr Rodar (who also spoke some English) could not refrain from imparting the information that they were proceeding to the luggage of the occupant of the famous Bismarck Suite of that crossing, and without so stating, gave the impression that he, Franz Rodar, was that occupant's manservant. This porter had once, two years before, on a *Europa* landing, drawn the voyager from this suite, who turned out to be a quite famous (or infamous) underworld figure, and had received a tip of a fifty dollar bill when the tier of baggage was delivered to the waiting, bullet-proof limousine on the street.

That had been his moment of grandeur, something to speak about with fond pride. That—and the fact that he was putting his son through Columbia.

A strange land—America!

The porter's face fell somewhat when he viewed the small trunk and the three bags of "Mr. Halka"; and their youthful, round-faced owner did not impress his sixth amount-of-the-tip sense as a cash-laden prospect, so he thought it best to subtly inject a casual statement: "I have once before had the pleasure of unloading a gentleman who crossed in the Bismarck Suite, sir."

The Bismarck Suite! That was the only part of the crossing the lad had not relished, this living in a false elegance, though he realized that the Herr Kommodore had placed him there from the most generous of motives and to treat royally any friend of Professor Anton Lavar. And it had enabled him to practice long hours on a fine pianoforte.

But when, in the street below, his trunk was securely fastened to the back of a bright yellow taxicab, and he and the valet with their few suitcases loaded inside, he realized subconsciously that this unhappy luxury-suite had raised its head to mock him.

It was obvious that the colored porter expected a very sizable *trinkgeld*—a gratuity—only something not of "trinket" but Bismarck-Suite proportions!

"I am a stranger here," said Stanislaus Joseph. "I do not really know what I should pay you for your most kind service. This is my first financial transaction in America—I want it to be generous—and correct."

He had taken out the gift wallet. Therein was, to be sure, the uncashed draft for five hundred United States dollars, but the store of cash money was pathetically small. In exchange for the five one-thousand-kronen notes he had been able to bring with him, he had received what he was told was twenty-five American dollars, that being their worth at that time.

He took out the five-dollar bill and the five ones still remaining of this store. A five-dollar bill he had given to the table steward on the boat. And to each of the five musicians of the ship's jazz band two one-dollar bills, for they had been most respectful to him. Only—*they* knew how he happened to be in the Bismarck Suite, and after hearing him play had given him the respect one humble and modest artist has for another.

To the porter Stanislaus Joseph continued, "You mentioned the Bismarck Suite and I think I should explain. I started this voyage in the Second Class, along with my friend here. I am a musician—a very humble musician. One of my teachers in Vienna had been a friend of the ship's Kommodore. I was moved up to that expensive suite as his personal guest. Like most folk who pretend to be what they are not, I fear I cannot live up to the obligations that the Bismarck Suite does and should promise."

And he held out to the startled colored man the remainder of his United States bills.

"Please to take what is proper," he said, "and if it is not sufficient, perhaps you will call at my hotel when I am settled there."

But this particular colored porter had heard something of even more interest to him than the size of his gratuity.

Unbelievable as it may seem, there are still scattered souls about the world to whom the *trinkgeld* is not the all-important thing, though such folk are usually found among the lower and uneducated classes.

The black man had heard the word "musician."

"Did you say, mister, that you are a musician?" he asked.

"Why yes," answered the somewhat surprised Stanislaus Joseph. "At least, I am trying to become one."

"Herr Dr. Halka is a very fine musician," interposed Franz Rodar sincerely and also feeling he must somehow make good his premature boasts about the evacuating tenant of the Bismarck Suite. "He is appearing next Sunday evening at your palace named Carnegie—a concert with the violinist Viktor Reimalsky."

And now the black man was truly interested. "You are sure giving a concert at Carnegie Hall?" he exclaimed.

"My friend exaggerates," smiled Stanislaus Joseph. "I play the pianoforte. I am the accompanist for a well known violinst, that is all. The concert is his, not mine."

"My son, who is in his second year at Columbia University, also plays the violin," said the porter. "He is taking a special course in it at the nearby Julliard School of Music. He has a scholarship. And he already earns money by playing weekends at a night club in Harlem, though it is not the kind of music he prefers."

"I also had a scholarship at the University in Vienna," said Stanislaus Joseph.

"May I shake your hand, sir," said the porter, "and please to put away your money. It is an honor to have carried your baggage, sir. Wait till I tell my son tonight that I served a great musician from Europe who is sure playing this Sunday at Carnegie Hall!"

"Permit me at least to do this," said Stanislaus Joseph. "I am entitled to two free seats for each concert. If you will write down your name for me, I will see that those seats are in the ticket sale office in your name. Perhaps you and your son would care to come."

"You will really do that!" said the porter. "Gee! I have never been in Carnegie Hall!"

"Most certainly I will," said Stanislaus Joseph.

A piece of paper was found, and the porter, writing against the side of the taxi, inscribed a labored "Henry Jackson and son."

"You will not forget it?" he added, still doubting that he was to be able to tell his son of this unexpected good fortune.

"I will not forget," said Stanislaus Joseph. "You are my first real acquaintance in America. I am most happy to be able to do you a service."

Thus a humble baggage carrier with a black skin, whose ancestors had arrived in America chained in the hold of a filthy "black ivory" frigate, gave to our Stanislaus Joseph an exhibit A of what America can do for those who had adopted her.

The driver of the taxi was not so gracious.

He turned and shouted through the open window behind his driver's seat. "When you two get through gabbing, I would like to get started! I have a wife and family to support, and I can't support 'em on gab. I hope you understand, mister, that the charge for trunks is fifty cents extra. Where do you want to go?"

"Don't mind grouch face," smiled the black man. "I'll bet he hates music."

"I do," said the taxi man. "Music and books. I'm trying to earn enough money today to take the missus to a wrestling match tonight. Wrestling is our dish."

America—all things to all men.

Franz Rodar had been told of an inexpensive hotel on the Avenue named *Seventh,* just opposite Carnegie Hall, and it was to this hostelry that they were driven. There they obtained a modest bedroom with twin beds for a dollar and a half per bed per day.

"This is not much like the Bismarck Suite—or even our Second Class cabin," observed Franz Rodar, as he looked at the faded wall paper, the clean but shabby coverings of the narrow beds, the two cheaply framed prints of "still life" upon the wall. Individual, artistic solace, doubtless, for each bed.

"It is homelike—I am happy," said Stanislaus Joseph. "I hated that Bismarck Suite—all except the pianoforte. I'm only sorry we shall be here for a few short days. I would like to remain in New York for a longer time."

Franz Rodar had to go to the Waldorf-Astoria, to unpack and lay out the wardrobe of his employer. He shook his head as he descended by the dingy, self-service elevator.

There were some things he could not quite understand about Dr. Stanislaus Joseph Halka. A nice fellow, but strange. Very strange.

✣ 2 ✣

FROM A CONVERSATION happening later that afternoon in the office of the American concert-tour manager, it began to appear that Dr. Halka was to have his wish of remaining longer than a few days in New York, if he so desired.

It was the American manager who was speaking.

He was a unique personage—this impresario—in the concert management business. He hated music. He despised musical artists. And yet—perhaps because of this attitude—he was a decided success.

He billed himself as "H. Rodman." *H. Rodman presents.* Those three words headed the show bills—the programs—of half the concert halls in America. No one seemed to have discovered what the "H" stood for. His business associates (and those transacting business with him) said it stood for "Hardboiled." Those who opposed him said it stood for "Hatchetman." He had not yet been accused of murder. But a little light mayhem, some delicate petty larceny (it concerned contracts, not money) had once or twice removed obstacles in his path.

When possible, however, he operated within the confines of interstate commerce laws. Some of the stories of his handling of temperamental artists bordered on the humorous. As for instance, how he had cured a certain hard-to-manage British-born prima donna, (who had an antipathy toward American hotels), of demanding a private-bedroom railroad car for her one-night-stands transcontinental tour—a demand that meant considerable extra expense and constant difficulty with the railroads, it being during wartime troop movements.

He could, of course, have booted her sizable rear from his stable of artists—he had once literally done that same to a famous tenor—but the lady's box-office receipts were also large, and he had use for his forty percent share of them. So, after her appearance one night in Atlantic City, and when the lady had retired, he arranged (there was always a suspicion that money had been passed to someone) to have this private car attached to the yard switching engine.

The temperamental lady spent that night being a bumper between the engine and the various freight and baggage cars which were being shunted to their proper tracks.

The lady's cries over the telephone to New York the next morning were heart-rending. H. Rodman was most sympathetic. But strangely enough, the identical thing happened the next night in Baltimore. And again in Washington. These American railroads! The lady decided from then on to patronize hotels, and travel by drawing-room—even by a plebeian Pullman chair when necessary—on regular trains.

H. Rodman had other and more drastic plans for her, had Washington failed to effect a cure, but, as it turned out, it was sometimes best to proceed politely and gently in dealing with temperaments.

H. Rodman's hatred of music and "artists" had a curious source that may be of interest.

As of today, he was in appearance a large man of blond coloring; large faced; small, hard eyes; small, tight mouth; heavy hands. Little if any hair. It was difficult to imagine, but he had been a child once—a so-called "child prodigy." Child of a pair of drunken parents—small-time opera singers—who had discovered that their offspring could be taught to play the pianoforte.

Taught he was to the full extent of his small endurance, and by the age of eight could appear in public. Appear with long blond curls.

The father (when sober) did the booking. The mother (when sober) continued the teaching. The lad had a thorough musical education; a thorough knowledge and acquaintanceship of the country's concert halls and auditoriums; but no childhood. He supported and continued to support this precious pair till an opportune railroad wreck bumped them off and out of his life.

He was then fifteen, and he hated them both with a consuming hatred.

He hated music, but he had a pretty wide knowledge of it. He also had discovered that silly, sentimental people would pay big money for "concerts" by alleged "artists." Artists even more phony than he felt himself to be, for he knew he was not really good. And he was getting too large to pass as a "boy prodigy."

He had an instinct for publicity and business dealings. There was more money in the handling of "artists" than in being one. Certainly than in being a second-rate one. He took on a violinist of some real talent. Then a harpist. Then two more violinists. He was one of the first to organize guaranteed tours. Persuade local committees of art-struck women—and men—to guarantee costs and box-office receipts.

He had now built up an empire on such bookings. He had some really great artists of course. He went to Europe each year to find them. But the local committees had to swallow the phonies with the greats. With his skill at publicity they did not know the difference anyway.

H. Rodman presents. It had come to mean sellouts, and forty percent of the receipts to the said H. Rodman.

To return to whereof H. Rodman was speaking, as he sat in his small, photograph-plastered office on Fifty-Seventh Street. The photographs—mostly of artists he managed or had managed—he sometimes referred to as the "Fakers Gallery." He was speaking to Herr Viktor Reimalsky and that gentleman's Vienna manager, both of whom had a knowledge of English—though it was English as spoken in London.

"Why, if I may ask," H. Rodman was saying, looking up from the pile of telegrams which told him of the exact receipts his enterprises had played to the night before, "do you want a new accompanist for your tour? It is of course your personal affair, only it seems that I must pay this new man, and in your case find him. Find him in two days. Absent for two months in your damned Europe, I have a few other matters on my hands." And he flicked the dozen or so Western Union sheets on his desk.

He had not troubled to keep a decided trace of annoyance from his voice.

After a week aboard ship in the proximity of his latest importation, he was just a bit "fed up." Not that he had spent much time in the violinist's company. It was not his habit to get chummy with his artists. And on shipboard he always tried to rest—stayed in his cabin playing solitaire and reading crime stories.

H. Rodman said the crime stories were a clean relief from the people he must deal with in his business life.

The Vienna manager cleared his throat. "Herr Reimalsky does not feel that the accompanist he has brought will meet the high standards of your management," he said, and waved a hand toward the concert notables that decorated the office walls.

H. Rodman smiled—a hard, unhumorous smile. He always smiled first, when he was especially annoyed.

"Rubbish," he said. "I heard your accompanist at the Prague concert. I heard him play with the Captain at the ship's concert. That duet of Schumann's in A Minor is difficult, and he played the most difficult part. I know. I used to have to play the damn thing myself."

"You are also an artist!" said the Vienna manager in considerable surprise.

"I *was* an artist. I reformed," said H. Rodman, and his listeners could not tell just how he meant that cryptic statement.

"Why don't you two be frank about it?" continued H. Rodman. "Surely you must know that I am not so unobserving as to be unaware of the Bismarck Suite incident and the incident of the Captain's table. 'Kommodore's table' I suppose they call it on those damn German boats. Both incidents struck me as being most amusing.

"I shall try to remember them when I some day write my memoirs. 'Asses and Artists' I shall name it."

H. Rodman permitted himself a short laugh.

Herr Viktor Reimalsky turned a slight purple and seemed about to burst. But his Vienna manager, seated beside him on the office couch, placed a tight grip on his arm.

"You are right, Herr Rodman," he said. "We gentlemen should be frank. "My client had come to dislike intensely——"

"Detest!" injected the bursting Viktor Reimalsky. "That *dummkopf*—" but the tightening grip of his manager caused him to stop.

"To *dislike* intensely our present accompanist," corrected the manager. "It will shatter his concentration and distort his technique. Make smooth appearances impossible."

"Well?" said H. Rodman.

"I might respectfully point out that under our contract we have the selection of an accompanist," said the manager. "A change back in Europe would be a matter of minutes. But we are strangers here. We will therefore need your cooperation. We are under the unfortunate necessity of asking you to kindly recommend another man."

"Suppose that I know no other accompanist?" said H. Rodman.

"That would be unbelievable," said the Vienna gentleman, waving his hand toward the walls completely hidden by photographs. "But—" he hesitated, then decided to play a bold hand, "in that case, Herr Rodman, we must ask you to release us from our contract. My client refuses to proceed on an extended tour with an accompanist so distasteful to him, whatever his reasons may be."

H. Rodman sat very quietly for a few moments. In business he only permitted himself to lose his temper when there was nothing else to lose—particularly dollars.

He had already plunged rather recklessly in the promotion of this violinist. First, because that season he had no really top-drawer string-artist to fill his subscription bookings. Second, he had sensed the possibility of a financial cleanup with a good-looking, sex-appealing "show off"; had already coined the phrase "The New Paganini" and ordered by cable some two thousand dollars worth of billing and posters.

The tour promised a clear twenty-five thousand profit, which was not "hay." Or rather—it meant considerable hay.

H. Rodman had use for hay—as we shall presently learn.

"Very well," he said finally. Without looking at it, he extracted the fifth telegram, counting from the top, and held it in his hand. "Fortunately for you I have under contract an experienced accompanist. For the last two seasons he was with—" (and he named a famous violinist now back in his native Italy), "—but this year he was foolhardy enough to want to make a concert tour alone. I gave him some open, speculative bookings.

"He has been out a week, and I think he is cured. His receipts last night in Hartford, Connecticut, were eight dollars and seventy-five cents. This in spite of a superior pianoforte talent. Talent—but no personality. No publicity angles. I could put him with you, Herr Reimalsky."

"You are most cooperative," said the Vienna manager.

"Not cooperative. Practical," said H. Rodman. "There are, however, several conditions which you must meet. As an accompanist this man received fifty dollars a concert—four concerts per week guaranteed. Your man we contracted for at twenty-five a concert. The extra twenty-five per concert will be taken from your share. Since I am guaranteeing you five hundred a concert you will doubtless not mind that pittance.

"Also, he cannot play your New York engagement. He is booked at a Y.W.C.A. in Boston Sunday night. You will have to put up with your lad from Vienna that one night. You will also have to rehearse with this new accompanist before starting your tour, which tour begins the following Thursday in Philadelphia. The extra rehearsals will cost about two hundred dollars, for the keyboard gentleman has a most mercenary Union. That amount also will be deducted from your share of the first week's take."

"If this man is as experienced as you say, we agree," said the Vienna manager, still gripping the arm of his about-to-violently-object violinist.

"He is fifty-five years old, scholarly in appearance, and plenty experienced; in fact, saved the bacon of several second-raters I've had out. Made them look better than they really were. You doubtless understand this. It's important with violinists. I will prepare a new contract covering these matters. And may I advise that you say nothing to your young Vienna pianist until after the Sunday performance.

"By the way, what was his name?"

"Halka. S. J. Halka," said the Vienna manager.

"This Halka person will have to be returned to Vienna. Under our immigration laws I have guaranteed that both you two, and he, will not become public charges, as we say. His boat fare back will be some three hundred dollars——"

"It was one hundred and twenty dollars coming over," interposed the Vienna manager, noticing that his artist was about to again erupt.

"Ah yes—I forgot—Second Class passage. Well, gentlemen, I must inform you that I do not knowingly travel my artists second class. Do not regard me strangely. No generosity or sentiment about it. Just business and business prestige.

"The steamship companies respect me. I can't afford to lose that respect. It will cost three hundred odd dollars to get S. J. Halka out of the country, plus whatever the railroad fare is to transport him from Bremerhaven to Vienna. This latter can be via second class. It is your known standing, not mine, that is at stake over there. Whatever the amount, it will also be charged to your share of the first few concerts.

"I will be generous, I will not charge you for bringing back to New York my piano player from Boston, though as a strictly business matter I should do so."

Herr Viktor Reimalsky was getting out of hand. That is, out of the hand of his Vienna restrainer. He had struggled to his expensively patent-leather-shod feet, "This is outrageous—" he commenced.

"Herr Reimalsky, please to be seated," said H. Rodman, and there was such a glint in the small eyes of the husky American impresario that the violinist thought it best to quickly comply. H. Rodman continued calmly, "You can of course avoid all this expense by retaining your first engaged accompanist."

The Vienna manager spoke. "I think that what Herr Reimalsky was about to suggest was that you might consider bearing half the expense. You must pardon his impulsive nature. That is one factor for his success with audiences, as you may have noticed in Prague. And he does not any too well understand the English language."

"He seems quite proficient in the matter of language," said H. Rodman dryly. "No, I will bear no part of the expense, though we are already practically sold out for the Sunday concert. A twenty-eight hundred dollar box-office. My subscription organization has taken care of that. So you can understand, gentlemen, it is purely a matter of business principle. Ethics—not money."

Conscientious H. Rodman paused to permit this factor of business scruples to penetrate. He continued:

"And one word of warning, gentlemen, if you will accept it. I give it to you free gratis. Do not become difficult with this new accompanist. He knows all the tricks. He will cooperate most generously under fair dealing, but he can and will wreck you if you resort to any chicanery."

"I do not understand the word 'chicanery,'" said Herr Viktor Reimalsky, but his tonal quality was suddenly weak in antagonistic vigor—a "twenty-eight hundred dollar box-office" not being without a certain impact, and well within his comprehension.

Also—he was simultaneously trying to convert this dollar amount into *kronen* value, and then to figure just what a sixty percent share of that net return would be, less ten percent of this sixty percent, the ten going to his Vienna manager. A problem that might well have set back Herr Einstein for at least a couple of moments.

Under such artistic mental preoccupation, anger cools.

"I am sure your personal manager can explain chicanery to you," said H. Rodman. "It is an international, bi-lingual word, often used in our profession. Both the word and its meaning."

"There is still another matter," H. Rodman continued. "Do not rise in alarm. It does not concern finance. There will be a press conference for you at this office tomorrow morning at eleven. Press and photographers. Please be here on the hour. And please, at this conference, cast no slurs on America. These newsmen are Americans, and might resent it. We need their help in our so-called business.

"Also make note that you rehearse at noon Sunday in Carnegie Hall. Again do not trouble to rise. I pay the expense of it. Pay the light bill and the janitor service, although less generous impresarios sometimes charge for that. Notify your Vienna accompanist to be there with all his music. Again I advise you to give no hint to him that his services end with—and that he returns to Vienna after—the evening concert. We want that performance to be an unhampered success.

"I should tell you that the new accompanist I am getting on for you once played an entire Tschaikovsky *Concerto* under the playing of a violinist's Mozart *Romance*—that violinist having irritated this accompanist by criticizing his pedal work just before the concert. It was most amusing. I laughed myself sick. They were of course both of them the artists of a rival concert manager at the time."

H. Rodman permitted himself a quite hearty, reminiscent chuckle, and then continued:

"That was how I came to first engage this accompanist. I liked his initiative and spirit. Now I do not think that your inexperienced Vienna lad would think of doing anything as novel as that—but you never can tell in this pleasant artistic business. It is full of little surprises."

By this time even Herr Viktor Reimalsky was completely stunned. Such horrors related as a matter-of-fact occurrence! A country surely without law and order, as well as completely lacking in any semblance of culture.

H. Rodman observed all this, and thought it best to now inject another note of cheer. "I hope you will approve the way I am billing you. I believe it has already fired the box-offices. We are calling you *The New Paganini.* You doubtless have heard of that violinist who died in the year 1840. Niccolo Paganini. Try to live up to this billing in your performances."

"The New Paganini!" gasped Viktor Reimalsky. "Oh, thank you, Herr Rodman!" He was on his feet by now.

"Don't mention it. The pleasure has been all mine," said that gentleman, and moved back in his desk chair.

He did not especially care to be kissed by the now overwhelmed artist.

When they were gone, H. Rodman spoke to his office manager. "Wire Frederick Arundel that his personal tour ends in Boston, which I think he will be glad to hear, as he has a wife and five children to support in Flushing. Tell him he goes on tour with a new Czech violinist next week. Mention that we are billing the guy *The New Paganini.* That will give poor old Arundel a needed laugh.

"And put with that stinker—you just saw him out—the toughest company-manager we have free. Bill Levy I think. Tell Levy anything goes, if the fellow gets fresh. Or his Vienna manager gets fresh. I think, however, they'll stay in line when they see the box-office statements. The pair seem to have no great abhorrence of American dollars."

H. Rodman opened the top side-drawer of his desk and took an expensive cigar from the box that he kept hidden therein. He lit that cigar, having first bit off the end and spat it in the approximate direction of his waste basket. After a puff or two he continued to his faithful office manager.

"*The New Paganini*—good idea, wasn't it? They'll fall hard for it right across the country. And the imbecile does have looks and sex appeal. Well, from what I read about that old time fiddle artist Paganini, he also was a pain in the neck. All the flashy box-office draws seem to be. Artists! What muck! I heard a beggar gypsy this summer in a cheap café in Budapest, that could fiddle circles around them all. Technique and soul. Some day I'll take on a guy like that—only he'll probably turn out to be a drug addict or a drunk. But some day I'll try it! Now get me the farm on the private wire. But first, let me wash my hands. Muck! Muck!"

This notation re H. Rodman. It was a complete secret as far as the general public knew. Only a very few intimates knew about it.

In a secluded section of New Jersey he owned a hundred-acre farm. The resident manager was an elderly veterinary and his wife was also a veterinary.

On this farm were fifty-six horses, a hundred and ten dogs, two hundred odd cats. They were all strays, and in the case of the horses—old, worn out, abused; they had come there suffering.

For years, H. Rodman had bought up old horses that he had seen drawing overloaded peddlers' carts, laundry wagons—animals obviously underfed; lame; with leg and collar sores.

He had once, on Third Avenue, pulled a profanely protesting brute of a junk dealer off the high seat of his cart with the crooked end of the cane he habitually carried—sent a bystander for a police officer—had the cart owner arrested; in spite of being swamped with work, had gone to court to appear against this man and for the underfed animal.

That animal had gone to his farm the same day—had become one of his special pets. "Third Avenue Mamie" he named her.

He picked up stray dogs. He rescued homeless cats. The S.P.C.A. knew him well, and could depend on him to give a home to any unwanted beast. And when—on free week-ends—he drove to that farm in his Cadillac convertible—these animals recognized him, as children know a kind father.

When the low, red car would pull up along the pasture that bordered the private road leading to the farm dwelling, horses grazing there came galloping, trotting, hobbling to the whitewashed rail fence, pushing to thrust soft nostrils against the coat and face of their friend.

He loved them all with a fierce, passionate, protective affection.

In H. Rodman's wallet was a picture. No one knew whose picture it was. Intimates said he sometimes would look at that picture for minutes at a time, and that when he did, the hard face became somehow kind and gentle. The small mouth lost its tightness. Even the eyes seemed larger.

It was supposed that it was the photograph of a girl. Maybe it had been an unrequited love affair that had made H. Rodman hard, sarcastic, ruthless.

Those intimates were wrong. It was a cheap snapshot of a little boy and a mongrel dog.

When he was ten, H. Rodman had found this dog half starved and lame and homeless on the street. He had taken it to the hotel where he lived with his parents. They had permitted him to keep it that summer, though complaining about the fifteen cents a day it cost to feed it—this despite the fact that they were living off the boy's winter earnings. That Fall a new tour started for the lad, and they refused to let him take the dog along.

They put it with a "friend," with the hint to "lose it." When the lad returned from off "the road" he was told that his dog had died.

That was another reason why H. Rodman hated his parents. He still hated even their memory.

He hoped that they were frying in whatever Hell was reserved for the meanest of God's creations.

So—over the telephone—H. Rodman could presently be heard saying: "That old horse with the harness sores—tell him his father can't come out this week-end, but he'll be there early Monday. You're going to be able to save the white mare with the spavined legs? . . . Good. Good. *That* driver got six months in the workhouse and lost his peddler's license. And tell all the old fellows to eat hearty. I don't want to see any ribs showing! The poor yellow cat I brought out last week—has she had her kittens? . . . Good! Fine! I'll have to think up four new names. Give every dog an extra pat. Tell 'em not to fight. Only lousy humans fight. See you Monday, Doc——"

Hardboiled Rodman. Hatchetman Rodman.

America.

❖ 3 ❖

Back in their suite at the Waldorf-Astoria, Herr Viktor Reimalsky was talking to his Vienna manager. They spoke in German when alone, but this reporter will take the liberty of putting their conversation into the English language.

"'The New Paganini.' Excellent! Perfect!" he was repeating. "And it fits me so exactly. Why couldn't you long ago think of something like that?"

The Vienna manager thought: "I would not care to be laughed at by my colleagues in Vienna," but aloud he said, "I am just a business man. Not a great publicist like Herr Rodman. Don't forget that I persuaded *him* to take *you* on. He is the most successful impresario in America. With your arbitrary stand about this Halka person we are lucky that he agreed to our conditions."

"You agreed to *his* conditions," countered Herr Reimalsky. "We have to pay for the outrageous expense of getting that bakeshop bastard back to Vienna. First Class! First Class! I tell you now that half of that expense will come out of your ten percent of my earnings. I refuse to pay for all of it!"

"Very well," said the manager. "Though I again remind you that young Halka was your man, not mine."

"Yes, you wanted me to bring your brother-in-law who can't even play a scale properly."

"My brother-in-law has gone with the Paris Symphony this season," said the manager quietly.

Even he was getting a little weary of "temperament." Like humble Franz Rodar, the valet, he was biding his time. If he kept Viktor Reimalsky in line, as he intended to do, maybe he could become the Continental representative of this clever American impresario! It was a goal worth striving for.

They already seemed to have one thing in common. A healthy contempt for artists. H. Rodman was going to have an apt pupil in this regard. Viktor Reimalsky would see to that.

So, as he had noted H. Rodman doing, he switched to a more pleasant subject. "I talked with the Rodman office manager," he said, "and we are going to do very well by this tour. More money than half a dozen years in Europe could produce. Keep that in mind when you become irritated."

"It *should* mean money to make up for having to stay in such a country," said Herr Reimalsky. "Did you get a look at this Carnegie Hall as they call it? Dirty brick! Fire escapes along the side! Food shops along the street floor; some sort of common, cheap drinking bar on its main corner! I think they are called 'drug stores.' Do you suppose the audiences will be sober?"

"Drunk or sober, they have already paid for a lot of seats," said the manager. "This H. Rodman is a wizard."

"I suppose my name had nothing to do with it!" sneered Herr Reimalsky. "And I hope this new accompanist is capable. And does not chew what these Americans call gum. Its manufacture must be the country's leading industry! By the way, what did the Rodman person mean by the word 'chicanery'? Is it an American musical term?"

"No, a Vienna one," said the somewhat wearied manager. "I think you can guess its meaning. And I think Herr Rodman's advice about what it means is excellent. Don't try it with him either—if I am any judge of character."

"I suppose I'll have to stand for Halka playing the Sunday night appearance," said Herr Reimalsky.

"I frankly feel a bit sorry for that young man," said the manager. "To be shipped back home after one show."

"*You* feel sorry for *me,*" snapped Herr Reimalsky. "And now, please, get a waiter. I hope the food in this place is edible."

And as his manager picked up the telephone to ask for room service, the violinist stepped into the bedroom of the suite and viewed his profile in the dresser mirror. "The New Paganini," he repeated. "Excellent! Excellent! I think, though, I'll let my hair grow a trifle longer."

He turned the knob of the radio (which each suite contained) and there was wafted out:

"Cartwright Pills will hit the spot!
Good for anything you got!"

He switched to another dial number and received

"Yes sir! She's my baby!
No sir! Don't mean maybe—"

He snapped off the instrument. "Some country we're in!" he said to the manager who now stood in the doorway. "But the women on the streets and in the hotel lobby seemed to be good looking. Maybe it won't be as horrible as I think."

❖ 4 ❖

DR. STANISLAUS JOSEPH HALKA was speaking to the valet Franz Rodar, who had returned about six o'clock to their hotel room. It was a repetition of his first conversation, only now in more detail.

For he had meantime walked down to a great whirling carrousel named *Times Square,* gazed up at the huge signs and the Paramount clock; been jostled by the swift moving crowds. He had watched the great, happy face of the Camel Cigarette man blow smoke rings across the square; gaped (and was not ashamed to gape) up at the plunging waterfall that was the background of a block-long advertisement for raincoats. Smiled at the antics of a monster Mickey Mouse with moveable arms and legs and eyeballs.

He ventured into a splendid gilded restaurant named *Automat* where the food was around the walls behind small glass doors; and by inserting American nickels in a slot, the door would snap open with a click, and a sandwich, a triangle of crusted sweet called pie, a little brown jar of sizzling, brown baked beans were yours to take to a table and eat—eat democratically, sitting alongside whoever else happened to be there!

He had gone over to a magnificent Avenue named *Fifth,* where a newly built Tower called *Empire State*—some ten blocks to the south—reached up to literally pierce the sky. But what he really marveled at was the stream of fine motor cars that flowed endlessly up and down—motor cars and buses and taxis by the thousands it seemed; and the shop windows with their brilliant and clever and almost living tableaux—making pictures more exciting than any theater shows of his native Vienna—and all there, just for the looking!

He stood directly before, and at the base of, the high, straight-lined building rising like a giant-tall soldier-at-attention from the main court of a beauty spot called *Radio City*—looked up at its seventy stories of steel and glass—and wondered that it did not sway—it seemed so slender and finely lined. He felt impelled to salute it and did, touching his hat as he would have done on the passing of a high official in a Vienna parade.

And just across from it the splendid Gothic portals of the Cathedral of Saint Patrick—an edifice that would have dominated any city of Europe, as Saint Stephen's dominated Vienna—and yet, here, was almost lost among the great department stores that surrounded it.

But most of all, it was the people all about him—folk of all shades and facial contours, of all life stations, all economic brackets, who rubbed shoulders and were proceeding to their tasks—or were just proceeding. But the faces were all eager, not weary like most of the countenances on the streets of Vienna.

The very air of this land seemed to cry Hope! Courage! Freedom!

"I love it all," he said to Herr Rodar, "and when our tour is ended I shall come back here. I shall try to get permission to remain here for a while. I could perhaps even bring my father over, if I could obtain employment. Maybe he too could obtain employment——"

"I also have some plans about America," said the valet. "My sister, who lives in a state named *Kansas*——"

But he decided he had best not say anthing about that matter. This nice lad had a long siege ahead of him with the Herr violinist. There seemed to be already some ill feeling on the part of their employer.

He must not make matters more difficult for the young man.

✣ 5 ✣

THE GUARDS EMPLOYED at the Cloisters, that branch of the New York Metropolitan Museum of Art located in Fort Tyron Park on the Hudson River, at the northern end of Manhattan, were mostly ex-service men. Their preferment in being given employment by the great Museum served well both the men employed and this unique treasure house of medieval art.

It gave worthy men, who had served their country, a fairly easy and lifetime job. It gave the Cloisters guards of known integrity and courage; courage if courage were needed (including a familiarity with firearms) to meet any emergency in protecting the priceless art objects on exhibition there.

Guard Dennis O'Rourke had been among those sent over seas with General John J. Pershing to fight the War that would end all wars. He had been wounded and captured by the Germans in Northern France.

He had escaped, but the wound hampered his complete escape. Picked up by a Nun in the grounds of a Convent, the brave Sisters had hidden him and nursed him until the Armistice. Hidden him in the Convent itself at the risk, if discovered, of having their Convent destroyed and the Sisters punished by death and worse.

It was called the Convent of the Virgin Mary. Corporal Dennis O'Rourke had acquired a love for that Saint. A quite understandable devotion.

So when, at its very beginnings, he had obtained this job, and was stationed at the Cloisters, he was especially happy. And when, finally, he was placed in a room called the Early Gothic Hall, that happiness was entirely complete. For that small room with its threc wide, thirteenth-century leaded windows overlooking the Hudson, was largely devoted to statues of the Holy Mother and the Christ Child.

At one end of the room, protected by a post-supported guard-rope several feet from its pedestal, was the gold clad life-sized monument of the Virgin from the thirteenth-century choir screen of the Strasbourg Cathedral, perhaps the most important Gothic sculpture on this side of the Atlantic. She gazed across the gallery at another life-sized figure of the Queen of Heaven which was set off by a crimson curtain background—this image with golden hair, and blue mantle lined in green, the blue drapery stenciled in gold to imitate brocade. It was considered the finest of the fourteenth-century Madonnas from the Ile-de-France.

Other figures represented a Deacon Saint; a Bishop (this carved in wood), his gilded robe ornamented with a long black stripe down its front on which the letters of Ave Maria in gilt were painted against a jet black background. The colors still very bright and arresting, even after six hundred years. There was a large fresco of the Man of Sorrows, the Cross in the shadows behind him, his outstretched hands showing the imprint of the nails. This was from a

Florentine monastery. There was a painting of the Adoration of the Shepherds. And there were a number of smaller statues of the Virgin and Child, placed around the walls and by the windows of this gallery.

But the favorite of Guard O'Rourke, though given only a single line of mention in the Cloisters guide-book (price one dollar at the office desk near the entrance) had been placed in the Early Gothic Hall at a very recent date. It had been the gift of a wealthy Brooklyn brewer and sportsman. It was said to have been in a Knights Templars monastery at La Celle, south of Paris.

It was the statue of the Virgin that had been transported to America on an early voyage of the liner *Europa,* commanded (as we know) by Kommodore Hugo Frederick von Steinburg.

Guard O'Rourke's interest—and solicitude—for this particular work of art was perhaps first stimulated by an act of its donor, who was himself present when the statue was installed. For this Brooklyn gentleman was also one of the owners of a famous metropolitan baseball club.

He had presented baseball fan Dennis O'Rourke with a season's pass.

But ex-corporal O'Rourke very quickly acquired an affection for this statue that had nothing to do with home-runs and no-hit games. It had probably to do with the fact that the statue constantly reminded him of the young French Nun who had rescued him, who had been his chief nurse through two months of feverish illness. He felt that in giving a special care to this new (to the Cloisters) Virgin and Christ Child, he was repaying in a small way that debt to the Sisterhood of Holy Church.

On his arrival each morning he went to this statue first. Having looked up at it and crossed himself, he inspected its wooden pedestal to be certain it was firm. If there was a single fleck of dust on the image, he carefully brushed it off with his clean handkerchief. Children (and older folk) who somehow must touch the priceless exhibits in museums, were sternly admonished and asked—ordered—to refrain.

His last inspection about the room at closing time was to be certain "his baby" was all cozy in every way—solid on its base, free of any slightest foreign particle. He always murmured, "Sleep well, Holy Sister," just before he left.

The statue from La Celle was in loving hands.

Guard O'Rourke had only just entered his Early Gothic Hall that morning, when he first noticed the strange happening we are about to record. It was on the morning of the arrival of the liner *Europa*—a trip that had been bearing a violinist and his pianoforte accompanist to these shores.

As Dennis O'Rourke had looked up at the statue, it had *seemed to be smiling.*

There had always been that mystic, heavenly trace of a smile which Kommodore Hugo Frederick von Steinburg had noticed. Which Stanislaus Joseph had observed in the framed photograph. But now—it was a different smile. It seemed a very human smile. A smile of real happiness!

Now Guard O'Rourke had dreamed the night before (as he sometimes did) of the young French Nun, and how she had smiled down at him as he lay in a secret closet, very near to death, and whispered, "Courâge! Courâge!" in her soft Latin accent.

He thought that must be the reason that he was imagining this uncanny and quite impossible idea.

He of course did not know that at that moment a young man, standing on the high bridge of the great ocean liner that was passing the towers of lower Manhattan, was trying to put into words to his companion, the Herr Kommodore of that vessel, his instant affection for this new city.

At the noon hour Guard O'Rourke spoke of this *human* smile to a fellow guard stationed in the Hall of the Unicorn Tapestries, and with whom he was accustomed to go to lunch.

"Listen, pal, you're going cuckoo in that 'Virgin Room,' " laughed his friend. "Completely cuckoo! Next thing you'll be telling me your dumb statues can talk! And walk! You better get yourself transferred to some other department. How many years have you been up there?"

"Going on eight years," said Guard O'Rourke, "and I would not want to be moved to any other room."

"O. K.," said his friend. "Stay there and get loco! Thank God my tapestries don't smile. They're flat on the wall and all about an old time sporting event—a Hunt. No damn religion. I sort of like the guy with the spear ready to give this crazy unicorn animal the coop de grace as they call it. But that spear fellow don't never smile at me! And he'd better not! If he did I'd beat it quick to an eye doctor. And that's what you ought to do. Or to one of them fancy psychiatrists. Waiter—I'll have another coke."

But that afternoon, around three o'clock, Guard O'Rourke happened to again glance toward his special statue. And again it seemed to truly smile.

It was just the guard's too vivid imagination of course, but at that exact moment Dr. Stanislaus Joseph Halka was standing in Times Square and thinking: "I like New York. I like America."

PART FIVE
THE CONCERT

❖ 1 ❖

THE CARNEGIE HALL CONCERT of violinist Herr Viktor Reimalsky came off as planned. H. Rodman made no mistakes about his initial New York concerts.

The rehearsal was not merely a partial going-over of the music; a getting-used to the great Hall's acoustics (which were excellent), and the tone of the Steinway concert grand (also excellent) that would play the accompaniment. It included also a proper lighting to secure the best possible effects for that particular artist. It included the hanging (and the shadowing lighting) of a huge tapestry depicting the Paganini period—a beautiful tapestry H. Rodman had managed to borrow from the Metropolitan Museum. It included the presence and rehearsing of some thirty hard-handed gentlemen who formed H. Rodman's own personal, highly-trained, experienced professional claque.

This claque was an all important cog in the perfect organization of his concerts. They were not just ignorant hand-clappers. Each member had a knowledge of music—could discuss that music admiringly (if advisable) with a seat neighbor. Even then, they were shown just where to applaud—and in what degree; just where to build that applause into an ovation. Cries of "Bravo!" (at the proper time) were included with the basic hand-clapping.

H. Rodman knew that audiences would follow these leads as so many sheep follow a Judas goat in a slaughterhouse. It always amused him greatly to watch such a chain reaction.

And for this particular concert he had thought up a brilliant innovation. He had one of his business managers also engage the entire professional claque then operating at the Metropolitan Opera House, it being a Sunday night when they were not practicing their noble profession at that temple of pure art. And when this claque had appeared, tickets in hand, at Carnegie Hall, H. Rodman personally had indignantly refused its members admittance—had in person seized all their tickets and ordered his box-office to refund their price.

"Members of a notorious claque! No such skullduggery is permitted at *my* concerts!" he had said, and said it so that newsmen heard it, or heard of it.

So this claque, completely mystified, as they had been paid in advance, retreated with a minimum of protest. Especially as the initial retreat was to the box-office each to receive a three-dollar ticket "refund." There *was* protest, for some of them felt it was not honest not to give services for which they had been paid; they felt that the integrity of their profession was at stake! It made a first page story in all Monday newspapers, and did no harm to the lily white integrity of H. Rodman and his unsullied artist, "The New Paganini."

H. Rodman's personal, private claque, already well distributed about the Hall, took good care that their worthy profession did not have a let-down that evening. So was honesty and prestige upheld all around.

It is not essential to record in detail Herr Reimalsky's performance. His appearance was striking, and if his technique was somewhat on the showy side it did not matter. One critic did say that he "would have preferred a little less vibrato." Another complained of "the liberties he took in matters of changes of tempo," but as a whole "he buffaloed 'em," as H. Rodman would have phrased it.

The private claque saw that the applause was long and spontaneous, and that there were many encores and bravos at the very end. The huge maroon-walled, white-balconied auditorium was completely filled—it was more the trademark of H. Rodman than the performer that had filled it—and that audience was there in a frame of mind to be entertained. The New Paganini was off to a running start.

Our interest is in Stanislaus Joseph Halka.

All went well with that young man who played modestly and humbly in the shadows while the violinist performed in the spotlight, so to speak. All went well until the long number which was Part III of the First Part of the program, and came just before the Intermission.

This number had originally been a Franck *Sonata,* but a veritable cloud of violinistic locusts (to quote a reviewer of the previous season) had descended to peck upon this composition.

H. Rodman suggested at the rehearsal that a change be made, and the replacement number chosen was the Brahms *Sonata Op. 108, in D Minor* (as it would read on the program), with which Herr Reimalsky was very familiar, but which Stanislaus Joseph had not played for some time.

However, as it was the practice to have the printed scores before the pianist on his instrument, and a man to sit by to turn the pages, this change presented no especial problem. The rehearsal of it went smoothly, the young man surprising all by his proficiency in the rather difficult piano score.

But when the rehearsal had finished—it was then about three o'clock—Stanislaus Joseph was not satisfied. It had always been his practice when serving as an accompanist to thoroughly memorize any music he must play—so that along with watching his keyboard he could keep an eye either on his singer or his string instrument player, and so follow them in any deviation of tempo, much as the players in an orchestra follow a conductor. He asked permission to take this Brahms score with him back to his hotel.

He had noticed that there was an ancient upright piano in the small parlor just off the lobby. He could not help but have noticed it, for when he and the valet had registered, it had been giving out with a fortissimo rendition of Mascagni's *Intermezzo Sinfonico* from *Cavalleria Rusticana* which was then—and still is—very popular with amateur virtuosi who, in the proximity of a piano, are unable to resist a display of talent that might otherwise remain hidden.

For the sum of three dollars, that same to be placed on his weekly bill, the amount being computed at the rate of one dollar per hour, S. J. Halka rented this room for the next three hours along with the use of its pianoforte.

There was, however, one condition.

"Who wrote this music that you wish to practice?" asked the clerk. "I will have to know that before I can let you have use of the premises."

Wondering why the name of a composer should matter, Mr. Halka replied, "Why, Brahms—Johannes Brahms."

"I guess he's not the guy, but I must be sure," said the clerk. "This fellow didn't by any chance write *Deep in the Heart of Texas?"*

"I don't think so," said Stanislaus Joseph. "That is a composition with which I am not familiar. Johannes Brahms was a German composer. I don't believe he ever visited America."

"Good!" said the clerk, and seeing the utter mystification of his guest he explained. "You see, sir, last week I permitted two musicians —they were in vaudeville—to use the parlor premises for two hours rehearsing. It seems they were learning a number entitled *Deep in the Heart of Texas.* They played and sang it fifty or a hundred times, and an elderly gentleman who occupied a room just above the parlor was taken to Bellevue Hospital in a straitjacket. Gone quite off his nut he had, sir. Wanted to commit murder. And he had lived here for a year, quiet and orderly like, and paid his bill promptly each week.

"There's an elderly lady there now, sir, and I can't take any chances. By the way, do you sing as you play, sir?"

On being assured that singing was not to be a part of his practicing, our Stanislaus Joseph was permitted to enter the parlor with his music, and the clerk hung a printed card, kept for that purpose, on its outside doorknob, which read "OCCUPIED."

So, for the next three hours, this humble parlor and its cheap, battered upright heard one of the great intellectual compositions of the ages—the *Allegro,* the *Adagio,* the *Un poco presto e con sentimento* and the final *Presto agitato* of the kindly soul who was of the three great B's in music—Bach, Beethoven, Brahms. I fear its classic chords had slight relationship to *Deep in the Heart of Texas,* and though not so momentarily popular as that striking composition, it may have a longer life.

Six P.M. came and there were no complaints. Stanislaus Joseph had gone over and over some parts of it—the difficult parts—but softly. He had known it all by heart once.

He was what stage-actors call a "quick study." He emerged at six with the *Sonata in D Minor* again completely beneath his belt.

Did the lad have some premonition that prompted him to again commit this Brahms work to memory? I do not think so.

He was of the fast disappearing school of artisans, whether it be a musician or the soda jerker in a drug store, who take pride in their trade, who want to do perfectly whatever thing they set out to do. Unfortunately public appreciation of such artistry has lapsed, and a fancy flip of the wrist above a piano keyboard or above an ice cream soda has taken the place of real talent.

❖ 2 ❖

As Stanislaus Joseph was committing to memory the Brahms *Sonata,* a scene was taking place in the Waldorf-Astoria apartment of Herr Reimalsky. A scene that would have frightened him.

The quiet assurance of the lad at the rehearsal, and the obvious approval of H. Rodman, ex-pianist, who recognized real mastery of that instrument, had further infuriated the violinist.

It crossed Viktor Reimalsky's jealous and biased intellect that his accompanist's excellent performance—and a flawless performance that evening—might cause the impresario to change his mind, and insist on this bakeshop, Bismarck Suite *gassenbube* (the word might be freely translated as *guttersnipe)* continuing for the American tour. He must find some real reason for complaint.

The newly inserted Brahms *Sonata,* which the lad would apparently have to play from the printed score, afforded an opportunity. It involved a risk but, as the atom-age statesmen now say, a calculated risk.

So opposite him now, in the Waldorf-Astoria, sat the page-turner of the rehearsal. Viktor Reimalsky had asked the man to come to the apartment.

He was a thin, elderly man, and the violinist had noticed that his clothes were worn. Not especially prosperous, he surmised. An extra fee might not be unacceptable.

Herr Reimalsky came to the point at once. "I want you to do me a special service and I will pay you for it," he said. "How much do you receive for this page-turning task?"

"I receive fifteen dollars a concert," the man replied. "I am a music teacher and my pupils drop off in the summer months. I am glad to pick up what I can in the early Fall, even in such an inconsequential task."

"Your task is not inconsequential," said Viktor Reimalsky, "especially in the case of an accompanist playing a composition that he has not yet committed to memory."

"If you are worried about the Brahms *Sonata* which has been put into your program for tonight, I can relieve your mind. I know that work well. It so happens that just lately I have been teaching it to an advanced pupil. I will make no mistake in my page turning—if that is on your mind."

"Suppose that I wish you to make a mistake?" said Viktor Reimalsky. And he awaited the reaction to this question. As the man just stared at him and said nothing, the violinist continued: "Suppose that I am willing to pay you fifty American dollars if you could manage to make a mistake."

The page-turner had several times received an extra tip from a performer *not* to make any mistakes, but never before to make one! It sounded very "fishy." But fifty American dollars—as this foreign gentleman stated it!

That was the exact amount of his overdue rent for the first-floor studio apartment in Queens with the tarnished sign in the window: "Music—Private Instruction." It was now thirty days overdue, and he had been served with a dispossess—answerable the next morning in the District Court. He had been in those three small rooms twenty years. He was rooted there. It was both home and business. He had felt that if he lost them he would be completely sunk.

Then there was the problem of his little dog—now ten years old—and how that dog would be lost without the tiny backyard. That was what really had kept him awake at night ever since he had received the dreaded dispossess.

Suppose he could not even find a place where he could keep a dog, much less have a backyard for him?

"Just what do you wish me to do to earn this fifty dollars?" he asked, and felt a cold sweat gathering in the palms of his hands. He had always been an honest man.

"Something very simple and quite likely to happen accidentally," said Herr Reimalsky. "When you reach the beginning of the *poco presto* section of the Brahms *Sonata*—that would be, as you doubtless know, about half way through it—I want you to turn two pages instead of one; and then, in the confusion, if the whole score could be knocked to the floor—well, in that case I would make it one hundred American dollars."

"But your accompanist does not know that number. He had to follow the score to play it just now! I was especially careful to not turn a page until the last measure on it, and then turn very quickly so that no fraction of a second would be lost. It is a humble job but I am expert at it."

"You have stated the case most admirably," said Herr Reimalsky, and waited further comment.

"But what will happen to the finishing of the *Sonata?* There is the difficult *presto agitato* as well as this *poco presto*——"

"I will play them without a pianoforte accompanist—I will play them alone. They will be much better that way than with this amateur *lausbube* playing them."

The humble page-turner was not so stupid as to not realize that here was a feud—a hatred. And he was being bribed to pull a very dirty trick. The accompanist had seemed very young, but he was no *lausbube,* whatever that meant. The violinist would doubtless fare all right, else he would not have this happen. The accompanist—well, it would show him up as not being familiar with his music. It might cost him his job. That was evidently the intent.

But one hundred dollars! It would pay two months' rent, and two months' rent was almost due. It would bridge over until the pupils started their Fall lessons. It would save the "studio" with the worn sign in the window.

Most important of all, it would save that garden for his little dog. That little dog—his one loyal friend—the one living thing that cared for him. The reason, for years, that he had kept up the struggle to exist.

Who were these two well-dressed, well-fed Carnegie Hall performers anyway? Two foreigners, coming over here to take money out of America. If you were from Europe, the ignorant public, the ignorant managers, thought you must be good. Americans could starve and be dispossessed. Why should he care what happened to either of them? Or what happened to a concert promoted by H. Rodman—that hard, close-fisted tyrant! What would H. Rodman understand, or care, about giving a poor little dog a home and a backyard to play in?

The page-turner steeled himself for what he was about to say. "To do this, I must have the hundred dollars in advance—now," he enunciated.

It was the measure of Herr Viktor Reimalsky's hatred for Dr. Stanislaus Joseph Halka that he accepted this condition without a quibble. He had changed a sizable sum of money into United States currency the day before. He took from his wallet five twenty-dollar bills, and carefully counted them over.

"I will pay you now," he said. "I suppose I can rely on you to carry out your part of our arrangement."

The page-turner took the money. He did not count it. He arose. He wanted to get out of that room as quickly as possible.

"You can rely on me," he muttered. And added, "I am an honest man."

"I will see you at your Carnegie Hall at eight," said Herr Viktor Reimalsky.

"I will be there at eight," said the page-turner.

He ignored the extended hand of the violinist. He took up his weather-stained hat (it had once been a fifteen-dollar Knox) and walked rapidly to the door and down the corridor to the elevator buttons. He pressed a signal button viciously.

As he waited for the gilded car that would take him down and out into clean air, he used an expression that had once before been applied to Herr Viktor Reimalsky. "The swine!" he said beneath his breath. "The foreign swine!"

He had substituted the adjective "foreign" for the adjective "cheap." One hundred dollars was not "cheap." Not when one hundred dollars was almost a matter of life and death.

When the page-turner reached the One Hundred Thirty-fifth Street station in Queens, he hurried down the platform steps. He almost ran the two blocks to the row of brownstone "walk-ups" where, in one of the front windows (its window frame badly needing painting), was the small sign "Music—Private Instruction."

The front door was not locked, but the moment he opened it he could hear the small paws leaping against the inside panels of the first door on the left. That was his door. A pupil whom he had left one day while he went to a nearby delicatessen had told him that Spotty had started to leap at the door many minutes before his master arrived. The dog seemingly knew exactly when that master had turned into, and was coming down, the block in which they lived.

He put his key in the lock. The play of small paws against the door increased. And to it was added a soft, joyful whine, and the rapid beating of a hard tail against the bare wood floor.

The door open, the animal was in the arms that he loved; was held tightly to a worn coat and licking a thin, worn face with a small red tongue. "My precious little fellow! My precious little fellow!" he heard.

It was a small, homely, mottled-brownish creature whose exact ancestry was doubtless a little confused. In the main he was *schnauzer*. A small, wrinkled, whiskered face. Large eyes. A tail almost bare of hair covering, but that could wag at a tremendous speed.

The page-turner had gotten him from the Bide-a-Wee Home for unwanted animals. Ten years before, it had been. The animal had repaid that page-turner by ten years of utter devotion and love.

The man had given of himself also. He had several times refused offers to go on tour as an accompanist. It would have meant leaving the dog in New York. He had more than once gone hungry so that "the little fellow" could be fed.

On that particular day, Spotty heard his master say as he held up five oblong pieces of greenish, crinkling, printed slices of paper, "We're safe, Spotty darling! You won't lose your garden. You won't lose your room with the box of cut paper in the corner! They won't put us out now!"

Spotty sniffed at the oblong slices of paper. They were sure sliced very thin! Sniffed at again, they seemed to have no eating flavor. No food value! But evidently they were precious. Humans took a fancy at times to strange objects!

He knew what was precious *to him*. He snuggled his small head against the chin of his god.

Maybe there is another God who provides special golden clouds with a box of cut paper in one corner thereof, and harps that can be played with one hand, leaving the other hand free to hold small (perhaps even large) soft, smooth, furry faces to one's cheek.

3

As STATED, the concert came off as planned, even to the page-turner's role, he now being clothed in his worn, but carefully cleaned and pressed, tailed evening coat. Dr. Stanislaus Joseph Halka, "at the pianoforte" as the program stated in very small type, wore for the first time *his* coat with two tails—"like the tails of a fine bull—if that bull had two tails," to quote the description of the Vienna slaughterhouse expert.

The Brahms *Sonata Op. 108, in D Minor?* After two pages of *Un poco presto e con sentimento* the page-turner, gritting his teeth, turned the next two pages of the piano score at one fell swoop.

Did Stanislaus Joseph proceed to play what was then before him, which would have been at complete variance with the notes coming from the violin; and realizing this—falter and collapse?

He most assuredly did not.

The fact was, he had scarcely been regarding the music sheets at all, for it had seemed to him that his soloist was fumbling; and when not concentrating on his keyboard the accompanist was watching the movement of Herr Reimalsky's bow as it shot up and down across the violinist's left shoulder, so as to synchronize his pianoforte chords with this sudden and unexpected nervousness.

For Herr Reimalsky, expecting the planned catastrophe, had himself, as a part of this catastrophe, planned to suddenly stop playing, turn to view the confusion of his accompanist, and after a magnanimous gesture for him to desist from an obvious wrong accompaniment, proceed alone to an individual triumph over clumsy ignorance.

So when, at the expected measure, no such discord occurred, and a furious Herr Reimalsky, thinking he had been double-crossed by the page-turner, did whirl around, it was to see that page-turner, acting out his second step—a supposed realization of his initial "mistake"—reach to the music sheets, and with a nervousness not entirely feigned, dash the entire piano score from its holding rack, so that it scattered beyond retrieval on the platform floor. Thus, at least, did this gentleman earn, to its last penny, his hundred-dollar blood money.

Stanislaus Joseph had glanced up at his music just after the pages were treacherously turned, and just before this final carrying out of the page-turner's bargain. He had instantly realized that the new page before him was not the correct one, and proceeded to play, on his own, the correct notes—for, as we know, he had only a few hours before memorized the note sequence. He had moreover studied it all through his dinner.

His trained, photographic mind—as far as music was concerned—did not now falter.

When Herr Reimalsky turned, Stanislaus Joseph feared for a moment that he might have made some error, but reasonably certain that he was playing correctly, he smiled encouragingly at the violinist, even nodding his head in tempo with the music as he played. He had before, in his work as an accompanist, pulled back wavering soloists to the correct line.

Then came the page-turner's final "frantic" gesture, and the scattering of the music sheets about the floor.

But Stanislaus Joseph continued to play, even placing a foot momentarily on the sheets, so that the man at his side could not add to the confusion by trying to replace them, and gesturing to him with a momentarily free left hand to disregard the whole matter. And Herr Viktor Reimalsky, unless he chose to make an utter fool of himself, was forced to proceed, for it was obvious that his accompanist was not in error, and proceeding properly.

Good God, the little fool really knew the Brahms *Sonata!* His reading from the score at the rehearsal had been mere pretense! And he, Viktor Reimalsky, had paid out one hundred United States dollars for absolutely nothing!

Worse than that, paid it to the glorification of this accompanist upstart, for it was quite obvious that discerning music-knowing patrons in the nearby audience rows realized that the lad was proceeding heroically, and apparently saving, singlehanded, a disastrous situation.

And if there was any doubt of what the audience thought and believed, at the end of several encore bows by Herr Reimalsky there were scattered cries of "Accompanist! Accompanist!" and the inwardly seething violinist had to extend a hand toward Stanislaus Joseph, and the young man had to rise and bow, before the concert could continue into the next number.

Could it be that the Three Fates were still concerned about our hero? Or Almighty God—in whichever you believe?

And that this time they had used a humble page-turner who loved his dog?

✤ 4 ✤

TWO VIEWERS of the episode were completely confused.

The page-turner was both confused and grateful. He had liked the boy and had been obliged to steel his heart before carrying out his shabby bargain. He had to conjure before his visual consciousness the image of the face of "the little fellow" waiting back in the Queens flat, before reaching for the music pages he intended to muff.

The other astonished viewer was H. Rodman.

H. Rodman had a habit of climbing to the so-called Dress Circle of the great Hall, which balcony, above two other balconies of boxes, extended in a great semi-circle around the back and sides of the auditorium. By going to its extreme end, he could look down directly onto the stage. He would station himself there especially when he had artists new to his management, for he could then watch the technique of their performance with an unobstructed and knowing eye.

He was standing at this vantage point for the playing of the Brahms *Sonata*.

His keen, experienced eyes realized instantly that the page-turner had taken two pages in his fingers at that particular moment. Deliberately done so, it seemed. He held his breath, but relaxed when the accompanist continued to play properly as if nothing had happened; and H. Rodman then noticed that it was Viktor Reimalsky, not the young man at the pianoforte, who became confused.

And the ensuing spilling of the music onto the floor seemed to be also a deliberate gesture of his page-turner. And it was all very curious that this accident—if it were an accident—had to happen during the playing of the one number that the young (and disliked-by-the-violinist) accompanist supposedly did not know. Or did he really know it? It seemed that he did!

Had the accompanist somehow connived with the page-turner to make himself a hero? Then why the obvious foreknowledge of the mishap on the part of the violinist?

H. Rodman did not fancy mysteries when they concerned his concerts. And the department of "chicanery" was one he preferred to reserve to himself. It was not a department for artists to mess into with a crude, unskilled technique.

It took no Sherlock Holmes to deduce that the one who would *know*—the fellow in the middle of all these strange occurrences—was the page-turner. Back in the Hall's box-office H. Rodman instructed his manager to bring this page-turner to the Rodman office immediately after the concert. He would go there anyway, or to the box-office, to collect his fifteen-dollar service fee.

Our page-turner would never forget that interview, or cease to wonder at its outcome.

Ushered into the presence of the great impresario—whom he had never personally met before—his courage had about deserted him. He could feel it oozing down from his stomach and out through the soles of his feet.

H. Rodman stood in the center of his office floor, and the small hard eyes seemed to bore right through the frail man who taught music in Queens. That man felt that guilt was stamped on his every feature.

"What exactly happened during the Brahms *Sonata,* sir?" the concert manager demanded. "I want the truth. I saw the entire incident myself, from the left side of the dress circle. I was looking right down on it. I have reason to believe it was not an accident."

The page-turner braced himself. "You may not believe me, Mr. Rodman," he said, "but I had made up my mind to come and see you in the morning and tell you all. I had never before, in fifty years, done a dishonest act. Today I was desperate. I accepted one hundred dollars to turn to the wrong page at the start of the *poco presto con sentimento* section of the Brahms *Sonata*. And then to see that the entire score was knocked to the floor."

"Who paid you the hundred dollars?" asked H. Rodman. "The accompanist?"

"Good heavens no! The honesty of that young man was what made me feel like the contemptible heel that I know I am. Thank God he was able to continue playing. He must have memorized it between the rehearsal and the evening performance. That is what he had done, he told me afterwards. And he did not even berate me for what he thought was an accident. Said it might happen to anyone. Sir, the bribe money was paid to me by the violinist, Viktor Reimalsky."

"When did Viktor Reimalsky pay you this?" asked H. Rodman.

"Late this afternoon, in his apartment at the Waldorf, where I was asked to go after the rehearsal."

"Why did you do such a thing? Don't you realize it might have wrecked my concert? Did you feel no responsibility to me as your employer?"

"From what the violinist said I felt the performance would go on. Anyway it was *his* performance. He said he wanted to play the last half of the *Sonata* alone. I realized of course that there was some feud between him and the young piano player. That was obvious all through the rehearsal. But neither of them meant anything to me. I—I was desperate, sir. Desperate for some money."

"Desperate about what?" said H. Rodman harshly. "Gambling debts? Maybe a sick wife?" There was a special sneer in the latter question. Broke musicians always possessed "sick wives."

"No sir," said the page-turner. "I do not gamble and I have no wife." He swallowed hard and continued. "It was a dog, sir. I know you will think me quite mad—quite insane—but I had been served with a dispossess of my studio in Queens. I live there also, and they let me keep my dog there. There is a small backyard where he can play, and when I have to be in New York I know he will not be hit by cars. He is quite an old dog.

"I—I love him, sir. I think he would die if he lost that home."

H. Rodman looked hard at this page-turner. The man's face was drawn. He seemed on the verge of breaking down.

"I hope you will not think it necessary to have me arrested, Mr. Rodman," he said, "for then my dog would surely die. I still have the hundred dollars at home. I intended to pay my overdue rent with it tomorrow morning in the Court. I will return it instead to you. You can give it to the violinist. I do not wish to ever see him again. I will try to find some other way to keep my home."

A music page-turner from Queens does not to this day understand the subsequent actions of impresario H. Rodman.

First, that gentleman laughed. It started with a chuckle, then became a loud guffaw. Then he sat at his desk, flipped open a large-paged checkbook and commenced to write.

"How do you spell your name? What *is* your name?" he asked.

He was given the name, and getting it, apparently filled it into whatever he was writing. He tore out this writing along perforated edges (it made a slight clicking sound) and handed what he had torn out to the page-turner.

"There is my check for one hundred dollars," he said. "That pays you for tonight and the eighty-five dollars balance can apply to future work for this office. There will be three more concerts this coming week. That will still make you owe us forty dollars, which can apply to the following week. I think we can give you several jobs each week."

"But sir, Mr. Rodman—I do not understand! But I will bring in the violinist's money—it is in twenty dollar bills—the first thing in the morning——"

H. Rodman again commenced to laugh. He had a very hearty laugh this time also. "If you gave back that money I would fire you on the spot!" he said sternly. "Have you arrested also!" And he dropped the sternness and laughed once more.

"But I do not understand at all!" gasped the page-turner. He looked down unbelievingly at the piece of pale blue paper he held in his hand.

"Don't try to," said H. Rodman. "Just see that you take good care of your damn dog. And get yourself a new concert evening coat. The office will advance you the money, if you haven't got it to spare. My regular employees must make a first class appearance."

"Regular employees!" gasped the man. "Mr. Rodman—I—I'd leave my right arm here—on that couch—if you needed it!"

"Don't do anything like that, please," said H. Rodman, and smiled for the first time. "You'll need that arm to turn music pages. Only —don't turn any more wrong pages, unless—" and he smiled again, "unless *I* instruct you to do so. It's a neat trick, and I thought I knew 'em all!"

"God bless you, sir," said the page-turner. He half extended a hand to grasp that of the impresario, but H. Rodman had turned his back and gone to his desk. The strange interview was at an end, the page-turner inferred, and he departed. For H. Rodman did not look up at him again. He had taken out his wallet, and was looking at a small snapshot that intimates thought must be that of a girl.

"I suppose I am a complete sucker," he said. "I don't suppose he really has a dog. Still, maybe he has. . . . The New Paganini nicked for a hundred bucks!" Again H. Rodman laughed.

His office manager entered and placed before him the box-office statement of the night's concert. Six thousand, two hundred and eight dollars. Absolute capacity. Forty percent of it to H. Rodman, less some expenses.

His manager was however somewhat surprised to hear H. Rodman's comment. "Tricksters all!" he said. "All muck! Muck!" And when the man had taken up his hat and left with a "Good night, sir," H. Rodman said to himself, "At least I can now start building the new addition to the horse barn. Get it done by winter sure."

✣ 5 ✣

H. RODMAN did have one friend—not of the animal kingdom—whom he respected and liked. It was a gentleman also in the "music racket" (as the impresario termed his art, unless he were talking to the press for publication), but this friend was in a somewhat different branch. He was the great voice teacher and coach, Albert Rouchard.

Like the page-turner from Queens, Mr. Rouchard had a studio on the first floor of the building in which he also lived, but there the resemblance ceased.

The building was a fine apartment house on the north-west corner of Broadway and Eighty-sixth Street. The studio was a spacious, triplex room which had been especially constructed so that its three-storied-high walls and ceiling were ideal for singing. It was sound-proofed and air-conditioned. There was a smaller reception room where pupils sat while awaiting their lessons.

There were pupils sitting and "awaiting" there from eight-thirty in the morning till sometimes eleven-thirty at night.

Mr. Rouchard's combination secretary and receptionist had her small desk in this room, which was the usual plebeian one story in height. Mr. Rouchard lived with his sister in the penthouse atop the high building, from the terraces of which he had a splendid view of the Hudson. That is, in such brief time as he had to view it.

He paid fifteen hundred dollars a month rent for the studio and the penthouse. He had never been in danger of being served with a dispossess.

For although there was no sign (worn or unworn) in the front window reading "Music. Private Instruction," Mr. Rouchard's problem was not how to get pupils, but which pupils to accept. The instruction that went on there was certainly in Music, and that instruction was private.

An observing person would have noticed that there was a marked difference in the appearance of the pupils who came from eight-thirty till ten in the mornings, and those who filled out the rest of the day till the dinner hour. Then from nine P.M. on, there was a return of pupils of the first category.

The pupils who came from ten-thirty till the dinner hour—Mr. Rouchard taking only a brief half hour for lunch—were (if female) dressed in sable coats and the smartest of Fifth Avenue gowns; and the men, except for an occasional Bohemian-minded eccentric, were so garbed as to indicate affluence or at least a steady income. Some arrived in chauffeured limousines, others in taxis. The women sometimes had their maids—and both women and men often had a manager or an agent with them.

They paid at the rate of one hundred dollars an hour for their instruction, and it was payable in advance across the desk to the secretary in the waiting room. They sometimes thought Mr. Rouchard grasping—quite a little "money mad."

But they paid it. He was the greatest voice coach in the great city.

He could get you up in a new role for the "Met" in a week. He knew the leading roles of practically every opera. Many "triumphant" first performances in the great building at Broadway and Thirty-ninth Street were due to his coaching. Many experienced singers—the so-called stars at that opera house—came to him regularly to keep their voices in trim. To keep from going stale in some well known role.

A producer of musical comedies paid him a flat five thousand dollars to "make sing" a great ballet dancer he wished to star in a musical play, and Albert Rouchard had accomplished the miracle in a month of daily lessons. The lady was no Lily Pons, but she did "get away" with half a dozen numbers most creditibly.

Sometimes wealthy society women took lessons just to amuse or amaze themselves, and to surprise their friends. These paid a hundred dollars for a *half-hour* lesson.

"Money-bags Rouchard" was the name they gave him around the "Met." "He must keep it in barrels" was another envious comment.

Albert Rouchard kept very little of it.

The pupils who came from eight-thirty A.M. till ten, and those who came in the evenings, did not arrive in limousines or even taxis. They wore no sable coats. They did not carry their music in hand-tooled portfolios. The men—mostly very young men—sometimes were even coatless or wore leather blazers. The clothes of the women were more likely to have been bought in Union Square.

Some of these pupils paid Albert Rouchard fifty cents a lesson. Some few as much as three dollars. Most of them nothing at all.

They paid what they could afford—or nothing. The secretary knew that Mr. Rouchard was paying the room-rent of many of them. Keeping them in eating money. Sending them to good concerts; to see performances at the "Met."

They came to him from teachers in the public schools located in the poorer sections of the city. From the personnel directors of department stores and factories. From Catholic priests and Jewish rabbis. From other teachers who could not afford to do, or had not the skill to do what Albert Rouchard was doing. From the choruses of musical plays whose musical directors felt that here and there was a real talent, but little money, and knew of Albert Rouchard's great heart.

His doctor and his sister also knew of that heart, and worried about it. He was fifty-two years old and working himself to death.

Not for money, as they thought around the "Met." He had been born, apparently, with a God-given talent for teaching. He had no false modesty about that talent. He knew he was the finest teacher of voice in New York. He was fearful that some deserving young persons would not reach the heights, would never even get started toward reaching the heights, because he could not give them of his knowledge and encouragement and financial help.

Of the young people who came to him he asked only three questions. *Did they sincerely care for music? Did they really want to study music? Was it a lack of money that was preventing their pursuit of this goal?*

One other question came later which he himself answered. *Did they have a talent for music?* If he found that they did not, he frankly told them so. Advised the females to get married. The young men to stick to that job in the shoe store.

But if they possessed the spark—he gave them all he had. One year he had ten of the more promising pupils taking post-graduate courses in Europe, paying all their expenses.

The hundred-dollar-an-hour pupils met the bills. So that all other bills could be met promptly, their fees were collected in advance.

"Money-bags Rouchard."

America.

He had been born and grew up in Paris. A boy singer. At eighteen, a leading tenor at the Opéra-Comique. Came to America for a short engagement in New York with that famous organization. Returned to Paris, and wanting to do more than merely sing in the profession that he loved—also realizing that his light voice was not going to last—he studied hard and became a conductor. Finally a conductor for two years at the Paris Opéra.

Still dreamed of America. Wanted to do *something* to create new singers. Felt that in America, with its vitalizing mixture of races, was the soil from which new, great singers were most likely to spring.

The father, a noted Paris surgeon, died. The son and daughter, now in their early thirties, were left a modest inheritance. Enough to migrate and settle in America. In New York, to carry out his dream. The fact that the father performed hundreds of difficult operations on poor folk for no fee, along with the large fees he obtained from wealthy patients, was probably where Albert Rouchard got the idea of "making the rich pay for the poor." That was how his father expressed it. The father who felt that he *owed* to his fellow man all the help his unique skill could give.

Like father—like son. The father in surgery. The son in music.

There are some people in the world who are cursed in that unique way. Feel that they owe something to the world! This reporter had a professor in rhetoric and English at Yale University who so felt. One of the eternal glories of that football famous institution. His name—Dr. John M. Berdan. There was another on the athletic fields. His name—Mike Murphy. No degree. Just a right guy with a heart of gold.

Arriving in New York, Albert Rouchard stepped into a sudden vacancy and continued for two years to be concert master at the "Met." He was especially welcome, because it was the season they were adding several French operas to the repertory.

He could have gone on to be a conductor. He chose the studio, where he would be his own master. Where he could make those dreams come true.

Albert Rouchard had never been very tall. When he sang at the Opéra Comique he had been slender, but now he was decidedly—as regards his body—on the portly side, with a round, friendly face. He detested exercise of any kind and loved rich foods, especially rich desserts. He was a connoisseur of, and loved, fine wines with his elaborate dinners—factors that also worried his doctor, if not his sister.

When not dining out at some expensive restaurant, that sister's greatest pleasure was to herself prepare the dishes her brother liked best, though they employed two maids and a cook in the penthouse.

He dressed immaculately, and there was always a fresh carnation in his coat buttonhole. And he worked at teaching and coaching twelve to fifteen hours a day, except on the occasional evening when he attended the opera or a concert.

One slightly humorous notation—humorous because of his friendship with H. Rodman.

He hated animals.

He had once refused a thousand dollar cash fee from the powerful "Met" itself, to quickly coach a great prima donna in a new role, because she insisted she must bring her dog to the studio. On her first visit with the dog he had asked her to leave. "Ordered her to leave," the indignant lady reported to the "Met." He had sent back her advance payment.

H. Rodman had presented him, one Christmas, with a small, framed, printed sign reading—

NO DOGS ALLOWED

to hang in the studio. Albert Rouchard did not hang it there, although the letters were engraved in gold, and it was most expensively framed. Not because he did not like the sign, or agree with and appreciate it, but because he felt that, aesthetically, it would be out of place among the Cézannes, the Renoirs, the Degas that decorated that studio's walls.

He thought H. Rodman just a little queer because of his love of animals—Albert Rouchard being one of the three or four who knew of the New Jersey farm.

H. Rodman thought Albert Rouchard a little "loco" because of his love of singers.

They were tremendous friends—these two.

6

THE SWITCHBOARD in H. Rodman's outer office was an extremely busy one during business hours. The male operator (H. Rodman would have no women around the office, although a man at the switchboard got double the salary of a girl) always said, "I will see if Mr. Rodman is in," meaning *I will see if he will talk to you.*

He did not say this when Albert Rouchard phoned. He had orders always to connect Albert Rouchard immediately.

At ten A.M. this Monday morning, the morning after the Viktor Reimalsky concert, the operator had practically no choice in the matter. For the well known tenor voice with the slight French accent said: "Give me that old humbug H. Rodman, and give him to me *immediatement*. Tell him it's the Federal Bureau of Investigation."

The Rodman operator was a potential editor. He condensed this message to three words. "Mr. Rouchard, sir," he relayed to his boss.

"Horatio—" (and here we learn for the first time what the "H" of "H. Rodman" stood for, and doubtless the reason for its concealment), "Horatio," said Albert Rouchard, "you heartless villain—I am reporting you to the S.P.C.C."

"What in hell is the S.P.C.C., Albert, you softhead?" said H. Rodman.

"The Society for the Prevention of Cruelty to Claques," said his friend. "What is all this phony nonsense on page one of my *Tribune* about your heroics in the Carnegie Hall lobby last night? You ought to be in the Tombs."

"In my business I've got to make the front page once in a while," laughed H. Rodman, "and it wouldn't do you any harm if you'd let me put you there at least once a year. Only you are so damn honest. You'll never be a success, my friend. Did you come to my concert?"

"God, no!" came the voice over the wire. "I might have though, just to see what new horror you are perpetrating on the innocent public. 'The New Paganini'! Sounds pretty dreadful to me. But I had to work all day Sunday and half the night. Getting up Fraulein Herta Sabora in *Salome* for a Tuesday opening. Her brain is as thick as her hips—some voluptuous siren she's going to be! But the *Jokanaan* weighs nearly two-eighty, so it will present a euphonious picture on the Met stage. I must battle with her some more this afternoon."

"Do you want me to have her bumped off? I have an ex-gangster company manager——"

"No. For she has a voice that is from Heaven itself. Why God ever gave such a woman such a voice I do not know! But there it is. I'm furnishing the brains. She the voice. It will be another triumph."

"For which you will receive no credit," said H. Rodman.

"I'm getting well paid," said Albert Rouchard. "Very well paid."

"What else is on your mind?" said H. Rodman. "Unless you just called me up to insult me."

"Two matters," said Albert Rouchard. "First—will you dine with me this Thursday? I'm going to take three hours off Thursday. Think I will deserve it. Dinner at Le Pavillon where that genius Henri Soulé has just invented a fresh strawberry *soufflé*. They say it's divine! Will you meet me there at seven sharp?"

"I had another engagement, but it's cancelled as of this moment," said the impresario. "I will be there."

"Good!" said Albert Rouchard. "I was afraid you might be over at that cursed farm eating hay and oats, or canned dog food. Now for request number two. It will keep me from going stark, staring mad if you can help me out."

"Just name it," said H. Rodman.

"Find for me but quickly, my friend, a piano accompanist that can play the operas. My own man sailed for Europe Saturday midnight. His mother is very ill in Milano. He's been wanting to go back for a year and I don't think he will return. I can play the scores myself, but I can't both play and teach properly."

"Will this fellow also have to play before dawn and into the night for all that riffraff you clutter your place with?" asked H. Rodman. "You know, Albert, you're going to have to answer some day for all the misguided youth you are encouraging to make screechy noises in an already too screechy world."

Albert Rouchard laughed. "Ah, my friend, you'll never understand," he said. "No, I have a piano player for the riffraff, as you call it. Two of them in fact. But they can't cope with opera. This job will be strictly union hours—ten-thirty till six, with half an hour for lunch. Double overtime if we have a rush case like this *Salome* task. Maybe you know someone——"

"Maybe I do," said H. Rodman. "I'll call you back later. Going to the farm this afternoon——"

"Oh God!" interjected Albert Rouchard.

"But maybe I can arrange it before I leave," continued the impresario, ignoring the interjection. "Sure you don't want the Salome murdered? For I can arrange that *right now*. Bill Levy, whom I am sending out with the 'New Paganini' that you so grossly malign, has just come into the office. I'd like him to have a little practice——"

"The law will catch up with you yet," laughed Albert Rouchard. "No murders. Just an opera accompanist. Hope I hear from you quickly, and don't forget—Le Pavillon, Thursday at seven. Goodbye, you old humbug. I must get back to work. Not a loafer like you who lives off the toil of others——"

The phone clicked off. H. Rodman tapped the glass top of his spacious, mail-cluttered desk for some moments which meant that he was debating with himself. Then he summoned his office manager.

"Get that piano player of last night's concert over here at once," he said. "He was to come in at noon, but tell him to come now. Immediately. Name of Halka. You must have the hotel address."

H. Rodman had an idea.

And some hundred and fifty blocks, north and west, in a room at the Cloisters overlooking the river Hudson, a Guard stationed in that room happened at that exact moment to look over at his favorite statue. "The lovely lady is smiling again!" he exclaimed to himself. "I may be going cuckoo—maybe I do just imagine it, but I could swear I saw it smile just now!"

And Guard Dennis O'Rourke crossed himself.

❖ 7 ❖

For almost the first time that he could remember, H. Rodman had not looked forward with keen pleasure to the firing of an artist. That is, if he had given a matter so inconsequential any thought at all. But the case of the young accompanist of Violinist Viktor Reimalsky had been disturbing his usual, self-centered calm.

It had not disturbed him after the initial interview with the violinist and his manager in the New York office, except in so far as it required him to find another accompanist, and that problem had been quickly solved.

The arranging of the transport back to Vienna of this Halka person, he would turn over to his own efficient office manager.

But since the actual concert, since the disclosure of the full infamy of what had been attempted at that concert as confessed by the unhappy page-turner, even Hardboiled Rodman had felt sorry for the lad. And he could not help but admire the way the young pianoforte player had carried on in the face of what seemed to be a real accident, and had tried, and really saved the program from being a disaster, if not for Herr Reimalsky, at least for the reputation of H. Rodman's perfectly planned performances.

That the boy—he seemed but a boy—had taken the trouble to learn the Brahms *Sonata* between the rehearsal and the evening performance—a herculean stint, even if one had once before known it—was a devotion to duty quite unusual in H. Rodman's experience with artists.

All this for a reward of twenty-five dollars! Twenty-five bucks and a swift kick in the pants! Fired! Sent back more or less in disgrace, as if he had not been equal to his task. And the lad had saved the show!

Such were the thoughts of H. Rodman as he walked from his office to his suite at the nearby Savoy-Plaza, the night before.

He always left all business worries behind at the office; at the Savoy-Plaza he was deep in the most exciting part of an new Ellery

Queen murder mystery which he intended finishing before going to sleep. Instead, he kept thinking about this wretched Austrian lad, and how, the next noon, he must inform him that he was being shipped home.

H. Rodman could still insist on the accompanist being taken on tour (the new arrangement was not yet signed up), but what kind of hell would he then be pushing the lad into? It would be as if he found an abused horse, and let that horse go on being abused simply on condition that the animal be fed regularly!

It is a compliment, not a disparagement of Stanislaus Joseph, that in the mind of H. Rodman the boy's welfare had become as important as that of some unprotected and helpless dumb animal. But the lad was far from dumb—at least in as far as music was concerned.

H. Rodman had never before felt that way about any human.

Then the telephone call from Albert Rouchard.

Perhaps—perhaps—but could the young pianist meet the exacting needs of his friend the voice teacher? How well did he know opera?

He could only send for Halka and find out. It was at least encouraging that for the moment a weight seemed lifted from his mind. He could conduct his business normally. Bawl out a printer who had made a mistake about some "heralds." Complain to the agent of the building about the impudence of a new elevator starter, and insist that the man be discharged.

If that Ellery Queen yarn were not parked back at the Savoy-Plaza he could catch up on it and even read another chapter then and there, in the office, before the young man could arrive.

Stanislaus Joseph, having been reached by the Rodman office manager, did presently arrive, not entirely unaware of the probable reason—the reason, as far as it concerned Viktor Reimalsky—for his summons.

For Franz Rodar, the valet, had blurted it all out on his return from the Waldorf late the night before, where he had been obliged to listen to a tirade from his employer, as the "New Paganini" was preparing to retire.

Back at his own hotel, Franz Rodar had exclaimed: "I can't keep it from you any longer, Herr Halka. A new American accompanist is going to be put into your place. You are not going on with the American tour."

Stanislaus Joseph was stunned. He had realized that there had been resentment about the Bismarck Suite and the Kommodore's table, but he did not dream it would come to this!

What would he tell his father, his patron the bakeshop owner, the workers in the bakery, his old teacher, the kind Professor Lavar who had written the Kommodore of the *Europa*, the good folk in the tenement who had bought him all those fine clothes? How could he face any of them?

At last he said, "I knew there was some feeling against me on the boat—I suppose I should not have moved to that fine suite—but I thought what I did at the concert tonight would make up for it."

Franz Rodar said, "Herr Halka, that was the final blow to Herr Reimalsky's vanity. Didn't you realize that the whole thing had been planned to discredit you? I did not know about that part of the affair until tonight, or I would have warned you. I surely would. You have been kind to me. I like you."

"How do you mean the whole thing had been planned?" exclaimed Stanislaus Joseph, incredulous of what he was hearing.

"The page-turner had been paid to do what he did," said Franz Rodar.

Stanislaus Joseph sat down on his bed. His world had suddenly collapsed.

"You would have been dismissed anyway," said Franz Rodar, feeling keenly sorry for the young man, and trying now to soften the blow. "It had all been arranged with the American impresario, even before the rehearsal. But you were not to be told until after the concert. Herr Reimalsky and his manager had an argument about that last night. His manager wanted you to be kept on, but Herr Reimalsky would have none of it.

"At least the American impresario is going to send you back First Class. I heard that much. He is to send for you and make the arrangements in the morning."

The boy was speechless and the valet continued. "Maybe you are lucky, Herr Halka. More lucky than I am. I have to go on with that conceited, selfish brute for a while. But when we reach a place called Wichita in the State of Kansas—" and he told the lad of his long laid plan.

"Look," he said at the end, "if you need money, Herr Halka, I have a little. Yesterday I changed the kronen I brought with me, and I have nearly a hundred American dollars. You are welcome to any part of it you need." And he took from an inner pocket his store of United States five- and ten-dollar bills.

The pale grey eyes of Stanislaus Joseph had been staring straight ahead into a vast void of blankness. What now? Nothing—nothing—nothing—perhaps presently a brink from which he could leap into a greater blankness and put an end to it all.

But suddenly, out of that blankness, came not a brink—a precipice—but vivid upstanding shapes—the Liberty Statue directing a symphony of towering long-stemmed notes that was lower Manhattan—the whirling crowds in Times Square, crowds now of eager folk all giant tall—the gilded entrance of the Automat—the great face of the cigarette-smoking man blowing his Saturn-like rings high above the heads of the surging people, the marvelous perpendicular building in Radio City, the hundreds of motor cars gliding lightning-fast, as if by magic, along the Avenue called Fifth——

It was not the offer of the money that had brought these idealized shapes from out the blankness. Stanislaus Joseph had scarcely heard that offer. It was what the valet had said just before that offer.

"You are staying in this America?" he asked, and into his eyes came a new, clear light.

"I am going to try to stay," said Franz Rodar. "My sister and brother-in-law think they can arrange it—they are already American citizens—I intend to become an American citizen——"

"I'm not going to go back, First Class or Second Class—at least not yet! I too am going to stay in America if I can!" suddenly declared Stanislaus Joseph.

"I'll tell you what," said Franz Rodar impulsively, "I'll write to my sister. Maybe she would invite you to come to this farm. I don't know whether they have use for music in this Kansas or not—I saw a film yesterday about the American West—all the men carrying guns, and a lot of savage folk called Indians—sort of wild-like it seemed—but if you could learn farming as I intend to do—my sister and her husband raise wheat——"

Stanislaus Joseph smiled. "You are wonderfully kind," he said. "I will never forget how kind you are. And generous. But I have some money. I don't need money. The fellow workers in my father's bakery in Vienna and the owner of the bakeshop gave me five hundred American dollars. I would not have taken it if I had known—the workers are just poor people—it's a draft that was hidden in a gift wallet—a draft on a bank here in New York. I haven't cashed it yet. Now I'm glad I have it. And what you say about your sister—she must be a wonderful woman—I hope some day I'll meet her—but it's right here in this city of New York I want to stay."

"Maybe, with your talent at the pianoforte, you can get work here," said Franz Rodar.

"I can at least try," said Stanislaus Joseph. Then, with another smile, "If I can't get that kind of work, I am an expert with the bakery *dressiersack*—the bakery men gave me one I had used—I have a letter to a cousin of one of the men who works on a street called York Avenue—works in a bakeshop there—I will look him up. The men gave it to me as a joke—but maybe it won't be a joke after all! What I do hope is that this American impresario will know of some other music job——"

"Don't count on him," said Franz Rodar decisively. "He's almost as heartless as Herr Reimalsky, as far as I can see."

"He can't any more than throw me out," smiled Stanislaus Joseph. "I didn't notice any music at the Automat Restaurant, but perhaps they would consider using a pianoforte player—and Franz—if you need any part of my five hundred American dollars—if you are discharged before you reach this Kansas—just let me know. I'll send you my address as soon as I find a more economical place to live——"

They talked a while longer about the wonders of this America, and then they both went to bed.

Stanislaus Joseph dreamed of a huge face blowing smoke rings over all the magic towers of Manhattan—sometimes it was a face —sometimes a huge *dressiersack*.

A hundred and fifty blocks away, more or less, a statue of the Virgin and the Christ Child *did* smile out through a leaded window onto the moonlit Hudson—only at that hour there was present no Guard O'Rourke to see her smile.

✣ 8 ✣

DR. STANISLAUS JOSEPH HALKA, graduate of the University of Vienna, sat in the office of H. Rodman.

Franz Rodar was right. Those small, hard eyes and that sullen blond face promised no friendliness. For H. Rodman had the bad news to deliver first.

"I have to tell you, Mr. Halka, that your engagement as the accompanist of Viktor Reimalsky ended with last night's concert. Your passage back to Vienna will of course be paid. When would you like to return?"

Stanislaus Joseph screwed up his courage. "I would like to stay in New York, sir, if that is possible," he said.

"Why?" said H. Rodman.

"I don't exactly know why," said Stanislaus Joseph, "except that I already love New York. I—I want to some day write a symphony about it all. Some day when I know New York better, and know music better. But meantime I will have to find work. Perhaps—perhaps you know of some other job in music, sir. I am not penniless, sir. There can be a little time. That is, if I am permitted to stay here. My passport says six months. But I understand you can apply to become a citizen if you are employed. I think I would like to become a citizen of your America, sir."

Stanislaus Joseph paused. He had not meant to say all of that! He had not even thought of all that. It just came out with a rush.

He hadn't in fact realized that he wanted all of that—but he knew now that his inner heart had spoken. *All that* was what he now really wanted.

And having stated it in so many words, he looked fearfully at H. Rodman. That case-hardened gentleman was himself surprised. He got up from his desk. He stood in the middle of the room. He towered above and frowned down upon Dr. Stanislaus Joseph Halka.

Was he going to be thrown out, as not quite right in his mind? So thought Stanislaus Joseph.

"My God, you little runt, you've got guts!" said the impresario. "But I might have guessed it from what happened last night at my concert. Before I forget, let me thank you, young man, for what you did last night."

"I—I did nothing," said Stanislaus Joseph. "Just tried to do my job, I fear not too well."

"Then you don't think you are the world's greatest pianoforte artist?" said H. Rodman. "If you don't, you are the first piano player I ever had in a concert who didn't!"

"I am just a beginner," said Stanislaus Joseph.

"Good God!" said H. Rodman. And then: "And you are not asking me to book you for a solo artist appearance in Carnegie Hall tomorrow night?"

"Now you are making fun of me," said Stanislaus Joseph.

H. Rodman went back to his desk. He looked hard at the young man seated on the same couch Viktor Reimalsky and his manager had occupied. "Mr. Halka, how much do you know about the operas?" he asked at last. "And now I am not making fun of you."

Stanislaus Joseph swallowed hard. For a great lump of what might be labeled "Hope" was obstructing his vocal chords. Was this powerful man really going to give him another chance? "I studied opera for four years at the Academy in Vienna under Professor Josef Kattnig," he said. "And in the studio of my first pianoforte teacher, Herr Dr. Gustav Emil Meyerhoff, who also coached singers, I played accompaniments for one year. I also played at the Ringstrasse Café where they had opera selections. I played there week-ends, sir, and some evenings."

"Kattnig is the finest opera man in Europe," said H. Rodman. "I know him well. You ought to know something if you worked under him." The impresario looked toward the baby grand piano half hidden in a far corner of the office. "Do you know the *Bolero* in Verdi's *Sicilian Vespers?*" he asked.

"I do not think I know that composition," said Stanislaus Joseph honestly. He felt his hopes fade.

"Good!" said H. Rodman. "It's on my piano. Go over, switch on the light, and play it."

Stanislaus Joseph uncertainly arose and went to the Steinway. He took up the music. The sheets were peppered with notes.

"May I look at it a few minutes?" he asked.

"Surely," said H. Rodman.

After a very little while Stanislaus Joseph said: "I'll try it now, sir."

He did. He played that most difficult piece with no mistakes. "I do not know that opera," he apologized. "I may not have given all passages the proper coloring."

"To hell with the coloring," said H. Rodman. "You never played it before?"

"No sir."

"Good God!" said H. Rodman again. And then, "Do you know the 'mother song' *Ah Mon Fils* of Meyerbeer's *Le Prophete?* It is also on the piano. Right under the *Bolero*."

"Oh, that I can play without the music—I often played it at the Café."

"Play it now," said H. Rodman, "and hand me the music. I will follow you."

Stanislaus Joseph did so. He played it note perfect.

"Good God!" said ex-pianist, ex-child-prodigy H. Rodman. And then: "Are you familiar with Puccini, Wagner, Richard Strauss?"

"I have studied and played many of their operas," said Stanislaus Joseph, "that is, played them as best I could."

"Play the duet in Act II of *Der Rosenkavalier,*" said H. Rodman. He took for granted that the young man knew that well-known selection. Stanislaus Joseph did—and played it.

H. Rodman picked up his telephone. "Get me Albert Rouchard, *immediatement,*" he said, and when the connection was made, "Albert, this is Horatio. Still looking for an opera pianoforte player? . . . Have I ever failed you? Can you see one now? *Immediatement?* . . . Good! He'll be there in twenty minutes or less, depending on the traffic lights. Name of Halka. From Vienna, but speaks English. Pupil of Joseph Kattnig. He looks very young. Is very young. Practically a baby. But hear him play. . . . First name? Damned if I know."

H. Rodman glanced at Stanislaus Joseph still seated at the piano. "Little fellow," he continued. "Very tight pants. Tightpants Halka will do. . . . Oh, don't mention it. Only hope he fits into your screech factory . . . What? . . . You go to hell! See you Thursday at Café Le Pavillon."

H. Rodman hung up and directed his voice to Stanislaus Joseph. He was smiling.

"Don't mind my calling you 'Tightpants,' " he said. "The trousers are O.K. Wish all my artists would dress as neatly. Now you take a taxi pronto—*immediatement* that is—and speed right up to Eighty-sixth Street and Broadway. Studio of Albert Rouchard. Finest voice teacher in America. In the world, I think. Needs an opera accompanist quick. If he likes you it will be a steady job. Hope he does.

"If you're hired you'll have to join the Union. See my office manager. He'll tell you what to fill out, and I'll vouch for you. As a musician I mean. Hope you don't get drunk, chase after women, or play the races. Leave your passport and I'll get it fixed so you can stay in the country a while. If you're serious about the citizenship and can stay out of jail I'll help you there too. O.K. your application."

He regarded the boy incredulously. "An artist who doesn't think he knows it all! Only one who ever landed here from dear, cultured old Europe and thought that way I guess. An artist from Europe who doesn't hate crude America! I live and learn!"

"Mr. Rodman," gasped Stanislaus Joseph, "I don't know how to thank you——"

"Don't try," said H. Rodman. "I'm doing it for Albert Rouchard. Just don't let me down with my friend. He already thinks I'm a little daffy. By the way, how come you were not surprised that you were cancelled out by Herr Viktor Reimalsky? How come?"

Stanislaus Joseph hesitated. He did not want to betray Franz Rodar. But he felt he owed this impresario some explanation.

"Give me your word, Herr Rodman, you will not divulge my source of information——"

"Cross my heart," smiled H. Rodman. "And please call me Mister, not Herr. If you're going to be a good American, you'll have to forget Herr."

"I'm sorry, Herr—Mr. Rodman. It was the valet, sir. You see, I live in the same room with the valet. He's a fine fellow. A gentleman. We were originally booked together in the same cabin on the *Europa*."

"Oh yes. I heard about that. Second Class. Most amusing, as things turned out. Tell me, how in hell does the valet stand for that violin genius?"

"He's not going to for long," divulged Stanislaus Joseph before he thought. "You see, when the tour reaches a place called Wichita, in a State named Kansas——"

Stanislaus Joseph stopped short. He had said too much.

"Go on," said H. Rodman.

"I suppose I must go on now," said Stanislaus Joseph. "The valet has a married sister there. He's quitting, when the tour reaches that city. He's going to stay there, sir. Become a citizen of America, I think."

H. Rodman burst into laughter. He laughed a full minute. "Thanks for letting me know that," he said. "I was going to cancel *Herr* Reimalsky after Chicago. I've spent advertising money up to that point. I'll now continue his tour on to Wichita. Got to get your room-mate settled in Kansas. I don't like crooked artists, Mr. Halka.

It's bad enough that most of them are phoneys. And I have a cable this morning that I can get back an Italian virtuoso that is a real master of the fiddle. Had him last year. This dago gent will be 'The New Paganini' after Wichita. That's the honest thing to do anyway, for the real Paganini was sure a dago."

H. Rodman permitted himself another laugh. Then he continued.

"Maybe I'll let Herr Paganini Reimalsky play just one more town beyond Wichita. Run his own bath—if he can get a room with a bath—and dress himself all alone in the next burg. Think it's called Pratt Junction. Palace Hotel. Business will be good and lousy. I'll see to that. Hotel ditto. Don't need to arrange *that*. A good place for him to get a wire he's through.

"And he'll be through, as far as America is concerned. I'll see to that also. Farewell with love and kisses.

"By the way, the office will pay you one hundred bucks—dollars that is—for last night. It was sure worth more than twenty-five. Come in tomorrow early and collect it. And if you don't land this job and have to return to Vienna, we hold your fare. First Class. Goodbye, Mr. Tightpants—and good luck up at Eighty-sixth Street."

So Tightpants Halka—the name was to get around and stick—somehow reached the street from the Rodman office—he had proceeded all the way on thin air—and took a bright yellow cab for the West Eighty-sixth Street address which Hardboiled Rodman had scrawled on a piece of pad-paper.

The Three Fates *and* Almighty God—let's include them both this time—had another chuckle.

PART SIX

INTERIM

1

MR. STANISLAUS JOSEPH HALKA remained in the employ of Albert Rouchard for a year and six months—for as long indeed as the voice teacher continued to instruct both the affluent and the struggling. For the great heart finally gave out—suddenly ceased to coach the rich in order to help the poor.

His man servant found him one morning, the mop of greying hair resting on the keyboard of his piano, where he had worked till midnight the night before, making a new musical arrangement for a penniless singer who had a chance to open in a night club.

Refusing to heed his doctor's warnings (when there were still poor students to be helped), he had literally worked himself to the state we label *Death.*

It is my belief that he proceeded straight to Paradise, and that the quality of the singing of the Heavenly Choir showed a marked improvement from that date.

For Stanislaus Joseph they had been happy months. But he had saved no money.

Not that he had not lived modestly, and well within his income. He had taken a small furnished room in a small family hotel on Amsterdam Avenue, near the Rouchard Studio, so that he had no carfares to reach his work. He ate at some one of the small "quick lunch" counters with which the neighborhood abounded. His one extravagance was to go to the Opera, and to an occasional concert at Carnegie Hall, or the more recently built Town Hall, and he justified the expense of these sometimes expensive relaxations by feeling that they were a part of his musical education.

For despite his Doctor's degree—which he did not use—he felt that he still had much to learn!

He soon discovered that he was endowed with another degree—"Tightpants." Tightpants Halka. H. Rodman had addressed him as "Mr. Tightpants"—and not unkindly—on several visits to the Rouchard Studio to hear new singers. The singers adopted it. They too—not unkindly.

His musicianship commanded respect. His always neat appearance also made a favorable impression.

Especially with Albert Rouchard. Mr. Rouchard's complaint about Stanislaus Joseph's predecessor at his highly polished, aristocratic piano was that employee's addiction to trousers called "slacks," which some arch enemy of neatness had invented; and to boisterous "sport coats," inventions of Satan himself.

It was an aesthetic relief to see those well-tailored trousers on his piano bench. He also felt that they blended better with Verdi and Wagner, not to mention Messieurs Cézanne, Renoir and Degas.

Stanislaus Joseph—"Tightpants"—had not saved any money because he had been sending more than two-thirds of his salary back, each week, to Vienna.

He was endeavoring to at least repay the financial debt he considered that he owed the bakeshop owner and his father. Most curious responsibility for a young man in this Age to harbor!

And he had returned intact the generous draft that had been tucked into his gift wallet. H. Rodman's payment of one hundred dollars for the single concert had given him immediate funds.

So it was a financial as well as a personal shock he received when he had appeared at the Rouchard Studio that morning. He was there at eight-thirty, for he had volunteered almost from the first, to play without pay for those poorer students who came at that early hour. He had offered to do this when one of the lesser accompanists had quit. He had continued to do it—and gladly—for months.

Albert Rouchard owed him no salary that tragic Monday morning that the great teacher was discovered dead. Stanislaus Joseph had received his previous week's wage the Saturday before, and already sent most of it back to Austria.

This remittance had completed the repayment for the spinet; and the boy had written his father and his patron to give that instrument to some new lad who needed one—as he had needed one. He was planning to try to find a small apartment, where he could install a Steinway baby-grand, which he would purchase "on time," and so have a place and an instrument where he could work at home, evenings, on his symphony.

Now, Albert Rouchard was gone. His job was gone. He had exactly fourteen dollars in his wallet, and some loose change in one side-pocket of the well-known tight trousers.

For three days he did nothing at all. Paced uncertainly, in stride and mind, along Riverside Drive, striving to evolve some plan.

Then, the day after the funeral, he went down to the Rodman office. No luck. H. Rodman was not there. He would not be there for several months. Not until the late Fall. The impresario was in Europe, arranging for the importation of an entire ballet troupe, and to find new artists for the next season's bookings. The office manager—remembering Mr. Halka vaguely—did not know of any pianoforte openings. "H. Rodman himself attended to such matters."

It was in the spring, and the various Rodman tours were all nearing their closing dates.

Stanislaus Joseph thought of cabling his father back in Vienna. But he knew only too well that his father would not have saved any money. He knew that the money he had been sending back had gone for *schnapps* and *schnapsen*. As he had indeed meant it should go. Was it not the father's only pleasure, as music was the son's only pleasure?

He debated cabling his patron, the bakeshop owner, to whom he had written each week, when he was remitting back the cost of his education. Asking him to please send, say, the equivalent of one hundred dollars, to carry on till he could find another employment. But Stanislaus Joseph did not like to do this, and before he could make up his mind to do it, he himself received a cable from the generous gentleman.

That week seemed loaded with tragedy for Stanislaus Joseph Halka. The lad's father had suddenly died. At least he had died happily. Dropped dead in his favorite café, and after winning a game of *schnapsen*.

Stanislaus Joseph had not yet reached the age when he would give much thought to Death. Death was something many, many years away. The writing-of-half-a-dozen-symphonies away. This was the first time that Death had intruded with grim reality into his personal pathway. His mother's passing had been long before the child could remember.

Albert Rouchard, his wonderful employer. The next day almost, the father—wonderful also in what he had done for the son; and that son's only blood relative. The boy had lately read a beautiful bit of verse. Had somehow been moved to cut it out of the newspaper column in which it was printed. It said—

I hail thee, happy, profitable Death
Sovereign physic for the pain of breath.
When my time comes, Goddess, I ask of thee
Let me not linger long in malady
Tormented on a bed. Since thou art sure
Let me find suddenly my sepulcher.
Guarding God's honor; fighting for my King;
My blood upon my own hearth issuing.

Well, at least these two had passed on in that quick and happy way. And in beloved surroundings. Albert Rouchard at *his* hearth—his pianoforte. The father at *his* hearth—the *schnapsen* table. Thanks to God at least for that!

The lad's "hearth" was now assuredly the City of New York. He still loved it. Had no desire to return to Austria. Austria seemed a land far away and in a dim past.

He had months before taken out his first American citizenship papers. Even if he had been provided with funds he could not have reached Vienna until after the funeral. It was before the day of trans-Atlantic planes.

So, with heavy heart, he cabled the bakeshop owner to please attend to all arrangements.

There was a vacant space beside the mother in the graveyard of the nearby village where both she and the father had been born. He, Stanislaus Joseph, would remit whatever the expense would be. And his gratitude for this service of his old patron would be eternal. He knew that his father's fellow workers at the bakery would also lend a hand.

So he sent his cable. It took eight of the precious fourteen dollars that he possessed.

He most certainly could not now also ask his old patron for personal help. He wrote suggesting that the simple furniture of the father's rooms be turned over to the widow Grete Ebenstein, she who had called the mass meeting that had provided the lad with his outfit of fine clothes. And that she give that furniture to some deserving family. If there was any rent unpaid for the top-floor 5D apartment he would send it as soon as possible.

He would be grateful if the father's watch—the watch that had been given to the grandfather by the Emperor Franz Josef—could be sent to him in New York.

❖ 2 ❖

THE NEED THEREFORE was for a new well-paying job, and that very speedily. The Vienna funeral expense would come to a lot of kronen. But Stanislaus Joseph found that such jobs did not grow on trees or hang on traffic-light posts, as the saying goes.

He applied at the several "Viennese Restaurants" which he knew about, and had occasionally patronized. They all used music, but were well supplied with pianoforte players. He looked in the daily want ad columns of the newspapers.

Under the "M's" were plenty of golden opportunities for Mail Clerks, Messengers, Managers, Map Makers, Mattress Stuffers, Machinists, Mill Hands, Mortuary Assistants, Masseurs, Multigraph Machine Operators; but no one wanted a Musician. Under the "P's" he found Paint Sprayers, Packers, Plasterers, Paste Mixers, Pharmacists, Photographers, Polishers, Plastics Extruders, Pressmen, Printers, Prong Setters, Proof Boys, Purchasing Agents; but no one advertised for a Pianoforte Player!

He went down to the "Met," but the opera season was over. The singers, for whom he had played—scattered.

This went on for a month. There were recurrent bills in his hotel letter box—bills presently with a red stamp—

"Overdue. Please Remit."

"All Bills Must Be Paid Weekly As Rendered."

He cut himself down to two meals a day, and budgeted each meal at twenty cents. He pawned his evening clothes to get money for eating. And the cuff links and shirt buttons that went with them.

He reached low point the late afternoon he returned after another fruitless round of restaurants that used piano players, and found that he could not open the door of his hotel room.

He was barred from that room by the insertion of a so-called plug in the door's keyhole.

Inquiry at the reception desk, back down stairs, brought the information that he "could not have access to it" unless he paid his bill in full, and that "such possessions of his still in the room would be held as security and eventually sold—see statute Number 583, Code of the State of New York for the protection of Inn Keepers."

Stanislaus Joseph, exhausted and discouraged, had walked to nearby Broadway, and sat on a bench in a small park for several hours. He was no quitter, but it seemed to be the very end of everything. Wrapped in his music and his interesting work, he had made no friend. There was not even a Franz Rodar to talk of a farm in Kansas.

He seemed to have reached a complete dead end.

At midnight he was still sitting on a bench of the tiny "island park" at Broadway and Seventy-second Street. The red sun had been setting behind the Palisades when he had first seated himself. Now he looked up and was conscious that there was a full moon overhead.

That moon also shone down on the River Hudson, and consequently also on that part of the river that flowed by the Cloisters perched on the high promontory that was a part of Fort Tyron Park. From one of the leaded windows of a west room in that building, a statue of the Virgin and the Christ Child had also watched the sun set, and felt the rising of the moon.

If Guard O'Rourke had been there, he would have imagined no happy smile on that statue's beautiful face. He had in fact noted something else just before he left for home.

Now there had been one other manifestation with regard to this statue, noticed not only by Guard O'Rourke, but also by the archeological experts of the Museum. It had to do with the stone from which the statue had been carved.

It was the same type of unusual stone from which the columns of the adjoining Cuxa Cloister had been formulated. It was a grey-white stone, but contained a mixture of mottled light red—one might call it pink. This stone was known to have come from a single massive mountain which lies between Ria and Villefranche in southern France, near the Spanish border. Only in this mountain was a rock of such curious and beautiful coloring to be quarried.

This stone changed in color from day to day. The pink would sometimes become bright red. This change was explained by atmospheric conditions. Damp weather caused the light-red blotches to become a much brighter crimson.

The La Celle statue of the Virgin, especially the bared breast of it which was not hidden by the carved and painted garments, was very sensitive to these changes of color. These changes in the moisture in the atmosphere.

But with respect to the statue there was a vague legend that the breast of the Virgin would become bright red at times other than when the atmosphere was saturated with moisture. That it became crimson at times of great calamity or sorrow in the world. That the breast became red at times of wars. Very red in the sixteen-hundreds, when the monasteries were sacked and many of them destroyed.

Red during the dreadful days of the French Revolution when the statue looked down from its bell tower at La Celle.

That evening, in the new-world city of New York, as Stanislaus Joseph Halka sat in utter despair on a park bench at Seventy-second Street and Broadway, the breast of this statue of the Virgin, up at the Cloisters, became very red. This, although the air was dry and clear, and a bright, full moon was shining overhead. Guard O'Rourke had noticed it changing color just before he left for home. At the exact hour (had he known) that Stanislaus Joseph Halka stood before a locked hotel-room door.

By the midnight hour of that day, Stanislaus Joseph was sitting on his park bench quite alone. Other late sitters had departed. Departed for their homes.

But he had no home.

He knew that he could not remain all night on that bench. A police officer had already passed across the tiny park several times, and eyed him suspiciously.

There was the short walk down to the river. There was a dock at the foot of West Seventy-second Street. Stanislaus Joseph had often strolled there to watch the boats at night, the great advertising signs flashing across the river. To observe the bright stars above—brighter away from the glare of the city street lights—and gaze upon the great black ribbon of the river.

Should he walk down to this dock, cross it, and keep on walking? The lad had never learned to swim. The end would come quickly. *I hail thee, happy profitable Death. Sovereign physic*——

He got up from his bench, and looked up again at the full moon. A cloud was passing over a part of it, so that the great ball became more of an oval than a perfect circle, and suddenly that moon took on another shape in the mind of the desperate, unhappy lad.

It took on the shape of a bright yellow, bakeshop *dressiersack!*

❖ 3 ❖

DR. STANISLAUS JOSEPH HALKA did not walk toward the river. He hastened northward to Seventy-ninth Street, where he knew there was a cross-town bus going to the East Side of New York—to York Avenue, which was in the Yorkville section. Great Central Park lay between, but there was a tunnel when the bus reached Central Park West that carried you to Fifth Avenue on the east border of the Park.

When he reached Seventy-ninth Street he found that the buses were not running at that late hour. So he started to walk eastward. There were all-night taxicabs still on the street, but he had only forty cents still in his pocket. He knew the exact amount because he had, several hours before, counted it carefully and allowed himself ten cents for his "dinner." A "hot dog" and a cup of coffee. He had better hold that forty cents in reserve.

On York Avenue was a "Viennese" bakery. A part of its working crew did their work at night, preparing the cakes, the confections for the next morning's trade. One of these men was that cousin of one of his late father's fellow workers.

Stanislaus Joseph had long ago looked up this cousin, and presented his note of introduction. He had seen the man a few times, not as often as he might have wished, for this worker, whose name was Hans Beuter, started his daily (or rather nightly) task at six P.M. and toiled till sunrise. The two had however eaten several Sunday dinners together; had gone to Coney Island on another Sunday; to Palisades Park on a holiday; and Stanislaus Joseph had been to the man's humble "diggings" where he lived alone in a one-room-and-kitchen cold-water flat near the bakeshop.

Hans Beuter was a simple soul, but kindly. He had been very proud of the fact that he knew the great "Herr Dr. Stanislaus Joseph Halka" who had played in Carnegie Hall! He also knew that the boy had been of late employed by the famous voice teacher Albert Rouchard.

Hans Beuter, white with baking flour, greeted his fellow Viennese with surprise, but with obvious cordiality. It was the bakeshop workers' midnight lunch hour. He insisted that Stanislaus Joseph eat with him and the six or seven other men—mostly also from Austria.

Our Stanislaus was glad to eat. He had eaten very little the past week. The almost two-mile walk across town was pretty exhausting.

After the meal, he took Hans Beuter aside and told him the full story. That he had been without employment for a month. That he had, that night, been locked out of his hotel room because of a month-old bill.

And Hans Beuter was still cordial.

"I cannot go to my place now," he said, "but I give you my key. We have a big rush job tonight and one of our men is sick. You go straight there, switch on the light, and make yourself at home. The bed is wide enough for two. Anyway, you will sleep at night—I sleep during the day! If either of us snores it won't keep the other one awake! *Groosartig! Wunderbar! Ausgezeichnet!* We should have gotten together and made this arrangement long ago!"

Both he and Stanislaus Joseph laughed. Stanislaus Joseph had not laughed for a month.

The young pianoforte player had been given a new lease on life. Literally given just that. After the laugh he was not ashamed of the tears that came into his eyes.

"Hans," he said, "Hans, I cannot tell you how much——"

"You tell me nothing," said Hans Beuter. "Tomorrow—the next day—next week—next month—you find some place to play pianoforte, I am sure! You should have come to me days ago. Tonight—you sleep. . . Wait a minute! Maybe tonight you *don't* sleep!"

He had reached out and snatched back his latch key from Stanislaus Joseph's still grateful hand.

"What is wrong?" gasped the lad. For Hans Beuter did not seem to be joking. At any rate, this was no time for that kind of frivolity.

"I just remember!" cried Hans Beuter. "My cousin write me way back when you first came to New York, that you were not only a great *musiker* but also a great decorator with the *dressiersack!* It is our *dressiersack* man who is sick tonight. Tonight of all nights—the poor slob! And we have a hundred large Easter cakes to deliver early tomorrow. I was going to have to write the *'Froliche Ostern'* and the *'Happy Easter'* on them myself, and me—I am a rotten *dressiersack* wielder! The very rottenest in New York! But maybe you are too tired out? No?"

But any feeling of weariness that had gripped the slender body of Dr. Stanislaus Joseph Halka, graduate *cum laude* of the University of Vienna, had suddenly vanished. He stripped off his coat, still the coat tailored by the finest craftsman of the *Karntnerstrasse.* He rolled up the sleeves of the stiffly starched shirt. A great apron was quickly tied about his waist to cover the striped trousers of immaculate fit. He seized the bakeshop *dressiersack* and held it, as his friend filled the bag with sparkling, red, flowing icing. And he set to work with a skill that he had not forgotten. *Frohliche Ostern! Happy Easter!*

From the lowest depths to the greatest happiness!

Stanislaus Joseph discovered—if he had not before discovered it—that service, even very humble service to his fellow man, is the supreme joy of being alive.

And to know that *someone* in this world wants you—needs you

❖ 4 ❖

STANISLAUS JOSEPH lived for three weeks with Hans Beuter.

During the first week, while hunting unsuccessfully for musical work during the daytime, he labored from six till midnight in the bakery, writing on and otherwise decorating cakes. Some very massive, some small.

It was the Easter holiday time—the shop, a small but famous one, was swamped with orders; and during that week of illness of the regular *dressiersack* operator, the proprietor was pleased indeed to have one of his men find someone skilled in the art.

That that someone was an Austrian also helped, for he had a large trade with German-speaking families who much preferred their sentimental wishes expressed in the homeland language. *Frohliche Ostern. Hoch Soll Er Leben.*

And this work enabled Stanislaus Joseph, without borrowing money from his room-mate Hans Beuter (although Herr Beuter offered to lend whatever was needed), to rescue his few belongings from the Code 583 protected, Amsterdam Avenue family hotel; to get his evening clothes and the cuff links out of pawn; to eat properly; and generally to regain his courage.

He had no luck about finding work till about the middle of the second week. And then it seemed to be under the theorem that Heaven helps those who try to help themselves.

He had gone to a restaurant on Park Avenue and Sixty-ninth Street, where he had once dined with a singer for whom he had played. He went there that day not to dine but to see if they needed a pianoforte player. This restaurant was across the street from one of the buildings of Hunter College.

They did not need a pianoforte player at the restaurant (an old, well-known story—alas!), but as the young man left he was hailed by a girl coming out of the College building—a girl who had been one of the "early morning" pupils of Albert Rouchard.

"Whatever are you doing over here, Mr. Tightpants?" she had asked.

Stanislaus Joseph had always been frank in reply to questions, even personal questions. "I am looking for a job," he answered with a wry smile. "I don't suppose you know of any."

"It just happens that I do!" cried the girl who was with several of her fellow students. "Girls—this is the wonderful piano player who was with Mr. Albert Rouchard. Gee, Mr. Tightpants—Mr. Halka, I should say—"

"I don't mind 'Tightpants,' " smiled Stanislaus Joseph.

"You're a little darling," said the school girl; and to her classmates, "Ain't he cute! And you ought to hear him tickle the piano!

If we could get him for our gymnasium class—but no—that wouldn't be your kind of music, Mr. Tightpants!"

"My kind of music right now is the kind that pays a salary," laughed Stanislaus Joseph.

"Do you really mean it!" cried the girl. "If you do, you come right back with me into the College office. The Spring and Summer gym class started today, and we had no music because the piano player didn't show up. Gone out with a jazz orchestra, we heard. I don't know what the College pays, but I think it's all right. Gee—if we could get a cute thing like you—and with your nifty talent!"

Stanislaus Joseph did not know whether the adjective "cute" in the American language was entirely complimentary or not, and the word "nifty" describing his ability at the keyboard of a pianoforte, would probably not have been used by an English-speaking member of the University of Vienna faculty, but both adjectives were obviously sincere.

And here, at long last, seemed to be one institution in the city of New York that, during the Spring and Summer months, needed a player of the pianoforte! Nifty or otherwise.

He got that job. To play afternoons from two till five. And three evenings a week from seven to ten. Salary, seventy-five dollars per week.

It was less than half what he had received from Albert Rouchard—but it seemed like a windfall after these weeks of sidewalk tramping and interviewing hard-faced, uninterested café managers. And it gave him his mornings and two evenings, as well as Saturdays and Sundays free. Free to work on his symphony, or to try to procure a real engagement for the coming Fall and Winter season.

His new-found luck did not end there. The woman instructor in the gymnasium got him another evening job.

Along with the endless repetitious playing of *The Blue Danube* and *Dardanella*—not to forget *Three O'Clock in the Morning,* during which the young ladies (while the instructor counted "One! Two! Three!—One! Two! Three!") bent sideways, bent to the floor, lay on the floor and raised shapely (and unshapely) limbs to the ceiling and Heaven, Stanislaus Joseph had one afternoon taken his courage in his fingers and played Claude Achille Debussy's *Golliwog's Cake-Walk.* A most startling departure from sacred gymnasium tradition, but it was liked!

The next day, on a slow movement exercise to "develop grace" (the young ladies raised arms in appealing gestures, at the same time taking stances of supposed beauty with the aforementioned lower limbs well spread), Stanislaus Joseph had ventured Peter Ilych Tchaikovsky's *Swan Lake* in the place of *Let Me Call You Sweetheart.*

When that particular session was ended, the instructress said to the young man, "My goodness gracious! You can really play!"

"I told you he was a nifty, very high class pianist," said the proud young girl who had recommended him, and who happened to be standing by.

The result of this revolutionary introduction of the classics to the Hunter Gym was that its instructress recommended our hero to a friend who had a ballet dancing class. By playing for this class on Saturday afternoons, nifty piano player Stanislaus Joseph Halka added another twenty dollars a week to his income.

All of which enabled the young man to carry out his former plan of a modest place of his own. He wanted no more hotel locked-doors.

He found such a place in an old residential building near the corner of Thirty-fourth Street on Madison Avenue. It was an excellent neighborhood, but because the building was ancient and a walk-up, the rents were reasonable.

He signed a lease for a tiny bedroom, a reasonably sized sitting room, a bath and a kitchen on the top floor front. Heat was furnished by the landlord who operated a restaurant on the street level.

The rent was thirty-five dollars a month, much less indeed than he had paid for one small room and no bath at the two hotels where he had before resided.

It was of course unfurnished, and at the first he bought the simplest of necessary articles at a famous Eighth Avenue installment-plan emporium that had started many a New York home to functioning with a bed, a four-drawer chiffonier, two chairs and a still life chromo showing a bowl of poisonously colored fruit beside a water pitcher. The young man brought deep sorrow to the heart of the earnest home-furnishing salesman by foregoing the chromolithograph, leaving an impression of a youth wholly oblivious of Art.

Stanislaus Joseph should have (but did not) explain that he had just received a letter from the late Albert Rouchard's sister telling him of the gift of one of his *Renoirs* in the voice teacher's will. That picture would have to carry on, for the time being, in his new home.

He also purchased the fundamental bachelor cooking utensils—

skillet, coffee-pot, saucepan, can opener, so that he could save money by preparing his own meals. The kitchen contained a small electric refrigerator.

But of paramount importance: because of his known connection with this same Albert Rouchard (he had several times visited their show rooms to help select a piano for a well-to-do pupil), the Steinway people were to let him have a fine, new, baby-grand pianoforte, which he would pay for at a modest rate each month. It would be delivered just as soon as he could make the first down payment.

So Stanislaus Joseph left the hospitable room of baker Hans Beuter—left it with a feeling of deepest gratitude—and one morning moved into his own home.

At last he felt that he was really and truly an American!

That morning, up at the Cloisters, Guard O'Rourke was certain that his statue had smiled. Smiled several times. No matter what others might think, that particular Queen of Heaven *did smile*.

And the very third night of his residence, coming home from a late gymnasium class, Stanislaus Joseph was certain that he had made a happy choice of a permanent domicile.

Ascending the steep and half-dark stairways, through a short, dark hall at each landing, he saw small, friendly eyes shining in the gloom. Shining for a moment and then scurrying away. Mice—maybe a rodent or two— just as there had been back in Vienna in the rookery where he and his father had lived so happily!

He had gone back out to a nearby delicatessen and bought some cheese, which he crumbled and placed in the corners of each floor landing. Blessed little fellows that made it seem for certain a real home.

He later discovered that an "Exterminator" gentleman came around on the first and fifteenth days of the month with various rodent-destroying fluids and formidable apparatus to squirt the same; so on the nights before these dates, Stanislaus Joseph made special trips down the stairs (if he did not return at a late hour), and if he saw any of the bright eyes he would sound a warning, saying: "Stay under cover tomorrow, little fellows. The Devil will be after you! Stay under cover."

Fortunately, the exterminator gentleman belonged to a Union that permitted its members to work only between the hours of eight

A.M. and five P.M. The rodents and the mice usually stayed in *their* secret apartments between such hours, being strictly on a night shift schedule.

So was there complete happiness at Madison Avenue and Thirty-fourth Street; and up at the Cloisters the La Celle statue truly smiled.

✣ 5 ✣

STANISLAUS JOSEPH HALKA had now been in New York for a year and almost eight months, and he had not yet visited the branch of the Metropolitan Museum of Art called the Cloisters.

After first seeing the photograph of the La Celle statue of the Virgin, on the wall of the quarters of Kommodore Hugo Frederick von Steinburg aboard the *Europa,* and hearing his strange tale of a happening, some years before, on the bridge of that liner, he had intended to seek out this museum on almost the first day of landing.

But the at-hand wonders of Times Square (including the Automat); the happenings at the Reimalsky concert; his dismissal after that concert; the immediate and most fortunate starting to work for voice-teacher Albert Rouchard; the long hours of that employment (he had played for singers from eight-thirty in the mornings till six at night—often playing evenings for the hard-working teacher), had given him no free time at such hours as the Cloisters, or any other museum, was open to the public.

During these busy days he had not entirely forgotten the matter. He had verified that he must go to the Cloisters between the hours of ten and five—but those were hours during which he was hard at his task. Sunday afternoons (the Cloisters was open from one till six P.M.) he had usually attended a concert, where he felt he would acquire some new knowledge for his life-work.

He had also often thought of the statue in connection with his friend the Herr Kommodore; of the Kommodore's request that he take a rose with him and place it on the statue's pedestal as a tribute from the ship commander who had transported the carving to America.

He had practically promised to do this. But he had constantly put off the visit to this somewhat distant spot.

It was now the morning of the arrival of his Steinway—a most important morning for the young man. There had been difficulty in getting this sizable instrument up the four flights of narrow stairs and around sharp turns into his rooms, but the strategy and superb technique of the four skilled truckmen—assisted by some colorful swearing—had seen this task accomplished.

When the legs and pedal supports were put back in place—they had of necessity been removed for this Heavenward journey, a journey otherwise designated by the sweating truckmen—and when he had made a few adjustments with his tuning wrench (grateful memories of his very first boyhood teacher!), he had at about ten A.M. sat himself on the mahogany bench and commenced to play.

The christening melody was Debussy's *La Mer*.

He had not really thought of just what he would first play as he seated himself in his own "American home" before his first, very own, regular pianoforte. Maybe it should have been *Yankee Doodle* or *Take Me Out to the Ball Game*. But the lad did not yet know these bulwarks of Americana.

His hands had slipped into the beautiful and stirring composition of Claude Debussy: a composition that has belonged to *all* lands which border on the Mother of Lands—the mighty Mother Sea.

La Mer. And to the lad, this Spring morning it brought a picture not of raging waters, but of handsome Kommodore Hugo Frederick von Steinburg filling his *meerschaum;* of a great baked Alaska moulded into the shape of an open pianoforte; and then, abruptly, of a small, framed photograph of a statue, which became as quickly a lovely lady standing on a high ship's bridge, and accepting from that Kommodore a rose.

The restless sea was there—all around them—but it was the restless surge of human souls that his skilled fingers brought to life, as his hands flashed across the black and white ivory keyboard, a keyboard like to the alternate black and white wind-swept crest of ocean waves.

At a softer passage he found himself descending with the Kommodore (as the Herr Kommodore had related) to the great vessel's strong-room, there to view the Virgin statue in its lifelike coloring—lifelike as it lay in a symbol of death—a coffin—and then he was back again on the bridge with the Kommodore and the Lady (was it indeed the same Lady!) as she said: *There is a golden cross in the great Record Scroll opposite your name. . . . A golden cross—not an iron one—Herr Kommodore Hugo Frederick von Steinburg—.*

He had completely failed his generous, shipboard friend! Two years—and no rose had been placed by him on the pedestal before the Lady up at the Cloisters!

Even now, at last, when some part of the daylight hours were his own, and had been for several weeks, he had done nothing. The conscientious lad felt a deep shame that he had failed to carry out this simple request.

And there was also a sudden tug, an urge that he did not quite understand, to himself view the image whose photograph and story had so stirred him.

Perhaps it was just this accidental playing of *La Mer*—what had the Kommodore said when they had performed it together on the Büttner and the Bösendorfer that evening? *We will play it for the Lady of the Statue—wherever she is—whoever she is.*

At any rate, Stanislaus Joseph looked at his watch—his late father's watch that had recently arrived from Vienna. Ten-thirty. His gymnasium class did not begin till two P.M. that afternoon. There would be time right then.

And it is an indication of the strength of those memories, and the personal urge, that he closed the lid of his wonderful new pianoforte (it seemed like Paradise to possess it at last!) and did what he did.

Stanislaus Joseph put on his coat. He took his Homburg from its hat box in the closet, the Homburg he had always carefully brushed and cared for as if it were a child. He spoke to his pianoforte: "You must excuse me—there is something most urgent that I must do."

And he descended the four flights of steep stairs, out onto Madison Avenue, and walked rapidly toward the Avenue named Fifth. There, he remembered, he had been told a bus would take him to Fort Tyron Park.

On the way across the Thirty-fourth Street block, he stopped at a fine florist shop. He asked to see the most beautiful rose in the establishment. He selected the one he liked the best. An excellent selection, the fawning salesman assured him, since it was the latest triumph of expert gardening and a Detroit rose-bush company, not apparently handicapped by any interference from Nature or God. The single rose was priced at two dollars.

No bus was arriving, or in sight, at the Fifth Avenue corner when he reached it, but there was an empty taxicab. He realized that the taxi fare, up to the distant Fort Tyron, must be considerable, but he took that taxicab. He would save money in some other way that particular week.

The Lady of the Statue was entitled to have her rose arrive in style! Also, he had only three hours before the gymnasium class, and he did not wish to be hurried when he reached the Cloisters.

The taxicab delivered him (and his rose) at their destination. Fare—three dollars and forty cents. The young man paid it, and a fifty cent tip to the driver. And he passed under the low, arched doorway of what looked like the "basement entrance" of a medieval castle perched high above. An entrance that could be blocked in time of attack. As indeed it was meant to represent.

The glorious harmonies of *La Mer* had carried Stanislaus Joseph to this point—rather than his legs or the wheels of a yellow taxicab. Those legs were now rushing him up the long, sloping flights of stone stairs enclosed under arched stone passageways—*to what?* To a beautiful, pulsating sweetheart, the thought of whom had "put wings on his heels" as the love song caroled? No. To something made of stone, as cold and lifeless as the tunnel's (it was like a rising tunnel) low, arched roof overhead.

He had better slow down. Several other early visitors, plodding slowly up the steps, regarded him with smiles, and he suddenly realized that he must be a ludicrous sight—running up those steps with face glowing, and with a flimsy, lengthy, cone-shaped package—obviously a bouquet—protruding before him.

He would deliver the Herr Kommodore's rose—for so he regarded it. He would pay his respects to the statue as the valuable art object it doubtless was. And his duty accomplished, he would get back quickly to his beloved, heart-throbbing music.

At the Cloisters' "office," off the oval room at the head of these steps, he purchased a Guide Book and inquired in what gallery were the medieval Virgin and Child carvings. The room, as we know, was called Early Gothic Hall; and in the Guide, after detailed descriptions of more famous images, was a line "there is a Madonna on the west wall of this gallery, said to have come from La Celle, south of Paris."

That must be the Herr Kommodore's Lady of the Statue. The Early Gothic Hall was on the same level as the office; several galleries beyond.

Stanislaus Joseph passed through these galleries, not pausing to examine the art objects that were on the walls, or about the walls; and came to a low, oaken door that gave entry to the gallery he was seeking. The door was closed, but a small printed sign denoted that this was the Early Gothic room.

The young man hesitated. All other doors had been wide open. Should he open this door, or knock. He decided that he should knock, and did so.

The guard stationed in the adjoining Cuxa Cloister, who had been regarding the faultlessly dressed Stanislaus Joseph with some amusement—the tight-fitting coat and trousers, the stiff, upstanding collar, the curved-brimmed, silk-bordered Homburg—("You sure got all kinds of characters in this crazy place!") called "Go right in, buddy. Them statues can't open no doors."

Guard Dennis O'Rourke, inside the Early Gothic Hall, could and did open doors, and was always pleased to do so. But at that moment he was crouching in a far corner where he had noticed some cigarette ash, flipped to the floor by a rules-breaking night watchman. He was brushing up the ash, and debating if he should report the matter. Before he could arise and answer this knock, Stanislaus Joseph had opened the door himself.

❖ 6 ❖

THERE—ALMOST OPPOSITE the doorway, across the narrow room—was the La Celle Virgin. And Dr. Stanislaus Joseph Halka needed no music of *La Mer* to make his heart beat faster.

He was not looking—as he thought he would be—at a grey image carved in cold, grey stone.

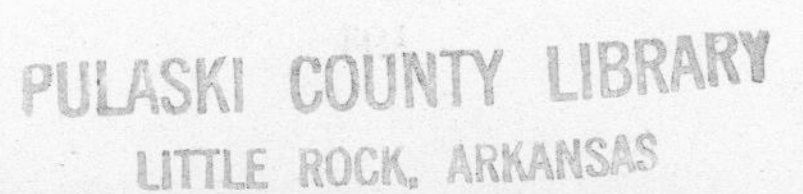

He was opposite a colorful young girl, and although she was motionless, standing on her waist-high wooden pedestal, she seemed to be of flesh and blood.

He moved directly to her, taking no notice of the other figures about the oblong room. He unwrapped the loose, cone-shaped paper covering about the rose, and placed that rose at the bare, flesh tinted feet that emerged from the graceful long folds of the figure's dull red under-garment.

By this time, Guard Dennis O'Rourke was on his feet, and suspicious of any visitor with a concealed article, had moved quickly to his side. But when he saw that the young man's package had contained, not some agent of injury, but a long-stemmed red rose, he smiled.

"You had me worried for a moment, sir," he said to the young man standing before the statue.

"I hope, sir, that I have not broken any rules," said Stanislaus Joseph quickly. "I have brought this rose, at the request of a friend. If I seemed in a hurry, I had promised to bring it here many months ago."

Guard O'Rourke did not seem surprised. There was no flippant remark like that made by the Cuxa Cloister guard.

"There were two other gentlemen, sir, who used to bring roses here for that particular statue," he said. "One was the donor—as they call it—of the statue. He was an elderly millionaire gentleman who lived in Brooklyn. He was a fine gentleman. He also owned a baseball club. He has been dead for seven or eight years—God rest his soul.

"The other was a German gentleman—he came one day in his uniform. He was a ship commander, I heard. I have not seen him for a number of months. I hope he has not died."

"I know of them both," said Stanislaus Joseph. "It is for that ship commander that I have brought this rose. But I think I shall bring other roses, for myself, if you do not mind."

"I do not mind, sir," said Guard Dennis O'Rourke. "She is my favorite statue. I call her my baby, and I hope it is not a sin to think of her that way."

"I do not think that you are committing any sin," smiled Stanislaus Joseph. "My name is Halka. And I would like to know yours, if I may."

"Dennis O'Rourke," said the guard. And then, "Very pleased to meet you, sir." And these two shook hands.

I have an idea that Almighty God gave His full approval to the somewhat informal attitude of both of them toward an image that represented the earthly mother of his Only Son.

The young man from Madison Avenue gazed up at the face of the image. It was as the Herr Kommodore had described it to him. A face of surpassing beauty—serene, courageous, utterly alluring.

The grey stone was painted—and so wonderfully painted that the colors had lasted through the centuries. The lips red, the cheeks delicately tinted, the elongated eyes a deep blue. And he especially noted the dark brown hair, parted in the middle, and a thick braid of it, seemingly drawn over the head under the small, gilded crown, and descending and drawn tightly to partly conceal the small left ear.

Like the Brooklyn brewer who had found her in the Louvre, like the German ship commander who had transported her, Stanislaus Joseph felt sweep over him a fascination, an admiration that, in his case, he had never felt before for any girl.

He talked at length with Guard O'Rourke. Told him of the *Europa* crossing and of what Hugo von Steinburg had related. Guard O'Rourke told the lad of his feeling that the statue sometimes truly smiled.

At twelve-thirty Stanislaus Joseph was still at the Cloisters. He took Guard O'Rourke to a brief sandwich lunch at a nearby restaurant, and returned with him again to the Early Gothic Hall. They chatted some more, but the young man could then remain only a few short minutes.

He did take time to pause at the office-reception room, to learn if they had any more information about the image beyond the brief single sentence in the guide book.

They knew very little. Not as much, it seemed, as Guard O'Rourke. Only the scanty information the Herr Kommodore had told him on the ship.

This statue had been bought from the Paris Louvre. It had come from a bell tower of a church at La Celle, just south of Paris. Before that, it had been in a Knights Templars monastery which was in ruins. It dated from the early twelfth century. It had been a gift of a patron of the Metropolitan Museum some ten or twelve years before.

He heard about the red-mottled stone of its composition, and the legend of how the breast of the image became crimson in times of great calamity. But there was of course an atmospheric explanation for the color change. Nothing about smiling statues from the austere office.

They did not have traffic with the fancies of simple-minded guards.

The young man, then and there, made up his mind to see if he himself could learn more.

Stanislaus Joseph knew an antiquarian who ran a rare bookshop on Fifty-seventh Street. The man was French—had been one of Albert Rouchard's friends. He had formerly been an assistant curator at the Paris Bibliotheque Nationale. That was the great State Library of French manuscripts and records.

Stanislaus Joseph determined to go to this man the next morning with such information as he had gathered, and see if, in any way, more could be discovered.

More was discovered, as we shall presently hear.

The boy was also able to purchase a stock photograph of the statue from the Cloisters office. A photograph much like that possessed by Kommodore Hugo von Steinburg.

During the following Summer months Stanislaus Joseph was to return often to the Cloisters—as often as he could find the time to make the journey to a Hundred and Ninetieth Street. He could reach it either by bus or subway. By subway almost as quickly as by taxicab.

I would say that he went there at least once a week.

He felt that he had made one more friend in America. In New York. The New York that he dearly loved. He had met *a girl.* So there became one more reason why the great, new city seemed to be his real home. There had been no "girl friend," as the young ladies of his gymnasium and dancing classes named it, back in Vienna.

"Now I have a best girl, and you already have a rival!" Stanislaus Joseph gaily told his Steinway, on his return to the Madison Avenue home that first evening. And he placed the photograph of the La Celle statue on the music rack, and played the first movement of *La Mer*.

One bit of confidential information, given him that first day by Guard O'Rourke, was just a bit startling. Startling at least when, later, he came to think it over. They had been talking of the red-mottled stone. Guard O'Rourke showed the young man the stone in the small columns of the adjoining Cuxa Cloister.

"I had often noticed this change of color in my baby's—I should say my Lady's breast," he told Stanislaus Joseph. "It would happen on a rainy day. But there was one night, just before I left for home—it was about a month ago—the breast of my Lady became *very* red. And it was a perfectly clear night! No 'atmospheric moisture' as them highbrows out in the office call it. I just call it wet.

"I remember that I went and looked at the Cuxa columns that are made of the same stone, and they had not changed color a bit. Only the breast of this statue had changed.

"I remember well what night it was. It was the Friday night before Easter. I might have thought it was because of Holy Week, but there had been ten years of Holy Weeks since the statue came here, and this had never happened before. Then I wondered if something had happened at my home—our youngest girl was ill when I had left home that morning. I was so worried I telephoned as soon as I got outside, but the wife said the girl was quite all right again. So it wasn't because of me. And there was nothing in the evening papers or on the radio about a bad accident or some other calamity—as they say. Even the Dodgers had won that day from the Giants. Won a double header! You see, I'm a Dodger fan, on account of the fine gentleman who gave my baby—I mean my Lady—to the Museum being one of the owners of that ball club.

"And that night there was nothing in the newspapers or on the radio about any flood or railroad accident, or no new strike called by John L. Lewis, or no new war being started or the subway fares being upped to ten cents, or any great athlete or any king or queen dying.

"Just nothin' at all had happened to make the breast of my Lady red!"

Guard O'Rourke paused in this lengthy listing of events that *did not happen*. He wiped his brow. He added: "But, Mister, something *must have happened* late that afternoon to upset my baby—I mean, my Lady!"

That had been (as we know) the late afternoon when Dr. Stanislaus Joseph Halka was locked out of his hotel.

When, but for God's grace, he would have proceeded to a contemplated self-destruction.

What, on the police blotters, is named *suicide*.

Stanislaus Joseph Halka had no feeling that he was of any special importance to the world. He was humble. He did not think for a moment that any tragedy that might occur to him would be world-shaking. Would cause any miraculous happenings.

He hoped someday to write a symphony—maybe several symphonies—that would have some merit. That would bring pleasure to lovers of good music, and cause those back in Vienna (and those in America) who had helped him, to be glad, and maybe even proud, that they had helped.

But that this symbol-of-disaster phenomenon, up at the Cloisters, had occurred at that particular hour, on that particular day; and that he was drawn to this particular image of a girl in carved and painted stone as he had been drawn to no other person, except perhaps his father; also that (it strangely seemed to him), on looking at this image, his devotion was returned——

Stanislaus Joseph, thinking of all this, was just a little puzzled and awed and shaken.

The young man had been in New York nearly two years, before the morning he had stood in the Early Gothic Hall, placed the Herr Kommodore's rose at the two small feet projecting from beneath a dull-red robe, and then looked up at the beautiful face with its gilded crown, and the thick, braided hair drawn down to hide a small left ear.

Two years, however, was but a tiny stretch in the great span of God's eternity.

That afternoon, when the strangely interested Mr. Halka had departed, Guard Dennis O'Rourke had thought again that "his baby" *truly* smiled.

Smiled whenever he looked toward her.

PART SEVEN

THE GIRL

❖1❖

STANISLAUS JOSEPH first saw the girl at a Florenz Ziegfeld chorus audition. The summer had passed and it was late September. He had started to work for the great musical-play producer around the first of that month. The gymnasium and the dancing classes had carried the "nifty piano player" through June, July and August. No complaints from either Hunter College or "Rachel Rosenblum's Academy of Greek Dancing."

Curiously enough, it again had been his bakeshop friend, Hans Beuter, who was indirectly responsible for this Ziegfeld engagement.

One day in August the bakery had been commissioned to make a huge birthday cake for His Eminence The Cardinal at Saint Patrick's Cathedral. The donors of the cake, the Holy Name Society, wanted to do better than a mere "Happy Birthday" greeting, written in red icing across its broad, top surface. "Hoch Soll Er Leben" would hardly do either, as the elderly Prince of the Church was an Irishman. Hans Beuter had an inspiration.

"I send for my friend, Dr. Stanislaus Joseph Halka," he told the shop owner. "You remember how he helped us out last Easter with the *dressiersack*. He has a swell *hochschatzung universitat* education. He will tell us what to say—and write it for us on the Herr Cardinal's cake. I guarantee you it will be an *erstklassiger,* humdinger job!"

Herr Beuter's vocabulary had now reached the intermediate stage where he combined, if not the King's, at least Broadway's English, with the best Vienna-bakeshop German.

So Dr. Stanislaus Joseph Halka spent another Friday night—this time from eight-thirty till four A.M.—at the York Avenue bakery, coat off, sleeves rolled up, his slender body completely incased in a huge white apron; but he spent those hours to great artistic purpose.

The "Herr Cardinal," to quote Hans Beuter, received a birthday greeting that year that he would not soon forget. Across its wide top, in cardinal red notes, with a thin-lined, chocolate musical scale for these notes to climb on, was traced the first eight bars of *Adeste Fideles* with the Latin words beneath the notes—

Adeste fideles, laeti triumphantes
Venite—venite in Bethlehem!

And there were Angels' trumpets in each corner, these drawn in gold-colored icing.

The much loved Cardinal was somewhat of a musician. And if not Stanislaus Joseph, the Holy Name Society of his New York diocese received a special blessing.

But His Eminence—a thoughtful man—did say a prayer that night for the workers who had made the cake, with a very special blessing on the head of the unknown artisan who had written out that noble hymn in colored sugar glaze. And who can deny that this prayer did not have its part in the next few steps of Stanislaus Joseph's career?

Step Number One. When that night's work had been finished at the bakeshop, Hans Beuter and Stanislaus Joseph had adjourned to an all-night restaurant for an American institution that, without fail, very early draws all immigrants as ardent worshipers to its shrines. Once tempted and indulged, they are lost beyond recall. One injection, by way of the mouth, and you are a confirmed addict.

Griddle cakes with Vermont maple syrup!

"How goes it all?" asked the bakery worker, as he loaded extra butter on his platter, already heaped with circles of Paradise Achieved.

"It goes very well for the moment," said Stanislaus Joseph, "only it is *all* going to end the last day of August.

"The Summer classes at the College will come to their final afternoon. There is a regular staff to take over for the Winter semesters. The Summer dancing class will end. Miss Rachel Rosenblum goes out with the All-Russian Ballet. I have been around and around, and around again, to the cafés. They need waiters and chefs, dishwashers and hat-check girls and doormen. They all *have someone* to play the pianoforte!

"Some of the singers for whom I played at Mr. Rouchard's will be back in New York in October," he added hopefully. "Perhaps I can secure some work with them. Mr. Rodman will return then also. Perhaps he will know of something—"

Hans Beuter had a new idea. This bakeshop worker, so full of "ideas," surely missed his calling.

As an advertising agency executive (especially if the agency were handling a cigarette or a ladies' "maiden form" brassiere account), he would soon have become a first vice-president in charge of Ideas, and a multi-millionaire with all regulation trimmings, including a residence in some lane called Old Mill or Water's Edge in Greenwich, Connecticut! But hidden in a bakeshop workroom, he was doomed to eighty-seven dollars and fifty cents weekly and York Avenue.

"Didn't you tell me that as a *musiker* you belonged to a Union—the same as I do?" asked Hans Beuter.

"Why yes, I had to become a member to play for Albert Rouchard—or to play in a café—if I ever again play in one! Mr. Rodman's office attended to it all for me. And I have been careful to mail in my dues, though I don't think you must be a Union member to play at the College where I now work."

"I was sure I remembered it," said Hans Beuter, "because I was a little worried that our Bakery Union walking delegate might come around the week you worked there steady. But I had it figured out what to say! That you already belonged to the *Musikant* Union, and that in Austria the *Musikant* Union was a branch local of the Bakeshop Workers Union. It would take him a long time to find out different—to write back to Vienna—to call a meeting of our Executive Board—"

Hans Beuter laughed, and asked for more Vermont nectar to slosh over his second "stack of cakes."

"In my case I think it was perfectly true," said Stanislaus Joseph seriously, and then they both laughed.

"But listen, Stanislaus Joseph," said Hans Beuter, "if I were out of a job, what would *I* do? *I would beat it, the very next morning, to my Union.* You bet you! They know where jobs are vacant. You bet you I would have a new job in one hour! Two or three new jobs!"

"I never thought of doing that," confessed Stanislaus Joseph. "Thanks! Thanks for the thought. You are my guardian angel, my life saver, Hans."

"You go tomorrow morning, and you tell them you are the finest damn *musiker* on the pianoforte who ever came to America!" cried the honest Hans.

Stanislaus Joseph laughed. "I won't tell them exactly that. They might have heard of Ignace Jan Paderewski, or maybe Sergei Vasilevich Rachmaninov. But I'll go to see them.

"I don't know why I did not think of it before!"

"Because you are a no-good business man," said Hans. "In America you must be a great *businesser,* as well as a great performer, whether it is on the pianoforte, or with the *dressiersack.*"

And in this, the humble bakeshop worker had stated a profound truth—unhappily the truth for a modest lad like Dr. Stanislaus Joseph Halka, who did not, even yet, at the advanced age of twenty-four, think that he had learned all there was to be learned!

But a "Herr Cardinal" was now on his side.

✣ 2 ✣

THE NEXT MORNING the young man did go to Local 802 Headquarters, on Sixth Avenue across from Radio City. The secretary took his name and address, along with those of half a dozen other new members—new to the office headquarters. There was no particular interest, and no promises were made. He was told (since he had no telephone) to come in each morning if he cared to, and if any "piano playing job came up," he would be informed about it. It was not very encouraging.

But after he had left, the fact of his connection with Albert Rouchard and H. Rodman came to the notice of the employment director, who also happened to be an Austrian-American.

In filing the young man's application (and verifying to see if all dues were paid), this official noticed these data recorded on the Halka membership card.

It also happened that this executive had been present (as a member of the Rodman private claque) at the Carnegie Hall Reimalsky concert, and had noticed and remembered the curious happenings there. He had occasionally wondered what had become of the heroic (musically speaking) little man who had carried on under such apparent difficulties.

So when Stanislaus Joseph appeared the next morning, he was given a special interview.

This union executive, as a young man, had been a member of a military band in Vienna—and as such, wore the red and blue Turkish Zouave costume which hide-and-slaughter-house expert Hans Hinterhofer had for a moment thought the young Stanislaus Joseph should wear on his journey to the distant America.

Stanislaus Joseph had heard about this suggestion, and related it to the executive. It cemented the executive's interest, whose clothes—alas—now came from a smart Broadway outfitter (two pairs of trousers with every suit), but where color schemes and cut were on a somewhat less attractive (and attracting) pattern.

"I've still got my Austrian uniform," he told the lad with a sentimental softening of unionized-hardened eyes. "I sometimes take it out and look at it. My wife says it was that uniform that swept her off her feet! And we have been very happy. I must see what I can do for you.

"Now if you could play the bass French tuba—I had a call yesterday—"

Stanislaus Joseph was obliged to admit that he was not an expert performer on the bass French tuba.

"Well—we'll stick to the piano. I hope you can play it good and loud! A technique that I surmise was not properly emphasized in the Vienna Conservatory of Music. It seems to be the main requirement of most of the calls we get here."

"I was taught a judicious use of *both* pedals," said Stanislaus Joseph hopefully.

"O.K.," said the executive with a smile. "I'll explain that to 'em, if we get a call. They won't know what the word 'judicious' means anyway. And by the way—aren't you the lad they call 'Mr. Tightpants'?"

"Why yes," said Stanislaus Joseph. "I suppose my trousers do seem a little snug. But they are like your *Bosniaken* uniform. I have a special regard for them. They got me to America, which I suppose might be called *my* wife. . . . I received my first American citizenship papers last week," he added proudly.

There was such fervor in the young man's voice that the executive reached out and shook his hand. It was a sincere gesture. "I myself have been a citizen for five years now," he said, "and I've voted every year! Voted *twice* one year—by mistake that was. Served on a jury every other year also. Good! Good! We'll see what we can do."

He made a special note on Stanislaus Joseph's card. *Has first citizenship papers. Expert in judicious use of BOTH pedals,* it read.

Step Number Two in the answering of the "Herr Cardinal's" blessing!

❖ 3 ❖

So THE YOUNG man went each day, and sat from ten-thirty till the lunch hour in the big Musical Union waiting room with others of his trade, all hoping there would be a "call" for a replacement, or a new job which their particular talents could fill.

Most of the others, while waiting, improved their musicianship with a careful reading of all details of the latest murder, as recorded in the tabloids, and an intensive study of a passed-around copy (since it cost ten cents) of *The Racing Form*. Tightpants brought a sheet of blank music paper and struggled with the *andante cantabile* movement of his symphony. He would have preferred to work at the keyboard of his Steinway, but it was necessary to secure some sort of salaried position before the afternoon gymnasium engagement ran its course.

A call did come through the last week of August. The final week of his steady job at the College.

And please to note that the call came through on the same morning that His Eminence, saying an early Mass at Saint Patrick's, where *Adeste Fideles* happened to be sung—for no reason at all unless it was the chanting of that hymn, thought of the handsome birthday cake of ten days before—the cake with the wonderful notes and words of that song in glorious red icing across its snowy top, and again said (in his heart): "God grant a special grace to the artisan who inscribed my birthday cake with a message of holy praise."

The "Herr" Cardinal was a thoughtful and ever grateful gentleman, as well as a holy one.

Who says that prayers are not heard and recorded?

Final and triumphant Step Number Three!

For the "special grace" was immediately granted, but I fear there was nothing "holy" in the wording of its earthly, mundane pronouncement. The call that apparently *was* in answer to that blessing, came through to the Musical Union headquarters, and was, I regret to report, even somewhat profane in its verbiage.

It came from the general musical director of the Florenz Ziegfeld Enterprises—at that moment a harassed and soul-tried man.

It was poured into the ear (via the telephone) of that Musical Union employment executive who was especially anxious to find a good job for piano player membership card Number 86,992 S. J. Halka.

There was some very choice, colorful, and mixed profanity to start with. The wire connection had been bad. Contact established, the Union executive heard the following, shouted rather than spoken, plea.

"Listen, brother! This is the Florenz Ziegfeld office. Maybe, by some wild chance, you've heard of it. And maybe there is, by an equally wild chance, among your several million of lousy card-carrying, paid-up members, one real piano player, whose repertory is not bounded by *Kitten on the Keys* and *Chop Sticks*.

"We want a piano guy who can play any damn piece ever written, whether by the late Harry von Tilzer or the equally late Johann Sebastian Bach, not to forget Peter Ilych Tchaikovsky, Victor Herbert, Ernest R. Ball, Richard Strauss, W. C. Handy, Ruggiero Leoncavallo, Giuseppe Verdi, George M. Cohan, and Carrie Jacobs Bond. *Play 'em all—at sight!* Mr. Ziegfeld is a quite up-and-coming lad in this business, and is liable to give employment to a couple of musicians in theater orchestras now and then. You ought to keep friendly with him. This genius piano fellow is needed for the auditions of the new Rudolf Friml operetta.

"For God's sake, and the sake of my job, who have practically from birth been a loyal Union man, send me such a card-carrying guy—if he lives and breathes in this cultural city of New York! And send him damn quick. Selah!"

So was the thoughtful Cardinal's prayer answered.

I believe that an all-understanding God—who must possess a sense of humor or he would not have created Man—pardoned the lack of reverence for Him in this sincere, urgent, straight-from-the-heart petition.

"O.K.," said the executive. "Stop worrying. That card-carrying guy is sitting right in our waiting room now. Sitting there waiting for your call, Tony.

"He can play all the lads you mention, plus a lot more that even you, my friend, have never heard of! Play most of 'em even without any music. Play 'em good and loud. Two-pedal expert. Albert Rouchard's accompanist for the last year and a half. He'll be at your low-down show factory in ten minutes. . . . Name? Halka. Mr. Tightpants Halka. Selah."

To the young man in the waiting room he said: "Tightpants, here's a real break for you. Right up your alley, and will lead to a permanent job.

"It's with the biggest and the best musical show producer in America. You start immediately, playing for auditions. Singer auditions—and if they like you, you'll get into the orchestra of the new operetta. Friml likes a piano in his orchestrations, which is not true of all of that ungrateful composer breed. Forget all about poor piano players as soon as they start to write shows. Rudolf is a great piano artist himself. One of the finest. Came to America as a concert pianist. Carnegie Hall—same as you.

"Here's the address. You can't miss it. Just up the street. The new Ziegfeld Theater.

"For the love of Mike and the glory of our Austria—not to forget both love and glory for Local 802—make good! You're too fine a musician to be sitting around here mornings with these *Racing Form* bums. Also, pretty soon, as you tell me, you'll fall behind on your dues. I've got to land you in a steady Fall job!

"And don't go highbrow on Florenz Ziegfeld. Not that he don't know good music. He does. And plenty. But play *anything* they put before you, even if it hurts. Give it plenty of pedal!

"One thing more. Don't tell anyone around that office you're writing a symphony! Keep *that* dark. Mr. Ziegfeld produced a show last year by a composer recommended because the guy had written a glorious symphony. Ziggie's only failure in years. Cost him two hundred thousand grand, *Variety* said.

"Mr. Ziegfeld is temporarily prejudiced about symphony composers."

Tightpants was hired and made good. For they had found a piano player to whom the *First Concerto* of Franz Liszt was a finger exercise.

And Stanislaus Joseph refrained from mention of his symphony. He wanted desperately to hold on to that home on Madison Avenue, four flights up, and the new Steinway.

He wanted to be able to buy an occasional two-dollar rose, and have bus fare to place it at the feet of the La Celle statue in the Early Gothic Hall up at the Cloisters.

4

ALL THE CHORUS auditions of the powerful musical-show producer, Florenz Ziegfeld, were a seething caldron for high aspirations and cruel despair.

The caldron was the large, bare stage of that producer's new, resplendent theater, designed by Joseph Urban, on upper Sixth Avenue.

Into it was poured by Hope, by Ambition, by Lust for Fame and Fortune, by Overdue Furnished Room Bills, sometimes by Hunger, the mass, if not seething, at least running to the hundreds, of young singers, dancers, show-girls, chorus men, that made up the always overcrowded profession of "ensemble artists."

They hailed from the bulletin board of the Chorus Equity; from the voice teachers (alas, from Albert Rouchard no longer); from the dancing schools; from the model agencies.

The more fortunate ones had homes; had fathers and mothers (sometimes husbands and wives) who could provide room and board during the periods of unemployment. The less fortunate issued from the boarding houses, the cheap hotels, that dotted the Times Square section and the Seventies and Eighties of the upper West Side.

Some were hardened, disillusioned professionals, who had given up all the hopes of advancement, of great achievement, and settled down to the mere hope of "a job." These did not stop to look at the billboards along the side-street wall of the theater: the billboards along the stage-door alley, proclaiming the great producer's several smash hits.

They did not pause (before turning into the stage-door entrance) and gaze up reverently at the electric signs that nightly flashed into certain magic names—names which meant sure box-office receipts—names that were once borne by unknowns, even like unto themselves!

But on the other hand, many in the mass cherished a Dream—a Dream newly born, or not yet killed by rejection and the failure to get a "second call."

The Girl, that morning, as she clutched her several song-sheets, was surely of this latter breed. I have no doubt that before entering the narrow stage-door, she had gazed at Lillian Faine's name in the electric bulbs, and knew how the glamorous Lillian had risen from the ranks. In her eager heart, *The Dream* was strong and vibrant.

And she was spurred to endeavor by a six-weeks diet of crackers and milk, and an inartistic and very commercially minded landlord, who had informed her only that morning that three weeks unpaid room rent was about as far as he could (without apoplexy) carry her.

The "call" had been duly announced in the theater columns, in *Variety, The Billboard,* and *Show Business.* Even, in the case of a Ziegfeld production, in the news columns of the daily press. "Ten-thirty A.M. at the Ziegfeld Theater. Bring your own music."

Some seven hundred appeared this first day. The jobs available numbered fifty-two.

Inside was the great high cavern of the stage, looking quite different from its appearance during a performance.

The scenery of the current show was stacked against the brick, fire-proof walls; twenty-foot high layers of flat, dead canvas, framed by narrow wooden strips, that each night, properly "set" and under the magic of lights, made *its* own Dream come true—dreams of palaces and tenements, of city squares and country gardens, of tall churches and low brothels. High overhead, and extending upward as great a distance again as from the floor to their bottom-bordering "battens," hung the vast "drops"—the "back cloths," the cycloramas—often the sides of rooms or house exteriors, when scene changes must be made quickly.

And alternating between "drops" were the rows of spotlights clamped on their iron pipes—Aladdin wonder-boxes that each evening, when rubbed by the current transmitted through dozens of snake-like cables, turned this darkened cavern into an enchanted fairyland reality.

No light sprang from them this morning at ten-thirty A. M.

There was a bare bulb at the end of a waist-high iron pipe, down front-stage-center, that gave out a hard, unfriendly glare. At the far side, two bare bulbs—one growing out of a pipe stationed by an upright piano—and one at the side of a small table. There was a chair in front of the piano keyboard, and a chair behind the table.

Across the dark gully that contained dead footlights gaped the shadowy auditorium—row on row of empty, teeth-like, seat backs.

Presently, in the depths of this horrendous maw, would seat themselves four dread, omnipotent figures—the producer Florenz Ziegfeld in person, flanked by his composer, his librettist, and his chief musical director.

In their hands rested the fate of the Dream.

At the table on the stage sat a lesser dignitary, the stage manager; sheets of paper and an ash tray before him: a pencil poised in his hand.

At the piano sat the more humble audition-accompanist.

5

THE ACCOMPANIST WAS Dr. Stanislaus Joseph Halka, already familiarly (and pleasantly) known to the Ziegfeld organization as "Mr. Tightpants."

The earlier weeks of the month, Tightpants had spent his days playing auditions of "principals." These auditions were held in the spacious private office of the producer, which was the top floor front of the building, reached by an elevator just off the lobby.

These auditions were not mass affairs, but by appointment.

The richly furnished office contained a great desk; a large cabinet phonograph-radio; a long bookcase containing bound copies of all the plays Florenz Ziegfeld had produced; and a concert-grand Steinway.

Alongside this Steinway postured the prima donnas, the ingenues, the leading tenors and baritones—sometimes a great bass singer—mostly artists who had risen above the herd and usually accompanied by their aggressive personal agents or managers, said agents or managers having arranged the time of their clients coming there.

Most of these singers were, of course, just as anxious as the chorus folk (some of them were just as "broke"), but they were trying out for leading roles. They had all supposedly had a certain amount of solo experience—some had already achieved a measure of success. Some were already stars.

Stars or unknowns—Florenz Ziegfeld insisted on "hearing them sing." The greatest voice in America might not fit the role this casting genius had in mind. All were anxious to exhibit their talents to the greatest star-maker of his day.

When they did not bring their own accompanist, Stanislaus Joseph did the piano playing.

He did most of it anyway. This at the request of Mr. Ziegfeld. This manager had perhaps a peculiar quirk. He preferred the audition music played by a stranger, rather than someone who came with the singer. For this "someone" was often the teacher of that singer, able, by clever playing, to gloss over defects in the singing, or at least give that singing a false value.

There were many stories of Florenz Ziegfeld's auditions. A new one was added by Stanislaus Joseph.

A somewhat arrogant prima donna, who had been one season with the "Met," appeared with her agent and accompanist. All were extremely vocal—vocal in praise of the lady, including herself. The general idea seemed to be that, after the "Met," she was very condescending to sing for a common "musical show" producer, and that this producer would be most fortunate if he could persuade her to join his cast!

Producer Ziegfeld became especially allergic to the visiting accompanist, and suggested that he preferred to have his own pianoforte operator—that same being Stanislaus Joseph—play the *aria* with which the lady wished to impress.

"But I do not think your accompanist could play this *aria,*" said that lady.

She did not realize the danger signal in the smile of producer Florenz Ziegfeld, "What ballad is it?" he had asked.

The accompanist spoke up. "The 'ballad' is the *aria*" (he corrected emphatically the terminology of this ignorant girl-show producer), "the *aria De Marina* from the first scene in Act III of *Boris Godunov,* an opera by a Russian composer Modest Petrovich Moussorgsky who died in 1881."

He paused to let this bit of information penetrate producer Ziegfeld's brain. Mr. Florenz Ziegfeld, who had a box each year at the Metropolitan—who had seen this opera performed in Moscow several times.

The lady's accompanist continued. "This *aria* is most difficult. Few accompanists can handle it. As indeed can few singers." And he now regarded with some pity the little man seated on the Ziegfeld piano bench.

Producer Ziegfeld spoke. "Mr. Tightpants, do you know that—" he turned to the lady's accompanist—"What do you call it?" he asked.

"Aria," said that gentleman. "In Grand Opera we call them *arias.*"

"I must endeavor to remember that word," said Florenz Ziegfeld, and then to his piano bench, "Mr. Tightpants, do you know that *aria*?" The producer here glanced at the outside accompanist for confirmation that he had pronounced the word correctly. He received that confirmation.

Stanislaus Joseph replied to the question. "I have played it, sir, not too well I fear."

"Play it now, please," said his employer.

One week of "Mr. Tightpants" at his concert-grand had disclosed to the astute producer the remarkably wide knowledge of his piano player.

The lady's accompanist spoke up. "I fear I do not have the score with me. You see, I know it thoroughly."

"Can you play it from memory, Mr. Tightpants?" asked Florenz Ziegfeld.

"I can try," said Stanislaus Joseph.

He did "try." The pupil of Josef Kattnig of the Vienna Conservatory played it as no one in that room had before heard it played on a pianoforte. Fortunately (or unfortunately), the lady had selected an aria that had been a special favorite of Herr Professor Kattnig. He had taught it to all his pupils with a complete measure-by-measure analysis. Tightpants needed no music before him for *that* composition.

Florenz Ziegfeld turned to the stunned prima donna.

"Now you have for once heard that little ditty played as it should be played," he said. "To me it seemed as well performed as when I listened to it, as a young man, at the Imperial Opera in Moscow, though I have heard it since at London's Covent Garden, and I think once in Brussels, which city at one time had the finest opera in Europe. And I hope you all profit by the rendition of my humble accompanist.

"And really, asking your indulgence, I do not think I want my thrill of hearing its lyric beauty marred by the sound of a human voice. So you may now depart. You see, madam, in my business we sometimes have to put up with idiots whom we have made stars—not knowing they were idiots. When we are forewarned, we do not deliberately engage one. You were, I believe, released from the Metropolitan Opera Company after one season. I think I can understand why.

"Good day, madam, and my gratitude for giving me all this valuable time of yours, and the time of your two most informative press agents."

The lady has not yet recovered. She spent her remaining days telling friends of the gross discourtesy of this "ignorant Broadway producer." She was speaking of a very kind and patient man, who, like our friends the Three Fates, abhorred pomposity.

The story got out. Was used by several newspaper columnists. "Tightpants Halka" received his first publicity. It embarrassed him exceedingly.

One other word about the Ziegfeld office. There were no framed pictures of the stars of plays, though he could have covered the walls of a dozen offices with the great ones he had made.

There were no photographs of any of the hundreds of beautiful show-girls he had launched to millionaire matrimony or cover-girl success.

There were two framed photographs only on his walls.

One was of his wife and child—the wife a great dramatic star in her own right—a star before their marriage.

The other, a very old woman—her face lined—her eyes tired—her hair thin and stringy. Hardly a Ziegfeld beauty. It looked as if it had been enlarged from a small tintype.

It was a photograph of Florenz Ziegfeld's mother.

He "glorified the American girl" in his stage shows. He glorified that mother in his inner heart.

✣ 6 ✣

WE RETURN to the bare stage of the Ziegfeld Theater, and the chorus audition for the new Friml operetta. The audition was about to start.

It was started in the usual Florenz Ziegfeld tradition. The slender, elderly stage manager, who had been with Mr. Ziegfeld for twenty years, arose from his seat at the table at the side of the stage, removed his cigarette and said:

"Ladies and gentlemen."

It then took several minutes for the assembly on the crowded stage to quiet down from the conversation of acquaintances—"What did you do last season?" "Did you like being in vaudeville?" "I've found a new boarding house on West Seventy-fourth Street—two bath rooms on every floor *and a shower.*" "Did you hear about Mazie's divorce? She should have known better than to marry an advance agent."

This important exchange of artistic information died down. Those still entering from the stage door were "shushed" by those nearest it.

Then the obviously bored stage manager continued. It was an old routine for him.

"Ladies and gentlemen," he repeated, "This audition is for singers only. No dancers or show-girls. Dancers go to the New Amsterdam stage where Mr. Busby Berkeley will interview you. Don't go there without your practice clothes. Mr. Berkeley's got to see your gams. Show girls will be seen here, on this stage, next Monday. Same time. Don't wear your falsies."

The elderly stage manager was an ex-comedian.

This announcement caused some two-hundred non-singers to make reluctantly for the exit. When they were gone, some five hundred still stood waiting—all supposedly vocalists.

The stage manager took a puff on his cigarette and continued. "I take it you are all singers. Now this is a Friml score, and to have a chance, you must possess a trained voice, and be a real musician. Don't embarrass yourself or Mr. Ziegfeld, not to forget any sensitive stage hands who may be present, if you haven't such a voice. You will each be heard in a song, but sing the refrain only. There are a lot of you to be heard.

"As I tell you to step forward, do so, and hand your music to Mr. Halka at the piano. Then go front stage, and sing out—out to the auditorium. When you have finished I will take your name and address. You will later be notified if we wish to hear you again. Everyone will be given a chance. So don't push. No contracts will be given for a week."

No singers left. None ever did. Trained or untrained, they all lived in hope.

The contraltos were heard first. They were always the smallest group, and the most difficult classification to fill. One by one, they came forward, handed their song to Tightpants, then moved to the front of the stage. The lights in a "border" above had been turned on—it placed the singer in a white glare, which made the almost empty auditorium seem more dark and fearsome.

The curved, hard, seat backs now looked like so many tombstones —a forest of tombstones in a graveyard, at night.

Tightpants said in each instance, as he took the music: "I will play you a very short introduction. Just a few bars. When I raise my hand, commence your refrain." And in each case he smiled. A kindly smile of encouragement. He realized what, in most instances, was at stake.

If a singer, through nervousness, made a false start, he would pause in his playing and say: "Start again. Do not be nervous." Sometimes he even added, "It was my fault."

It was never his fault.

He was a kind lad, as we know. So was Mr. Florenz Ziegfeld. Mr. Ziegfeld had noticed this trait in his new audition player, and was not displeased by it.

But kind or unkind, the great producer had decisions to make. In each case, after the singer had finished, he arose and said: "Thank you very much. Give your name to Mr. Dixon."

But Tightpants had noticed that stage manager Russ Dixon peered down into the auditorium as each singer was approaching his table to leave name and address. And that producer Ziegfeld gave stage manager Dixon a signal.

It was a very simple signal, but it meant life or death to the chance of an engagement.

If Mr. Ziegfeld held up one finger, it meant that singer was to be classified as A. To be sent for in audition finals. Two fingers meant class B; to be sent for, if, in the final trials, all the A's were exhausted.

Three fingers meant that the singer was *out*.

Tightpants noticed that the stage manager carefully wrote down the name and address of even this last classification, but as the singer turned her (later it would be his) back and left, that address sheet was deposited in a capacious waste basket underneath the table.

So, ingloriously, ended most of the Dreams.

The mezzo-sopranos were reached by mid-afternoon. Those were the girls whose voices lay between the contraltos and the high sopranos. The several hundred male singers, it being evident they could not be reached that day, had been dismissed at the lunch half-hour—told to come back the following morning.

And now *The Girl* was motioned out from the mass, perhaps about the twentieth of this mezzo group. She stepped to the piano, and handed Tightpants the music she wished played.

There are times, in the experience of human souls, that two people see each other for the first time, and know, without rhyme or reason, but without the shadow of a doubt, that here is *the only one*. One second before, these two did not even dream of the existence of each other.

An explanation? Perhaps the theory of reincarnation. Perhaps, over mysterious waves, a rushing together of a chemical coordination. Perhaps just the mercy of Divine Guidance.

Fortunate are they to whom it happens in early life, before the false magnetism of an ankle, a curving bosom or a manly carriage, a rugged profile, have led to a mistake. Fortunate beyond all the wealth of the world and all its swiftly passing glory and honors. Fortunate of the greatest blessing of Almighty God.

For He permitted to be evoluted (if there is such a word) a gangling, longitudinal creature with a muddled bunion named Head at one end, and two unsightly, stumbling bunions named Feet at the other. But in between, in His divine wisdom, he placed a true, clear-seeing organ named *Heart*—sometimes called *Soul.*

✣ 7 ✣

AN OBSERVER, sitting with Florenz Ziegfeld, would have seen only another girl step forward—a very slender girl in an immaculate, stiffly starched, brown and white summer dress. Stanislaus Joseph, not much concerned with women's dresses or figures, raised his eyes somewhat wearily from his keyboard (he had been playing steadily for five hours)—and looked into this girl's face.

It was a very beautiful face. Beautiful with a sad beauty—oval—a firm mouth—a perfect nose—eyes wide apart—they seemed slightly elongated—and of a very deep blue.

It was a face of foreign origin—Slavic or French he thought—such as he had sometimes seen in Vienna—the faces of women coming from nearby Poland or France.

But it was the frame—as it were—of that unusual face, that first held and stirred something deep within him. I mean the hair: the soft, brown hair that was drawn down firmly and hid and disappeared just below where the ears would be. It was heavy hair, and started from a clean, white part at the exact middle of her head just above a wide, smooth forehead.

And this hair was not bobbed as was then the fashion among young girls. It was obviously richly long, for two parallel braids of it lay flat and curved downward across the very top of the head.

They were like a soft, tilted coronet—a semicircle of pure beauty more lovely than any jeweled diadem.

This girl, as was true of most of the girls on that bare but glamor-haunted stage, wore no head covering in the still warm, Summer-Fall weather.

All this Stanislaus Joseph Halka saw, as he took from her small hands a sheet of music; and still fascinated by what he saw, placed the music automatically on his piano rack.

And then, like a sudden clap of thunder, like a flash of blinding lightning, came a realization of where he had seen a facsimile of that face before.

It was the face and figure of the La Celle statue up at the Cloisters.

He passed his hands across his eyes. This would not do. It was just an hallucination. It could only be a remarkable resemblance. This was no painted stone statue. But neither had the painted statue at the Cloisters seemed, at first view, to be a stone carving! But this was surely just another chorus girl, trying out for a place in a new Ziegfeld-Friml operetta. As indeed it seemed to now be, for when he looked again he realized that there was an expression in the eyes that he had never seen in the eyes of the La Celle image.

It was an expression of fright; a brave fright, to be sure, but those eyes were frightened. There was also weariness.

It was just a girl—the "next girl" of the audition who had been standing for nearly five hours. This chorus girl before him. Her thoughts were written in those eyes. *The desperate moment for a job had arrived. Would she be equal to the test?*

What this girl then saw I do not know.

No great, heroic lover, it is certain, in the round, small head below her, with the blond hair and the slightly upturned nose. But I think she saw something in this strange man's eyes that conveyed to her an understanding—a reaching out to comfort and help. Perhaps a recognition that she also did not understand.

Stanislaus Joseph was jerked back to reality and his task by a sharp exclamation from the Ziegfeld stage manager.

"Well?" this gentleman directed at the accompanist. And he glanced significantly at his watch on the table before him. It was three-thirty. There were still a hundred or so singers to be heard.

Tightpants had not yet looked at the music. He spoke to the girl as he now did so—spoke automatically his customary line.

"I will play you a very short introduction. When I raise my hand, commence your refrain." Then came the smile, but this time he added a new line.

"Do not be afraid."

His heart added still another line, unspoken, conveyed only by his eyes. "Don't you know that I would lay down my life to help you!" it said. Did *her heart* hear it? Who can tell?

I do know that many blocks away, up at the Cloisters, Guard O'Rourke (I have talked with him about it) again imagined that "his baby" was truly smiling. The illusion—if it were an illusion—was more intense than ever before. It really startled him.

The Girl's audition was a complete catastrophe.

The song she had brought was the well known *Sylvia*. It was not a good selection for this trial. Too quiet. And she had bought it in a key too high for her mezzo voice. Also, it had no refrain as such—must be played and sung in its entirety, so that it seemed very long. She was extremely nervous, and not a little tired.

The Girl had had no breakfast or lunch that day. Breakfast and lunch cost money.

With his month of audition experience behind him, Stanislaus Joseph realized some part of this, as he played and listened to a sweet, low voice trying hard to reach notes much too high. He did his best. He played as he had not played since the Carnegie Hall concert.

But it was the singer, not the pianist, that the manager out in the empty auditorium was judging.

Producer Florenz Ziegfeld was also getting a little weary. He arose and spoke, almost before this girl had finished. "Thank you very much. Give your name and address to Mr. Dixon."

And looking down into the dark, graveyard void, Stanislaus Joseph saw the fatal three fingers raised in signal to the stage manager. Nevertheless (as before explained) the stage manager was carefully taking down this girl's name and address on a sheet before him.

The girl's name was also written in ink—in longhand—at the top left corner of the *Sylvia* song sheet which Tightpants still held. Her own handwriting doubtless. Stanislaus Joseph read this name, and the address beneath it, and photographically memorized it, as he was trained to memorize the notes of a composition he must learn.

The words he memorized were:

Olga Lasenka
Hotel L'Esplanade-Plaza
West 46th Street

Now the girl had left the stage manager's table; she stood by the piano, and was taking back her music. Even as she again approached him, Tightpants saw the stage manager's sheet, with its carefully written name and address, dropped into the table wastebasket.

The Girl was speaking to Tightpants for the first time. "Thank you, sir. I fear I sang it very badly. But I have never heard it played so beautifully. Oh, I know I did not do it well."

The speaking voice was low and beautiful. She really *had* a voice, Stanislaus Joseph thought.

And the little man on the piano chair handed her back the song. His heart was pounding. His brain was throbbing. But he said only five words.

"Be brave, Miss Olga Lasenka."

To repeat the name aloud would help him in remembering it. He almost repeated *Hotel L'Esplanade-Plaza, West 46th Street* for a like reason. But he checked this. And before he could add another word of courage, the next singer, having been signaled to come forward, was pushing her sheet of music into his hands.

She was a self-assured, seductively dressed lady, who fancied that she knew how to handle *men*. Bending down, so that Stanislaus Joseph would have an eyeful of curving breasts and curving hips, she said, sotto voce: "You have my sympathy—playing for these silly amateurs."

The lady never knew why that accompanist took her music without a word—a copy of *My Hero*—brazenly transposed its key, and played it so loudly and with such changes of tempo that she made an even worse impression than Olga Lasenka.

It was the first time Stanislaus Joseph Halka had ever committed a deliberate, unkind act.

Accompanist "Mr. Tightpants" needed all his musician's skill to play the remaining two hours of that audition. For before his eyes, and pushing itself between those eyes and the successive sheets of music, was a sad, oval, French and Slavic face, slightly elongated eyes and brows, with the soft, brown hair pulled down hiding the ears, and two thick braids slanting across its top.

And instead of printed lyrics beneath the black notes on the music sheets, there was an endless repetition of *Olga Lasenka, Hotel L'Esplanade-Plaza, West 46th Street—Olga Lasenka, Hotel L'Esplanade-Plaza, West 46th Street——*

❖ 8 ❖

THE WORDS L'Esplanade-Plaza denote some thing or some place, wide and spacious. The entrance to this hostelry, on West Forty-sixth Street, was a single door, scarcely three feet wide.

Originally this somewhat ancient building, now tucked in between more modern office structures, had flaunted a double-door entrance, leading into an equally wide lobby, but the temptation of lush rentals for store space on a busy crosstown street between Sixth Avenue and Broadway was too much for the real estate department of the bank that now owned it.

The wide entrance and the wide lobby went the way of most purely decorative efforts in this section. A delicatessen and a barber shop crushed the entrance of Hotel L'Esplanade-Plaza down to a single door, and compressed most of the lobby into a narrow hall.

At the end of this hallway was retained a four by six space for "reception," and an equally small space for a "parlor," both planted in the rear of the delicatessen. A rattling, self-service elevator was at the very end of the hall.

But so that, in this struggle for survival, the hotel's identity would not be completely lost between dill pickles and clipped hair, there were two outside signboards; one on each side of the single sidewalk door, which signboards trespassed on the outside walls of the aforementioned shops.

Each board read:

HOTEL
L'ESPLANADE-PLAZA
PERMANENT
and
TRANSIENT
RATES REASONABLE

It had once been a good, middle-class hotel. A sentimental original owner had refused offers of sale when tall office buildings replaced older structures flanking it. This owner had, of course, eventually lost it to a bank, and the bank continued holding the property looking to a sizable profit when more office buildings would be imperative for defence measures like bar supplies, wholesale millinery, stock-market brokerage boards, theatrical agencies.

The bank apparently had not read about the desperate New York housing shortage, else (with the well-known philanthropic attitude of banks) it would have made any sacrifice to do its bit in an hour of public need.

It was a housing shortage especially felt by theater and night-club people employed in the district. So Hotel L'Esplanade-Plaza was bulging with chorus girls, waiters, bartenders, small-time gamblers, hoofers, and assorted Times Square hangers-on.

The Girl had come in "off the road" when a vaudeville picture-house act had closed six weeks before. She was a stranger to the big town. A fellow trouper had told her of this hotel, where rates were "reasonable."

The Ziegfeld audition that day was called off at five P.M. by the producer. He had a cocktail engagement with a Wall Street backer at the Sherry-Netherlands.

Tightpants hurried out of the theater and indulged in an unusual extravagance. He took a taxi to his Madison Avenue apartment. He ran up the four flights of stairs. He hastily changed to a clean, stiff shirt and immaculate collar, and carefully brushed his best coat and the Homburg. He gave his black shoes a quick polish with a strip of flannel cloth.

He had no idea about the Hotel L'Esplanade-Plaza, but from its name it must be a fine place. He must look his best.

His mission was not only to find *The Girl.* To hear her speak. To look at that haunting face so like the face of the La Celle statue. He also had a plan.

Despite what had happened at this first audition, he believed he knew how to help this girl secure the job which obviously meant much to her.

It did cross his mind that she might not see him. That she might not want to see him. After all, he knew nothing whatever about her. If he tried to tell her that she resembled a statue up at a museum called the Cloisters—a resemblance that must be pure accident—she would either think him insane, or an especially inventive "wolf" with a new technique to meet a stranger victim!

But if all this were true, if she were going to refuse to even see him, how could Heaven let him feel the excitement, the tenderness, that was surging through every nerve of his frail body, and making a bonfire in his brain?

He was nearly twenty-five years old, but he had never before felt love for any woman. Never been attracted to one. Music, and music only, had been his love. One might say—his mistress. And here he was, about to force his presence on an almost stranger of the female sex!

There was—in sanity then—this plan to rescue that female's name (figuratively speaking) from out of that stage manager's waste basket, and onto the "A" list of producer Florenz Ziegfeld. He believed he knew how to cause her to make good at another Ziegfeld audition. There would be a final try-out for the "A's" in another week's time.

He must take the chance that she would see him.

He boarded another taxi and arrived before the L'Esplanade-Plaza. The entrance door dismayed him. It was not even as genteel looking as the two hotels at which he had lived, and they had both been on the shabby side.

He found himself in the half-dark, narrow hallway, having in his haste stumbled over three inside steps; and the only visible object ahead was an open, cage-like, empty elevator!

He turned back and went again to the sidewalk. Perhaps he had entered by the wrong door. This was some sort of delivery entrance. But there were the door-flanking signs. It was the main—the only entrance—to the Hotel L'Esplanade-Plaza all right.

He entered again (not falling over the inside steps this time), and found that at the end of the short hallway, to the right of the elevator, was a tiny reception office. A semi-circular, narrow shelf fenced off a corner, with room for a stool and a mail-box rack behind the shelf.

A husky, very black colored man sat on the stool behind the shelf, and in front of the rack of letter-receiving pigeonholes above and at his rear. The colored man was checking the racing tips in a tabloid newspaper that on its editorial page was campaigning against "race-track gambling."

Stanislaus Joseph stood before this shelf, tipped his Homburg (an European courtesy gesture that even two years around New York had not eradicated), and addressed the dark-complected student of "the improvement of the breed."

"I beg your pardon, sir, but is Miss Olga Lasenka in residence at this hotel?" he asked.

The colored man looked up from his computations as to who would win the final race at a California track. There was still time, before the deadline, to phone the two-bucks bet to his bookmaker.

He had looked across that shelf at strange characters since his employment at the L'Esplanade-Plaza, but never had he seen one quite like this. The funny, round face above the stiff white collar. The black Homburg. The Ascot tie of another era. The coat collar with its black-taped edges.

"Is you a friend of Miss Lasenka's?" he asked, not unkindly.

"I am a friend of hers," said Stanislaus Joseph Halka, and he found himself adding, "An old friend." Why had he added that? He could not have told.

"Well, boss, that young lady sure needs an old friend right now," said the colored man. "As for her being 'in residence' at this hotel, she *is* and she *ain't*."

"What—what is wrong?" gasped Stanislaus Joseph. His heart had paused in its beat.

"I guess that she found the keyhole of her door plugged when she went up there a little while ago," said the colored man. "I know she did, because I had to plug it myself. Didn't like to, boss, but them was the orders from the manager. 'Three weeks unpaid bill,' he said. A singer she was, and told me she hoped to get an engagement today. Only I guess she didn't get it. She owed me three dollars personal, but I didn't mind that. I never minded locking out some of the fresh girls who live here, girls who have a different 'husband' every week end. But I did hate to lock a nice, sweet child like her out of her room."

Stanislaus Joseph turned pale, long before this voluble recital had finished. His blood chilled. As we know, *he* knew the utter, bleak horror—the utter despair—of such a situation.

Knew it well.

You are sick with financial stress. You have only a few pennies in your pocket—maybe this girl had no pennies at all! You have pawned everything pawnable—your extra clothes, your watch, your cuff links. And you go back, at the day's end, to your one refuge from a hostile, outside world—back to *a door;* and find a metal plug (which must have been invented by Beelzebub himself) inserted by some evil method in the keyhole of that door!

Your key, which, in your eagerness to reach the haven of your room, is already in your hand, cannot be inserted in the lock.

You therefore *have no door of your own! No home!* No place to remove the shoes from your tired feet. No place to curse. No place to laugh bitterly. No place to weep.

No place to pray in humble privacy for the help of Him who promised to provide even for the sparrow.

When it had happened to Stanislaus Joseph, around five o'clock that day on Amsterdam Avenue, and he had sat till midnight on a park bench at Seventy-second Street, it had been the one and the only time of complete despair. A time that he had even contemplated self-destruction.

A walk to the river. A walk across the high dock that bordered that river—*and keep on walking*.

So this knowledge of the plight of this young girl actually froze his blood. He seized the arm of the colored hotel clerk. He said: "Good God! Where—where is she now?"

In his mind was a horror picture of this lovely child with the tender elongated eyes, the hair-braids across her head, crossing a river-fronting dock, looking down at the sewage-tainted water. Then—a few steps more—what did it all matter——

There were river docks at the end of Forty-sixth Street; at the ends of all the city streets, the same as at the end of Seventy-second.

On Forty-sixth Street it was made easier. Whether you walked a few blocks *east* or *west*, you came to a river.

The colored man understood that tightening of fingers upon his arm. A respectable male guest, in this same situation, had shot himself the week before in that very lobby. He was only surprised that the fingers of this slight little gentleman were so strong.

"Rest easy, boss," he said. "I've kept my eye on her. She's sittin' in the parlor there, right now. I told her to sit and rest for a while. She came down the elevator all broke up like. She didn't look very happy even, when she came in. Guess she didn't think she'd got that job.

"I had in mind to ask her to come home with me tonight. I'm off in half an hour now. My missus would not mind, and my two kids—they'd love her—though of course we live in a colored tenement in Harlem. She could stay with us till her luck changed—that is, boss, if she didn't mind livin' with colored folks."

"God bless you, sir!" said Tightpants Halka. At that moment this colored man, with his black, sweaty face, was the noblest gentleman he had ever met.

The black man's eyes were suddenly focused beyond the little man in the Homburg. And Stanislaus Joseph turned.

The Girl stood in the doorway of the "parlor."

9

OLGA LASENKA stood there, slender and beautiful. Only her eyes were a little red from recent tears. But her head was raised proudly, it seemed to Stanislaus Joseph. Again the resemblance to the La Celle statue was utterly startling.

She then spoke in that soft, low voice he remembered from the audition.

"I would be proud and grateful to live at your home, Mr. Freddie," she said to the Negro hotel clerk. She had been standing there, unnoticed, and heard what he had said.

And only then did she realize the identity of the young man to whom the colored clerk was talking. Stanislaus Joseph moved to her and took both her hands in his. So relieved was he.

He almost crushed her hands in his—those remarkably strong hands of a professional pianoforte player.

The Girl did not withdraw her hands. She did not seem surprised. She simply said: "It is you."

She had, then, even back at the voice audition, felt the pulsing current.

She knew.

"It is I," said Tightpants in his painfully correct English, "and I have come to arrange these matters, Miss Olga Lasenka, if you will permit me."

"I—I had hoped you would come," said The Girl.

And so, simply, with no sentimental declarations, with no protestations that so often are but of the moment, are but the desire for a momentary possession, did these two *know*—for that moment, and for eternity.

Stanislaus Joseph turned again to the colored clerk, who had given up entirely as to whether he should phone a bookmaker friend and lay two dollars "across the board" on *Blazing Pomp* or play *Wise Mike* straight "to win," at the Santa Anita track, 7th race.

Right before his eyes was more exciting drama.

"This matter of a bill that you mentioned," asked Tightpants. "Just what is the amount of that bill?"

But before the colored man could reply, a door opened behind him, and a new figure appeared beside the clerk.

It was the manager of the L'Esplanade-Plaza.

This manager was a hard-faced gentleman with a perpetual glint of suspicion in his narrow eyes, and he was not in the best of tempers. He had just emerged from a purely personal quarrel with the lady he called his wife, and her penetrating voice pursued him as he emerged through the door.

Her exact words need not be recorded. They referred specifically to his paternity and (in her opinion) his general character.

This gentleman hastily kicked shut the sound-emitting door behind him, and addressed himself to guest Olga Lasenka. It was her ill fortune that at that moment he detested *all* women; detested the admirable real estate department of the bank that employed him; detested the management of hotels. And he was regretting bitterly that he had ever left Buffalo, N. Y., where he had had a good, non-ulcer-creating job managing an undertaking business. It was not a very swell "mortuary parlor"—it catered to middle-class working people—but the women he accommodated there were *dead*. Happy recollection!

Alas—the fatal urge to migrate to the Big City!

"Well, lady," he sneered, "are you waiting to pay your account, or just to make some new excuses?"

It was Stanislaus Joseph who answered. He had removed his Homburg when he had seen Olga Lasenka standing behind him. He therefore could not tip it respectfully as he addressed this new figure. But he bowed slightly.

"Sir, the lady is waiting to pay whatever is owed your hostelry," he said. He had no idea how much was owed, but he had his previous week's salary in his wallet—one hundred and twenty-five dollars. He hoped that would be sufficient to cover the indebtedness.

Never before—even on that Seventy-second Street park bench—had mere money been of such importance.

The Hotel L'Esplanade-Plaza manager regarded Stanislaus Joseph, the sneer changing to a genial smirk.

"Of course, if I had known she had a gentleman boy-friend—" he commenced.

Dr. Stanislaus Joseph Halka had been experiencing an entirely new set of emotions since he had first looked up at Olga Lasenka at the Florenz Ziegfeld chorus audition. To these assorted emotions was now added another—anger—and the anger was reflected even in his pale eyes, so that this hardboiled hotel manager stepped back a little.

"I meant no offense," he said quickly. For the little man in the stiff collar was reaching for his hip pocket. Could it be he carried a gun? There had been newspaper stories of late about a certain dapper baby-faced thug who dressed immaculately, and had appeared quite harmless, but who had conducted several financial operations in the Times Square district not exactly sanctioned by the codes of the Federal Reserve Commission.

But gangland Stanislaus Joseph was not reaching for a "rod." He was taking out his wallet, the wallet given him in Vienna when he had left for America, and which he had of late been carrying in his right-rear hip pocket. He now held the wallet in his hand, and the statement he made indicated that he had gained control of any anger. After all, to one who did not know, he probably did appear to be a "boy friend."

Nevertheless, the statement that he made was a surprising one.

"This lady," he said quietly, "is my affianced wife." That surely answered the hotel manager completely.

What of the Girl? Like all young girls, Olga Lasenka had doubtless dreamed her Prince Charming; dreamed a marriage proposal in some rose-scented garden, or, if it were indoors, at some ball during a dance. At the worst, it would happen in a darkened movie as the lovers watched Clark Gable do his stuff.

Well, it had happened in the cubbyhole lobby of a cheap hotel, well-scented from the adjoining delicatessen. Her romance had started only an hour or so before, on a crowded, bare-of-romance, scenery-stacked stage.

She was to think often of the beauty and wonder of it all.

But Tightpants (that was how he felt he must appear to her), having made this statement so boldly, turned in momentary apprehension.

He need not have feared. She moved closer to him, and placed a hand again in his. The pressure of her hand, and the look in her eyes, said as plainly as any words: *"Of course. How could you think it would be otherwise?"*

The hotel manager had still one more barb. Stanislaus Joseph's wallet did not look unlike a check book.

"I ain't takin' no checks from strangers," he said, with what was meant to be a masterly, executive tone. And he used a double negative to give it the proper emphasis.

In the otherwise ideal Buffalo undertaking parlor, it had been necessary to use the utmost caution in the matter of checks. They sometimes "bounced," even in the payment of sacred funeral obligations! And he was very miffed at his momentary show of fear for this little shrimp's toward-the-hip-pocket gesture. For the lady of his choice had entered through the door behind him, and had been watching.

The curve of this lady's well-rouged lips denoted amusement and contempt. Contempt for his fearful backing away. A forceful executive should not be cowed by any mere gesture. At least, not before his lady love. The managing gentleman was having a very bad day.

A brief note about this lady. To create a bit of sympathy for this unhappy hotel executive. And the admission that an unimportant but patriotic writer, in America, should not scoff at the all-important profession of "management." For in our larger corporations, "management" gives employment to hundreds of stuffed-shirts who might otherwise be "on the counties."

So, be charitable. Make allowance that the lady was large and blond. Luscious is, I believe, the proper descriptive adjective.

She wore a very low-cut, red blouse. She did not wear, and needed, no "falsies." Her glance at slender, virgin-breasted Olga Lasenka was somewhat pitying. But the dapper little man looked interesting. And prosperous. She turned slightly, to give Stanislaus Joseph a profile view. She had been told that her profile was like that of Lillian Russell.

But Stanislaus Joseph was concentrating on the manager. "We will pay in cash," he said, and opened the wallet.

Stanislaus Joseph was fully conscious that he had not said "I" or "she" will pay. He had said "we." He somehow knew it would be "we" from then on. On and forever.

Olga Lasenka's three week's bill was thirty-six dollars and sixty cents. Twelve dollars per week for the overdue room-rent. The girl protested the additional sixty cents. An indication, as Tightpants afterwards knew, of her carefulness about money.

The hotel manager made an irritated explanation. "You had been using your electric iron again. Can't you read? There is a sign on the inside of all doors which says: *Positively no cooking and no ironing with electric current allowed to occupants of this room.* The Bank that owns this hotel can't pay out *all* its money for chorus girl's electric bills! When you break that rule we make a sixty cent charge for electric current. I know you did it today, because when I inspected your room there was your iron still connected with the light plug!"

But while making this statement of indisputable fact, he had been viewing the contents of Tightpants' wallet—a very handsome wallet—and the hundred and twenty-five dollars in tens and fives looked to be much more than it really was. "Of course," he added, "if she will pay her back bill, and something in advance, I could consider letting her remain."

"Thank you, but Miss Lasenka is going to her home," said the little man in the stiff collar and the black, silk-edged coat.

Olga Lasenka ascended in the elevator, accompanied by the lady in the low-cut blouse, and the colored clerk. The clerk to remove the door plug. The lady—on stern, masterful orders from the manager, to see that the departing guest "didn't snitch nothing that didn't belong to her." "We been missin' too many towels—and even sheets lately," he added. And then: "The Bank is complaining about that also."

A purist in grammar might have noted the use of a *triple* negative in a part of this instruction. It was for triple emphasis.

Tightpants had smiled and said: "I believe I can safely guarantee your Bank that none of your towels or sheets from this room will be absent at roll call. I can be reached at the Florenz Ziegfeld Theater if they are."

"My—er—wife will see to that," replied the manager. The Florenz Ziegfeld Theater meant nothing in his life. Oh, for that peaceful, Buffalo, N. Y., undertaking parlor!

Olga Lasenka's few belongings were quickly packed in her small trunk and single suitcase. The manager's lady made a valiant effort to elicit information from the girl regarding her "fiance." Even to the hint that she would not notice the "snitching" of a couple of towels.

It was not surprising, however, that Olga Lasenka was less than even usually communicative. All she really knew about said "fiance" was that he had been the piano player at the Florenz Ziegfeld chorus audition. That—and that he was her predestined man!

"He seems like a kind and generous gentleman," finally commented the fact-seeking defender of the towel and sheet supply, "but don't trust them, dearie. I know. The whole damn lot of them are that way before you give your all, and go to live with them. Take it from someone who knows."

With the help of the colored clerk and a taxi driver, Olga Lasenka's meager baggage was carried out of the Hotel L'Esplanade-Plaza. Stanislaus Joseph Halka shook hands with the black man, and pressed a bill into his hand.

"But I can't take a tip like this, boss—" commenced the clerk.

"It's not a tip," said Stanislaus Joseph. "One does not tip one's friends. It's a spare ten-dollar bill that I'm happy that I have. Three dollars to repay the advance you were so kind as to make to Miss Lasenka. The rest to buy a present from her to your two children. I hope we both will have the honor of someday meeting them."

Tightpants and the girl entered the taxi. Where was she bound for? The girl did not know. Her thoughts were whirling, and she did not hear the address Stanislaus Joseph gave the driver. The young man had told the clerk that she was going *to her home*. That was enough for her to know.

They sat together on the wide taxicab seat, both looking straight ahead. Finally the girl spoke.

"I should explain about the sixty cents charge on my bill. I had washed and ironed my best summer dress for the Ziegfeld audition. I wanted the wide collar starched stiff, and the laundries don't do it properly. Besides, I was out of money. I wanted to look my best."

Tightpants said, "That's quite all right. I like a well-starched collar myself."

Silence again. Then Stanislaus Joseph said, "I want to ask you something, Miss Lasenka. Did you ever live in France?"

"No," said the girl, "but I am often asked that question. Maybe

I look a little French, though my father was Polish, as you could guess from my name. But my mother was French. Here—" and she opened a small locket about her neck. "Here is a picture of my mother. I think she was very beautiful."

Stanislaus Joseph looked at a small, tinted picture of another girl. Again it was the face of the La Celle statue.

"It was taken in Paris when my mother was a young girl. She came to America when she married my father. I was born in America."

"Did your mother live in Paris?" asked the young man.

"Oh, no," said the girl, "but it was not far from Paris. She lived in a little village near Fontainebleau. It was called La Celle. It is on the river named Loing. My mother used to tell me about it. There was a very old church there, and the ruins of a Knights Templars—I think that's what she called it—monastery."

"I know," said Stanislaus Joseph.

But did he know? In his heart was a great wonder.

Again silence. Then, suddenly, as the taxicab swung around a corner, their hands touched. And quickly, spontaneously, those hands clasped tightly.

Stanislaus Joseph was looking straight ahead. He did not dare look at the girl.

Finally she said, "Sir—my dear one—please tell me your name. I ought to know your name."

10

THE TAXICAB containing Dr. Stanislaus Joseph Halka and Olga Lasenka drew up at the Madison Avenue address. The rent of the fourth floor front was paid, and had been paid promptly on the first of every month. Thank God for that! God willing, it would always be so paid.

So thought the lad, and almost said it aloud. He had discovered that you could be a refugee, even in the land you called home. In the city you called home. In the dwelling you called home. If the small matter of rent were not paid. A little word that could mean Heaven or Hell.

The taxi driver helped Stanislaus Joseph carry the small trunk up the steep stairs. The lad thought—this was the second very precious burden to make that four-flight trip. The Steinway had been the first.

The girl had carried her suitcase. At the fourth floor landing the young man paid off the driver. He would manage the trunk into the apartment alone. He wanted to open his door, alone with the girl.

Tightpants unlocked his door, and they entered. Light still came from the four small front windows, but he snapped a magic-trigger-like button by the entrance, and the electric lights flashed on.

"This is where I live—where you now live," he said simply.

"Where *we* live," said the girl. And she added, "It is beautiful."

Perhaps her standards of beauty were not those of, say, Sloane and Company of Fifth Avenue. But after the accommodations at Hotel L'Esplanade-Plaza, and a series of like accommodations "on the road," it doubtless seemed a paradise.

There is no doubt but that the presence of a grand piano—even a baby-grand—gives to any room an air of cultured grace. It can transform an attic into a Louis XV *saloon*. Particularly if its great, broad top is open, held up at a beautiful angle, like a slanting roof of mahogany, by the slender wooden prop that is hinged just above the strings. For in being open, it declares that music lives there. That in that room, no matter how humble, also dwell some immortals named Bach and Beethoven and Debussy. Or maybe Lehar, Victor Herbert, Richard Rodgers, Rudolf Friml, Sigmund Romberg, Jerome Kern, George Gershwin.

No room that sometimes hears great music—melodious music—can be a lonely room.

One other attribute gave Stanislaus Joseph's "parlor" distinction. The four windows looking down on to Madison Avenue were not hard, graceless, square holes in the west wall. They were quite small windows, for the ceiling was low. Their distinction was that their tops curved in a quarter semi-circle, which gave them a graceful quaintness. A softening of unrelenting, straight lines. They gave a blessed kindness to the whole interior.

The girl seemed to notice this (as had Stanislaus Joseph when he first found the apartment), and to notice how the graceful, curved sweep of the piano's highly polished sides seemed to synchronize with the smaller curves of the window tops. She had moved to the piano, touched its curved box lovingly as if it were a living thing—then stepped to one of the windows and ran her fingers along a bit of the curved sweep of the upper part.

She turned again to view the room. Of furniture, there were only a few pieces, but they were worthy to keep company with the baby-grand and the curved-top windows.

To her right, against the opposite wall from the piano, was a William and Mary secretary-desk, and beyond it a studio couch. The young man had picked them up in auction rooms at a small fraction of their value. The glass-fronted bookcase which rose above the back of the narrow desk and was a part of it, disclosed a number of volumes along its shelves.

The writing lid of the desk was pulled down, and strewn with manuscript music. On the couch were also scattered sheets of music. Stanislaus Joseph had himself stained the walnut woodwork of both desk and couch, to match the mahogany of the piano.

There was a narrow table, along the left wall coming away from the piano, which was also well littered with music—some printed, some manuscript. And in the far corner from the pianoforte stood a small radio cabinet, that was at the same time a phonograph. Some dozens of records were in the open, lower part of that cabinet.

There was a straight-backed chair before the desk, and two other more decorative chairs (intelligently selected from the auction rooms) against the walls.

Through an open door, up by the windows, she could see his tiny bedroom—a bed; a chiffonier; a chair; these necessary articles having come from the Eighth Avenue installment-plan shop, and selected for practicability rather than beauty. They had been the only original furniture—these and the piano in the living room. Other things had been bought as he could spare the money.

A dark maroon rug covered most of the sitting room floor.

The walls of yellow plaster were almost bare. Close to the piano hung an enlarged photograph of his first teacher and the bakeshop owner, one standing, one seated at that teacher's pianoforte. The lad had had it enlarged from a small snapshot.

On the same wall, in smaller frames, were his diploma from the University of Vienna and his Doctor's Degree from the Academy of Music. Over the couch was a framed show-card of the Carnegie Hall concert of two years before: *H. Rodman presents,* and bearing the small, printed line—

Stanislaus Joseph Halka, Accompanist.

The Renoir of Albert Rouchard hung on the wall above the Steinway pianoforte. It was a painting of the busy Paris Boulevards, which the lad had always admired.

But the girl now perceived, as she stood, her back to the four windows, the open door on the opposite wall leading into a tiny, narrow, box-like kitchen.

She could see the gas stove with its raised oven, the whole being set atop the square, white refrigerator; and the adjoining box-like trough that was the sink, for there were water faucets projecting out above it. And above this, shelves for dishes—though the dishes reposing there seemed to be very few. An iron skillet hung from a nail, and a bread toaster. A brown broom-handle projected upward in a narrow space between sink and gas stove—humble symbol of cleanliness.

A kitchen! A real kitchen! A kitchen of her own! She had not possessed her own kitchen since her father died.

"Oh, it *is* beautiful!" she exclaimed. "God is so good to me!"

So these two stood alone in the walk-up, fourth-floor-front, of Dr. Stanislaus Joseph Halka. "Tightpants" Halka, piano accompanist of the Ziegfeld staff. Olga Lasenka, chorus girl, trying for a humble place in the great producer's new operetta.

It was the first time any woman had been in that apartment since the young man's occupancy.

They looked at each other for a moment, uncertain what to say or do. They were quite alone for the first time—just they two. No dozens of other singers; no hotel clerks or managers; no taxi drivers. A short three hours before each did not know that the other was alive. The girl was not even certain of the man's name—it was such a long name as he had repeated it in the rumbling taxicab. "Stanislaus Something Halka." It sounded foreign, like hers.

She wondered if he were Polish.

Their eyes met, and the girl, sensing his bashfulness, his inherent courtesy, suddenly went to him. She was a modest girl. She also had never had a real "boy friend," but she placed her arms about his head and drew that head to hers. Their lips met, and she felt herself clasped so tightly in his arms that it almost hurt. Even then he did not speak.

"Duszka," she said, "my duszka." It was a Polish term of endearment, so like an Austrian word that he understood. It meant "little soul." It meant "my dear one."

And then Olga Lasenka burst into tears. Tears of such happiness as only tears could express, and Tightpants held her close. He kissed her eyes—he kissed the braid across the top of her head. He kissed her face and the smooth, rounded Slavic cheeks. Then he took her two hands and kissed them, and led her to the studio couch.

They sat, holding each other closely, seemingly fearful that even now they might lose each other.

11

FINALLY THEY spoke again.

Stanislaus Joseph now took command. "We will be married as soon as it is possible," he said. "I wish—I wish it could be tonight. But that cannot be. In this city you must first go to a physician and obtain a blood-test certificate. Then you go down town to a large building near the Brooklyn Bridge subway station. You take an elevator to the second floor of that building, and if you are of foreign birth, like me, you must show your citizenship papers. I have my 'first papers.' You present the blood-test certificates and apply for a license.

"I know all this, because I helped a musician acquaintance who was married last year. He worked for the same voice teacher where I was employed."

"I leave it to you, my duszka," said the girl. "I have never been married before." And she smiled.

When she smiled it caused her face to light as if the sun had suddenly burst from a cloud. It was typical of the Polish women he had seen in Vienna. Sad faces in repose. Brilliant when they smiled. Symbols, he had always thought, of the oppression of the race—and its courage. Sometimes her face seemed entirely Polish. Sometimes more that of a Latin.

"You—you were born in America?" he asked, for her speech, unlike his own, had no trace of accent. "I should tell you that I came from Austria—from Vienna.

"But I am now a citizen of America," he added proudly. "At least, I think I am."

Said the girl: "I was born in America. A city in Pennsylvania where there are coal mines. My father worked in one. He is dead. So is my mother. They are buried in a beautiful cemetery just outside the town—on a hill. There is a space for me also. There is—" and she paused a moment, "there is a space there too for 'my husband,' as my dear father would always say, when we went on Sundays to visit my mother's grave. But I would say, 'There will never be a husband, because there will never be a man in the whole world as good and kind as you are.' "

The girl now looked straight at Stanislaus Joseph and smiled again. "You are like my father. You try to help people. And you wear collars like he wore on Sundays, when we went to Mass, and then to the cemetery. His Sunday coat had beautiful black silk binding around the edges. Like yours. His coat had been made in Warsaw, and he only wore it on Sundays.

"I am glad you wear stiff collars. I used to wash and starch and iron my father's collars. He said no one could do them like I could. I will wash and starch and iron your shirts and collars from now on."

Then Stanislaus Joseph told Olga Lasenka something about himself—about Vienna and his father and his patron there; about the trip to America; about the concert in Carnegie Hall and the two years that followed.

"I haven't been able to save any money," he said sadly. "But now, at last, I seem to have steady employment with a solid management, as they say up at the Union. When this new musical piece opens, the conductor has promised that I will play pianoforte in the orchestra. There is going to be one number in which a celesta only is used, and that instrument is very like a pianoforte. I make one hundred and twenty-five dollars a week."

"And I am afraid I'm not going to be much of a helpmate to you," said the girl. "Last season I worked—traveling around the country with a picture-house 'unit.' That is what they are called. We had a comedian and four girls who made up a 'sister act.' We weren't any of us sisters really, but we were supposed to be sisters. One of the girls was the comedian's wife.

"We finished our route six weeks ago in a New Jersey town, and I came to New York for the first time. The comedian and his wife and the other two girls live in Chicago, and returned there. I could have gone with them, but I wanted to come to New York. Something drew me here. It must have been you."

"I believe it was because of you that I was drawn to America," said Stanislaus Joseph. "When I think that if I had not ever found you—"

"And you've only found a penniless failure who couldn't even pay her hotel bill!" said the girl seriously. "But I *have* earned money —my salary with the act was fifty dollars a week last season! That was a lot of money for a girl to earn, I know, and you'll think I am a spendthrift. But it cost so much to live on the road, changing towns every week, sometimes twice a week. I could only save a very little.

"I had hoped to get into some New York show right away—just in the chorus, of course—but—well, you saw what happened today. Maybe I belong out on the road. But I just must get something to stay in New York. To stay here with you, and yet not be a burden to you!

"There will be some other musical shows being produced. I'll go to their auditions. I'll keep on trying. I mustn't be a dead weight— a millstone——"

12

THEN ONLY DID Stanislaus Joseph remember his plan. But first he said to the girl: "My darling, you do not have to work at all. You will never be a burden. When the new operetta settles down, I think I can earn extra money. Playing during the daytime for singers. Copying music."

"But I want to work," she said. "I don't want to give up trying to be a real singer. But I would not again leave you. Some other girl would find you——"

"No other girl wants me," said Stanislaus Joseph with a smile, "and I can hardly yet believe that you do, my dear one. And I think I know a way where we can both hold tight to each other. I think I have a plan to get you into this new Friml operetta."

But he discovered that the girl had an artist's pride. "No," she said. "I won't let you ask them to give me a place as a favor to you. Besides, it might make you lose your job, too, and then where would we both be?

"If I can't get a job in some theater, I can maybe find work as a clerk in a five-and-dime store. I worked in one in Wilkes-Barre, Pennsylvania, before I went with the picture-house unit. That's where the five and ten cent stores started—in Wilkes-Barre. Oh, I am a very expert five-and-dime-clerk—not an amateur, the way I am about show business."

"Hush—hush!" interrupted Stanislaus Joseph. And he touched her hair tenderly with his sensitive fingers. "The most beautiful girl in the world is not going to work in a five-and-dime store, as you call it. Though I once had to play a song for a musical-play singer who had come to my employer to be coached. It was a song about that. *'I found a million dollar baby in a five and ten cent store!'*

"I hated most of those kinds of popular songs I sometimes had to play, but I liked that one. Now I know why I liked it. Maybe you were working there when I was playing it! I was certainly lucky you waited till you got to New York before letting yourself be found!"

"My duszka," she repeated. "I was waiting for you."

"And you don't have to work anywhere," he repeated. "I am also writing a symphony that maybe some publisher will take and some great orchestra play——"

But he paused. There was such a hurt look in her deep eyes.

"You have said that twice," she said, "that *I don't have to work.* You don't believe—you don't believe I can sing at all—my duszka. I can't say that I blame you—the way I sang this afternoon! But I can do better than that. I really can."

Without her telling him, he knew then how much she really wanted to sing—wanted desperately to sing—not just for money, but because, in her heart, as well as in his, was the quenchless urge of expression—the urge that could lead to great happiness or great despair. Yet without that urge in some human hearts, what beauty and happiness the world would have lost. He already had tasted some of the bitterness of this urge.

But he was glad that she was that way. It was another tie to bind them. And now, if disappointments came—they had each other.

It was also, he felt, another opportunity by which *he could* add to her happiness.

He could not give her sable coats or motor cars or diamonds, but he could teach her some of the things he had learned when playing for Albert Rouchard. During that year and a half, he could not have helped but absorb many of the fundamentals of voice technique.

And so, for the next fifteen minutes, he became the not unskilled, professional musician. "Come to the piano," he said, and she stood beside the white and black keyboard as he sat on its bench and struck some chords.

"We'll first try some scales."

The girl sang "La la" up and down the scales, as Stanislaus Joseph hit a starting chord in various keys. She did not have a big voice, but it was clear and true, and there was a deep but soft resonance in her notes that was most pleasing to the ear.

"You have studied?" he asked.

"In high school, in Wilkes-Barre," she said. "My father put me through high school and I specialized in music. But of course that isn't like studying with a great voice teacher in New York."

"Maybe it is better," the young man said. "So-called great teachers have ruined a lot of fine natural voices. I heard them when they came from the wrong kind of teachers to Albert Rouchard. You have an excellent natural voice. You are a true mezzo soprano. I think you have been trying to be a lyric soprano. You must not try to sing too high.

"Many songs are more beautiful in lower keys. They were written to be sung in lower keys. The song you brought to Mr. Ziegfeld's audition was in the wrong key for your voice. And the wrong key for the song, in fact. Had I known, I would have transposed it and played it in a lower key, but it was too late to do that after I had started, and you had sung the whole of the opening."

"I was also very tired and pretty frightened," the girl said, and then she added, after a moment of hesitation, "I hadn't eaten anything before I came to the audition. My money——"

"Good Lord!" he said. "Here I am just showing off how much I think I know about singing, and you are starving! I should have taken you to eat before we came here. I didn't think—came straight here because I usually cook my own dinners—mostly out of cans—but I'll not take time to even do that now. We'll go right downstairs to the restaurant on the street floor. I hope you like Italian cooking."

"I like it," she said, "but we mustn't start out by you spending all your salary taking me to expensive restaurants! And after what you had to pay out for me today! I can wait till you cook—out of the cans—or let *me* cook out of them! I am a good cook—with or without can openers.

"I cooked all the years for my father. He said I was a very fine cook. He did not die of indigestion!"

"There will be lots of dinner times for you to cook for me, and me to cook for you," he laughed. "Tonight we go downstairs and eat spaghetti and meat balls. Not out of cans! They make them fresh, and the best in all New York. Tonight I just want to look at you and hear you talk. And I don't want either of us cutting ourselves with can openers! Those tools are dangerous to hands, as well as to stomachs!"

So they went down the steep stairs (in his excitement he forgot to snap out the lights, but he noticed that Olga Lasenka did not forget), and at a little checkered-clothed table in a corner, between the spumoni and the black coffee, he told her of his plan.

✣ 13 ✣

STANISLAUS JOSEPH's plan was a very simple one. It concerned a famous Old World song. Songs can have their part in human destiny, as we have before noted. This one—the first few bars of it—are for example carved on a certain stone——

Of this we shall learn in due time.

"Do you know *Als Die Alte Mutter* by Dvořák?" he now asked the girl Olga, and added quickly, "I should have said 'Songs My Mother Taught Me'? Those are the English words."

"I know it," said the girl. "My voice teacher in Wilkes-Barre had it. But why do you ask me if I know that special song?"

Stanislaus Joseph smiled. "Because that song is the favorite song of producer Florenz Ziegfeld. Of course, it's a beautiful number with its haunting Gypsy melody, but I think Mr. Ziegfeld must have some special reason for liking it. Maybe it was a song *his* mother sang to him when he was a child. Maybe he loves his mother."

And Stanislaus Joseph told the girl about the photograph in the Ziegfeld office. "I never knew my mother," he added. "She died when I was very small."

"My father loved *his* mother very dearly," said the girl. "She also came to America, and lived with us when I was a little girl—until she died."

Tightpants continued: "I've been playing for Mr. Ziegfeld for a month now. At his office, for the people who wanted leading singing roles. And, truly, a lot of them didn't have voices as pleasing as yours. But I noticed if anyone sang that song—they were 'in.' Mr. Ziegfeld was their friend. I remember he asked me if I knew it, the first time I sat at his concert-grand pianoforte. I did know it, and I played it. He made me play it several times while he sat looking up at that photograph on his wall. I really believe that's how I got *my* job right away.

"That song had been a favorite of one of my teachers in Vienna. That teacher had known Anton Dvořák. And he played it exactly as the great Bohemian composer meant it to be played. I was taught to play it that way. Perhaps that is one song I play entirely correctly."

"I know you can play many songs entirely correctly, my duszka," said the girl.

She hummed the first eight bars. The melody suited her exactly. Again Stanislaus Joseph felt she had a voice. And he was enough musician to divorce his intense feeling for her from his judgment of that voice.

"It will be perfect for you," he said. "Florenz Ziegfeld is going to hear his favorite song sung as he never heard it sung before! I will teach you exactly how the great Dvořák felt it."

"But my chance of Mr. Ziegfeld hearing me sing *any* song has come and gone," said the girl. "I know without your telling me, that I will not be sent for again. I have been through this kind of thing before. The considerate managers take your name and address. They don't want to humiliate you before the other singers. But you never hear from them again."

"There will be the final Ziegfeld chorus auditions next week," said Stanislaus Joseph. "I will give your name to the stage manager and you will be called."

"But suppose that stage manager remembers that my name was one of those not wanted? He wrote it all down. A foreign name like mine. He might remember."

"You are forgetting," said Stanislaus Joseph, "that by next week, God willing, you will have another name. It will not be Olga Lasenka.

"Your new name, which I will give the stage manager, will be Olga Halka."

✣14✣

THEY WENT BACK up to the apartment on the fourth floor front. And they sat and talked of many things. But all the events that had gone before, now seemed only a prelude to this day.

Those events had all happened so that he would be the accompanist at a Florenz Ziegfeld chorus audition, and so that she would be one of the girls trying out at that audition.

"I've been a sort of professional singer for two years," she told him. "My Wilkes-Barre High School music teacher thought I had a good voice. I sang at school exercises. School entertainments. I sang the *Star Spangled Banner* at a meeting of the Lions Club, and they paid me ten dollars. I sang at an entertainment to raise money for the Girl Scouts. After school, and on Saturdays, I had a part-time job at the five-and-dime store, because I wanted to also take dancing lessons, and those lessons had to be paid for.

"Then my poor father died, and I had to earn my own living. They put me on regular at the five-and-dime.

"I was very mixed up then in my mind as to what I wanted to do. I knew I did not want to go on just working in the store. Most of the other girls there were looking forward to getting married, or meeting a boy friend who would want to marry them.

"I—I didn't like the boys I met. They'd take you to a dance, and then want to get fresh. I couldn't stand in a doorway and let them kiss me and pinch me. I couldn't drive out into the country and neck—that's what they called it—in a parked auto. I didn't think I was better than the other girls—I just somehow couldn't do it. These boys would only take me out once. They wouldn't ask me again.

"I sometimes thought I'd like to be a nun. I loved to sit in the church, especially at night, when there was no one there. Or almost no one. Just sit and look at the candles, and the great high altar, and the images of the Saints. Yet I wasn't especially what you would call religious. I hope I'm a good Catholic, but I didn't care especially for the Masses. I just liked to sit there in the church alone. I'd think about my father, and about my mother who died when I was very young. I'd take out my locket and look at her picture.

"I hope I didn't commit a mortal sin to think that my mother was a blessed Saint.

"But what I really loved was music. In the house where I boarded, on West Main Street, there was an elderly man who gave singing lessons. It was fifty cents a lesson. I started to take three lessons a week. I took two dancing lessons each week. They cost more—a dollar each. Both my dancing teacher and my singing teacher said I should go to New York, and try for a Broadway show.

"I began to save money to be able to do this. But it was a little discouraging. I could only save six dollars a week, after I paid my board and my lessons. I thought I ought to at least have a hundred dollars before I came to New York. And I needed to have some better clothes.

"Then, fairly early one morning, a man and three girls came up to my counter in the five-and-dime. I was on the millinery counter. I sold ribbons. There weren't any other customers around, and I was humming a new song that I was trying to learn. Humming it very softly while I was arranging the various items along my counter.

"That was the way I would practice new songs. Hum them to myself when the store wasn't busy.

"These four people stopped and stood looking at me, and listening to my humming. I didn't know they were there! We had some awfully pretty ribbons just come in—all colors—and I was grading the colors, like in a rainbow, to the song I was humming. When I realized I had an audience, and was not attending strictly to business, I was very embarrassed. I stopped humming quick.

"I said: 'I beg your pardon. What can I do for you?'

"One of the girls said: 'Tom, doesn't she look like Nellie?' And the man said, 'She sure does! A spittin' image.' And then he said, 'Go on with that melody, kid.'

"At first I thought he was joking. Or trying to be funny or sarcastic. One time before, I was humming, and didn't know a customer was there, and a woman in a hurry had said: 'Don't let me disturb you, Galli Curci, but if it isn't too much trouble, I'd like a spool of 40 thread.'

"I guess he realized my feeling for he repeated: 'Go on, girl. I mean it.'

"Well, I went on very softly. And then the man said: 'A mezzo too. Girl, are you a professional singer?'

" 'I hope to be one someday,' I said, 'and also a dancer. But what can I do for you now, sir? These ribbons are just in, and a very fine bargain——'

"But they didn't pay any attention to my sales talk. One of the other girls said: 'She's just Nellie's size. She could wear Nellie's costumes. No alterations.'

" 'Ye-ah,' said the man. 'Ye-ah. I noticed that too.'

"He leaned over the counter like, and looked me up and down. 'I hope her legs are good for the pink tights in the finale,' he said to the girl who had just spoken. I found out afterwards she was his wife.

" 'You forget about them legs,' said this girl. 'She says she's a dancer. Her legs will be O. K. I'll attend to all the leg inspections, Mr. Gallagher.'

"They all laughed, and then the man said to me: 'Look here, kiddo, we came into this damn store to buy some ribbons for costumes, but maybe we've found God's gift to vaudeville—voice and legs and all!' He laughs again, and pulls out a card and pushes it at me. It read—

Tom "Wow-Em" Gallagher
and
The Four Rosebud Sisters
Sensational Comedy and Singing Act
Now Playing R. K. O. Time
Permanent Address
1503 Sherridan Road, Chicago, Ill.

"I'll never forget that card! And my heart was beating fast by that time. I knew all along, by their clothes and accents, that they weren't Wilkes-Barre folk. They were real theater people, and they were talking to me!

" 'How would you like to join our act?' the man said, just like that. And he didn't laugh. Very serious like. And the girl I afterwards found out was his wife said to him: 'It will save us a carfare from Chicago, and the wiring back to our agent for a new girl.'

" 'Ye-ah, we got to get another girl quick in Nellie's place,' said the man.

" 'You really mean that you want me?' I asked. 'You're not making fun of a poor small-town girl?'

" 'Sure we mean it,' the man said. 'We're playing this week at the Colonial. Tom Wow-Em Gallagher and the Four Rosebud Sisters. One of our girls got ill, and we had to ship her back home to Chicago this morning. She'd been sick all along, and had to miss shows. We aim to please—that's our motto—and the house managers complained there were only *three* Rosebud Sisters, when our contract and billing guaranteed *four*. The salary is thirty-five dollars a week. What do you say?'

"I was getting twenty-two fifty a week at the five-and-dime. Thirty-five dollars! It sounded too good to be really true! And the Colonial was the best picture and vaudeville house in town."

Olga Lasenka then told Stanislaus Joseph that she had given up her lunch half-hour that day, and gone to a church near by to pray. Pray that all this wonderful good fortune would really come true—that she could be one of the Four Rosebuds! And that God would make her thin legs look good in pink tights!

"I was pretty worried about my legs," she said. "They were sort of thin like.

"I then went into the rectory, and spoke to the priest," she continued. "I had talked with him sometimes about becoming a nun. I asked him if it was all right for me to join a vaudeville act.

"The priest was a singer himself. Although now an old man, he still had a fine baritone voice. He told me to do it. To go on with my career. He knew how I wanted to sing. I didn't dare tell him about the pink tights. Only God knew about that."

That night she had gone to the Colonial, where Mr. Gallagher had left a pass in the box-office, and she had watched three runnings of the feature picture and three sessions of the act. The comedian told jokes, sang songs, and played a violin, standing on his head.

"That standing on his head sounds a little silly, I know," said Olga Lasenka, "but it somehow isn't silly when I think of it now.

Mr. Gallagher told me afterwards he was the only performer in the entire world who could do it perfectly. I think if there was something I could do, like no one else in the entire world could, I would have a right to be proud too!"

The three girls filled in behind Mr. Gallagher with several costume changes, and they sang three numbers with a jazz harmony.

After their final show, Olga had gone back stage and rehearsed for an hour in the simplest numbers. She had tried on Nellie's costumes, and they were a perfect fit. She was to report at ten-thirty the next morning for more rehearsing, and join the act for the first afternoon show; that is, if she could arrange with the five-and-dime manager to let her quit her store job immediately.

"That store manager was a most kind gentleman," she told Stanislaus Joseph. "I guess it helped that he was a member of the Lions Club, where I had sung the *Star Spangled Banner*.

"He not only let me quit that morning—it was a Tuesday—but he paid me a full week's salary, and called up the local newspapers about it all. There was a front page story with headlines—FIVE-AND-DIME GIRL JOINS STAR VAUDEVILLE ACT AT THE COLONIAL. LOCAL GIRL, SAID TO HAVE REMARKABLE SINGING VOICE, IS LATEST SENSATIONAL FIND OF TOM 'WOW-EM' GALLAGHER, WHO HAS DISCOVERED MANY STARS.

"I don't think Mr. Gallagher had really discovered anybody, except the three other Rosebuds. You found out today how much of a discovery I really was!

"But all this—true or false as they say—made business bigger both at the theater and at the five-and-dime. So everybody was happy. One of the other clerks at the five-and-dime told me people came in to ask at which counter I had worked! It made me very excited until I thought that maybe they came because the store was rid of me. Me and my humming!"

Stanislaus Joseph said: "They came because the loveliest girl in the whole world had worked there—like to a shrine."

"Duszka, you're going to make me very up-stage," smiled the girl. "But I'll lose any vanity after a few more New York auditions!

"Like I lost most of it when we left Wilkes-Barre that Saturday, and played a week in a picture house in Pittsburgh. The home town publicity, as they called it, didn't mean anything in Pittsburgh!

One paper there said 'A very poor stage-show' and I felt so sorry for Mr. Tom Wow-Em Gallagher who had been so kind to me.

"I guess in Wilkes-Barre I thought I was a star already—especially that Saturday night when the Lions Club came in a body, and at the end of our act shouted 'We want Olga Lasenka!' And I had to sing the *Star Spangled Banner* just as I had sung it at their club luncheon.

"But in Pittsburgh I was just one of the Four Rosebud Sisters, and probably the worst of the four! Nobody wanted to hear me sing the *Star Spangled Banner!* The big applause came when Mr. Gallagher stood on his head and played *Hearts and Flowers* on a violin while we girls held up his legs. That was where I wore the tights. Two Rosebuds were in pink tights, and two in green ones.

"But they were kind, good people—that man and the three other girls. Like children they were. I suppose I felt older and acted older, because I had grown up, always looking out for my father. Cooking for him, and keeping house for him, and keeping the clothes in repair, and starching his collars for Sunday, I mean. And I'd gone through high school.

"The other three girls were practically born in the theater. They knew no other life but those vaudeville and picture houses.

"I have worked steady with the act for two years. Everywhere across the country. Except New York. I guess we just weren't good enough for New York. The nearest we got to New York was Bayonne, New Jersey. That's where we closed the season, two months ago.

"They wanted me back this season, but I'd made up my mind to try my luck here. Oh, I do want to get into a real musical play! Maybe, if I start at the bottom, in the chorus, I can someday get an understudy—then a part. It would please my father so. He would be so proud of me! I believe that he will know."

As the girl said this last, her face became so like the face of the La Celle statue that Stanislaus Joseph was again startled.

But Olga Lasenka added quickly and with a smile, "I hope you don't have to wear pink tights to get in a Broadway show. In spite of all my prayers, my poor legs are still too thin to look really good in them."

So that was her simple desire. Her Dream. Just to gain a part in a Broadway operetta. Not to be a star at the Metropolitan Opera, as he had heard so many silly women rave on, women with money or backing, for whom he had played at Albert Rouchard's studio—women without one-half the talent and charm of this child.

Just to sing one song perhaps, and hear the applause, and know that she had touched an audience.

That, he felt, he could do for her. He could try. Beyond that—no one knew. But he felt that he would give his soul's salvation to make her happy.

His own Dream? He must start again to practice more regularly. At least an hour every day on Debussy, Chopin, Brahms. Maybe he could, in a year or so, give a concert of his own.

And he must work intensively on his symphony.

He had put the symphony completely aside since playing for the Ziegfeld office. There it lay neglected about his room. The long hours of voice trials for a new show gave him little time. As had the long hours when he had played that year and a half for Albert Rouchard. He must now do something to make *her* proud of him.

She must not just be the wife of Mr. Tightpants Halka, accompanist.

15

Stanislaus Joseph Halka went to his pianoforte. It possessed a beautiful tone. He had selected it after trying some twenty instruments on the Steinway floor. And he kept it in perfect tune, for he had a sure ear for pitch; and with the aid of the precious wrench, given him by that first boyhood teacher along with that first spinet, he could instantly correct the slightest error caused by temperature or use.

Each day he dusted it with a soft brush and a silk cloth. It had the care given to a baby.

It *was* his child. He now touched the keys lovingly, as if each white and black slip of ivory was a living soul.

"These will be your only rivals," he said to Olga Lasenka. "I fear I shocked a kindly priest in a church near here—a priest I talked to once or twice this Summer, when I was feeling low. He would say to me, 'Go to your home, my son, and read the greatest comforter of all the Ages—the Twenty-third Psalm of David.'

"That great writing was comforting, but I told him that for me there was something even more comforting. These black and white symbols that could sound courage and solace and faith more vividly than any mere words.

"I think he thought me a complete pagan until he remembered that David played to his holy words on a golden harp. So he gave me his blessing and said: 'Go home then, and sit at your piano, but have God's image in your heart as you play.'

"I wonder what that priest would think, if I now told him it would be your image I place before me as I play; that is, if I try to play great music that was written from the heart. But he soon will meet you and see you and understand. He will be the one to marry us, if he is still at that church."

"He will think that I am a very ordinary girl, and that you are quite unbalanced," smiled Olga Lasenka, and she came and stood beside the pianoforte. "But I am happy that you are unbalanced, and please don't ever become really sane again, my duszka. Please play for me now. Just for me. Play for me your favorite music. I know it will be something different from what you have to play for the auditions. How you must hate *One Fine Day* even if it was written by Puccini, and *I Love Life,* and *My Hero!* And *Kiss Me Again.* I did try to bring something that everyone else did not sing. But play now—something you really love to play."

So the little man with the fingers of steel, but fingers as sensitive—when need be—as the gentle touch of a summer breeze, began to strike those black and white symbols with the guidance of his artist's brain and soul.

He played from Bach and Handel and Gluck and Haydn. Mozart and Beethoven and Schubert and Mendelssohn. Schumann and Chopin and Liszt.

He introduced the girl, as it were, to these immortals that had been his friends—it seemed his living friends—back in Vienna.

And the young girl with the face of the La Celle statue was deeply moved and thrilled.

She had never really heard a great pianoforte artist play. She had had no realization of the music—almost like an orchestra (as Liszt had said)—that could come from those steel strings in their sounding box of mahogany. And she had innocently complimented him on the playing of her simple song!

"What you must have thought of my presumption!" she said, "When I told you I liked your playing of *Sylvia*—"

"Hush," he said, "it is as difficult to play properly a little song as it is to play a symphony. If that song is great music, and expresses a great thought. I love Tchaikovsky's *None But The Lonely Heart,* as the English words say it. I will still love it, but I shall not have to play it ever again as expressing my own loneliness. Now that I have found you."

And he played the beautiful ballad of the greatest of the Russian composers. The girl started to hum it very softly. "Sing it please, if you know it," said Stanislaus Joseph, and she did—timidly, but very well.

She really had a voice, he thought.

"What composition do you love the most?" she asked him finally. "You who know so much of music. Is there one single piece that brings you the greatest happiness to play?"

The young man said: "There was never a single piece until two years ago—the year I came to America." And he first told the girl a little of the voyage to America, and how he had traveled in the Bismarck Suite, because of the friendship of Professor Anton Lavar for Kommodore Hugo Frederick von Steinburg. "That piece is called *La Mer,* which I do not perhaps need to tell you means *The Sea.* It was the favorite piece of my friend, the Herr Kommodore. I played it with him—I have come to love it—someday I will tell you why. I will play you just a part of it now."

And the young man played the second part—*the conversation of wind and wave.* A part that made you see a great stretch of waters that might well be the answer to all eternity.

And the girl, Olga Lasenka, then said a strange thing to him. The girl from the Wilkes-Barre five-and-dime who had come from a cheap hotel to the audition of a Florenz Ziegfeld operetta, where he was just the humble piano player.

"I have never really seen the sea," she said. "And when I did look at it once, near Los Angeles—our act was playing in picture houses there—it frightened me. It was so vast, so unending. And I certainly have never been aboard a great ocean liner such as the one on which you came to America, or on any great ship. I have seen pictures of them, of course. Still, I have sometimes had a strange dream—a very strange dream for me to have who know only trains and buses—maybe a rowboat on the Susquehanna River at Wilkes-Barre.

"I have dreamed that I was standing high on the front of a great ocean liner, such as I have seen in the pictures, and I was looking far out at the sea. I heard music in this dream. I did not know that music. I think now it was the music you have just played. Who wrote that music?"

"Claude Achille Debussy, who died only a little while ago," said the young man. "He was French. Maybe your mother knew that music. Maybe that is why you thought you had heard it before."

But through the mind of Stanislaus Joseph Halka was racing another thought. The tale the Herr Kommodore told of the Lady of the Statue on the bridge of his *Europa*. This resemblance of the girl to the Madonna at the Cloisters—the statue that had been brought to America on that ship!

No. He must not wander off into utterly wild fantasy. The girl was from Wilkes-Barre, Pennsylvania. She had worked in a Five and Ten-Cent Store there. She was now trying to be a singer in a Broadway show. She was flesh and blood and no sainted Madonna.

He loved her. He was going, God willing, to make her his wife, as soon as the laws of the City of New York would permit.

16

So Stanislaus Joseph Halka pushed mad thoughts away. And suddenly he looked at his watch. Midnight. And the Ziegfeld audition for the next morning was called at ten!

"It is very late," he said. "It is now after twelve. You were tired when we came here, and I have tired you more."

"I have never been so wide awake," said the girl. "I never dreamed I should find such enchantment—such elation. And most wonderful of all—you are 'my man,' as the song says! My own duszka! Me—from the five-and-dime, and a picture house act! Will you play for me every evening—if you are not too tired?"

"I will play for you every evening, if you wish it," he said, "but now I must go, so that you can sleep. I must sleep also, for there is another long chorus audition tomorrow."

"But this is *your* home. Where—where do you go?" she asked.

"I have a friend with whom I can stay," he said.

"But it is late. Your friend will be asleep. Or maybe not even at home."

"He will not be asleep, and he will not be at home," smiled Stanislaus Joseph. "He works all night in a bakeshop. I will go there and get his key. My dear one, I also know what it is to be locked out of your room. This good friend took me in. I think he will take me in again. I know that he will."

"But—but—you are not locked out of *your* room tonight! Cannot—cannot we both stay right here? I want to be in your arms, my duszka. Now and for always."

Stanislaus Joseph had risen from his pianoforte bench. He held her close for a long moment. He kissed the blessed braids of her dark hair.

"I also want you—always and forever," he said. "God has been very good to me that I have found you. That I have found you when I have employment and a home. So we will start our lives together with God's blessing. I will come back early in the morning. At eight o'clock, if that is not too early for you. We will have our breakfast, and then go to a doctor I have met. That will get the blood tests started, so that the next morning we can go down town to the license bureau and attend to that.

"Then, the next day or the next, we can be married. I think the priest that I know will consider it an emergency—we are soon leaving town with a theatrical attraction, and he will permit us to omit the announcement of the banns—as I think they call it. My musician friend who was married managed it that way, as he and his bride were leaving for Europe."

But there was real fear in the girl's blue eyes. "Suppose—suppose you cannot find your friend. Suppose something should happen to you. In that room is your bed. I can sleep on the day couch. I can sleep in one of the chairs. Oh, I have often slept all night in a chair—not even a chair—a hard bench, in some railroad station, when we had to take a five A.M. train for the next town; and since our last show was near midnight we would give up our hotel rooms to save the two or three dollars. We will stay here together. I cannot, I must not lose you now."

There was a great yearning—a great desire in his heart also, but he conquered it. "You can unpack and put your clothes in the closet off the bathroom. They, at least, will be near to mine tonight."

He moved to the desk and took from his pocket the remainder of his salary money. He kept a five-dollar bill, the rest he put in a small drawer.

"Here is our fortune," he said and smiled. "It's about eighty dollars. It belongs to both of us now. Use whatever you need of it. I've been working at the Ziegfeld office for four weeks, but I was behind all around, and had to pay up my debts. And a down payment on the pianoforte. Everything is all clear now. I will come back early—eight o'clock—and fix our breakfast."

"You will do nothing of the kind," she said. "*I* will have the breakfast ready when you arrive here, Mr. Halka! Do you like bacon and eggs?"

"I like bacon and eggs, Miss Lasenka," he said and laughed, "but I usually only have eggs and coffee."

"Tomorrow we have bacon and eggs—and waffles—that is, if you like them."

"I would love waffles," he said. "But I don't know if there is any bacon in the icebox, or any waffle flour. There is a waffle iron. It's in the empty oven. I've tried to make them sometimes on Sunday mornings, but there is a conspiracy against my making an edible waffle!"

"Waffles are my luckiest dish!" she laughed. "I'll be up at seven, maybe earlier. At six-thirty! There must be stores near here. I'll find out what supplies you haven't got, and get in whatever is needed. It will be the happiest—the most exciting marketing I have ever done! I'll keep track of the money I spend and what I spend it for. How do you like your coffee—strong?"

"Quite strong," he said with a smile.

"I know," she said. "That's how my father liked it. It will be as if I were again cooking for my father. Only—only I think I love you even more than I loved my father. Is that wicked of me, I wonder?"

Again he took her in his arms. Then he said: "Now I must really go. Here are the keys. One is the front door, down stairs. Sometimes it is locked. This smaller key is the apartment. Tomorrow we will have duplicates made. When I come in the morning, if the down-stairs door is still locked, I will press the button by my name. I'll press it three times. Then you'll know it's me, and not someone else who has heard that the most beautiful girl in the world is living here. That button by our door will unsnap the lock. You press it when you hear my signal."

"I'll stand by it from seven-fifteen on," she said, "and only press the door-opening button for three rings! It would be terrible if someone else found out how beautiful I was and got up here by mistake!" And they both laughed.

"Duszka," she said, "there's just one thing more. I call you 'Duszka'—that is what my father always called me. It is Polish, but I guess you know what it means. 'Dear one.' But your real first name. It is a fine name, but it seemed very long. Stanislaus. My father had a friend—a Polish miner—with that name. He was called Stan by his friends, but I don't like Stan for you. What shall I call you, duszka?"

And Dr. Stanislaus Joseph Halka heard himself saying: "There is another name by which I am known. It was given to me here in America, soon after I came.

"At first I hated it. I thought the people who used it were making fun of me. Perhaps they were—at first. At the very first. But afterwards I realized they meant no unkindness. I believe they also thought Stanislaus was pretty much of a mouthful. And when they called me Halka, it meant they did not know me very well—did not want to know me.

"In America, if you haven't a nickname, as they call it, it usually means that no one likes you.

"The name I was given came about because of my trousers—the way they are styled, I suppose you would say—a way that is out of fashion here, but I've always worn that style—had new pairs made exactly that way—in memory of the kind neighbors back in Vienna who paid for my first fine suit of clothes when I came to America. And besides—although I haven't been much of a success, I felt that those trousers were a sort of badge of courage—kept up my courage—didn't let me completely forget what I had hoped to become.

"At the Musical Union, around the studios where I had work, the people who know me well, and I hope don't dislike me, all call me Tightpants."

He paused, a little fearful of what he had told her; fearful that she would laugh; that this nickname would destroy the respect she had for him.

The girl smiled, but she did not laugh.

She took her eyes from the kindly, homely face, and let them scan the trim, black-taped coat, the trim, snug-fitting pants of striped broadcloth, ending with the carefully polished shoes. Shoes that he polished each morning himself before leaving home.

The trousers were such as her father had worn—on Sundays—when they went to Mass together.

"My duszka Tightpants," she said.

If Guard O'Rourke had been at his post in the Early Gothic Room up at the Cloisters at that hour, he would again have seen his statue truly smile, as that statue gazed out of her leaded window to a starry sky and the dark, moon-streaked waters of the river Hudson, and the black line of the distant Palisades.

A river excursion boat was returning from a moonlight sail to Bear Mountain. Lit up "like a grand hotel" as Rudyard Kipling so wonderfully said. The deck jazz band was playing, and the notes came clear and poignant over the silent water.

The jazz band was not playing Bach or Schubert or Debussy. It was playing a new popular melody, but the statue's smile seemed to approve. It was playing *Without a Song* by a modern genius of the pianoforte. Vincent Youmans by name.

I'll never know—what makes the rain to fall;
I'll never know—what makes the grass so tall;
I only know—there ain't no love at all
Without a song.

He paused, a little taken aback at what he had told her, and afraid that she would laugh; that [illegible] would [illegible] the [illegible] she had for him.

The [illegible], but she did not laugh.

She took her eyes from the kindly, homely face, and let them scan the [illegible] cheap suit, the [illegible] [illegible] pants of striped broadcloth, ending with the carefully polished shoes. Shoes that he polished each morning himself before leaving home.

The trousers were such as her father had worn on Sundays—when they went to Mass together.

"My dadda Highpants," she said.

If Guard O'Rourke had been at his post in the Early Gothic Room up at the Cloisters at that hour, he would again have seen his statue truly smile, as that statue gazed out of her leaded window to a starry sky and the dark, moon-streaked waters of the river Hudson, and the black line of the distant Palisades.

A river excursion boat was returning from a moonlight sail to Bear Mountain. Lit up "like a grand hotel" as Rudyard Kipling so wonderfully said. The deck jazz band was playing, and the notes came clear and poignant over the silent water.

The jazz band was not playing Bach or Schubert or Debussy. It was playing a new popular melody, but the statue's smile seemed to approve. It was playing *Without a Song* by a modern genius of the pianoforte, Vincent Youmans by name.

I'll never know—what makes the rain to fall;
I'll never know—what makes the grass so tall;
I only know—there ain't no love at all
Without a song.

PART EIGHT

THE LEGEND

1

THEY WERE MARRIED that Sunday. All legal formalities had been completed by Friday, but the pressure of auditions gave accompanist "Mr. Tightpants" no free time the entire week. On Sunday at noon, they went to a side chapel of a little Catholic Church on Second Avenue at Forty-seventh Street. Stanislaus Joseph had made arrangements with the elderly priest who had advised him to read the Twenty-third Psalm.

"Father, I have found the key to all happiness, to all immortality," he said.

Who can say he was not right?

That little church is now torn down. Demolished by all-wise city planners to make way for a grand "plaza" to give a properly impressive entrance to the exalted buildings housing the United Nations. At least, that is what the organization is named. The great diplomats who function there, who roll over the site of that church in their shiny black limousines, do not even know of its existence. May the white-walled tires of their great cars absorb and transmit to the souls of those diplomats only a modicum of the charity, the wisdom, the humbleness, the true happiness which that tiny house of worship had brought to hundreds through its life span!

The best man at the wedding was—you have guessed it—Hans

Beuter—to whose night-empty bed Stanislaus Joseph had hied himself to slumber since he had brought Olga Lasenka to his own bed. The bride was "given away" and attended by a colored gentleman and his wife. The colored gentleman was employed as a clerk at a hotel named L'Esplanade-Plaza on West Forty-sixth Street.

After the short ceremony, the five of them went for a wedding luncheon at the King of the Sea on nearby Third Avenue. It was a friendly place Stanislaus Joseph often frequented, when he felt the need of a not-out-of-the-can meal, and he had already discovered that he and Olga Lasenka—now Olga Halka—in addition to music had another all important passion in common.

They both had an emotional fervency for sea food. In this instance the King of the Sea had an additional merit. Its proprietor was not a secret member of the Ku Klux Klan. He welcomed patrons of all races, so long as they were a credit to their race—the human race—as someone has already said.

And at the King of the Sea you were expected to eat hearty and with abandon. When you were seated at one of the plain pine tables, scrubbed to a shining cleanliness, the waitress carefully tied a great white bib about your neck.

A veritable escutcheon it was, with a glorious oriflamme emblazoned on its front, that same being a huge red lobster. It not only raised you to the nobility, but, unlike most such honors, it had a real usefulness.

Clothing, collars, and neckties—if not ears and fingers—were fully protected. The rich, melted-butter sauces could splash at will!

On this day the tall, colored head-waiter greeted Stanislaus Joseph with his usual friendly smile, and a barely noticeable eyebrow-lifting at the size of his party. Ordinarily, the little man came in alone, and having deposited his Homburg with the queenly hat-check girl, would wait until he could sit at a small table by the Third Avenue windows, through which he could gaze out at the passing sidewalk strollers as he ate a frugally selected meal.

Waitresses were anxious to serve him, because it was known that no matter how small his meal-check, there would be a dollar bill left on the table as a tip. In a place always crowded, the weekly comings of this curiously dressed, lonely man were looked forward to. "It is such pleasure to serve a genuine, honest-to-God cultured gentleman," said one of the female food-servers, and that expressed the unanimous opinion of the employees of the King of the Sea.

On this Sunday, no little table by the window would suffice. And their regular patron would obviously have no need to gaze out of a street window for company. An air of built-in festivity radiated from all five, from the broad smiling face of the colored man, resplendent in a new sports coat and a green necktie (he had had a good week—via the telephone—at Pimlico track) to the very beautiful young girl who clung to the arm of the man they had heard was called "Mr. Tightpants" around Broadway.

The head-waiter himself escorted them to a large table in the center of the long main room, with its bar at the rear, and the walls frescoed with fantastic, slightly rampant fish. The head-waiter himself snapped his fingers for an assistant to take the "gentlemen's" hats, and himself presented the huge four-page menus, which were not only covered with red and black printings of every conceivable inhabitant of ocean and stream (properly steamed, baked, poached, broiled or fried), but had clipped around their edges, a multitude of small cards announcing the "Specials."

Abundance added to abundance!

There was this novelty also for a fairly expensive restaurant. The names of the foods were printed in the English language! Not in French. It is a wonder the King of the Sea had been the complete success that it surely was!

The girl and their three guests looked in some confusion at this multiplicity of alluring (and understandable) names, and Stanislaus Joseph took the matter in his hands.

"With your permission," he said, "I will order for all. I have been here often. Everything is good, but some dishes are better than good."

Then to the waiter he said: "We will start with Amontillado Dry Sherry, and with that bring a Lobster Bisque and I think several orders of Imported Russian Caviar. We might also have some stuffed celery with Roquefort cheese, and some olives—the ripe ones, not the green variety.

"Then—let me see—a Crabmeat Cocktail all around, and then Lobster all around—the large fellows—with the melted-butter sauce you make so well. And bring three side orders of your Deep Sea Scallops—sauté—bring them sizzling in the metal dishes in which you cook them—and in case any of my friends do not like scallops, bring two orders of Poached Halibut Steak with lobster sauce. And with this main course a white Burgundy—you have a Puligny-Montrachet year 1927. Bring that. And a salad—you make an excellent one with lettuce, tomatoes, cucumbers, radishes, chicory, escarole—you know the kind I mean—an egg sauce dressing—and oh yes—hot biscuits—plenty of hot biscuits.

"The dessert we will decide on later—I think it will be Strawberry Shortcake and Lemon Chiffon Pie."

By this time two of his listeners were breathless. The head-waiter, who sensed that this was not just some ordinary meal; the girl, who had taken up her copy of the menu and at least located the prices of two of the items—Russian Caviar $2.25 a portion; Broiled Live Lobster—large—$3.50 *up*. Her training in the "five and dime" enabled her to make some lightning calculations—five times two twenty-five. Five times three-fifty and probably *up*—maybe even four-fifty! Twenty-eight dollars and seventy-five cents for just two of the items! And all the other things—and the wine—

"Duszka! Duszka!" she said, leaning to his ear.

Stanislaus Joseph read her thought. Caring for his purse. Fearful perhaps that he did not have all that money.

"Sh— sh—," he said quietly, and gently touched her lips. "We are only married once—you and I, my darling."

The head-waiter, at the young man's elbow, could not help but overhear.

"May I, sir, may I offer my humble congratulations, and wish you happiness," he said; and to the girl: "We are very fond of your husband at the King of the Sea. We are honored that he should come to us for this occasion. I will tell the people in the kitchen. It will all be the very finest we know how to provide."

And so it was. No chef on Park Avenue could have done better. Or perhaps as well.

For into each basic ingredient, into each sauce, along with the butter and pepper and herbs, went a portion of comradeship, of regard and rejoicing for the new happiness that had come to a fellow man.

The first toast was with the Amontillado, and the liquid seemed to be a burnished gold as they held the slender glasses to the light of the overhead electric fixtures. The white Burgundy was like ambered silver. And after the strawberry shortcake—great layers of egg-filled pastry and huge red, crunchy berries between, the whole mountain high and crested with snow white whipped cream—two waitresses brought a huge magnum of chilled champagne and the glasses to pour it into, and a card bearing the compliments of the manager.

Stanislaus Joseph called the head-waiter. "You are most kind," he said. "I do not know how to thank you. May I do just this? May I buy another magnum? May all your waitresses—the two men at your bar—the good folk in your kitchen whom I do not see—drink a health with us?"

And so that also was. There were ten waitresses in the restaurant. They stood around the room. The dozen kitchen people with their white aprons and white caps came to the door of their service pantry. The two hat-check girls stepped out of their recess. The uniformed doorman was called from the sidewalk outside. And they drank to "Mr. Tightpants Halka" and his bride.

The other guests at other tables, entering into the spirit of the event, stood up and drank their various drinks.

Suddenly, a sound familiar to the ears of Stanislaus Joseph Halka came through the doorway leading out of the kitchens. Happy, full-throated, uninhibited notes that could clear any atmosphere of gloom; that could add extra joy to any atmosphere of happiness.

An accordion! And those in the kitchen doorway made passage for a young Italian dishwasher, a very large accordion strapped to his chest and stomach; above it a face with a smile as wide almost as the spreading bellows, and nimble dark fingers racing up and down the piano-like keyboard along one side of the bellows.

He was playing the *Wedding March* of Felix Mendelssohn-Bartholdy with the greatest gusto that march had ever received. *Forte Fortissimo, Abbandono, Accelerando,* with a full measure of *Appassionato* to show that there was no coy holding back in that restaurant's musical well wishes!

There was tumultuous applause (as the political speech news reporters say), and the dishwasher musician went into a gay Italian *Tarantella*. Then another toast to the young married couple was proposed and drunk all around.

Self-appointed press agent Hans Beuter could not resist the temptation to proclaim the talent of his friend. He mounted a chair and cried, "Let the Herr Bridegroom play just one piece for the glory of Austria! Don't you know he was the best damn accordion player in all Vienna!" And, reluctantly, Stanislaus Joseph had to permit the transfer of the accordion to his own chest and stomach, and he played for them an old Austrian folk ballad.

Hans Beuter—that multi-sided genius—opened still another faucet of accomplishment, and sang it in an enthusiastic (if slightly off key) baritone voice.

Still, thought Stanislaus Joseph, it was all a good omen. His musical career had started with an accordion. His marriage was starting out to the music of an accordion. Maybe accordions brought him good fortune.

How his bakeshop-owner patron would have smiled could he have been there!

So, at last, bridgegroom Mr. Tightpants took up his check. A formidable listing that ran over on to two regular-sized check tabs. He left five dollars on the table for the girl who had served them. Five dollars for the head waiter, and five for the accordion artisan. He proceeded to the counter, where stood the owner-manager by his cash register.

"I have to thank you," he said, "for your generosity about the champagne. It was wonderful."

Again the girl was perturbed. She had not seen the check, but she knew it must be very sizable. Stanislaus Joseph felt secure. He had in his pocket his salary money of the past week. It would surely be enough.

The manager picked up the check as "Mr. Tightpants" produced his roll of bills. The manager seemed to be doing something to the check. Perhaps seeing that the long additions were correct. He impressed a rubber stamp across it. Doubtless his "O. K." of this addition. Then he spoke to the young bridegroom across his cash register.

"I'm sorry, sir, but this check cannot be paid," he said sternly. "It is strictly no good. You did not look at it very carefully, I fear."

Loyal Hans Beuter stepped forward, *his* past week's wages in his hand. If his friend was short of cash money——

"What—what is wrong?" said Stanislaus Joseph. For the first time *he* was a little fearful.

He looked at his checks, which the restaurant owner had handed back to him. Stamped across their face were the words

Do not pay this check.

It was a stamp used on waitresses' duplicates, so that checks would not be counted twice.

"I do not understand," said Stanislaus Joseph.

"I was married once myself," said the now smiling manager. "It was in Russian Poland. In the ghetto. It had to be in a cellar. In secret. My people were being persecuted. Soon after, my Rachel and I fled to America. America received me. Has been kind to me. Let me repay just a little. You owe me nothing, sir. And I wish you and the beautiful lady every happiness. Tomorrow, my lady and I—she is a grandmother now—will go to our synagogue and ask a *borocho* —a very special blessing for your special happiness."

America!

✣ 2 ✣

MR. AND MRS. STANISLAUS JOSEPH HALKA returned to their top floor front on Madison Avenue, but only for a brief fifteen minutes.

"We are now going on our honeymoon," said Tightpants, "and I have a surprise. We are going to France and Spain. If the shoes you are wearing are not comfortable for walking, put on a pair that are. We may do a bit of hiking. We must leave at once, for there are some things to be seen, and we have a special date with a sunset at about eight o'clock."

The girl knew, of course, that he must be joking about a trip to France and Spain. He had been rehearsing her each evening in the Dvořák ballad *Songs My Mother Taught Me,* so that she could try again at the final Florenz Ziegfeld chorus auditions the very next morning. Auditions that started at ten-thirty. But she played up to his remark.

"You must have chartered a rocket plane, such as I've been reading about in the comic weeklys, that travels faster than sound," she laughed. "And the reckless way you are spending your salary! I think I'd better take charge of the family money! My father always said, 'When you are married, Duszka, make your husband save his money. You will someday grow old, like me, and also—there may be children coming——' "

Olga Halka stopped. She threw her arms around Stanislaus Joseph Halka's stiff-collared neck. She held him very close.

After a while she said, "We don't need to go on any honeymoon journey. No place in all the world can be as lovely as this room."

"Just the same we are having a honeymoon," he said to her. "There is a special reason, in addition to the important matter of the sunset. Darling, I hope you will forgive me, but I have kept something from you. Before I met you I had a sweetheart—a girl friend as they say. She was foreign born, like myself, and finding a new home in America. Perhaps that was one cause of my being so drawn to her. It was only here in New York that I met her face to face, though I had heard of her and seen her photograph before."

"You were engaged to her?" asked the girl who had been Olga Lasenka. And she did not know whether to smile or to cry.

She was worldly-wise enough to know that men were seldom single lovers, and also knew she had no right to assume that this man, thrown by his work into the paths of attractive women, had never before been attracted to some one of them. Perhaps by several of them.

Still, somehow, she had thought that she was the first. The only one. Just as he had been the only one in her own life. But he was older than she was by at least five years. Five years of maturity—of susceptibility—

"We could not become engaged," said Stanislaus Joseph, replying to her question. "There was a reason why we could probably never be married. I am taking you now to meet this girl."

The girl who had been Olga Lasenka was also not a woman to glory in a triumph over some other woman. Had her happiness wrecked the hopes of some other girl—a girl perhaps who was ill—or tied in some unfortunate and tragic web?

"Duszka," she said, "do you think this is wise? Did you love her very much?"

"Very, very much," said Stanislaus Joseph, and although the sincere unhappiness in her eyes tempted him to explain, he only added, "and you will love her also. Just wait and see."

Then he changed the subject abruptly. "About your handling the money—that also is wise, and here is our family capital, except what may be still left in the desk drawer——"

"I have kept careful account of all that I have spent of it," she said seriously.

"I shall call in an auditor at the end of each month," he said with a smile, as he handed her the roll of bills he had expected to be much reduced at the King of the Sea—"Take it all, but you must allow me to keep back twenty cents."

"Twenty cents?" she questioned. Her husband was strangely mysterious. Did all husbands suddenly become that way?

"Yes," he said, "for twenty cents will be our transportation cost to where we are going to meet this girl."

"But you said we were going to France and Spain," she said, her spirit reviving at this most satisfactory and economical solution of one mystery! "And you will have to have forty cents!" she added. "You must have the return fare. I don't want to stay forever in France and Spain. We must get back here tonight."

"To France and Spain and back again," he smiled, "to meet your only rival. I think she is French, though I was never quite sure. French or Spanish. And now I think that perhaps her father was Polish—just as yours was. You will see. Ah, she is very beautiful."

"As beautiful as I am?" said Olga, with a little smile.

"As beautiful as you are, my duszka," said Tightpants Halka solemnly. "In fact, you are very much alike in many ways."

"I hope you are not going to regret the choice you have made," said the girl who had been Olga Lasenka. "We folk of Polish blood are sometimes very stubborn and temperamental."

"I am fully reconciled to all that," said Stanislaus Joseph. "I know that I shall lead a dog's life!"

And he held her close in his arms again.

✣ 3 ✣

As RECENTLY as half a dozen years ago, there existed in the City of New York an institution as basic for liberty, democracy, and the pursuit of happiness as the Yankee Stadium, the Metropolitan Opera House, the Bill of Rights, the Automats, and Coney Island.

It had its very roots in our doctrine of equality—"all men born free and equal"—and by means of it all men, regardless of race, creed or color, and no matter how lowly or "common" (not to forget women and small children), could literally be elevated to the heights. It was, at one and the same time, a solace for the sorrowful, a spur for the adventurous, a reward for the laborer and an excuse for not laboring—and as a veritable cradle for the nurture of honorable romance, it was doubtless the main reason for the rapid increase in the population of the great metropolis.

One would believe that such an institution was beyond challenge; that, if necessary, angry protests and mob violence would arise in its defence; but alas, it is no more. And boiling in hot oil would be too slight a punishment for those officials—public or private—who had a hand (and an absolute lack of heart) in its abolition and destruction.

We refer, of course, to the open-upper-deck Fifth Avenue buses.

So, fortunate Mr. and Mrs. Tightpants Halka (the bride having changed to her walking shoes) proceeded across Thirty-fourth Street to Fifth Avenue, and mounted to the open top of a northbound Number Four bus, that being their rocket plane to France and Spain. They had stopped briefly at a florist's shop where Stanislaus Joseph purchased *two* two-dollar roses, extracting a hidden five-dollar bill from a vest pocket in payment therefor.

"Already you are holding out on me," said the girl. "I see I will have to go through all your pockets on salary day."

"Each salary day there will be four dollars held out," smiled Stanislaus Joseph. "A rose for each of my two girl friends." And one of the roses, its long stem clipped, was pinned on the girl. The other he carried in a lengthy, cone-shaped wrapper.

They were going, of course, to that bit of the middle ages of Spain and France that is a part of New York-on-the-Hudson. To the Cloisters at Fort Tyron Park—a place with which we already have a passing acquaintance.

Right here it should be stated (I apologize for not stating it before in this chronicle) that the existence of the assorted and legally (I trust) incorporated Standard Oil Companies of many states are fully justified by the existence of this place.

Mr. John D. Rockefeller, Jr., had made possible this romantic gem.

The roof of this bride and groom's front bus-top seat was the blue sky, (it being a bright September afternoon), which sky view perhaps made partial recompense for the fact that they could not spend the journey (as do more fortunate honeymooners today) studying overhead, roof-bordering signs describing the beauties of certain brassieres, nylons, laxatives and blended whiskies.

Even Fifth Avenue, that thoroughfare of great shops and clubs and apartment dwellings, with presently the park called Central along one side—a street only equalled but not surpassed by the Avenue des Champs-Elysees of Paris—gave the girl a new vista and thrill. In her brief few weeks of job hunting from the Hotel L'Esplanade-Plaza, she had never ventured north of Fifty-ninth Street!

At One Hundred and Tenth Street they turned west—past colorful Harlem, up the hill skirting the great, perpetually unfinished Cathedral of St. John, to the Drive named Riverside because it borders the noble Hudson. The girl had never even seen this river!

No theatrical casting agencies had offices that far west in her Times Square district.

"I thought I knew New York," she said to the little man who was holding her hand very tightly. "I had visited Macy's and Gimbel's. I did not know about this river."

"Wait and really see it from where we are going—where lives the other girl with whom I was in love," said Stanislaus Joseph.

Again this French or Spanish girl! But the excitement of the ride did not permit Olga Halka to continue to worry. Stanislaus Joseph Halka was hers now. For ever and ever.

No River Girl could steal him away from her.

Presently they slowly crossed the long viaduct, after passing the dome-topped tomb of an Ohio farm boy named Ulysses Simpson Grant, and the Gothic, sky-reaching Riverside Church. And there, ahead, was an eighth wonder of the world: a delicate, thread-supported sky pathway, yet more mighty and breathtaking than the Colossus of Rhodes, as it straddled the broad river to the Jersey Palisades. The great river-bridge named for the Father of his country.

At One Hundred and Thirty-fifth Street they turned east again, back to the ancient Dutch cow-path named Broadway, now exhibiting every language and complexion of the globe in the Sunday sidewalk strollers; the loungers on the benches set in its middle strip of grass; the small-shop owners that stood hopefully in doorways. Upper New York's great private melting caldron, from which emerged *Americans.*

West again their bus rocket-ship journeyed to the river and the great Medical Center (Stanislaus Joseph fortunately did not know how he would come to have intelligence of *that* location), and north through streets of fire-escape-fronted apartment homes, till a sudden turn whirled the motored wheels away from tawdry modernity into a lovely, narrow roadway bordered by spreading trees, whose lower branches were only slightly above the heads of the bus-top passengers.

And with another sudden turn into a rampart enclosed courtyard, you were opposite the lower, now open portals of a towering, hewn-stone, middle-ages Monastery that might—and in fact was—for the greater part, brought stone by stone from ancient lands.

The "last stop!" cry of the khaki-shirted, visor-capped bus conductor, his head and shoulders appearing at the top of the vehicle stairway, seemed entirely incongruous. He should have been clad in a vermillion, velveted, great-sleeved doublet, a plumed hat crowning his wig-bordered face; and his cry should have been *"Avante!"*

Stanislaus Joseph and the girl climbed down, and with their several fellow travelers entered the low doorway into the small, six-sided, vaulted lobby. Then up a long, steep and vaulted stone-flanked passage, with short flights of steps alternating numerous landings.

There were crenellated window openings, high up on the stone walls, and the girl noticed that these windows had curved casement tops. Like the windows in Stanislaus Joseph Halka's humble Madison Avenue room. She stopped a moment to look up at them.

"They are like our home," she said.

"I'm glad you noticed that," he replied. But he had known all along that she would notice it. A girl who looked like the La Celle statue could not fail to notice it!

And he remembered how he had made this climb the very first time, carrying before him Kommodore Hugo Frederick von Steinburg's rose, (he must write the Herr Kommodore telling him of this new happiness), little dreaming that so soon he would be making this climb with the Lady of the Statue come to life!

What if—when he and the girl reached the Early Gothic Room—the statue were no longer there! What if this girl *were the statue!*

Or would there occur some sort of metamorphosis by which the late Olga Lasenka, now Olga Halka, would become that statue; would fuse with it, and he would have lost her forever!

❖ 4 ❖

It is perhaps a pure coincidence that at that very moment when Stanislaus Joseph Halka gave thought to his ocean voyage friend, the Herr Kommodore, that gallant gentleman was about to mount his newest, prize-steeplechase thoroughbred for the day's final, gentleman-rider's race, at the famous *Champs de Cources d'Auteuil,* located in the great Woods of Boulogne, near Paris. This race *cource* a part, in fact, of that wide stretching city.

And that the Herr Kommodore should also think of the young musician who had crossed the sea with him, and wonder if the lad were still in America.

The Kommodore had not been on the Bremerhaven-New York run for the past six months—his ship was making an around-the-world cruise. Two weeks of vacation, and he would be off again to New York harbor.

He must try to look up the lad.

His memory had perhaps been jogged by the name he had given this race horse. She had been christened the *Lady of the Statue.* There was no disrespect in giving the animal this title—it was the most beautiful creature in his extensive stable. The most beautiful horse he had ever owned!

But in one respect the name was a misnomer.

The animal was anything but "a statue" except in outward appearance. The Herr Kommodore was the only person who dared ride her in a race.

The trainer was, at that instant, giving a word of caution to his employer, who was now garbed in his jockey uniform—the gold and crimson colors of his riders' silks and cap giving him the appearance of a much younger man than when he wore the uniform of a commander on the bridge of his beloved *Europa.*

But these racing silks were equally dear to the heart of Hugo Frederick von Steinburg.

"Have a care, sir," his trainer was saying, though he knew he was wasting words to caution this daring and expert horseman. "She nearly killed two grooms last week. I took her over the jumps myself yesterday morning, and it was all I could do to control her. A wonder horse, but dangerous—dangerous."

The Herr Kommodore laughed. He touched lovingly the quivering nostrils of the proud head; and the beast, held tightly at arm's length by two grooms with a taut line from each bit-side (and they were also keeping well clear of lightning-striking heels)—this half-wild creature seemed to understand her master. The animal did not bare white, dangerous teeth but whinnied softly, and then lurched at the restraining halters, eager to be off.

And the Herr Kommodore said to his trainer: "It is just you who do not understand 'My Lady.' Like myself, she is born of *La Mer*—the untamed Sea. When landsmen try to steer her, she rebels—as my ship would rebel if one of you undertook to command. My whip—and give me a leg up! And I hope you have placed a sizable wager. We will outdistance this field as my *Europa* would leave behind a fleet of sailing boats."

Hugo Frederick von Steinburg swung into the saddle and whirled out upon the race course.

"Good luck and Heaven protect you!" shouted the trainer.

And he fervently crossed himself.

✣ 5 ✣

WE LEFT Stanislaus Joseph Halka and the girl who had been Olga Lasenka near the end of their lengthy climb up the stairs of the tunnel-like approach to the main floor of the Cloisters, built on the cliff above the roadway.

They now made a sudden turn, and after another short flight of stone steps were inside a larger, roundish, eight-sided vestibule.

It was the main entrance hall on the top floor level of the building, and its vaulted ceiling was several stories high. A large, circular window-opening, high up just below the vaulting, showed the massive thickness of its outer walls. Walls that outside rose far above, to make the square, symbolic monastery tower.

The grey limestone walls of this vestibule were severely plain. Only on one side, head high, was a simple bronze tablet, giving credit to the kindly gentleman of oil millions, whose generosity had made it possible to "give reality to the past," as the bronze letters read.

There was a uniformed guard stationed on each side of this entrance hall. There was an open alcove which formed the office with its counter; the rack of guide books and photographs; and young ladies working at typewriters on the several desks beyond. There were other visitors standing about.

This was (said Stanislaus Joseph to himself) *just a museum*. It was filled with eight-hundred-year-old stone statues. Some of the statues were painted wood. But all of them were cold and most decidedly *dead*.

The girl beside him was warm and breathing. No miracle of transformation was going to happen. Still—there was that incident on the bridge of the liner *Europa* as related by Kommodore Hugo Frederick von Steinburg, a very practical and credible gentleman!

Stanislaus Joseph took a firmer hold on his wife's small hand. He did not push forward so impetuously to the Early Gothic Hall. Maybe he should not have brought this girl to the Cloisters at all!

But they had now walked deep into this "past-reality"—through an arched doorway that had graced the chapel of Knights Templars at Baume. He could not very well turn back, for it was evident that the girl was completely fascinated by her surroundings.

This first gallery was called the Romanesque Hall. The girl from the Five-and-Dime in Wilkes-Barre, from the Hotel L'Esplanade-Plaza on West Forty-sixth Street, paused and stood and gazed in excited wonder. She had read of such things in High School, seen drawings of them; but in her busy, money-earning-of-necessity life, she had never viewed them in reality.

Stanislaus Joseph had never really noticed them. He had always pushed through to the Early Gothic Hall, just as a big-city worker, day after day, goes down familiar streets to an objective, and could not tell about the buildings on left and right.

On that day he also paused for the first time—paused with the girl who was now his beloved wife.

The objects were worth pausing for.

On their left, a great wall fresco from the Spanish monastery of San Pedro de Arlanza, founded in the eleventh century by a conquering Visigothic king. It pictured a huge, fantastic lion, painted and carved on the flat stone nearly a thousand years ago by some unknown sculptor-painter-architect-poet-satirist Michelangelo.

This artist also had a bit of Ham Fisher in his makeup. Perhaps he was the very first cartoonist! The great beast's face is quite humorous in its genial ferocity (there is a mustache curiously prophetic of that embellishing the countenance of a late Russian gentleman, symbol of world comraderie, world peace, world thought control. With a dash of world mayhem and world larceny added, so that mankind will not become over-soft in his complete Utopia).

But the master stroke is a great tail, curving upward and backward to make a huge S ending over the animal's neck and head.

What a pity the so-called human race lost its tails. So decorative and so expressive! Here it is as if a monster dog were wagging a "Greetings, comrade!" But look lower; the stiff, strong legs and powerful, clumpy claws cry out, "Beware!," and below this creature of good will and terror is a wide border of fish—not unlike the fish that disport themselves on the walls of the King of the Sea.

Could it be that they were the "peepul" swimming about blissfully under benevolent authority? Could it be that the expression "poor fish" here originated?

That Visigoth king, I think, and his royal artist had a private sense of pictorial irony for the foibles of mankind.

"Let them guess what we mean," I can hear the warrior monarch say, with a great chuckle in his beard. "Let the generations wonder (or learn) while you and I laugh."

Directly across, on the opposite wall, another Lion, but this one was three-dimensional and realistic, its face not debased to look like man's, and carved in the living stone.

It is trampling a serpent, the symbol (it seemed) of Satan, while behind it spread a crowded background of smaller human figures—Christ forgiving Mary Magdalene; St. Michael destroying the Evil One. There had been no frivolous satire in the makeup of *its* churchman patron, or in its monk-hooded sculptor. It had been carved for the solemn task of guarding the main portal of a cathedral in Spain.

The Lion (so read the modern, small placard beneath it) was "The Lion of the Tribe of Judah."

Farther along, and its back to the left wall of the chamber, set high over another priceless doorway, was a group of four near-life-size statues, representing the Adoration of the Magi. Carved about the year 1188. Amazingly lifelike and human, as if they could, at any moment, step down into the room.

One of the Kings has lifted his garment to bare a deformed foot. Who was he? What sin had caused his deformity? Did his journey to the stable of Bethlehem make his limb miraculously whole?

Was that the *first* of the divine Christ's miracles? So mused the girl, her mind reverting to the Sunday School lessons of her childhood.

And these stone gentlemen, from their high place above their doorway, gazed across to the other wall, where hangs, nailed to a great cross, mankind's eternal (it sometimes seems) answer to divine love. The answer given in Asia; in Europe; in America.

His name was Jesus Christ, the carpenter of Nazareth. In Europe it was a woman who tended geese, named Jeanne D'Arc. And in America, another man named Lincoln—profession, rail-splitter.

The *Cross;* the *Fire;* a *Revolver*. But the *Answer* was one and the same.

Here in the Cloisters, the Christ is just a painted wood torso. The head is in the Paris Louvre.

But no head is needed to convey tragedy, and touching beauty beyond mere words. Only this frail, headless body—painted flesh color, a loin cloth of red and blue-green! And in the side, the gaping spear wound.

The girl felt that she should kneel before it, as in a church. And she *did* kneel, for just a moment, and crossed herself.

"I could not help it," she said. "I have never before seen anything so wonderful."

Stanislaus Joseph was to one day pause again before this torso—a day he would not soon forget.

On each side of this headless image, two wooden figures of red pine: one—the Blessed Mother who bore Him; the other—that Saint named John who baptized Him. Even their drooping garments manage to express agony and sadness beyond the power of human tears.

Who knows what armored Knights and Noblemen and Kings had, sword in hand and great shield at side, knelt before this group in a Knights Templars monastery at ancient Lavaudieu, before setting out to the Crusades? This thought in the mind of Stanislaus Joseph Halka, more versed in history than his companion.

There are those unfortunate ones who can remain unmoved in the presence of the glories of antiquity. Not so this simple girl. Surely the Wilkes-Barre "five-and-dime," the horrors of endless second-string "picture palaces" and second-rate hotels, had not prepared her for an appreciation of the beauty that was of medieval France and Spain.

Perhaps there had been an ancestor in ancient Crakow who had carved in stone, who had painted images of Saints on the stone walls of nunneries, and who now, reincarnating himself through her wide eyes, came with her on this day, and to this room, in the city of New York.

Or maybe there is still a hope for our youth in their own puzzled souls, born into a world of radio and television comics and bubble gum.

The girl could have remained there for hours. But Stanislaus Joseph brought her to the present, and their real reason for the journey.

"We must hurry on," he said. "The Cloisters closes at five. We will come again, I hope, and often, to see all these wonders and many more. I have never really looked at most of them myself. So eager was I to get to the presence of my former sweetheart—the girl I could not marry."

Let come what will, he would bring face to face the girl who was Olga Lasenka, the girl who had dreams of standing on an ocean liner (although she had never been to sea), and the statue so marvelously like her in appearance that had really crossed *La Mer;* the statue that perhaps had lived that dream in a reality!

"This other girl—she works here?" asked Olga Halka, for she had noticed the young women behind the office counter at the entrance gallery.

"She lives here," said Stanislaus Joseph, and gave no further explanation.

✣ 6 ✣

THEY PASSED THROUGH a sculptured archway and were out-of-doors—at least so it seemed to the girl, for she could see the blue sky overhead. And yet they were surely still inside the Cloisters!

They were under one of those narrow, arcaded passageways which bordered each side of the open-to-the-sky squares that were the very heart of all the ancient monasteries—the true "cloister" part of them—the enclosed walks for study and meditation, exercise also.

The babbling world shut out by high walls, but God's sky above. For these walks surrounded an open court, where flowers and grass and even trees could thrive.

Ideas likewise thrived there; ideas and ideals not entirely concerned with how to make the sharpest sword blade and the heaviest captive chains!

In the center was always a fountain.

Stanislaus Joseph became the musician. "It was in such a courtway as this," he said, "that black dots with stems were first written down against straight lines drawn across gray parchment; written by its churchmen composers, or by equally talented performers, so that other musicians could read it, and play it exactly as the composer meant it to be played.

"Perhaps that wasn't as great an invention as motorcar assembly lines, or death dealing airplanes or super-duper washing powders I hear of on the radio, but it has brought its humble benefit to mankind. Just think—if a way of writing down musical notes had never been discovered, you couldn't have brought a song sheet of those notes to the Ziegfeld audition! There wouldn't have been anything before me with your name written on it. And then—you would have come, and sung, and gone; and I would never have seen you again!"

"I think we would have somehow found each other," said the girl with a little laugh, for the boy had spoken with such earnestness. "Maybe the stage manager, who did write down my name, would have remembered I was the girl who sang the worst—the worst of all of them!"

They both laughed. Then she added, "I'm glad that it's with you I have first seen this beautiful place. Do the stars shine down here at night? I'd like to walk here—with you—beneath the stars."

"I am told the stars shine down," smiled Tightpants, "but I'm afraid the authorities—even Mr. Rockefeller—wouldn't let us come here, just so that we could walk beneath them."

"This beauty spot should be open at least one night a week," said the girl, "so that young lovers could come here and be blessed by the stars!"

"I'll speak to Mr. Rockefeller the next time I meet him on the street," smiled Stanislaus Joseph. And then, most seriously, "You have no feeling that you have ever been here before?"

"How could I have been here?" asked the girl. "I had never been in New York before. I most certainly have never been in France where the guide book says these stones were first set into cloisters and monasteries.

"In New York I don't believe I've ever been north of Fiftieth Street until today. When you are desperately hunting a job, you do not search out places like this. But if I had known about it, I believe I would have gone without a meal to see it. Or pretended that was the reason I had gone without that meal," she added with a grim smile.

"I suppose I do not mean 'have you been here in Fort Tyron Park, in New York,' or 'over there somewhere in France,' " said the young man. "I mean, have you been here in your dreams—just as you once told me you dreamed that you stood on the bridge of a great ocean liner?"

The young girl who was now his wife looked at the man curiously. "I dreamed that dream again last night," she said, "but, duszka, why did you remember about that dream? It's surely just a silly young girl's fancy. I was never really on an ocean liner. I have never crossed the sea."

"I wonder?" said Stanislaus Joseph. And in his heart he said, "Perhaps I shall soon know."

With the newly introduced "daylight saving time" in New York, it was then near six P.M. at the *Champs de Cources d'Auteuil* in the outskirts of the city of Paris. Time for the final race of a protracted, eight-race Sunday card; and thirty steeplechase thoroughbreds were galloping to the starting line of the *Grand Prix de Cources d'Auteuil.*

It was a gruelling four miles and eight hundred yards, calling for some thirty-six jumps, many of great hazard. Twice over the course, shaped like an eight, and passing twice before the grandstand.

Hugo Frederick von Steinburg was in tremendous spirits.

He had won a race "on the flat" earlier in the afternoon. The evening before he had received a telegram from Anton Lavar—Anton having (wonder of wonders!) happened to look at the sports page of his *Kronen Zeitung,* and there was a photograph of Kommodore von

Steinburg astride his new steeplechase sensation, the *Lady of the Statue,* and mention of the next day's "gentleman rider's great race."

"Please come to visit us before you go back onto your trans-Atlantic run," the wire ended.

Kommodore Hugo Frederick would do just that—with the gold cup of the *Grand Prix de Cources d'Auteuil* to show them!

"My sweetheart," he said in the ear of the beautiful animal swinging forward beneath him, "we'll show these French and English landlubbers how to sail through a jumping race. Ahead are just a lot of green waves, and over we'll go like a sea wind!"

The great beast seemed to throb at her master's voice and touch. They were a picture—these two—worthy of the fresco around a Greek vase, as they sped with the galloping pack that late afternoon across the green turf to the running start of the *Grand Prix de Cources d'Auteuil.*

✣ 7 ✣

So at this hour, in distant New York City, Stanislaus Joseph Halka and the girl stood before the small oaken door leading off a cloister's border passages into the Early Gothic Room.

The door was closed. For some reason it was always kept closed—possibly because of the great value of the art objects within, so that they would not be exposed to drafts from the open space of the adjoining Cuxa Cloister.

Stanislaus Joseph had knocked on this door his first visit, and he had continued to knock on subsequent trips, to the continued amusement of the outside Cuxa Cloister guard, the man who had that first day advised: "Go right in, buddy. Them statues can't open no doors." There is a species of the *homo sapiens* to whom a stiff collar and a courteous approach to closed doors are a matter for hearty mirth.

I fear his inability to burst in through doors that were closed, would always be a grievous handicap to Dr. Stanislaus Joseph Halka.

Guard O'Rourke, however, within the Gothic Room, understood, and had even mentioned to his wife that "at last a real polite gentleman had come to his bailiwick, by God!" Without doubt this admiration for politeness was due to the hang-over softening influence of those war weeks at the French nunnery. An evil influence for rugged Americanism.

Thank God, most American youth in a Howdy-Doody, Kick-'Em-In-The-Face Age are not so exposed!

So on this Sunday afternoon Dennis O'Rourke opened his door, knowing full well who was there. Unless indeed some other "polite gentleman" had by some mistake arrived at the Cloisters. And the guard had been somewhat concerned about his friend Mr. Halka, whom he had not seen for several weeks. Numerous Ziegfeld office-auditions had taken place on Sundays, and Stanislaus Joseph had been unable to make his weekly pilgrimage to the stone image by the leaded window.

"I'm sure glad to see you again, sir!" exclaimed Dennis. "I've missed you, sir, and I think my baby has missed you also. I hope you have not been ill."

And then Guard O'Rourke realized that Mr. Halka was not alone. He looked hard at the girl. He rubbed his eyes unbelievingly.

"Good God!" he said, and hastily crossed himself. Like Stanislaus Joseph, he shot a glance across the gallery to be certain the La Celle statue stood on its pedestal.

It was still there—calm and serene. It had not vanished because its counterpart in the flesh stood in that doorway.

And the girl who had been Olga Lasenka did not vanish because *her* counterpart stood in profile by its leaded window, and gazed at the river Hudson far below. It did seem to Guard O'Rourke that "his baby" was truly smiling—but he had become used to that small miracle.

"This is my wife, Dennis," said Stanislaus Joseph; and to the girl, "Olga, this is my good friend Dennis O'Rourke, who has been taking very good care of the lady with whom I was deeply in love before I met you."

And he put his finger to his lips meaning that Guard O'Rourke should be silent about the fantastic likeness of two women in that room.

The girl who had been Olga Lasenka did not at first see the La Celle statue.

She noted the three noble windows directly opposite which looked out upon the distant Palisades across the Hudson, tall graceful windows of the thirteenth century, formerly in the wall of a French church near Chatellerault.

And she noticed the square-hewn wooden beams of the ceiling overhead that had come from a hall at Carcassone—beams of wood—that blessed material of *the Cross*—instead of the hard, stone vaulting of the other galleries they had passed through; and the wooden beams seemed to give this particular room a warm, home-like atmosphere.

This room did not seem a Hall in a museum. It was a room where folk *had lived*. Where folk still lived! For the girl's wondering glance now lowered to the painted statues about this chamber, images that had been born and lived for centuries in great cathedrals, in busy Knights Templars preceptories—ageless—for they all radiated youth and indescribable beauty.

Except in the Paris Palace of the Louvre, there was probably no other such collection of colorful Madonnas.

And the girl now understood—if she had not guessed it before—that it was a statue her husband had meant, when he said he had loved another woman whom he could not marry. And there vanished forever a jealous hurt that had still lurked in the back of her mind.

"Oh, duszka," she said, with a little laugh of entire happiness and relief, "they are all so completely lovely! I will gladly share you with all of them. So long as I am the favorite of my husband's harem. But I don't know how I have managed to win out over *that* lady—" and she was looking at the Virgin from the Strasbourg Cathedral, "—or that other one opposite," and she turned her gaze to the Madonna from the Ile-de-France, which was considered the finest perhaps in the world.

Stanislaus Joseph took his wife's hand. "Dennis," he said, addressing the guard, "we will now take my wife to meet the *real one*—'your baby' as you call her—my first infatuation until I met another girl only a short week ago. It was only today that that girl and I were married, and this is our honeymoon."

"Had I known, I would have had *my* wife here today," said Dennis O'Rourke. And the three of them moved—not to the left or to the right—not to either of the two famous figures that dominated the chamber, but to a smaller image by a central window.

They stood before the Madonna from the Knights Templars monastery at La Celle.

At first the girl said nothing. But it was obvious that *she knew.* How could she help but realize the resemblance, unless she had never looked into a mirror, or into a shop window "as she passed by," to quote the song from a favorite musical play. She had done both of course. What young girl has not?

The wide forehead, the slightly elongated, almond-shaped but large eyes, the perfect mouth and rounded chin, the cheeks of Slavic oval. There was a gilded crown on the head of the statue, but it did not hide the carved and painted hair, hair parted tightly in the middle, drawn down to hide the ears, and the thick braids across the head, one of them slanting down across the hidden left ear.

But what the girl said was unexpected. She said: "It is my mother—my sainted mother as I always think of her."

Stanislaus Joseph said: "You say that for two reasons, my dearest. First, because the statue is very beautiful. Second, because you are extremely modest. The statue is *you*—it could only be you."

"But I showed you the picture of my mother in my locket—here—look at it again," and the girl unfastened the ornament she habitually wore and handed it to Stanislaus Joseph.

Looking at it more closely than he had in the taxicab, the face within the locket *was* the same, but not quite the same as that of his wife, and the statue.

The face in the locket was almost entirely Latin in contour, while Olga Lasenka's face was Slavic in the turn of the cheeks and in the touch of sadness—when in repose—of the eyes and the mouth. It was the parting of the hair and the thick braid across the top that slanted down over the left ear that caused the most characteristic resemblance.

"Tell me," said Stanislaus Joseph, "where did you learn to do your hair in the striking way it is arranged? I never noticed hair arranged in just that manner before."

"It was as my mother always did her hair," said the girl. "She said *her* mother before her had so dressed her hair—it seemed to be a sort of family tradition, going way back. The girls at the five-and-dime used to joke about my long hair, when it was the fashion to have hair bobbed, and worn in bangs in front. But I never changed it."

"I am glad you always kept it as it is," said the young man, "for as you can see, that is how the young girl of La Celle who posed for this statue must have worn it."

"The young girl of La Celle—of La Celle in France!" exclaimed the girl who was now Olga Halka. "The very town where my mother was born!"

"That very town, I am sure," said Stanislaus Joseph.

"You knew this girl who posed for this statue?" asked Olga Halka.

"I'm afraid I did not know her at exactly that period," said Stanislaus Joseph with a smile. "She was born about the year 1100, and that was just a little before my time. But I know *about* this girl."

Guard O'Rourke sensed that it was best these two be left to each other. But as he left for his station at the room's far end he said: "I forgot to congratulate you both. I do so now. May you both be very happy. I know that My Lady is happy for you—she smiled—she truly smiled, Mr. Halka—as you first came in. Please come back often to see her and me."

As she continued to gaze at the statue—her exact counterpart in stone—the girl from the Wilkes-Barre five-and-dime and the cheap motion picture houses became just a little frightened. Frightened, but with a strange lift in her inner soul. And this guard had said—not jokingly—but in a meaningful earnestness—*the statue had smiled when she and Stanislaus Joseph had come in.*

"What did the guard mean—his statue truly smiled?" she said to her husband, whose arm she now held very tightly. "Was the guard joking—that the statue smiled?"

"Dennis O'Rourke believes that 'his baby' really smiles when she is happy," said the young man. "And there is still another manifestation when she is sad. I will tell you of that later. But I have something else to tell you now. Something even more strange. It is the reason I believe that statue is somehow a part of you. That you perhaps—in some way—are a part of the girl who posed for it over eight hundred years ago!

"You spoke of a dream—that though you had never been at sea, you dreamed you were standing high on the front of a ship, gazing out at the wide ocean."

"Yes," said the girl, "but what has this statue to do with that?"

"I came to America on the same ship, and with the same commander, that had transported this statue from the Paris Louvre to New York. That commander had a photograph of this statue in his cabin. And when I admired it, and was somehow drawn to it, he had a most strange adventure to relate to me.

"He thought that he had *talked with the Lady who is that statue* one night, on the great high bridge of his ship, although the stone image that is that statue was fastened tightly in a coffin, deep in the strong-room of his vessel."

And Stanislaus Joseph related in detail what Kommodore Hugo Frederick von Steinburg had told him about that strange occurrence.

At the end he noticed that the girl was trembling. "I think I will have to sit down for a while," she said. "There is something that I did not tell you. I did not tell you, duszka, because in this dream I was not always alone. Sometimes I was standing beside a man.

"It was not you, duszka, it was a very tall man. He wore some kind of uniform. And I was saying to him, *There is a golden cross in the great Record Scroll opposite your name—a golden cross—not an iron one.*

"It seemed so meaningless that I should say words like that! What would I know of golden crosses—iron crosses—and now, with what you have just told me—Duszka, I am afraid.

"Take me out into the sunshine. I am terribly afraid."

8

IT IS SAID THAT the racing of horses was first introduced in the Olympic Games of the ancient Greeks. The first scene of *The Clouds* by dramatist Aristophanes indicated the extent of the Greek passion for the sport.

But it is my opinion that primitive man, long before the dawn of any history, and just as soon as he had tamed the breed called woman, next turned his attention to the *equus caballus* and was speeding atop a horse from point to point in competition with his fellow *genus homo*.

Wagers? I'll wager that these also came speedily into being—quite possibly some woman being the payment of these early gambles. And professional bookmakers doubtless arrived very quickly on the prehistoric scene.

But it remained for Christian civilization to invent the most terrifying horse-race in the books. A race called *steeplechase*.

This very name, indeed, had a Christian beginning, when owners of hunters in England, in Ireland (blessed land of fine horse flesh, and would that they would send more of it across the sea in lieu of politicians, bus drivers, and labor leaders), these owners raced to the goal of some prominent landmark, such as a neighboring church steeple. There is an early record of such a match race of four and one-half miles "from the Church of Buttevault to the spire of St. Leger Church."

So let churchmen cease their clatter about horse-racing, just as some of them should refrain from damning the theater, an institution which also had its founding in temples dedicated to Almighty God.

Which brings us again to the *Grand Prix de Cources d'Auteuil,* a steeplechase, late this Sunday afternoon. It was at the tenth barrier —a hedge five feet high, on the approach side of which gardeners had turned every shoot "inside." This horticultural trickery (and triumph) made it a stone wall, if an animal attempted to burst through; or a steel spring that snaps at legs which do not clear it cleanly, and throws the animal precariously balanced above those legs, into complete confusion.

There was also a six-foot ditch to clear on the far side of this hedge.

It was the second time around the frantic course, laid out in the shape of a figure eight. And it was here that the Herr Kommodore planned to give free rein to the untiring animal beneath him, and leave the field—what still remained of it—trailing behind "like a fleet of sailing boats."

And he and the Lady of the Statue would have so managed, but six animals with their riders, and one minus a rider, took the jump at one and the same moment. The riderless horse, his hoofs touched by the spring-like top of the fearsome hedge, crashed the Lady of the Statue in midair. Even then, Hugo Frederick von Steinburg would have righted her, and held her to the *cource,* but the horse on the other side was in the process of turning a complete somersault, with five others partly in the path.

Well—you probably have seen blood-curdling scenes of it in the news reels, picturing the running of almost any British *Grand National,* the most famous of this type of race. Here at Auteuil a cluster of half a dozen trailing contestants pitched madly over into the first melee.

It made for an exciting but not a pretty sight.

A clanging ambulance rushed Kommodore Hugo Frederick von Steinburg (and two other "gentlemen riders") to the nearest hospital. The Herr Kommodore's only concern (although horribly injured himself) seemed to be for his horse named the Lady of the Statue.

They did not tell him the animal had had to be destroyed.

9

STANISLAUS JOSEPH and the girl who had been Olga Lasenka sat on the low stone balustrade, which was the outer part of the sheltered cloister walks, and gazed through the open arcades into the central garden. The tiny, central garden of the Cuxa Cloister from which one reached, by a closed door, the Early Gothic Hall.

An apple tree—with its ripened treasure, *malus pumila,* now most universal of all God's fruits through nature—flourished near one of its borders. Blessed fruit that came from the old world, to help beautify and feed the new. Homely, simple antidote that can counteract all hatreds, all fears.

No garden with an apple tree can countenance that lowest form of malevolence—intolerance.

The girl was calm by now, and wished to know all that Stanislaus Joseph had discovered about the La Celle statue within the Early Gothic Room.

"The people here at the Cloisters knew very little," he told her. "It was bought from the collection of the Paris Louvre. The French Republic has been kind enough to permit some of these matchless wonders to come to America. Even the Louvre simply knew that this image had been in a bell tower in a church, at your mother's village of La Celle, and before that, in a Knights Templars preceptory now in ruins. Fortunately the statue had been removed to a church, when the preceptory was finally and almost completely destroyed during the French Revolution. The very stones were used for paving streets! Such can be man's fury. That was all that was known.

"Through the French voice teacher, for whom I played the pianoforte, I had met an elderly Paris gentleman here in New York, who dealt in rare books and manuscripts.

"I told him about this statue. I brought him here one Sunday. He became interested. He sent a photograph of the statue back to a friend in Paris at the great Bibliotheque Nationale. He also had a friend at the Cluny Museum.

"Between them (these two experts about such things) they made a magnificent discovery. It has not yet been given to the public. They want first to present it at an important meeting of world antiquarians at the end of the month.

"What these two men had discovered was a manuscript. A parchment that had been buried in the tomb of one of the great Knight Abbots of that ruined Knights Templars Preceptory. The stone tomb had been rescued from the Preceptory, and eventually taken to the Cluny Museum.

"This manuscript—reposing in the vaults of the Louvre—had been sewn in the linen cloth that covered the bones of the dead soldier-Abbot.

"You may have noticed that the extended right hand of the statue in that room is missing. Hands—feet—sometimes even heads of these medieval carvings are often gone. Broken off somewhere through the years. Usually that right hand of statues representing the Queen of Heaven held a small scepter. Or maybe a Sacred Heart or a rose. Or it would be raised in a gesture of blessing.

"It was always a symbol of peace, of gentleness, of forgiveness.

"The right hand of this Queen of Heaven statue held a sword! A mighty, two-handed sword. The only statue of the Virgin, so far as is known, that held a sword.

"The statue (so said this parchment) was called the *Madonna of the Sword.*

"I must show you one other matter that has to do with this effigy, before I read to you the contents of that ancient manuscript. I have brought a translation of that parchment with me today. To read it to you here. But what now I wish you to notice is just where we are sitting.

"Look behind you at the small stone columns that support the arches of this arcade. The gray body of the stone is mottled with a pale red. All of the columns in this particular cloister are like that. It is a special kind of stone from a special quarry in a great mountain in southern France. It is said there is no other stone in all the world quite like it.

"This stone changes in color. This pale red sometimes becomes a bright red. It is explained by changes in the moisture content of the atmosphere. On a rainy day, the red in these columns becomes quite crimson. Almost like blood.

"The La Celle statue was carved from this same stone. No other statue has been found made from this quarry. So that our statue would also be expected to undergo these atmospheric color changes. And so it apparently does; but because of the several coats of paint applied to the carved garments—the tinting of the hair and face and the remaining hand which holds the Christ Child—and even the feet—such changes would not show through.

"The left breast of the image is not so painted. It is the raw stone. So that these color changes are visible on that breast, the same as on these columns.

"But there is a legend—and the reason therefor is explained in the parchment—that the statue's breast becomes quite red at times other than when there is dampness in the air about it. That it becomes red because of sorrow—red if something happens that would cause the Lady grief.

"Guard O'Rourke tells me it has happened here. Happened on a bright, dry day, such as we are having now. Happened when the red of the columns in this cloister *did not change color*.

"It happened—," the lad hesitated, then decided to speak of it. "It happened not long ago, on a day when disaster had descended upon my humble head, and I felt there was no use trying to go on. It frightened me a little—just as your ocean dream has frightened you. But I thought afterwards it must have been just a coincidence.

"Somewhere else in the world there must have been an event of more concern to this Lady than any of my silly troubles. Or the whole incident was just this guard's imaginings.

"And now—I will read you the parchment—my copy of what was written about the Madonna of the Sword by the Knight Templar Abbot who had caused the image to be carved, and which writing was buried with him in his tomb."

Stanislaus Joseph took from his pocket a typed sheet. "You must imagine," he said, "that this is a voice from out the past—perhaps you had better just read it yourself."

"You read it, please," said the girl. "I wish to hear it first with your voice."

But the girl did not hear the reading of the contents of the parchment at that time.

A voice very much out of the present came to them as the oak door leading into the Early Gothic Room swung open, and Guard Dennis O'Rourke appeared. Dennis was very excited.

"Come quickly, if you will, Mr. Halka," he said. "It is happening again, and you will see for yourself that I am not just imagining it! The breast of My Lady is becoming very red. It started to turn crimson a little while ago—right after you stepped outside. I did not know if you were still here. . . . No—the pillars are not red, as you can see. There is no atmospheric moisture as they say out in the Cloisters office. But My Lady's breast——"

It was night in western Europe, and through that night a giant Mercedes-Benz motor car was plunging over the Berlin-Paris road at seventy miles an hour. It was fortunate that this was at night, when the great through highway was comparatively free of other cars.

At the wheel was the Berlin chauffeur of Kommodore Hugo Frederick von Steinburg, this chauffeur being an ex-racing driver who had been in three Paris-Madrid races and had won two of them. But never had he driven so rapidly or so recklessly.

In the body of the car sat a single passenger, an elderly, gray-haired professor of music at the University of Vienna. Name—Anton Lavar. Professor Lavar had been located in Berlin where he was unexpectedly attending a convention of music teachers—located by the frantic butler of the von Steinburg apartment, who in turn had been telephoned to by the manager of the von Steinburg estates in Bavaria.

"Kommodore Hugo Frederick von Steinburg was near death in a Paris hospital. He was asking for Anton Lavar."

The Paris night train had already departed. This race-driver chauffeur would get Professor Lavar to the French capital before the next express would leave.

The gentle man in the rear seat of the car spoke into the communication tube.

"Can't you go faster—faster!" he said.

The grim-faced race-car driver upped his speedometer to eighty-five miles an hour.

10

FOR A SHORT WHILE LONGER, Stanislaus Joseph and the girl had remained in the Early Gothic Room. And then it became five o'clock, and visitors must leave at this hour. The breast of the stone counterpart of the girl, the breast of the image that gazed out upon the Hudson, was still red. They just stood before it and talked of the matter in low, hushed tones.

Why it was crimson they did not know, although we who read this history can perhaps conjecture as to its reason.

Conjecture if this special statue-legend were really true. For Guard O'Rourke had gone several times to look at the outside pillars in the Cuxa Cloister, and they had not changed in color. Why should they when the day was dry and clear?

"Perhaps it is going to rain tomorrow," said Guard O'Rourke. "Perhaps this stone from which 'my baby' is carved is more sensitive than the stone outside. At any rate, I do not think she is sad because of us. My children are in very excellent health, and my wife won a jackpot last week in a radio contest. It was a wrist watch and a cigarette lighter, and she is most pleased and happy, though she would have preferred to win the washing-machine."

Thus simple, kindly Guard O'Rourke, his mind centered on "his own"—as indeed it should be.

And he did not forget a word of cheer for the bride and groom. "I don't think it has anything to do with your happiness either," he added. "I am certain that My Lady truly smiled when you two came into the gallery. And I believe it is good luck that your missus is so like the statue. One of our guards has a cat that looks exactly like the cat pictured in one of the big tapestries. He brought it here one day in a container, just to be sure; and the very next week—which was last week—that cat had four kittens, and all doing well!"

So, on these words of cheer, Stanislaus Joseph and the girl who had been Olga Lasenka departed from the Cloisters building. But they were very silent as they walked upward around the cliff on which this building stood, to come to that portion of the hilltop which overlooked the great river.

There is a spot closed in by trees, and there are benches where one can sit and watch the sun go down behind the dark-green Palisades.

These two sat on one of these benches. The girl was the first to speak.

"I am not afraid any more, duszka," she said. "I will never be really afraid again, as long as I am with you. Your friend, that nice Cloisters guard, is doubtless right that the reddening of the statue's breast has nothing to do with us, but I do hope that his story of the cat who discovered her counterpart in the tapestry and immediately had four kittens does not mean that you and I—I love children, duszka; but quadruplets!—I hope we both have jobs before anything like that should happen!"

They were alone in this tree-enclosed space, and she held him very close for a little while.

Then the girl said: "Now I wish to hear the rest about the statue—the parchment you said was found, that told of the girl who was its model. Please read it to me now, duszka. Here in this lovely spot, with the great ball of the sun watching us from over there in the west sky.

"I love the sun. It always gives me courage. And one seems to see it so little in a great city."

Stanislaus Joseph said: "My darling, perhaps you have not known where to look for the sun in New York. It is at this time of day that it is most wonderful. At the time of sunsets I mean. And that is why I brought you here—though it is just as wonderful from a place in Times Square."

"But one would never see a sunset there!" exclaimed the girl.

"Ah, but you are wrong," said Stanislaus Joseph, "though I can understand. I never noticed the sunsets back in Vienna. But in New York, Nature has provided a special effective setting. A special frame, as it were, for sunsets.

"Those high ridges called the Palisades that we are now looking at. They form a hard, dark line—it's like the heavy, double bars at the end of a musical composition—and that great actor, the sun, can here make a dramatic, blazing exit.

"Just look to the west, down any New York crosstown street at this hour, if you are at the center of Manhattan Island. On Broadway, for example. There the sunset has a complete frame, and its shimmering ball of fire is often as wide as the whole distant street end! The clouds above it are all rose and vermillion through the city's horizon haze. Even the windows of the buildings along the distant street-end play their part—they reflect this magic like a corridor set with ten thousand flashing diamonds."

"And to think that I have never noticed it!" said the girl. And then: "I'm afraid by sunset time I was thinking about which Automat to go to, and just what six nickels would buy, and whether there would be another rent-demanding bill in my letter box when I got back to the hotel."

"From now on I'll worry about the nickels and the rent bills," laughed Stanislaus Joseph, "and you can stand in the middle of the street and look at sunsets. If what we now will soon see were on the stage in Mr. Ziegfeld's theater, folk would stand in line to pay seven dollars—or at least six-sixty—to view it. Because it is free, every Autumn evening, most of the seven million living and working here will never notice it.

"I even liked an elevated railroad on the avenue named Ninth, before they tore it down. It was like a black music bar across the red face of a huge flaming descending whole-note! One thunderous note to end the symphony of Day.

"And now, before it really happens—before that great note reaches the border of those Palisades—I'll read to you what was on the parchment found in the stone tomb of Hugh de St. Omer, Abbot of the Knights Templars monastery at La Celle, which monastery had been founded by his predecessor, the great Duke Godfrey of Bouillon, who led the First Crusade to the Holy Land and brought back a fragment of the True Manger to place in the altar of that monastery's chapel.

"I think it is fitting, duszka, that you hear this in a sunset. For it was in a sunset that Sir Hugh, on his death bed, dictated the document to a clerical monk, who afterwards transcribed it."

Stanislaus Joseph again took from his pocket the printed sheets which had been sent from Paris, and read aloud to the girl—the girl who, as far as outward appearance went, might have been the girl of the ancient document.

That strange, true story of the *Madonna of the Sword.*

11

THIS IS what the young man read to the girl who had been Olga Lasenka.

"In this year of our Blessed Lord, the year 1167 counting from the Death on the Cross, I, Hugh de St. Omer, Knight Abbot of the Preceptory of St. Michael the Archangel located at La Celle-sur-Loing in the Kingdom of France, which Preceptory was founded by the Sainted Godfrey of Bouillon when he returned from the First Crusade, the capture of Jerusalem, and the freeing of the Sepulcher of Christ from the foul hands of infidels (may their souls ever burn in the lowest Hell); I, Hugh, surnamed Hugh of the Bloody Hand, having passed the allotted age of four score and ten winters and being confined to my bed and sorely ill; and as I can plainly see Master Death grinning and beckoning before me, do desire to have set down in fair writing by the clean hand of our Chaplain Monk here seated at my bedside, the true and awful facts leading to my surname, and to the creation of the Statue of Our Lady that I long ago had carved and painted and placed in the Chapel of our Preceptory. The Statue named the Madonna of the Sword.

"For I do believe with all my heart, and do know, that Almighty God, (before whose Judgment Bar I soon shall naked stand), while He punishes mortal sin, will also forgive that sinner, if true repentance hath been made.

"It is well known that though (for cause I shall here divulge) I am known as Hugh of the Bloody Hand, having indeed but one hand—my left—with which to wield a sword, I took full part in the Second of the Crusades. It is known that I have slain in battle combat at least two hundred infidels to Christ's glory, and that—since the most grievous event I shall herewith set forth—I have kept all vows of chastity, obedience and poverty, and that I have ruled this Monastery in strict accordance with the sacred code of our Order. And I have faith that all this will be taken into account when I am judged.

"But to proceed to the crime I must confess, before you who may this read, weary of an old Knight's wordy memories. For dastardly as this crime had been, I believe it has brought something of goodness into the world, including the salvation of my own then wicked soul; and that with and by the aid of blessed St. Michael, Archangel, the Patron Saint of this Preceptory, I will leave to the world a new conception of Our Lord and His Blessed Mother, and most of all, that I have perpetuated in indestructible stone the memory of a humble girl whose mortal body and immortal soul should now dwell among the Saints; who during her too brief years on this earth, by skillful nursing did save many lives of wounded Knights (including indeed my own) else would I have died a death of utter infamy one certain day.

"For I do know for a surety that her carved image, placed in our Chapel to represent the Queen of Heaven, which image bore an insignia never before held by the Virgin (said insignia being placed there at the direction of St. Michael himself, as I shall relate); this Image hath sent and is sending many hundreds of tall fighting men to the Holy Land, imbibed and inspired with a flashing courage and an eternal faith.

"Being a younger son of a noble house, I very early decided on becoming a Knight of the Temple, feeling that here would be my future advancement with an active and adventurous living. And so I fought against the Spanish Moors and on the First Crusade, and with such prestige and success in arms that on my return (although I was but thirty years of age) I was made Knight Abbot of this Preceptory.

"I here confess—though that seems hardly a necessity—that I had taken my early vows very lightly as regards my mode of life. I paid small or no heed to words regarding chastity and humility. Only in the matter of Arms did I uphold the honor of the Order. I say with shame that I was especially given to vile and open lechery, never being able or even attempting to resist the lure of woman; but except for the damnation which it brought to my own unclean soul, I do not believe I occasioned much added sin therewith into the world, since the ladies of my acquaintance, both those of noble and of humble origin, were (God forgive them as I do hope he shall forgive me), of loose character, and more tempting than to be tempted.

"And then, one fatal day, I did lay lascivious eyes on the daughter of the tanner in the village of La Celle, and Satan himself must have entered my black heart to create therein a lust for this tall, clean girl.

"The loveliness of her was like to that of a forest rose. It was a beauty quite apart and different from that of other village girls that I had known. For her father was a skilled artisan that had migrated from the East—from the ancient Kingdom of Poland which was ruled by a lusty fighter Boleslaus III, a Christian prince who did much to convert his land to the Kingdom of Jesus Christ. They were a proud people, and their women were especially beautiful—a beauty different and more subtle than that of the women of France. That was one reason, I believe, why I was so inordinately attracted.

"But this pure girl would have naught of my advances, repulsing them gently but firmly. Caring for her widowed father's home at night, she was already serving during the day as a nurse in the adjacent Nunnery Hospice, and I think had planned to become a member of their Order. I would see her going back and forth along the road, and my hot blood leaped at the stark beauty of her.

"Came the night of a great banquet in the Great Hall of our Preceptory, and I became flushed with wine. I could only think of this girl's face and figure; and an evil, all vile plan entered my befuddled mind.

"The maid was most devoted to her father—her mother being lately dead—and the long banquet over, I ordered two of my roughest personal serving men to proceed to the tanner's abode, seize the poor man and bring him before me. In my chambers I told him I must possess the girl, and ordered him to return with my men and fetch her forthwith to me.

"But this Polander, although a peasant and a commoner, was of a proud mind and soul, neither was he lacking in the courage of his race; and he defied me, cursed me for a Judas Iscariot to my Order and my Vows; and in a great fury at this rebuff, the greater fury because I knew it to be the truth, I did strike the man, and struck him again and again, so violently in my insane rage that he suddenly dropped dead before me.

"This should have been the end, but it was not; for my passion only urged me on to greater crime. Crime and most evil cunning. For I had the body removed and hidden, and sent the serving men back to themselves bring the maid. And when she was brought to me, I told her that I held her father in our prison dungeon, and would forthwith see that he was executed as an alien heretic, unless she would that night submit to my embraces.

"This pure girl loved her father, and when she saw that my insane will was adamant, and knew that I had the power to carry it out, she wept a little, then said that to save her father (although he was no heretic but a true believer in Christ Jesus) she would agree; but first—I must go with her to the Chapel and swear on God's altar that having made her sacrifice, I would not be false to my given word, but return her parent in safety to their home.

"It mattered not to me at that moment of lust and passion that my oath would be a false one. I proceeded with her to the adjoining Chapel where the altar lamps were always kept burning, and with her stood before the altar, which altar not only contained the blessed Sacrament, but a fragment of the True Manger brought back from Jerusalem by the sainted Godfrey.

"And here I should explain that high above that altar, just beneath the vaulted roof, and held by two short chains of solid gold, was hanging the great two-handed sword of Godfrey—the sword used by him throughout the First Crusade—the sword that had aided in the recapture of Jerusalem and Christ's Tomb. This mighty sword which had been blessed by Pope Urban II himself.

"So I stretched out my right hand and placed it on the altar, and did commence to repeat the words: *'I swear by my knighthood and by all that I hold sacred to keep the pledge given to this maid—'*

"I got no further in that most false and unholy blasphemy. For overhead there was suddenly a flash of blinding lightning, and then a sound of the breaking of chains, and the great sword of Godfrey of Bouillon crashed down upon the altar he had built, which altar contained a fragment of the True Manger (as I have heretofore stated)—crashed across my extended wrist and severed my right hand from that wrist so that the hand fell to the Chapel floor. And a furious spurt of red blood rushed out from my gaping wrist, so that it spattered all the breast of this maid, and turned the altar top into a pool of crimson.

"This much only I saw before my reeling senses left me. Left me from agony and sheer terror.

"I was stretched in my bed when next I recovered my full faculties—a surgeon monk who was a member of our Order working at my wrist with a basin of heated water and sundry bandages and blood-stopping drugs, and this brave girl assisting him. It seems that when this act of Heaven's justice had occurred—for surely it was that—she had not fled or lost her lucidity. With the knowledge gained in her nursing at the Nunnery, she had bound up the open blood-veins, tearing strips from her linen bodice, and then she had calmly gone for help. Else would I have bled to my death, for it was late at night, and all other members of the Order were in their beds, except some still drunken revellers lying prone and cursing beneath the tables of the banquet hall.

"Through God's infinite mercy and the nursing of this girl, I in due time regained my full health and strength. She stayed by me night and day, even when I had to tell her that her father was no more. Need I say that from that hour on, my life was different. This girl went to live with the Sisters of the Nunnery, and would doubtless have taken full holy vows, but that she was struck down by a heathen fever which she contracted nursing those returning wounded and sick from the Holy Land. But she did not depart this earth before I could do (praise be to God and St. Michael) at least one deed of retribution.

"There was no image of the Queen of Heaven in our Preceptory. I sent to Italy for a great sculptor whose patron had been a fellow comrade Knight in the Second Crusade. And this sculptor carved an image of the Holy Virgin, using this sainted girl as his model for that image. His was a perfect skill, for he made it in an exact likeness, even to the curious manner in which the maid arranged her long hair—wearing it with two thick braids drawn across the top of her lovely head.

"The image was then painted to cause it to be lifelike—painted by the greatest artist in all France. And it stands to this day in our Chapel—and so I pray will always stand—a shrine to the bravest maid, I think, who ever walked this earth.

"There is one thing more. As the statue was being carved, I swear that on several occasions when I was at prayer I heard the clear voice of St. Michael say: 'Hugh, place in the right hand of your Virgin a great, two-handed sword. For it shall serve two purposes—it will be a reminder to you of your great sin and the necessity of living a life of service and penance for that sin. But also it shall proclaim to the world that the Queen of Heaven is a fighting Saint—as her Son, Christ Jesus, is a fighting man. Not a weakling, as some would preach. Never cease to fight strongly for the Faith—and you shall be rewarded in the Kingdom of God.'

"So, in this record, do I bear witness to God's great mercy, for indeed my spurs should have been hacked from my heels, my sword belt cut, and my sword broken in twain on that day when I had so grievously sinned.

"But I have been permitted to live, and even to go on fighting for Christ's cause—since I taught myself to wield my sword with one hand—and that one the left—and many infidels could bear witness to the double measure of strength given to me therefor.

"That my statue was granted a divine grace was early apparent. For the breast thereof, which was not painted, would sometimes become bright red. The red of my sin—of my blood as it had spattered the pure breast of that pure maid. Therefore—red if there were sorrow in the world—if there were cause for grief.

"This, then, is my statement. Given this day of our Lord in the year 1167. Would that I could depart on the new Crusades soon to commence, but that task must be left to younger men. I can only watch the sunsets across the river Loing, and pray God to receive me, a sinner, who hath tried by living in faith to redeem my early life of guilt. And I do think that pure maid will speak for me on the Day.

"And I do desire and decree that two true and faithful copies of this document be made—one to be placed in the archives of the Preceptory, and one to be buried in my coffin, which coffin, although unworthy, will rest beneath the Chapel with those of all Abbots of this Preceptory dedicated to the glory of St. Michael the Archangel."

✣ 12 ✣

STANISLAUS JOSEPH PAUSED.

"That ends the parchment's writing," he said. "There were some signatures—that of Hugh de St. Omer and two witnesses. And the seal of the Order."

Then both he and the girl were silent. One would have said that they were watching the miracle of the Palisades and the setting

Sun God; watching it until the great fire ball had disappeared, and the cloud ships above slowly turned from crimson to pearl gray.

But I do not think they saw much of that particular sunset.

Their eyes and thoughts were fixed on a monastery in a French village—a monastery that was no more—its statues, its tombs even, scattered or destroyed—but still living in the ancient parchment whose content the young man had just read aloud.

And living most vividly in a statue gazing from a leaded window of a building just a short distance away.

Was it living, still more vividly, in the young girl with the slightly elongated eyes and the dark hair with its crowning braid that hid her left ear—the girl that sat upon that nearby Fort Tyron park bench in the glow of a New York sunset?

Presently the young man spoke.

"Hugh de St. Omer died the very next day at the age of ninety-one. That death record, also, these Paris searchers discovered in a sort of day-book of the Preceptory, now in the Louvre. The tomb of this Knight who fought in two Crusades, and lived to almost see a third, is in the Cluny Museum, a life-size stone effigy of him as a fighting man in full armor (as was the custom) lying atop the coffin-like sepulcher. His hands are crossed above a great naked stone-sword, and the right hand is severed at the wrist. I believe he found forgiveness up there among the eternal stars. Perhaps he has been a captain in the army of his beloved Saint Michael these many centuries."

"I *know* that he found forgiveness," said the girl, and then, realizing what she had said, "Oh duszka, I do not know why I should know, but I seem to know."

"The maid of La Celle was also a Polish girl," said Stanislaus Joseph. "Her blood is in your veins."

"I have much to live up to," said the girl who had been Olga Lasenka. "My duszka, I will try so hard to make you happy."

And then she voiced the thought that still disturbed them both: "I do not think the breast of the statue became red this afternoon because of either you or me. Unless it was just because you were to read to me the parchment writing, and it was so that we would both understand.

"Understand and believe."

For she could not then know that in a white-walled private room of a Paris hospital, a tall man with whom that statue was not unconcerned—a man not unlike Hugh de St. Omer in athletic stature—lay on an iron bed and "saw Master Death grinning and beckoning."

Two nurses and three physicians were in attendance, and their grave faces and whispered conversation told that hope had been abandoned. But they had learned of the importance of their patient, chief Kommodore of the great German steamship lines, and a sportsman and patron of music known over all Europe. Telegrams were already pouring in from high officials, from the hundreds of folk who knew him, and who had read the evening papers.

The President of the Republic had called in person and left his card. And the British, the German, and the American Ambassadors.

But the man on the bed with a broken back and other injuries did not show interest in all this. He asked repeatedly for one person, Anton Lavar, and they told him Herr Lavar was on his way, having received that message from Berlin.

It seemed that Kommodore Hugo Frederick von Steinburg only clung to the slender thread of life until this humble personage could arrive.

Out on the Berlin-Paris road the Mercedes-Benz was now racing ninety-five miles an hour.

Word had been telephoned to villages and towns to clear the path; and a swift police escort had been sent out to meet the car and rush it through the Paris suburbs, through the Paris streets to the courtyard of this hospital.

The gentle man alone in the passenger seat of this car only said from time to time to the chauffeur: "Faster! Faster!" and then to his God:

"Let Hugo live. Oh God—let Hugo live."

✣ 13 ✣

STANISLAUS JOSEPH HALKA and the girl walked slowly back, through the gathering dusk, to the Fort Tyron Park entrance. They walked hand in hand.

The boy was thinking: *Should I have read this parchment legend to the girl?* The girl thought: *Come what may I have found my man.* And they both thought: *We have found each other—that is all that really matters.*

She is now my beloved wife.

He is now my husband.

Their hands clasped very tightly. And then—as if she read his first doubting thoughts—the girl said: "I am glad that you read it to me. I am not afraid."

They were now at the park entrance and the boy hailed a passing taxi. The girl protested this extravagance, and this simple, blessed gesture, so characteristic of her concern for him and for their future, brought them both from out the tragic middle ages to the hope-filled today.

The boy said again: "Duszka, you and I are only married once." And then: "I wanted to bring you here on an open bus top, but now it is night time—there is nothing to show you on the way—we travel in style, by private coach, to our wedding bed."

And later that night, in the top floor front on Thirty-fourth Street and Madison Avenue, just before they went to sleep, the girl said: "My darling, I am thinking about the Madonna of the Sword. About her blood-red breast at a time of sorrow.

"Duszka, what miracle occurs when something happens that brings her great joy?"

"Guard Dennis O'Rourke tells me that 'his baby' truly smiles when she is especially pleased or happy," said Stanislaus Joseph, "but I have never myself seen this happen."

"If you were there now you would see that miracle," said the girl. "The statue is smiling now, my duszka."

And so it was, as the stone image gazed out through her leaded window to the star-sprinkled sky. Truly smiling, with a smile of infinite happiness, and yet—her breast was blood red.

A double miracle!

14

AT THAT EXACT MOMENT, a man sitting in a chair by a Paris hospital bedside was clasping with both hands the hand of the man who lay prone beneath the white bed-cover.

The man on the bed opened his eyes. His pain-racked face seemed to clear of agony. *He* smiled.

"Anton," he said, "dear blessed old Anton. They wanted me to send for a priest, but I told them I wanted no priest. I wanted only you."

"Hugo, it were well to have a priest at this time," said Anton Lavar.

"A man can die without a priest if he has his friend," said Hugo von Steinburg. "All my life I have lived without a priest. Lived hard and sinned hard and laughed—had sorrow also—but you shall bear witness, as they say, that I have never denied Jesus Christ. For my mother's sake I have always remembered Him. Ah Anton, it is good that you are here. And Alma—she is well?"

"Alma is well," said Anton Lavar. "And I am glad that I was nearer than Vienna to Paris. I had been called to Berlin to speak to fellow musicians. I was intending to try to find you in the morning. To surprise you. And now—now——"

There were tears in his tired gray eyes. "O God—O Almighty God—" he said, and bowed his head to the hand he was clasping.

"Do not weep for me, my friend," said Hugo von Steinburg, "One must sometime die—I have often thought of it—and I now thank God that it will be with you at my side."

"But you must not die!" said the old music teacher. "You must get well and go back to Vienna with me. Alma and I will care for you at our home—there is a room looking out upon her garden—there are flowers still blooming there, and birds in the early morning——"

"No, Anton," said the other man. "It will never be. These doctors have told me—I forced them to give me the truth." And for a moment he closed his eyes, as new pain shot through his body. His will conquered the thrusts, and presently he continued.

"This is how I should die—unless it were aboard my ship. Flower gardens—tranquility—were never meant for me. I would have won that race, Anton, and I intended to come to Vienna and bring you the gold cup—then we would have made a night of it—the Prater—the Ringstrasse Cafe—I wonder, could I still drain the great stein at one breath."

"Ah Hugo—Hugo," said the other man, "we can still do all of that."

"No. Not that—but there is something you can do, Anton," continued the dying man. "There was a pupil of yours who crossed with me—you wrote me about him—I meant to look him up when in New York, but never did. Is he still there, Anton?"

"I heard from him only a week ago. He is still there. I think he is remaining there."

"That is good. It is a great country for a young man. And this is what I wish you to do. He knows about a statue of the Virgin that also crossed on my *Europa*. An hour ago I seemed to see that statue —or rather, the Lady who was that statue—see her again, as I once saw her on the bridge of my ship—it was at night—this lad will know.

"She told me there was a golden cross opposite my name on a great scroll, out there—somewhere—I believe she also will speak for me to our Lord—ask the lad to take a rose to her image—as I gave her a rose on my ship's bridge that night. This boy will understand——"

And Anton Lavar, though he did not quite comprehend the meaning of this request, answered:

"Hugo, I will do as you have told me."

"And tell Alma," the man on the bed continued, "that there was never really anyone else—no one else except perhaps this Lady of the Statue and the Sea—*La Mer*——"

The man suddenly raised himself in his bed.

"Anton," he said, "I hear that music now—*La Mer*—you remember —I played it—we played it together—only I always played too loudly —'Too much pedal!' you would say. But the sea is loud, Anton, not gentle as you are gentle—Anton—Goodbye—Goodbye my dear—my only true friend——"

The man in the chair at his bedside said: "Hugo, there are many friends. The hospital tells me the calls have been legion—it was in the newspapers it seems—ambassadors—musicians—people of your racing and shipping world—folk who crossed the ocean under your protection——"

But Hugo Frederick von Steinburg had dropped back to his pillow. He closed his eyes as if he were very tired. He had not heard all that his friend was saying.

He was not even there. He was galloping through the stars astride a valiant horse named the Lady of the Statue. That horse, with flaming eyes, had been waiting in the outer shadows—not quietly—but eager—plunging—pawing the winds——

Does man, in his arrogance, think that he alone possesses an immortal soul?

"We will win this race, My Lady," the rider of that horse was saying, and Anton Lavar felt the tall body give a final stiffening—that reflex that the muscles will give after the soul has departed. Anton felt this, as he held the large, cold hand.

"Doctor! Doctor!" he cried, and then, "Oh God!"

The night sky outside was filled with sparkling stars. And presently, somewhere—up there—a rider pulled up with a great swerving rush at a golden gate. Perhaps Saint Michael himself, the fighter-Saint, was waiting with that cross to pin onto the bosom of his newest captain. Perhaps Hugh de St. Omer was there too, fully armed with mighty two-handed sword and shield emblazoned with the Cross of the Crusades, to bid welcome to a fellow warrior.

And perhaps, for a brief space, the spirit of a statue whose breast in a carved image had, at that moment, been blood red, was also there, her breast now purest white—her smile now one of radiant welcome and gratitude.

And perhaps the Choir of Angels—that part of it that accompanies on golden harps—was playing a composition named *La Mer,* which means the Sea.

In a room in a Paris hospital, a white-haired teacher of music was sobbing like a child.

So—in a top-floor-front on Madison Avenue, a street of the new world in the City of New York—and in a room of a hospital in Paris

—an ancient city of France—did Life and Death commence at one and the same hour.

So always do Joy and Sorrow sit at the same board in this whirling speck we name Earth.

Our solace? That there is no such thing as Death. A Life named Jesus Christ was sent to us for that purpose.

All we need do is to *Believe*.

PART NINE

THE LIFE

❖ 1 ❖

UNLIKE THIS DEPONENT, Stanislaus Joseph Halka did not, as he ate his breakfasts, first look carefully at the inside final page of the first section of his daily *New York Times,* which newspaper he obtained during a customary walk around the block each morning before "fixing" that early meal. We refer to that page called *obituary.* A word from the Latin *obire* meaning to *go down.*

Whether those there listed went *down* or *up* could be judged from life records which the news "morgues" had recorded.

One thing seemed certain. They had gone. Were dead.

The young man had not reached the age (as heretofore noted) when Death was striding ruthlessly through the ranks of his acquaintances, and filling that page with names not unknown to him.

In fact, Stanislaus Joseph usually did not look at this special page at all. And thanks to Heaven and the Musical Union he no longer must peruse another mortuary page whose columns were headed *Help Wanted—Male.*

A glance at headlines on Page 1 to keep posted on newest strikes, murders, domestic political corruption and international suspicions and bickerings; a detailed reading of the reviews of concerts and other musical events; the review of a new book (if it concerned a musician or music); a glance at the standing of the baseball clubs of the National League—(without having ever seen a real game he had become a Dodger fan—this ball club, like Richard Strauss waltzes, having a universal, irresistible appeal); such was our hero's journalistic morning stint.

What he saw first, this first new morning of his wedded life, was the photograph.

The Herr Kommodore was wearing his heavily braided officer's cap and uniform, which emphasized the vigor and authority of the strong-featured face. And there, beside it, was the black headline:

HUGO FREDERICK VON STEINBURG, 56
KOMMODORE OF THE EUROPA

and in smaller headline type beneath this:

German World War Hero,
Musician, Sportsman, Dies
In Paris As Result Of
Steeplechase Accident

There followed a full column of detail cabled by the Paris correspondent. "Special to The New York Times." For a phrase in the first sentence read, "known to hundreds of Americans who had crossed on his liner."

The girl had risen from her chair to pour Stanislaus Joseph his second cup of coffee. She looked over his shoulder.

She, also, saw the photograph.

Of sorrow there are various categories. That comrade Sorrow which all-wise Cervantes wrote was "man's only faithful companion."

There is the kind that stabs the heart—that breaks down even the physical control of the tear ducts of a grown man. A sorrow that becomes, for the moment, acute anguish. Such was the sorrow of Anton Lavar in that room in a Paris hospital. And there is the kind, of equal depth, that momentarily stuns, that shocks. You cannot believe that what you see, or hear, or read about, has really happened. And yet—you know that it has.

Stanislaus Joseph read the obituary of Kommodore Hugo Frederick von Steinburg with this latter sorrow.

The girl stood silently by him as he read. She sensed that it meant more to her husband than just the death of a well-known personage. And she had a question also, not of sorrow, but of suppressed, excited amazement.

The young man laid the half-folded newspaper on the table cloth. For *a table* and a table cloth had now become an adjunct to his breakfasts. Previous to the advent of Olga Lasenka he had eaten perpendicularly—standing—his table being the white metal surface of the shelflike, non-sink part of the kitchen sink, that same being directly (and conveniently) adjoining the gas stove. But the girl had revolutionized all this! Each morning she cleared the living-room table of manuscript music, ashtrays, erasers, ink and pens; purchased two tablecloths and two napkins at Macy's—thus transforming an uncivilized bachelor quarters into a civilized *home*.

"That picture?" said the girl. "The man with the braided cap. Duszka—who is he? Did you know him?"

"I knew him," said Stanislaus Joseph. "He was a very great and a very kind gentleman. He was especially kind to me—a mere nobody—who had been booked in the Second Class on his great ship."

"That is the man," said the girl who had been Olga Lasenka, "who stood beside me high up on a ship in my dream. To whom I spoke about a golden cross. That great, strong face—I am certain that it was that man. Oh, Duszka—again I am a little afraid."

✣ 2 ✣

LIFE, HOWEVER, MUST GO ON, and it is often fortunate that Life's demands give little time for contemplative grief. Or, in the case of Joseph and Olga Halka, for speculation as to why this girl, who had never been on shipboard, should have dreamed that she stood on a great liner's high bridge and talked with a Kommodore who had just died in Paris.

The final auditions of the new Friml-Ziegfeld operetta would commence one hour from then. Much of their happiness would depend on the outcome of her voice trial at that audition.

So they finished their first breakfast as man and wife, washed up the dishes and the coffee pot (Stanislaus Joseph doing the "wiping," as he had insisted on doing the past six days), and once more they went over, at the piano, Anton Dvořák's *Als Die Alte Mutter*.

On that day she probably could sing it as well as any singer in America. The little accompanist had been coaching her the entire week about it.

They took a taxi to the theater, Stanislaus Joseph insisting on this extravagance. The girl must not be physically tired, as she was at the first (and wholly disastrous) voice trial.

To this audition had been called only those singers marked "A" the week before. Stanislaus Joseph explained to the stage manager that this girl was a friend of his, and he would be grateful if she could be heard.

So she was motioned to step out the very first one. She moved to the piano, and handed her music to the accompanist. And that accompanist noted with a smile that this sheet *Selection of Song Favorites* with the check opposite *Songs My Mother Taught Me: Medium B* (a sheet he had himself selected and bought at Schirmer's) had written in its upper corner in a firm, round handwriting:

Olga Halka
179 Madison Avenue

The girl had secretly written this just before they left home. And he thought of how he had desperately memorized the same handwriting only a short week before! The last name and the address were then different.

He had no need to memorize this new address.

Stanislaus Joseph said, as he had said that week before: "I will play you a very short introduction. When I raise my hand, commence." Then the smile, and this time the line—softly—for her ears alone: "You'd better make good, Mrs. Halka. Your husband's reputation as a coach is at stake!"

Florenz Ziegfeld was seated with his advisers in the darkened auditorium. And before the girl was half way through, the young man at the piano could see the great producer holding up the one finger that meant that the singer—at this final audition—was "in."

And it was not entirely because of its being Mr. Ziegfeld's favorite song. Olga Halka sang it beautifully. She would have been a poor learner from Stanislaus Joseph Halka, Doctor of Music of the University of Vienna, if she had not.

One other thing helped her, which she did not speak of to Stanislaus Joseph till much later.

Out in that darkened auditorium, and apart from the Ziegfeld group, seemed to stand a tall figure of a man. The overhead stage light just caught a reflection on the heavy gold braid of his coat cuffs, and on the visored cap he wore at a jaunty angle. And to touch the gold of a cross upon his left coat breast along with the several medals and rows of service ribbons. And he appeared to say, as Stanislaus

Joseph played the introduction, and just before she started to sing: *"God bless you, and the fine lad who is your husband. This time, My Lady, you will clear all barriers!"*

As for the girl who had been Olga Lasenka, only the astute and observing Ziegfeld stage manager discerned that she had sung and been rejected the previous week.

"Put one over on us, didn't you?" he said to Tightpants at the lunch hour. "I remember that girl. Damn attractive kid to look at, but couldn't sing for a hoot-in-hell last week. And she seems to have changed her name, along with her voice! 'Halka.' Relative of yours?"

"She did change her name the past week," said Tightpants. "She is now Mrs. Halka."

"Well—well! Congratulations!" said the stage manager. "Only why the hell didn't you tell me last week she was your fiancée? I'm not half as mean as I look. I'd have helped you then—let her slip by—only you don't seem to need help. That tear-jerking 'mother song'! I guess you've spotted one of the boss's few weaknesses."

"She wasn't my fiancée last week," said Stanislaus Joseph.

"Well! Well!" repeated the stage manager. "Strange events sure do happen around the Florenz Ziegfeld auditions! And me just getting a divorce from my third wife! I'll be damned!" And he added: "Better luck to you, old pal."

Stage manager Dixon did not get to congratulate Olga Halka until the following week, when rehearsals started. The girl had gone from the audition to the Ziegfeld business office, to sign and receive her contract. She and such others as were finally selected.

Olga Lasenka, late of the Five-and-Dime and the Four Rosebuds, was, at last, in a New York show.

✣ 3 ✣

THERE CAME a period of content and great happiness for Olga and Stanislaus Joseph Halka. They did not set the world aflame with their talents, but, like the old ballad, there was a flame in their hearts.

By the end of that week the new operetta was fully cast. The grind of rehearsals followed. Five weeks of intensive work.

Tightpants played the piano from ten in the morning till ten at night. The musical conductor found that this young man could help about copying the orchestrations and the chorus parts. Stanislaus Joseph would often sit up two more hours at night at these tasks, taking home music which must be ready by the following morning; and for this he received extra pay at so much a page.

He was glad to earn this extra money.

Sometimes he played for the so-called principals. Sometimes for the chorus. Sometimes at the ballet rehearsals. There were two other pianoforte players now steadily employed, as rehearsals were often going on at three theaters or halls at the same time.

Mr. Ziegfeld always required that *all* singers learn all musical numbers, whether, at the beginning, they would seem to be concerned with them or not. A straight solo might become a duet. A number in which the chorus did not at first participate might have the chorus on-stage in the final staging. A number that started out as a dance might become a song with a lyric added. And when the operatic *finales* were reached, with everyone on stage, these *finales* were bound to be made up of well-planted numbers.

There was no haphazard guesswork in the thoroughness of the producing of a musical play by genius Florenz Ziegfeld. His continued success was not just a matter of good luck, as certain envious imitators sometimes attempted to explain.

There was one outside interruption for Stanislaus Joseph and Olga during this routine. One morning a letter arrived from Vienna. A letter from Professor Anton Lavar.

This was the letter from the boy's old Conservatory teacher.

"My Dear Stanislaus Joseph:

I know that the sad news of the death, by a racing accident, of Kommodore Hugo Frederick von Steinburg must be known to you. Both the *Kronen Zeitung* and the *Volksblatt* sent reporters to interview me, and later I saw copies of New York newspapers in the *Volksblatt* office. His tragic demise was recorded around the world, they told me. His great modesty was typified by his feeling that he had no friends. I am certain that thousands mourned his passing.

"So I will not enlarge on facts of which I feel certain you are already aware.

"I thank God that I was with him at the end. He died peacefully, his brilliant faculties clear. Music was in his last thoughts. He spoke of one of his favorites—Debussy's *La Mer*. Ah, he would have been a great artist had he pursued our profession! But he lived—and died —I believe, as he would have wished to live and die. That, only, comforts me.

"He made a request in his final minutes on this earth that concerns you, my one-time pupil.

"He asked that I write you and request you to go to a statue that is in the city of New York, and place a rose at the feet of that statue. He said you would understand. He said that he had—in his last hours —seemed to see the Lady who was that statue—a statue of the Holy Virgin it apparently was—that he had once transported to New York on his *Europa*. He said that this Lady had told him of a Golden Cross—'Up There'—that 'Up There' she would speak for him, he believed.

"I hope that you understand fully just what it was that Hugo wished. There was no time, at that tragic moment, to question him further about it all. Personally I believe his own fine, unselfish life will speak for him before his God.

"There was a state funeral in Berlin. A simpler one in Bavaria, where he is buried beside his mother. My heart is too sad to write you more at this time. I have lost my dearest friend who was more to me than a brother. Please carry out Hugo's wish, if you understand it.

"Your old (and rapidly growing older) teacher,

Anton Lavar

"P.S. Along with his Berlin attorney, I was made the executor of his will. He left a large sum to form a Foundation for poor music students, which I am to administer. He left my wife and myself a considerable annuity (and it was like him to say nothing of all this to me directly), which will give us comforts all our lives, and free us from material worry. He provided handsomely for all who had served him faithfully.

"He wished that you have a framed photograph of this statue which was on his cabin wall aboard the *Europa*, and the copy of Debussy's *La Mer* which he said you had used on his ship, when you had played it together with him. This as a remembrance. I will send them to America when his personal effects reach me here in Vienna.

A. L."

Stanislaus Joseph paused. That was the letter's end.

It was then that Olga Halka told her husband that she had seemed to see Kommodore Hugo Frederick von Steinburg out there in the Ziegfeld Theater auditorium, the morning of her final audition.

"The golden cross was shining on his breast," she said.

Stanislaus Joseph, having carefully (and sadly) folded the letter, was about to replace it in its envelope.

Then only did he notice that there was still another sheet of paper which was lodged in the envelope, and had been folded separately from the main letter.

There was writing also on this sheet. He extracted the paper, and read this further communication from Professor Anton Lavar.

"P. S. No. 2. There was a codicil to Hugo's original will. His attorney told me the Kommodore had added it just before he made that last around-the-world cruise, which was his final voyage, and on his return from the last trip he had made over the Atlantic to New York. I have separately copied this codicil, so as to send it to you in its exact wording. You will see that even in his busy life Hugo had not forgotten you. And I think he must have liked you. The codicil reads:

" 'To Dr. Stanislaus Joseph Halka, graduate of the Vienna Conservatory of Music, whom I believe to be in America, but whose address I do not have, which address I think will be known to, or can be discovered by my co-executor, Professor Anton Lavar of that Conservatory, I do bequeath the sum of five thousand American dollars, said sum to be realized by the sale of securities to that amount, and transmitted to the legatee (if he is still in America) in the form of a draft drawn on a responsible New York banking house.

"I do this in gratitude for a week of music spent with this talented and modest youth when he crossed to New York on the ship of my command, the *Europa,* some two years ago; and also to repay him for a cash outlay he would have had to make, to carry out a request I then made of him; and which request, being a sincere lad, I am quite certain he carried out.

" 'I had asked him to purchase a rose, and take it to a statue of the Queen of Heaven which is exhibited at a museum called the Cloisters located in the northern section of Manhattan, City of New York. Roses, in any section of that new world city are, I happen to know, very expensive. I wish that he therefore reimburse himself for the expense he was subject to, in order to carry out my request, and that he keep for himself whatever is left of this sum of five thousand American dollars over and above that expense, to use and benefit from it as he sees fit.

" 'Perhaps also, he will sometimes play a composition by Claude Achille Debussy named *La Mer,* and think of me, his friend and well wisher.' "

This P. S. No. 2 was also initialed "A. L.," and there was added—"This money will be sent you by the Berlin attorney, as soon as the estate is settled."

It was Stanislaus Joseph Halka's turn to wipe a tear from his eyes, as he handed this paper to the girl who had been Olga Lasenka.

They had to rush quickly to their rehearsals that morning. But at the lunch hour Mr. and Mrs. S. J. Halka took a taxi to the little church on Second Avenue. They arranged with the priest who had married them to have a Mass at seven the next morning.

And that next morning, after this Mass and a hasty breakfast, they took a fast taxi to the Cloisters which opened at ten, taking with them a rose, which they placed at the feet of the La Celle Lady.

Guard O'Rourke well remembered the Kommodore, as the "tall, foreign gentleman in a uniform who had himself once brought a rose." And he now understood why the breast of "his baby" had been crimson that late afternoon, two weeks before.

"But the next morning My Lady's breast was pure white again," he said. "So we know that this fine gentleman is at peace. I will myself light a candle for him when I reach home tonight, and I will light one in a church near here, when I have my snack at noon. And say two *Hail Mary's*. And except for this sad news, I know that you two have been happy. My Lady has truly smiled each morning when I came in, and before I left at night. I hope she will have no more cause to be sad."

They could stay at the Early Gothic Room only a few brief moments. Must hasten back to very modern Broadway and the tasks of the day. Their rehearsals that day started at ten-thirty, else they could not have journeyed at all to the Cloisters that morning.

So did the hurly-burly of life go on.

However, at the noon hour that day, in a bare rehearsal hall, where Stanislaus Joseph was playing for the first time a new and difficult Friml ballet for the premier dancers and the dance director, and when these folk had left, he lingered at the piano and plunged into a composition by Claude Debussy called *La Mer.*

The room was otherwise quite empty (an observer would have

said)—only the cheap chairs around the walls and the battered, cigarette-burned, rehearsal-hall piano; for it is not yet given to most of us to see a personage who has departed this life.

But I do believe that suddenly, back to back with the cheap upright, was materialized a great, shadowy, highly polished Bösendorfer concert grand, at which pianoforte was seated a tall and handsome gentleman now wearing a loose smoking jacket, and his strong teeth clamped onto a well stained meerschaum.

And that strong, and skilled fingers joined with the lad, in the playing of the *Second Part* of this composition—a part named *Conversation of Winds and Waves.*

✣ 4 ✣

WHAT OF THE GIRL?

The girl from the Wilkes-Barre five-and-dime, the girl who had been the humblest of the lowly Four Rosebuds, the girl who had been Olga Lasenka, was moving in a complete Paradise.

She was rehearsing in a New York show. Actually a member of a big, new, operetta company! A Ziegfeld-Friml show! Just in the chorus, of course, but it was a production for Broadway!

Unbelieving, she would repeat that, over and over to herself!

And she had found her man out of all the world. Out of all the Ages, if she let her mind dwell on the implications of her resemblance to the La Celle statue!

So when, at last, she and Stanislaus Joseph were in each other's arms around midnight, this hectic world seemed a very glorious place to be alive in. Even to be asleep in!

They had to eat in restaurants, for there was little time to market and to prepare meals at home. The girl did not like this unthriftiness, but they were both earning money. Her rehearsal salary was twenty dollars a week. Stanislaus Joseph made one hundred and twenty-five with his playing. Some weeks he made another fifty dollars with the music copying.

The girl opened a joint account at a savings bank just a block away from their apartment. She managed to save nearly a hundred dollars each week.

"When this piece really opens we will really save money!" she said. "My salary will be forty dollars, and we won't have to eat lunches and dinners out. I'll find the best places around here to shop. I'll cook you better meals and they will only cost about half as much. Why, we can live on my salary alone, and save all of yours!"

Stanislaus Joseph laughed. "I've certainly found a treasure," he said, "a girl that wants to support me! You'll even be planning to pay my Union dues and buy my cigarettes, and don't forget I'll need money for a hair-cut, once a month, out of what you earn!

"No, darling. No. When this piece opens, and if it is a success, you're going to have some nice new clothes and shoes and all the *agitato arpeggios* and *doucement cadenzas* that go with 'em—*everything* a girl as beautiful as you are should have! You're going to be the finest dressed lady in the City of New York!"

"I see that you want to make me look like—and sound like—what we call a steam calliope!" laughed the girl. "And, duszka, I wouldn't want to hurt the feelings of the great society ladies that I read about who are voted *the ten best dressed women in America* each year! Suppose one of them committed suicide because you made me edge her out of this class? How would you feel then—and how would I feel?"

They both laughed, but the boy said seriously: "You forget. We will have all that money the kind Kommodore has left us——"

"He left it to you," said the girl, "and you are going to save it. Or I am going to save it for you. I'm going to put it deep in *another* savings bank, as far away from here as I can find! I hear they have savings banks across the East River in a place called Brooklyn. Or maybe there's one in that Bayonne, New Jersey, where we closed the picture house act! I want it in a place that I will hate to journey to, so there won't be the temptation to spend it if I see a diamond bracelet at Tiffany's that I think I ought to have!

"And you'd buy it for me," she added, "even if it cost the whole five thousand. Or if that were only the first down payment. I know!"

Stanislaus Joseph took her in his arms. I think he realized the beneficence God and a Ziegfeld chorus audition had bestowed on him.

After a little while the girl said, as soon as she was permitted to talk again: "And, duszka, we haven't received all that fortune yet. We may wait a long time to receive it.

"My father's brother died in Poland, and it was a full year before my father had some money left to him. And in some of the countries of Europe they do not allow large sums of money to be sent abroad, as they say. I know all this from hearing them talk around the five-and-dime.

"Oh, you are married, duszka, to a very great financial genius, skilled in both domestic and foreign finance!"

"You are of course right," said Stanislaus Joseph. "We must not yet count our unhatched chickens, as they say over here. And big musical plays have a way of sometimes failing. I hear talk about that around the Union—of pieces costing thousands that rehearsed five or six weeks, and closed in two——"

Here the girl was the optimist. "How can you even think of such a thing about this operetta!" she cried. "Aren't you the principal pianoforte player? Am I not the fourth girl from the right in the opening chorus?"

And then, quite seriously, she added: "I go every day with one of the other girls who is a Catholic, and pray for its success at a church near here. And every day I ask that Guard O'Rourke's Lady of the Statue up at the Cloisters—the French-Polish girl of the manuscript your friends discovered in Paris—to intercede for this production, and for us.

"I think that peasant girl must be in Heaven—like Bernadette Soubirous, or Joan of Arc. I do not think that she will fail us."

Stanislaus Joseph thought to himself: *Is that girl in Paradise, or is she here—in the person of the girl who had been Olga Lasenka—now speaking to me?*

For this fantastic possibility had more than once occurred to him.

5

WHETHER IT WAS the prayers of the girl who had been Olga Lasenka, and the intercession of the Lady of the Statute (*whoever* she might be); whether it was because Kommodore Hugo Frederick von Steinburg and Hugh de St. Omer were keeping a watchful eye;

whether it were The Three Fates or Almighty God (in whichever you believe)—all these meantime getting a quite sizable "assist" from a composer named Rudolf Friml and a producer named Florenz Ziegfeld, not to forget a costume and scene designer named James Reynolds, a scene painter named Robert Bergman, a producing assistant named Roy Cutter, a conductor named Anton Heindl, a director named Richard Boleslavsky, a lyricist named Brian Hooker, a writer of words named Justin Huntly McCarthy; the rehearsals reached a seemingly triumphant conclusion.

The new operetta—this musical entertainment which could be shown in two and one-half brief hours, but on which skilled hands had labored for two years, was ready for the final court of approval (or disapproval), the ticket-buying public. And the company and producing staff went by special train to Philadelphia for a two-weeks "breaking in."

In Philadelphia, there was an all-day Sunday and all-night Sunday dress rehearsal. Tightpants sat at his piano keyboard with the rest of the forty-man orchestra, for twenty straight hours.

Olga Halka, along with the thirty other singing girls, was wearing her six changes of costume (Thank Heaven, no pink tights!), and to the little man in the orchestra pit, who looked up at her occasionally from his piano and celesta (placed next the conductor), she appeared more beautiful with each change.

She received an unexpected "break" at that marathon rehearsal. The adaptor of the book put in a new line in the Tavern Scene, and the friendly stage manager gave the "Halka girl" that line.

It was merely *Red wine, you said, because my lips are red!*—but it meant that Olga's name would go opposite a "character" on the printed programs. She would be listed there "in the order of her appearance," as well as under "Ladies of the Singing Ensemble."

So the stage manager informed Stanislaus Joseph at a fifteen-minute rest period, when they all stepped out into the stage-door alley for a breather and a cigarette.

"And tell her not to go high-hat on me about it," he said to Tightpants with a smile. He added: "I don't think she will. She's a good worker, and a fine kid—that wife of yours. Why the hell can't I find someone like her! My second wife was in a chorus, and she lost us both our jobs when I gave her a line to speak. With Georgie White's Scandals it were. Thought she ought to be starred or something! The prima donna finally refused to go on, if that silly girl stayed in the show.

"She had a grand shape too! But no brains. No brains at all. Seems it's impossible—not to say improbable—to find both in one and the same female!"

Stage Manager Dixon sighed heavily at Nature's utterly unfair and niggardly distribution of feminine attributes.

The piece opened the next night. Everyone, from Mr. Ziegfeld to the humblest stage hand, "all in" and "dead on their feet" at seven-thirty P.M. Most of them had not taken time for a so-called dinner.

But at eight-fifteen, when the assistant stage-managers announced "All on stage for the opening chorus," and the music of the overture floated through the lowered house-curtain, and the stage lights were blazed on from the great switchboard at one side, those hundred and fifty "dead on their feet" folk were like so many race horses at the barrier—fired with boundless energy, determination, enthusiasm.

From where obtained? Just one of the miracles in that crazy jamboree named "show business." That blessing to mankind named "theatrical entertainment."

The theater was crowded, and many friends of the producer and the cast came over from New York. The performance was far from perfect—no first performance out-of-town ever is perfect—but success was vibrating in the atmosphere of that playhouse.

It seemed certain Mr. Ziegfeld was headed for another smash hit.

Although most of their waking hours were now spent in the Forrest Theater (what with performances, as well as constant rehearsals of new numbers, scene changes, the general "tightening up" in preparation for New York), the company and staff could not *sleep there*. But there were nights when they were almost weary enough to drop down and attempt it. Only it seemed that there were fire-prevention laws, made by non-understanding, non-show-business city councils, which forbade such a practice.

Therefore "Mr. and Mrs. S. J. Halka" (so Stanislaus Joseph signed the hotel register) for the sole purpose of *sleeping* were in residence at a small hotel, already known to some of his road-hardened fellow musicians—a hotel which gave "professional rates."

That initial Saturday midnight, on the company's arrival from New York, was the very first time Tightpants had signed a hotel register with a woman companion.

He had, as we know, signed very few hotel registers in any capacity.

He was slightly flustered as one of those formidable, ledger-like books then in use, was pushed out before him. For once, the presence of the girl and her assuring smile and supporting nudge toward his register-signing hand did not help. For the girl who had been Olga Lasenka of the Four Rosebud Sisters had been obliged to sign on many such date-headed, slightly soiled, register pages in a multitude of picture-house cities.

Amateur Stanislaus Joseph first started to write *Mr. and Mrs. Tightpants Halka,* for that was how they were known, and not unkindly, by the operetta company.

He actually penned the first three letters of "Tight." He had to cross this out, and hastily decided on the "S. J." "Dr. Stanislaus Joseph" or even "Stanislaus Joseph" seemed too pretentious, considering his humble position with that organization.

The knowing, though not hostile (it would rather be termed bored) look on the hotel clerk's face, because of the young man's fumbling, was not especially complimentary to the morals of the young lady at his side.

And an entirely erroneous interpretation could be placed on her assurance and encouragement in the situation.

How was that clerk to know that she was a veteran of many such dreary lobbies with their books of registration, in which she had inscribed "Olga Lasenka, Wilkes-Barre, Pa."? And Mr. Tom "Wow-'Em" Gallagher had been greatly pleased, if his girls would also write "of the Four Rosebuds now at the Capitol (or the Celestial or the Rosenberg Continental) Theater."

The more obscure and dingy the picture "palace," the grander the title!

So the little musician felt the necessity of saying, with some dignity: "I assure you, sir, this lady is my wedded wife. It is—it is the first time we have traveled since our marriage. We were never married before, hence your hotel register confused me."

It was on this clerk's tongue to reply: "Don't worry, brother. We don't ask to see marriage licenses around here," but he took a second look at the man who took the trouble to make such a naive statement. And not denying his initial smirk, he said very sincerely—said for the first time he could remember ever emitting such startling words: "I am sorry."

He *was* sorry.

There was something very genuine and clean about the two young people across his counter. Their presence and patronage made his tarnished hostelry seem a little more sanitary and decent.

He must have given them a thought the next day also, for when Mr. and Mrs. S. J. Halka came back to their room in the dawn of that Monday morning (it was after the dress rehearsal), there was a large bouquet of roses in a vase on the routine hotel dresser.

The girl exclaimed: "Oh duszka, you should not have spent this money!" but Stanislaus Joseph had to admit they were not his gift.

"Already you have an admirer," he said. "I see where I'm going to have a difficult time holding my wife, now that she is a Ziegfeld beauty!"

And then they found the card which was under the vase. It read:

"May a dumb wise-guy, who thought he knew all the answers, again say 'I'm sorry.' And may he wish you every happiness, and a nuge success to the new show you are with."

On the reverse side was the name of the night clerk. Assistant Manager was his title, printed below the name of the hotel.

Stanislaus Joseph said to the girl: "Your America is a wonderful land. I thank God I discovered it. I thank God that I am now an American."

Forgotten were the heartbreaking weeks after the death of Albert Rouchard. Forgotten those hours on the Seventy-second Street park bench.

The whole great, friendly world was just a *dressiersack,* filled with a sparkling liquid called *Good Will!* And with God's help, and the help of this wonderful girl at his side, he, Stanislaus Joseph Halka, would write with this *dressiersack* on his life's cake—*Success—Happiness.*

6

There was, during those days and nights, only one imperfection in this Utopia set geographically on the north bank of the Delaware. Not that they ever saw this river, but there was a rumor that it existed. A Forrest Theater stage hand claimed that he went fishing there—the fish being of the genus *craw* that navigated backwards.

Laughter-seeking, low comics of radio and burlesque claimed this habit had been acquired by the otherwise intellectual fish through observation of the citizenry of Philadelphia.

The gag was especially popular in adjoining Camden. Philadelphians said the Delaware was placed there by God as a defense against said Camden.

Stanislaus Joseph and the girl longed for another river named the *East* that defended the east side of Manhattan from Queens and Brooklyn.

Although every hour of the next two weeks seemed crowded with either rehearsals or performances, they missed that top-floor-front of Madison Avenue and East Thirty-fourth Street. That humble place that was their symbol of home. This girl who had known no home since her father died; this lad who now realized how utterly lonely his life had been.

Two people who had not had a home for too many years.

They missed especially the breakfasts in that apartment—she the preparing of them, he the sheer magic of what was placed before him.

She had soon discovered that Stanislaus Joseph cared more for breakfast than any other meal. And he had become completely American about it. No more Viennese horrors of ink-black coffee and boiled skimmed milk, even if it were camouflaged on the top of the tall glass by a dash of whipped cream; no more hard, dry *Kaiser semmel* rolls as the only solid-food part.

Even as a bachelor (as soon as he acquired that Madison Avenue kitchen) Stanislaus Joseph had started with a large glass of orange juice—or what he liked still better, a canned apricot "nectar." Then a toasted hot cereal which he had invented himself by the mixing of two well advertised brands (both "breakfasts of champions"), one of oats, the other of wheat. On it, plenty of sugar and heavy cream.

Then eggs—two of them—boiled four minutes—with a chunk of butter in the cup before he broke the eggs into it (having first held the hot, shell-enclosed treasure under the cold water faucet so that he could comfortably grasp them; break the shell with a spoon rim; and run the spoon around the inner edges of each half-shell).

And when eggs and butter were well broken up together, a *furioso allargrando* of black pepper straight out of the tin in which he bought it.

With this—toast; but not thin slices put into some patented electric contraption that, at a set moment, popped up brick-hard squares of bronzed dough. *His* toast was put over the open flame of his gas burner—the flame turned low—half a dozen slices of thick, fresh bread, so that the outside only was crisp and flame-stained, while the inside remained soft and spongy-delicious! On this perfect morsel—butter. Plenty of sweet butter.

Such were his high ideals. He did not always achieve this fruition.

For when your mind was on the *andante cantabile* motive of your great symphony, *you would forget to look at your watch* when you dropped the eggs into the boiling pan of water. You might even rush to the pianoforte to try a new chord or tonal progression.

By the time your wandering brain had returned to the really important matter of eggs—said eggs were "ten-minute eggs." In the heart of a true egg-lover I know of no other abrupt discovery that can create such cold ferocity.

At the other extreme, suddenly thinking of your eggs and not knowing just what second you dropped them in the water—you find that you have "two-minute eggs"; raw and unpalatable. For once the shells were broken, it was too late to boil them some more. The Rubicon had been crossed. "The saddest words of tongue or pen—et cetera."

The girl had banished such morale-destroying disasters.

When she boiled eggs she concentrated her excellent intellect on the sole subject of eggs. She purchased a small clock with a second hand. She placed it above the gas stove. Four-minute eggs thereafter, were *four-minute eggs!*

And there was no more completely burnt toast, due to sudden *allegro molto* inspirations.

As already recorded, Olga Halka had contributed that invention of the angels—waffles. Under her expert hands, the fragrant, golden squares that came from the indented irons were like pieces cut from the glowing sunrise Tightpants sometimes went to his roof to watch, as the sun came up over the East River slaughterhouses. At least, that was what he told the girl they resembled.

And as if all this were not enough, Olga Halka added an item called buttermilk biscuits. They had been her father's favorite bread.

I cannot describe these biscuits except to say that they literally melted in the mouth. Especially if spread with raspberry jam.

Describing the handiwork of a clever girl over a New York apartment two-burner gas range, with a tiny gas oven above it, should be left to the greatest poet of the Age.

I have omitted a discussion of the coffee. It was certainly not like the diluted, pusillanimous liquid obtained at most lunch counters. Enough that an ample heap of sugar was first deposited in the bottom of the cup, and over it poured the rich, flowing, copper coffee-as-is-coffee that became a golden brown when just enough heavy cream was added.

Sometimes Stanislaus Joseph had three cups of it.

Such breakfasts were not found by economy-minded troupers in the drug stores of Philadelphia—or of any other city! Not even in New York. And these two missed New York—just New York—that cold, friendly; terrifying, comforting; ugly, beautiful; sordid, clean; inspiring, discouraging; utterly unique town that took to its heart all peoples of all other cities—of all lands—and held them with some magic of fanatical, maternal attachment.

Like the tramp in the great O. Henry tale who had been in Manhattan only a single hour, New York was their "home town."

In Philadelphia also the girl did find opportunity to go almost daily to a church, and light a candle for the success of their musical play. Not forgetting to thank God for her job; for her husband; for all the material good that had made life cease to be a fiscal nightmare.

There was an extra ten dollars in her pay envelope the first Saturday, this because of the "line" she had been given to say. And this first week of playing, Stanislaus Joseph earned an additional seventy-five dollars for the copying of orchestrations of new music—new songs that were put in—a new *finale* to one of the acts.

Most of all, *he* was grateful that even in their work, he and the girl could be together. He was a "quick study" of his piano score, and could often look up from his place in the orchestra pit, even while playing his pianoforte, to see the girl he loved, when the ensemble was on-stage.

That first Sunday, after a week of both giving performances and rehearsing, the entire company was granted a much needed day of rest. And immediately after the Saturday night performance most of the show people took a one A.M. train for New York. New York was only two hours away, and with no rehearsal call on Monday they could have almost two days in their beloved city.

Perhaps only a dozen of the some hundred and fifty players, musicians, company working crew and staff were born there. But New York was their home, whether it was a real house in a suburb on which mortgage payments seemed to become due with an uncalendar-like and unexplainable rapidity (nothing can speed the months like a galloping mortgage!), or simply a tiny but familiar hotel room.

To these wandering professionals, it was their nest of happiness. Their hearthstone.

✣ 7 ✣

STANISLAUS JOSEPH and the girl did not take that A.M. train.

He had a half day of new music-copying to do, and he planned to do it Sunday morning. And for Sunday afternoon and night they had been invited by the wise-guy-who-thought-he-knew-all-the-answers hotel clerk to go to his home in a Philadelphia suburb, and meet his wife and children. It seemed that he had a home and a wife and children!

It might be stated in parenthesis that much as the girl Olga wanted to be back on Madison Avenue, it is doubtful if she would have agreed to a journey to New York for this single day and night. They must pay their own transportation on such a trip, and she had secretly figured carefully that it would cost eight dollars and forty-two cents more to make this journey than to stay in Philadelphia.

Olga Halka was determined that she and her man should become economically solvent. Wise girl in a very unwise world! She had not so soon forgotten the blank-wall, dead-end horror of that locked hotel-room door at the L'Esplanade-Plaza on West Forty-sixth Street.

At the end of a station wagon ride out on "the Main Line" the next afternoon, Stanislaus and Olga had another surprise.

The roses that had been placed on their hotel bureau were grown in this clerk's own garden and small greenhouse. And having been asked to stay the night in the guest room of his bungalow, they awoke the next morning to look out on a garden wall covered with green vines and red-and-blue morning glories.

And when they sat up in the broad bed with its hand-embroidered cover, the wide picture-windows gave them a view of a small garden filled with flowers, stretching its distance to this wall.

Stanislaus Joseph said: "In your America one can never guess about the real life of the folk you meet! Here is this, as you would say, hard-boiled assistant manager and night clerk at a theatrical hotel. The last thing his surroundings there would suggest would be an interest in horticulture. You would think he would spend his spare time in a poolroom or at a race track; and if he didn't live at his hotel, it would at least be in an apartment in the most hectic part of the city.

"We find that he raises roses, and has a garden wall with morning glories!

"He told me yesterday he's taken prizes with his roses. And he doesn't dislike his hotel job! He also told me he likes *people*. Only that sometimes he wishes he could—before they register—spray a lot of them with a plant disinfectant—spray especially the loud-talking, self-important kind.

" 'I don't mind the phony morals of some of them,' he said to me. 'What gets me jumpin' is *phony talk*. Flowers can't yap, thank Heaven. They just grow beautiful and don't have to boast about it. Or if they don't bloom, they don't blame the capitalistic system, the Democratic Party, or the income tax. And thank Heaven, they don't write books! Them authors are the worst! I've had experience! Every year we get a Book Convention here.'

"Well—that's your America," continued Stanislaus Joseph. "A ship-dock porter with a son in Columbia. A commercial-hotel clerk with prize roses. My news dealer, in his sidewalk cubby hole on Lexington Avenue, told me his son was studying to be a doctor at a University named Cornell. Anything and everything is possible here. And I am thrilled by it.

"To succeed in America just takes a little courage."

The girl said: "When you finish your symphony and it is played by all the great orchestras, and you have become rich and famous (*and I'll see that you don't boast about it*); and when I am a great operetta star, and making a thousand dollars a week (*and you will see that I don't boast about it*); do you want, my duszka, that we have a bungalow and a rose garden—in the country—like this?"

The young man had to think a few moments before he answered that question—this boy born in the slums of Vienna—living here in cheap hotels and a tiny, cooped-up New York "apartment," where anything larger than a hall bed-room is named "apartment."

This child of the city, surfeited with city noises and city crowds and city smells. At least, so one would think.

He looked out again at the garden wall—so different from the crowding, soot-tarnished wall of an adjoining building opposite their hotel-room window; he listened as a song bird made a serenade to the sun; he took a deep breath of the flower-scented air. And he said to the girl:

"No.

"Not unless you very much wish it, my duszka. It's all right for this one morning. It would be all right for a morning now and then. But this silence—silence except for that bird song—frightens me—stifles me.

"Once, when I was a little boy, a well-meaning charitable society in Vienna sent a lot of the children from the poorer quarters to the Tyrol country for a week. They took us in big, chartered busses. We each had a tag around our neck, with our name and the name and address of our parents written on it. And a small *rucksack* strapped to our backs, with a change of underwear and an extra shirt.

"I cried when I had to leave my father. And I think I sobbed all the way on that four-hour ride.

"I was frightened when I looked out of the bus window. No houses. No tram cars. No people. Just big, empty fields and maybe a house—way off in the distance. The villages even that we passed through looked lonely and empty.

"Of course I didn't cry all that holiday week. We went to a sort of camp by a small lake. But I was very unhappy. There was a Wayside Calvary out on the roadway near the camp. It was Christ Crucified, high up on a tall cross, with a flat board backing, shaped like a triangle, behind the figure, and the wide part as wide as the arms of the cross.

"On this board the country people would fasten various emblems of our Saviour's death. I remember that there was a Roman soldier's spear; the purse that contained the thirty pieces of silver; another spear with a sponge on its end; and a small wooden cock sat on one arm of the cross—the cock that crowed after Saint Peter had three times denied Jesus.

"That roadway shrine was the only thing I liked about the beautiful mountain country," continued Stanislaus Joseph. "I would slip away from the other children and go there and pray that I would get back safely from this silent, lonely wilderness; back to the street hawkers and the church bells and the bump-bump of the tram cars and the people quarreling or laughing in our courtyard, and the blare of the big horns in the military-band parades that I could hear every day, when the guard was changed at Schoenbrun which was the old Emperor's castle, and they would march through our street on the way to their barracks.

"My duszka, I think I even missed the smell of the open garbage wagons, and I missed terribly the old man with white whiskers who sold *kastanien* which were hot roasted chestnuts, on the corner, right by our tenement. I used to pray that he would not die before I got back to Vienna from all this desert loneliness! He looked like the pictures of the Emperor Franz Josef, and he always wore some medals he had won in the old wars. And he had looked so old and feeble the morning we left, and my father had given me some kronen to buy a little bag of his chestnuts to have for the journey.

"I know I've never prayed so hard for anything since, as I did every day at that shrine—prayed just to be back again in a big, noisy, people-filled city!

"I even missed climbing the stairs at night to the safe top-floor, where my father and I lived in one room. Oh, I was very, very afraid at night, out there under the blazing, pressing stars. No roof to protect me! No gas lamps to light the black roadway!

"No, my duszka, as you have taught me to say. Your husband is hopelessly a city bird. A gutter street-sparrow, who'd rather eat after the generous horses have trotted by, than to pick fresh berries from forest bushes with sharp thorns! I can feel those dreadful thorns now, against my legs and hands—and the kind camp-counselor thought he was giving us a grand time to take us up the mountain side to pick those berries!

"Does all this absurd dislike of mine for the country make you unhappy, duszka?"

The girl drew the face of the man she loved to hers. At first she pictured the lonely little boy, kneeling in desperation before the wayside crucifix. But soon it was her husband—her lover—equally lonely. And her heart cried, *You will never be lonely again.* And after a while she said:

"I believe I also have come to love cities best. Wasn't it a great city that brought us together? There never would have been a Florenz Ziegfeld audition in a rose garden in the country.

"We will make our life success in cities—in places where there are many people. We should live there—among many people.

"I confess that I do like hills. My father and I would go on Sunday afternoons to the hill country around Wilkes-Barre. The cemetery there, where my mother sleeps—where I want to sleep at the end—is on a hillside. But I believe I was always glad to get back down into the town.

"I like people. I liked the five-and-dime because of all the people who came in and out. It was just that I didn't like that kind of work so well. But if I hadn't been working in the five-and-dime, Mr. Tom Wow-'Em Gallagher would never have discovered me, and taken me for one of the Four Rosebuds! I wouldn't have made even *that* start in the theater, strolling down a country lane!

"And if I hadn't been one of the Four Rosebuds, I would never have had the courage to come to New York and go to a Ziegfeld audition!

"So when I think of all that cities have given me—you—this fine job; and to possess it all I don't even have to wear pink tights——"

In special gratitude for this latter negative blessing, she again held her husband close to her heart.

❖ 8 ❖

THEIR HOST HAD PLACED another bouquet of roses (at this time of year from his small greenhouse) on their bureau, and as they were dressing, the girl took up the vase and buried her face in the fragrance of the petals. And she looked out again at the morning glories on the garden wall.

"I do like flowers," she said, "and I believe I have a solution for that desire."

"I will buy you flowers every day when we get back to Madison Avenue," said Stanislaus Joseph. "I am very stupid. I should have been doing that each day since we were married! There is that florist right along Thirty-fourth Street——"

"Then we *would* be headed straight for bankruptcy!" laughed the girl. "At two dollars a rose! No, my duszka. You'd have to write a new symphony each week! I'll settle for morning glories, and we can have those right in our own garden at our apartment.

"Window boxes! Window boxes in our four beautiful front windows. I knew there was some one thing missing in our home, and that is it! We always had window boxes in Wilkes-Barre—my mother tended them when she lived, and my father kept them going in memory of her.

"And it won't be just morning glories," she added. "We can have geraniums and fuchsias—fuchsias are a wonderful bright bluish-red, and begonias with the leaves as well as the blossoms colored, and pansies, and petunias—which bloom into all the colors.

"And the morning glories shall have real vines to grow on! We'll put latticed trellises at the ends of the boxes. These trellises can follow the line of our windows, and arch up high over the boxes, so that some of the vines will hang down across the window openings. "*Our* country bungalow, duszka, will be right off Broadway, four flights up!"

At breakfast they told their host about this plan. And the hotel clerk rose-fancier looked across at his wife, who seemed to guess his thoughts before her husband spoke, for she nodded before he said:

"Let us do all that for you. When you get back to New York, send me the exact measurements of your windows. I'll build you the boxes and their trellises. I'll put just the right kind of soil in the boxes—soil from our garden here. It's a loam and leafmold, with some dried cow manure and bone meal. The loam should have a little sand. And we'll start you off with the plants that will grow best out-of-doors this time of year."

"But all this will cost you a lot of money, besides the time it will take; and how will you get them to New York?" said the practical Olga. "My husband would pay you, of course, for what it costs, but we really can't let you go to so much trouble——"

The rose-loving hotel clerk interrupted.

"Just you try to prevent me from doing it! And just you try to pay me! Hell—I was already growing old—old and sarcastic and cynical at forty. So help me, didn't believe you two fine people were married when you walked up to my hotel register! That's getting pretty far gone! The past week—just watching you two coming in and out of that dump has made me young again. My wife out here even noticed the change in me. . . . I know that my roses noticed that change," he added with a smile. "They've been blooming like crazy!

"I'll get a couple of days off soon. My wife and I will drive to New York in our station wagon—made the last payment on it last week, so that now we can have painted on its side ROSEDALE FARMS—and in the back will be loaded your complete garden for *your* BROADWAY FARMS!

"You may have to hire an outside handy-man to help us attach the boxes and lattice-work to the windows. You may have to borrow a hook and ladder from the New York Fire Department. I'm sure they won't mind and will gladly cooperate! We'll just turn in an alarm if we need 'em. Maybe I'll let you pay the fines for that—but only if your show is a big hit on Broadway.

"Listen—to do this little thing for you two, is going to give me the greatest pleasure I've had since I saw my first home-grown rose bloom!"

"But," said the girl Olga, "we only have a room and a kitchen. A little bedroom—yes—but there's just one tiny bed. We can't return your wonderful hospitality——"

"That is nothing for you to worry about," said the hotel man. "Our hotel belongs to a chain. There's one of our houses in New York, and not far from you, on East Twenty-eighth Street. I get no bills when I stop there. They'd better not give me a bill!"

"But the gasoline you will use up to travel to New York and back, just for us," said the girl graduate of the Wilkes-Barre five-and-dime.

The host laughed. To Stanislaus Joseph he said: "You are a damn lucky guy! You have found a wife who figures out everything. And can count the costs. I'm lucky that way too. If it wasn't for my darling here, I wouldn't have this house and our garden. She made me save my money. Then we went to the Liberty Bell Savings and Loan.

"We had a pretty big mortgage at first—used to keep me awake at night—I'd see that damned legal paper I'd signed, damned neatly folded, marching back and forth across my bed chanting:

I'll get you yet—I'll get you yet!
You'll never, never be out of debt!

And it was hard to resist the can't-lose tips I'd hear about around the hotel every day—what was it the old song used to moan—

Sure tips on the races bring many long faces.

I think I saved enough, just *not playing* those can't-lose tips, to meet the interest and carrying charges! But the mortgage is now nearly wiped out. Another year, and this half-acre will be all ours!

"I know what I'll do," he continued, "just to show you I'm not soft. I'll make you two *give us* a mortgage on your window boxes, for the cost of the gasoline used, going and coming from New York, and the wear and tear on the tires. And I'll not forget the toll charges through the Hudson tubes. Six percent interest. Quarterly payments. See that you do not default, for I can be hard and grasping, as well as completely looney over two swell people!"

And the hotel man put on a very fierce look over his coffee cup.

They all laughed.

Stanislaus Joseph said: "Apparently the only thing you're going to permit us to do, is to take you to dinner in New York. My Olga cooks one dinner for you. Maybe I cook one. Then we take you out for one. And if you make any move to reach for the check, I'll twist your hand right off. I have very strong, pianoforte-playing fingers.

"And I'll have seats for you in the Ziegfeld Theater—in the front row—if I have to see Mr. Ziegfeld himself to buy them! We two are not very important there. I am—fortunately for the audience—out of sight, down in the pit with the orchestra. Olga is in the chorus——"

"Fourth from the right in the opening chorus, and I have a line in Act I," broke in the girl.

"I'll learn to count up to four—and we'll be waiting just for that line," said the hotel clerk.

"The dramatic suspense of the whole act depends on it!" laughed the girl.

And that was how it came about that Mr. and Mrs. S. J. Halka, some weeks later, had window boxes and flowers along the fourth floor front on Madison Avenue that were so striking that the aggressive press agent of the newest Ziegfeld "musical smash" landed a special story, with pictures, in the magazine section of the *Journal American*.

9

THERE IS ONE OTHER incident, occurring before the New York run, that perhaps should be recorded. It happened in the city of Boston, Massachusetts.

After the two weeks in Philadelphia, it was decided to take the new piece to another city before the New York opening. The Colonial Theater in Boston was available, and it was there the company went for an additional two weeks of polishing.

Besides being the site of Faneuil Hall (the "Cradle of American Liberty"); the Old North Church, from whose steeple Paul Revere took the signal for his famous gallop; the Battle of Bunker Hill; the Old Howard Burlesque Theater; the Jordan and Marsh Department Store; and the place where fish cakes, baked beans with molasses, and the writings of Henry Wadsworth Longfellow originated; this great New England metropolis has within its confines several institutions devoted to the higher education of our youth.

This latter fact did not lessen the prestige of Boston as a stopping-off place for musical plays.

For it seemed that a careful study of such productions, particularly with regard to an analysis of their feminine pulchritude, must have been—and doubtless still is—a required course of each curricular seminar. Attendance at Exhibits A, created by the Master of such an exacting science, Mr. Florenz Ziegfeld, were practically compulsory. Like morning chapel. Or the wearing of baggy pants.

Performances were viewed with a proper reverence and critical documentation of curves, except on the nights after an important athletic contest, especially if that contest had been won by the learned representatives of the local University.

On such special occasions, youthful exuberance would sometimes overcome a natural scholastic reserve, and things would get a bit out of hand in the local playhouses.

The throwing of confetti, a lusty joining in the choruses of musical numbers, gratuitous advice as to hats, lines, the technique of love scenes were a frequent academic occurrence.

But show people—being basically children themselves—usually accepted it all with an understanding good humor.

Such a night came to pass at the end of the first week of the Boston engagement—it being by then the month of October, when a game which concerned an inflated, pigskin-covered (*pig—origin doubtful. Skin—sku—Sanskrit, to cover*), melon-shaped ball, sometimes handled by *"that segment of the limbs of a vertebrate creature upon which the body rests in standing"*—in short, *the feet* of the participants—was the seasonal scholastic escape valve.

Our Stanislaus Joseph—Mr. Tightpants—had been rushed to New York by sleeper after the performance the night before. Mr. Friml, back there to make an album of piano recordings to be released at the time of the New York opening, had written a new *overture.*

Tightpants could hear the operetta composer play this composition, could make expert note of all tempos and shades of expression, and then return with the manuscript by sleeper Saturday night. The piano player of the Boston house-orchestra would take his place for that Saturday matinee and evening.

So Stanislaus Joseph and Olga were separated for the first nights since their marriage.

He took her back to their small hotel Friday around midnight, before having to board his New York train. He ordered her to take a taxicab the following night—they usually walked—and he would be on hand again early Sunday morning. He worried that he had to leave her alone, and asked his friend the stage manager to be sure she had the taxi after the Saturday evening performance.

The girl had laughed at his fears for her safety. "My goodness," she said, "I've trouped all across America with that picture-house unit. Nobody is going to try to kidnap me! You're the only one, my duszka, who wants me. To keep you from worrying, I promise to take a taxi to the hotel after the night show tomorrow, but it's a dreadful waste of our money. A needless waste."

"You're just all I have in the world," said Stanislaus Joseph. "I'd die if anything happened to you."

"You stop worrying," said the girl. "Put that wonderful musical mind of yours on Mr. Friml's new music. I'm very proud that it's you they are sending. It shows they think you are the only one who can explain just how Mr. Friml wishes it played. Unless of course our conductor could go, and he's needed here."

This conversation at the hotel, as he was leaving for his one A.M. sleeper.

"And don't worry that I'm going to step out to some night club as soon as you are gone," she added with a smile. "I promise I'll go straight to bed."

"Now I know you are joking," said Stanislaus Joseph. "Just the same, I won't be comfortable till we are together." And he kissed her with a tenderness that touched the girl deeply. For in her heart she was of course happy and proud that he worried, and that he cared so very much.

And that night she said a special prayer. "Dear God, don't let there be a railroad wreck or any other harm come to my duszka. I'd just die too, if anything should happen to him."

So Stanislaus Joseph was not alone in his worrying. But this fine, loyal girl did not wish anything to interfere with his work.

She *was* proud that he was sent to New York. It did mean that her duszka-Tightpants was considered the best musician in the Ziegfeld orchestra.

10

THE SATURDAY NIGHT performance arrived. Harvard had won. In all Boston places of amusement, the victorious students took charge of proceedings.

Stage manager Dixon, who had experienced these nights in several previous seasons, gave the Ziegfeld company a word of advice.

"There are a lot of crazy Indians out front tonight," he said. "But they have paid for their tickets, so let them have their fun. So long as it is just fun. If they yell for you to take off your hats—do so. Put them back on, if they immediately want them back on again. If they want to sing a couple of the choruses with you—let 'em do it. If they razz a love scene—cut to the end and go right on. Cut the big emotional love scene in Act II completely. Just go into the song. Don't mind a little confetti. Dancers, just be careful you don't slip in it.

"If there's any real trouble, I'll ring down the curtain—but I won't do that unless there's real danger to you, or damage threatened to the scenery and clothes. This show is so good I think they'll behave reasonably well for celebrating college boys.

"Show 'em you are real troupers and can take it, as well as dish it out."

And it was not beyond-expectations bad.

The college boys were won over by an occurrence soon after the opening chorus. A football was tossed onto the stage from somewhere in the front rows. The chorus boy who expertly caught it had been a player on his High School team in Omaha. And he made an expert drop-kick return of the ball far back into the auditorium.

A purist might have thought this an incongruous act for a character dressed as a fifteenth-century Paris tavern habitué, but it brought forth a concerted cheer. And the show went on with an added respect from the future B.A.'s and Ph.D.'s out front.

Maybe these chorus men were not as dumb as they looked! Maybe some of them had a feeling for culture—had a real, advanced education also! Maybe they were even gentlemen!

Rah! Rah! Rah! as they would say in the Greek and Latin classics.

It was after the final curtain of the performance, and in the long, dark stage-door alley, that any real difficulties occurred.

Half a hundred of the young enthusiasts for the dramatic arts from the other bank of the River Charles were not satisfied just to study this newest Ziegfeld spectacle from across the footlights.

They decided to seek a more intimate knowledge of stage dynamics, by making the personal acquaintance of a few of these Ziegfeld professionals—in particular the feminine exponents thereof. And a number of the more hardened chorines were not adverse to proceeding to a night club or a private "party" without the benefit of formal introductions to their escorts.

Olga Halka, dressed for the street, finally emerged.

Stanislaus Joseph had always before been waiting for her in the small entrance with its company mailboxes, and the pipe-smoking stage-door men; the entrance room was on the street floor at the foot of the steep, winding stairway that led up to the dressing rooms. Stage Manager Dixon, still out on the now darkened stage to be certain that all was in the clear for the night, had noticed her and called, "Be with you in a minute, Mrs. Tightpants."

He had not forgotten his promise to see her to a taxi. But Olga had said: "Thanks—but please don't worry about me. I'll find a taxi all right."

And she had stepped alone into the alley.

Some half dozen husky and vociferous celebrators were waiting there, just for her. They had noted from across the footlights her unusual type of beauty. They felt that they should pay a special homage to it—said homage to take the form of a gay party at a nearby hotel room which two of them had especially engaged, said room having waiting an elaborate supper and plenty of champagne. And her fatal line in Act I had identified her beyond mistake.

"Yah! Red wine you said because my lips are red!" went up from half a dozen already well lubricated throats, as she appeared.

The girl was frightened. Any girl of her nature would be, when seized on each side by none too gentle hands, and propelled—almost carried—down the alley by six or seven young men shouting, "Red wine, you said, because my lips are red!"

"Boys, I can't go with you. I must go straight to my hotel. I promised my husband—" was drowned in the vocal exultations of her captors. Finally she cried loudly, "Help! Mr. Dixon! Help!" and a silencing hand was clamped across her mouth.

It was then that it happened.

A huge figure of a man appeared from nowhere. He was not dressed in the habiliments of this enlightened century. He seemed to be wearing chain armor such as is seen in museums, and on his great head was a round, pointed metal cap, while attached to its rear circumference was a flexible, flowing chain cape that covered his neck and broad shoulders, and was fastened tightly beneath his chin. There was a small gold-colored cross on the front of this headdress. The face was bearded; the eyes deep and brooding.

He uttered not a word. He seized, and then struck.

Single blows from that mighty mailed fist were enough. In seconds, the stage door alley of the Boston Colonial Theater was littered with fallen bodies of amazed collegians. When they attempted to rise, they were knocked down again by this whirling apparition. Fellow students, attracted by the turmoil and the hurt cries of victims, rushed to the rescue and were added to the slaughter. A policeman at the end of the alley blew his whistle. Other police came running. The students—such of them as could get up from the concrete—fled.

And by the time the officers of the law were on the spot, this gigantic figure had disappeared. Vanished. Mr. Dixon had come running to find the girl unharmed but shaken.

Who was this man?

Several members of the Ziegfeld company, who had been approving witnesses, had to admit it was certainly no one of that company. No actor or singer in this Ziegfeld production wore such a costume, or in any way resembled this terrific battler in appearance. Since the girl's protector was in costume, it must have been an actor.

Across the alley was the stage door of another theater—the Shubert. A Shakespearean revival was being presented there. Soldiers were in it—Roman soldiers. But no one could be found who resembled the opportune defender of a Ziegfeld chorus girl. The police were mildly, if not sympathetically, interested, because two of the young gentlemen from Cambridge had broken jaws and had to be taken to a hospital. One other was completely "out."

Another somewhat amazing bit of information came to light.

All witnesses (and some victims) testified the giant man struck out *with only one fist*. The left. Why—if he intended to wreak such havoc—he should use but one arm, was an unexplainable mystery.

One thing was certain.

He sure could use that one arm expertly. He was *some* southpaw fighter!

The girl pleaded ignorance as to the identity of her defender. But Olga Halka knew who it was. And why he fought with one arm only.

The deep-eyed, bearded man in the chain-mail armor had but one hand. His right hand was missing—severed at the wrist. The only person in the midst of the slaughter and not blasted, she had observed this strange deformity with startled eyes. She had observed it when the first blow had been struck. She had observed it as she sought to thank him, and the man had vanished before her eyes. Vanished as suddenly as he had appeared.

It should be stated that these college lads probably meant no serious harm to the girl. Nothing more than a couple of hours of gaiety. That is, unless she herself had otherwise wished it.

At heart they were young gentlemen.

She was not going to be submitted to a "fate worse than death," as the old-time melodramas phrased it.

But it should be forgiven gallant Hugh de St. Omer that he did not know this. He was just a simple-minded soldier. And remember, he had lived his earthly life in a rough and violent Age.

In his day, the forcible seizure and abduction of a woman meant only one thing.

It is perhaps fortunate that this gentleman left behind in Paradise—so hasty was his departure to this scene—his faithful and trusty two-handed sword!

And that night, up at the Early Gothic Room of the Cloisters in the northern tip of Manhattan, City of New York, the breast of the La Celle statue did not turn red. Or even a slight pink. Rather (if Guard O'Rourke had been there) he would have observed a slow smile that became almost laughter.

That a group of college lads, even though several of them were six-foot members of the varsity crew, should think for a moment that they could compete in battle witth a veteran of Odessa—of Damascus—doubtless aroused the risibilities of even an image of stone!

So our Lady of the Statue, despite her customary serious view of the life on this planet, permitted herself the luxury of laughter.

❖ 11 ❖

THE NEW OPERETTA reached New York. I will not attempt to create suspense as to the outcome of that endeavor. It ran that season and the next. Two solid years.

Musical plays with scores by Mr. Rudolf Friml and produced by Mr. Florenz Ziegfeld had a way of doing that sort of thing.

It is human nature to take life easily, to coast along, when all goes well, and there is a sure salary envelope each Saturday.

Stanislaus Joseph did, however, work each day on his symphony. He had a new idea about it all—it would be a musical progression from the Old World to the New. From old Vienna to new New York. He discarded all he had written before. He spent weeks on single passages.

His wide knowledge of music was such that he had to be careful he did not unconsciously copy something written by another composer. Sometimes he wrote pages that seemed very fine. The girl thought them fine. Then he would discover that they were like a little known composition by Brahms.

"But there are only eight notes in the scale!" Olga would say. "If you count the half tones—five more. What if it is a little like something else? Most of the songs I have learned sound a little like something else! I'll bet that Johannes Brahms had in his head music that was written before his time—and that he sometimes borrowed it, with the added touch of his own genius."

"That may do for other writers, but not for your husband," said Stanislaus Joseph. "What I compose must be entirely my own. Mine and yours. I must be honest in my work or I could not put my name to it. I will find another way to express that passage." And carefully worked out pages would be destroyed, and a new start made.

And sometimes, as she listened to her husband playing intricate strains and strange harmonies, the girl's level mind became a little concerned about the practical value of it all.

Even when it was finished, would it be understood? Would he find a publisher? Would he be able to persuade some important symphonic orchestra conductor to play it? Wouldn't it be better if the young composer started with something less involved, something with more of what her humble Wilkes-Barre voice teacher had called "the melodic line"?

Why couldn't her duszka write just a song?

The idea came to her in the middle of the night. She suddenly sat up in bed.

"That's it! That's it!" she cried, and switched on the light just above the bed headpiece.

Stanislaus Joseph, awakened from a sound sleep, sat up also. He was alarmed. "My darling, what is wrong!" he said.

"Duszka," said the girl with great earnestness, and then she suddenly stopped. A new difficulty occurred to her. A song was not just music. Unlike a symphony, it must have words. Often the words came first. Shakespeare's lyric for the *Sylvia* of Franz Schubert. Lord Alfred Tennyson's *Sweet and Low* which became a beautiful lullaby.

But whether first or last, *words* were an essential part of the composition. And much as she admired her young husband's talent, there was no indication that he was also a poet—or even a rhymester.

And so the inspiration in her face died, and she shook her head and switched out the light.

"Nothing. Nothing," she said. "I thought I had a new great idea for you. But it wasn't as good as I thought it was. Maybe I'll tell you tomorrow. Tonight—I'm just glad that you are you, and that I found you out of all the world."

Here was a thing he had not fully realized. The girl worried about him—*about his work.* He must accomplish something to make her proud of him. He knew that she wished this, not for her sake, but for his. But her anxiety was there. He must redouble his efforts about the symphony.

Aloud he said: "You must stop worrying about me. And maybe you are tired of these performances every day—tomorrow we have two of them. I am earning enough for both of us. I could arrange for you to have a vacation——"

Manlike, he had made an entirely wrong suggestion. So seldom does a man really comprehend an utter devotion. (He is just as stupid in the comprehension of feminine treachery.) The girl said:

"Hush, hush. I love my work. Maybe I'll get a chance to go on some night in the understudy role Mr. Dixon has been so kind as to rehearse me in. I just wish you didn't have to play every night, after working all day on your symphony."

"I'd miss the nightly playing," said the boy. "And I am near you—can look up at you."

And held close in his arms, they both forgot, for some moments, all else but their eternal devotion.

12

BUT HAVING THOUGHT of this idea of Stanislaus Joseph writing a song, the girl could not banish it from her active day-time thoughts.

Perhaps she could think of some great poem suitable for a song, and not yet set to music. As Kipling's *Road to Mandalay* had been scored. Or Ben Jonson's immortal *Drink to Me Only with Thine Eyes.* She threw her memory back to her High School days, and tried to recollect some verse that could be used. But the stanzas she could recollect were all too lengthy. Or were not suitable for a ballad. And the stories they told were of long ago.

The girl wanted to find something for the present. Something that would touch folk *now.* Something—and she was not ashamed to think of it in that way—that would have a chance of becoming popular. That would, in fact, bring in royalties. The low influence, doubtless, of the five-and-dime. But there it was! A small-part girl in their show had written a popular song, and it was selling—being sung on the radio. Phonograph records were being made of it.

That week, Stanislaus Joseph was doing some outside orchestral arranging at a radio station (work obtained through his Union), and Olga went to the public library and pored over Keats and Shelley and Browning and Ella Wheeler Wilcox.

She could not find just what she wanted.

And suddenly, one day, in a flash, it came to her. Why not? If another girl in that Ziegfeld show could do it—surely she could. At the least, she could try.

As a young girl in High School, even in Grammar School, she had written little verses for the school paper. She had once sent a "poem" to the Wilkes-Barre *Times-Leader* and it had been published. The paper had paid her seven dollars for it! She did not think that she could compose the music—but maybe she could write words. *The words of a song!* And Stanislaus Joseph would set those words of hers to musical notes!

And she had an idea as to what to write about—something that concerned her duszka.

So the young man presently noticed his wife industriously scribbling on sheets of paper—crossing out words—adding new words. She did not volunteer what she was doing, and he did not ask. She would tell him when she wished to tell him.

And after about a week she did tell him. One afternoon when they were both at home, she looked up at him—he was at the Steinway deep in the intricacies of the newest *allegro* movement of his new symphony—page 72—and said:

"Duszka, did you ever think of just writing the music for a song? For just what I am afraid you would call a popular song? You know it might be easier and quicker to get a simple song before the public. I've—" and she took her courage in her hands and swallowed hard, "I've written the words for one, and it is *you*."

"About me!" said Stanislaus Joseph, looking up from his piano bench. "So that's what you have been frowning over, with all those sheets of paper, the past weeks! No wonder you're making lines on that lovely forehead, and if that's what it's all about, you must stop.

"I can think of nothing more futile or indeed impossible than to write a song about *me*. Unless it's a comic song, and I don't think you're going to make fun of me just yet a while. Songs must have beauty—romance—adventure—qualities that I am absolutely lacking in, as I well know."

He turned to his manuscript music on the piano before him and continued, "Now listen to this, darling, and see if you think it's good. I don't pretend it has beauty or romance—but maybe there is adventure. I think I've at last found an entirely new progression."

And he played for the girl a short passage of strange harmonies that did indeed have a fascination, but was not likely to make any "hit parade."

"You are the most beautiful and the most romantic man in the whole world," said the girl with a smile, "and I think you are the most talented musician in all New York—except perhaps our Mr. Friml who gave us the lovely songs in our show. But even Mr. Friml has someone else write the words for his music—Brian Hooker, Otto

Harbach, Oscar Hammerstein—and while I'm just a hopeless amateur, I've dared to write down some words. It's a song about the way you think about a certain thing."

"If it's how I think about you, there might be beauty and romance," said Stanislaus Joseph. "The great German poet, Heinrich Heine, wrote a song I learned in school. Robert Schumann set the words to music. The first two lines were:

Du bist wie eine Blume,
So hold und schön—und rein,

In English it says: 'You are so like a flower, So fair and pure and bright.' Only Herr Heine's song goes on to tell that 'sadness comes, when the poet looks at his love.'

"I don't feel sad when I look at you, my blessed one. You have brought me only joy and happiness."

"I'm afraid I'm not the great poet Mr. Heine was," said the girl, "but I did get part of my idea from flowers. From looking at our window boxes——"

"Then, if it's about me, it won't be true at all," laughed Stanislaus Joseph. "It is you who love the flowers and take care of them. It is you who thought of having them. I can't even remember their proper names!"

"I know," smiled the girl. "You'd rather have a perpetual sunset in each window, or a New York harbor skyline. Or maybe just a nice, big, beautiful Manhattan garbage can! To please you, duszka, I had thought of planting what we call sunflowers—but they bloom at the top of stems six feet tall, and I don't think the man underneath would let us move our boxes to his window for starting those stems. He's already complained about my plant watering.

"My song doesn't say you are like a flower, which please God you are not! It's what you said that morning, over a year ago, when the show was being tried in Philadelphia, and we woke up, looking out at that kind hotel clerk's garden wall.

"Remember that morning? My song is about how—Oh, I'm bad at explaining things. Here it is. It isn't, of course, exactly the way you would say it. I'm afraid it's the way what they would call a Tin Pan Alley songwriter would say it. But the Tin Pan Alley songs get popular and make money. They give happiness to lots of people.

"I hope—I hope you won't dislike it too much, my duszka."

This is what the girl had written on her several sheets of paper. Written in her round, firm, school-girl handwriting. The same handwriting that had been on that song sheet at that first Ziegfeld chorus audition, and which the boy had so desperately memorized.

Song For My Duszka
entitled
"Bungalow on Broadway"
By Olga Halka

Verse

Yes—I've heard about "the cottage in the dell"
With the "rambling roses" and the "wishing well"—
When I'm rich I think I'll build another kind.
I'm a city guy—with something on my mind!

Refrain

I'll build my Bungalow on Broadway
Right close up to Old Times Square!
Where the lark song's made by taxis—
(Honk! Honk!)
Motor buses scent the air.
I want to gaze out on a garden
Where sweet subway kiosks grow—
And instead of flapping roosters
Let me hear the newsmen crow!
(Extra! Extra!)
I'll thrill to buildings reaching skyward!
No dull mountain tops for me.
And a Sanitation sprinkler
Is my idea of the sea.
Give me noise and smells and laughter—
Give me crowds all night—all day!
And I'll need no other Heaven
If my Bungalow's—Broadway!

2nd Refrain

I'll build my Bungalow on Broadway
Where the Automats are near!
(Click! Click!)
You can take your babbling brooklets—
Just draw me a blessed beer!
(Here's how!)
And those so-called "moonlight evenings"—
Stars that mess around the sky—

(Twinkle! Twinkle!)
I prefer to watch the bright lights
And a blimp that's soaring by!
(Drink Pepsi!)
Give me lawns of nice dry concrete—
No damp greensward dew for me!
And the traffic poles with street-signs
(Next stop—42nd Street!)
Are much nobler than a tree.
(Strain of *Trees*)
Some may like to hear the crickets—
Give me jazz bands—moanin' low—
(Band effect)
And a girl who loves the city
(boy)
For my Broadway Bungalow!

Dr. Stanislaus Joseph Halka read the song lyric. The girl watched him fearfully. Would he be hurt by her audacity in putting his thoughts (as it were) into a Broadway jargon?

He did love the city passionately. Everything and all things about the great, hurrying, noisy town. But she guessed that "jazz bands moanin' low" would not exactly be his choice of city music!

The New York music that her husband liked was the occasional Sunday-night symphony orchestra recital at Carnegie—the playing of some great violinist (vivid memories of his own first appearance there as an accompanist!) or a talented performer on his own instrument—the pianoforte.

And the sweeping, tug-filled Harbor, and not a "Sanitation sprinkler" was his idea of *La Mer*. And as for the line about "traffic poles being nobler than trees——"

The little man at his piano read the song verses through a second time. Then he got up, went over and kissed the girl he loved more than life. Almost more than the music that had been his life up until the time he had found her.

How could he make her understand that other love of his—his deep love of fine music? His doubtless completely old-fashioned idea that music should only be coupled with great thoughts.

"Duszka," he said, "it is clever verse. It does say, in its way, what I feel. But I would not want to set it to music, even if I could. There is, I know, a strange, new kind of music in the city noises—the taxicabs—the street cars—the subways—the garbage wagons even. There is a music in the giant buildings and the electric signs. Someday, perhaps, I can write a symphony about all that. About the soul of the city. I know that it is stupid and dull of me to feel this way about my music; but music, as I feel it, should only be used to express the greatest of emotions. It should uplift as well as entertain.

"I'll tell you something that may sound hopelessly fatal for a professional musician to feel—I never liked the organs in motion picture houses; organs used with the 'soap operas' (as they call them) on the radio; organs on the crime programs. The instrument made great by Bach, by Handel, belongs in a more important place. In great cathedrals. In the concert hall. In a village church or in a city attic—if there is a reverence there for tonal beauty and inspiring harmony. I'm afraid I even feel that way about the pianoforte.

"To be sure, I have often had to make my living by playing music of little consequence. I was not ungrateful for those jobs. I thank God for them, especially as they led me to the finding of you. And I do not mean the lovely music I now play at Mr. Ziegfeld's theater.

"Rudolf Friml has the gift of great melody. He is probably the greatest living composer of pure melody. Some of his songs will be sung as long as songs are sung. But I do not have that gift, which was also given to Franz Schubert, to Schumann, to Liszt, to the American Victor Herbert.

"When Mr. Friml has to compose a whole long operetta he must put in some light, inconsequential music. But then comes a great inspired melody. *Toujours L'amour. The Indian Love Call. Only A Rose. Waltz Huguette.* And the lyrics of those songs are real poetry.

"I am glad that Mr. Ziegfeld was producing such an operetta when I came to him, and not a so-called revue.

"So, someday, I hope that I can both earn a living and write a noble music. A music that might gain the approving nod of Debussy, of Mozart, of Franz Liszt.

"Perhaps that is a wild dream, but it is my dream. I can only try—and keep on trying. Can you forgive me, duszka,—your stupid, old-fashioned husband who maybe lives in an impossible dream-world of ideals? Without those ideals I would not worship you as I do. And I do worship you, as I think you know."

So the girl who had been Olga Lasenka took back her "Bungalow on Broadway" song. She was disappointed, but she understood.

"Maybe—someday—I can write a song lyric that you will care to set to music," she said very seriously. "I shall try—someday. When I have read more and studied more, and heard more fine music. I will try. I promise you I will try."

Dr. Stanislaus Joseph Halka was to remember that promise. Remember it and seize upon it at the supreme moment of his life.

And the song about a "Broadway Bungalow" was also to play its humble part in their life story.

✣13✣

BUT THAT DAY Stanislaus Joseph returned to the intricate harmonies of his symphony. And the girl to her household tasks and her voice lessons. For he had insisted that she take voice lessons from a teacher he had found—and whose methods he approved.

She took four lessons a week, on the four days on which there were no matinees.

The girl liked to "keep house." The two rooms and its kitchen were spotless. She lovingly washed his shirts, even his socks and underwear, although the young man protested, and tried to have that latter task for his own selfish masculine satisfaction—the same as he had gloried in it for years.

"I may fall short of knowing all there is to know about music," he said, "but when it comes to sock-washing, I lay claim to being the world's greatest expert!"

"You're just a schoolboy amateur about it," the girl replied. "I thought my father held the booby prize in sock-washing, but it passed on to you years ago!

"*You* have been using the same soap you use on your face; you don't know how to hang them to dry properly; you never iron them —and as for your sock-darning, you haven't even graduated from kindergarten! I find black socks darned with tan wool, and tan with black. And the lumps! It's a wonder your feet are not covered with big blisters!

"And those patches on your B. V. D.'s! I've thrown all those in the ragbag and you'll find new ones in your drawer. If Mr. Ziegfeld even guessed how you looked underneath your famous tight, broadcloth pants, I'm sure he would never have hired you! A Ziegfeld production indeed!"

"Mr. Ziegfeld glorifies his girls—not his accompanists," laughed Tightpants, but he submitted meekly to this out-of-sight refurbishing, although the expertness of that patching had been a source of much secret pride.

The laundry and suit-pressing industry of Madison Avenue and environs was also dealt a body blow. The girl bought a long, collapsible ironing board. She delighted to starch and iron his stiff open collars. She pressed his trousers.

And she especially enjoyed cooking for him—to surprise him sometimes with a new Polish way of fixing a dessert, or making a gravy for the meat.

It was an event the night she served potatoes which he thought were simply browned whole, without the skins, and they were so utterly delicious that he ate a whole plate of them!

"Where in the world do they grow potatoes like these?" he had exclaimed.

Then she told him what she had done. Cooked them, mashed them with milk and butter and a little pepper and a touch of garlic. Then moulded the mass into small, potato-like shapes and dipped these shapes in a bowl of beaten eggs and flour and cream, and finally fried the ovals from Heaven in a very hot skillet well greased with bacon fat.

Tightpants had an expression, "You can't buy food like this at a drug store!" A not too happy memory of too many flavorless meals at pharmaceutical counters.

On Sundays they both felt entitled to a holiday—he from his symphony writing, she from her cooking and laundry and pants pressing.

They would sleep late, then go to eleven o'clock Mass at the little church where they had been married. After the church service, they would have a combination breakfast and lunch at some small restaurant. And in the afternoons—some one of the many pleasures New York folk can enjoy: pleasures that have little or no cost.

They went often to the Metropolitan Museum.

It always amazed Tightpants that while New Yorkers who had been abroad had immediately rushed to the Palace of the Louvre and spent hours there; found the National Galleries and the Tate Museum in London and, guide book in hand, gaped at the pictures and manuscripts; yet they had never been inside their own free storehouses of art treasures!

He especially liked to wander in the rooms of the Frick Collection, housed in the beautiful town house of its founder, that Pittsburgh steel molder who loved fine paintings and fine furniture. For its treasures were on a single floor, so that one did not tire from the mere mileage of journeying from gallery to gallery.

It still seemed to be what it really was—the private home of a hospitable, kindly gentleman, who beamed a welcome from his life-size painting over the fireplace of his library.

Stanislaus Joseph was always finding beautiful paintings of females that he said reminded him of the girl.

In this mansion it was the Romney "Lady Hamilton," the amazing, tragic lady who was a blacksmith's daughter, became the Ambassadress to Naples and the mistress of Lord Nelson. And finally died in poverty at Calais in 1815. He said she had his Olga's sad smile; and the blue and silver bands across her hair reminded him of Olga's braids.

And to make amends for seeing her likeness in a somewhat notorious beauty, he also likened Olga to a saintly figure in a small gilded religious panel by the monk Fra Filippo Lippi; for here, the lady painted in the year 1400 had a golden halo, and was the angel bringing the Annunciation message to Mary, Mother-To-Be of our Blessed Lord.

Not to be outdone in the matter of gallant detection, the girl found a figure she was certain was like her "Tightpants Duszka." The Rembrandt called "The Polish Rider." Tightpants laughed when Olga stood him before this painting, and tried to point out a similitude.

"Number one—I was never on a horse in my life," the lad said. "Number two—this young Polish adventurer is a vision of daring and courage. That's hardly me!"

"It is exactly you!" said the girl. "The horse is simply a symbol. It represents your music. The sheath of arrows are your pens. And as for daring and courage—didn't you have the courage to put me into the Ziegfeld finals after I'd been turned down—didn't you dare, before that, to go to the immaculate Mr. Ziegfeld for your own job, with patches on your B. V. D.'s!"

Tightpants laughed. "Shall I show you who I think is really me in this museum?" he said. "Yes. I think I will. I found this lad a long time ago—my first visit here. And he's still here, I'm sure."

So he took the girl to a corner of the room, where hung the great Goya called "The Forge."

"But there are three figures in it," she said. "Which one are you?"

"I hope I don't yet look like the old man peeping out around the stalwart about to swing down the huge hammer," said Stanislaus Joseph. "And I fear I'm not muscular enough to be that blacksmith with his sturdy legs and hips—so sturdy even, they are bursting from the knee breeches and the drooping stockings. And that bared, strength-bulging left arm, and the fist that holds the hammer—no. Not your duszka.

"I'm just the scared little guy—as they would say around the theater—holding the piece of metal in place on the anvil before the hammer crashes down, and pretty fearful and suspicious about it all. Maybe that hammer will come down on his hands! Or head.

"That's how I used to feel the world was waiting to get a good free-arm whack at me and my symphony composing—felt before I met you," he added.

And that was the only time the girl ever heard Stanislaus Joseph speak of fear. She was more certain than ever that her husband was a brave and gallant gentleman—like the Polish Rider—even if he had never been astride a horse! And she told herself that she must never fail him in encouragement about his music—the kind of music he felt he must try to write.

She was to have a problem in that matter sooner than she thought.

Some Sundays, when the weather was fine, they simply walked up Fifth Avenue and looked at the windows of the great stores. They felt there was often as much Art in the figures and arrangement of those windows as in the museums.

Stanislaus Joseph was always fascinated by the mannequin figures in their gorgeously smart dresses and curiously alluring postures. He would have been afraid to stare at a real woman as he did at these figures. They somehow satisfied his male interest in feminine beauty and attire and seduction. And did he not now possess, as his very own, the most beautiful girl in the world!

"There are your only rivals," he would say to the girl at his side. "I think I would be afraid of any other live lady but you!

"When I first came to New York there was a mannequin in the

window at Russek's—I first saw her in a Russian outfit—furs it was—I was told it was called Persian Lamb—I followed her through all the seasons' changes falling deeper and deeper in love—she was very, very fascinating also in a Palm Beach bathing suit—but one sad day she was gone——"

"Maybe she married the boss's son and retired," laughed the girl.

"Something like that," said Stanislaus Joseph. "I was quite desolate for a while. Till I found another girl in a window of Arnold Constable's. Now, it is really you that I see in all these striking costumes. Just as I see you in every fine painting. I can only wonder that you are satisfied with a man as ordinary as I am."

"I certainly would not trade you for any of the figures I see in the men's furnishing store-windows!" laughed the girl.

And seriously: "I think you know that it is just you that I desire. I knew it when I first looked at you—your funny, dear face at the Ziegfeld audition. I knew it when I looked up from my weeping, and saw the back of your trousers standing at the shelf they call a desk at the Hotel L'Esplanade-Plaza. Where in the world did its owners find that name?

"When I hear the boy-friend troubles—the husband-troubles—of the other girls in the big chorus dressing room—*Gee! How lucky I am!* I say to myself."

Sometimes on Sundays they attended High Mass at St. Patrick's. The boy loved the music from the fine organ, and the color and pomp of the service against the great, towering altar, often with a red-robed Cardinal seated on his high-backed throne at one side.

After the service, they would step across the Avenue into Radio City. Watch (in the Winter) the skaters skimming around the sunken ice-pond; or in the Summer sit on the low stone borders of the gardens, and presently (if the young man had earned extra money that week) have their luncheon under one of the green and white umbrellas that transformed the now macadam-floored, skating pond into an open air restaurant.

And when they were finished, they would gaze up at the sight just behind them, a sight not equalled anywhere else in the world unless one could stand at the very base of Mount Everest!

That great, central Rockefeller Center skyscraper—then just completed—that really does "scrape the sky" with its seventieth story, building-wide pinnacle. No phoney, synthetic "tower" here, to make for an alleged height.

This modern Tower of Babel, (*Gate of God,* the word really means in the Assyrian), not ending in a jagged, uncompleted confusion but in a smooth, level, completed *unity*.

A poem of steel and glass and concrete, that amazes all foreign-born from cities where eight to ten stories is the legal height of any structure, except a church.

The workmen who made it—its true builders?

Catholics, Protestants, Jews, perhaps a Hindu and a Mohammedan—black men and brown men and white men; men of all faiths and colors and language—but of a single courage and determination and freedom that is named *America*.

Or these two would journey a few more blocks northward, where they could sit on the rim of a fountain in a broad Square that might be of Paris or Rome, with its stately buildings on three sides, and the park named Central to the north, bringing rural greenery and brown rocks and shining lakes to the very heart of the city.

Of course they went often to the Cloisters. And there (as witnessed to by Guard Dennis O'Rourke), the Lady of the Statue continued to truly smile at least once each day.

A period of content and happiness for Mr. and Mrs. Tightpants Halka.

PART TEN

THE DEATH

1

THE FINAL NEW YORK PERFORMANCE of a great theatrical entertainment—its Death, so to speak—is at the same time an evening of both gaiety and sadness.

A "great show" of course will never die. The next season it will go on tour. It will afterwards be produced by the many Summer companies—usually in the open air—of various cities. Its music will live via the radio and the concert hall. Some of its songs will live forever.

But that last performance of the original production in New York is the death of an inspired effort—a perfection of beauty of scenery and costumes and lighting, a perfection in the casting of the various roles, that will never again be quite equaled.

James Reynolds' costumes, Richard Boleslavsky's direction, the *Villon* of Dennis King, are never quite duplicated.

And no matter how great its New York success, this Saturday night, that is the last, will come.

For many of the players, this New York closing—even after two solid years—is a dire financial tragedy. For on the following Saturday there is no Saturday matinee and night, between which the company business manager sits at his little table back-stage, and passes out small, brown salary envelopes.

There may not be salary envelopes for many, many Saturdays to come.

Theater folk are children. In spite of knowledge and past experience, they live up to that weekly salary envelope, as if it would go on forever. Living expenses outside the theater land-of-make-believe do, unhappily, go on forever, whether the show does or does not. Rent and sustenance cannot be eliminated until the next and often distant engagement.

Such money difficulties did not face Olga and Stanislaus Joseph Halka on that final New York Saturday night of this Ziegfeld production.

The girl had managed to save at least a part of their joint earnings—save close to seventy-five dollars a week. She could have saved much more, but Tightpants insisted that she take the weekly voice lessons with the best teacher he could find. These lessons cost thirty dollars per week.

He insisted that she buy herself some new clothes, and buy them often. Olga told him she had found a bargain place on Fourteenth Street, but her young husband would have none of it.

"My wife is going to be dressed as nicely as any girl in the company," he said. "With both of us working, I won't have the other girls—and the men—thinking I am too stingy to buy you the very best of clothes. And anyway—I want you to have the best."

So she had dresses from Bergdorf-Goodman's, shoes from Miller's, and when cold weather came, a beautiful fur coat from Russeks.

Tightpants partly paid for this latter with extra money he had made by music copying. The conductor of the Ziegfeld Theater had recommended his work to a radio program producer, and the pianist received some five hundred dollars for a couple of rush jobs, which he did in a part of his spare time.

"It's my misfortune to be married to the most beautiful girl in New York—in all America!" he smiled. "She must have clothes to match. It's your fault entirely. You should not have such a lovely figure and be so good looking!"

And while the girl's saving nature fought this "outrageous extravagance," she was secretly pleased that her husband took such pride in her. What young wife would not be?

And the clothes expenditures—the "outrageous" expenditures—were not entirely at his insistence.

She made the little man buy a new supply of the white, pleated shirts he liked so well—shirts made up to his order—and the stiff, open-faced wing collars to match. She took three weeks of her own salary to get him new cuff links—platinum, set with small chip diamonds. Those, she said, were her wedding present to him—her Polish dowry—of which she had been unfortunately lacking at the time of their marriage.

And shortly after the first Christmas, when he had a windfall of some more radio copying and orchestration work, the girl had thought up an immediate and absurd (in the opinion of Stanislaus Joseph) use for it.

One of the Ziegfeld "Members of the Ensemble" had a boy friend —a Wall Street broker (so it was reliably reported) who would call for her each night in a great Cadillac. This man was a "swell dresser" as well as a "down-town big shot"—to quote the other girls—and Olga pried from the show girl the name of her gentleman friend's tailor.

It was a most exclusive shop, hidden away in an office building in the upper Fifth Avenue district (most exclusive as to prices also), but the girl Olga made Stanislaus Joseph go there—the name was Gellman Ltd.—for three new suits of clothes. They were styled in the tight, broadcloth trousers and the silk-faced black coats like his precious Vienna-made suits. In fact, the older brother of this custom establishment, Ed Gellman, had learned his trade in Vienna—knew exactly what the young man desired.

Even Burg-Theater actor, Herr Otto Woltner, could have found no fault with these successors to his original, personally supervised, Viennese creations.

The girl also had Stanislaus have fitted a new tuxedo to wear in the orchestra pit at night. And a new black Homburg from Knox that cost thirty dollars. The young man wanted to take one for ten, but the girl, who bargained for every penny in her household buying along Third Avenue, would not hear of it.

"I can't have people around the theater thinking I made you spend all your money on me!" she laughed. "And if your friends back in Austria could send you to the best tailor, I'll not have them hearing that I made you go to a cut-rate clothing-chain store! What would they think of me!

"Besides," she added, "someday you're going to do something wonderful. I feel it! Become famous over night. All the newspaper photographers and the news reel men will be around to snap your picture. There just won't be time then to have new clothes made. You must be ready for it!"

"I will want nice clothes the night I sit in the pit, or maybe in the audience, and watch your debut as a great prima donna," he said. So his scanty and somewhat worn wardrobe was replenished, along with hers.

But the career "breaks" that they both dreamed of, did not seem to happen.

The girl had an understudy part of the ingenue role in the operetta. With the other understudies she rehearsed this part every two weeks. It meant five dollars more per week in her pay envelope, but the principal player for whose role she was the protection seemed to need no "protecting." Seemed to have a cast-iron constitution and a cold-proof larynx. The lady never missed a performance.

Stanislaus Joseph struggled with his symphony—composed and re-composed. Never entirely satisfied with it.

Only in their complete devotion to each other did their lives seem (and were indeed) complete.

Who shall say this was not really the greater achievement? The greater consummation.

✣ 2 ✣

So came the final week of the New York run, late in June, almost two full years from its beginning.

And at the end of that final performance it was to be the task of the humbler folk of the company and the working crew to provide an entertainment. A "company party" (with refreshments), to take place on the stage of the theater immediately after the final curtain had descended and the final paying audience had departed; New Yorkers to their homes; out-of-towners (including Hollywood luminaries) to the night spots.

The audience for this party entertainment would be the principal players, the entire companies of the several rival musical plays then running, and the staff of the Ziegfeld organization, including the great producer himself.

Merriment was to be the keynote of the proceedings. Merriment and a friendly, finger-pointing satire.

For Mr. Ziegfeld would laugh the loudest when a tall, not unpersonable stagehand, dressed exactly like the producer in the typical light-colored tweeds and contrasting dark lavender shirt, "interviewed" the famous prima donna, counterfeited by the broad and hefty head wardrobe mistress; and when this lady tried to explain that she had studied voice with DeReszke and Emma Eames demanded, "Voice—hell! How are your legs? Come back tomorrow in a one-piece bathing suit."

Mr. Friml would applaud and chuckle as the stage manager, made-up as the great composer, could not write a love aria without three shapely chorus girls seated above him on top of an upright rehearsal piano, and his counterpart demanded that skirts be lifted "a little higher" to provide a proper inspiration.

Mr. Reynolds would cry "Bravo!" as another stagehand of slight build and attired in the black derby and the pearl-grey gloves that the designer fancied, tore an offending dress from a girl at the horrified costumer's, because its color was "robin's egg blue," not "hen's egg white," as he had ordered.

And the great director, Richard Boleslavsky, would collapse his two-hundred and forty pounds into the aisle when a rotund property-man, imitating his Polish accent, showed the prima donna just how to play an impassioned love scene!

And a tall Sherlock Holmes-looking chorus boy would appear as master lyricist Brian Hooker, with a Rhyming Dictionary (so it was labeled in foot-high letters) that was fully four feet square.

The chorus boys, dressed in the girls' ballet costumes, would perform their version of the great Act III ballet. A version that I doubt would have met with the approval of the late Anna Pavlova, or the directors of the late Imperial Russian Ballet.

And finally, there would come a more serious part in which the members of the chorus, the working crew, and the staff displayed talents heretofore unsuspected and undiscovered.

A chorus boy, whose hobby was "magic," revealed a mystifying agility at card tricks. Another gave quick-change imitations of leading public figures. One brought his dog, whom he had taught to howl dolorously as the master sang *Asleep in the Deep,* his pet taking the final low note with a horrifying growl.

The girls mostly sang—seriously or comically—and it was here that Olga Halka had been persuaded to attempt a thing that she did with much misgiving. Almost with fear and trembling. Because, for the first time since their marriage, she had done something that she had not discussed with Stanislaus Joseph. Something which she had kept from his knowledge.

It should be explained that stage manager Dixon had met frustration not only in holy matrimony, but in the equally bewildering domain of music. Unlike Stanislaus Joseph, he wanted to write songs. To write *a song*. A popular song. Even a low-down, popular song.

Although considered the best musical-show stage manager in America, he was no graduate *cum laude* (or *sans laude*) of any Academy of Music. He had never taken a music lesson in his life. He "played the piano" by ear—in one key only. But then—so he had heard—did the great Irving Berlin. He had composed numerous "tunes" in the above mentioned key—for his own amazement, as he said—but one might have noted a trace of sadness in his jest.

He would have liked to "amaze" others also.

His difficulty was the matter of words.

He was not a Master Poet. And though "in the business," and knowing a number of lyric writers, he had had no luck in inducing them to set words to his tunes. Or to permit him to set tunes to their words.

Unfairly enough, they all preferred to work with piano players like Mr. Friml, or Victor Herbert, or Hugo Felix, or Jerome Kern, or Sigmund Romberg. Also there was the obstacle that these professionals were usually under contract to write only with certain professional wielders of words.

So tune-writer Russ Dixon's melodies were born, languished and died (so to speak) on the inspirational vine.

His newest candidate for wife Number Four (and the reason for the urgency of a divorcement from Number Three, who had recently eloped with that lowest form of theatrical worker—a tenor), this newest charmer, sat next to Olga Halka at one of the long, chorus make-up tables. They became friends.

Like many another more experienced writer, Olga Halka had felt the need of friendly criticism even before showing her "Broadway Bungalow" lyric to Stanislaus Joseph. Did not the great Molière first read his plays to his cook? So when she had written this verse weeks before, she had read it to her theater make-up neighbor.

Unlike Olga's husband, this show girl thought it "swell." That her interest and praise was sincere was evinced when she several times solicitously inquired about its fate.

Olga Halka had been evasive. "Her husband was very occupied with other work." "He was in the midst of writing a fine symphonic composition."

But this men-wise chorus girl suspected the truth. At least, the basic truth, that Olga's husband did not wish to "set" the song.

"Husbands are all alike," she said. "Selfish pains-in-the-neck. I know. I've had two already. They don't give a wife credit for any talent. Take me. I was married first to a circus acrobat. That dope could have made me famous as a slack-wire performer. Did he? I give you three guesses! I just rode an elephant in the Opening Parade, and was the Sultan's Favorite in the Pageant of History. I've told our stage manager flat that if he wants to get anywhere with me, he's got to land me a part in a show. Then I might agree to marry him—that is, if he can get his divorce, and I can get mine."

Olga Halka did not attempt to explain that Stanislaus Joseph's reluctance to compose music for her verse was based on a somewhat higher plane than wife discrimination. And she realized the girl did not really think Stanislaus Joseph a "selfish pain-in-the-neck"—that this description was a generality, resulting from a life of disillusionment about the genus male. So the matter was glossed over and forgotten.

But when the preparation for this final-performance party was under way, this girl remembered.

"Look, Olga," she said, "You never did nothin' with that Bungalow Song of yours, did you?"

"No, I didn't," said the girl who had been Olga Lasenka, and there was a noticeable shading of regret in her tone. But she quickly added, "I guess maybe it wasn't as good as we thought it was. I'm trying to write something more poetic——"

"More poetic my eye!" said the Ziegfeld girl. "That lyric was good. It was better than good. It was swell! And I've got a plan about it."

"What kind of plan?" asked Olga Halka weakly. For in spite of her respect for Stanislaus Joseph's opinions, she had liked her little old "Bungalow" verse.

"A terrif, whamming good plan," said the Ziegfeld girl, with true *Variety* emphasis. "Mr. Dixon is putting together a show for all of us to give after the last performance, a week from Saturday. He can write music. Not music like Mr. Friml's, or the music you tell me your husband composes, but it's whoop-de-doo and sockeroo catchy.

Let Mr. Dixon set your verse! It's right up his avenue! Smart and topical. Then he plays it, and you sing it, as your stunt at this party. I'll bet it makes the wham-bam hit of the night!"

The temptation was overwhelming. *Her own little song—with music—and she could sing it right out on a real stage! Just a private party to be sure, but there would be an audience there to hear it—*

"But—but—" Olga commenced.

"Mr. Ziegfeld will be at the party," said the temptingly wise chorus girl.

"My husband will be there also," said Olga Halka. Her tone expressed apprehension.

"Oh God!" said the other girl, and the exclamation denoted anything but alarm. "Listen, kid," she expounded. "You're still young. He's your first, isn't he? I thought so. When, like yours-truly, you've had a couple of those louses cluttering up your bed, you'll stop worrying about what husbands think!"

"But I love my husband," said Olga Halka.

"Sure you do," said the other girl. "I loved mine too. Both of them. Else I wouldn't have married 'em, the dopes! My second was a real gentleman, like yours. Swell dresser, on and off. He was in pictures at Fort Lee. Did he get me a job in them 'silents'? Not on your life! I had to work in burlesque that season. And I would have been swell as the 'menace' in them *Perils of Pauline!*"

A sentimental recollection momentarily softened her voice. "But he *did* shave every morning. And kept his nails manicured and trimmed the hairs out of his ears. I couldn't get that stupid acrobat to shave only twice a week. Don't ever marry no guy what won't shave. A sure sign he's not a gentleman. Now that's one nice thing about our stage manager. I've noticed that he shaves."

"But—but suppose, in spite of daily shaving, Mr. Dixon doesn't want to set my words to music," said the sorely tempted, but still hesitant Olga.

"He'll want to set it *or else!*" said the husband expert. "I ain't yet said that I'll marry him. Listen. He'll set it, and jump out of his pants to do it. Ain't he goin' around in circles tryin' to find a lyric writer? *Me. This show. A lyric writer.* Them are his life passions now. . . . Come on, kid! Take a chance. And I don't think you'll lose your man. I've seen enough of your Mr. Tightpants around this show to know he's a real high-class gent. No louse, like some I've known."

Olga Halka had to smile. Her friend was in such deadly earnest.

"No, my duszka is no louse," she said, "and maybe he won't mind. If I only were *sure* he wouldn't mind!"

"He'll be proud of you!" cried the girl. "And ain't he and Mr. Dixon good friends! I've noticed that too. That's one reason I'm thinkin' of takin' on Mr. Dixon as my third. He's good friends with the *nice* people around this show. Don't chum around with the half-wits and the phonies.

"Listen, kid, I've got another idea! I'll ask Mr. Dixon to ask your husband to do something at the party-show. What can he do besides just play the piano in the orchestra?"

"Why—why—" and Olga Halka also had an idea. "He plays an accordion. A friend of his here in New York says he was the best accordion player in Vienna. He played it at our wedding party."

"Swell! Swell!" cried the other girl with real enthusiasm. "I love accordion music. Everybody does. It will be just what is needed to pep up the party! After two years of a whinin' orchestra. And don't you see—your husband won't feel that he's left out of the show! He'll be a hit in it too! Only don't let him play no Mozart or Beethoven or any of those guys."

"My husband plays some wonderful Austrian folk songs," said Olga.

"That's the ticket!" cried the chorus girl, and she had an additional inspiration in this moment of great inspirations.

"All this will help in another way," she said. "You won't have to tell your husband what you are doing. Because why? Because *you are not allowed to tell him!*"

"I don't understand," said Olga Halka.

"Don't you see," said her friend, "I'll tell Mr. Dixon that your husband's accordion playing must be kept a secret. To surprise even you—his wife! And so—your song with Mr. Dixon will be kept a secret. To surprise even him.

"That's the whole idea of these parties. Surprises. Mr. Ziegfeld is going to be surprised. And Mr. Friml. No one is to know beforehand what will happen. Your husband will surprise you. You will surprise him."

So with dire misgivings, but with the thrill of the prospect of her "Broadway Bungalow" coming to life, Olga Halka let herself be persuaded to agree.

After all, Stanislaus Joseph had turned down her lyric. However high his motives, and however kindly phrased, he had turned it down. And he and the stage manager *were* good friends. Mr. Dixon could not be suspect of being, in any way, a rival for her affections.

She knew that this stage manager had helped her to get her present job, and helped her because of his instant liking for "Mr. Tightpants." For if he had disclosed, at that final audition, that he recognized her as a singer who had tried and failed at the earlier voice trials, she would not have been permitted to sing at that final trial.

This conversation between Olga Halka and the chorus girl had taken place during a Saturday matinee. The orchestra conductor asked Stanislaus Joseph to come up to the Ziegfeld office after that matinee, to play a new musical score just received from London by Mr. Ziegfeld. The score of an English success the producer was thinking of presenting in New York.

"Keep dinner open, for I'll take you to dinner afterwards, Tightpants," the conductor said. "We'll probably go with Mr. Ziegfeld himself. He will want to discuss this English score. The big boss is leaving for Hollywood the next morning after we close, to work out a picture deal about his Follies. So tell your nice wife she'll have to eat tonight on her own."

So did Fate play into the hands manipulating this daring song plan. The hands of a hard-boiled show girl, unselfishly trying to help two friends.

It was (as we know) not her fault that *husbands* were beyond the pale of her charity.

Olga Halka went to dinner between the matinee and night that Saturday, with her chorus-girl friend and the stage manager. She wrote out her lyric for Mr. Dixon. Mr. Dixon liked it. He started to hum a melody even as he was reading it for the first time.

Mr. Dixon, however, had not forgotten his friend. His masculine friend. That often inconvenient loyalty by which some men are handicapped from birth.

"What about Tightpants?" he asked.

"Tightpants turned it down," said his girl friend quickly. Too quickly, thought Mr. Dixon. He turned to Olga Halka with the question in his look.

"My husband turned it down," said Olga Halka.

Mr. Dixon, experienced with the handling of hundreds of show girls (not to mention three wives chosen therefrom) may be pardoned if he pressed the matter further. He saw in this song lyric his chance—an unexpected, heaven-sent chance—but he had a real affection for "Mr. Tightpants," and a respect for his ability as a fine musician.

"Mrs. Halka," he said, "do you give me your word that your husband really turned down the writing of the music for your song?"

Again the decision for Olga Halka was a difficult one to make. She was surely only telling the truth—and yet—. Her show girl friend had taken her hand and was pressing it hard.

"I give you my word," said the girl who had been Olga Lasenka. "He said—he said it wasn't his kind of song. I shall try to someday write a more poetic lyric that he will like. But this one——"

"O. K.," said the stage manager. "I just wanted to be sure. I like that little guy you are married to. He's tops in my book. I don't cut in on the province of my friends. But damn it all, I do like that lyric! O. K. Tightpants turned it down. O. K. Here we go to hell!"

Decision made, his enthusiasm mounted. "Just let me get at a piano! I have to pound things out on a piano. Key of F sharp. At least, that's what I think it is. Damn it, I've been searching for a lyric like that for years. Give me one short hour at a string box and I believe I'll have it! Have it for you tomorrow, kiddo. Just let me at it!"

So the fat was in the fire, so to speak. Mr. Dixon would suggest to Tightpants (as the show people knew him) that there was a rumor he could play an accordion, and that it would be a welcome novelty if he would perform on that instrument at the party. He would caution the accompanist to keep it as a surprise even from his wife. And not to play Mozart or Ludwig van Beethoven.

"Ask him to play Viennese folk songs," said Olga, as she had said before to the show girl. "They are lively. They are beautiful. I've never heard anything so fascinating."

"And I will have him do one other thing that I'm sure will please him," said the resourceful Mr. Dixon. "As an encore I'll ask him to play that *Songs My Mother Taught Me* with you singing it. That will please Mr. Ziegfeld also. Damn it to hell, this is going to be *some* party!"

Mr. Dixon made one condition. "When your husband hears our song—if he's still alive by the end of it—and if he don't like my inspired melody—if he can and will write a real one for you—I bow out. Bow out with no hard feelings. Agreed?" And he held out his hand to Olga Halka.

"Agreed," said the girl. "Gee, but you are a nice man."

"O. K., O. K. But please don't fall in love with me," said the stage manager with a smile. "My fatal Casanova attractiveness for women has gotten me into enough trouble."

It all sounded very "merry and bright," as the show girl phrased it; but the girl who had been Olga Lasenka sought out a Catholic Church off Sixth Avenue on Forty-seventh Street after the dinner, and said a most ardent and solemn prayer before the shrine of the Queen of Heaven in that church.

"Dear Holy Mother," she prayed, "please intercede for me with my duszka. For I love him more than my life. But I would so like to have my poor little song come to life. Everyone will know it is not his type of song. And if Mr. Dixon and I could get it published, I could then help him to get his finer music published. Please, most of all, don't let my singing it at the party hurt him.

"And please, Holy Mother, make the people at the party like my little song."

✣ 3 ✣

STANISLAUS JOSEPH HAD LEFT HIS ACCORDION with Hans Beuter, baker, up on York Avenue. The young, symphony-composing husband had no immediate need for it, and the energetic Hans had expressed a desire to woo the Muses (if not his neighbors) via that instrument.

"I never told you that I also started out to be a professional *musiker!*" he had said. "As a small lad I earned money in the Summer vacations by turning the organ crank on a merry-go-round in the Prater. The owner said I was the best damn crank-turner he'd ever had! Maybe it isn't yet too late for me to become a great artist! With my fine natural singing voice, if I could play an accordion with my hands and arms, and a drum with my feet, and maybe between songs a flute with my mouth, I could give a symphony concert all alone at Carnegie Hall! Whoop-*ee!*"

And the expert baker had roared with laughter at the picture he was presenting.

"I sometimes think all that is just as sensible as what I am doing," Stanislaus Joseph had said soberly.

It was during those days when he was playing for the girls' college gymnasium classes. And he thought of this as he journeyed up to

York Avenue the next Monday afternoon, while Olga was occupied with a voice lesson.

His symphony—even now—seemed to be getting more and more involved. As involved as Hans Beuter's accordion and drum and flute! He had now reached page 103. And there was no end in sight.

Well—in another week, when the Ziegfeld show closed, he would work steadily at that symphony all day and all evening. He would take in no outside copying or arranging.

He would reach the long delayed day when he could present to the world his masterpiece.

He was glad to see Hans Beuter. At four P.M. Hans was just getting up, in preparation for his all-night work at the bakery. Stanislaus Joseph had of course seen Hans since the wedding luncheon at the King of the Sea. He had bought the baker seats for the operetta several times, and several times he and Olga had taken their friend to a Sunday dinner. But the fact that the bakery employee slept during the day, and worked all night, made social get-togethers difficult.

And there was that curious geographical separation of the great city that seemed to make it more difficult to see a friend four dozen blocks away than one living in another town!

"So that nice girl hasn't thrown you out yet!" cried Hans. "Well, you'll always have a place to come to when she does. Me—I can't seem to find myself a steady girl at all. As soon as I have to tell them that I work all night and sleep all day, they leave me flat. I had my eye last month on a fine plump waitress in an all-night restaurant, and she seemed willing. But one day I find out she is a widow with six small children!"

Hans Beuter looked very comically sad as he recalled this awful discovery.

"I've come to borrow back the accordion," said Stanislaus Joseph. "Or rather—to practice a bit on it, and then borrow it for next Saturday night." And he told Hans Beuter about the stage party.

"I'll have to come here to practice," he explained, "for they want me to keep what I will do a secret, even from my wife. Everyone is to do something crazy. It's a good thing our stage manager doesn't know about a *dressiersack* or he'd have me writing something with sugar frosting on the big stage curtain!"

"And you'd write it *ausgezeichnet* swell!" said loyal Hans. "*Frohliche Fourth of July* would be the words to say now!"

And when Stanislaus Joseph had the accordion strapped to his shoulders and between his arms, an instrument he had not touched for almost two years—not indeed since his wedding day at the King of the Sea—a feeling of keen nostalgia swept over him.

Those old days in Vienna—they were not so bad! And it would be pleasant to see Professor Anton Lavar again, and his first boyhood teacher Herr Dr. Gustav Emil Meyerhoff, and his patron the bake-shop owner, and all those kind folk who lived in the old tenement. Was the old actor, the one who had been the inspiration of his fine clothes and who had supervised their making, Herr Otto Woltner, still alive? And the widow Frau Ebenstein, and the slaughterhouse worker Hans Hinterhofer?

Sitting there on York Avenue, in Hans Beuter's little room, and playing again the Viennese folk songs with their gypsy melodies—it would be *ausgezeichnet* grand to see them all once more!

Perhaps, when this Ziegfeld operetta closed, he could take a trip back—take back for a visit the girl who was now his wife! He would be so proud to show her to all those kindly people——

And then there was the legacy left him by Kommodore Hugo Frederick von Steinburg. Olga had been right about that. There had been a long delay in the settling of the complicated estate. More delay about money being sent out of Germany. Perhaps that matter could be settled at the same time.

But no. He must not return until he had accomplished something. All these people had had such a firm faith in him. The violinist Herr Viktor Reimalsky had doubtless well advertised that his accompanist had been dismissed after the first New York concert. He must have his symphony finished—finished so that he could play it in its entirety.

As Stanislaus Joseph played over the familiar folk melodies, Hans Beuter, almost as though he could read the thoughts of his friend, said: "Stanislaus, how is the symphony progressing?"

"Slowly. Slowly," said the young man. "But after this next week I shall be able to give all my time to it. Olga and I—mainly Olga—have saved some money. I won't have to do other things for a while at least."

But Hans Beuter had a reason for asking about the symphony—a form of musical endeavor that was just a name to him, but something that he feared—as did the girl Olga—was a little visionary and pretty "highbrow"; and that even when finished, might not become a credit item either in money or in fame for years to come.

Hans had, in fact, mentioned the matter of a symphony to another Austrian acquaintance of his who played traps in a jazz band, and that noise-expert had declared: "A symphony! Good Lord! A guy who writes one of them things has to be dead for a hundred years before the poor boob or his composition gets a break! Me—I can't wait that long. I got a nifty song that Rudy Vallee's going to croon."

Hans Beuter did not wish to utterly discourage his friend by such a direct quotation from the horse's mouth (as they said at a nearby pool room where he sometimes spent unprofitable afternoons instead of profitably bed-sleeping), but as he listened to Stanislaus Joseph playing the catchy folk music—and playing it exceedingly well—he had a word of advice not unlike that given by the girl Olga.

"Stanislaus Joseph," he said, "did you ever think of writing a song?"

The young musician looked at his friend suspiciously. Had he been talking with Olga? For he had not forgotten the girl's suggestion about a song, and her obvious disappointment when he did not care for her rhyme about a bungalow on Sixth Avenue. Or maybe it was Broadway. But no—there could not be any collusion. Here was just another friend trying to be helpful.

"Why do you ask me that?" said Stanislaus Joseph.

"Because I want you to be a big success as a *musiker!*" said the frank Hans. "This symphony—it's going to take a long time to get it finished—not?"

"It may take a long time," admitted Stanislaus Joseph.

"And when it is finished," persisted Hans Beuter, "maybe it will take another long time to get it published—to get it played—whatever it is you have to do about symphonies—not?"

Stanislaus Joseph had to smile. "'Not' may be the answer," he said. "But one must try. One must try to do something fine and lasting—even if you fail. Your bakeshop—you try to make only the finest cakes—not?"

But Hans Beuter replied very seriously: "A cake can be fine, even if it is just a little cake—not a great big one. When I learned the trade, I started making fine, *little cakes*—just what we call in America 'cookies' they were. But they were the best damn 'cookies' in Vienna!

"Look, Stanislaus Joseph," he continued, "our shop here in New York makes a tiny tart—a round macaroon with jelly in the middle—that sell for ten cents each. Just a couple of bites—but the shop gets ten cents for them! They are famous all over the town. We ship them out of town to customers who have moved away. We sell hundreds of them. And the big cakes—the 'symphonies'—we make them good too—but only for holidays like Easter or Christmas, or for a wedding or a birthday. The shop would soon go out of business, if it did not make the little confections."

This baker man had stated a profound truth, whether it applied to commerce or to Art.

"Hans," said Stanislaus Joseph, "maybe you are right. I have not forgotten that it was because of your advice that I went to the Musical Union, and procured my fine engagement with Mr. Ziegfeld. And my Olga—she said the same thing to me a while ago. She had even written the words of a song. And I know that I hurt her, when I would not even try to write music for those words."

"There you are!" said Hans Beuter. "I'm just a dumb baker—not?"

" 'Not' is certainly the right word here! You are far from dumb!" said Stanislaus Joseph. "I know what I will do. I shall 'not' stop working on my symphony—that must still be my big cake—my *Frohliche Ostern* cake—but when this operetta has closed, and after this closing-party is over, I'll speak to my Olga about her song. I'll see what I can do!"

"Now you're talking! Now you'll get somewhere!" cried Hans Beuter. "If you can write something half as fine as any one of those old folk songs—I wouldn't trade any one of them for all the grand symphonies ever written! You just try it and see! And I'll bet a month's wages the answer won't be 'not'!"

So that week Stanislaus Joseph journeyed each afternoon to Hans Beuter's to practice the folk songs on his accordion, and planned the week following to tell Olga that he would try to set her song. And he pictured how her beautiful but sad Slavic face would light with that smile that was like sunshine breaking through a cloud. It was something to look forward to!

And the girl who had been Olga Lasenka was going those same afternoons to the hotel of the chorus girl, where stage manager Dixon would meet them; and they would go over her song as the stage manager played his music on the show girl's small rented piano.

It would seem that there was going to be a real surprise in store both for the girl who had been Olga Lasenka and for Dr. Stanislaus Joseph Halka of the University of Vienna, alias Mr. Tightpants.

✣ 4 ✣

THAT FINAL PERFORMANCE CAME, and was vocalized into Broadway history. At its last curtain, the whole company lined the footlights and sang *Auld Lang Syne,* many of the audience joining. That last audience was pretty much composed of patrons who had seen this operetta many other evenings. Like an opening night, the house could have been sold out a dozen times over.

Then—at midnight—came the "farewell-party show."

After the burlesque "first part"—the climax being the actual appearance of the two-hundred-and-forty-pound wardrobe woman in a one-piece bathing suit, while the frail counterfeit leading man, brought on by a nurse in a wheel chair, sang *Love Me Tonight* to her, only he prefaced the immortal first phrase by the line *Alas! Why did I let you!*—after this good-natured foolery, company and guests adjourned to the basement underneath the stage, where four mighty kegs of a cooling product of hops and malt were waiting to be tapped by experts from the Rheingold Breweries. This rite being consummated—there were heaps of sandwiches also—all returned to the theater proper for the more serious display of the talents of the chorus people.

Mr. Dixon, as master of ceremonies, made an announcement.

"The public and the critics," he said, "believe, in their crass innocence, that this show has run two full seasons because of the talents of its principal players. They believed that our ensemble was here, simply as a background—for decorative purposes!

"Ladies and gentlemen, that chorus—and several members of the hidden, back-stage staff—will now show you what was really the hidden pulse of this operetta. That radiation of abilities which the audiences unconsciously absorbed and responded to.

"I can speak of this knowingly, because, among other disclosures, you will be startled to find that we have a composer, a lyric writer, not to mention voices that should, by rights, be down the street at the Metropolitan, and dancers that belong with some Imperial Ballet. And where else in the entire world will you have found such a concentration—yes, such a *saturation* of both feminine and manly beauty? I give you my own profile as an example—but modesty forbids further delineations.

"On with the show!"

So, amid laughter and applause, the party-performance resumed.

Olga Halka felt her knees grow weak as she heard the announcement of a "lyric writer"—she wondered if Stanislaus Joseph, in the orchestra pit, suspected.

She could not see her husband from her place in the wings. But she steeled her courage, and whispered a little prayer.

Perhaps, after all, her song would fall flat—would "lay an egg," to quote Mr. Dixon. That gentleman, to tell the truth, was also a little fearful of the initial emergence of his secret talent before an audience that included Florenz Ziegfeld and Rudolf Friml! It must be reported, however, that he breathed no prayer.

You always were a damned idiot—now the whole world will know it, he said to himself. But a glance toward prospective wife Number Four, and her not discouraging smile, stiffened his hoping-for-the-best. That lady also was about to tempt Fate, in search of high glory or ruinous descent into the depths. Literally so. For attired in spangles and tights, she was going to walk across a swaying slack-wire borrowed from circus friends who were playing their vaudeville act in Jersey City, and which the Ziegfeld stage crew had been instructed how to mount.

Walking a slack-wire thirty feet above the stage was surely a much more hazardous venture than to sit at a piano and punch out a melody!

Stanislaus Joseph was put in a friendly frame of mind. Early in the proceedings he was called upon to perform on his accordion, and the strident melody of that uninhibited instrument in the hands of an expert could not be denied. After the first three short numbers, the entire company did an impromptu dance to the fourth. Had they known the words of the Viennese songs they would have sung them.

It gladdened the heart of the little piano player. He repeated to himself that he would speak to Olga about the writing of a song.

He had no suspicion of what was presently to come.

And producer Ziegfeld made a mental note that an accordion interlude would be a novelty for the next Follies. An entire orchestra made up of accordions! This versatile Mr. Tightpants to train it, and be its soloist.

Unfortunately, he had not been so impressed by the slack-wire act of the show girl—though that also gained its full share of surprised applause from all present.

So—finally—acting a manner of nonchalance which he was far from feeling, stage manager Dixon made this announcement.

"And now, ladies and gentlemen, we are about to permit you to hear, for the very first time on any stage, a new song. That of itself, I well know, is no novelty. Hundreds of new songs are written and composed. They all have to be sung *some place,* and for a first time.

"But this song is a homespun product of the tremendous hidden talent of this theatrical company. I prophesy that the music of this number, once given to the sound waves, will engulf, will literally overwhelm, the entire country! Mr. Friml may withdraw, if he feels that he will suffer embarrassment. I know whereof I speak, for I have been singularly privileged to be the very first unbiased, critical ear to hear this melody.

"Did I mention the fact that I composed that melody myself? I fear, in my well-known humility, I did not. I do so now."

There was great laughter—but it was kindly laughter. Mr. Dixon was liked. Mr. Friml, far from leaving, stood up and applauded.

"I should further state," continued stage manager Dixon, "that any resemblance to the works of Beethoven, Brahms, Debussy, Franz Liszt, Chopin, Tchaikovsky, Stephen Foster, Victor Herbert, George M. Cohan, is purely accidental and coincidental. Also inconsequential. After all, these so-called composers had a head start on me in the use of the musical scale."

When more laughter and applause had subsided, Mr. Dixon continued:

"The lyric of this song is quite another matter. Now I am not joking. I believe that it was written with real talent. I believe—and I can give it no higher praise—that its writer will some day become another Brian Hooker.

"This lyric was penned—most likely penciled—by a young lady of our singing ensemble, and she herself will sing it. So I give you a girl that we all love and admire—the wife of a right guy whom we also love and admire, which admiration you have already most enthusiastically shown. I give you Olga Halka—Mrs. Tightpants Halka!

"The name of her song is *Bungalow on Broadway,* and we both apologize for keeping its composition a dark secret, and sincerely hope that her husband—her talented husband—will approve of our humble efforts. For our song is dedicated to him, and his well-known affection for our great city, although he was born in a far distant land."

✤ 5 ✤

IF A BOMBSHELL had exploded beneath Stanislaus Joseph's chair as he sat in the orchestra pit, he could not have been more startled.

That there was a hurt, he could not deny. And yet—and yet—he had turned Olga down about her song. Turned her down decisively. How was she to know that he had been thinking of changing his mind.

He knew that he must rise and make some response to Mr. Dixon's announcement. To this—it must appear—most thoughtful dedication to his sentiments. He did so, his mind whirling in a kaleidoscope of conflicting thoughts.

And as he looked up he met the eyes of the girl he loved.

There had always been between them that thought transference—that knowledge of what the other felt, without the use of words. And in her eyes he now read, not defiance, but a tragic plea for understanding; for forgiveness—if there was anything to forgive; for hope that he would understand. That she would even now not sing the song, if he disapproved.

It was then that he experienced for the first time—perhaps the only time—the illusion that personages now dead and gone were present. It was at the same time a startling confirmation that the remarkable resemblance of his wife to the La Celle statue up at the Cloisters was something more than a mere likeness of form and feature.

The stage manager-composer, having made his announcement, had led the girl to the front of the stage, while two stage hands were pushing a piano from the wings so that Mr. Dixon could do his part of the new song's debut. And as Stanislaus Joseph gazed up at her, and read the message of her eyes and face, two figures appeared on her other side, one of them holding her free hand.

They were most certainly not ensemble folk of this Ziegfeld operetta.

It was only for a moment that they appeared. But long enough for the young man to observe that one tall gentleman was clad in a red surcoat apparently worn over a suit of armor, on the front of which coat was embroidered a large golden cross; while the other—a modern—wore the dark blue, double-breasted jacket of a naval officer, including the heavily gold-braided cap.

It seemed fortunate that the figure next the girl and holding her hand was clasping that hand with his own left—for his right arm stopped abruptly at the wrist of his chain-armored sleeve.

There was nothing either tragic or serious in their aspect. In fact, both figures were smiling. It was as if they had been present the entire evening, and had absorbed the festive spirit of the occasion.

Only the equally tall man in the maritime uniform spoke. He seemed to say in Viennese, *"Komm, Stanislaus Joseph! Seix doch ein bisschen grosszugig"* which might be freely translated to mean, "Come, Stanislaus Joseph! Be a good sport!"

The young man said—said to those on the stage of that Ziegfeld Theater and those seated in the audience—said to those two formidable figures he somehow knew were only visible to his eyes:

"I have always believed that I was fortunate of Heaven to win a most unusual and talented girl. An exceptional girl. And I am happy that my good friend Russ Dixon has found a way to set a melody to her clever lyric. I'd insist on being the accompanist—as I have served for most of you with your songs—only these two have kept it all a secret from me as well as you.

"God bless them both—and good fortune to their song. May I be humbly worthy of its dedication."

So Stanislaus Joseph heard his lips speaking. The words he repeated were eminently proper and polite. But did he really mean them?

He was still stunned and confused in his mind and heart, and not a little awed by this visible proof of the girl who had been Olga Lasenka's connection with the legend of the twelfth century maid who had posed for the La Celle statue; of Olga Lasenka's dreams of an interview with Kommodore Hugo Frederick von Steinburg on the bridge of his ship, when that ship had transported the Queen of Heaven statue to the new world.

Was it all his own imagining? His own guilty realization of how much Olga's little verses had meant to her, and how he had fallen short in this one request that she had made on his talent as a musician?

But there was no time given for contemplative speculation. Mr. Dixon had seated himself at the piano. An ex-comedian, he could not resist a sweeping gesture backwards through his thinning and short hair, as if they were the locks of a famous virtuoso. But the gesture was not just for a smile. It subtly told the audience that he did not yet think he *was that*. It put them on his side.

He played an introduction. The girl was singing her *Broadway Bungalow* song.

And the music was not bad. Stanislaus Joseph realized that it was much better, in its way, than he could have done, with his erudite attitude toward all music. There was a mock sentimentality in the verse—

"Yes—I've heard about "the cottage in the dell"

With the "rambling roses" and the "wishing well"—

and the refrain proceeded with a lilting arrogance and sophistication, and yet a sincerity, that was most intriguing and "catching." Stage Manager Dixon might never write another melody, but in this simple song all of his forty years of Broadway, show-wise experience found expression. And he, too, loved the great city of raucous noise and raucous smells, and underneath—a sentimental tenderness.

The applause was spontaneous. The kind of applause that skilled managers and artists know impels hands to clap and vocal chords to shout "Bravo!"

Not daring to look down at her husband, the girl went on to her second refrain.

Dr. Stanislaus Joseph Halka did not hear the exact words of this refrain. He only realized that this highly professional audience was again being pleased—being enthused—by both melody and words.

For again, his own mind was in a turmoil of doubt, of self-recrimination. Was it not a heinous crime to stifle a talent just because one did not understand it—just because its standards were not exactly his exalted—maybe quite stupid—standards? Music—song—were meant to give pleasure; to take folk out of themselves; and perhaps, in final reckoning, a simple words-and-melody in the popular vernacular would count for just as much as a soaring symphony of intricate chords and progressions!

He himself had received only encouragement toward his goals—from his old patron, from his teachers, from Kommodore Hugo Frederick von Steinburg, from H. Rodman (Hardboiled Rodman who had not forgotten to send him a wire the opening night of this Ziegfeld operetta), from this loyal girl, his wife. And he, perched on his pinnacle of lofty ideals (and as yet having accomplished absolutely nothing), had felt that *his* ideals were the only goals worth aiming for.

His ideals were not wrong ideals, but should he not have a tolerance for the goals of others? And—thought most disturbing—was he not only failing to be a help, but actually a dragging millstone tugging to drown the talent of the girl who had linked her life to his?

Again, these thoughts were interrupted by wall-echoing applause.

✣ 6 ✣

AND THIS WAS NOT the end of the "Bungalow on Broadway" presentation.

There was a surprise in store for even stage manager Dixon, a surprise that had been secretly engineered by the lady of slack-wire aspirations.

She had learned from her religious weekly reading of the show people's Koran—*Variety,* that Mr. Busby Berkeley was in town from distant Hollywood.

Mr. Berkeley, now a leading film producer, had been the dance director of this Ziegfeld production two years before. He was also a friend of Mr. Dixon's. And he was the kind of showman willing to give the other fellow a boost.

The show girl had made an extra copy of the song. Mr. Berkeley—using the ballroom of his Hotel Warwick just across from the theater—had put his clever, number-producing mind at work the afternoons and after-midnights of all the previous week—with the ensemble people sworn to secrecy as far as Mr. Dixon, Olga Halka, and Olga Halka's husband—Mr. Tightpants—were concerned.

So when the applause for the second refrain ended, the retiring-to-the-wings and startled stage manager was pushed back onto his piano stool, as a Floradora Sextet emerged singing and strutting from those wings—the six boys and the six girls alternating in the chanting of the lines.

They were properly costumed with picture hats and parasols for the ladies, morning coats and grey toppers for the men. And they sang the refrain with an entirely British accent!

More applause and laughter, and (Mr. Dixon again being pushed to his keyboard) Busby Berkeley himself—an expert tap dancer—dressed as the greatest Broadwayite of all time, George M. Cohan, led out a regiment of male choristers all made up as George M's!

With tilted straw hats and slender canes they sang and danced the song, with the well-known mannerisms of that symbol of Broadway when he had been a star in vaudeville.

You may be certain that here the accents were an authentic and properly nasal *American*. Blessed, homely twang, that we joke about but love!

There was a trick lighting effect at the end of this sequence—the stage darkened except for a special "flood spot" from the balcony, so that the hats and canes only appeared (these having been painted with an iridescent fluid, to alternately show green and red and gold under the proper filters of the "flood"); the hats and sticks seemingly doing an entirely unsupported and comically weird, fantastic dance

By this time the almost-overcome Mr. Dixon could cease his key thumping, for the orchestra in the pit took up an unrehearsed and impromptu, without-written-music-sheets playing of the catchy melody. There may have been a wrong note sounded now and then but that mattered little in the general enthusiasm and hilarity.

And Mr. Busby Berkeley's "production climax" was still to come

While the lights were out, a background curtain that had been borrowed from another musical show was quietly lowered.

It pictured Times Square at night: lights sparkling, huge blazing advertising signs; and as the by-now almost breathless Olga Halk again sang her first refrain at the instigation of Mr. Berkeley, stag hands in spick-and-span new overalls emerged with pieces of pre-fitte scenery (this the work of the expert Ziegfeld property men unde Frank Koetzner) and swiftly and with a humorous, stylized timin to the music and singing, constructed a dainty, miniature bungalow its painted brick chimney going into place with the exact fina note!

Then, as the orchestra played very *forte,* since by this time the had become quite proficient in the simple melody, the whole stage suddenly filled with traffic policemen, newshawkers, a jumble of men and women pedestrians.

One girl brought on the chorus boy's trained dog who dutifully relieved himself against a traffic light-post, thus confirming a cityite's preference of lamp-posts to trees! And a great tangle of honking, miniature vehicles, borrowed from the toy department of a famous Herald Square department store—children's motor cars, trucks, buses, a fire engine, a sanitation sprinkler spouting real water—all these whirled about, while overhead sailed a toy blimp and a dozen circling airplanes.

At the very last, two puppet figures appeared at two adjoining windows of the "bungalow" and expressed by comic grimaces their complete ecstatic content and happiness.

Once more Olga was called upon to sing her song from the beginning, the entire company and most of the audience joining in the refrain. And then—the stage cleared—she and stage manager Dixon had to respond with many bows to sincere cheers and approving laughter.

Stanislaus Joseph had emerged from all this, a man who had inwardly been groping his way through a blinding snowstorm. Outwardly he had appeared calm enough. The accompanist who had not been flustered when a page-turner pushed his music to the floor; the lad who had early learned that first rule of a public performer—*If in trouble, do not telegraph it to the audience*—had played his orchestra pianoforte, along with the others, in perfect rhythm and control.

And at the end he did emerge, calm and not a little proud. His Olga had moved this entertainment-wise audience to cheers, not only with her singing, but with the creation of her brain. It was his own self-made misfortune that he was not more a part of it all. At the end, he was applauding and cheering with all the others.

Mr. Dixon had also emerged, and was no less shaken. A song with his music and apparently a hit! At least, a hit at that try-out performance.

He managed to thank the company, his friend Mr. Busby Berkeley, and that audience of fellow theater-workers. No wisecracks this time. There was a catch in his voice, as he spoke his little speech of gratitude.

He also said: "The credit should go entirely to Olga Halka. It was *her* lyric—her idea—that commenced it all. A great little kid, for whom I predict a future both as a writer and a performer. Her husband, our Mr. Tightpants, is a lucky guy."

It was fortunate that Mr. Tightpants—*our* Stanislaus Joseph—was also by now a rational being. For stage manager Dixon had not forgotten what he had planned to be the *finale ultimo* of the evening.

"My friends," he said, "for the closing number we will hear a song with *real* music—a truly great song that is the favorite of our very great employer. Tightpants—come up onto the stage. For this time the accompanist is to be a real artist at the pianoforte. Mrs. Tightpants—Olga Halka—come out from the wings.

"I need not tell you that I did not compose this song. It was written by Antonin Dvořák, a fellow Bohemian countryman of our own great Rudolf Friml. Olga Halka will sing—Mr. Tightpants Halka will play—*Songs My Mother Taught Me*. I hope they have not forgotten it. I know damn well they haven't!"

They had not forgotten it.

Stanislaus Joseph had often played it at the Madison Avenue apartment, and Olga had often sung it—because they liked it, and as a memory of how the girl had obtained her Ziegfeld engagement.

They needed no rehearsals for that song.

Tightpants played it beautifully. She sang it beautifully.

So the evening ended in a triumph for them both.

And that was not all. Mr. Ziegfeld said, before all the company: "Mrs. Halka, if there is a role for you, I promise you a part in my next operetta. And Mr. Dixon, maybe I can find use for your number, with Mrs. Halka's lyric, in my next *Follies*. We shall see."

Mr. Florenz Ziegfeld did not make promises that he did not keep.

✤ 7 ✤

Both Olga and Stanislaus Joseph were unusually silent as they rode home in their two A.M. taxi. Going up the dimly lit stairs, there were more than usual sharp eyes shining at them from dark corners. Stanislaus Joseph had forgotten to bring some cheese, and he went back out to an all-night delicatessen to feed his tiny friends—fugitives from the highly unionized Exterminator Industry. This simple routine somehow seemed to completely clear his thoughts. To fix the part a real artist should play in this warring world.

He must not be an exterminator. He must help, in every way—even as he had been helped.

They were in bed before the silence between them was broken.

"Duszka—do you forgive me?" said the girl, and burst into tears.

She had been close to tears several times before during that evening. Tears of worry. Tears of elation. Tears of happiness. Tears of gratitude to Mr. Dixon for asking Stanislaus Joseph to have a part in that final-curtain song. But all elation and happiness would be canceled out, if her husband—her man—were hurt or angry about her song.

Stanislaus Joseph kissed those final tears away. "It is I who should ask forgiveness," he said. "I have been stupid and dull and self-centered. But it has turned out for the best. I could not have written a proper setting for that song. Mr. Dixon could. I would have made a dull, highbrow failure of it.

"But maybe there will be a song of yours that I *can* set to my stupid kind of music," he added. "I shall try. Give me another chance. And I have something very strange and wonderful to tell to you.

"You remember the legend on the Knights Templars monastery parchment, which I read to you that first day that I took you to the Cloisters. The legend of Crusader Hugh de St. Omer?

"Hugh de St. Omer was there on that Ziegfeld stage tonight. He held your hand with his good hand. He and Kommodore von Steinburg were there beside you. I saw them as plainly as I now see you.

"I had better be good to you, my darling, or I will have two very husky protectors to contend with!"

And the girl who had been Olga Lasenka was again happy. Happy but for one disturbing thought.

There was something else she had not told her husband. Two things, in fact.

One—that her defender in the Boston theater alley had been this same Hugh de St. Omer. Stanislaus Joseph had of course heard of the incident, and along with most of the company, taken for granted it was some modest member of the Shakespearean troupe across the alley, that had in its cast players garbed in chain armor.

He certainly had not connected that modern stage-door-alley happening with any moldy, parchment legend.

The girl did not tell him now.

She did not tell him, because the very next day was her twenty-second birthday. And there was a tradition in her family—the La Celle side of it—regarding *that particular year* of the oldest daughter's life—a tradition that she hardly dared to think about.

And linked with this tradition was something she also remembered having said, in her recurrent dream of standing on the bridge of a great ship, with the man she now knew was the late Kommodore Hugo Frederick von Steinburg. A tragic something that she had said, having to do—perhaps—with her own present destiny.

Stanislaus Joseph's mention of these two figures who were already dead brought to the girl who would become twenty-two years of age the next morning, a vague alarm.

But for that night she lay close in her husband's arms. And the La Celle statue at the Cloisters (had Guard O'Rourke been there at such an hour) seemed to be "truly" smiling. Truly happy.

❖ 8 ❖

THE LEGEND, or rather the tradition of the girl Olga's family in France, was this. That the first-born girl would die during the twenty-third year of her life. It seemed to dip back into the dim past—to a daughter who had in some manner been connected with a monastery of the neighborhood. The family had descended through the younger sister of this maid.

Olga Lasenka's mother, who had also been a younger sister, had felt impelled to speak of this to her only daughter just before she died. Her older sister, who had become a nun in France, had died at that age.

The tradition also was—that some day there would be but a single daughter, and with this daughter the La Celle family and the legend would pass into history.

At the time of her mother's death—the girl Olga had been but ten years of age—she had paid little attention to the tale. In her school and occupational life she had almost forgotten it. Ambitious Youth does not concern itself with "profitable Death."

Profitable Life—even unprofitable Life—is too filled with high hopes and ambitious dreams.

But now came this identification with the La Celle statue—with the legend as recorded by Hugh de St. Omer. That girl—according to the legend—died when she was twenty-two. But what especially disturbed the girl who had been Olga Lasenka was something of more modern moment. Namely, her dream about the great ship.

Because there was one other saying, besides that referring to a golden cross, that she always remembered speaking to her companion of that dream. That saying was this: *"Ah, Monsieur le Capitaine, it is hard to die when one is only twenty-two. One does not then know that it is not Death to be feared. Only Life. Only Loneliness."*

The girl who was now Olga Halka had conquered loneliness. She had found her mate. Death was something very much to be feared. She wanted *to live.*

And this matter of a career seemed to be at last beyond the dreaming stage. A role—even a small role—in a new Ziegfeld show would put her feet firmly on the success ladder.

And if her song, to which she owed this start, could really go into the next Follies! That was the goal that even experienced song writers would not scorn.

With all this, she had not forgotten that the *real* start occurred when her husband had taught her that Dvořák song, by means of which song, under his coaching, she had obtained her part in the Chorus of the piece just finished.

Her worry was on his account much more than on her own.

Not that the young husband would fail to have employment. The Ziegfeld conductor had already told Mr. Tightpants there would be a place for him in the Fall, as soon as Mr. Ziegfeld returned from California and started a new enterprise—whether it be a new Follies or the English musical play he had decided to produce in America. And as before, his work would commence with the month-long auditions which would precede the regular rehearsal period.

But the girl knew that Stanislaus Joseph wanted to be more than just a regularly employed accompanist—that the young man's heart was set on the completion of his symphony, and the prestige that would be gained by it, and she seemed so utterly helpless in regard to such a composition.

She could only listen each night to the page or two that he had struggled over all day, and then, more than likely, discarded.

She constantly tried to think of some new song lyric that he might like to set to music, such a song to give him an immediate start as a composer. But what she would write seemed trivial.

She destroyed as many pages of verse as he tore up unsatisfactory pages of black-noted manuscript.

Could it be that she was doomed to write one song-lyric only—and that the *Broadway Bungalow?* She knew that there had been one-song song-writers, just as there were *one*-play playwrights, *one*-novel novelists, *one*-role actors.

Meantime Stanislaus Joseph was very definitely helping *her*.

He insisted that she take a voice lesson every day. He would sometimes go to these lessons with her—would play the accompaniment, especially if it were a foreign song that he knew. And he would go over scales with her at home, before each lesson. Her excellent natural voice became more full and mellow; she learned phrasing, breathing; acquired an assurance that she had not possessed.

She would be ready for whatever Mr. Ziegfeld was courageous enough to entrust her with.

9

THEN, LATE ONE JULY Friday afternoon, came the news that stunned Broadway; stunned the entire amusement world.

One did not need to wait to see the obituary pages to learn of it. The men at their news-stands were shouting it. The clicking teletype machines were spelling it out. Even the Wall Street ticker tapes took note, between the fall of the price of steel and the rise in the price of copper.

And the lagging news sheets (as soon as they were off the throbbing presses and into the streets) carried it in black headline type (one paper printed the words in red) across their first pages.

FLO ZIEGFELD OF THE FOLLIES DIES

The great producer who "ruled the stage as the world's premier showman" had suffered a sudden heart attack in distant Hollywood. He had died even before his wife Billie Burke, who was working in a picture there, could reach his side "still in make-up," at the

Cedars of Lebanon Hospital, to which hospital he had been rushed.

Stanislaus Joseph and Olga had heard the shocking news as they emerged from the subway at Park Avenue and Thirty-fourth Street. He had gone with her that late afternoon for her voice lesson. Returning, he had been telling her that he thought he could borrow the score of the English piece from the Ziegfeld conductor—the piece it was expected the producer would first put into rehearsal in the Fall. She could thereby become familiar with the singing numbers, if she were so fortunate as to obtain one of the roles.

And an already hoarse voice from the news-stand at the top of the stairs was shouting:

"Read all about it! Ziegfeld dies in Hollywood!"

These two, whose theatrical destiny at that moment depended on this personage, stopped in their tracks and looked helplessly at each other.

"How dreadful!" said the girl.

"How very sad!" said the young man.

For them, and for many others in the great town, it was both dreadful and sad. Sad because he was a much loved gentleman. A considerate employer. A producer who had helped hundreds reach the top. Dreadful because these two well knew, as did many others, that dreams were ended by this sudden death.

For the theater, made up of the collaboration of many talents, has at the heart of each enterprise one single man. Or sometimes woman.

When that heart stops its beat, the pulsing life of the enterprise dies. Plans do not proceed as they would in an automobile manufacturing company or a department store. For it is an Art—whether it be a picture-house act, a burlesque show, a Victor Herbert or a Rudolf Friml operetta. The artist who painted with these many talents has died. He may, of himself, have possessed no one of these talents—that of composer, librettist, scene designer, director, singer, actor, comedian, financial genius—but he could select and combine all these into one great artistic entity; he could select, and then say "No" or "Yes," and on his "No" or "Yes" rode the success of the entertainment.

Stanislaus Joseph and the girl walked the block to their home in silence. At the street door the young man said: "I think, dear, I will go to the Ziegfeld office. Others of the staff will be there. By my presence I can at least express my sorrow and gratitude."

"I will go to our church and light a candle," said the girl. "That isn't much to do, but it is all that I can do. God rest his great, generous soul."

At the spacious Ziegfeld office were gathered those of the staff and the working crew of the theater who were still in the city. They did not speak many words. Miss "Goldie," the secretary of many years, was sobbing. The others stood about. The head electrician tightened a light bulb that seemed loose and flickering in one of the wall brackets. The cleaning woman brushed the top of the desk chair with her apron and then burst into tears. A great comedian sat disconsolate on the sofa and talked in low tones with the wardrobe woman. When Tightpants entered, stage manager Dixon said:

"There was one song that Mr. Ziegfeld loved above all others. It had to do with his mother. I believe he would be pleased if our Mr. Tightpants would play it now—for him and for his mother whose picture we all well know. Afterwards I will lock the piano. It will not be played upon again."

So Stanislaus Joseph sat on the familiar bench and played very tenderly the great song by Antonin Dvořák, and Mr. Dixon closed the lid of the Steinway and turned the key.

And the general manager said: "We will send a telegram to Miss Burke—all of you will sign it—his family here in New York—and then I will lock the office. I'm not much on religion—only thing I ever knew in that department was the Lord's Prayer—and I've maybe forgotten that, but let's all stand and say it as best we can. His mother, up there on the wall, will forgive any mistakes we make, I am sure."

And so it was done, and each filed by the empty desk-chair where had sat a great—and of much more importance—a good man.

The next morning, Stanislaus Joseph again turned first to the page called Obituary in his *Times*.

On that morning one personage occupied more than half its eight columns. The late Florenz Ziegfeld. There were photographs of him, his wife and daughter; the detailed story of his career from the management of a sideshow at the Chicago World's Fair to the Follies series and the great musical plays like "Kid Boots," "Sally," "Rio Rita," "Show Boat," "The Three Musketeers."

But what most interested Stanislaus Joseph appeared in a small box at the bottom of one column. A special wire dated from Chicago, where the producer had been born. It read:

"All the world knew today that Florenz Ziegfeld was dead, except his mother. She may never know.

"The white-haired old woman, so idolized during his lifetime by the Broadway producer that even his last hours found him trying to telegraph or telephone to her home here——"

So it continued.

Florenz Ziegfeld's aged mother was near to death herself, in an upper room of the old family house from which Florenz Ziegfeld Senior—Dr. Ziegfeld—had operated the Chicago Musical College; where the showman son grew up against a background of Beethoven, Schumann, Bach.

Reading this, Stanislaus Joseph was glad that he had so studied as to properly play Dvořák's *Songs My Mother Taught Me.* That he had been able to play it in that studio-office above the theater on Sixth Avenue, the late afternoon before.

Could it not be that his ability to play perfectly that touching Gypsy song at that tragic hour—that this alone justified his years of study; and this alone would place beside his name on that Great Scroll mentioned by the Lady of the Statue a golden cross, a cross that no symphony of many pages could gain for him? Who—in meagre earthly wisdom with its false evaluations—can with certainty tell?

For perhaps the Chicago reporter of the great *New York Times* was not correct in writing *That mother may never know.*

Perhaps, even if that mother did not know of the death of her famous son at its instant, she had heard the playing of that song; and through the penetrating magic, the thrusting impact of the divine fire that is great music, she then knew that her son had thought of her, and reached out to her with his final heart beat.

And perhaps, for a moment, the photograph with the lined face, the tired eyes, the white hair, became young again.

The most beautiful girl Florenz Ziegfeld had ever "glorified."

PART ELEVEN

THE TRIUMPH

✣ 1 ✣

NEITHER STANISLAUS JOSEPH nor the girl who had been Olga Lasenka had given any thought to their employment for the coming season. That employment had seemed assured. But now there would be no more Ziegfeld productions. The theater was in fact very quickly leased to a motion picture company by the real estate corporation that controlled it.

For the girl: other producers would be producing other musical plays. There would be auditions. Five hundred singers appearing for each thirty jobs. If she asked to try for a so-called part, there would be the eternal question "What have you done?"

She had done nothing at all within the meaning of that question. A cheap picture-house act. The chorus of a show. Even the chorus of a Ziegfeld show.

"Leave your name and address. We will let you know if there is anything" would be the eternal comment. There apparently never was "anything." Too many experienced girls were in the market—the always overcrowded, heartbreaking market of theater employment. More correctly—*un*employment.

The young man—well, he remembered the drab look of the big "waiting room" at the Union headquarters, with the hard benches and the unemployed musicians sitting about waiting for a "break." Fine musicians—ten of 'em for every possible call. For this was before the rapid development of radio and television somewhat lessened the lack of work for piano players and violin and brass and wood-wind exponents. He had not forgotten the weary round of restaurants.

He had not indeed forgotten that locked hotel-room door.

It might not be so difficult for him as for the girl. His talent was above the ordinary. And he did now know well a few more musicians than when he had first gone to the Ziegfeld office. Still—he had taken for granted that the dreary days of looking for employment were over. That the Ziegfeld job would continue to pay for food and clothes and rent, until the great symphony was ready for the world.

But neither of these two was lacking in courage. They were not quitters. Stanislaus Joseph had each Summer turned down the offer to again play for the Summer session at the Hunter gymnasium classes. The next Monday he telephoned the director there.

A bit of good fortune—at least for Stanislaus Joseph. Their piano player was ill. They would be glad indeed to have him for the remainder of July and the month of August. By September there would be new theater productions. Or maybe the orchestra of a radio program—off the air for the Summer—for which he had done some "arrangements."

The girl did not wish him to do this work. "We have saved some money," she said. "We can get along for a while. You must work at your composing. I'll watch *Variety,* and go to all the chorus auditions.

"And there are two dozen five-and-dime stores in New York," she added. "I've not entirely forgotten how to sell ribbons and make change. I'll go back to that before I'll let you waste your time and talent on hack work."

"You'll do nothing of the sort," said Stanislaus Joseph. "I'll play at the gymnasium. It's only a few hours each day. That will keep up the rent and meals. The money we have saved is your money. If anything should happen to me, you will not be penniless."

He added with a smile: "In September, if I can't find work in some theater, I haven't forgotten how to use the *dressiersack.* I think I can still paint red hearts and green-stemmed roses on birthday cakes. I can still spell out *Frohliche Ostern* with gold-colored sugar icing. Hans Beuter, up on York Avenue, will get me into the Bakery Workers Union, and give me a job."

And he added seriously, "Sometimes I think my father was right.

I should have studied and worked at the baker's trade. People have to *eat,* and they don't have to listen to music!"

With this—alas—only too profound observation, he put a period on the subject of gainful employment; but it brought another matter to his mind.

"Speaking of birthdays," he said, "when is yours? You have never told me. I'm not even sure how old you are, my precious darling, except that when we applied for the marriage license, you said you were twenty. That would make you twenty-two by now.

"The last time I saw Hans he told me to find out the date of your birthday, so that he and his men could make you a great *Sachertorte*—which is a real Vienna cake with chocolate flavor—Oh delicious!—and I could write on it with their *dressiersack.*"

"That will have to be for another year," said the girl, and the boy could not understand the shadow that crossed her face and was reflected in her eyes. "My birthday was several weeks ago. At the time of the theater party. I was then twenty-two."

"And you did not tell me!" said the young man.

"My real birthday was the day I first saw you at that Ziegfeld audition," said the girl.

So she did not tell him of her secret dread of that twenty-third year. *Would there be a twenty-fourth?*

Stanislaus Joseph took the college gymnasium job. He played again for a dancing class at night. It interfered with his work on the symphony, but it kept them from dipping into the account at the savings bank.

The money left them by the late Kommodore had not yet materialized. There was a difficulty, it seemed, about sending such an amount out of Germany. It would come eventually (so the Berlin lawyer wrote), but international heritage laws were slow and complicated.

The lad again thought of going back to Vienna for a few weeks. But that would dig deep into their savings. It would also take them away from New York at a time when engagements for both of them for the coming season must be obtained—if they were obtained. That trip might not even permit the bringing of this legacy money to New York, even if it facilitated their obtaining it.

And there was the matter of the still unfinished symphony composition. Stanislaus Joseph dismissed a trip to Europe from his mind.

The girl cut her voice lessons to two a week. They were expensive lessons with a fine teacher that cost ten dollars each. Stanislaus would not let her entirely stop the lessons, and would not consider a less expensive and less able teacher.

The girl could not banish the matter of the family legend from her mind.

One day—the night before she had again had the dream of standing on the bridge of the great ship and repeating the fatal words—she journeyed alone up to the Cloisters. It was on an afternoon that Stanislaus Joseph was occupied with his gymnasium-class playing. She did not tell her husband that she was going there.

Guard O'Rourke was on his yearly two-weeks vacation. For this she was grateful, because she did not then have to pledge him to secrecy. A strange guard was stationed inside the Early Gothic Room, for whom she was just another visitor.

"Dear Image of the Queen of Heaven," she whispered as she stood before the stone carving, "If I am you—if I am the girl from the La Celle village who posed for your making; please do not let this legend happen to me, as it has to the other daughters of my family. For I am not now alone in the world.

"I have my husband whom I love very dearly. I believe that he needs me. I know that I cannot change God's will—that I cannot alter my destiny—but please let me go on living with him. I must cook for him, and work for him, and starch and iron his shirts and collars, and give him my true love.

"And perhaps I can write the words of a song that will help him in his career. I don't want it for myself. I want it all for him."

But the statue remained cold and unresponsive in her presence.

There was only the fixed, mystic, unearthly smile. There was no human smile such as Guard O'Rourke had been accustomed to believe he could detect. There was no reddening of the breast as had happened on the afternoon when Kommodore Hugo Frederick von Steinburg had failed to clear the tenth barrier of the *Grand Prix de Cources d'Auteuil* steeplechase.

The painted eyes gazed out upon the sunlit Hudson with no change of expression. No change to compassion, or compliance, or denial.

And so the girl who had been Olga Lasenka left the Early Gothic Room as she had come there. The very fact that the statue remained impassive, unmoved, brought her a degree of comfort.

Perhaps it was all just a legend—an old wives' tale—and she had no need to fear for words written in an ancient parchment—words spoken in a crazy dream.

But when she had gone, the guard who was filling Dennis O'Rourke's place happened to pause before this special statue and look up at it. He had been asked by Guard O'Rourke to give it special attention.

The leaded window through which the statue gazed, as were the other windows of the room, was swung half open, for the day had been oppressively hot. There had been an occasional rumble of thunder over the great river; and low, dark clouds above the Palisades indicated that it might be raining there.

Suddenly there was a brisk, light rain outside and against the open window panes, although the sun was still shining. And this guard perceived two glistening drops on each cheek of the statue which Hugh de St. Omer had had carved for his Knights Templars preceptory at La Celle in the Kingdom of France, more than eight hundred years before.

"Gee! I'd better close this window damn quick!" he said to himself, but aloud. And he did so. Then turning to the statue, "I beg your pardon, Lady. Your pal Dennis O'Rourke would sure give me all hell if he knew I let you get wet!"

And as he wiped away the two drops with his handkerchief: "Funny. They sure look like tears!"

✣ 2 ✣

As EACH DAY CAME and went, the girl felt more and more keenly that she must do something to help the man she so dearly loved—help him in his career. That just cooking for him and washing his socks were not enough. And what she felt that she could do—*if she only could*—was to write the lyric for a song that would be words for his kind of music.

With stage manager Dixon, she had visited the offices of several music publishing houses about their *Broadway Bungalow* opus. She had sung the song, and Mr. Dixon had played it for their professional managers.

There was no mad scramble to buy it.

It was obviously a "production" song. Meaning that it should be first sung in a stage production. If Mr. Dixon could place it with some manager producing a new musical play or a revue, publishers would be interested.

That, the resourceful stage manager was now trying to do. But here he encountered another obstacle. The new attractions were usually written by composers and lyric writers under contract to a producer for the entire show. These writers objected to outside musical numbers being interpolated into their scores.

It would have been different with Florenz Ziegfeld—where both Mr. Dixon and Olga Halka were already members (as it were) of his staff. Neither of them were now members of any producer's organization. Mr. Dixon had to find for himself a new engagement as a stage manager, and even that task was not a simple one. Other producers had their own stage managers. He had been working for Mr. Ziegfeld for many years, and had no close acquaintanceship with any other producer.

It seemed that you not only had to write a song, but you also had to *sell* it. And the selling part was more difficult even than the writing task! Frustration had barred the path of many another and experienced song-writer. Some of the greatest "hit numbers" had at first been refused by half a dozen publishers.

That fact buoyed up the hope that springs eternal.

There was one type of song that publishers did seem to be looking for. That they would publish *just as a song.* No stage production required. That would be a song based on the eternal relationship of the sexes. In short—on love.

It could be true love or untrue love. It could be triumphant love (the kind that rhymed *surrender* with *lips so tender*), or unrequited passion that rhymed *desire* with *raging fire.* Just so long as it concerned that supreme joy, or hopeless anguish, that was brought about by that emotional disturbance which draws a boy to a girl. A man to a woman.

It was as one successful publisher phrased it, although that very morning he had left his Riverdale apartment, smarting from an uproarious row with his wife. And during the journey to his office, silently cursed all women.

"Listen, kids," he said to Mr. Dixon and Olga Halka, "The world wants Love! The guy has found the right girl, or the girl has got her peepers on the right guy, and is going to hook him good. Or maybe the girl has left him or vice versa, and he or she is sobbing their heart out—the poor saps.

"Them novelty songs, like yours, is all right for a show. But for a straight popular song, someone's got to be going nuts over someone else!

"A song using a girl's name wouldn't be bad right now," he continued wisely. "We ain't had a hit like *Sweet Genevieve* for years. Or *Jeanie with the Light Red Hair*. Or maybe it was *brown* hair. I hate women's hair. It gets in the breakfast cooking. And don't bring me no song about any Henrietta."

Henrietta was the first name of the gentleman's wife.

This erudite counsel from the song-publisher past-master in the science of metaphysics gave Olga an idea. Stanislaus Joseph had already planted the idea.

"Darling," he had said one day, "why don't you write a verse using your name? I love your name. *Olga*. That name has come to mean all happiness—all Heaven to me. I believe I could write the music for a song called *Olga*. It would be writing about yourself, I realize. But imagine that you just aren't yourself. That you are someone writing about a beautiful girl with whom a man like me is in love. I think I could give such a song a musical soul."

So, a few evenings later—Stanislaus Joseph was playing at his dancing-class stint—Olga sat herself before a sheet of blank paper and wrote at its top:

A Song Describing How I Hope My Duszka Thinks of Me.

And then, on a single line, she wrote a title

OLGA

The first two lines came immediately into her mind. They were a rhythmic paraphrase of words her husband had said to her. Words that he had first spoken months before, and because he knew they pleased her, had often repeated in one form or another. She wrote these two lines quickly with her black leaded pencil.

Olga—whose eyes were violets—
Olga—whose tears were pearls—

She noticed that she had put the verbs in the past tense. *Were,* not *are*. She made a mental note to change this; but as her inspiration seemed to surge forward, she wrote on as rapidly as she could form the letters on the paper before her.

For that miracle was happening which every writer has experienced—which I believe every inventor, every painter, every creator of something supposedly *new* has experienced. There must be, of course, a certain fundamental knowledge and technical skill in the matter at hand, but the immediate inspiration seems to come from beyond. From some outside force.

You are, for the moment, simply the instrument through which that force is operating.

So it was with Olga Halka as she wrote her song called by her own name, "Olga." Her song that would describe her husband's thoughts about her.

This was that song—as she pencilled it, in the next ten minutes, on a single large sheet of paper.

OLGA

(Whose Eyes Were Violets)

Olga—whose eyes were violets—
Olga—whose tears were pearls—
Olga—how soon the world forgets—
One pause for vain regrets,
Then onward whirls.
Olga—that grave among your hills
Where come the whip-poor-wills
As shadows fall—
Somehow—I know it cannot be
A final Destiny
Beyond my call!
For every Springtime there are hilltops crossed with violets—
And every Springtime brook will flash its pearl-like tear—
And I can hear a voice that whispers in that Springtime—
"So long as Love remembers, I am always near—"

Olga—whose eyes were violets—
Olga—whose tears were pearls—
Violets and brook-tears cry
That someday—somewhere—you and I
Will meet—and mingle violets and pearls!
Olga!—Olga!—Olga!

Having so written it, she took up the paper to read the completed lyric, as if that lyric were the work of a stranger.

She read the words with a certain elation. They seemed much better words than she had ever written before! It seemed like real poetry! Maybe Stanislaus Joseph would really approve of this. Would like it. How soon would he return, so that she could show it to him? Or read it aloud to him?

And then—as if she were emerging from a fantastic dreamland—

she realized that she had written about herself *as if she were dead!*

Her first impulse was to destroy the verses, and destroy them quickly. Before Stanislaus Joseph could come back and see them. Before anyone could see them.

But she thought better of this, and read it again. It dealt with Death—or what the world calls "death." But it also dealt with Life—that greater life beyond the grave that was the basis of her Faith. And the added promise that even though Death intervened, "so long as Love remembered" those who so love would never be really separated.

And that "someday—somewhere" they would be physically united again.

The girl who had been Olga Lasenka had a simple religious faith. If one led a clean and upright life, one would proceed to Paradise, and live in the company of the Blessed Saints. But now that she considered it, did she wish to live in the company of the Blessed Saints? Sanctified as their company might be—would it be the place for her?

Would she not—and the thought was with no sacrilegious intent—be utterly bored?

About what did the Saints converse as they sat on their golden thrones? Theology? Its synthesis—the combination of its various elements? The philosophy of religion? Of man's relationship to God? That might be Heaven for the elderly priest in Wilkes-Barre who had been her special confidant; but for her—she feared she would not even understand the meaning of most of the words they used!

And would they not be utterly bored with *her* company?

Her chatter about the Wilkes-Barre Five-and-Dime, and the Four Rosebuds, and the Ziegfeld operetta, and popular song writing? Maybe she couldn't even get into the Heavenly Angels Choir, for she had never been partial to hymns! She liked sentimental songs. Waltz songs. Even light, humorous songs.

She had learned the *Ave Maria* as a school girl, but would that be enough?

In Paradise—if she reached it—she would like to see Hugh de St. Omer again, and really thank him for that Colonial stage-door-alley rescue back in Boston. She would like to meet the great Kommodore Hugo Frederick von Steinburg, and tell him that she really talked with him on the bridge of his *Europa*. And thank him for being so kind to her Stanislaus Joseph.

She would like to see her father. His dear, tired face. The courage and patience in his eyes under a more or less humdrum existence. His hopes for her.

Her father would be very proud that she knew intimately such people as Hugh de St. Omer and the Kommodore! And he would like Stanislaus Joseph. She wondered if her father now had the expensive electric razor he had always wanted, but never felt he could afford to buy. And if there was anyone around with whom he could play his favorite game of chess.

No. What she wanted in Heaven for herself was just what she was now having on this earth!

To be with her husband. Her "duszka Tightpants." To work with him in a show—she on the stage; he in the orchestra pit. Maybe Florenz Ziegfeld was producing new operettas there!

But would there be open-top buses when she and Stanislaus Joseph were free in the evenings—Sunday evenings—so that they could take long rides and finally come to a great bridge like the one named *George Washington?*

Would there be a restaurant like the King of the Sea for special sea-food dinners, especially if Hans Beuter was their guest? For she loved to listen to Hans and Stanislaus Joseph talk about Vienna.

She, too, hoped that someday she and her husband could pay a visit to that romantic city across the sea.

But Hans had a habit of sometimes swearing fearfully, although always in Viennese. Would that bar Hans from their company? Maybe the angels would not understand Viennese!

All of which meant that she wanted Paradise to be exactly as she had been having it on this earth since she had met her husband, even including a tiny apartment four flights up, with mice on the stairs late at night that sometimes frightened her. Some place where she and her duszka Tightpants could be entirely alone when the day's tasks were done.

There would be no Paradise without that.

The thought of her father brought to mind that she had never taken Stanislaus Joseph to her native Wilkes-Barre. They could go there by bus early one morning, and come back the same night. Or if they stayed the night, return by early bus the next morning.

She could show her husband where she had been born: the Five-and-Dime where she had worked. She would take him to meet the old priest who had advised her to keep on with her singing and not become a nun. Would he still be alive? And then they would go to the lovely cemetery just outside the town, in the hills above the town. She could take him to that hillside where both her father and mother now slept—where her father had wished her and *her* husband to sleep beside them.

Her father had not thought other than that she would continue to live in Wilkes-Barre, and find her man there, and at the end, die there.

This Death—was her unconscious writing of that song lyric a further warning that it was near, as the legend had foretold?

At least—if it had been written as a message from Beyond to her—it was a message of hope. "As long as Love remembers."

She had no doubt of her husband's remembrance.

But she must not show that song to him now. She would wait till the fatal, twenty-third year had passed—if it did pass!

The girl had a cardboard, box-like letter file in which she kept receipted household bills—any letters also to Stanislaus Joseph that should be preserved. The letters from Professor Anton Lavar and the letters from the lawyer in Berlin regarding the Kommodore's legacy.

She carefully folded the song lyric and put it in an envelope. On the outside she wrote: *A song I hope my husband will care to write the music for.* She placed the envelope in the compartment under the letter "O."

Under the first letter of her name and the name of the song. "Olga."

On her twenty-third birthday she could hand it to him; tell him then of the legend, and smile at her fears; and he could set the words to an inspired melody.

If she should die, she must tell him of the song before her final breath. And he must then set it to music in her memory.

✣ 3 ✣

THEY MADE THE TRIP to Wilkes-Barre a couple of weeks later.

Being theater-habituated, they did not exactly leap from their bed at the hour of five-thirty A.M., at which hour they had to arise in order to have breakfast and make a seven o'clock bus at Fifty-first Street and Eighth Avenue. But they made it.

Hans Beuter had been commissioned to arouse them by telephone, since that was the hour when he was quitting his night's work at the York Avenue bakery.

Hans also appeared at the bus station. He brought them a large box of the macaroon jelly-centered cookies so that they would not be hungry on the long, five-hour ride. Cookies fresh from the night's making. Loyal Hans who could be depended on to think of everything!

"And don't let yourself get captured by Indians in that wild Pennsylvania," he cautioned. Hans's knowledge of America outside New York City was mainly gained from forty-cent movies, and everything west of the Hudson was peopled by knife-carrying Red Indians, and gun-toting desperadoes.

"I was born in the Pennsylvania Territory and will protect Stanislaus Joseph from the natives. The deputy sheriff of the totem pole village of Wilkes-Barre was a friend of my father's," laughed Olga. "And I'm sure with all these wonderful little cakes we can bribe the Wyoming Valley Indians not to scalp us!"

So Stanislaus and Olga climbed aboard the great Martz Line bus, were honked down busy Eighth Avenue (busy even at that hour) and into the newly built Holland Tunnel.

Then westward and slightly northward for an hour or so, along one of the great New Jersey turnpikes, heading for a smaller roadway bordering the River Delaware; which after another hour they had crossed, and were out of the State of New Jersey and over into Pennsylvania.

Now came one of Nature's wonder feats—the Delaware Water Gap, where the river had spent five million years—or perhaps it was six—cutting through a mountain ridge so that on each side of the stream bed there now arose two great perpendicular cliffs—one named the Devil's Slide, the other the Indian Maiden's Leap. For from the sheer top of this latter, the legend told of a beautiful Indian girl who had jumped a thousand feet to her death, because her father would not permit her to mate with a warrior of a hostile tribe.

"And here's where I will come to 'end it all' when you leave me for some tall and willowy, blonde show-girl," smiled Olga Halka.

But her pulse was beating a little faster to see the hills again—the blessed hills whose memory even a towering city like New York can never completely erase from the heart of one who has been born among them.

Stanislaus Joseph also was not a little thrilled. He had never before seen this type of American countryside, his journeys being confined to the trips to Philadelphia and to Boston—and that by leveled-off, easy-riding but scenery-avoiding railroad tracks.

They were quickly into the long central street of the cozy town of Stroudsburg, and here their swaying carrier stopped before a counter restaurant, where passengers could gulp a cup of coffee and visit the welcome rest rooms. And as they sat on high stools at the long, oval-like counter, a well-dressed gentleman opposite eyed the girl Olga curiously.

"I think the man over there wearing the Panama hat wants to speak to you, and is not quite sure if he knows you," said Stanislaus Joseph. "He hasn't taken his eyes from you since we came in. And he doesn't look at all like the deputy sheriff you spoke of your father knowing," he added with a smile.

Olga directed her eyes to this man, and the gentleman—he was obviously a gentleman—arose and came rapidly around to them.

"I can't be mistaken—you are Olga Lasenka from Wilkes-Barre!" he exclaimed. "And don't tell me you have forgotten me, although I'm not now a celebrity and a great musical show star like you have become!"

"Why—I—I—" stammered the girl, and then it dawned on her with a rush. The lean, kindly face, with the close-cropped mustache and the shrewd grey eyes.

No apparition this, but a very alive personage, though out of an antiquity that seemed centuries ago—so much had happened in the past four short years. "You're Mr. MacPherson, the manager of the Wilkes-Barre Five-and-Dime!" she exclaimed.

"That same, in the flesh and in person! Positively no facsimile!" laughed the Woolworth Store executive, his face alight with excitement and obvious pleasure.

"And this is my husband, Dr. Stanislaus Joseph Halka," said the girl, and Mr. MacPherson seized the hand of the little musician in a warm, friendly grasp.

"Glad to know you, and may I say—a mighty lucky fellow!" he said. "Got one of the best girls that ever worked in our store! And now I know why I wasn't sure it was you my wife and I saw in that big beautiful Broadway show last Winter. For I looked on the program and it said *Olga Halka*—it was the only 'Olga' on the program, and yet I knew you as Olga *Lasenka.* Thought, if it *was* you, you'd taken a stage name, as I believe they call it. And it was only because you were married! Well! Well! And to a doctor! It's a fine profession, sir! Surgeon or general practice, sir?"

This latter question was directed to Stanislaus Joseph. Mr. MacPherson had early learned that a successful executive should express an interest in the other fellow's profession.

Before the somewhat flustered Stanislaus Joseph could answer, Olga spoke for him.

"My husband is a Doctor of Music," she said proudly. "A graduate of the University of Vienna in Austria. He is one of the finest pianoforte players in America, and is now writing a symphony. He was the leading member of the orchestra of the Ziegfeld-Friml operetta you and your wife must have seen."

Mr. MacPherson again shook the young man's hand warmly.

"Excellent! Wonderful!" he said. "Always wanted to go into the Arts myself, had a talent for it, but my father insisted I enter trade. It's fine—simply fine!—when two young people can work together. My own wife was a cashier in our store before the children started to come. Now she's busy at home. *Very* busy."

Mr. MacPherson gestured the progressive height of five offspring. "I expect you yourselves will soon be finding out!" he added jovially.

"Nothing like a happy marriage to keep a woman out of mischief! Ha! Ha! . . . Gee! But you were great—*positively great* in that show, Olga! What was that big scene you had? *Red wine you said*——"

Mr. MacPherson hesitated, apparently fearful of quoting incorrectly that immortal declamation.

Olga Halka laughed, but she was pleased and thrilled that her old boss remembered her humble contribution to the thundering drama of that Justin Huntly McCarthy libretto.

"Because my lips are red!" she finished. "And it wasn't a very big scene, as you well know, Mr. MacPherson," she laughed again. "I was just in the chorus of that show. But my husband——"

"Tush! Tush!" interrupted the Five-and-Dime executive. "You were the star singer, as far as me and my wife were concerned! And the star actress! And you were the most beautiful girl on that stage filled with beautiful girls! I always knew you'd reach the top, ever since I heard you sing the *Star Spangled Banner* at our Lions Club. And in that pleasing vaudeville act at the Colonial. What was it called? Don't tell me. . . . *The Four Carnation Buds!* That was it! Remember it because it has the same title as a great condensed milk we sell a lot of in our grocery department. And to think that you were on the ribbon counter of our Five-and-Dime, as they call it!"

Over his face came suddenly a look of utter inspiration. So must the countenance of Napoleon Bonaparte have changed when he first conceived the idea of conquering all Europe. So must Michelangelo Buonarroti's face have brightened in that first ecstasy of inspiration for the idea evolving the decorations of the Sistine Chapel.

Mr. MacPherson jerked out his heavy-chained watch, and snapped open its gold cover.

"Excuse me," he said. "There's six minutes and thirty seconds more before the bus leaves for Wilkes-Barre, and I've got to do some quick telephoning. Headed back there myself. Over here in Stroudsburg yesterday to get a new branch started. See you both on the bus. You *are* on your way to Wilkes-Barre, aren't you?"

"My husband has never seen where I was born," said Olga. "He's been only a few years in America."

"Good! Good! You'll see one of America's great metropolises, Mr. Halka!—I should say Dr. Halka!" corrected Mr. MacPherson. "Population 86,236, and growing by the minute. Queen City of the Susquehanna!"

Again Mr. MacPherson consulted his watch. "Don't make any luncheon engagement, you two. You've got one at the Lions Club. Sterling Hotel. One P.M. This is the day we meet. That's why I'm rushing back this morning. I'm its president now—but maybe you've already heard!"

And "these two" watched Mr. MacPherson's well-tailored back disappear quickly into a telephone booth at the far corner of the lunch room, and the booth's folding door snap-to with a bang—the door-closing of a man who knew what he wanted, and got it!

"He's a grand, kind gentleman," said Olga Halka to Stanislaus Joseph. "I'll never forget how he paid me a week's full salary, although I joined the Four Rosebuds on a Tuesday, and how he got the Lions Club to come in a body that Saturday night, and how he put big stories in the local papers! At least there's one person in Wilkes-Barre who didn't forget me."

"There are probably many of your friends there," said Stanislaus Joseph.

But they both might have been slightly alarmed had they guessed the implications of the beginning of an authoritative conversation from that corner phone booth.

"Listen!" Mr. MacPherson was saying, when he had obtained a quick long distance connection with his Wilkes-Barre Five-and-Dime. "This is MacPherson. Talking from Stroudsburg. Give me our advertising manager and give him to me quicker than quick! This is the biggest thing our store—not to mention the sovereign City of Wilkes-Barre—has ever had!

"Step on it, for I've got to also phone through to City Hall and the Mayor, all before the next bus pulls out!"

✣ 4 ✣

AGAIN OLGA AND Stanislaus Joseph Halka were aboard the speedy Wilkes-Barre bus, Mr. MacPherson in the seat behind them, he having barely made its closing entrance door by a last-minute sprint from his phone booth after a pregnant conversation with his close friend, the publicity-minded Mayor of this city of eighty-six thousand, two hundred and thirty-six souls.

And soon these three and their fellow twenty-eight passengers—were passing through the pine-scented Poconos; onward and westward for another two hours into the almost-mountains that would presently give them a view of that great and beautiful valley called Wyoming, the cradle of their destination.

Along with an enthusiastic running commentary on the scenery, and the vitalizing freshness of the Pennsylvania ozone (as compared with that of less fortunate States), Stanislaus Joseph absorbed a detailed description of the civic glories of Wilkes-Barre, including its lately installed sewage system, "the finest, sir, of any city in America, bar none!"

Mr. MacPherson was also President of the Wilkes-Barre Board of Trade, and neglected no opportunity to advertise the unparalleled cultural and economic assets of his native town.

And now they were winding through its suburban thoroughfares; reached a main street of the city; and presently turned abruptly into a wide alleyway, at one side of which was the embarking (and disembarking) entrance of the Central Bus Terminal. Through the wide, open doors, and across a ticket-selling lobby and waiting room, was the central Square of the town on which the front of the Terminal faced.

But it was this alleyway and the parking lot just beyond the bus terminal, and on the opposite side of the alley, that seemed to be the scene of unusual excitement.

"Unusual" is not quite the word. "Tremendous" would better describe it.

At a spot where a dozen travelers, or folk expecting travelers, would ordinarily be waiting, was a sea of eager, smiling and excitedly chatting faces. The bodies below these faces packed the alley, thronged the open waiting room, spread out to cover the acre of parking lot!

The late edition of the *Morning Record* estimated a crowd of "over one thousand." The *Evening News* placed the number at "well over fifteen-hundred." The next day's *Sunday Independent,* carrying photographs, said the police called the crowd one of twenty-five hundred. And as the New York bus drew up to a halt (police having kept an open lane so it could reach the Terminal doorway), a full-throated brass band burst into a rousing march.

That march was not unfamiliar to the ears of the girl who had been Olga Lasenka, and to Dr. Stanislaus Joseph Halka of the University of Vienna.

"Stanislaus—they're playing Mr. Friml's *March of the Musketeers!"* cried the girl. "I wonder what is going on!"

"They must be expecting the Governor of the State, or maybe the President!" said Stanislaus Joseph. President Roosevelt had paid an official visit to Boston when the Ziegfeld operetta was there, and the young man had been late at a rehearsal because he could not get across Boylston Street.

"I can't imagine what this is all about!" said Mr. MacPherson, Manager of the Wilkes-Barre Five-and-Dime, with a twinkle in his shrewd eyes, in reply to the question in the voices of these two, and the directly vocal and amazed questions of the other passengers who were straining their eyes through the windows as they pushed toward the bus exit door.

The occupants of that bus were not long in the dark.

As the girl who had been Olga Lasenka of the Woolworth ribbon counter emerged and while she still stood on the top step of the bus doorway, a great shout went up that almost drowned the now energetic playing of another equally famous Friml march, the *Song of the Vagabonds*.

"Olga Lasenka!" "Our Olga Lasenka!" cried a thousand voices (or fifteen hundred or twenty-five hundred—depending on which newspaper you read), but there was nothing problematical about that shout, as the girl recognized in the front ranks of the shouters some hundred of her former fellow workers at the Five-and-Dime!

And opposite her, held high over all heads, and stretching twenty feet between two stout flagpoles, was a strip banner bearing in great red and gold letters (the colors of her store signs):

WELCOME HOME OLGA LASENKA

and behind it, another banner with a double line of blazing words

ZIEGFELD'S NEWEST STAR
OUR OWN OLGA LASENKA

There were several news photographers with cameras held high to focus on her face, and a constant flashing of their light bulbs. A news-reel camera was grinding from the top of a radio truck parked opposite.

The shouting, smiling enthusiasts who crowded that bus terminal alley, the terminal waiting room, the big adjoining parking lot? Delegations of clerks and other employees not only from her own Five-and-Dime, but from its rivals—Kresge's, and McCrory's, and Neisner's; clerks and executives from the big Department Stores—Isaac Long; Bergman's; Fowler, Dick and Walker; Lazarus; The Hub; Pomeroy's; Zimmerman's; clerks from the great markets—the A and P; the American Stores; the Grand Union; half the office force from Stegmaier's great Brewery.

Hundreds from the stores were young girls in their natty store uniforms, and the market men were in their white. Humble store workers there to salute the courage of a fellow humble worker who had ventured out fearlessly into a great world and made good.

It should be recorded that there were a dozen ushers from the Colonial Theater in their gold braided jackets, hoisting their own special banner:

WELCOME TO THE FAIREST OF THE FOUR ROSEBUDS!

On the more conservative side was a representation from the Lions Club; the Rotary Club; the Kiwanis Club; the Advertising Club; the Women's Club.

The entire cheering Central High School population was there, for although it was a Saturday, there had been a school rally that morning for their baseball team. Pupils and teachers were on hand to greet a famous graduate!

One might also have noticed an elderly priest, who stood off at one side, and wiped a tear from a happy eye.

The young advertising manager of Mr. MacPherson's Five-and-Dime, knowing that the girl was a Catholic, had not forgotten to "contact" the clergy, along with the Retail Store Employees Union, the store executives, the newspapers, the two radio stations, the High School rally, the presidents of the various Clubs.

It was not till afterwards he learned this particular priest had come of his own accord. The Cathedral, to which the store advertising man had telephoned, had dismissed the notification as "publicity." An actress looking for notoriety. More of this incident later.

The music at the bus terminal was by the American Legion Band. And they had now gone into the complete score of the last Ziegfeld-Friml operetta.

It perhaps ought to be explained that Mr. MacPherson's young advertising assistant was a Wilkes-Barre ex-newspaper reporter, who had, the summer before, been the press agent for a small traveling circus. He had hopes of becoming a big-time theatrical press agent.

It would seem that his hopes had a certain basis of native ability. He had accomplished this well organized "welcome" in two short hours!

"Duszka! Duszka!" cried the girl who had been Olga Lasenka. "Whatever shall I do?"

"I told you that you would have some friends here!" said Stanislaus Joseph. "How could a girl like you think otherwise!" And the young man was remembering the generous send-off given to him, when he had taken that train from Vienna to Bremerhaven.

He was a very proud young husband as he stood beside the girl.

Olga Halka did not have to worry about what she should do. She realized, of course, that all this was due to her old employer Mr. MacPherson. The first thing she did do, was to impulsively throw her arms around that gentleman's collar and kiss his well-shaven cheek, Mr. MacPherson being somewhat taken back and embarrassed for the first time in his aggressive, executive life.

Thereafter, the girl was swept onward by forces quite outside her command.

The grand parade around the adjoining central Square and down

Main Street was led by the Military Band, three motorcycle policemen at its head giving it official sanction. Behind them marched the delegated employees from the various retail stores—three hundred each from Pomeroy's, and Fowler, Dick and Walker alone—a hundred and fifty from her own smaller Five-and-Dime; each store bearing its designating banners.

Then came the pupils of her Central High School led by their own drum and fife corps, this latter having at its head four shapely and skillful drum majorettes hurling thir batons high into the air.

The ushers of the Colonial Theater followed with their "Four Rosebuds" banner. Then, in a large, open convertible with Mr. MacPherson, the President of the City Council (the town's official "greeter" who was also the President of a great Mining Company), and the editors of the two leading newspapers, rode a completely overcome Olga Lasenka and Dr. Stanislaus Joseph Halka.

Olga was made to sit perched high on the raised back of the car, so as to be seen by all.

Other open motor cars followed, conveying the officers of the various Clubs, the superintendent and principal of the High School, officers of the Miners Union of which Olga's father had been a member, representatives of the American Legion in their distinctive caps, the Chief of Police and several squad cars of the State Police.

And the waving and shouting hundreds who lined the sidewalks (for it was the noon lunch hour) were not ignorant as to who she was.

An early, special edition of the *Times-Leader* was already out. The Mayor had proclaimed that day "Olga Lasenka Day." Two local radio stations had been broadcasting at fifteen-minute intervals "spot announcements" of this fact, including the vital (and paid-for information) that Miss Lasenka, "the newest Ziegfeld star," would be at her old ribbon counter at the Five-and-Dime from three to four that afternoon. "A most gracious and democratic gesture from a Wilkes-Barre girl who was now the Toast of all Broadway!"

One need not be told that all citizenry—both male and female—were anxious to get a close view of the local girl that the late Florenz Ziegfeld had, as almost his last managerial gesture, "raised to stardom." It attracted much more attention than the presence of any mere Governor or even President. Perhaps the appearance of Champion Jack Dempsey or screen vampire Theda Bara might have drawn an equal throng along Main Street—it would have had to be celebrities of such caliber to approach its friendly curiosity and hurrahing enthusiasm.

This parade reached its climax at the bunting-decorated City Hall, where the Mayor himself (having rushed home and donned his official-greeting morning coat and pearl-grey vest) awaited the young lady with a symbolic key to the city and a brief welcoming speech, which speech did not fail to mention the now proven and obvious advantages of starting life in that fair city!

What the young lady said in reply did not much matter. She was too excited and overcome to talk coherently.

From City Hall the motor cavalcade (this time behind screaming police motorcycle sirens) rushed to the Hotel Sterling and the Lions Club luncheon.

This luncheon had been hastily expanded (on orders from its President then in Stroudsburg) to the hotel's largest ballroom, and included many outside guests and the wives of its members. Olga and Stanislaus Joseph sat at a special raised speakers table beneath an excellent copy of Marie Rosalie Bonheur's "The Horse Fair," and along with the Mayor, the Club President, and the invited Presidents of the other Clubs.

A concert-grand Steinway had been placed just below and at one side of this table. And after the meal, and several speeches, she was called upon to sing the *Star Spangled Banner*, the public singing of which for this very Club four years before, had been "the true and prophetic start for her meteoristic climb to Broadway stardom," to quote one of the more conservative introductory speeches.

Her audience stood as she sang the bombardment-inspired Francis Scott Key verses—sang them somewhat better, I believe, than she had four years before—so that after the applause there were insistent cries for more songs—why not the music of the Friml operetta of which she had been the "star?"

The honest girl was happy to oblige, but she did again try to correct this "star impression" before she commenced her recital.

"I know, and I think you all know, that I was not a star in that last great Florenz Ziegfeld production," she protested. "I was a very humble and unimportant member of that operetta company—but of that even, I do not deny that I am very proud. Proud to be chosen for the ensemble of such a fine production.

"As a member of that ensemble I do know all its lovely Friml songs, and I will try to sing some of them for you, if you really wish it. Fortunately my husband, Dr. Stanislaus Joseph Halka, was a member of the orchestra. He will play for me and for you. And if these songs give you pleasure, it will be because of his great talent in interpreting Mr. Friml's genius as a composer, and not my poor endeavor."

But Mr. MacPherson was on his feet.

"Don't you believe a word she says!" he cried. "Except, of course, that her husband is also a great artist. My wife and I saw this show in New York. Our Olga Lasenka was the loveliest and most talented member of its cast. I have a program at home to prove that she was not just a 'member of the ensemble.' Her name is there, opposite a leading character—*the* leading character as far as my wife and I could see, and I flatter myself that *I know* about the theater.

"That program says 'Olga Halka' which is now her married name. But for us, her girlhood friends—and I hope her nice husband will forgive us—she will always be Olga Lasenka. She is just modest—that is all—a failing that all we Wilkes-Barre people have, because we know we come from the finest city in the entire land, bar none!"

There was kindly laughter and more applause. These good folk knew that Olga Lasenka was not yet a star in Broadway parlance, but she was something much greater to them.

She was their own home-town girl who had gone out into the world and *not failed*. She personified for them courage—success. That was enough—and more than enough. Let poor old New York have its phoney luminaries! Wilkes-Barre *knew*. And maybe they were right!

✣ 5 ✣

So the girl Olga sang the *Waltz Huguette* and *Someday* and *Love Me Tonight* and *Tomorrow* and the immortal *Only A Rose,* and sang them well. Mr. Rudolf Friml would have approved. Mr. Florenz Ziegfeld would have approved.

And then, when there was applause and demands for more songs the Dvořák *Songs My Mother Taught Me.*

And Stanislaus Joseph arose and said: "My wife, as Mr. MacPherson says, is most modest. She herself has written the words of a song with music by the stage manager of our operetta. Fortunately I believe I can play it. It's about New York, but maybe you'll permit her to sing it here.

"I think that someday she will write a song about your Wilkes-Barre—among your hills—they were her first love, and still her true love I have long suspected. This New York song is simply a practice number for that greater song which will be nearer her heart. So now—would you care to hear her Broadway song?"

There were shouts of "Yes! Yes!" and Olga sang a stanza and chorus of her *Broadway Bungalow*. But as she sang it this time, she wondered if Stanislaus Joseph suspected she had already written a song about Wilkes-Barre, as it were—a song that had to do with her beloved hills. Her "greater song."

He would know—in time.

And after *Broadway Bungalow,* she, in turn, asked if they would care to hear her husband play an instrumental number; and Stanislaus Joseph said: "My wife is of Polish descent. I understand that many of your forebears were also from that land. I will try to play a Chopin *Polonaise* that I love. That you doubtless know and love."

And the young musician gave them the stirring composition in *A-major* that the great Polish composer had written for his beloved native land—the composition about which he said "the nobility of his native Poland seemed to march before him in review, as if going to battle" as he was writing it.

Olga was half an hour late getting to the Five-and-Dime where she had worked.

That store, on Main Street, had a great "WELCOME HOME OLGA LASENKA" banner across its entire front, and extra police were keeping the waiting crowds in line.

Mr. MacPherson himself proudly escorted the girl to her old ribbon counter, where she insisted on again taking a hand at selling its merchandise to the eager-to-meet-her shoppers. Its well-stocked counter was completely exhausted in the first twenty minutes.

At four-thirty she and Stanislaus Joseph were rushed to the Auditorium of the Central High School, where it had been announced by radio and in the early newspaper editions the girl would meet her old classmates, and sing several of the songs "from her great New York success."

The huge auditorium was crowded—I fear with as many parents

as "classmates"—but she did find a lot of her old school friends and all of her teachers. The Superintendent of all the schools welcomed her and introduced her—"a shining example of what study and hard work could do for all young people," and Olga again sang most of Mr. Friml's fine score and Stanislaus Joseph played Debussy's *Clair de Lune* and several of the Brahms *Hungarian Gypsy Dances*.

At the end, Olga sang the ballad her class had adopted as its own special song—Victor Herbert's *Toyland*. The simple, charming lyric by Glen MacDonough brought a mist to many eyes.

> Toyland! Toyland! Little girl and boy-land,
> While you dwell within it—You are ever happy then.
> Childhood's Joyland, mystic merry Toyland!
> Once you pass its borders you can ne'er return again.

And for this song, her old music teacher played the accompaniment.

Most of the younger folk now pressed forward to obtain her autograph—it seemed she had been signing her name ever since her arrival! Signing it on slips of paper, in autograph books, on menu cards. Camera men and reporters from the newspapers (one, she was told, even from the Associated Press) had also accompanied her all along the line.

Shortly after five, she and Stanislaus Joseph, tired out but happy, were permitted to retire to a room at the hotel which the Five-and-Dime store had engaged for them.

Mr. MacPherson sensed that they might now wish to be alone—these two who had taken a bus in New York for a quiet day at Olga's home town! He knew that the girl wished to show Stanislaus Joseph where she had lived—the church which she had attended—the cemetery where her father and mother rested.

He said to them as he deposited them in the hotel lobby: "A great day! A great day for Wilkes-Barre! A great day for the Five-and-Dime! Mr. Halka, we sold more merchandise in our store this afternoon than all of last week put together! I ought to pay your wife a handsome commission. The store can at least do this—a room in this hotel is yours for as many days as you can stay."

"You are most kind," said Olga, "but we have to return to New York. We really planned to go back tonight. But I think now we will stay here the night, and take an early bus in the morning. If I stayed much longer, Mr. MacPherson, I'd begin to really believe all the wonderful things you and everyone else have been saying——"

"There you go again!" said Mr. MacPherson. "Belittling yourself!

Stop it! I wouldn't be where I am if I hadn't believed I was the best retail store executive in America! You just start doing the same. I always did think New York was over-rated. Stay around Wilkes-Barre a while and find out how we do things here!"

"I've sure found out today!" said Olga. "And I'm grateful. I can't tell you how grateful. But I know that my husband must be in New York to play at Hunter College at four P.M. tomorrow—it's a graduating class exercise."

"Then, *if* you must, you can take a nine o'clock bus in the morning," said Mr. MacPherson. "I'll tell you. I will come at eight, and have breakfast with you. I would ask you to have dinner at my home tonight, but I think you have things to do that you wish to do alone."

A sentimental softness suffused his executive-sharpened eyes. He permitted himself to reminisce.

"My wife took me to Shenandoah, where she was born and raised, a year after we were married. Folks wanted to entertain us every minute, but we wanted to see some places alone together—the street where she had gone from door to door selling soap, so that she could get money for a new dress—the neighbor's yard where she mowed the lawn so that she could have ice cream soda money.

"A clever business girl—my wife! Sorry she couldn't be at the luncheon. But very, very busy now. Five little ones, and another on the way! Very busy. Very busy indeed.

"But that is her happiness," he added quickly as his eyes brightened and he shook off a slightly doubting mood, "just as hard work and success in business is mine! But I've never forgotten what a dreadful time we had breaking away from well-meaning friends that day in Shenandoah. So you see, I understand how it is. Good night and thanks. Many thanks! See you at breakfast."

And energetic and hard-working Mr. MacPherson was gone. Gone doubtless to be certain there was no new addition to his family after two days' absence; and if there had been, to assure his wife's continued happiness by wasting no time in commencing operations for the next.

"He is really a grand, kind man," said Olga Halka again to her husband, "but still, my duszka, I'm sort of glad I married you instead of him!

"And now there *are* some places I want just to show to you—all alone, my dear one. I think we will go to our room and freshen up. Then we will go to my church. I believe I saw my old priest in the store this afternoon, and before that in the bus station. I hope he was at the luncheon."

"I think he was," said Stanislaus Joseph. "I saw a priest, way back, at one of the tables."

A desk clerk approached them, and handed them the evening paper. Half of the front page was covered with their pictures—their arrival; the parade; standing with the Mayor on the City Hall steps; the crowds around the Five-and-Dime; Olga behind her old ribbon counter.

"Whatever would Mr. Ziegfeld think of all these exaggerations—these falsehoods about my being his newest star!" said Olga. "I hope, wherever he is, he is not too angry. I tried my best to tell those wonderfully friendly people otherwise, but they just would not listen."

"I think that Florenz Ziegfeld was very pleased," said Stanislaus Joseph. "And Hugh de St. Omer, and Kommodore Hugo Frederick von Steinburg. I only wish Hans Beuter had been here!

"We must take back some newspapers to show Hans, or he will never believe it! By the way, where is his box of cookies? We might have a couple before dinner. We should have offered some to Mr. MacPherson. Given him the whole box. All those children and his busy wife!"

"Good Heavens!" said Olga Halka. "The cookies! I must have left them on the bus!"

But I believe that even Hans Beuter would have forgiven them, had he been at the Wilkes-Barre bus station that day, and followed his two friends through that afternoon.

6

THE OLD PRIEST sat alone in his study. He was wondering if th[e] young girl, whose name and photographs had monopolized the eve[ning] paper and local radio news commentaries, would remembe[r] him—would come to see him.

He felt very old and very much alone.

He had felt that way for the past year. Could it be that on

sometimes lived too long upon this earth? That one outlived all usefulness?

Maybe it was just that his little church—the building that was that church—had outlived its usefulness. It was in a poorer quarter of the town that had once been a prosperous one. The finishing of the new Cathedral, the swing of the population away from the river, had drained his parish—his congregation.

Most of his old friends were dead. He had not made many new ones.

Attendance at his Masses had dwindled to a few scattered worshipers. He had, on several occasions, at a regularly scheduled Mass, entered his sanctuary and turned to make the sign of the cross—and made it to empty pews. Three Sundays before he had preached his sermon to only his organist in the small choir loft and a parishioner who stood at the rear to take up the offering. Take *it* from empty seats.

He had had to ask help from the Bishop in nearby Scranton to maintain his expenses. He had heard rumors that his church property was to be sold, and what was left of his parish combined with a nearby larger church, headed by a young and energetic priest. What would happen to him he could only surmise. There was a monastery at Mount Hope to which he could retire.

That might have suited some, but it did not suit Father Joe, as he was called.

He had been called that ever since he had served as a chaplain in the Spanish-American War. Served in Cuba, and later in the Philippines. He had been the youngest chaplain in the United States Army. And one of the most popular. He had been cited for bravery by Colonel Theodore Roosevelt, and given the Distinguished Service Cross. "For Valor" was on the small scroll, below the eagle and the bronze cross.

There had been a grand homecoming reception when he had returned from these campaigns. He had been given this church—then new—as a sort of reward for service and popularity. His company and his sermons had been sought after and, he felt, enjoyed.

He had immediately volunteered when America entered World War I—had wanted to go overseas, but younger men were selected for that service. He did give his friendship—his talks—even his voice, for he was an excellent singer—to Army Training Camps all across the land.

Again there was recognition and popularity when the war was over and he returned to his parish. He was made Chaplain of the Pennsylvania State Police.

But now—well, he was well over seventy. No one seemed to remember, or care any more.

He easily recalled this Lasenka girl. She and her father had lived in his parish. When her father died, she had talked to him about becoming a Nun. But he had heard her sing. He had encouraged her to keep up her lessons and go out into the world. To find success in her work. To meet a man that she would love and who would love her. A husband.

He wanted no other person to experience the loneliness he was already commencing to experience.

Now she was back in Wilkes-Barre for a day. Apparently happily married and a success. He had heard about her coming on his radio. He had gone to the bus station, but finding that huge gathering, remained in the background. He had gone to the Five-and-Dime and watched her from a distance that afternoon.

He had not been at the luncheon. Stanislaus Joseph had been mistaken about that. He had not gone because he had not been invited there. It was a priest from the new Cathedral whose Roman collar the young husband had seen at one of the tables in the Sterling Hotel ballroom.

So now he sat alone in his study. This would be a sort of test if he was completely forgotten. For this young girl, after her father had died, had seemed to rely on his spiritual—yes, on his worldly—advice.

But so had many others in the old days. They were all dead, or had forgotten.

His doorbell rang. But it was only the evening paper that his housekeeper brought. He had already seen the paper. Bought one on the street when he had returned from the Five-and-Dime store. The doorbell rang again, and the voice was that of a young girl.

The girl he had known as Olga Lasenka and the man he had been told (and read) was her husband were ushered into his study.

"Father Joe!" cried the girl. "Dear Father Joe!" and she seized the wrinkled hand and kissed it. "This is my husband, Dr. Stanislaus Joseph Halka, and you will like him, for he also is a musician." And to Stanislaus Joseph, "Father Joe has one of the finest baritone voices I have ever heard. He encouraged me to be a singer. But for his encouragement I would never have found you. Father Joe and

Mr. Tom 'Wow 'Em' Gallagher! Do you remember him, Father, and the Four Rosebuds?"

The old priest found his voice. There had been a sizable lump in his throat.

"Do I remember him!" He continued with a laugh, "I remember him well; and how I worried about him, especially when I heard that he was a Presbyterian!

"But it's all turned out for the best. I said many a prayer for you, my child. And I confess I was sitting here wondering if you would remember me with all your triumphant day and your fine husband." And he shook the hand of Stanislaus Joseph. "God bless you both!" he finished.

"And I came to Wilkes-Barre just to see you, and have my husband meet you! And of course to see my father's and mother's graves. How can you think I would forget you! We are going to the cemetery, after a talk with you."

"Again—God bless you," said the old priest. "You don't know what your remembering has done for me."

So they chatted about the old days, and Father Joe seemed to grow younger and younger. He had been complaining of rheumatism and arthritis for the past month, but he was soon striding the floor as he had done in the past, when there was something to excite him.

"I've done so terribly much preaching," he used to apologize, "that I have to be on my feet when I talk!"

"And how goes the Church?" said Olga innocently. "Father Joe is the most popular priest in Wilkes-Barre," she said to Stanislaus Joseph.

The priest paused in his floor-pacing. He seemed to be old again.

"Not good. Not good." he answered. "I think they feel a younger man should be here—or my blessed church should be closed entirely." There was an infinite sadness in his voice. And the terrible acceptance of defeat.

"No!" said Olga Halka. And she also was on her feet. "No! No!" The girl's eyes were flashing. Stanislaus Joseph had never seen her in such a fighting mood.

And it was then that Father Joe had what he afterwards called a *blessed visitation*—an inspiration from Heaven itself!

"Olga, do you still sing the *Ave Maria?*" he demanded.

"Why yes," she said, "I could still sing it, I am sure, though I fear

I haven't practiced it lately. Certainly I can sing it! But why do you ask? Listen, Father Joe. I will write to the Bishop in Scranton. As soon as I get back to New York I will write him. Maybe he will pay attention to a letter from New York. I once met the Bishop. He came to our school——"

Father Joe broke in. "Olga, will you—will you sing the *Ave Maria* at my Masses tomorrow? Not the early ones at five and six, but maybe the ones at nine and ten and eleven o'clock?"

"Why—we were going to take the nine o'clock bus back to New York. My husband must be there by four in the afternoon. But maybe—perhaps—" and she looked at Stanislaus Joseph anxiously.

"Certainly she can stay and do it," said the young man. "I must go back, but Olga can take a later bus—that is, if you really wish her to do this."

"Do I wish it!" said Father Joe. "It will save my church. It will save my life perhaps. Now I think I can go on living and working! I will telephone the Sunday newspaper. Its editor is a friend of mine. An old war buddy. About the last of my old friends.

"They will find out if my little one-horse church is through! That, I know, is what they have been saying about it."

So it was arranged. Stanislaus Joseph would return alone on the nine A.M. bus. But Olga would stay to sing at the High Mass at eleven, as well as two earlier ones.

The girl and her husband departed for the cemetery. Father Joe, after a busy fifteen minutes at his almost unused telephone, sat at his desk to write a sermon of new faith, new hope, new courage.

I believe that a Divine Hand guided his pen as he set down words of flame and passion—a sermon that all Monday papers asked for, and printed in full—their newsmen having attended the High Mass because of the presence of Olga Lasenka. Their reporters and photographers, and a throng that overflowed and packed even the small street from nine o'clock till noon! That Sunday newspaper editor saw that the modern town criers—the radio stations—were also fully informed of Olga Lasenka's church appearance.

It was near sunset as Olga and Stanislaus Joseph Halka stood by the two graves on the great, sloping, hillside cemetery down West Main Street, at the far end of the town. A hillside that looked toward the west.

Far across a wide valley rose the mighty mountain range which was in reality a part of the Appalachian system, extending from Quebec to Alabama. And beyond these framing, dark-green mountains, they viewed a sunset quite as breathtaking—and on a larger scale—than that performed each clear evening behind the Hudson-bordering Palisades.

The same great crimson fireball, the same rose-tinted clouds in a sky of blue-green—clouds that gradually became a coral grey, and then merged with the sky in an almost blood-red black, as the earth gave itself entirely to the impassioned night.

All this they had experienced in New York, as the boy had first pointed out to Olga two years before. But then came something that New York and the Jersey Palisades did not possess. A sound-chorus of infinite beauty and restfulness.

"What—what is that?" asked the young man.

It was what the girl who had been Olga Lasenka was waiting for. What—she remembered—was in the song that she hoped her husband would some day write.

The song she dared not yet tell him about.

"It is the crickets and the whippoorwills," she answered. "Something that only my hills can give. Duszka, perhaps now you can understand why, when my time comes, I want to be buried here. I want to work and live in the city, along with you; but here is the place to sleep."

And the boy understood. They walked back slowly into the town. They went to a small restaurant where the girl had eaten when she had worked in the Five-and-Dime. Even there she was recognized, and their excited waitress and several customers requested her autograph. She could not deny that it warmed her heart.

Afterwards they went past the house where she had been born, and the nearby house where she had boarded after the death of her father. And they walked by the Colonial Theater where she had started her career as one of the Four Rosebuds.

Up in their hotel room—for they must again arise early—they turned on the small radio which operated by inserting a quarter into a slot at its top. News from a local station was coming over, and it dealt largely with the girl's reception and progress of the day. At the last it said:

"An important announcement. We just have word from Father

Joe O'Conner of the Church of Our Savior, that Miss Lasenka will sing the *Ave Maria* at all Masses tomorrow, starting with the one at nine A.M.

"Father Joe's church is a small one, and we advise our listeners to get there early, if they wish to hear this talented artist's remarkable voice—a voice that has thrilled Broadway for the past two seasons, and that many of us were privileged to hear today at the Lions Club luncheon, and at the High School Auditorium."

"Duszka," said the girl, "I quite forgot to tell dear Father Joe that all these stories about my being a great star were just made up by Mr. MacPherson. Do you think I ought to phone him now, and maybe not sing at his church? It doesn't seem quite honest——"

Their telephone rang. It was the young advertising manager of the Five-and-Dime.

"Been trying to find you all evening," he said excitably. "The Choir Master at the Cathedral wants Miss Lasenka to sing there tomorrow at their noon High Mass, but she will have to wear a black dress, and no facial make-up. I told them I didn't know if Mrs. Halka had brought along a black dress——"

It was Stanislaus Joseph to whom he was talking. Tightpants did not think it necessary to consult his wife.

"Thank that Choir Master very much," he interrupted, "but my wife is singing tomorrow at *three* Masses at the church of a priest named Father Joe. You probably know which one it is. And Father Joe doesn't care what color dress she wears—red, blue, green or yellow—or if she's plastered with make-up. *Plastered!* Just so long as she is there. And I don't think his God will mind either.

"Tell that Choir Master to wake up, and turn on his radio, and he will hear all about it!"

And to Olga he said: "We'll not worry about your being, or *not being*, a star! I think that courageous old priest needs your help. I'm only sorry I can't stay to help. And to watch you wham 'em, as *Variety* would say.

"You just give 'em all Hell—as I've heard Mr. Dixon tell the Ziegfeld company—give 'em *Ave Maria* as they've never dreamed it could be sung! Then maybe a red-hot, ripsnorter *Hallelujah Chorus* as Georg Friedrich Handel meant *it* to be sung. He once said it seemed as if 'all Heaven and Earth were lying open to his gaze' as he composed it. And I believe that Hugh de St. Omer will be standing right close behind you, to raise his two-handed sword *with one hand* on the high note!

"Wow 'em, my darling! Wow 'em—*ausgezeichnet!*"

As we know, Dr. Stanislaus Joseph Halka could sometimes lose his temper. And from Hans Beuter he had been acquiring an Americanese-Viennese vocabulary.

PART TWELVE

THE MIRACLE

⁂ 1 ⁂

BY THE MIDDLE OF September they both had jobs with another management. He to play the pianoforte in the orchestra, she as a member of the singing ensemble.

Their old conductor was the leader of this orchestra, but it was not like a Ziegfeld show. It was a solid success, but an "extravaganza," with inconsequential music, and depending on the antics of two popular vaudeville clowns for its box-office draw. Stanislaus and Olga were not very happy about it, but it was work at the union scale, and they were together.

They both hoped to get with something better—that is, more musical—before the season progressed far.

The young man continued to work at his symphony. The girl took up her singing lessons once more, and continually tried to find another idea for a song that her husband would like—but a song in which she was most emphatically *not* "dead."

When she was alone in the apartment, she would take out the "Olga" song and read it over. She liked that lyric, but why had she been inspired to write verses with such words?

She still worried sometimes about the legend affecting the twenty-third year of her life.

The theater where they worked was on upper Broadway, and they would board a bus down Broadway to Thirty-fourth Street to return home each night. Then walk east to Madison Avenue. One night—there had been both a matinee and an evening performance that day—the girl suddenly stopped half way across the long block.

She stopped because she suddenly could not walk.

Stanislaus Joseph hailed a passing cab, although the distance to the apartment was but a few hundred yards. He carried the girl up the four flights of stairs. Slight of build, he was surprisingly strong. He frantically telephoned Hans Beuter at his bakery—the hour then being eleven forty-five P.M.—asking if Hans knew a doctor.

As soon as Olga could lie down, she was not in pain; but if she tried to walk, even across the room, severe pains seemed to shoot up and down her legs.

A young doctor from Vienna was living in the same house as Hans. He was in America for special research and study at the great New York Medical Center. He was on leave from the Wiener Allgemeine Krankenhaus, the greatest hospital in Vienna.

Hans phoned back that although his friend had retired for the night, he was getting up, and would hurry to the Halka address.

"His father was a baker, like yours," said Hans, "and he came here with a letter to me. Wanted to live near someone from home, so he took a room in the house where I live. Although still quite young, I hear he is considered a brilliant Herr *doktor* and surgeon."

It would seem that the baking industry of Vienna was a special breeding-ground for professional talent!

This doctor arrived. He was a young man of about thirty. His knowledge of English was none too fluent, and he had to have Stanislaus Joseph put some of his questions into English, and get Olga's answers via the same medium. He examined her limbs, and asked especially to examine the base of her spine. When he exerted a slight pressure there, the pain in her legs was renewed.

He took Stanislaus Joseph into the next room. Olga lay on the bed of the small adjoining room.

"Well?" said Stanislaus Joseph.

There was such anxiety in his voice and face that the doctor hesitated. He had not yet become hardened to human emotions. And he felt for this fellow Viennese who seemed so humble and so gentle. Hans had told him that his friend was a very fine musician. And a very great gentleman.

"I will speak to you in German," he said. "I can express myself better, and it is best your wife does not understand.

"I should tell you first that I was sent to America by my Vienna Hospital to work for a year with the great scientists here about a special disease. I was fortunate to make some progress about it in Vienna, and my superiors felt that I should add to that knowledge—and impart my knowledge—to some great hospital here, where millions of dollars are being spent to solve this malady. They have welcomed me at New York's fine Medical Center Hospitals. I consider myself still only a student, so I hesitate to give an opinion.

"What disease is your specialty?" asked Stanislaus Joseph.

"The disease that has baffled the medical profession for years, Dr. Halka—I understand you also are a Doctor. A Doctor of Music. That disease is now called cancer."

"Oh God!" said Stanislaus Joseph. He had heard and read in a general way about cancer. The Foundations that were being subsidized for its study. The great buildings that were being erected for its special research. No one who read a daily newspaper could be entirely ignorant of it. Or listened to the radio.

A great athlete had died of it. A great writer. There was already a large Fund of nation-wide subscriptions in the name of one of these men.

"Do not yet despair, for I am not yet certain of your wife's ailment," continued the young doctor. "Tomorrow I will arrange for her to be admitted to the Neurological Institute, which is the branch with which I am directly associated. More experienced and older physicians will examine her. X-ray photographs will be taken. Only then will we surely know.

"Please God it may not be what I suspect it is."

"But my wife is only lame—it is only her legs that pained her tonight. I know nothing of medicine or this dread disease," cried the young musician, "but from what little I do know, cancer is of the stomach or the throat or the lungs."

He was fighting off this calamitous pronouncement with what weak knowledge he possessed.

The young physician shook his head. "Cancer is a malignant tumor-like growth of cells that may start in almost any part of the body," he said. "As you say, it is usually in the torso, and that is where I fear this growth has started, and has been growing for a long time, in the beautiful body of your dear wife. It is no respecter of beauty."

"But why, then, is she lame?" said Stanislaus Joseph. "The legs, as I understand it, are not the torso."

"Mrs. Halka is lame," said the doctor of medical science, "because there is apparently a small internal growth—I cannot say yet that it is cancer—at the base of her spine.

"That growth is now pressing on the nerves that descend from the spine into her lower limbs. I have had several such cases in Vienna. There too, physicians at first thought such physical collapses simply ailments of the leg nerves. Now we know better."

"There is a cure—surely there is a cure!" cried the shaken boy.

"Perhaps," said the man who already felt Stanislaus Joseph to be his friend. "If it has not progressed too far. That is the tragedy of this disease. We do not yet know why these tumors—these cell growths—start. And we are too often not aware of them until it is too late. Your wife, for example, has only become aware of some disorder when she experienced a difficulty in walking.

"And the spine—ah, that worries me greatly! We can operate—we can remove a part of the lungs or the intestine or the breast or the throat. We cannot cut off the base of the spine."

"Oh God!" said Stanislaus Joseph. "Oh merciful God!"

The young doctor came to him. He placed his hands on the boy's shoulders.

"Do not despair," he repeated. "It may be just a small tumor, near but entirely free of the spine. Only the X-ray can show that. Thank God for this discovery of a great German physicist Wilhelm Konrad Roentgen. Their proper name is *Roentgen Rays.* The disease can also be treated by so-called X-ray therapy. I myself have been working on an antibiotic serum——"

He was conscious of the agony of the man before him. "Would to God that it were fully tested and perfected! Would to God that I had worked harder and longer hours upon it!" he said, and clenched his lowered fists. "I must find the answer! I *will* find it!"

"Can we get my wife to this hospital tonight?" asked Stanislaus Joseph. "I have money. I can meet any expense."

"It is now after midnight," said the doctor. "A period of a few more hours—a few more days even—does not matter. Your wife will not suffer if she remains quiet. I have brought a sedative, and will give her a mild one. She will sleep. Tomorrow morning I will make arrangements. I think she should go in an ambulance, although she could come in a taxicab."

"She will go there in an ambulance," said Stanislaus Joseph.

"I will then myself be here with it at nine o'clock," said the doctor. "And I think I can arrange for a semi-private ward."

"Arrange for a private room," said Stanislaus Joseph.

"A private room is expensive," said the young doctor. His tone was kind and solicitous.

"I have money, doctor. Thank God I have money," said Stanislaus Joseph.

"Very well," said the doctor. "Before I go I would like to ask your wife one question. I hesitated, for I did not wish to unduly alarm her. It is this. *Did either of her parents die of cancer?*"

"I think we should leave that till tomorrow," said Stanislaus Joseph. "It cannot be of any help tonight, can it?"

"No. Nothing can be of help until we take the X-ray films," said the doctor.

He said goodbye to the girl. He gave her a powdered sedative in a glass of water. "I will be here at nine," he said. And at the door he said to the young husband, "Be brave. The finest physicians in New York are at the Neurological Institute. I can humbly say they like me, and I believe they respect my work although I am a very young man. They will give me any service I ask. I know now why I looked up our friend Hans Beuter when I came here. It was so that I could serve a fellow countryman, even in America. Good night. Courage."

"What was all your talk about?" said Olga, when Stanislaus Joseph returned to her. "What stupid thing is the matter with me? Am I going to have to miss the show tomorrow night? I hope not. I think I feel better already."

"Do not worry about the show," said Stanislaus Joseph. "It will go on just the same if you have to be out a night or two. You are going to a fine hospital tomorrow morning for a thorough check-up, as I think they call it. This young doctor—in whom I have every confidence—advises that."

"That will be expensive," said the girl, "but I suppose he knows best. I'm glad my best dress is back from the cleaners. I must wear my best dress."

"Yes. Wear your best dress," said Stanislaus Joseph. He hesitated, but anxiety drove him on.

"Olga," he said, "do you know of what your father and mother died?"

"What a question!" said the girl. "My poor father died as the result of an accident in the mine. Not in the mine, but as a result of it. A heavy beam had fallen across his chest. It affected his lungs.

He lived for a year after it, but could not again do hard work."

"And your mother?" said Stanislaus Joseph.

"I was a small child then," said the girl. "I think—I think my mother had something the matter with her spinal cord. They called it a tumor or something like that. I remember now—she could not walk—Oh duszka! You don't think—the doctor doesn't think——"

But her voice trailed off. The sleeping powder was making its merciful effect.

"I am—so very sleepy—" she said. Olga Halka slept.

Stanislaus Joseph Halka fell on his knees beside the bed. He prayed as he had never prayed before.

After a while he was calm. He went to his all-comforting pianoforte, raised the keyboard lid, played very softly Dvořák's *Als Die Alte Mutter.* He thought of the notes in the literal meaning of the beautiful Bohemian Gypsy lyric:

Als die alte Mutter
Mich noch lehrte singen,
Thranen in den Wimpern
Gar so oft ihr hingen—

When my ancient Mother
Still taught me to sing—
Tears in her eyelids
Were often strangely hanging.
Now I myself am old enough
To teach those life-songs—
And my own tears flow,
For *I* now also know Life's sadness.

Then he sat by the open window for a while, where the night wind blew in a fragrance from the geraniums Olga had newly planted in the window boxes for the Fall. He arose every once in a while, and stood by the bed, and gazed down at the sleeping girl. Thank God she was asleep and not racked by worry. Or maybe pain.

He took off his stiff shirt and collar, and put on a dressing gown Olga had bought for him. But he did not further disrobe. Although weary from a morning rehearsal, two hours' work on his symphony, and two performances at the theater, he did not lie down or sleep at all that night.

And that midnight, there had been two glistening drops below the painted eyes of the La Celle statue, standing in the Early Gothic Room up at the Cloisters.

And *that* midnight it was not raining through any open, leaded window.

✣ 2 ✣

STANISLAUS JOSEPH "fixed" the breakfast the next morning. He had apparently managed to doze off at around five o'clock—to sleep two brief hours from pure exhaustion—for he awoke with a start at seven. He was sitting in the morris-chair by the window. The girl was still asleep. He took a quick shower, shaved, then changed his clothes. He made cereal, soft-boiled eggs, and coffee. No waffles that morning or hot, buttermilk biscuits! At eight he gently awoke Olga.

She did not at first seem to remember, and then it came back in a flood.

Her lameness! That doctor! The question as to how her mother had died. She was to be taken to a hospital. She must wear her best dress.

Maybe it was all just a dream! She sat up in the bed, and again came the sharp pains shooting down into her lower limbs.

It was not a dream.

And into her awakened consciousness came another driving impact. The legend that concerned the twenty-third year of the oldest girl in each generation of her mother's family. Was it happening now to her?

She was on the point of telling it to Stanislaus Joseph, of blurting it out; but his tired, worried face that he tried to conceal with a smile and a kiss, caused her to remain silent about it.

She looked at the pillow by her side. It had not been slept on. The covers of that side of the bed were even and unruffled. Her husband had not been to bed.

"Duszka!" she said. "Where did you sleep? Or did you sleep at all? You should not have stayed up all night. This is terrible! You must be exhausted."

"I had a good night's rest in the morris-chair," lied Stanislaus

Joseph. She knew it was not true. His eyes were red around the lower eyelids.

"I—I had an inspiration, and did several hours' work on my symphony," he lied again. This, Olga thought, might possibly be true, but she doubted it. Stanislaus Joseph had once or twice risen up in the middle of the night to put more black notes on his music paper.

"What a trouble I am," she said. "I will try to get up and fix our breakfast."

"Our breakfast is ready—such breakfast as I could make," he said. "I will bring yours in to you. You are not to get up. Then I will bring you water, and a mirror, and your comb, and you can arrange your hair. I don't know if you should dress or not. We will see. You have plenty of time. A whole hour. The doctor is coming with an ambulance at nine."

"Duszka, you will go with me!" she cried. "You will not let me go to this hospital alone!"

"How could you think that!" said the boy. "I will ride with the driver. Or take a taxi, and don't you frown about the expense a taxi will be!"

The girl pulled his face to hers and held him tightly. "God has been good to me," she said. "I found you. That is all that really matters. Where would I be if I had not found you!"

They ate their breakfast. "You've not forgotten how to boil eggs and make good coffee," smiled the girl.

"I have not forgotten," said Stanislaus Joseph, "and this morning I watched your clock. Four-minute eggs! Exactly to the second!"

At eight-thirty—as Stanislaus Joseph was holding the small mirror so that the girl could arrange her hair—their downstairs buzzer rang. "Oh dear," said the girl, "and I am not ready!"

"The doctor said nine o'clock," said the boy. He looked down out of the window. There was nothing that appeared to be an ambulance on the street below. Again the buzzer rang insistently.

Stanislaus Joseph pressed the button that released the downstairs entrance door, and stood in his apartment doorway waiting. There were heavy footsteps coming up the stairs. The top of a familiar figure rose into sight—a figure with a bag slung over his shoulder. The postman.

"Registered letter for Halka!" was called from the floor landing below.

"Here," called back Stanislaus Joseph. "Another flight—front apartment."

He signed for the letter. It was a foreign letter. From Berlin. A letter from the Berlin law firm of the late Kommodore Hugo Frederick von Steinburg.

"I brought you another letter also," said the postman, "as long as I had to bring this one up."

The other letter was addressed to Mrs. Olga Lasenka Halka. It was from a Parish House in Wilkes-Barre.

Olga took her letter. Stanislaus Joseph opened his.

His contained not only a letter—a typewritten letter in German—but a long slip of bluish paper with perforations at one end. It was a draft from a Berlin bank on the Irving Trust Company of New York for "five thousand American dollars." The letter explained briefly that the Kommodore's bequest had at last been cleared, and "hoped the long delay had not inconvenienced Herr Dr. Halka."

Herr Dr. Halka's eyes filled with tears. "I think the Herr Kommodore must know," he said. "God rest his generous soul." Then to the girl as he showed her the bank draft, "Now I surely have taxi money."

"You will take that paper straight to the Savings Bank—today—when we get back—and you are not to spend it on me for taxis or anything else!" said Olga.

But to the young musician it meant the lifting of one worry. Whatever was ahead, they would be able *to pay*. Their some five thousand dollars of savings. This opportune bequest. Stanislaus knew the tragedy of trouble and no money. This world was not unkind, but a little money always helped! Now he and Olga were reasonably secure, come what may.

Again he thanked the gallant Kommodore who had not forgotten him.

The girl had read her letter. Tears also filled her eyes. They too were not tears of sorrow. She handed the letter to Stanislaus Joseph. It was on the stationery of

The Parish House
The Church Of Our Savior
Wilkes-Barre, Pa.

and it read as follows:

"Dear blessed Olga,

Forgive me for not writing you sooner. You who have given me new life. I need not tell you about that unbelievable Sunday. You saw the crowds that even the police could hardly keep in line. My church would have been filled five times over—ten times—at each Mass.

"And I told you then how beautifully you sang. I know fine singing, my child. Did I not recognize your voice, even when you were a young girl here? I have heard very great singers in my time. Adelina Patti, Christine Nillson, Lili Lehmann, Lillian Nordica, Emma Calve. No one of them could have sung more beautifully than you did that miracle Sunday. Our young organist has never stopped talking of it. I prophesy that someday your name will also become great. Olga Lasenka—as I know it.

"But no more on the subject of your voice, or you will become a victim of vanity. I must tell you something that I did not tell you when you were here.

"My church was definitely about to be closed. My parish combined with a larger one. That danger is now past. There is not a day now but that I have several christenings, and there have been nine large weddings. My Masses are crowded. I am asking Scranton to send me an assistant. They come partly, I know, just to see where you, the great New York star, stood and sang.

"My waiting room has several folk there all through the day, and late into the evenings, to ask my advice—my consolation. I am in demand to speak at public gatherings. I am heading a large Catholic Charity Drive, because it is thought my personal popularity will bring in funds! The American Legion has made me their Catholic chaplain. I think *I* am the one in grave danger of the mortal sin of vanity!

"Believe it or not, my arthritis and rheumatism are entirely gone! Young people have difficulty in keeping up with me along the street! My doctor says it is a miracle.

"It *is* a miracle. The miracle brought about by a girl who did not forget. And you were that girl. God bless you and keep you. I remember you each day in my prayers.

"Yours gratefully in Christ Jesus

"Father Joe

"P.S. You write me that you are not really 'a great star' or any star. That you were only 'in the chorus' of that New York operetta. About that I do not know. I believe, in God's Heavenly recording, you are a star of the brightest magnitude. You have already brought new joy and a new hope to hundreds in this city. I hear it and see it in the faces of those who ask me about you.

"Again—God bless you—and my blessing also on your husband,

J."

Stanislaus Joseph returned the letter to the girl on the bed. That letter also gave him a new faith. A new hope. And a happiness for what it must mean to this loyal girl.

Olga Halka placed this letter in the bosom of her nightgown. Just above her heart.

❖ 3 ❖

THE YOUNG Viennese doctor and the hospital ambulance arrived at nine. Two white-suited interns also, to carry Olga down the steep stairs. Stanislaus had helped her to dress—the "best" dress—and had packed a small bag with her toilet articles, two nightgowns, extra stockings and bed slippers, and the kimono.

"I'll be back by night," protested the girl. "I don't think I need all those things."

"You will have to remain in the hospital for several days at the best," Stanislaus Joseph had said. "They make X-ray photographs. They make tests that I do not understand. You must be a good patient. They will head off any serious illness."

Would they? Or had the fatal cancer—if it were that—gone too far? The young doctor had said the night before—*often we do not discover the ailment until it is too late.*

Safely in the ambulance, the girl's sense of humor did not desert her. She lay prone on the bed-like slide. The doctor and Stanislaus and one intern sat ranged along the side, in the row of straight-backed, chair-like seats that ramped the bed. The other intern rode with the driver. The vehicle was a new one, bright in glass and varnish.

Olga said: "The press agent at the Winter Garden should know about this. One of his girls in such a swanky outfit! Four attendants and a driver! We should whirl twice around Times Square with a banner *Laugh Yourself Sick at the Winter Garden.*"

But Stanislaus Joseph did not smile. Her drollery "laid an egg," as Mr. Dixon would have said.

Was there a fifth attendant riding in that ambulance? Did Cancer—the Specter of Cancer—ride with them also?

The ambulance proceeded up Fifth Avenue with the right-of-way given to such carriers—gained by the use of its authoritative gong. At One-Hundred-and-Tenth Street it crossed up the gradual incline past Morningside Park to Broadway, and then straight north to One-Hundred-and-Sixty-eighth Street, where the great hospital development fills several blocks, stretching clear to the Hudson River.

Stanislaus Joseph could not help but remember that a major part of this route was the same the buses traversed to reach the Cloisters.

They turned down this numbered street, going a short block to Fort Washington Avenue, where was the comparatively smaller building of the Neurological Institute, one side of which bordered the great river.

The girl was carried to a room on the fourth floor, which the Viennese doctor had already bespoken for her. Stanislaus Joseph meantime went with this doctor to the ground-floor business-office, to register Olga; establish their address; his relationship—and responsibility for the bills.

The room engaged for the girl was ten dollars per day.

"I can still place her in a semi-private ward. That will cost you five dollars," said the Viennese doctor in German.

"I realize that you are trying to help me," said Stanislaus Joseph, "but Olga and I have some money. We can pay. I would sell my Steinway before I would let her have anything but the best."

So presently they were with her in a single room overlooking the river. Like her counterpart in stone, further north at Two-hundredth Street, she could see the Palisades if she gazed from her window. Even from the high hospital bed she could see them plainly.

The attending nurse had already assisted the girl to undress, and she was now in a hospital-style nightgown which opened down the entire back, and she lay between the white sheets of the bed. They were awaiting the arrival of the floor doctor and the great specialist whom the Viennese physician had arranged to see her at ten.

"What a wonderful room!" said the girl. "And I know, duszka, that you are paying much more for it than you should be spending."

"Stop worrying, my darling," said Stanislaus Joseph. "We must do everything to get you well again."

"But I had hoped I could go home this afternoon," persisted Olga. "I must be at the theater by seven-thirty tonight. The manager-star does not like it if the girls come in late. And I've just remembered! *You* have a rehearsal at eleven this morning. The dance director called the ballet. It was on the bulletin board, and you were to report to play the pianoforte!"

"Thanks! Thanks for remembering it," said the boy. There was a telephone on the small table by the bed. "I will call the Union at once. They will send a substitute player."

"You know very well that no substitute can play that music at sight!" said the girl. "No, duszka. You go. I feel better already. Then you can return after the rehearsal. I hope they will have found that I am all right by then. Perhaps you'd better tell the stage manager I might be out just for tonight." She looked at the young Viennese doctor for confirmation.

This doctor shook his head. "I am very sorry, Mrs. Halka," he said in his labored English, "you must remain here for several days at least. The nurses will give you every care. But Dr. Halka—you may go to your rehearsal as your wife suggests. I would have to ask you to leave as soon as the physicians arrive.

"We will take Mrs. Halka to the X-ray room. That, with a thorough examination, will take several hours. You would only worry, sitting here or downstairs in the waiting room. Worry yourself and worry your brave wife.

"Come back at four this afternoon. By then we can report to you. It is simply photographs that we will be taking, and making certain nerve tests. It is best that you attend to your theater engagement. Surely you feel that your wife is in expert hands. In my case, the hands of a friend, as I hope you feel that you are mine."

"Yes," said the girl. "Please, duszka, go to your rehearsal. I will be causing the show enough trouble to be out a night or two, without your missing an important rehearsal."

Stanislaus Joseph went to the bed and kissed his wife. The girl threw her arms about his neck and held him close.

Then she said softly: "Do not worry, duszka. I do not worry so long as I have you. So long as I have your love."

Her heart was beating out the words of her song—*so long as love remembers*——

The great physician entered as the young man was about to leave. He was introduced. He was a large, kindly man. The boy noticed especially his hands. Great, sensitive hands. Hands whose skill and sensitivity had saved hundreds of human lives.

Stanislaus Joseph realized that he had heard or read of this physician's name before. Dr. Thomas Brooks Attwater, the greatest cancer surgeon and specialist in New York.

Specialist of the brain and of the spine.

✣ 4 ✣

STANISLAUS JOSEPH WENT to his rehearsal. Like the trained professional artist that he was, he managed to play the ballet music as if nothing out-of-the-ordinary had happened. He told the Winter Garden stage manager that his wife would be out of the cast the remainder of the week. That he had taken her that morning to a hospital.

When the rehearsal had finished, he was told that one of the famous comedians—and the co-owner of the show—wished to see him in his dressing room. The man was a strict disciplinarian, and the young musician expected he would be told his wife need not return to the cast, if she was missing performances. That had happened to several other chorus people.

He knocked on the closed door. The "Come in!" did not sound friendly.

The comedian-producer was going over back-stage expense accounts. He was marking with a red pencil where he thought they were excessive. There were a lot of red marks on the sheets before him. He looked up with some irritation at the interruption.

"Oh, it's you. The musician they call Tightpants," he said.

"You sent for me, sir," explained Stanislaus Joseph. Perhaps he also was to be given his notice.

"The stage manager informs me your wife can't be here tonight" was barked at the boy.

"I'm sorry sir," the young musician said. "I had to take her to a hospital early this morning."

"*What* hospital?" said the comedian. His tone would seem to imply a not-concealed doubt of the veracity of musican Tightpants' statement.

"The Neurological Institute at the Medical Center," said the boy. He did not like the tone of his employer, but he supposed the man did have a right to ask the question.

"Serious?" asked the actor, whose fame—and sizable earning power—had been attained by his ultra "rough-house" manner of getting laughs. "Anything for a Laugh" they called him.

"I fear so," said the boy. "It may be cancer."

But *why so many questions?*

The boy was in no mood for further unsympathetic questions. This "comic" would get no new gags—as he called them—to use in the show, from the details of Olga's illness. The actor's partner had once missed a matinee because he had been hit by a taxi, and at that performance this jokester had elicited numerous "belly laughs" from the audience, by reading fifteen-minute-interval bulletins on the damage *done to the taxi.*

"Have you any money?" barked the comedian.

"I have some," said Stanislaus Joseph, restraining his temper. "If my wife's absence will cause you any expense for the altering of costumes for another girl, I will repay you. Or you can deduct it from my salary."

The comedian looked hard at the little musician. He lit a fresh cigar which he carefully extracted from a long, glass, cork-stopped tube. His cigars were so cased because they cost one dollar and fifty cents each.

He frowned as he blew a critical smoke-ring. The cigars were not up to standard lately. He again gave his attention to Stanislaus Joseph.

"Hospitals are expensive," he said. "My wife had to be in one, part of last year. I sent for you to tell you if you needed money, the company manager will advance you against your salary. I'd noticed that girl. A damn good worker. Minds her own business. Keeps her mouth shut except when she's singing! And they tell me you can play Chopin. I like Chopin. God, how you must hate the music of this show! But we have to please the public, not ourselves.

"Someday I want you to play some Chopin—just for me."

"Why—why," gasped Stanislaus Joseph. "I'd be happy to. I will tell my wife what you have said, sir. It will cheer her. And about the money. Though I fortunately do not need it, you are most kind to think of it."

"Kind hell! I'm the meanest guy in the business," said the comedian, but there was a twinkle in his eyes. "I'm mean when they try to put one over on me. Out of the show because of a party. Drunk. You and your pretty wife—top bananas! Tell her I said to get well quick. And if you need anything—just yell. You have to yell around a show like this, or you won't be heard!"

Dr. Stanislaus Joseph Halka did not hate the Winter Garden music quite so much as he played it that night.

Even the alleged music that accompanied an episode in which the two comedians belabored each other with bags bursting with bread flour. And then engaged in a battle with lemon meringue pies.

5

BUT BEFORE THAT NIGHT'S PERFORMANCE Stanislaus Joseph had returned to the Medical Center.

Before returning, he went to a branch of the Irving Trust Company on Forty-eighth Street. He did not cash the Berlin draft. He opened an account there with it. A checking account. He had never had a checking account. He knew now that he might be writing checks unless he carried more currency with him than he usually did.

He was supposed to pay the hospital a week in advance. His introduction by the Viennese doctor had not made that necessary. However, when he reached the hospital, he first went to the business office and drew his first check for seventy dollars. One week's charge for Olga's room.

Again he breathed a silent word of thanks to the late Kommodore.

He went up the elevator to the girl's private room. A nurse had been assigned to her; she opened the closed door when he knocked. She put her finger to her lips. Olga was asleep.

She had just been brought back from the examination clinic. She was still under the influence of an anaesthetic they had given her, so that various injections could be made into her spine.

The Viennese doctor arrived shortly. He was now in his white laboratory coat. He took the girl's pulse, and then met the anxious eyes of the young husband. He again spoke to him in German.

"We do not yet know," he said. "The X-ray films are not yet developed. Certain extractions from her spine are yet to be analyzed."

"I asked her the question that you hesitated to ask," said Stanislaus Joseph. "She remembered that they said her mother died of a tumor—a tumor near her spine."

"That will not be important now," replied the doctor. "I was then seeking a verification of my own hasty examination. Tomorrow we will know exactly what is wrong. Not my knowledge alone, but the knowledge of several much greater physicians of this Institute."

"Tell me frankly, what do you now think?" asked the young man.

"I think that there is no doubt but that there is a malignant growth," said the doctor. "We know now that such growths are usually of a cancerous nature. Has this growth penetrated her spine? The X-ray photographs will show. And the fluid extractions we have made. Can we operate and not destroy the life of the patient? We do not yet know. Whatever the course of action, there will be a preliminary treatment. With radium, with X-rays, with drugs.

"As I told you yesterday, do not despair. You are in the most efficient hands in America. My poor knowledge is also yours. Tomorrow we shall know and decide what course to take."

"If this girl dies, I will not believe that there is a God!" cried the young husband. "What harm has she done? Why should she die just as her life has begun?"

"That question I cannot answer," said the young doctor quietly. "I am a humble scientist, not a theologian. In my work as a physician in great hospitals, I have had to observe what we call Death a hundred—yes a thousand times more—than falls to the lot of the average man. If I permitted myself to believe that this Death—this stoppage of the physical functions of the body—was the complete end, I would come to regard the world in the words of Sir Rabindranath Tagore, the Hindu poet, as a 'huge charnel-house.' Eight thousand Americans die yearly of the ailment of cancer alone. Many more in Europe, which does not have the health services you have in this great country.

"But despite this knowledge, this personal observation, I do not believe that the Spirit dies.

"The Spirit, the Soul, the Mind—whatever you choose to call that God-given attribute that transcends these heartbeats, these arteries, these livers, these intestines, these lungs that are provided for our physical existence on this earth. The break-down of these earth-organs is but a passing phase of a greater Life.

"Did it ever occur to you," the young doctor continued, "that your agony is perhaps a purely selfish agony? If you are honest with yourself, you want this girl to live, because her so-called death will deprive you of her comradeship, of her love. It is not primarily for *her* sake.

"How can you know that it is not best for her that she quit this earth at this time? That her mission has been accomplished? What disappointments, what tragedies may lie in wait for her? Suppose you are soon destined to die. Is it best that *she* then be left alone instead of you? Do you wish that anguish, that sorrow, to fall on her, instead of on yourself?

"May I tell you this more. I first looked down at the girl I loved on a hospital bed. She loved me, unworthy as I am. We were married in that hospital ward two days before she died. I knew that she must die. That every day—every hour longer—that she lived meant another day, another hour of suffering. I did all I could to save her life. That was my task on this earth. But I believe that she waits for me somewhere Out There. That our marriage will be consummated in a greater Life. Perhaps it happened so that I would dedicate all my life here to the work God has given me a special talent for.

"I asked no sympathy when that brave girl passed on. I needed none. She is with me every day. God, in his wisdom, knew what was best for us.

"In His wisdom, He will decide what is best for you, and for the girl who is sleeping on that bed."

The young doctor left the room to visit his other patients. Stanislaus Joseph sat in a chair by Olga's bed. The nurse also left, to return periodically to see that all was well.

Was this young scientist—this young doctor right? Was his agony for his own happiness?

No. For the unthinking moment perhaps. But in his deepest heart——

"Oh God, do not let her suffer," he said almost aloud. "If she must go, do not let her suffer." But he added: "Oh merciful God, please do not take her from me."

Olga awoke about six. The simple meal was brought to her on a tray—the food she should eat while various tests were being made.

"They are wonderfully kind here," she said. "I am in good hands. I was a little frightened when they wheeled me under the great X-ray machines, and I looked up at pointing, black tubes that appeared like small cannons! But all they shot were pictures—pictures of my back. Not one of my face!

"Do you think the Winter Garden can use some pictures of my poor back, duszka?"

Stanislaus Joseph tried his best to smile. Then he told her of the episode at the theater with the great comedian.

"I am glad that I am liked and you are liked," said the girl. "Tell them all I will be back at the theater just as soon as I can walk again," she said as the boy left at seven, to stop for a hasty snack at a restaurant on upper Broadway near the hospital, and then take a subway down to the theater for his evening performance.

He could not see her again that night, as visitors were not allowed after ten o'clock, unless there was a crisis in a patient's illness.

The nurse promised to telephone him if there was a need. He left the theater phone number, as well as his own. There would be no need that night, the nurse assured him.

The great specialist, who came to the room just before he left, also gave Stanislaus this assurance.

At the Winter Garden, the comedian sent for the boy after the performance.

"Your wife?" he asked.

"They do not yet know," answered the musician.

"Chin up!" said the comedian. He called to his dresser who was putting out his street clothes. "In the right hand coat pocket. A piece of paper." To Stanislaus Joseph: "I copied something to give you, out of a book I own. In case the news was bad."

Receiving the slip of paper, verifying it, he handed it to the young musician. He said to Stanislaus Joseph: "You have looked so depressed the last two days—and I think not entirely due to the music you have to play here! I want to see a smile."

The boy took the slip of paper. He hoped it wasn't a "gag." "Anything for a laugh."

It was the well-known habit of this actor to write new jokes he had invented on slips of paper and ask his friends if they seemed to be really humorous. Stanislaus Joseph was not exactly in the mood for hearty laughter.

He read—

Do not despair when Darkness brings the Night—
We move eternally toward greater Light.
There is a Sunrise, glorious and bright—
Bright Destiny!

The comedian commented: "My wife says it's simply a highbrow version of a song she sang in burlesque—we were in burlesque together—a song called *Wait Till the Sun Shines, Nellie*. But I guess the guy who wrote that bit of philosophy didn't lift it from Tin Pan Alley. He lived and died in the years around fourteen hundred. Quite a guy. Had troubles in plenty. Francois Villon. Greatest poet of his day. I'm a sucker for these poet guys. By the way, if you need any help of the kind I suggested, just yell. Yell good and loud. And don't forget. We have a date when you will play Chopin—and maybe a little Debussy—if you play him too."

The comedian held out his hand to the young musician. "I want to see a smile," he said.

The handclasp was warm—sincere—even though the face still wore an absurd character make-up which included a broad putty nose and a "fright" wig.

Stanislaus Joseph smiled. If not a smile of cheer, a smile of deepest gratitude.

✤ 6 ✤

STANISLAUS JOSEPH HALKA needed help the next morning, but not financial help. He was at the Neurological Institute by ten o'clock—the hour he had been told to come. The Viennese doctor took him into the small consulting room which he was using as his office.

"The news I have for you is not good news," he said.

"You mean?" said the young musician.

"I mean that your wife has a cancerous growth in her lower spine. I have the X-ray films here," and he took four dark, laboratory films from his desk drawer. Two were quite large, eighteen inches in length. He held them in rotation to the light.

One film showed the entire spinal column—the bone structure standing out white against the dark background that was the girl's back. The other film disclosed the base of the spine and the pelvis—a life-sized spread of the basin-like structure joining the lower limbs to the body.

In both films, there was a small, white bulge, that did not seem to be a part of the regular, duplicated, right and left bone formation.

"That white bulge is the growth," said the young doctor. "The tumor, as we used to call it."

Next he showed the lad two smaller films—close-ups of the spine base, with this white bulge blotting out entirely one of the vertebrae.

"This is the cancer," said the young doctor. "It has been forming for at least two years. Your wife only realized its presence when this growth began to press on the nerves that start at this point, and extend downward into her lower limbs."

The boy had taken the smaller films in his hand. He again held them to the light of the window. His hand was unsteady as he replaced them on the doctor's desk.

"What then do we do?" he asked. His voice was dull and hopeless. His face expressed an utter helplessness.

"At first," said the young doctor, "we will treat her with X-rays. With radium. With injections of a powerful serum. We will attempt to kill these malignant cells."

"How long will such treatment last?" asked the boy.

"For some two weeks," said his Viennese friend.

"Will she be in pain during this treatment?" asked the boy.

"It will be relatively painless," said the doctor. "We apply a local anaesthetic. During this period the patient must be absolutely at rest."

"And if this treatment is not successful?" asked the young man.

"If we cannot burn out—dissolve the cancerous cells," said the doctor, "we will try an operation. We will attempt to remove this growth by use of the surgeon's knife. In that case, pray God the growth has not penetrated the tissues of the spine itself."

"I will ask this," said Stanislaus Joseph. "Is it necessary to tell my wife that it is cancer?"

"No," said the doctor. "That is not necessary, if you so wish it."

"Please do not tell her then," said the boy. "So far as I know, she suspects and dreads only a tumor. Let her believe it is only that. Something that can be removed. I do not think she knows anything of medicine. But every schoolgirl has heard the frightening word cancer.

"Do not terrify her by that word, if you can avoid it."

So it was left. The girl bore up bravely under the news that she must have hospital treatment for at least two weeks. She worried more about the expense of her private room than about her ultimate recovery.

She worried about not cooking for Stanislaus Joseph, and the washing and ironing of his shirts and collars. That he would forget to water the plants in the window boxes. That *his* worry for her would interfere with his work.

She felt that she would soon recover, for she seemed to be in such expert hands as those of the doctors and the nurses of this institution. Each day she was wheeled by white-coated interns to the laboratory. Placed under the powerful X-ray which would, if possible, burn out the dangerous tissue of the growth.

She slept a great deal. Mild sedatives were given her, so that she would sleep.

It was the Saturday night of the second week that she again had the dream.

She had not experienced that dream for several months. Again she stood on what she now knew was the bridge of a great ocean liner, and said to a man she now knew to be the late Kommodore Hugo Frederick von Steinburg: *"Ah, Monsieur le Capitaine—it is hard to die when one is only twenty-two."*

She had awakened with a start, so vivid had been the scene, and called out for Stanislaus Joseph—"Duszka! Duszka!"

A floor night-nurse was passing in the hallway—the girl was not yet considered a serious enough case to have a special nurse in constant attendance. This floor-nurse entered the dimly lit room quickly.

"Mrs. Halka! What is it?" she said. "You have only to ring your bell, and someone will be here directly." There was a boxed pressure-button at the end of a cord that always lay alongside her bed cover.

"I'm sorry," said Olga. "I was dreaming. And when I awoke I thought I was at home."

"The word you were saying—it seemed such a pleasant word. Was it a name?"

"Duszka?" said Olga.

"That was the word," said the nurse.

"It is Polish," said Olga. "It is what I call my husband. It means 'Little Soul.' "

"You and your nice husband are well liked around here," said the nurse. "I wish all my patients were like you. We all pray that you will recover soon, though we will hate to see you leave us."

"There will be great gratitude in my heart to all here when I leave," said the girl Olga.

When she left. How would she leave? On her two small but sturdy feet or in a long box? For the daily visits to the laboratory—the serious faces of the doctors who worked over her—she would have to be very dumb not to realize that something was really wrong with her spine.

She had gotten up one night, and tried to cross the small room to the wash basin. The pains in her legs were like stabs. She had to crawl back into the bed and ring for a nurse. She was cautioned not to make such an attempt again.

And her dream had caused the legend of her mother's family to recur vividly to her mind. That twenty-third year in the life of the eldest girl.

Then there was the quite unexplainable matter of the song lyric she had written—written as if she had already died.

She slept only fitfully the remainder of that night. Most of the time she gazed out of the window opposite her bed. It was an "elevated" hospital bed, and she could see the distant Palisades through her window—a black line against a moonlit sky.

The black line reminded her of the distant mountain-line she had so lately viewed from the hillside graveyard in Wilkes-Barre.

But there was no pleasant song of crickets or whippoorwills. Just the hoarse call of a steamer passing; the honk of an all-night taxi on the drive far below; and the low, never completely dying, coherent yet undecipherable murmur of a mighty city.

❖ 7 ❖

STANISLAUS JOSEPH HAD SPENT two desperate weeks. He stayed at the hospital as many hours of each day as possible. He continued to report to the theater and play the performances. The girl insisted on his doing that.

Several events at the theater did, in fact, comfort him.

The first Saturday he was handed *two* pay envelopes. One, his own salary. The other marked "Olga Lasenka." The girl had gone back to this as a professional name—I think to please anyone from Wilkes-Barre who might by chance see the Winter Garden piece.

Stanislaus Joseph was asked to sign for both envelopes. The girl's contained her full week's salary which was forty dollars.

The musician said to the company manager: "There is a mistake. My wife has not been here all week." The company manager said: "No mistake, Tightpants. It is by order of—" and he mentioned the name of one of the comedian partners of the enterprise.

The young man went again to that gentleman's dressing room. It was just after the matinee.

That day the comedian-manager was in no mood for quotations about "bright Destinies," and his thoughts were not on Chopin *Etudes*. A newly inserted comedy scene had "flivved." "Flivved" badly. He was still in its costume, wearing an oversized plus-four suit of loud plaid, and a cap of the same material, two feet wide.

"My orders of course!" he shouted at the lad. "Who the hell else gives orders around here? My partner and I will continue your wife's salary until she is well. Any damn Musical Union rules against that? We're playing to capacity. What kind of heels do you think we are, Mr. Tightpants! Get the hell out of here, and give that sweet girl my best wishes. And yell if you yourself get short of cash, like I already told you."

Stanislaus Joseph had a feeling this actor-producer would really discharge him if he refused to take Olga's salary money. Discharge *him* and continue *her* salary!

Too bad the actor-producer could not see Mr. Tightpants' face as the musician softly closed the dressing room door.

Stanislaus Joseph really smiled.

He had carried that salary in its envelope to the hospital the next day, handed it to the girl, and she had cried a little as she took it.

"Show folk in America are like that," she told the boy. "Put it in the savings bank account. When I am well, we will give it to the Actors Fund. It will go to help some poor singer who really needs it." And she wrote a note to the comedian, thanking him and his partner for their thoughtfulness and generosity.

The boy also had brought her a large, long box, and when she opened it she found it was filled with American Beauty roses. They were from the other girls of the chorus. A rose from each girl. Thirty-five roses in all.

Olga kept half a dozen of them. She sent the others to one of the wards.

"Give each woman or girl there a rose, and if there are not enough to go around—take some more from mine here," she had said. And to Stanislaus Joseph: "Tell the girls in the show I did this. I am sure they will not mind. I must share my happiness."

Another small incident happened at the theater that brought comfort to the young musician. The theater cat, who lived in the boiler room underneath the stage, gave birth to four kittens. Apparently this animal loved music—even the Winter Garden brand of music—for she chose the orchestra pit one night as their birth spot. Directly beneath Stanislaus Joseph's baby-grand pianoforte at one end of the pit. The engineer carried them back down to his boiler room, but the mother cat returned them, one by one, to their slightly more artistic birth-spot.

This transition occurred three times. The engineer was frantic, for he loved that mother cat. Stanislaus Joseph asked that the little family be left beneath his piano. The other orchestra men did not mind. They said it was good luck. Tightpants liked the feel of the small furry bodies as they would climb across his feet while the show was going on.

They were his children.

He and Olga had no children, as we know. They had taken no measures to prevent this. But the girl had learned from a Chorus Union doctor, whom she had visited, that her womb was slightly turned. A minor operation would be necessary before she could become a mother. Both she and Stanislaus had thought it best not to have this performed until they were both farther along in their careers.

The boy told Olga about the kittens. One day he carried one of them to the hospital in a small basket to show to her. The little, plump body with its big eyes cuddled close in her arms.

"When I am well, we will take them all home to Madison Avenue, if the theater engineer will permit it," she had said. "They will be our children. I have always wanted a cat at the apartment—we had a beautiful one at home in Wilkes-Barre when my mother lived. But I knew how you loved the mice in the hallways. I was afraid to suggest a cat."

"We will keep the kittens right in the apartment," smiled the young man. "We'll not let them out. There are no mice to be gobbled up in the apartment.

"The kittens in our apartment—the mice in the hallways! So we will prove to the world that we are free of all bigotry—truly tolerant Americans!"

❖ 8 ❖

IT WAS THE SUNDAY after the night when she had again dreamed the dream, that Olga told him.

She really had not meant to tell him. But Stanislaus Joseph had spoken about going up to the Cloisters late in the afternoon, before that museum closed; then return again to the Neurological Institute. The Cloisters was only some thirty blocks away, up Fort Washington Avenue to the George Washington Bridge, and then on to Fort Tyron Park.

He had in mind to say a silent prayer to the La Celle statue for the girl's recovery.

She told him first of her dream, the nature of which he already knew. But he did not know about the line *Ah, Monsieur le Capitaine—it is hard to die when one is only twenty-two*.

She told him for the first time about that line, spoken to Kommodore Hugo Frederick von Steinburg; and about the legend that the eldest daughter in each generation of her mother's family would die during the age of twenty-two—a legend that apparently went back to the girl who had been the first flesh-and-blood counterpart of the La Celle statue now at the Cloisters. The French-Polish girl who had posed for that statue.

And in this burst of disclosures, she also told Stanislaus Joseph that she believed it had been Hugh de St. Omer who had come to her rescue in the Colonial Theater alley in Boston, two years before.

She realized quickly that she should not have told all this to her husband. He said not a word, but his strained face hardened, and there came a fixed look in his eyes.

What was going through the mind of the young musician was this. It was *not* God's will that the girl who had been Olga Lasenka should fall ill, and perhaps die at this time. It had nothing whatever to do with God. With any "bright Destiny."

It had to do with a cursed, Dark Ages destiny, established eight hundred years before; with a legend and destiny that started in the village of La Celle in France at the time of the blood-spilling Crusades.

It had to do with a wicked Abbot of a Knights Templars preceptory; with his lust for an ancestor of this innocent girl now on that Neurological Institute Hospital bed; and finally, with a stone statue of the Queen of Heaven that had brought with it all this medieval sorcery straight to the very heart of the modern city of New York.

This statue with its reddening bosom; its smiles (if Guard O'Rourke were to be believed)! Instead of something holy to be revered, it was a symbol of disaster—a treacherous effigy of Death.

And into the anguished mind of the lad came a fearful idea. If he could somehow destroy this image—break it up—demolish it—put it out of existence—would such a deed perhaps put an end to this trail of Death through the centuries, this *dark* Destiny that seemed now to have fallen on the one girl that he loved?

Hugh de St. Omer had saved her from the trivial matter of a few college boys bent on nothing more than an evening of merriment. He had seemed to appear on the stage of the Ziegfeld Theater the night of the closing-performance party, over the equally trivial matter of a song. To ask him, Stanislaus Joseph, not to be angry. The Knight Templar could perhaps protect her from *the living*—from any *mortal* hand that was raised against her, or mortal thought that would hurt her.

But when the protagonist was from Beyond the Veil—was he helpless? Since he himself was also a Shadow, and of that Beyond, ruled by Fates whose laws were his laws, and before whose callous heathen might, he was powerless and impotent?

Was it only *a mortal* who could end this earth projection of an unearthly terror? This death-ray that seemed to strike once each generation, because of a mortal's likeness to a statue carved from earth's stone.

If some *mortal* dared to break this spell; utterly destroy its source; would its then-victim be spared?

Stanislaus Joseph said suddenly: "I am going to the Cloisters. No twelfth-century legend is going to take you from me, my darling."

He had seized his hat, and was gone before she, in utter amazement, could speak. They were alone in the hospital room at the time. She rang desperately for the floor nurse. When the nurse came running, she cried: "Please stop my husband and ask him to come back."

The nurse said: "Are you all right, Mrs. Halka?"

"I'm all right," said the girl. "It is my husband. He is upset regarding something I foolishly told him. Please! Stop him before he leaves the hospital. Hurry! Bring him back to this room."

The nurse ran down the hall to the elevator. The up-car was just arriving, and the down-car had just descended. She entered the arriving car.

"Rush me to the ground floor. It is an emergency," she said.

She was too late. The other car had also had a quick descent. Stanislaus Joseph had been the only passenger. When the nurse emerged at the entrance floor, and rushed to the doorway, the doorman told her that a grim-faced gentleman had hailed a passing taxi going north.

He had seemed to be in a great hurry, the doorman said.

9

THE NURSE RETURNED to Olga Halka's room and gave her this report.

"Please do not excite yourself. It is not good for you," she said. And she added, "If you know where your husband went, I will get permission to go after him. That is, if you wish it. I have got to know him fairly well. I believe I could persuade him to return here, if that is what you wish."

"You are kind," said the girl on the bed, "but that would not help me. I have a friend where he has gone. Please find me the telephone number of the Cloisters, which is a branch of the Metropolitan Museum at Fort Tyron Park. Please find it as quickly as you can."

The nurse found the telephone number. She dialed it. When an answer came, she handed the receiver to Olga Halka.

The girl tried to, and did speak calmly.

"My name is Mrs. Dr. Stanislaus Joseph Halka," she said. "Please get the guard stationed in the Early Gothic Room to the telephone.

His name is Dennis O'Rourke. He knows me well. The matter is most urgent."

The museum operator said: "It would be quite irregular to bring one of the guards to the telephone. Give me the message. I will have it sent to Mr. O'Rourke. Or I can ask him to call you back at his lunch hour, if I have your number."

"Please," said the now almost distracted girl, but she still managed to keep her voice at a sane level. "I must speak to Guard O'Rourke directly, and at once. I am on a bed in a private room at the Medical Center. It is most urgent for him, for me, and for the welfare of the Cloisters."

The mention of the Medical Center swayed the operator. And the "welfare of the Cloisters." If it were some female crank, this guard would know. A wealthy patient at Mt. Sinai Hospital had once called on his deathbed, asking for a special Guard in the Treasury Room, in order to leave to the Museum the most valuable Altarpiece of his collection; and to do it through his friend, the guard of that room.

The name also carried weight. *"Mrs. Dr. Stanislaus Joseph Halka."* It sounded important.

The operator decided to break rules and send for Guard Dennis O'Rourke.

Perhaps Stanislaus Joseph had received his degree of "Doctor" so that it could be used by Olga at this desperate moment.

Guard O'Rourke came in haste when he had the message, first however asking the Cuxa Cloister guard, on which his gallery opened, to stay in the doorway of the Early Gothic Room till he returned.

Mrs. Halka in the Medical Center! They had been to his room—she and the husband he considered his friend—one Sunday only three weeks before.

"Dennis," said the girl whose voice he immediately recognized, "listen carefully and return quickly to your room. I have been for two weeks at the Medical Center. Some mysterious illness. My husband thinks it is because of your statue. You know my resemblance to it. There is no time to explain further. He is on his way there. Might reach the Cloisters any moment. I do not know what is in his mind. You are his friend. Do not let him commit any rash act. Do not let him near the statue. I fear he means to harm it. He will listen to you. Restrain him, but please do not harm him. Thank God you are still the guard in that room and are on duty today."

Ex-G.I. Dennis O'Rourke, ex-paratrooper of World War I, had a level head.

"Thank you, Mrs. Halka," he said. "Trust me. Trust me absolutely. I must now hurry back to my room. Goodbye."

"Well?" said the operator. "Was it important?"

"The most important call I've ever had," said Guard O'Rourke.

When he reached the Early Gothic Room, he took his heavy service revolver from a small desk drawer, and slipped it in his trousers belt, beneath his coat.

He stationed himself at the only entrance to the Early Gothic Room.

"God grant I have no serious trouble," he said and crossed himself. He had grown very fond of Dr. Stanislaus Joseph Halka. But his primary devotion was to "his" statue, and to his duty to the Early Gothic Room.

He had noticed that the breast of "his baby" had been tinged with red all the previous week, although the weather had been clear and dry.

"Do not fear, my Lady, I will protect you," he said to the stone image that gazed out across the Hudson to the distant Palisades.

✣10✣

STANISLAUS JOSEPH sped straight northward on Fort Washington Avenue in the taxi which had been passing the Fort Washington Avenue entrance of the Neurological Institute, as he had emerged from that building.

After he had directed the driver: "The Cloisters Museum in Fort Tyron Park, and hurry," he had sat, repeating to himself in a kind of dull frenzy—if a frenzy can be so described: *"The La Celle statue must be destroyed. The La Celle statue must be destroyed."*

If one repeats to one's self enough times some resolve, that resolve becomes almost an accomplishment.

And after several blocks, his brain commenced to plan the method of its accomplishment. The same trained brain that could lay out and plan just how he would perform a difficult musical composition.

He certainly must not rush into the Early Gothic Room like a madman, stride to the statue by its window, seize it and dash it to the stone floor—although that might indeed bring about the desired result. There would be other visitors in the room. There would be Guard O'Rourke. They would seize him; send for the police; place him under arrest. He would be taken to a jail or an asylum. Olga would be deprived of his company and help, and he would be deprived of hers. It might wreck both their lives.

And Guard O'Rourke, for whom he had a genuine affection, would surely lose his job. For this innocent guard, whose duty it was to protect from harm all the priceless art treasures in the gallery, would have no suspicion of the harmful intent of a man who had brought "his baby" roses for the past two years!

No—it must be made to appear to be the result of an accident. Just as the dashing of the music sheets of the *poco con sentimento* section of the Brahms *Sonata* to the floor by the page-turner of Herr Viktor Reimalsky's Carnegie Hall concert had been made to appear an accident.

That was it! It would be exactly like that incident! Only there would be no eagle-eyed H. Rodman around to detect the deception. And no artisan present to restore the broken pieces, as he, Stanislaus Joseph, had restored from memory the pieces of that musical composition as they lay scattered on the platform floor.

Broken stone would be broken stone. It was not of the mind, like great music.

The window! That would be the way! The day was warm, and the window would without doubt be open. He would greet Guard O'Rourke, as he usually did. He would even first knock on the door before entering. He would pass the time of day. Speak of the mild weather. He would tell Dennis of Olga's sudden illness, and of his fears for the girl's recovery. The inference would be that he also wished to say a silent prayer to the statue for his wife's restoration to good health.

He would move to the front of the statue. The high, open window would be directly behind it. The window that swung open from hinged sides. Therefore, open its entire height. The base of the statue, on its pedestal, was about even with the window's lower sill.

He would pretend a sudden dizzy spell. He would throw out his arms and lurch his full weight against the statue. It would go crashing through the open window; crash to a concrete path five hundred feet below. Be dashed into a hundred—a thousand pieces. The entire Cloisters, as we know, was perched on a high plateau-like promontory, the highest spot in New York City.

Having done this, he would have to pretend a kind of faint. Such as he had seen the character *Cavaradossi* do in the opera *Tosca.* There might be some difficulties afterwards, but there would be no evidence of deliberate and premeditated destruction of the statue. He was simply under the understandable stress of a husband who knew that his wife had cancer.

It would seem to be a perfect plan. The "perfect crime," as the detection novels say.

The hour was twelve-thirty noon, when Stanislaus Joseph arrived at the lower entrance of the Cloisters.

At that hour it was exactly five-thirty P.M. in the distant city of Paris, Republic of France. Consequently it would take no expert in the world system of time reckoning to say, without fear of contradiction, that the exact hour in a certain corridored Salon of the Palace of the Louvre was also five-thirty P.M.; that "most splendid palace in the world" and "Treasure House of the Masters," first built as a block-house (that being the meaning of the word "Louvre") outside the walled City of Paris by Philip Augustus; completely reconstructed by Pierre Lescot, architect of Francis I in 1541, to become the world's finest and most extensive royal residence (covering and enclosing an area of forty-nine acres) at the very center of the by then expanded city.

There were uniformed guards in this vast, now-museum, not unlike the guards stationed about the Cloisters; guards who were responsible for the safety of the paintings, the statues, the manuscripts, and every manner of ancient and near-modern art objects that were gathered there to be freely viewed, during fixed hours, by a public that came from every corner of the globe.

In a longish gallery, called the *Salle du Moyen Age;* a gallery overlooking the River Seine, which once had witnessed the marriage of Margaret of Valois to Henri of Navarre—also the somewhat less holy revels of Mistress Jeanne d'Etioles, better known as the Marquise de Pompadour—was stationed such a guard.

And in this room, along with the ancient Crown Jewels (including *The Regent,* the finest diamond in the world); a vase of jasper considered the most exquisite of Benvenuto Cellini's craftsmanship; altar-pieces; tapestries; there was a special glass case which contained a very special treasure.

Its maker was unknown, but it was held to be by the Louvre authorities (and by this guard) of greater value than even the Regent diamond or the Cellini vase.

Like Dennis O'Rourke, this Paris guard was a veteran of the great World War (now called World War I, to apparently differentiate it from an endless series of such conflicts); and like our faithful Dennis, he took his museum guardianship most seriously.

At five-thirty P.M. each day his gallery closed—as did the entire great stretches of Louvre *Galeries, Pavillons, Salons, Salles;* and before leaving each night for his home and family in the suburb of St. Denis, he always went to this special glass case to be doubly certain all was well regarding its priceless content.

Also—since he was a good Catholic—to make the sign of the cross.

So, on this late Sunday afternoon, the signal for closing time having sounded, this guard moved to this special glass case, the case that contained his special treasure.

I have said "contained." To the horror of ex-sergeant Pierre Roudelle (wearer of the *Croix de Guerre* for courage in the defence of Hill 304 in the long siege of Verdun), the object was not there! Just the crimson pillow on which it had lain, and lain only a short five minutes before, when he had been speaking of it to a French-speaking American visitor.

Sergeant Roudelle did not lost his head.

He called to the two guards at the two exits of the oblong gallery, to prevent anyone still there from leaving. He crawled under the raised showcase to be certain the object had not in some manner been jarred out of its resting place. He rushed about the room to see that it was not in some other case. All this in a matter of seconds; and then he turned the key of a small box at one end of the *Galerie.*

The turning of this key sounded a clanging alarm connected with every exit of that vast wing of the Louvre Palace. It meant that all exit doors were immediately locked—all guards alerted—no one would be permitted to leave the wing until the reason for this signal was communicated.

Guard Roudelle telephoned this reason to the central office. An art treasure was missing. Had perhaps been stolen. It was small enough to permit concealment under the coat of a man or the skirt or blouse of a woman.

The treasure missing was a twelfth-century carved and painted wood head of the Christ, that had come from a ruined church in

Lavaudieu, near Brioude, in southern France. It was considered the finest example of such wood carving in existence. So lifelike indeed was it that to Guard Roudelle it had always seemed to *live*.

It had been broken from a full figure of a life-size Christ-on-the-Cross. Broken, it was said, by the wicked Count Berenger, Lord of Castelnau, leader of a band of military adventurers who had devastated the countryside around Brioude in the year 1361, using that city as his headquarters.

This titled "Captain-out-of-Hell," as he was called, had torn the whole sacred effigy from its place in the church at the village of Lavaudieu, and struck off the head with repeated hackings of his sword. This to prove to his followers that he was mightier than the Christ.

But even these hardened ruffians were horrified by such sacrilege, and were seen to fearfully bless themselves. And one month later Count Berenger had been found murdered in his blood-soaked bed, *his* head severed from his body.

It was said that a repentant mistress had killed him as he slept after a drunken revel. That she had thus hoped to redeem a life of sin.

To return to the Christ effigy—head and torso had been gathered up and hidden by the priest of the tiny Lavaudieu church. This priest had died within the year, still fearful of disclosing the hiding place.

Two centuries later *the torso* was found, when a monastery, now occupying the house of this priest, dug a well in their cellar. The torso was in a crude, coffin-like box. The lower limbs had been eaten away by termites, also the extended arms, which were not protected by the torso-incasing box.

There was no head.

The monks set up the torso in a corner of their chapel. It was a carving of such pathos and beauty.

And there sprang up a legend about it. The Christ head, which had not been found, would sometimes miraculously appear, and appear joined to the body of the Christ figure! Its appearance usually caused some minor miracle in behalf of that person who *saw* the head. A negative miracle, so to speak.

Some crime was prevented.

A monk who had intended to kill his blood brother, because he felt that the wickedness of this brother was damning that brother's soul's chance of salvation, had paused before it and been deterred by the sadness—the plea—in the painted eyes of the suddenly appearing head.

A novice nun had not proven false to her vows when she had been drawn to it, and looking up, perceived that a face of great compassion was gazing down at her from the always headless body.

All this in the fourteenth and fifteenth centuries.

Came the French Revolution, when an invention by a friend of one Doctor Guillotine, made severed heads a matter for very little concern. The Monastery at Lavaudieu was burnt in that frenzy against all intrenched authority, including the Church. Its treasures were destroyed or scattered. Including the Christ torso.

But as if to compensate for this temporary loss, the Christ head was found!

In the desecration of a Catholic cemetery, near this same Lavaudieu, a carved wooden Christ head was dug up. It had been most carefully packed in a metal casket, made waterproof and termite-proof by expert wax sealing. It was in a perfect state of preservation.

The priest of the Lavaudieu church had taken a care about that head that he had not given to the torso.

The local deputy for the Commune had been an art lover. He took the head to his office, and kept it. Kept it because of its beauty rather than out of any religious reverence. Like every loyal Patriot, he hated all religion, but his art-loving soul could not permit the destruction of such a treasure.

So this head came into the hands of civil authorities rather than ecclesiastical; and eventually, when the Palace of the Louvre became a *Musée National,* found a permanent haven there.

The torso was also eventually found—it had been rescued by another free-thinking citizen—this time a tavern keeper who had placed it for a while in derision behind his bar. *He* had sold it to a dealer in antiques. It passed through various collectors' hands, to come eventually to America.

To the Cloisters, in fact, as readers of this epic have long since guessed.

It of course had been discovered that the painted and gilded Christ head in the Louvre belonged with the torso in the Cloisters—or vice versa. Some effort had been made to negotiate a deal between the two museums, whereby one or the other could obtain the entire Christ figure, but nothing came of it.

Each side, understandably, was loath to part with such a perfect treasure.

There was, needless to say, no miraculous joining of head and torso, as had been reported to have occurred for the salvation of the fourteenth- and fifteenth-century monk and nun. This was the enlightened twentieth century. Miracles were now only performed by scientists and the manufacturers of dish-washing powders.

The days of silly religious miracles had passed.

✣ 11 ✣

STANISLAUS JOSEPH paid for and dismissed his taxi; entered the low, arched doorway from what might be called the Cloister's lower courtyard; proceeded up the long, tunnel-like passage that would bring him to the main floor of this building whose very stones had been brought from Europe, and were as old as the treasures they protected.

He paid no attention to the symmetric beauty of the high, curve-topped, deep-set windows of the passage (windows that he always of late had paused to admire), or to its vaulted ceilings.

One thought was pounding through his mind with the rhythmic beat of a jungle tattoo. In his case—like the beat of the reversed pendulum of a giant metronome.

The La Celle statue must be destroyed!

It was the Sunday opening-hour, and almost no one was yet there. The domed, circular "first Entrance Hall," with the office in an alcove at one side, was vacant except for its two guards. He passed through the arched twelfth-century doorway whose soft white limestone was intricately carved with the figures of fantastic beasts, on into the oblong hall called Romanesque.

The Lions on either side—the great painted wall-fresco beast on his left—the stone-carved beast on his right—did not attract his attention. Neither did he gaze up, as he and Olga usually did, at the Adoration of the Magi group—the four life-size stone figures of the Two Kings, the Virgin Mother, and St. Joseph, which were placed high on the wall above the doorway leading into the Cuxa Cloister.

The La Celle Statue must be destroyed!

It was to the opposite wall that the young man's eyes were drawn as if by some magnetic power. And at the same instant his feet were halted as though they had met a barrier they could not pass!

He was before the painted wood torso of the Christ with the red and blue-green loin cloth, and above this the flesh-colored body, its anatomy almost a living, breathing chest and bowels in death agony —yet having an infinite grace and beauty; and in its side the gaping spear wound made by the Roman soldier's spear.

He remembered how Olga, on her first visit to the Cloisters, had knelt for a moment before this wooden image, as she would kneel before a shrine in a church.

But it was something higher on the figure than the torso he had seen so many times, that drew his purpose-fixed eyes; drew *his* eyes to other eyes.

The painted head of the Christ was there, looking down at Dr. Stanislaus Joseph Halka—Tightpants Halka—just as it had miraculously gazed down at a monk and at a novice nun five hundred years before!

And then came the sound of distant bells—though these were doubtless from some church in the great valley of tenements and streets that lay beyond the high ground of Fort Tyron Park—a church somewhere in the vast stretch of the Bronx that on that quiet Sunday noon hour was summoning the faithful to a Mass.

Stanislaus Joseph could not meet those eyes in which seemed reflected sorrow, compassion, understanding but which said as plainly as if the words had been spoken: *"I gave my life because it was the Father's will. I gave my life so that you and yours might have eternal life. Did I die in vain, Stanislaus Joseph? Must I be crucified again and again and again to make the world understand? To make you understand?"*

The young musician had lowered his eyes. He raised them again to explain why he must do the deed he had set out to do.

But the Christ head was no longer there. The sound of the bells no longer came to his ears. His step was no longer impeded.

He was free to do as he wished. Without explanation. Without hindrance of any kind. No towering Hugh de St. Omer blocked his way with a two-handed sword. No Kommodore Hugo Frederick von Steinburg stood in his path with a lead-loaded riding whip. He did not, of course, know of Guard Dennis O'Rourke in the doorway of the Early Gothic Room, his service revolver in his trousers belt.

Only the mental picture of those sad, compassionate eyes that reflected all the sorrows of the world. And the questioning words: *Must I be crucified again and again and again?*

Did this miracle really happen? Could it not simply have been the inner corrective conscience of an upright and kindly man? That conscience that at one time or another has prevented the noblest of mortals, born in sin and laboring under some terrifying emotional stress, from a deed they would spend a lifetime regretting?

Or could it not have been the mystic answer to the frantic, fervent prayer of a girl on a hospital bed who was repeating: *Oh blessed Jesus—save my Duszka from any dreadful crime! For the fault is mine—mine.*

What then of the happenings in the Paris Louvre?

Well, suppose it *was* a real miracle? Suppose it really happened?

There are those who doubt the Flashing Presence that asked one Saul of Tarsus: *Saul, Saul, why persecutest thou Me?* There are those who doubt that *He* appeared to His disciples in that upper room. Appeared after the martyrdom of The Cross.

Who has the divine wisdom to say? Or judge?

This reporter only sets down truly what he was told by a World War nurse at the Medical Center to whom the girl Olga had talked.

Sets down what he learned from a Guard in the Palace of the Louvre who wore the *Croix de Guerre.*

I do know for certain that Dr. Stanislaus Joseph Halka retraced his steps; back through the doorway that came from a twelfth-century palace in Southern France; back through the circular Entrance Hall that let into the long, winding passage to the roadway below.

There was a bus loading there which he knew went past the Neurological Institute. He boarded it.

Only then, as he sat in his bus seat, did he realize that he had read in a Cloisters guide book that the head of the Christ torso of the Romanesque Hall was in the Paris Louvre.

At this same Paris Louvre, the searching of all visitors now leaving the long, many galleried-wing that bordered the Seine was in full methodical operation. A crowd of five or six hundred Sunday supposed "Art-lovers" had been trapped there. Three motor car loads of *agents de police* had arrived, and their presence somewhat, but not entirely, quieted the violent protests of innocent tourists.

There had not been such excitement since Leonardo da Vinci's *La Gioconda* had one day been stolen. Word had reached the newspaper offices, and reporters and photographers were on the way.

Frantic Guard Pierre Roudelle had made several desperate rounds of his showcases, hoping against hope that the Christ head would be somewhere about. He made another round.

On its crimson pillow lay the painted and gilded head! Just as it had lain, fifteen minutes before, and immediately before he had discovered its disappearance.

Guard Roudelle was taken to a hospital suffering from acute nervous prostration. A strange seizure to come to a veteran of Hill 304 at Verdun. His honesty (and sanity) could not be doubted—the two other guards in the adjoining salons had verified that the head had been missing. And just as suddenly reappeared! The matter was utterly unexplainable.

Some weeks later, the authorities at the Cloisters received a communication from the historian of the Paris Louvre, asking if on a certain date there had been any unusual occurrence having to do with a particular Christ torso in their possession. If, in fact, *the head* belonging in the Louvre had been seen as joined to this torso, of which it had once been a part?

This historian had been delving back into the history of the Louvre Christ head, and had come across the fourteenth- and fifteenth-century legends we have recorded.

The Cloisters replied that nothing unusual had occurred. "These Frenchmen!" the young secretary who had answered this letter had exclaimed.

Dr. Stanislaus Joseph Halka had been the only one to see the joining of the head to the torso. He had told only his wife about it. And she had spoken of it only to her favorite nurse.

PART THIRTEEN

BUT—THERE IS NO DEATH

✣ 1 ✣

ONE WEEK LATER the hospital staff decided to operate. Such antibiotic serums as were then known were not destroying the malignant cell growths. The doctors had projected to these cells as much lethal energy as they dared—streams of electrons from the powerful X-ray machine. Further treatment of this kind might burn out other vital tissues of the spine.

The surgeon's knife must be tried before the growths reached a vital spot where such surgery (called *carcinectomy*) would be impossible; or before the growths penetrated the blood stream with their fatal poison.

The interns wheeled Olga Halka to the operating room at ten A.M. that morning. The girl was frightened, but outwardly calm. She was more worried about Stanislaus Joseph than about herself.

He, of course, could not go to the operating room with her. He sat on the chair in her private room and waited.

The Viennese doctor had assured them both that there was no danger of death on the operating table. The girl's heart was in good condition. The operating surgeon was the finest in New York—perhaps in America—for any ailment that concerned the spine. A professional blood-donor who had Olga's type of blood would be present in case of necessity.

For all this Stanislaus Joseph realized that he had to thank Hans Beuter. Simple, kindly Hans, whose bakeshop *dressiersack* had literally saved *his* life one desperate midnight; whose advice had secured for him the Ziegfeld engagement, the consequent meeting with Olga, and now the skill and advice of this young fellow-countryman doctor whose interest had in turn enlisted the services of the great surgeon.

Stanislaus Joseph did not know that Hans was at that moment sitting in the waiting room of the entrance floor, waiting to go up and be with his friend through whatever crisis might ensue; for the Viennese doctor had told him the day before of the pending operation. And that day Hans had planned to visit his favorite pool parlor, to watch the odds and place a sizable wager on a "long shot" he had been following for weeks in the racing sheets! Instead, he sat on a waiting room bench of the Neurological Institute.

Greater love hath no horse-player!

At eleven, Hans took the elevator to the fourth floor, and went to the small private room that overlooked the river.

He clasped the hand of his friend. "I am here," he said, "but you will not need me. The Herr Vienna *doktor* assured me last night that Olga would pull through this operation."

"I know," said Stanislaus Joseph. "It is I who am weak, not she. God bless you for coming. Now I think I shall bear up. A wife like Olga, and a friend like you. It is more than any one man deserves."

And so they sat in silence—waiting—waiting.

Stanislaus Joseph was not much given to religion. Music was his religion. But he did say a prayer or two.

Hans Beuter just wished with all his great heart that Olga Halka would pull through, with an occasional straying thought of what the odds now were on *Galloping Sal* in the first six-furlongs race at the track named Laurel, State of Maryland.

At the Cloisters, the breast of the La Celle statue was blood red. But then so were the pillars in the outside Cuxa Cloister. The air was filled with moisture. "Humidity ninety percent and climbing. A Four M day—moisty, muggy, morbidious and mind-you-take-a-bumbershoot," said pithy Charles F. McCarthy on his seven-thirty A.M. broadcast.

It was not until two P.M. that the hospital interns wheeled Mrs. Dr. Stanislaus Joseph Halka back to her room. She was still under the influence of the powerful operating-table anaesthetic. But her breathing was regular. She had been given two blood transfusions during the operation.

She lay very white on the hospital bed. The attending nurse—a special operating-room nurse—took her pulse every fifteen minutes. Presently the young Viennese doctor and the great surgeon appeared.

They talked with the nurse, and studied the chart—a sheet of ruled, data-recording paper clipped to a small holding board that hung at the foot of the bed. This chart had recorded her heartbeats—her blood pressure—her temperature during the operation and since she had been returned to her room.

"Have no immediate fears," said the surgeon to the young musician. "Your wife came through nicely, and her pulse is even and strong. It will be at least twelve hours, however, before she fully regains consciousness. That is as it should be. She must have the absolute quiet of sleep."

"I do not know how to express my gratitude," said Stanislaus Joseph.

The physician saw the relief that came into the worried face of the young man before him. He hesitated—but he was an honorable gentleman—as well as a great surgeon. He had to say what he had to say. Only, he would not say it there, in the presence of the girl, although she was in the deep sleep of drugged unconsciousness.

"Do not thank me yet," he said. "Come with me to my consulting room. My colleague from Vienna will come also, since I understand he is also your friend as well as mine. Your wife is his patient. I am only the surgeon who has been called in to help."

Stanislaus Joseph introduced Hans Beuter. "I would like Herr Beuter to come," he said. "He is my faithful fellow-countryman. It is through him that I have obtained your help—your very great help."

"Very well," said the surgeon. "It is well to have a friend. A faithful friend is sometimes of greater value than a scientist."

❖ 2 ❖

THEY WERE SEATED in the consulting room of the surgeon. "I am not to be interrupted," he told his secretary in the adjoining entrance-office.

The surgeon spoke from behind his small desk. "I could not accept your gratitude, for I must tell you, Dr. Halka, that the operation was not successful.

"I cut as deeply as I dared. Had I probed deeper I would either have killed the patient, or left her with a complete paralysis from the hips downward. Some of the cancerous cells are still in her spine. Their growth has been momentarily halted. She will seem to get better. There will not be such a pressure on the nerves going to her lower limbs. But as your wife gains in strength, those cells will flourish again. They will spread. A second operation would not be possible."

"And then?" said Stanislaus Joseph dully. And he noticed that Hans Beuter had moved to his side, and stood with his strong, dough-kneading hand upon his shoulder.

"And then," said the surgeon, "she will die. The virus will reach the blood stream. Reach her heart or brain. She will not die suddenly. We will have warnings. From now on there will be a relay of nurses in constant attendance. She will not suffer. We will apply a local anaesthetic to prevent that.

"It is hard for me to tell you this, but I would be less than honest if I did not. I understand you are a fellow scientist. A scientist of a great art—the art of music. I speak to you with the honesty of one scientist to another. I know that you will understand."

I believe that the mention of music helped the young musician to bear up. Franz Schubert died at thirty-one. Wolfgang Mozart at thirty-five. George Gershwin, a very young American, had just died. Great women like Jeanne D'Arc had left this world at nineteen.

Of the blessed Saints there was Elizabeth of Hungary, she whose apron of bread for the poor had suddenly become roses, when an irate and parsimonious husband demanded what she was carrying, and she had answered, "Roses." She died at twenty-four.

Teresa of Lisieux, blessed Little Flower of Jesus, died at twenty-four. Young Saint Adelaide, back in the year 1250, who through suffering that included blindness, leprosy, paralysis, saved many souls in purgatory before an early death.

There were perhaps other things of more value than mere years.

So the brave lad only said: "Is it necessary to tell her this—that death is near?"

"She will not be told," said the surgeon. "She will not be told if you so wish it."

"I wish it so," said Stanislaus Joseph. "And this also, that I be warned, so that I am here when the end comes."

"We will know in time to give you warning," said the surgeon.

❖ 3 ❖

DURING THE NEXT FOUR WEEKS Olga Halka seemed to improve. The incisions in her back healed rapidly. As the pressure on the great sciatic nerve which controlled the muscles of thighs, legs and feet had been relieved, she no longer felt the pains in her limbs.

She believed that she was on the way to full recovery.

But new X-rays (which of course she was not shown) disclosed that a new metastasis—meaning a spreading—of the cancer cells was occurring. It was but a question of days when it would strike at a vital organ. Or penetrate the blood stream, and so reach her heart.

Stanislaus Joseph continued to play his performances at the theater. To have given that up would have disclosed to Olga her true danger. And his salary—and hers—were not unwelcome—his weekly union scale of eighty-four dollars, hers of forty. A nurse was now constantly at the girl's bedside. Three nurses each day, serving eight-hour shifts. Twenty-four dollars a day. With X-ray expenses and periodic blood transfusions, his bills at Neurological Institute ran close to three hundred dollars weekly.

The great surgeon had told the Viennese doctor he would make no charge for his work, but Stanislaus Joseph wanted no charity. He paid a nominal fee of five hundred dollars for these services. And fifty dollars per week to the young Viennese doctor, who visited Olga's room half a dozen times daily—again a nominal fee.

Each morning, after his breakfast, he sat at his Steinway and played some part of *La Mer,* and gave silent gratitude to Hugo Frederick von Steinburg.

But for that draft of five thousand American dollars (diminishing only too rapidly), his worries would be near tragedy.

Then he would walk crosstown to the Eighth Avenue subway and proceed by it to the Neurological Institute, so as to be there at its earliest visiting-hour of ten A.M.

Except on matinee days, he would remain at the hospital most of the daylight hours.

The girl slept a great deal, due partly to the medication she received. She hoped each week that she could go home, and if not strong enough to report to the theater, she could at least cook their meals, iron his shirts and collars.

Each week they managed to put her off till the next. So she lived on and in hope.

She talked a great deal of Wilkes-Barre; of that wonderful day there. "When I become well and strong, we must go back for a day or two." The boy was grateful that Olga had had those few hours of glory, of adulation.

The old priest wrote her another letter, a letter of hope and courage for himself, and of what she had done for the people of the town. Neither she nor Stanislaus Joseph had informed him that the girl was in a hospital. The young man thought of sending for Father Joe to come to New York to see the girl, and then decided it were best not to do so. She might suspect that her husband knew her days were numbered. And Olga did not want Father Joe to be worried. She wanted him to surely come when they were back home.

Stanislaus Joseph spent so much time at the hospital that it almost seemed they were both living there!

The boy could not return to the hospital after his evening performances, and he took to going for a while to Hans Beuter's all-night bakery. He gave the hospital that telephone number, along with that of the theater and the Madison Avenue apartment.

At the bakery Hans would let the young musician write on the wedding cakes—the birthday cakes—if these were a part of the night's work. The bars of shining music that crossed some of the larger cakes even became a little famous. Cakes that had the opening measures of some great opera *aria* in white and gold icing!

This humble work took the mind of Stanislaus Joseph momentarily from the dread of what he was told he must soon face.

He said one midnight, after he had added a bit of *Madame Butterfly* to a great party-cake: "You know, Hans, perhaps my father was right. He wanted me to be a great *dressiersack* artist. Maybe I could have been that. So, at least, I think it is pleasing my poor father that I have not forgotten how to spell out the sugar icing!"

"You will be a great composer," said Hans, "and a hundred years from now some *dressiersack* artist not yet born will be writing *your* music on cakes! Stanislaus—if you would only write songs—as I have urged you—as Olga urged you! The symphony? It is finished?"

"I do not think it will ever be finished," said the young musician. "I take music paper to the hospital, and try to compose. What I write I tear up the next day. You speak of a song. Olga was going to write me a lyric that I could set. But now—it is too late—unless the doctors are wrong and a miracle happens."

He did not know that the song—the words of a song—was already written, and lay in the cardboard letterfile under the letter "O."

The girl thought of that strangely written song often, but she did not tell her husband of its existence. She would think of it whenever she watched the young man frowning over his music sheets of the endless symphony.

She was feeling much better. The pains in her legs were almost entirely gone.

She would show the "Olga Song" to Stanislaus Joseph as soon as she was out of that hospital, and safely back in Madison Avenue.

✣ 4 ✣

ANOTHER FOUR WEEKS went by. Weeks devoid of untoward incident. Except that one day H. Rodman sent for Stanislaus Joseph. The young musician's name was now in the New York telephone book. Stanislaus Joseph Halka. He left out the "Dr." in this listing. The Rodman office could also have obtained the address from the Musical Union.

"Sort of lost track of you, Tightpants," said the great impresario, looking up from his daily sheaf of telegrams and box-office reports. "Hope you've been keeping up your pianoforte practice. Have you?"

"Yes sir, I have," said Stanislaus Joseph. "And I have not forgotten your kindness to me about the Albert Rouchard engagement. I often think of it and of him."

H. Rodman's eyes hardened. "The greatest voice teacher in the world—killed himself helping a lot of useless, worthless, screeching singers—the worst medieval torture chambers would be too mild a fate for that riff-raff. They murdered my dearest friend——"

The impresario threw off the bitter mood. Became what—for him—was friendly. "Well—anyway—you didn't let him down with your playing. Thank you for that, Mr. Tightpants."

He shook off this second mood of near sentiment. These moods were all most unbusinesslike. But H. Rodman could be pardoned. He was a little weary and not in his best office-interview form.

He had been up all night with a sick mare at the New Jersey farm.

He returned to his initial question to the young pianoforte player. "You're certain you've kept up your Debussy and Bach? I hear you've been messing around with Broadway theater trash for a couple of seasons. That never has been a noticeable help with Czerny technique."

"I practice every day," said Stanislaus Joseph.

"O. K.," said H. Rodman.

He pressed a button that brought in a male secretary, and handed the man a dozen of the wires. "File these," he said, "and wire Bill Levy in Kansas City that I'll have a new pianoforte player on to him in forty-eight hours. Join the tour in Denver."

He turned to Stanislaus Joseph. "You know Robert Schumann's *Toccata—the* Toccata?" he asked. He had mentioned one of the most difficult of the great Saxony-born pianist and composer's compositions. Few musicians could really play it.

"I know it," said Stanislaus Joseph. "I was playing it the other night. That is, till the tenants below me pounded on the steam pipe, and I had to stop. I hadn't realized it was two A.M., sir."

H. Rodman laughed. "That one would surely wake 'em up!" he said dryly. "Well, there's the pianoforte. Play it for me, Tightpants. Give it all the pedal that you wish. To hell with the folk in the office underneath. That piece is sure liquid fire."

The truth was that the young man was really starved to play for someone who had an appreciation of such a composition.

Since Olga's illness, he had had no audience for the pieces he loved. Hans Beuter liked the folk songs. That was as high as his musical appreciation could rise. The boy had played some Mozart and some lighter Debussy for the Winter Garden comedian between a matinee and night. But not a composition of pure technical beauty as this *Toccata*.

He played it now. H. Rodman could find no fault with its playing. That, from him, was the highest praise.

"I have a piece here by the Hungarian Ernst von Dohnanyi," he said, taking from his desk drawer a manuscript. "Think you could play it?"

"I used to know that composer's *Pierrette's Veil.* It's a pantomime, as you doubtless know," said the young man.

"Yes, I know," said H. Rodman. "I had to learn it when I was twelve. And I hated it. Well—this is a manuscript just discovered. I tried to play it, but I'm out of practice. You try it."

Stanislaus Joseph took the ink-dotted manuscript. It was an *Etude.* Not too difficult, he thought. He played it, having only to pause where the manuscript was blurred. Even there, he provided notes. "This is what I believe Herr Dohnanyi meant," he said.

"O. K.," said H. Rodman. "Tightpants, you leave tomorrow morning for Denver. I've already sent the wire. Perhaps you heard me. Took a chance you hadn't forgotten how to play. You join a violinist we have out there—a real performer—no phony Viktor Reimalsky. I can give you a season till June. Salary two hundred dollars weekly and travel expense. By the way, what are you doing now?"

"I am in the Winter Garden orchestra," said the astonished Stanislaus Joseph. "But, Mr. Rodman, I cannot—"

"No buts, young man. I'll fix it with the Union. And I know that theater management. Earning only the theater minimum scale, aren't you?"

"Yes sir," said Stanislaus Joseph, "but they are fine people. Only lately——"

"Tightpants, I'm a busy man," interrupted H. Rodman. "My office will arrange everything. Send the Winter Garden a piano player that will be much better than you for the junk they play. I know the conductor. Friend of mine. He won't stand in your way. Go pack your bags. Take evening clothes. Come in tomorrow for transportation and instructions."

H. Rodman returned to his desk papers. The matter was settled. The interview was closed.

"Mr. Rodman," said Stanislaus Joseph. "I must ask you to hear me. I am grateful. More grateful than I can tell you. I was beginning to lose confidence in myself. In my so-called talent. You give me hope again. But I am married——"

"Married! You married! Good God!" said the impresario, staring with a smile at the lad before him.

"Yes. I know it is difficult to believe that any girl would marry me," said Stanislaus Joseph. "But I am married to the most beautiful girl in the world. I could not leave her, sir."

"Well, take the damn woman along," said H. Rodman with a shrug. "We'll pay her railroading also. But keep her away from the concert halls. Women can louse up any tour. Fall for the other soloist. Think *you* are falling for some dame in the hotel. I know."

Stanislaus Joseph did not get angry. He had heard from Albert Rouchard about H. Rodman's background—his dislike, almost hatred, of all women, because of the memory of a drunken mother.

"My dear wife is ill at the Medical Center. She is not expected to live. I am again most grateful to you, Mr. Rodman, but I cannot leave New York at this time."

H. Rodman was, as we know, accustomed to having his own way. He had no sympathy whatever for "sick wives." Sick wives or healthy wives. He had thought this lad had some common sense. Along with an unusual talent. Well, he had been wrong. He held out his hand to Stanislaus Joseph.

"Goodbye, Mr. Tightpants," he said. "Too bad. Too bad a fine pianoforte player like you has to get messed up with a sick woman. Any woman. Thought you had more brains. Nevertheless, good luck to you."

Stanislaus Joseph left the Rodman office, but he was neither depressed nor angry. He could still play the pianoforte! Play well enough to please even this exacting critic.

Maybe Olga would get well. Maybe the doctors were wrong. Maybe a fully recovered Olga and he could go on and do fine things together! Even H. Rodman would not hate his Olga Lasenka.

Someday, when she was well, he would take her to the Rodman office.

It is one of life's strange and crazy coincidences that there had been another barrier to Stanislaus Joseph's going out on the road—a matter that had entered his thoughts and which he had immediately dismissed as being utterly non-understandable to this hard boiled concert manager. And yet—a mention of that barrier-coincidence would have changed the entire attitude of H. Rodman!

Dr. Stanislaus Joseph Halka would not have wanted to leave the four small kittens who climbed lovingly over his feet during each performance in the Winter Garden orchestra pit. *His children.*

Tightpants did not know about the picture in the impresario's wallet—the cheap snapshot of a little boy who had once been H. Rodman. The snapshot of a little boy and his mongrel dog. Or about the animal-crowded farm hidden away in deepest New Jersey.

✣ 5 ✣

But no miracle of recovery for the girl who had been Olga Lasenka was destined to happen. Several more weeks came and went, and she suddenly began to show signs of sinking. An unusual, strong vitality and a will-to-live were all that kept her alive.

The Viennese doctor had worked frantically on his vaccine. But it had not reached the point where he dared to test it on a human.

His concern for Stanislaus Joseph caused him to delay imparting this state of affairs to the young man. The young musician was at the hospital at all possible hours without it.

The doctor did verify that he had all possible telephone numbers at which he could reach the devoted husband.

It was on a Wednesday that the girl seemed near an end. Stanislaus Joseph had been there early in the morning, and left for an eleven o'clock rehearsal. Then he played a matinee. At seven forty-five that evening the doctor decided—although he realized it was near the hour of his friend's evening performance—to reach him.

The Madison Avenue telephone did not answer. Stanislaus had come and gone. They rang the theater box-office.

It should be explained that the employees of a theater at the "front-of-the-house" had no connection with the performing company. They were employed by the theater owners. A show was just another show. Playing the theater on a percentage of the receipts basis. Shows came and went.

Box-office employees would know the names of the stars—of the leading players. They knew the company manager who counted up each night when all receipts were in. They usually knew the press agent. All others were simply so many robots.

In particular, the members of the orchestra whose names did not even appear on the printed program.

The first delay in finding Stanislaus Joseph originated in the Winter Garden box-office.

Sammy Rosenberg, the young and efficient assistant treasurer (just lately promoted from head usher and keenly feeling his importance), got the first call. The Neurological Institute at the New York Medical Center wanted one Mr. S. J. Halka to come there at once. His wife, in private room B, fourth floor, was sinking.

The very busy Sammy (there was a long line, money in hand, at his box-office window) curtly informed the voice from the hospital that there was no such person employed at the Winter Garden, and returned to the more important task of taking six-sixty per seat for the evening performance of a smash hit.

But in another five minutes there came through another and more insistent call. This time it was the head nurse of the Fourth Floor. The Viennese doctor felt that his imperfect English had perhaps not been understood.

Sammy Rosenberg was really sore.

"Listen, lady," he shouted, in his best theater box-office courtesy voice, "Ain't I once, already, told somebody who can't speak English right, that there ain't no actor in this company by the name of S. J. Halka or any other Halka!"

Sammy had had one of his girl assistants check the program after the first call. No such name listed there.

The female voice at the other end broke in before Sammy could slam down the receiver. This floor-nurse had grown fond of Olga Halka and her "nice" husband. She was not to be put off by very youthful arrogance at some playhouse.

"Listen, young man," she took a chance on the age of the male voice, "this is a matter of life and death. Do you want me to telephone the police? Mr. Halka—Dr. Halka—is not an actor. He is a musician in the theater orchestra. He left this number where he could be reached evenings, except Sundays, from seven-thirty to eleven-thirty. Get word to him at once that he must come to the Neurological Institute Hospital if he wishes to see his wife. She may not live more than an hour."

So it was a damn musician that was causing all this annoyance! "Dr." Halka my eye! Musicians were even a few notches lower than actors in Sammy's opinion. Both, necessary nuisances around a theatrical enterprise. It *would be* a musician who had to have a wife dying, just as the night window-sale was the heaviest!

Undoubtedly also, this S. J. Halka—"Dr." Halka—was a foreigner. All musicians damn foreigners! Especially those who stuck a phony title ahead of their silly names. They ought to be kept out of the country.

Sammy often forgot that *his* father and mother were immigrants who arrived at Ellis Island just in time for the young Samuel Abraham to be born under the Stars and Stripes.

But Sammy Rosenberg was not an unkind soul. Just annoyed that trivial people and their trivial troubles so often interfered with an important matter like commerce. Like the night the prima donna had insisted on getting a veterinary to attend her sick dog back in the dressing room.

Getting help for a sick dog when tickets were being sold!

So Sammy turned his busy window over to a girl assistant, and journeyed down through the dark auditorium to the orchestra room underneath the stage.

Here there was further delay. No one seemed to know who S. J. Halka was. Certainly there was no "Dr." Halka. The contractor (the flute player who hired all musicians) had not yet come in. Nor the conductor. The contractor did come presently and identified "S. J. Halka" as the piano player. There was a general belated recognition.

"Tightpants!" "It's Tightpants that you want!" went up from a chorus of voices. "Why the hell didn't you say so in the first place?" asked the bass fiddle player, who sat next to Stanislaus Joseph in the pit. Sammy's answer cannot be recorded in a book that hopes to make the public libraries.

This "Tightpants" had gone to the telephone pay-station booth, located in the stage entrance hallway. He was trying to get the Neurological Institute and getting only a busy signal. Worried and wishing to ask regarding his wife's condition before reporting for his evening's work.

Sammy dug him out. Back to the musicians' room to report to the contractor that a substitute would have to be summoned from the Union for that night's show. Then a rush to the sidewalk outside, to decide whether subway or taxi would take the frantic husband more quickly to One Hundred and Sixty-eighth Street.

And here Sammy Rosenberg proved that he was a real New Yorker, worthy of his Ellis Island birthright. That his heart was bigger than his mind.

The anguish of the little man in the tight, striped pants and the tight, silk-taped black coat, topped with the funny black Homburg, got under the skin of the hard-boiled ticket dispenser.

"Kiddo," he said, "I see a police car across the street. The cops in it know me. Have been bothering me for weeks for a pair of passes to this show. Maybe I won't get fired if I promise a couple of pairs of free ducats for tomorrow night, even though we are selling out. Follow me, Dr. Kiddo."

The two cops also had a heart. Tightpants, crowded into the seat between them, was rushed, with siren screaming, up Broadway through all traffic, faster even than the subway would have taken him.

Back in Sammy's box-office, the girl assistant asked: "Well, did you find the guy?"

"Ye-ah," said Sammy wearily. "Guy named Tightpants. Damn musician. Funny looking, damn foreigner."

But it is my belief that the Angel who recorded Good Deeds in the great Ledger made that day a golden check—if not a cross—against the name *Samuel Abraham Rosenberg.*

And all this was why that night, for the first time in his theater-playing career, Tightpants Halka missed a performance.

The mother cat and her four kittens missed him. There was no saucer of milk and bits of liver between the second and third acts. No familiar, loving feet to climb over.

The *adagio* dancers sure missed him when they had to do their spinet-accompanied "lifts" without the proper dramatic pauses in the music.

And the dog-loving, but self-centered prima donna registered a strident complaint with the stage manager, and demanded that somebody be discharged when her big number went wrong because the hastily summoned substitute piano player from Musical Union 802 started to play the wrong theme for her series of screechy, coloratura trills in the first act *finale.*

Only the pie-slinging comedian-star telephoned the hospital switchboard at the first intermission.

"Tell a guy named Dr. Tightpants Halka to yell if he needs any help of the kind I once mentioned to him," was the message he left.

❖ 6 ❖

WHEN STANISLAUS JOSEPH opened the door of the private room, he faced, not the bed and Olga lying on it, but two tall, white screens.

His heart almost stopped, for he thought he had arrived too late; but the raised finger of the nurse and her calm face reassured him. And there were voices from the other side of the screen.

One of the voices was Olga's. She was repeating lines which were first said by a male voice.

Stanislaus Joseph knew that the male voice was that of a priest.

"O Holy Lord, Father Almighty, Eternal God, we earnestly beseech Thee that the most sacred Body of our Lord Jesus Christ, Thy Son, which our sister hath now received——"

Then the voice of the girl repeated the words, the end of the phrase being—"may be to her an eternal remedy both of body and soul. Who liveth and reigneth with Thee, in the unity of the Holy Ghost, one God, world without end. Amen."

There was a silence. The boy knew that the priest was blessing her—that he had administered to her the last rites of their Faith; and presently his voice came in the final benediction, "The blessing of God Almighty, the Father, and the Son, and the Holy Ghost, descend upon thee, and remain with thee always."

And both voices repeated, "Amen."

The black-clad priest emerged. He was replacing the tiny silver lid on the thimble-like oil-stock container—the holy oil with which he had anointed the girl—and removing the narrow, ribbon-like, purple and white stole from about his shoulders, the symbol of his authority as a priest.

Stanislaus Joseph had met the priest. He was a tall strong-featured, middle-aged man from a nearby church. He visited the Medical Center daily to give spiritual consolation to its Catholic patients. He had talked with Olga a number of times before.

"Courage, my son," he said kindly to the distraught little man who stood by the nurse. "I have administered the final rites. You have a good wife. A true daughter of the Faith. Her life has been without sin. She is devoted to you. She has been asking if you were here."

"Thank you, thank you, Father," Stanislaus Joseph managed to say.

Then he was inside the tall screens, and looking down at the beloved face so still and motionless against the white pillow case.

She had never, it seemed to him, appeared so beautiful. And her brown hair was not loosely combed as it had been that morning, but carefully parted in the middle, drawn down tightly, and a thick braid curving across the top of her head.

More than ever before like a halo, it seemed to him.

Her eyes were closed—the prayers had taken of her physical strength—but even before she opened them, she seemed to know of his presence, for she spoke.

"Duszka—my duszka," she said very softly, and then she was looking up at him. "I have been asking for you."

"Your hair—your lovely, lovely hair," he said. And he touched the braid tenderly, reverently, as if he were touching something holy.

"Now I know that you are a saint," he said.

The girl smiled. "I am your wife," she said, "and that is all the sainthood I desire. I had the nurse fix my hair after you left this morning—arrange it the way I know you like it. I did it just for you. Duszka—this is goodbye—goodbye for a little time——"

"No—no!" His voice broke. There was a chair by the side of the bed, but he ignored it. He fell on his knees and seized her white hand that lay outside the cover of the bed. He held that hand as a drowning man might hold a life line reaching to a solid rock of safety. Only his rock was a frail girl whose end he knew was near.

During the weeks since he had known the worst, he had tried to brace himself for this final day, but now that it was here, all resolves of courage, of calmness, were swept away.

"I should never have left the hospital this morning," said the boy. "Why didn't they send for me before? Why? Why?"

"Duszka," said the girl softly, "they wanted to reach you, but I knew you had a matinee. I would not let them telephone. All that does not matter now. The doctor was at my side most of the afternoon—we would not have been alone. And then the priest came because of what the doctor had to tell him.

"They knew, duszka, and somehow I knew. I think I have known for quite a while—only I would not admit it to myself. Or to you. Now we must not waste time. There are things I wish to tell you before I go."

"You cannot go—you must not go—Oh God—Oh God!" said the little musician.

"Duszka, we are not children," said the girl. "I know that I have only a few hours more—maybe not that long. Something about the hormones within my blood stream. It does not matter what. We will not spend that hour or two weeping.

"I am not afraid to die, my duszka. Only distressed that I must be separated from you. First—about what the good priest said. He wished to make me reconciled to this passing. Spoke of a city of pure gold—a Heaven with Angels' voices singing, and me in a spotless white robe in the presence of the Blessed Lord."

She paused a moment, lifted his hand to her cheek, and then continued.

"Duszka, I have thought about all this before. I hope I am a good Catholic—I have faith—I believe sincerely in Jesus Christ—that He died on the Cross for you and for me—but I have sometimes wondered if all this Heaven-story were really true. And now—when the priest says I may soon be there—I don't much care, duszka, whether it is true or not true.

"About the golden sidewalks, I mean—and the long, white robes. I want to live on—yes—beyond the thing called Death—where you will some day join me—but I don't want to live in a glittering golden city with great Angels and all the Blessed Saints.

"I had thought it all out—I just want to again live simply, and with you—maybe they'll let us have a little room off to one side somewhere—just you and me—and I don't want you to wear a long white robe or even a gold one. Just your own tight, broadcloth pants and stiff shirts—and I'll just have on my old house dresses, with maybe my best dress for Sundays.

"And maybe they'll let us have one pianoforte instead of two harps, so that you can play Chopin for me. Ah, duszka, I think that if ever the Blessed Lord heard you play Chopin, He'd let you give a concert—for all the Angels and the Saints——"

She paused and closed her eyes. He could only press her hand against his cheek.

Presently she opened her eyes and continued.

"And about your playing, duszka—I know that I have held you back, here on earth. Oh yes, I did!

"If you hadn't met me, and used all your efforts to help me, and wanted to be where I was working—where we could both work at the same theater—you might have been giving concerts—you might have made a great name for yourself; and instead of that, you were wasting your talent in a theater orchestra where I was a chorus girl—just to be near me——"

The boy broke in. "Olga darling, no. It was all the other way. I kept you back—always at your heels—I know how theater managers think about a beautiful girl with a husband always being around—'We've just got to take *him* if we use her.' I believe at first I was helping you—but I didn't help, except at the very first.

"If I hadn't always been there, some playwright, some great manager or agent might have taken an interest in you; someone who could do more than just get you into a chorus line——"

The girl raised her hand and put it over his lips. "That just isn't true, duszka," she said softly, "and besides, I'd rather have had you than all the great playwrights and producers in America and Europe; not only because you were you, but because some day—now that I will not drag you back—you're going to make the grade—finish your symphony—go on concert tours——"

"No one wants me or is likely to want me to go on concert tours. They have to have big names," said the lad, just a little sadly.

"Duszka—duszka," said the girl. "You are not good in making up a falsehood. I know that Mr. Rodman wanted you, two weeks ago, to go on tour. A fine salary. In large cities. It would have been a new start for you. And you turned it down because of me."

"How did you know that!" demanded the boy. "If that impresario annoyed you here about it—."

His eyes were flashing. He was truly angry.

The girl laughed. A sweet, low laugh that he well knew.

"Oh duszka, I believe you really do love me," she said. "No—don't rush back downtown and strangle poor Mr. Rodman. Or the man who told me about it, either. For that man is the best friend you and I ever had. Hans Beuter.

"And Hans didn't mean to tell me. You know that matinee day he knew you couldn't come up, and he came and brought me some roses, and to the nurses, a big cake? He mentioned quite innocently that you had told him H. Rodman had sent for you. He thought I must already know about it. Then he realized he should not have told me, and I dragged it out of him. What happened, I mean.

"So you see, my duszka—I know. I know how you have sacrificed for me."

The girl closed her eyes for a while. The Viennese doctor came in, took her pulse, listened to her heart with his stethoscope.

Stanislaus Joseph stepped out into the room, as these tests were made. And a strange, new urge swept over him.

For there are miracle moments when the most beaten, the most humbled of human spirits feel that, in spite of all vicissitudes, there must be a year—a day—an hour—of destiny. Else why were given hopes and dreams? Why a soul—mortal or immortal?

Who never feels this has never really been alive.

Maybe that day in Wilkes-Barre had been such an hour for this girl. Thank God for it. But there must be a greater hour!

So, at the most tragic moment of his life, the almost dead embers of Tightpants Halka's soul were blown upon by the fresh, strong wind of a new determination.

This determination was not just for himself. It was also for this girl. This girl whose faith in his talents was living even beyond what we call Life.

✤ 7 ✤

HE COULD SCARCELY wait to speak to her again—as he did as soon as the doctor left. The doctor who said to the young husband in German: "Your dear wife's time is short. I would say one more hour. I will leave you with her. You two should be alone, I know. I will be in the sun lounge at the end of the hall. My day's work is done. Call me if you need me."

"Duszka," said Stanislaus Joseph, when he was again at Olga's side and she opened her eyes and looking up, had seen in his eyes that glow—an inner glow that made one forget the unimpressive face, "Duszka, I know now, at last, what I can do, what I *must* do, to make your name famous, to make your name live! So that all America, all Europe, will know it! Your name of *Olga. Olga Lasenka—*"

"My name need only matter to you, my dear one," interrupted the girl.

But Stanislaus Joseph went on, as if not interrupted. "My symphony. I've been trying to write about the wrong thing for me to write about. Big world events like wars, and the curse of dictators, and social injustice; all involved with the history of Vienna and Austria—ancient and modern.

"Duszka, the Vienna I knew, the Austria I knew and my people knew, isn't there any more I hear; and anyway, that story has all been told by greater composers than I can ever hope to be!

"*My* symphony will be just America—about an American girl—about *you,* my duszka—about sacrifice and loyalty and courage and faith and beauty. The *Olga Symphony* I'll name it—and you will be known, not because you were foolish enough to fall in love with me, but because your name is linked to what, with God's help, will be a *meisterwerk,* as they would say in Vienna.

"I think I will start it with the arrival here of your immigrant father and mother—the Statue of Liberty—the great, towering buildings—they go to a small inland city like your Wilkes-Barre to bravely start a whole new life in this new land—you are born—you grow up—go to what you call High School—work in what you call the Five-and-Dime—but all the time you dream of a great career in Music—in this Five-and-Dime you are found humming a melody—but found by a *great impresario* like H. Rodman or the Director of the Opera like Guilio Gatti-Casazza—he brings you to New York—again, in the music, the wonders of this great city, but now through the eyes of an American girl in contrast to the emotions of your immigrant father and mother—you are the understudy at the Metropolitan for the *Carmen* role, and one night the great star is ill. You step into the role—a triumph—an instant triumph——"

The girl on the hospital bed could not but smile. "And you would then have me meet and marry a millionaire! Oh, I know.

"But, duszka, I'm glad it didn't happen that way at all. I'm glad I was found by Mr. Tom 'Wow-'Em' Gallagher and became one of the Four Rosebuds, and finally reached the L'Esplanade-Plaza Hotel where I couldn't pay my bill, and went to try out for a Ziegfeld chorus job, and looked down on a piano stool and there were you—my own duszka!

"Oh, I know that you could write it all the other way, but, duszka, while I have been here I have had a great deal of time to think. We are perhaps just little people, meant to do something wonderful, but something *small.* Not large like the Statue of Liberty and the Empire State Building. And maybe, in the end, the small things are really the large things. I am not worthy of any great symphony."

And now came her opportunity. She would tell him about *the song* under the letter "O" in the cardboard letter file down on Madison Avenue.

"Duszka, if you want to please me; if you want to do something to make my name live; just write a song. A simple song like *Alice Ben Bolt* or *Sylvia*. Duszka, I did not tell you before——"

"No—no!" Stanislaus Joseph interrupted. "It will be a great symphony—if it is the last thing I do! I'll only live and work for that. With God's help I'll do it! I'll forever link your name with a noble, soaring symphony—it will have its tender moments also—I'll start it with a *fugue* which will be the theme——"

The nurse had suddenly joined them behind the screen. It was time to take again the girl's pulse and temperature, and the truth was she had thought there was a quarrel, for in the fervor of his new idea, Stanislaus Joseph had raised his voice.

"Careful—careful, Dr. Halka," said this night nurse, who was an experienced, middle-aged woman.

Tightpants did not at first understand, but Olga did, and she said quickly, "It is all right, nurse. We won't talk so excitedly. It's just about a song my husband is going to write——"

"A symphony!" said Stanislaus Joseph firmly. "A noble, soaring symphony—if God gives me the talent to write it."

The nurse thought: *These theater people. Even in the face of death, centered selfishly on their work. Doesn't the stupid man realize that his wife has only a few hours to live?* But aloud she said, "I think Mrs. Halka should rest a little while. You can speak with her again, after she has some minutes' rest."

So Stanislaus Joseph moved into the hallway, leaving the door ajar. He felt, which was the case, that the nurse had some intimate duties to perform. As he walked back and forth he tried to form a prayer, "Oh God, she must not die!" but even as he repeated the words over and over, there were notes on white, black-lined paper forming before his eyes, and a soaring melody was coming to his ears.

So God, in his mercy, eased the terror and pain of this good man.

The nurse presently came out and asked him to come again to the bedside. "Your wife seems to have something on her mind. Please say nothing to excite her. I fear the end is near. Any excitement would only hasten——"

"I understand," said Stanislaus Joseph. "I will talk no more of my work." And his sad smile made the nurse understand that *he* understood.

But the girl who had been Olga Lasenka had Stanislaus Joseph's work very much on her mind. She had not yet told her husband of the "so long as love remembers" song. And she was feeling very tired. So very tired.

And there was coming a strange sound to her ears. It was not the confused noises of the city, or the whistle of a night boat going down the great river. It was—it surely was—the song of crickets and whippoorwills!

Her husband was again standing beside her bed. Her duszka Tightpants. He was kneeling now beside the bed. He was holding tightly to her hands. He was repeating "Olga—Olga, my darling. You must not die."

The girl who had been Olga Lasenka tried to focus her thoughts. What was it she must tell her husband? *The song. The song that she had written for him.*

"Listen carefully, duszka," she said, but the words came so faintly that he had to raise himself to be nearer her lips to understand. "Back down at Madison Avenue—you will find it—" and then, as her mind wandered, she commenced to repeat the lines

"Olga—whose eyes were violets—
Olga—whose tears were pearls—"

"What is it, my darling?" cried the boy. In his voice was agony and utter devotion and desperate, stark entreaty.

But Olga did not answer. Her breathing had stopped. Her eyes became glazed.

Stanislaus Joseph called wildly for the nurse.

Again, at such an hour, there was no one in the Early Gothic Room of the museum named the Cloisters, further up the river Hudson. Had Guard O'Rourke been there, he would have perceived the breast of the La Celle statue, which had been blood red all evening, turn suddenly to purest white.

The Spirit of the statue was also at complete rest.

8

THE DETAILS OF THE FUNERAL of Olga Halka are not material to this humble saga.

Stanislaus Joseph made the sad journey to her native Wilkes-Barre with the body. Loyal Hans Beuter took two nights off from his bakery, and accompanied him. Stanislaus had telegraphed Father Joe to arrange for an undertaker to meet the train, and the coffined body was taken to his little church for a Mass. Then to the hillside cemetery, where her remains were laid to rest beside the graves of her father and mother.

And so, her freed spirit could hear the nocturnal song of the crickets and the whipporwills, after watching—if it so desired—the glorious sunsets beyond the distant mountains.

"Here is where I wish to be brought when my time comes," the boy told Hans Beuter. "To lie beside Olga. As a matter of fact, it's the only real estate, the only plot of ground in America that I own. Olga's father left it to her. As her husband, it will come to me. And she often told me that her father, who must have been fine, like her, wanted 'her man' to also be buried here. So you are destined, Hans, to make at least one more trip to the Territory of Pennsylvania."

But Hans Beuter said very soberly: "I hope that such a trip will be long delayed."

And then he added, with the smile that even a funeral could not banish, "We need you around the bakery to write greetings on special cakes. Those music bars with the real notes of great pieces are getting much in demand. I'm going to put you in the Bakers' Union so there will be no trouble over it if the walking delegate finds out who writes them.

"Don't let me be calling you up some midnight and find you dead! The Bakers Trade needs you."

And this jest—but a jest half in earnest—did help Stanislaus Joseph to bear his great sorrow. He was really wanted—*needed*—in a world of sorrow and indifference.

There had been sorrow but no indifference at the Mass at Father Joe's little church.

The interest had of course been kindled by that memorable ovation some months before, but Olga's High School mates, her fellow workers from the Five-and-Dime, her old teachers, a delegation from the Lions Club, were there in sincere solicitude and as a mark of deep respect.

One might have noted many young folk in the gathering who had not really known her. Father Joe in his brief and touching talk at the graveside spoke of the very great lift her life had given to the young people of the city. For almost the entire church gathering had also gone to the cemetery.

The floral tributes had filled three motor cars, and Stanislaus Joseph, after their symbolic journey to the grave, had asked that they be sent to the City Hospital—to the wards there. He remembered how Olga had distributed her Winter Garden company roses to the ward at the Neurological Institute.

And the evening papers carried full accounts, one of them having an editorial in praise of her modesty, her industry, her saintly life.

Father Joe said to the young man when they returned together to the parish house: "Your wife, Dr. Halka, always reminded me of my own favorite Saint of the female sex—the Blessed Imelda. *She* died when but a child of twelve, but her example of courage and virtue has lived, and will live forever.

"Who knows but that your Olga may sometime perform miracles! I shall tend her grave myself. I shall say a Mass for her each morning. And why not? She gave me a new life. She gave my blessed church a new career."

And so, in his heartbreaking grief, Stanislaus Joseph also felt a great pride.

In his new symphony he must introduce a religious theme. A great chorus of heavenly voices that, at the end, would welcome his Olga to Paradise.

And he was able to tell Father Joe that the girl had never forgotten him. The nurse at the hospital found a letter in the bosom of Olga's nightgown. It was the letter Father Joe had written her, and which she had received the morning of her departure for the hospital. Stanislaus Joseph had instructed the undertaker in New York that this letter was to be placed next her heart, in the bosom of her burial dress.

It was a colored woman who had gone from the Madison Avenue apartment to the New York undertaking parlor with the girl's burial dress, and to see that her hair was arranged as it had been at her death. And to be sure this letter was so placed.

A colored woman who had been at Olga's wedding, and to the King of the Sea wedding luncheon—the wife of a colored clerk at a hotel named *L'Esplanade-Plaza* located on West Forty-sixth Street.

The presence of this letter in her coffin and on Olga's bosom, was most likely why a certain superstition sprang up in Wilkes-Barre. A superstition that if a child or a young girl greatly desired something, or needed help, a letter slipped into the small urn at the foot of Olga Lasenka's grave would bring that help, if it were worthy.

For Father Joe, with the pardonable pride of an old man, had spoken of *his* letter in a sermon the following Sunday, and told his friend the newspaper editor about it, and about its being next the heart of this saintly girl. And Mr. MacPherson had placed a small bronze tablet at the side of his ribbon counter in the Five-and-Dime, recording that "here, for two years, the blessed Olga Lasenka sold ribbons, before becoming a great singing star."

Let sceptics be told that it was Father Joe who salvaged such urn-placed letters, and if, on investigation, the requests were worthy and sincere, then, with the help of the American Legion and some wealthy members of the Lions Club, "a doll," a "dress for communion," a "puppy dog," a "new ironing board for my mother," mysteriously found their way to hopeful, believing hearts.

PART FOURTEEN

THE SYMPHONY

1

DR. TIGHTPANTS HALKA CONTINUED to play the piano and the spinet in the orchestra at the Winter Garden. He sent the some twelve weeks of Olga's salary, that had been paid her since her illness, to Robert Campbell at the Actors Fund of America, that admirable charity that saw that no member of the theatrical profession was ever buried in potter's field. That is how the girl would have wished it to be used.

Thank God the legacy of Kommodore Hugo Frederick von Steinburg had cared for her, even to the grave.

Stanislaus Joseph continued to live in the apartment on Madison Avenue. He kept her dresses hanging alongside his several suits in the single closet. And her shoes, neatly lined in their trees, in the pocket-divided shoe container that hung on the inside of the door. Her stage shoes and her street shoes.

Olga had liked nice shoes. They were her only extravagance. She had once told Stanislaus Joseph: "In Wilkes-Barre I never could afford more than one good pair. Now that we have a little money ahead, you mustn't mind if I have a dozen pairs of shoes. I will save money on other things. And they will last longer when I only wear each pair once every two weeks."

"Mind!" His one complaint had been that she would not let him buy her all the dresses and suits and blouses he thought she ought to have. Her one concern was that *he* should be always faultlessly clothed. The young man's several pairs of shoes rested along the floor of the closet.

Olga seemed to be with him often.

Not physically—there was no ghost of her standing before the waffle iron (he again made most unsatisfactory attempts to create with this stubborn implement), nor was she sitting in her chair darning his socks or just listening as he played the pianoforte. Rather, her spirit seemed to hover in the atmosphere. To permeate the entire apartment with a sense of devotion and encouragement and divine tenderness.

Her physical appearance was rather always before him with a dozen or so photographs, which he had framed and hung about the walls.

Like all girls of the theatrical profession, her likeness had been taken numerous times. Stanislaus Joseph sought out the studio which had photographed the last Ziegfeld production. They went over their films and managed to find a dozen or so of his wife. Some in costume—some in evening clothes. There had been photographs taken of various members of the ensemble of the present Winter Garden show. He found a number of his Olga.

So she looked out at him from all the walls of his two rooms. In most of them her hair was done in that distinctive style of the La Celle statue—parted in the middle, drawn down tightly, a thick braid drawn across her head and slanting down to cover her left ear.

In some of the photographs she smiled. In some she appeared sad. Always there was that exotic Slavic beauty that was the heritage of her Polish father and of the Pole who had fathered the girl who had posed for Hugh de St. Omer's statue of the Virgin.

The Winter Garden extravaganza ran the entire season and through the following Summer. Indeed into half of the season following. Tightpants was at least fortunate in this respect regarding his theater engagements. They lasted. He heard from fellow musicians of years when they obtained a total of ten or twelve weeks only. A couple of shows that failed. The remainder of the time: sitting around the Union waiting room. He had been spared that.

And his salary had been raised above the "Union scale," as H. Rodman had phrased it. One of the violin players obtained another engagement as a conductor. He had been the "librarian" of the Winter Garden orchestra. The man who collected and distributed the music each performance, and was responsible for keeping it in good order. Tightpants was given this additional task. It increased his wage to one hundred and ten dollars weekly.

At least once a month he made a trip to Wilkes-Barre. He would take a bus early of a Sunday morning. He would arrive in time to attend Father Joe's noon High Mass. Then, after a simple meal in the parish house—the Father's literal break-fast, the young man's luncheon, they would walk together down the long street to the hillside cemetery.

Stanislaus Joseph had had erected a simple headstone. On it was carved "Olga Lasenka Halka, beloved wife of Dr. Stanislaus Joseph Halka." And the years of her birth and death. But this headstone was unique in one respect.

Across its base, just above where the grass hid its sinking into the brown earth, was carved a bar of music. Three brief measures, and one note in a fourth.

A singer would know it to be the first ten notes of *Als die alte Mutter,* a song that had become her favorite as well as Florenz Ziegfeld's.

"That song by the great Anton Dvořák made possible, you might say, our lives together," Stanislaus Joseph told Father Joe. "Through it, we were able to work together that first two years in New York. Through it, Olga obtained the engagement that gave her that wonder day here, among her friends; here, where I believe her father and mother were happier that she should have had her triumph than if it had happened in New York or Paris or Vienna. For New York and Paris and Vienna forget very quickly. But here—they do not forget."

"I will never forget—and there are many others like me," said Father Joe.

And it was probably because of these stone-carved bars of music, that on one of their visits to the cemetery, Father Joe and Stanislaus Joseph found in the urn, at the other extremity of the mound of earth, a note that was to do much to make live the name and memory of this girl of a Ziegfeld-Friml chorus.

This and another song—the words of which Stanislaus Joseph had not yet discovered in the cardboard letter-file under the letter "O."

The note in the urn, on ruled, tablet paper in a schoolboy hand, read:

Dear Blessed Olga Lasenka,

I am a young boy ten years old. I am in the eighth grade. I play the harmonica. I have a fine harmonica. It cost two dollars. I want to learn to play the piano, and maybe the violin. But my father cannot afford to let me take lessons and besides, we have no piano or even a violin. I have five young brothers and sisters, and my mother says it takes all the money to feed us and buy us clothes and pay the rent. Will you help me to take music lessons, blessed Olga? My mother says you are in Heaven and only help little girls. I am sorry I am not a little girl, but I can't help it.

Sincerely

Robert Ladusky.

P.S. I am Polish like you. I go to Mass every Sunday.
P.S. No. 2. My mother told me how to spell harmonica.

There was an address in the poorer quarter of the city.

Father Joe handed the letter to Stanislaus Joseph.

"We can take care of the simple requests," he said sadly, "but things like this—it breaks my heart to have to ignore them."

And it was there, standing above his Olga's grave in the bright sunshine of a springtime Sunday afternoon, that Tightpants Halka had his great idea.

"Listen, Father Joe," he said, and in the voice of the young musician was an excitement the old priest had never before perceived, "you are not going to have to ignore this request, if it is an honest one. Or any request like it that comes to my Olga about music.

"Since Olga and I were married we were both fortunate to have employment. We saved a little over five thousand dollars. It was mostly due to her carefulness and clever management. That money is still intact in a New York savings bank. I'm going to turn that money over to you, Father——"

But Father Joe was also having an inspiration.

"The Olga Lasenka Music Fund!" he cried. "A great Fund to help poor and deserving boys and girls who show talent, and really wish to go forward in the musical arts. Your generous gift, Stanislaus Joseph, will be its foundation——"

"Her gift," said the young man.

"Olga Lasenka's and your gift," repeated the music-loving priest. "And with this to start—to start in the helping of harmonica playing," and he looked at the signature on the ruled tablet paper, "Master Robert Ladusky—who knows? This pulsing city with its foreign population—Poles, Russians, Italians, Czechs, Hungarians, Finns—maybe we'll be helping another Rimsky-Korsakov—another Mascagni—another Sibelius—another Paganini or Paderewski or Liszt——"

It was Stanislaus Joseph who was the conservative in this little scene by Olga Lasenka's grave, probably because he remembered how she would have regarded it.

"Olga will be quite happy, Father," he said, "if it helps a few young people to gain pleasure and give pleasure with a musical talent. As she once said to me—'what we do doesn't need to be the Empire State Building or the Statue of Liberty'—and her five thousand dollars will not go very far—I wish it could be much more——"

"It *is* much more," said Father Joe. "Just as her singing the *Ave Maria* in my church was much more than just a song. For with this start, I will go to several wealthy men here whom I know—a steel company owner—a hotel operator—a great brewer—the head of a big salt company—a tobacco merchant—a shirt manufacturer; within a week I will have a fund of a hundred thousand dollars, all because of your generosity and regard for the memory of your blessed wife——"

And so, indeed, it happened! The "Olga Lasenka—Father Joe Music Fund," for Stanislaus Joseph insisted that the priest's name be also used.

A Fund of *two hundred thousand dollars* it soon became, because a young girl had been saving; had lived in courage and in faith; and because a young man, whose love for this girl seemed only just beginning with her so-called death, had not forgotten how he had been helped.

Who says that either of them had lived to no purpose? *Death,* not this girl, had died.

"So long as love remembers"—her song, the song Stanislaus Joseph did not know about, had said.

2

ONE HUNDRED THOUSAND DOLLARS of this Fund had been the gift of one man. It was in dividend-paying securities, so that the principal need not be touched.

Some seven thousand dollars yearly would be available to the Fund, with the basic gift still intact.

This man was the wealthy president of the anthracite coal company, in one of whose mines Olga's father had been employed. He had come to Father Joe when he had read in the newspapers of the organization of this fund.

"I'm not even a Catholic—I'm a lowdown, heathen Scotch-Presbyterian," he had said with a smile, when he called on Father Joe one morning with the bundle of securities. "And I'm not musical—don't know one damn note from another. But I remember last year when that Polack girl was here. Read about her in the papers and saw her at that Sterling Hotel luncheon where I was an invited guest. For I'm Rotary—not Lions Club. I liked her modesty and her pluck."

He took the stock certificates from their envelope and flipped them through his fingers.

He continued: "My father came to America as a Scotch laborer. A miner. He knew about coal. Took over an abandoned coal patch. It had been completely given up. Designated N. G. Had a hunch there was a layer of bottle green ore, with low ash content, farther down.

"He was right.

"He didn't have any money. Fifty dollars was his starting capital. Did all the work at first himself. Worked with a pick and shovel all day. My good mother worked beside him, sorting and picking. At night he loaded the day's work in a wheelbarrow and peddled it from house to house. Had a mechanically minded friend who was making a fool contraption called a steam shovel. It came through. Could do the work of ten men. This friend went in with my father. The beginning of what we now call surface strip mining. . . . Well—here I am.

"I'm for that poor Polack kid that had the guts to get out and dig. The Five-and-Dime and cheap vaudeville, I hear; and then into a New York show.

"Maybe she wasn't a big star—she said herself she wasn't—but she had guts. Mighty sorry when I read of her death.

"So here you are, Father. These securities are worth a hundred thousand hard cash, any time—any day. I know about you also, and your church, and what you say this girl did for it. My Scotch ancestors behind the kirk in Glen Rothes are turning over in their graves that I'm trusting a Catholic. But maybe they'll survive the strain.

"Good luck to you, Father Joe. You're made of the right stuff too. Top-grade, hard, pure anthracite. No lousy ash content. Call me up if I can do anything more."

❖ 3 ❖

THIS REPORTER has long debated the advisability of recording the following incident which occurred in this saga of Tightpants Halka. Because it may quite reasonably strain credulity—perhaps already strained to the limit—by happenings outside the customary fixed orbit of this mundane life.

Of confirmations and explanations (one must, it seems, have them) the Wilkes-Barre mine owner has assured me that First Mate August Sandburn, Registration 12489, is a sober, reliable seaman, not given to either hard liquor or soft day-dreaming.

Also—that his strange letter had the later confirmation of some forty seamen (all properly registered in the Maritime Union) and the owner's two young sons.

And there was no doubt of what the *S. S. Susquehanna* had been through when she arrived at Bremerhaven. She could not have made port except *by a miracle*. Lloyds of London does not pay out fifteen thousand pounds sterling for storm damages because of a bad dream.

Later in this present chronicle you will have Father Joe's comment, when the letter of the First Mate was brought to the priest's attention. But Father Joe, a Catholic, may have been, and doubtless is, biased.

Actor Otto Woltner, my personal friend, had perhaps the wisest solution, when I told him about the alleged incident some years after its happening, on my last trip to Vienna.

This gentleman (and scholar) said: "Have you forgotten that your magnificent English speaking dramatist wrote:

There are more things in heaven and earth, Horatio
Than are dreamt of in your philosophy."

Herr Woltner knew those immortal lines well, for the speech had been addressed to him nightly by the great Sir Johnston Forbes-Robertson as *Hamlet* to Herr Woltner's *Horatio*.

But alas, I have already admitted that Herr Woltner's world was entirely a dream world, and that besides Master Shakespeare he was living under the cultural influence of the Messers Grimm and Andersen. Also, at our last interview, he was nearing the age of one hundred years.

His faculties—and voice—were however as clear as ever.

But all this aside—the incident happened on *La Mer*.

What do landlubbers know of the wonders of the Sea—the Sea older by far than the Earth—as old, perhaps, as the Heavens? The vast, unending, ageless, inscrutable *La Mer*.

At any rate, it is the duty of a true reporter to set down all that he hears and observes that even remotely concerns the hero of his recording.

And so—St. Michael and Hugh de St. Omer protect me from the brickbats of the realists and the doubters! Here goes!

Like the oil companies with their tankers, the great coal companies have their fleets of sea-going vessels. Carrying cargoes of black, carbonated energy to Amsterdam, Le Havre, Bremerhaven—yes, even to Liverpool and Newcastle.

The saying "carrying coals to Newcastle" has become obsolete. American fuel is used around the globe.

One month later, a vessel of some six thousand seven hundred tons, belonging to the great American company of which this Scottish-American was the president, and loaded with some hundred and ten thousand dollars worth of anthracite (ship and cargo being worth in excess of $ two million), was headed through the North Sea for Bremerhaven.

Besides the crew of forty-one men, there was aboard two passengers—the two young sons of this company president. One fourteen, one seventeen years of age. They had chosen to spend a part of their vacation in this way. A sea holiday, and at the same time to get an inkling of their father's business, into which they expected to enter when school and college were finished.

May this reporter cut short this episode by reprinting the brief, amazing, but factual letter received by trans-Atlantic airmail (it was the beginning of that service) by the coal company's president at the office in Wilkes-Barre?

The letter was from the first mate of this vessel, on its arrival at Bremerhaven, after a voyage that barely escaped disaster. It read:

Respected Sir:

I report to you the safe arrival of your vessel *S.S. Susquehanna,* now docked at pier No. 24 in the port of Bremerhaven, and tomorrow morning, our papers being cleared, we will discharge cargo onto barges of the Berlin Kohlen Syndicate, as per bill of lading.

I have already informed you by cable of the unfortunate loss of Capt. John H. McGill, who was swept into a cyclonic sea during the night of Nov. 1st, latitude 53.9°, longitude 4° East, when a gigantic wave, during the worst Atlantic storm I have ever encountered, shattered the wheelhouse, and swept it overboard.

There were two waves—the first causing the structure to crack, even extending down the vessel's side some distance, and immediately followed by another mountainous flood that swept all before it. It is my opinion, sir, that the wreckage of some other unhappy vessel was born on the crests of these waves, acting as an irresistible pile driver; so only can I account for the demolition—the shambles made of the entire structure!

Fortunately the wheel itself was practically intact, and on hearing and observing this disaster (I was climbing up from the chart room at the moment), I rushed along the rail to the spot, and took over, as was my duty.

I should have said that we had fair weather the first ten days out of Norfolk, as you will see by the copy of the log, which I enclose. Wind velocity an average of 15 to 25 miles an hour, seas smooth.

But on the morning of October 30th, we having passed through the English Channel, the barometer fell suddenly, and we plunged into heavy, rolling seas, with sustained winds well over 60 miles an hour; with gusts reaching up to 100 miles an hour. It was the beginning of a three days' storm—the worst (as I said) I have ever encountered in the North Atlantic. I have learned that dozens of small craft were washed ashore, and three other large vessels were sent to the bottom during this hurricane.

On October 31st the No. 1 hatch forward was beaten in; huge waves constantly swept the entire deck structure; and we began to list badly and roll dangerously. The forward auxiliary pumps were in constant action. All hands were on 20-hour duty out of each 24.

So heavy were the seas and the furious head winds that we made little progress, and half the hold was speedily filled with water above cargo, which had shifted badly.

I wish here, respected sir, to commend your two fine sons, who took their places with the crew at whatever tasks they were able to perform. You can be proud of them, respected sir.

As I said, it was the night of Nov. 1st that we encountered terrific gale weather. I estimated the force of the wind at 120 miles per hour. Seas rising to a height of 50 to 80 feet. It was exactly eight bells midnight when the wheelhouse collapsed and our captain perished.

Unfortunately I was not too familiar with these North Sea waters. I knew that we were off the West Frisian Islands, latitude 53.4°, longitude 4° East, and we seemed to be setting to starboard and sweeping toward the shore at an alarming rate. The radio operator was desperately sending out S.O.S. (he had had no rest for 40 hours), but with no response. Many other vessels in the area were in trouble also.

Now I come to a part of my report that is beyond belief.

For suddenly, at three bells after midnight, when I had ordered all crew to stand by with the life boats, and was fearful of complete disaster—for it was doubtful if a single boat could have been launched; also, with a sudden change of winds we were now sweeping out toward the treacherous Dogger Bank where the maps said the depth was often as shallow as 13 meters, there appeared at my side by the wheel a tall, powerful man in the uniform of the German merchant marine.

From the wide gold stripe on his sleeve, and the heavily gold-braided visor of his cap, he was a high officer.

He pushed me aside, and forcibly took over the wheel. My physical exhaustion was such (I had had no sleep for fifty-two hours) that I fear I could offer little resistance. And I ceased to protest when I saw that this stranger was an experienced navigator with a seeming complete knowledge of these waters, and was bringing us back onto our proper course!

He carried us through the night with such an exhibition of skilled seamanship as I have seldom witnessed. At about 8 bells the morning of Nov. 2nd we were out of the storm and riding an even keel. There was no doubt but that we would now safely resume our proper course and reach harbor. He then motioned me to take over the wheel.

He had said little except to give sharp, meaningful orders now and then to members of the crew, and to shout an occasional proper instruction down the speaking tube (which tube was miraculously still intact) to the engine room. He spoke good English, but with a marked German accent.

When he returned the wheel to me, I attempted to express my gratitude, and ascertain his identity, and how he came to be aboard our vessel. He cut me off sharply. I can only report to you, respected sir, what he said. It was this:

"My name does not matter, and do not thank me. Tell your damned Protestant owner in Wilkes-Barre, State of Pennsylvania, to thank one Dr. Stanislaus Joseph Halka. I came to your rescue solely because of your owner's kindness to this gentleman."

Having said this—I hesitated, respected sir, to repeat his profanity, but think it my duty to give you an exact report— he saluted, laughed most heartily (I fear referring to his religious slight), lit a very black cigar, and utterly disappeared. Vanished before my eyes! I assure you I was cold sober, respected sir, but he vanished into thin air. Or seemed to.

I can only account that he had been a stowaway, and that after this service to us, he had leaped into the sea. My almost physical exhaustion may have confused my vision.

One of the crew men—also a German—said that he greatly resembled his former captain of a submarine during the great World War. Swore indeed that it was none other than this man. By name Captain von Steinburg. That this captain had later become a kommodore in the German merchant marine—the commander in fact of the Norddeutscher-Lloyd liner *Europa*.

But that Kommodore had been dead for two years! Killed in a steeplechase horse-race in France, this German seaman said he remembered reading.

So of course this seaman's idea was utter nonsense. As a Bible-reading, God-fearing man, I have no traffic with supernatural idiocy. And I apologize to you for such nonsense from any crew member of your employ.

If you know anyone by the name of Dr. Stanislaus Joseph Halka, probably a Catholic—I am certain that was the name—you can doubtless learn a logical solution of this mystery.

For myself, I can only thank this German stranger (although his aforementioned orders to my crew were sprinkled with oaths I would not report verbatim in a letter to you, respected sir); nevertheless thank him, and Almighty God, that I am here to write you this communication.

And you can thank him, and Almighty God, that your two sons are safely here with me!

I am having all proper repairs made to the vessel, and I trust the expense will be moderate, and meet with your approval. Without a doubt they are covered by our insurance, but mere money cannot immediately replace a fine ship or its cargo.

I will see that the vessel is in a proper condition before our return voyage, of that be assured, respected sir.

Advise me, sir, by cable, if I shall bring the vessel home, or if you desire to send on a more experienced captain.

Y'rs respectfully,
August Sandburn
(First Mate *S.S. Susquehanna)*
Registration 12489.

This reporter repeats—the preceding is submitted with some reluctance. But in a true saga, *all* facts must be recorded.

4

TIGHTPANTS did not accompany the Winter Garden extravaganza when, in January, it departed for a Chicago run. Because of his superior ability at the piano he was asked to go, although it would have been customary for that instrument (as were most of the others) to be handled by local Chicago musicians.

He did not go for several reasons.

First, he was on the last lap of his new symphony. He had already orchestrated a part of it. He felt it would be necessary to be in New York, if he hoped to place it with a publisher.

Next, he now had certain commitments in Wilkes-Barre.

Twice each month, on alternate Sundays, he took an early morning bus for the hard-coal mining metropolis. For in the afternoons, under the auspices of the Fund, he gave a piano recital and a talk, each appearance having to do with a special composer.

One Sunday it would be Franz Liszt. Another, Debussy. Another, Schumann. So on through the great ones. These recitals had started in a very small way in Father Joseph's small parlor, the Father having there, however, an excellent baby-grand piano. They were supposed to be for the dozen or so young pupils studying under the money paid out for them by the Fund.

But soon their fame spread. Parents of these pupils desired to come. Also the local music teachers. And the patrons of the Fund. Very soon it was necessary to engage the ballroom of the Sterling Hotel to accommodate all.

The owner of the hotel was a patron of the Fund, and gave the use of the ballroom without charge. Stanislaus Joseph gave his services. No mere money could have paid him for the pleasure, the sincere appreciation these kindly provincial folk gave his playing. And he was helping to keep the name of Olga Lasenka alive.

There was another small matter but one which he had to admit gave him personal satisfaction.

Stanislaus Joseph could not possibly be charged with any personal vanity. Whatever his faults, vanity was not one. Rather, he was too self-effacing. Too modest in a horn-blowing world.

But it did please him to be addressed as Dr. Halka.

"Tightpants" was all right around the theater—as he had told Olga, he never resented it, realizing that it was a term of comradeship and not derision—but it was pleasant twice a month to be addressed by a title he had worked hard to gain, and to which his knowledge of music surely gave him full sanction.

And the young man did not wish to be away for any length of time from the Madison Avenue apartment.

Wilkes-Barre spoke of Olga and printed her name often in the newspapers in connection with the Fund concerts; and Father Joe and her girlhood friends did not forget her; but it was back in New York, four flights up at Thirty-fourth Street, that it always seemed to him his Olga really lived.

And it was at the King of the Sea, when he would dine there with Hans Beuter, that Olga would seem to be in their company.

That was why, by means of his new symphony, he must make her name really live again in the greater city on the River Hudson.

One more tie now bound him to Madison Avenue—a tie that might seem absurd to many who have never known the devotion of a small, helpless animal to a lonely heart.

In this case it was the devotion of *five,* not one, and sometimes not-so-helpless pets. Like the time they managed to force open the door of the shelved closet above the sink, and scatter over the kitchen as well as the living room floor a fragrant mixture of coffee, pepper, sugar, waffle flour, cleaning powder, headache pills; or the Sunday they discovered that fairly heavy manuscript-music papers were super-excellent for scratching and claw sharpening, and completely obliterated all signs of a completed orchestration of the *Fifth Movement* of the *Olga Symphony* which Stanislaus Joseph had forgotten to lock up, and had left on his working desk.

I will keep the breathless reader in suspense no longer. The dearly beloved ones—the culprits—were a mother cat and four kittens. The animal-loving engineer at the Winter Garden had died. His successor disliked "domestic quadrupeds," to quote Mr. Webster. There were rumors of a telephoning to the S.P.C.A. to send its black Maria whose destination was a gas chamber, unless adoption occurred within ten days.

Tightpants Halka stepped into the breach. He removed the small family in a sizable basket with a shutable and lockable lid, to 179 Madison Avenue. They became *his children* in fact as well as fancy.

Thereafter, Hans Beuter discovered one of the penalties attached to a binding friendship. He was given a key to the top floor front. And on each Sunday evening and Monday morning that Stanislaus Joseph was in Wilkes-Barre, it was Hans's sworn duty to go to Madison Avenue and see that "the damn cats" were fed. The quoted expression is Hans's. Not Stanislaus Joseph's.

For like unto Albert Rouchard, Hans Beuter did not love dumb animals.

It should be recorded that on Stanislaus Joseph's part there was no fickleness or disloyalty to his first loves—the mice on the hallway stairs. They also were rationed regularly, and the cats kept confined to the apartment, except when, on sunny mornings, Tightpants would take them all to the roof to frolic and absorb ultraviolet energy.

He felt that Olga fully approved of the new adoption.

So, for all these weighty reasons, the young man chose to stay on in New York City.

✣ 5 ✣

TIGHTPANTS obtained another theater engagement almost immediately. It had circulated among playhouse orchestra contractors that he was an especially excellent pianist for auditions. Several new big musicals were about to start casting.

But he now had a taste of the unhappy side of theater employment.

Two successive pieces, for which he was employed at auditions, then rehearsals, then two weeks of out-of-town tryouts, failed miserably. One of them had a lame run of three weeks in New York. The other came off after the first five metropolitan performances, so damning were the all-powerful newspaper reviews.

To be sure, these engagements had given Tightpants four months of steady work at a good salary, but they had consumed his entire time. Working at the theaters from ten in the mornings to midnight—with rehearsals and performances—he had no brain or vitality left to complete his *Olga Symphony*.

Worse than that—for the symphony had yet quite a way to go before completion—he had to cancel most of his Sunday Fund concerts in Wilkes-Barre.

He had managed to get off for only three of them in the entire sixteen or seventeen weeks. He had journeyed up from a Philadelphia tryout for one. For two others from New York.

And he also knew that two-weeks-at-a-time of steady cat-feeding, morning and night (the weeks of the out-of-town tryouts), were placing a severe strain on his friendship with Hans Beuter! He valued that friendship highly.

The Ziegfeld-Friml operetta and the Winter Garden piece with the box-office-drawing comedians had been time-consuming work for the first few weeks; but then had followed months in New York of having to go to the theater only in the evenings, except on matinee days, and when an occasional rehearsal was called.

So he declined the offer of a third new-production, theater-orchestra engagement. He went to the Union headquarters, and had a talk with his Vienna-born executive friend there.

He had sometimes thought of teaching the pianoforte. But that required a studio, and a slow, hard build-up. And in the end—not much reward, unless you were an Albert Rouchard. Besides, he had no great desire to be a teacher.

He was a perfectionist—he felt that he was still *teaching himself*—and feared he would have little patience with amateur efforts. He wanted to help sincere students—yes—witness his trips to Wilkes-Barre—but he was there helping students by perhaps showing them what real music could be achieved—if one studied hard and practiced hard.

The torturing detail of the teaching craft was not for him.

He had thought of calling on H. Rodman again, but any engagement through the great impresario would surely involve a months-long, out-of-town journey. Even the very famous ones gave only a single concert in New York each season.

It perhaps should be recorded that he did attempt a concert for profit, more or less on his own. A teacher in Nanticoke who had heard some of the nearby Wilkes-Barre recitals, persuaded him to play in her town in the High School Auditorium "for the benefit of the Fund." Admission to be charged. The Wilkes-Barre engagements were free.

Stanislaus Joseph paid out a hundred dollars for the Nanticoke hall, twenty-five dollars for the printing of tickets and programs, two hundred and fifty dollars in advertising. The gross receipts were two hundred and five dollars.

Those who came were enthusiastic—that is, those who understood fine music. The others were mystified. The young man realized that it took an H. Rodman to promote financial success in such undertakings. He was not anxious to go through the experience again.

No. What he wanted was some sort of steady living wage, with employment that would enable him to live on Madison Avenue, and still have enough free time to work at his composing.

If his symphony were completed, and being played by all the great symphonic orchestras, then perhaps a concert tour of its composer would draw at the box-office.

It was necessary that he have an income. The savings had gone to the Fund. He was never unhappy about that. It was doing for Olga's name what his personal work had not yet been able to do. And in order to continue that personal effort he must have a steady salary check each Saturday.

So the young musician proceeded one morning to the Local 802 headquarters. He explained his problems and desire.

He did not mention the five cats, but their welfare was also in the back of his mind. He feared the Union might not quite understand *them*.

"The solution of your headache, Tightpants, is a night-club job," said the employment-wise union executive, "though you've had such good luck I ought to let you remain out of work a while, just so you don't get too damn independent. Two steady years with a Ziegfeld show—almost two steady years at the Winter Garden! Good God, man! That's a lifetime career in this business!"

"We sure miss Ziggie," he continued sadly. "We and the Stage-hands Union and the Chorus Equity. Never—almost never—a failure. They don't make 'em like him any more, though there's a couple of new lads named Rodgers and Hart that will bear watching. If they have a new show I'll remember you."

He hummed a few bars of a Rodgers and Hart melody that was sweeping the town. He returned to the matter at hand.

"To get back to this night-club racket—we got a call yesterday—spot named the Horse and Buggy—regular gold mine—been operating for five years now—will go on for another twenty-five I guess—they want a piano player for what they call their classical stuff, Heaven help us!—meaning by that *In the Shade of the Old Apple Tree, Wait Till the Sun Shines, Nellie, I Wonder Who's Kissing Her Now, Will You Love Me in December As You Do in May*. I think you could somehow manage to meet their high standard of technical requirements! Want to try it?"

"What is the salary, and what are the hours?" asked Stanislaus Joseph.

"My God, but you've gotten Americanized!" said the Viennese-born executive. "You told me you had your first papers when the Ziegfeld job came up, but I didn't expect a complete indoctrination!"

"It isn't that, sir," said Stanislaus Joseph, laughing apologetically. "It's just because I have certain expenses to meet every month. Five little mouths to feed, and I would like to save a bit, if possible, against a rainy day——"

The executive had raised his eyebrows at the "five little mouths to feed" but he asked no questions. He thought: *Good God! These little guys sure can work fast!* He replied aloud: "The salary is O.K. One hundred twenty-five a week. And they tell me there are tips.

"Don't be offended if some free spender wants to leave a twenty-dollar bill on the piano because you've played at his request 'After the Ball.' Or 'On a Bicycle Built for Two.' It was probably played at his wedding!"

"I have a special charity that I'll turn over such money to," said Tightpants with a smile.

"The hours are O.K. also," continued the Union executive. "Not much worse than the theater, and no matinees. Eight P.M. to four A.M. That gives you the whole daytime clear. You can orchestrate, copy music, teach, sleep, try to pick winners at the tracks, do whatever you wish."

"I'm working on a new symphony," said Stanislaus Joseph. "That is one of the main reasons I want to stay in New York."

The Union executive thought, *Good Grief! Hasn't he got that waste of good sleeping time out of his system yet!* But aloud he said: "You'll have all your daytime hours for symphonic musing," and he added mentally, *and all your lifetime hours too, poor lad!*

He had known other moonstruck musicians who were writing symphonies. They often came to 802 to get financial aid from the Musicians Relief Fund.

At least this Tightpants guy understood the necessity of coming down to earth to earn a living—rent and meal money—and had the ability to do so!

"There's one thing more," said Stanislaus Joseph. "Could I get off two Sundays a month? I have a commitment in Wilkes-Barre, Pennsylvania, for those Sunday afternoons."

"I guess we can arrange that," said the executive. "You're entitled to one day a week off. They may wrangle about it being Sundays—that's a big night for them—but if it's only two a month—I'll phone 'em you're especially reliable and very classical, and they had best grab you before you take on another big Broadway hit like this last one—the five-day one! Don't laugh, my friend. That's why I was damn happy to get a desk job here instead of tooting a French horn. Oh yes, there's another fine print contract clause. You have to agree to wear a costume—way they were supposed to dress around the year 1893—Chicago World's Fair period, they call it."

"I won't feel any more uncomfortable than I did summer time at the Winter Garden—white jackets and a blue sash so that the audience would look at us and think the cooling system was working!" said Stanislaus Joseph.

The Union executive thought: *Hell, maybe they'll let him dress just as he looks now! A nice guy, but slightly cuckoo. Still writing that symphony! Too bad.*

So it was arranged.

Mr. S. J. Halka, Union card No. 86,992, called by appointment at the office of the Horse and Buggy Night Club, Inc., and after being heard to play their pianoforte—if it could be so called—by the critical Mr. Kennedy—whom we have met—was signed up.

The 802 Union executive said to his wife that night: "I had a strange one in today. Funny little fellow named Tightpants. Came originally from Vienna. Plays the piano like all hell. And is apparently good, too, in other ways.

"Says he now has five little mouths to feed! And he can't have been married more than three years! Must be two sets of twins and a single the off year. Probably two more on the way!

"You'd never dream it if you could see him. Some busy worker! I'll sure keep him away from you, sweetie pie!"

6

STANISLAUS JOSEPH did not find the Horse and Buggy Night Club, Inc., too difficult to take.

Its atmosphere was not as difficult, indeed, as a theater engagement would have been for him. In a theater orchestra pit, looking up at a stage without his Olga thereon, brought constant pang.

The singer with whom he was now coupled on the small platform for the six or seven performances each night had a pleasing voice and was a lady, and the old songs had real melody. He grew to love the Stephen Foster songs, which he had not known. He found a charm and a certain pathos in even *After the Ball. Me and My Shadow* struck a personal chord of his own loneliness.

They were like his Austrian *lieder*—the true folk songs of the America he had come to love.

He found himself taking a pride in playing these songs with the simple, naive sincerity with which they had been written; in applying his undoubted skill to bring out any beauty that rested in their melodic line. It was no false statement when co-proprietor Kennedy told partner Levine, "Some night listen to his *I Wonder Who's Kissing Her Now* if you want to hear real melody."

Perfectionist Dr. Stanislaus Joseph Halka did well whatever he did on the pianoforte, whether it was the incidental music under a Winter Garden pie-slinging scene or a Chopin *nocturne*. With such an accompanist, the singing of Annette Blair became much better also.

But Stanislaus Joseph never mentioned his Doctor of Music degree to his fellow performers. As in the theater orchestras, he was known as Tightpants Halka. It was only known that he was a graduate (as it were) of playing in Broadway shows.

When Annette one day, after they had both reported early to rehearse a new number, asked him: "Tightpants, where did you learn to play so beautifully?" he had simply said: "I was fortunate to have some good teachers back in Austria, where I was born. I played in several Vienna cafés. I was one of the accompanists for voice teacher Albert Rouchard here in New York. He taught me a very great deal about how to play for a singer."

He would not have dreamed of lording it over these kindly, humble performers. As the Four Rosebuds and Tom "Wow-'Em" Gallagher had appeared to Olga Lasenka, so they appeared to him. They were children. They could be forgiven for boasting of their somewhat pathetic "triumphs." Their professional lives were behind them.

Stanislaus Joseph felt that his life—his artistic life—had not begun. It would begin when he finished his *Olga Symphony*.

At the end of one year he finished that symphony. One hundred and forty-seven pages of the carefully black-noted music sheets. The so-called *conductor's score*. He was now ready to interview publishers.

There had been one good omen. The week before, Mr. Dixon telephoned him one noontime at the Madison Avenue apartment. He had some wonderful news. The *Broadway Bungalow* song was to be used in a new revue. "Could Mr. Dixon come with the contract, and a contract just signed with a music publisher?"

The excited stage manager arrived. Beside the two contracts, he handed Stanislaus Joseph a check for two hundred and fifty dollars.

The lyric half of the five hundred dollar publisher's advance for the song.

How the little musician wished that Olga were there! He held up the check—it was made to Olga Lasenka, the name used on the song—before his favorite wall photograph of her. Then exhibited it to all the other photographs. He cried: "You see, my darling! Your name will now be famous all up and down Broadway! Not only in Wilkes-Barre, but all over America! How proud I am of you!"

Mr. Dixon was somewhat more conservative concerning immediate national fame, but he did perform a tap dance that was his outlet for bursting emotion.

Stanislaus Joseph went to his piano and played Mr. Friml's rousing *Song of the Vagabonds* as a sort of triumphal paean of exultation, because it was that great show which had brought Mr. Dixon and Olga together. And the two men sang, with a not too harmonious choral effect, the stirring words:

Sons of toil and danger—
Will you serve a stranger!
And bow down to Burgundy!
Sons of shame and sorrow
Will you cheer tomorrow
For the Crown of Burgundy!
Onward! Onward! Swords against the foe!
Forward! Forward! The Lily Banners go!
Sons of France—Around us!
Break the chains that bound us!
And to Hell with Burgundy!

"Burgundy," in this case, meant *opposition* of any manner or kind—opposition or indifference.

Onward! Onward! Swords against the foe!

Then Stanislaus Joseph made Mr. Dixon sit and play the *Broadway Bungalow* song. It might not have possessed Mr. Friml's pulse and fire—but it *had arrived*. Would soon be sung in a real performance before real audiences! Maybe soon be on the hit parade!

Stanislaus Joseph said again: "Olga, my darling! You have arrived!"

He had one more task about it.

He took Mr. Dixon to the office of a young lawyer in the next block, to whom he had gone when settling some matters regarding Olga's death—the releasing of their joint bank account—the proof that he was her sole surviving heir. He had the song and production contracts changed to give the lyric copyright ownership to the Olga Lasenka-Father Joe Music Fund of Wilkes-Barre, Pennsylvania, and endorsed the check so that it would be payable to that Fund.

The theater production contract would pay Mr. Dixon and the lyric writer twenty-five dollars each week that the production ran. What would come from the publisher's contract depended on the sale of sheet music and phonograph records, over and above this advance payment, which was against royalties.

That these monies should accrue to the Fund, Stanislaus Joseph was certain was the way Olga would have wished it. It was most certainly the way he wished it.

Stanislaus Joseph's sole selfish regret—that Olga was not still there to write a lyric for which *he* could supply the music! He suspected that she had been working on something of the sort. Her illness and her death had, alas, cut short any career she might have had as a great lyric writer.

But his great *Olga Symphony* was now ready. Her name would live, both on Broadway and in all the concert halls of America! Of the world!

He must use her full name.

The Olga Lasenka Symphony.

7

STANISLAUS JOSEPH had not been to the Cloisters since his almost tragic journey there, the month before Olga's death.

He had been a little fearful of going when he thought of what he might have done except for the miracle—if it were indeed a miracle and not an optical illusion of his then tortured mind—with respect to the joining of the head to the appealing Christ torso.

Olga had never told him of her frantic telephone call to Guard Dennis O'Rourke. So far as the young musician knew, Dennis was not even aware of her illness, much less of her death. She had in reality telephoned Dennis the following day, and told him that her husband had returned without even entering the Early Gothic

Room. And that she expected soon to be out of the hospital and on the way to full health recovery.

Stanislaus Joseph had intended to call on a music publisher the day following Mr. Dixon's visit. But that day was a Saturday, and he decided it would be a bad morning for such an important business conference. So he put off this visit till the following Monday.

Instead, he steeled himself for a trip to the Cloisters and the Early Gothic Room.

And so, a few minutes after the opening hour, Dennis O'Rourke heard the familiar knock on his closed door leading out to the Cuxa Cloisters. It must be Dr. Stanislaus Joseph Halka! The musician was the only visitor who always knocked, and waited for the door to be opened before entering.

Guard O'Rourke had often wondered what had happened to the young gentleman and his beautiful wife with her remarkable resemblance to "his baby."

Probably they had both gone out of town with the Winter Garden show which he had read was in Chicago. He was a little hurt that they had not paid him a visit to say goodbye. Ah well—museum-visiting friends came and went. He sometimes did not see frequent visitors for months, and suddenly they would bob up again.

He started to open the door, and then hesitated. The girl's telephone warning of over a year before came back vividly. *Do not let him*—meaning this Dr. Halka—*near the statue*. Should he again get his service revolver from its place in the small high desk before opening to this knock?

He decided that he could handle any situation without firearms, and opened the door, just as Stanislaus Joseph knocked the second time.

Guard O'Rourke need not, of course, have been fearful. Stanislaus Joseph did not make a rush toward the La Celle statue by its window. He held out his hand to his friend.

"I'm so very glad to see you again, Dennis," he said. He was glad.

"And I am so happy to see you, sir, and in good health," said Dennis O'Rourke.

There was an awkward pause, each wondering how much the other knew. They were alone in the room, alone with its company of priceless statues. It was too early for any other visitors.

"And how is the missus. I—I heard she was in a hospital," said

Guard O'Rourke. He was still careful to keep between Stanislaus Joseph and the precious statue.

But the young man did not move toward the leaded windows. There were two chairs at one side—in case any visitor might become ill or museum-tramping weary. Stanislaus Joseph indicated them. "Can we sit there, Dennis, and talk?" he asked. "I think I need to be sitting down to tell you what I have come to tell you."

"If I jump up suddenly, don't be alarmed," said Dennis, and now he was comfortably smiling, no longer alarmed. "It will be because some supervisor has appeared. We are not supposed to sit during visiting hours. If any harm should come to any of the statues—."

He stopped suddenly. He had not meant to bring up that subject.

"If any harm should come to any of the statues," repeated Stanislaus Joseph. "Dennis—" and sitting there, side by side, Stanislaus Joseph related all to him. Not sparing himself, or attempting to condone his wild plan of one Sunday noon a year before.

Only once did Guard Dennis O'Rourke interrupt. That was when he learned of Olga's death. He said: "Oh God. Oh blessed God!" and crossed himself. And then he reached over and took the hands of his friend in his own hands. "God rest her loyal soul," he then said.

And this humble, gallant gentleman breathed no word to Stanislaus Joseph of Olga's telephone calls, for she had obviously not disclosed them to her husband before her passing.

He did have this to tell the young man.

"I feared sometimes that something was wrong. My statue seemed cold and lifeless. As if her soul had departed, you might say. She never smiled again. Her breast never became red. I was glad that her breast did not redden. But I was a little worried because she never smiled.

"Not till yesterday, in all the past year, did she smile. At noon yesterday, I thought I saw her smile."

It had been at noon exactly that Mr. Dixon had telephoned Stanislaus Joseph about the *Broadway Bungalow* song contracts!

Perhaps the spirit of the La Celle statue, the spirit that was also the spirit of the girl who had been Olga Lasenka, had returned to earth from Paradise for a brief moment. Only the Three Fates or Almighty God (in whichever you believe) could with certainty tell.

It is known, however, that the simplest of earth joys are often the most pleasing to the Saints.

❖ 8 ❖

THE FOLLOWING MONDAY MORNING Stanislaus Joseph carefully tucked the one hundred and forty-seven manuscript pages of his *Olga Lasenka Symphony* into a portfolio, and started for the offices of a great publisher whom he had once met when he had worked for Albert Rouchard.

This firm specialized in operettas, grand operas, and the compositions of the famous classical writers. The publishers who had taken the girl's *Broadway Bungalow* were strictly popular song exponents.

But he had used the deal Mr. Dixon had made with this latter firm as a gauge to measure what he should ask for the publishing rights of his own composition. Five hundred dollars for some four pages of music. Applying the science of mathematics, that would be one hundred and twenty-five dollars per page. One hundred and twenty-five times one hundred and forty-seven was eighteen thousand, three hundred and seventy-five dollars.

Although his figures were numerically correct, he felt that such a price might be a little high. He knew, however, through his association with the Ziegfeld office, that operetta composers like Mr. Friml and Jerome Kern received as much as twenty-five thousand dollars advance against the publication of the numbers and score of a new musical play.

But such a composer was well known, had had many successes, and there was a production, using the music, guaranteed.

He felt that as a new name, it would be fair—most fair and generous on his part—to ask for only ten thousand dollars advance. So he settled on that modest figure in his mind. One should not demand too much. It was best to mention a sum that would be agreed to at once.

He did not wish a work of art to become a matter of petty bargaining.

One other mistake he avoided. He carried his "work" in a plain, brown cardboard portfolio, tied with a single tape. It had cost twenty-five cents.

He was aware of the publisher-producer superstition that when an author arrived with his effort incased in an expensive, hand-tooled, silver-buckled portfolio, the contents were usually pulp stuff. Rudolf Friml had delivered one of his biggest hit numbers to the Ziegfeld office (Tightpants had been present) in a delicatessen store envelope which had contained his favorite smoked sturgeon. The composition itself was written on the back of a restaurant menu.

The use of Albert Rouchard's name got the young man immediately to the seventh floor of the famous building on West Thirty-fourth Street, with the retail store on the ground floor.

The private secretary came out to escort Stanislaus Joseph into the drawing-room-like private office with the richly upholstered furniture and the concert-grand piano.

Looking about—the window curtains were like priceless tapestries—the young musician decided he had best not insult the great publisher by asking only a ten thousand dollar advance.

Twenty thousand would be more in keeping with the atmosphere of that office.

The greeting was cordial, and after a few words about the fine character of the late Albert Rouchard, the publisher said: "Well, Mr. Halka, what is on your mind?"

Stanislaus Joseph was probably, as we know, the most unmercenary musician in all New York, but what was on his mind at that moment was that perhaps even twenty thousand dollars was too modest a figure for his *Olga Lasenka Symphony*. But he realized it would be very crude to start the interview with the matter of money.

That would come along as a subsidiary, and quite secondary, consideration.

"I have just finished a new original symphony, sir. I hope it has some merit. I have worked on it a year and a half. I have it completely orchestrated for one hundred and five instruments, and have with me the full conductor's score."

Stanislaus Joseph would have been most unobserving if he had not noted the sudden disappearance of a smile from the elderly publisher's countenance on the mention of the words "original symphony." The look that replaced the smile could not be termed horror, but it most certainly did not reflect an inner delight and approbation.

Perhaps the gentleman had doubts about the young man's ability to compose such a work? After all, the publisher only knew Stanislaus Joseph as an accompanist.

The young composer decided here was a time and place that he should reveal, without false modesty, his true musical background.

"I am a graduate of the University of Vienna, sir," he said. "I hold a degree of Doctor of Music. I have studied the pianoforte since I was ten years old. I studied music theory, harmony, counterpoint and composition with the finest instructors at the University. If I could play several passages of my work for you, I believe you would not doubt my musical knowledge."

The publisher was not an unkind gentleman. He indicated the open pianoforte.

The young man played, not some of the passages which possessed a real melodic character, but several of extreme technical difficulty in which the progressions were almost discords, and yet conformed to strict classical usage. For he felt that by so doing he would banish from this publisher's mind any misgivings about the performer's knowledge of musical science.

Perhaps it were best, after all, that he should only ask an advance of ten thousand dollars.

The older man said nothing at the end of this miniature recital. How should he put it? The blunt truth was perhaps the best. And the kindest.

"Young man, how much money have you to spend?" he asked.

"How much—*to spend?* I do not understand," said a completely mystified Stanislaus Joseph. Surely he had not heard correctly.

"You are undoubtedly an accomplished musician," said the older man. "I should have known that, or you would not have been Albert Rouchard's operatic accompanist. And you have there some hundred and fifty pages of doubtless perfectly technically correct music.

"You say it is orchestrated for one hundred and five instruments. That is the correct number for a full symphonic organization. There are about five of them in America. It will cost, in round numbers, some two thousand dollars to extract the parts so that such an organization could play it—provided of course we could persuade any one of them *to play it*. They would probably pay us one hundred dollars for the use of the symphony—provided, I repeat, we could persuade them to give it a showing.

"Fifty dollars of that fee would go to you and fifty dollars to us.

"I do not advise you to do so," the publisher continued, "but granted we do accept your work, and attempt to lease it—are you in a position to put out nineteen hundred and fifty dollars for the necessary parts? I regret that I could not advance such an amount personally, as we are a corporation and I am responsible to my stockholders."

"You mean—you mean that you do not *pay for*—that you do not *buy* a new symphony, if one of merit is brought to you?" gasped the young man.

"We have to buy what we can sell," said the publisher.

He felt very sorry for the young man before him. Just as he had felt sorry for other young musicians who had worked one year—two years—ten years—over some Grand Opera or, like this young hopeful—a symphonic composition.

"It is most unfair and unjust," he added, as Stanislaus Joseph sadly commenced to replace his music in the cardboard portfolio. "We undoubtedy have many fine composers of classical music in America. Almost once a month someone comes to see me. And I have to tell them the same as I am telling you, Dr. Halka.

"You see, we cannot *print* a hundred and fifty pages of a symphony as we would print a song or an operetta—or even a grand opera of which a production was guaranteed at the Metropolitan Opera House or in a similar theater in Chicago or Philadelphia. And since it would not pay us to print it—what have we to sell?"

"What then do you do—if you find a composition such as mine that may have merit?" asked the young man.

"We put it in our library," said the publisher. "Then we try to persuade some symphonic orchestra to play it. If we succeed in this difficult endeavor, and if by then we have ready the extracted parts, we can tax them one hundred dollars for its use. Maybe even a hundred and fifty dollars.

"But it is most difficult to get any of them to perform a new and unknown composition. That is, unless it is by a nationally—I might almost say internationally known figure; and then it is the name of the composer, not the composition, that makes the leasing.

"You see, the audiences which support such orchestral organizations want to hear the great classic works. The well-known works," the publisher explained. "They find novelty when some new great conductor gives a new interpretation of Bach or Beethoven or Handel. If you were a friend of some great symphonic conductor, that would help. I take it you are not. I am sorry. Really so very sorry. Now if you would come to me with a song—do you think, Dr. Halka, that you could compose a new song?"

"I had my opportunity to do that and passed it up," said the young man. "And thank you for your courtesy. To answer your first question, I haven't got two thousand dollars. Maybe I will extract the parts myself. I have the knowledge to do that. But it will take many months more——"

"It is a long task for one man," said the publisher kindly. "If it were done here, we would put half a dozen experienced men to work over it. But they would have to be paid for their work, at so much a page."

Stanislaus Joseph rose to go. The great publisher shook his hand. "Come to see me if I can be of any other service—if, for example, you ever write a song," he said. "I will be glad to hear it. Or some simple, short composition that we can print and sell.

"And do not feel depressed. Chopin, Mozart, Haydn, Beethoven could not pay for board and lodging with their symphonies. Could not get them played even in their lifetimes. So you are in good company. It is not a cheerful thought, but perhaps after you are dead, some great orchestra will play your work—it may cause your name to suddenly live again."

"I wanted to cause another name to live—but no matter," said the young man. "Again I thank you for telling me the truth. I suppose you think me very stupid that I did not know."

Dr. Stanislaus Joseph Halka went down the elevator. He went out through the store—a great music store in which dozens of folk were buying old and new popular songs—songs displayed on every counter and counter rack.

Well, maybe little old *Broadway Bungalow* would soon be there. At least Olga Lasenka had not lived entirely in vain, but no thanks for it to him.

9

BECAUSE HE WAS not a quitter, the young man did try another publisher. In the Ziegfeld office he had met one who was more of Broadway, who published many of the better musical shows. At least his Ziegfeld connection would enable him to see this man.

He did see him, in his somewhat more plain and businesslike office in Radio City.

The answer was the same.

"Tightpants," said this gentleman, "if the angel Gabriel walked into this office with his golden wings on, and a symphony in a star-studded briefcase, I'd have to turn him down. And it's really a disgraceful shame. I'm just a lowdown popular song and popular show publisher trying to keep out of the red, but I've often thought if some big millionaire music patron wanted to really help, he could put up a fund to encourage serious composers to finish works like yours. Pay the big orchestras to take a chance, and once in a while play the worthy ones. Put up the dough to have orchestrations made and parts made——"

"Yes, I know," said Stanislaus Joseph.

"Listen, kid, one of the heads of the music department of a great university, no less, is finally getting a symphony he wrote played—played after three years of peddling it around to every conductor in America! And I'll wager he became discouraged and is *paying* to have it performed. So what chance have you? Now if you ever write a song——"

"Yes. I know about that too," said Stanislaus Joseph.

"You gotta die to get a symphony played," said this publisher with a laugh. "And you don't want to croak yet, kiddo. I hear you're very good at the Horse and Buggy. Will drop in myself some night, though I don't often stay in town. Get that five-ten for Scarborough where the air is cleaner. But we're bringing out a new number that maybe you could use. Great title 'I'll Cry Till I Die When You Tell Me Goodbye'! It'll blast 'em! And don't forget. If you yourself can think up a good hot, sad song——"

But Stanislaus Joseph was departing down the hallway to the elevators.

Well—that was that. *Finale Ultimo.*

He took the *Olga Lasenka Symphony* back to Madison Avenue, and put it, in its brown container, high on the top shelf of the clothes closet. Just above where Olga's dresses hung. At least it would rest near her.

He went to his piano. He played the first movement. It *was* good. He knew somehow that it was good. But what was the use?

He took the portfolio down from the closet. He took out the

one hundred and forty-seven pages of manuscript. He went with it into the kitchen, and lit the gas burners.

He was on the point of feeding it to the flame, page by page.

Then something, he knew not what, made him decide differently. He went to his working desk—the desk where he had spent hours, days, months over these sheets of music paper. Completely wasted hours. He brought the cardboard portfolio from the bedroom where he had tossed it on the bed, and replaced the *Olga Lasenka Symphony* in it. He carefully, and very tightly, tied the tape.

And he took his pen and wrote viciously on the cover in large, bold letters

To be played after I am dead

Stanislaus Joseph Halka

He underlined the bitter words. Then he replaced the portfolio high in the top of the clothes closet. He laughed. A long, hard, bitter laugh.

But as the first publisher had said, he was in excellent company. Mozart, Chopin, Haydn, Beethoven had probably done the same.

His Olga had been fortunate. She had died before bitter disappointment came.

PART FIFTEEN

THE SONG

1

THERE FOLLOWED A YEAR of a sort of numb depression for Dr. Stanislaus Joseph Halka. Annette Blair, his singer at the Horse and Buggy, noticed the change the night after his interviews with the two music publishers. It was especially noticeable because of his high elation of the week before—the week of the news about *Broadway Bungalow*.

On that night she had said to him: "How beautifully you are playing tonight, Tightpants. You almost made me break down and cry when I sang *Take Back Your Gold.*"

"I've had some very good news. A friend of mine is about to have his first song published. *Two* friends of mine. I am so happy for them," the young man had replied.

"When the song comes out, let me have a copy. If it's in my range, maybe we can sing it here," said the kindly Annette.

"It's to be in a new Broadway revue. I don't know if they can release it at once," said the piano player proudly. "If they do, I will surely be very proud to play it and to have you sing it."

But the following Monday night! A complete change. Stanislaus Joseph did not play badly. He was too trained an artist to do that. But something had obviously gone wrong for him. Music critic Mr. Kennedy would not have thrilled at his routine playing of *I Wonder Who's Kissing Her Now*. It seemed to have lost its poignant zest. And when it came to *Take Back Your Gold,* its title seemed to Tightpants so absurdly tragic that he gave it a flippant rendition that almost upset the singer of the classic words.

"My goodness, Tightpants, what has happened?" she said at the finish of their first show.

"I'm sorry," said Tightpants. "I should not let my personal disappointments show up in my playing."

He looked at the still attractive face of the night club singer, her still excellent figure, and he somehow, and for the first time, realized that she also had her tragedy. She had not started out in her career, expecting at fifty to be singing sobby ballads in a place like the Horse and Buggy. She also must have dreamed of perhaps the Metropolitan Opera, or at least a glamorous career on Broadway. And unlike him, she was no longer young.

At fifty—where would *he* be? Wasn't it better—far better—to be dead. To be beside his Olga on the beautiful hillside of the outskirts of Wilkes-Barre.

He said to the singer: "I sometimes think this art of music that I love, and to which you and I have given our lives, is not a blessing but a terrible curse. I want to write something great. Something that will make the world a nobler place, as great music can do. In my case, something that will also cause the name of someone I loved very dearly to live. And I fail.

"It were better that I did not live at all than that I go on just eating, sleeping; working to be sure, but to what purpose? To what end?

"Folk who do not have this dreadful creative urge are happy. I know a hotel clerk in a cheap hotel. A colored man. He is raising a family. A contented family. He earns a living wage. Beyond that, he gets a supreme thrill if he picks what he calls a long-shot winner at some racetrack. I envy him. I hear the business men who come to this place for relaxation. Maybe they have played a round of a game they call golf that afternoon, and lowered their score by four strokes, as they say. They are content with life. The electrician at this night club. He wanted to get a certain lighting on my playing and your singing of the Stephen Foster songs. He achieved it. He is happy. I envy him. But you and I——

"I know you are not content," he finished. "That you had dreams. Ambitions. For you have an excellent voice. Where are those dreams? What has happened to them in this rotten world?"

It was then that Annette told him about the son at Harvard and her plans that this son would go on to be a great surgeon. "He had the highest marks in his class last year," she said. "You have no family, Tightpants?" she asked. "No one besides yourself to work for?"

"The one I worked for died," the young man said. And then, with a smile, "My family consists of five cats. And some mice on the stairs outside. I am grateful to God that I have money to feed them. A roof to give them physical comfort. They give me all they can—their devotion. That, I suppose, should bring me happiness. They make my lonely rooms seem like a home. Someone is waiting for me when I come to that home.

"But there is also this curse to write great music. My beloved pianoforte is also waiting there."

Unhappily, our Stanislaus Joseph did not yet have that assurance that he could write greatly, the assurance that poet Charles Baudelaire possessed so that when days were the darkest and creditors the most pressing he could say: *I will go to my room and with God's help write a quatrain that will live forever.*

Was there, at the top of his clothes closet, such a quatrain, so to speak? One hundred and forty-seven pages of "quatrains" that were destined to live? Only the Three Fates and Almighty God could then tell.

"Why don't *you* write a song?" said Annette at the end of this interview. "You play so beautifully. I would try to sing it beautifully."

"You are very kind," said Stanislaus Joseph. "But I fear if I introduced here a song I had written, I would be discharged. And you would be discharged.

"No. I will not be the cause of your son having to give up his career!"

The words *Why don't you write a song?* haunted him however. But a song required words. His kind of song, a poet—or a near-poet.

Stanislaus Joseph was no poet.

He did presently pull himself out of his doldrums.

He got into the habit of going to Hans Beuter's bakery when he finished his night club work at four A.M., partly for Hans's company, partly because there was usually some work that he could do. He became the official decorator of all special cakes—cakes for weddings, cakes for birthdays, cakes for the holiday trade.

Hans had Stanislaus Joseph made a member of the Bakery Workers Union, so there would be no difficulties on that score. He was at least a recognized expert with the *dressiersack!* He felt that his dear father, at whatever café in Paradise where he was playing *schnapsen,* would be pleased.

The bakery owner insisted on paying the musician for his work—at the union rate for the hours he worked. Stanislaus Joseph sent this extra money to Father Joe, to add to the Olga Lasenka-Father Joe Fund.

And the trips twice a month to Wilkes-Barre were a morale-saver—a life-saver. There, he was Dr. Stanislaus Joseph Halka, admired and looked-up-to musician.

In this connection he even commenced to write music again. He discovered that the exercises used by the local teachers for new pupils—those also for advanced pupils—were extremely dull.

After one trip, he went to his Steinway and wrote an exercise. It contained little passages that would give the fingers of the pupil "stretching technique." That would give them practice in difficult fingering. But at the same time it was an interesting melody. The pupil would feel that he—or she—was learning a real composition. Not just laboring over a dull, monotonous hitting of piano keys.

This *Exercise* was an instant success. With his permission, the teacher to whom he first showed it had mimeographed copies made. They went to all the teachers in Wilkes-Barre. To the teachers of music in the public schools.

Stanislaus Joseph was urged to write more of them. He did. He finished some eighteen.

The newspaper publisher friend of Father Joe—one of the humbler patrons of the Fund—found out about them.

This publisher had the *Exercises* printed and bound in a music-sheet-size, paper-bound booklet. On the cover it said:

SERIES OF EXERCISES FOR THE YOUNG
By
Dr. Stanislaus Joseph Halka

And listed below—I, II, III, IV, et cetera—were the eighteen compositions. The editor had had them played for him. He had given each exercise an appropriate name. *Early Morning. Sunset. The New Doll. In a Church. The Café. Gypsy Dance. Bird Song. Sadness. Happiness.*

The booklet would sell for one dollar. The price so that it would be within the means of all. At the bottom of the cover it read:

Published By The Olga Lasenka-Father Joe Music Fund
Wilkes-Barre, Pennsylvania

Father Joe and the editor kept all this a secret from Stanislaus Joseph. When the first printing of two hundred copies was ready, Father Joe placed it on the piano at the young man's next Sunday afternoon recital. He announced:

"We have today a series of new, short compositions by a new composer. I am asking Dr. Halka to play them. If he makes mistakes, you must excuse him. He has never seen this book before."

The little musician would never forget that afternoon.

There had been one other moment in his life when he had looked up from a piano bench, and been thrilled to his very toes on the pedals. Thrilled to his finger tips as they approached the pianoforte keys. The time he had looked up at a Florenz Ziegfeld chorus audition and gazed into the face of a young girl whose hair was parted in the middle, and a thick braid of it drawn tightly across its top and slanting down so as to conceal her left ear.

This was another such moment.

After he had played the *Exercise I,* played it with an emotion he had not even experienced when he had first played *La Mer,* and the applause had subsided, Father Joe again arose and announced:

"I forgot to tell you that the composer of these little masterpieces —there are eighteen of them in the book—is our own Dr. Stanislaus Joseph Halka. He wrote them out of the kindness of his great heart for the pupils studying under the auspices of the Fund. Some of us felt they should have a world-wide circulation. They are on sale at the door. One dollar each.

"I need not tell you that the proceeds will go into the Fund. We haven't yet obtained Dr. Halka's permission to do this, but if he does not approve, the Fund has a good lawyer on its board who will fight him clear to the Supreme Court!"

As for Stanislaus Joseph, he was completely speechless.

His work—the notes from *his* brain—in print! Published! His name on the cover of some music!

There *was* an all-loving God in Heaven after all!

Two hundred copies had been printed. They were sold in exactly fifteen minutes after the recital—after that audience insisted that he play all the eighteen *Exercises.* Orders were taken for three hundred more copies of the booklet.

That afternoon, up at the Cloisters, in the City of New York, once more Guard Dennis O'Rourke imagined that "his baby" was truly smiling. The happiest smile he had ever seen on her lovely face.

And I think that maybe, that afternoon, the real Olga was standing back in the shadows at one side of the Wilkes-Barre High School stage, *her* beautiful face aglow, the light from a high window striking the thick braid so that it indeed became a halo.

And by her side, and holding her hand, stood a little Viennese mother whose last appearance had been in the drab room of an Old World top-floor tenement, when a little boy had found a small spinet over against the wall.

✣ 2 ✣

ANOTHER YEAR CAME AND WENT.

Stanislaus Joseph counted his years from Fall to Fall. As did most theater folk. Their seasons started in September. They ended in June, unless they were fortunate enough to be in a holdover success. The new season commenced the next September.

As the Union official had told him, the Horse and Buggy flowed —or rather rolled—on forever. For that he could be grateful. If he so chose, he was apparently settled there for life.

We have recorded the several incidents outside the routine grind. He tuned the piano "on his own time." He went to Molly Dorcey's Christmas party, (his holiday companion, Hans Beuter, had been out of the city that particular Christmas for a catering assignment on Long Island). There was the episode that concerned R. H. Bankhead, Esq., President of the Syracuse Nut and Bolt Company.

Incidentally, Night Club proprietors Levine and Kennedy found it cheaper to bribe a city inspector than to alter some factors at the club building that were a building-code violation. More of this later.

As Mr. Kennedy had mentioned, besides Tightpants' fine playing of *I Wonder Who's Kissing Her Now,* the young musician was most dependable. S. J. Halka never missed a performance.

As heretofore noted, he arrived promptly each evening at seven. He executed the routine of the timeclock (sacred Idol of the God Efficiency) in the lower basement entrance. He proceeded to the male performers' dressing room and changed into his costume. With his singer, Annette Blair—also dependable—he did his eight shows nightly at their appointed hours.

The work was not such a hardship as it might sound, since each performance, as far as these two were concerned, lasted only fifteen minutes.

Hit 'Em Hard and Fast was the motto of the Horse and Buggy.

At three-thirty A.M., having given his final show, Stanislaus Joseph changed to his street clothes—his famous tight, broadcloth pants and black, silk-taped coat—his black Homburg—and having again recorded his presence and now departure on the timeclock, departed.

He seldom went directly to Madison Avenue.

He took a taxi to the York Avenue bakery where Hans Beuter was employed. That taxi cost sixty cents. It was part of his deal with the bakery proprietor that if there was work that he could do—i. e., cakes to be decorated—he was reimbursed this sixty cents, in addition to his two-hour Baker's Union wage.

For he would work at that trade till six A.M. Then, with his friend Hans, he ate breakfast at a nearby lunch room. Sometimes Hans went with him to Madison Avenue, and they had their breakfast there, which Stanislaus Joseph would prepare. Then Hans departed for his home and bed, and Stanislaus Joseph retired to rest.

With the blinds down, the musician-baker slept till noon. Five hours of slumber was his nightly—or we should say, daily—requirement. The afternoon was then his own.

These afternoons were the most difficult. No longer did he have a symphony to work upon. That prodigious, misguided effort reposed at the top of the clothes closet, with its bitter, sarcastic marking:

To Be Played After I Am Dead

Some days he did not open his Steinway at all. Would just sit in utter dejection, and go over the events of his life.

The days in Vienna, the trip to America, that first concert at Carnegie Hall; H. Rodman, Albert Rouchard, Florenz Ziegfeld.

When he reached the hour he had looked up from his piano stool and first looked at Olga Lasenka, he would pause. He would gaze long at his favorite photograph of her among the many on his walls.

He was desperately lonely for her. He felt sometimes that she was desperately lonely for him.

He would go to the piano and play *Als die alte Mutter.*

Those days were the tragic days.

He was not sorry for himself. He was not ungrateful to life. He had had more than his share of opportunity, he felt. It was simply a tragic loneliness.

And on those days a pall of inertia seemed to enfold him. A pall of frustration. He was glad when it was time to go for a humble meal at some nearby restaurant, and then to the Horse and Buggy.

The five cats seemed to understand his loneliness. They would climb onto his lap and atop his shoulders and snuggle there. His children. His only children, alas.

On other days he would play the pianoforte frantically. All the most difficult pieces that he knew. Then indeed, like Baudelaire, he felt he was doing something as well—perhaps a little better—than anyone else in all New York.

But to what end? Only the five cats were his audience.

He did have one definite task before each alternate Sunday. He would select and practice the classical numbers he intended to play for the recital in Wilkes-Barre.

Those trips to Wilkes-Barre were his only real comfort and pleasure. And he composed another booklet of *Exercises* for the music teachers there.

A thousand copies of the first book had been printed and sold. Not only in Wilkes-Barre, but in Scranton and Nanticoke, and other nearby towns. The Fund had been enriched another five hundred dollars from the profits of these sales. The music teachers told him there was a sudden remarkable willingness on the part of their pupils to practice. A quite amazing interest and willingness which meant that the *Exercises* were *good*.

He had changed the title on the booklet to

THE OLGA LASENKA SERIES
OF EXERCISES FOR THE YOUNG

At least, his Olga's name was known in one section of one State in the Union!

The Wilkes-Barre part of his life was completely unknown to the other performers, the owners, the patrons of the Horse and Buggy. As were indeed the hours at the York Avenue bakery. All this belonged to what he thought of as his "Life In Art."

Humble as it might be, it was his and Olga's alone. It had nothing to do with the drab earning of a livelihood.

One employee only knew something of the outside activities of

Tightpants Halka. He was the "show electrician" at the night club. Familiarly known as Bennie.

We met Bennie—and Mrs. Bennie—at Molly Dorcey's Christmas party, and mentioned that both he and his wife were short and wide and friendly. Tightpants had been drawn to Bennie because when he had offered to pay for his help about tuning the piano, the electrician had refused to take any money therefor.

"I like your playing, Mr. Tightpants," he had said. "I look forward to listening to it every night. I'm trying to make my lights and color effects fit each song you play. I think you've noticed it. I was going to do that with the other acts, but they just want a bright 'spot.' Complain if they get anything but amber! No real feeling for color. And it's a shame the way they abuse that poor piano! My oldest daughter is studying piano. Maybe you'll hear her play some day. Count on me to help you any time and on my own time, Mr. Tightpants. I know a real artist when I see one. I also used to work in big Broadway shows."

And several other occasions arose when Bennie's assistance was asked for.

On two of the Sundays of trips to Wilkes-Barre, Hans Beuter was out of the city visiting a cousin in Bridgeport. Tightpants asked Bennie to feed the cats; had him come to the Madison Avenue apartment and gave him the keys. He had discovered that Bennie and his family lived quite near, in a flat on Lexington Avenue.

Another time there was trouble with proper lighting at the York Avenue bakery, and Bennie had gone there with Stanislaus Joseph one night, to advise the kind of new lights to install. And later helped to install them.

Of more consequence perhaps—Stanislaus Joseph had one Sunday taken Bennie with him to Wilkes-Barre, to advise about some better lighting in the High School auditorium, when the more advanced pupils of the Fund gave a recital of their own. Bennie went one Sunday for a rehearsal, and the next Sunday (even borrowing some special equipment from a supply shop where he sometimes worked daytimes) for the actual performance.

Bennie's professional lighting did its part in the success of that performance. Again he had refused to take any money for the work.

So Bennie knew about Olga; about the bakery; about the Fund activities in distant Wilkes-Barre; about the fact that Tightpants

Halka had the right to be called Dr. Stanislaus Joseph Halka of the University of Vienna.

Tightpants swore him to secrecy about it all.

"Please don't say anything regarding all this around the Night Club," Stanislaus Joseph had asked. "I don't want the folk there to think that I imagine I am any better performer than any of them. I'm not. I just had a little more chance of study, that's all."

Bennie had his own ideas about that, but he respected Tightpants' wishes.

Stanislaus Joseph now had two good friends. Baker Hans Beuter. Electrician Bennie.

If he only were as expert in his profession, as they were in theirs, he sometimes thought in moments of depression.

✣ 3 ✣

It was about five p.m., of one of the "tragic days," that he found *The Song*.

He had been especially depressed. Especially lonely. Scenes from his life with Olga had passed through his mind. Sitting in the Madison Avenue room, it was as if he were viewing a motion picture made up of those scenes.

Their meeting at the Florenz Ziegfeld audition. His desperate memorizing of her name and address on the cover of the song she sang so badly. The lobby of the L'Esplanade-Plaza Hotel on Forty-sixth Street. The trip to that very Madison Avenue address in the taxi, when she had asked him his name.

Their first meal together in the small restaurant on the ground floor. Her life story up to then, as she had told it—her schooldays in Wilkes-Barre, the death of her father, the Five-and-Dime, the Four Rosebuds, the fruitless hunting for a theater job in New York.

Their marriage, the wedding luncheon at the King of the Sea, his teaching her *Songs My Mother Taught Me,* which was Dvořák's *Als die alte Mutter,* the singing of it at the final Ziegfeld audition, and her consequent contract for the chorus of the Rudolf Friml operetta.

Their complete happiness working together during that long engagement—happiness in their work, in the trips up to the Cloisters, the bus-top rides, the walks up Fifth Avenue.

Most of all, their contentment in the very rooms in which he sat. He working on the first symphony he had attempted to compose, and had never finished. She preparing a meal, darning his socks, ironing his shirts and collars, or just listening as he played her favorite Chopin.

The little bed in the adjoining room! He sometimes took his rest on the couch outside, because he could not bear the pain of its poignant memories, of her complete devotion and tenderness.

He realized that he should be grateful for a love that not every man can find. That few men find.

The statue of the Virgin at the Cloisters and its legend, and her apparent connection and identification with that statue—this he could not fully understand.

If, to round out some plan of Destiny, she had to die at twenty-two, why could he not have been taken also?

Those phantoms of some World Beyond—Hugh de St. Omer, then the great Kommodore—they were *friendly also to him.* The mine owner in Wilkes-Barre had shown him the letter from his First Mate of the *S. S. Susquehanna.* He had told this mine owner just who was the "Captain von Steinburg," of his own ocean-crossing with this Kommodore, of the Kommodore's connection with the La Celle statue that Olga Lasenka had so resembled.

They had together taken the letter to Father Joe, and the priest had said:

"Our blessed Lord Jesus saved his fishermen apostles in the storm on the Sea of Galilee. It is not beyond my humble belief that He could have sent this deputy to save the lives of your two sons; you who have helped perpetuate the memory of a Saint. For I have believed for some time that this girl, Dr. Halka's wife, was a Saint. This is her first miracle. Or rather, her second. For is not our Fund a miracle? There will be other miracles."

So, in his memories on that particular afternoon, Stanislaus Joseph arrived at the hour of her death at the Neurological Institute.

It was an hour he did not like to remember, to reconstruct in his mind. When it did come to mind, he tried to dismiss it as quickly as possible.

But that day it persisted, and he seemed again to hear her saying,

"Listen carefully, duszka, back down on Madison Avenue—you will find it—" And then the quite unexplainable words:

"Olga—whose eyes were violets—
Olga—whose tears were pearls—"

It was repeating, in a sort of meter, words he had said to her in describing her eyes—her tears. Only he had said *are,* not *were.*

The girl had been trying to tell him of something "back down at Madison Avenue."

What something?—And what did the two lines of almost-poetry mean?

He had long since gone over her few papers that were about the apartment. Letters, her theater contracts, the programs of some concerts they had attended, her High School diploma she had intended to have framed. These were tied with a ribbon she had sometimes used at night for her hair, and were on the top shelf of the clothes closet. The shelf that held his *Olga Lasenka Symphony.*

He had the urge to look at this ribbon-tied bundle again, and on reaching for it, noticed for the first time the cardboard, box-like letter file which had been pushed to the back of the shelf.

He took down this letter file.

He had seen it often before, when Olga was alive. He knew that in it she placed the receipted rent bills, telephone bills, grocery bills, bills from the cleaner's and the laundry. He remembered she had told him that in it, under his initials, were the lawyer's letters from Berlin.

It was a sort of business file. The unbusiness-like young man had never troubled to open it.

He now opened the metal, hinge-like clasp, folded back the top cover so that the compartments spread out fanlike, their contents easy to see and remove. The contents was mostly what he had thought—small sheets of paper that were deep down in the lettered compartments. Bills.

But under the letter "O" was a longish white envelope. It did not look like a bill. It looked like an unopened, unmailed letter. He took it out.

On that envelope he read, in her firm, round handwriting

*A song I hope my husband will care
to write the music for.*

His fingers trembled as he opened the envelope. It was unsealed. He extracted the single sheet of paper. Across its top it said—as we indeed know:

A Song Describing How I Hope My Duszka Thinks Of Me—and below this, the song.

OLGA

(Whose Eyes Were Violets)

There were the two first lines that she had spoken with her final breath:

"Olga—whose eyes were violets—
Olga—whose tears were pearls—"

The young man was on his feet. He read the entire song. His heart was pumping like a motorcar engine. His brain was flaming.

Dr. Stanislaus Joseph Halka strode to his Steinway and opened its key lid. He placed the sheet of Olga's handwriting on the music shelf before him. He ran his expert fingers over the white and black ivory protrusions.

They were *not* just the keys of a pianoforte. They were pieces of ivory each attached to a great harp—harps that extended up beyond that simple room; beyond the towering skyscrapers of the great city that surrounded that room. Harps that reached to Paradise!

He played as he had never played before. He played notes that fitted to the words on the paper before him. I think that his old shadowy friend of the Vienna school days, Franz Schubert, stood on one side of him and Franz Liszt on the other.

He rushed to his desk and tossed out papers till he came to some blank, ruled music sheets. He dipped his pen in the black ink and jotted black notes, separated by music bars, on those sheets.

When he had filled three sheets of music paper with the notes, he returned to his piano to see if he had written correctly what he had played. Written at least the "lead sheet." The melody.

Now he knew why he had not died when his Olga had died! What there had remained for him to do, before *he* died!

His telephone rang. It was Guard Dennis O'Rourke up at the Cloisters. Dennis was leaving for home after his day's work.

"Dr. Halka," he said, "I had to tell you. At five o'clock tonight my baby suddenly smiled. Each time I looked at her she smiled. Just as I left some minutes ago she was smiling again. I have never before known her to seem to be so happy.

"I thought I ought to tell you, sir. I hope it is a good omen for something you are doing."

"Thank you, Dennis," said the young musician. "Something has indeed happened! I will tell you when I next see you. I will show you. You are most kind to phone me."

He was late that night arriving at the Horse and Buggy, although he had not taken time to go for his dinner. At seven-thirty he had suddenly realized the hour, and rushing down the four flights of stairs, jumped into a taxi for the Night Club. But no harm was done, as he and Annette Blair did not "go on" until the third section of the first show.

The night club singer noticed his excitement. *Take Back Your Gold* had never been played so passionately in its entire career. *I Wonder Who's Kissing Her Now* assumed a new stature. At the end, there was extra applause, obviously for the humble piano player.

Annette graciously indicated that Stanislaus Joseph should play alone. He gave them the Schumann *Toccata—the* Toccata he had last played for H. Rodman, and they liked it.

"Whatever has happened to you, Tightpants?" asked the girl, as they went down the hall to their between-shows resting quarters. "I've worried about you all week. Tonight you seem like a different person!"

"In a week I'll have a new song for you to try," said Stanislaus Joseph. "You have been kind to me. I think the one for whom I wrote this song would be pleased to have you sing it first."

He took his usual taxi to the bakery at four A.M. There was a big order of special cakes to decorate. He had blue icing made, and covered their tops with sugar violets. Only violets.

And he made borders of drops of white icing. Pearl-like sugar tears.

At six he took Hans Beuter to Madison Avenue. He played him the song. He sang it in the voice that always gained laughter delivering *You Made Me What I Am Today* in the midnight show at the Horse and Buggy.

Hans Beuter did not laugh when he heard the *Olga Song*.

"Christ!" he said. "Christ!"

I do not think the Recording Angel put a black mark against Hans's name for this profanity. It was the only way simple Hans knew to adequately express how he was moved.

✣ 4 ✣

Stanislaus Joseph spent the next four days writing a proper accompaniment for his new melody.

It had been a late Monday afternoon that he had found the *Olga* lyric. His skill as a pianoforte player enabled him to give it a very beautiful background; here and there a counter melody which was, and yet was not, the true melodic line.

At the very beginning and the very end, under the phrase that said the name "Olga," he invented an especially haunting strain. In each instance it was only a few notes, but they gave the composition a strange, weird beauty.

On Thursday morning he visited the office of the Ziegfeld music publisher in Radio City.

"You suggested that I come to see you if I could think up a 'good, hot, sad song,' " he said to this publisher with a smile. "I don't know how hot this one is, but I hope you will like it."

"What is the title of your composition?" asked the publisher.

"It is quite simple—just the name of a girl. Olga," replied the young composer.

There was a surprising reaction from the musical show publisher. The mere name of a girl—any name—would not have ordinarily caused any particular glow of interest or enthusiasm. There was no novelty in a girl's name. George M. Cohan's *Mary* had been a real success for this firm. It had been in that actor-composer's *Forty-five Minutes from Broadway*. *Irene,* from the show of that name, had also caused a stir. *Charmaine,* sung back in World War I. Mr. Friml's *Rose Marie* of more recent date.

But it was not a recollection of girl's-name-songs that had stirred this cold, unemotional business man.

At the mention of the word "Olga," Stanislaus Joseph had seen the hard eyes of the man behind the desk—and behind the half-smoked cigar—soften. Those eyes shifted to a small, framed photograph on his desk. The only photograph there. It was apparently the picture of a mother and a young daughter.

The eyes of the publisher moved back to Stanislaus Joseph. Now there was suspicion in them.

"How did you find out that my daughter's name was Olga, Tightpants?" he asked.

"Why—I did not find out at all! I did not know you had a daughter!" said the surprised Stanislaus Joseph.

"Did you select that name just at random?" asked the publisher.

"The lyric is not my work," said the boy. "It was written by a girl whose name was also Olga. That girl was my wife, sir. She is now dead."

The publisher took up the small, framed photograph on his desk. He handed it to Stanislaus Joseph. It pictured a middle-aged woman and a girl of about twelve.

"My daughter is also dead," said the publisher. "She died the next year after this photograph was taken. Our only child.

"I would not want to publish a frivolous lyric using that name."

Stanislaus Joseph had in his cardboard portfolio—a new twenty-five cent one bought for that purpose—his piano copy of the song and the lyric sheet in Olga's handwriting. He handed the lyric sheet to the publisher.

"My late wife wrote this before she died. I did not find it until two days ago. I hope, sir, you do not find it frivolous."

The publisher read Olga Lasenka's little verses. He read them several times.

There was a flower bed on the lawn of the fine estate in Scarborough, where this music publisher had lived many years. Lived there since his first big publishing hit. He and his wife—both now over seventy—would sometimes stand by that flower bed in the Spring. It contained only violets, because they always thought——

The publisher shifted uneasily in his chair. He did not like to appear deeply moved. It wasn't proper to feel that way in Radio City. But somehow Stanislaus Joseph felt this music publisher did not find the lyric frivolous.

"Play what you have written, Tightpants," he said. He blew his nose a little too violently. "Your wife was a poet, Mr. Tightpants," he added.

"She was a saint," said Tightpants Halka. This publisher would probably have laughed if any other composer had spoken of his wife as a saint. He had had dealings with composers' wives. He did not laugh at Tightpants Halka.

"Play your music," he said.

The piano in this office was not a concert grand. Just a small upright. The young man took his place before it. This publisher's concert grand was at the home in Scarborough.

"Shall I sing the words as I play?" asked the young man. "I am no singer. My voice is not very good."

"I think it is better that I follow the lyric as you play," said the publisher meaningly.

"I also think that will be best," said Stanislaus Joseph.

He played his song. He played it very well. The best he knew how. The young man whose teacher had been a pupil of Anton Dvořák knew how to play a song. The young man who had been Albert Rouchard's accompanist.

There was no doubt but that this publisher was excited. He lit a fresh cigar. He pressed a button on his desk. Pressed it till a secretary came running. When she appeared, he said: "Get Mr. Watters in here at once. At once!" he repeated.

The secretary beat a hasty exit. Mr. Watters was the firm's professional manager. He dealt with the singers—the recording companies. Mr. Watters had picked numerous hits.

Mr. Watters came.

"This is Mr. Tightpants Halka, who was a member of the Florenz Ziegfeld staff," said the publisher. "He has written a new song."

To Stanislaus Joseph he said: "This time, sing it—or better, just talk the words as you play. Mr. Watters has no daughter by the name of Olga. Maybe my own judgment is biased. I think it probably is."

Stanislaus Joseph played, and spoke the words as he played. Mr. Watters also had the girl's lyric sheet in his hands. He asked the boy to play the song again, without any words.

He looked at his boss.

"Well?" said the publisher.

The professional manager raised his hands indicating surrender. "Why pretend otherwise?" he said. He paused before making the next fatal statement. He had rarely been wrong about a song.

"Dammit to hell! It's great stuff!" he exclaimed. "Loveliest thing I've heard since the last Rudolf Friml score."

He spoke directly to Stanislaus Joseph, "How the hell did *you* manage to write such a song! Just to be sure, play that melody with one finger. You play so well, Mr. Tightpants, maybe you have fooled us with your very clever arrangement, and your skill as a performer. I have been fooled in that way several times."

Stanislaus Joseph played the melody as requested. It was, in a way, more poignant and beautiful than when dressed up with the magic of a fine accompaniment.

The professional manager must have known about Hans Beuter, though how he could have known, I do not know. "Christ!" he said. "Christ!" And again I do not believe that the great, all-understanding Heart resented the use of His name.

"You think then it is worth publishing?" said the publisher. There was a smile now in the hard eyes.

The professional manager was on his feet. He had gone to the piano and taken the music sheets in his hands. He looked up from them.

"You know damn well it's what all the record companies—all the disk jockeys—are praying for right now! What—" and he named four great recording singers—"are down on their bare knees praying for! A new, real, black-and-white hit number. They'd give their blasted souls——"

By "black-and-white" he meant the customary format of printed cover for that type of song. A song neither lowbrow nor highbrow.

A well-known operetta composer had called them *middlebrow*.

It was the type of song most difficult to find. A song that would have a chance of becoming immediately popular—and yet *last*. Not washed up and washed out in a month or six months. Or six years.

Some of the songs of Rudolf Friml, of Victor Herbert, of Jerome Kern, would be sung as long as songs were sung.

The publisher opened the wide, shallow drawer just before him and just under his desk top. He took out a large, square, flat checkbook. He opened the book, dipped a pen in the inkwell on top of the desk, and commenced to write.

He was writing with almost the same haste and excitement as Stanislaus Joseph had used and felt, when he had seized the blank music sheets from out of his desk in Madison Avenue, the afternoon three days before; the afternoon he had first discovered the *Olga* lyric, and rushed from his pianoforte to that desk.

❖ 5 ❖

STANISLAUS JOSEPH WENT FROM RADIO CITY to the York Avenue house where Hans Beuter had his room. He woke up Hans to show him the check. It was for one thousand dollars.

He wished Hans to see it, before he mailed it to Father Joe in Wilkes-Barre, to put with the Fund.

Hans viewed the piece of paper critically. "Only a thousand dollars!" he said. "You should have asked for five. Ten."

But Hans did not understand the deal regarding a song.

"This is just a payment against first royalties," Stanislaus Joseph explained. "They are making out a contract which I will get tomorrow. I receive so-much on the sheet music sales; so-much on the sale of phonograph records, if they can make a deal with record companies; a royalty if it is played by orchestras. And even if the song should fail to sell—this first thousand dollars is mine. 'Non-returnable' they call it. The publishers take a chance that royalties will at least reach that amount."

"A hell of a chance they're taking!" said Hans, "and I still think they should have paid you more of an advance, as you call it.

"And I don't think you ought to send all that good money to Wilkes-Barre," Hans continued. "Suppose you get sick? Suppose you get piano-players cramp—or whatever it is piano-players get! You've got whatever money I have, you know that—but I been having rotten luck at the tracks lately. I don't understand it at all. Horses that *can't* lose——"

Stanislaus Joseph had to laugh at his baker friend's long face. "I'm not going to get sick," he said. *"Musicians* never get sick. They can't afford to!"

"No. You'll probably be hit by a taxi or a beer truck. Going about with your head in the clouds over your fool symphony and your fool cats—I don't know which is the biggest waste of time——"

Hans was immediately sorry he had so spoken of the symphony. That was still not a laughing matter to his friend, he realized by the expression on the musician's face. And Stanislaus Joseph for the first time told Hans of its fate. The interviews with the publishers; the stacking it on the top shelf of the clothes closet.

Despite the thrill of having at last composed a song that would see publication—a song with a lyric by his Olga—there was a sharp hurt whenever he thought of the greater work. Greater, at least, in the thought and time he had spent on it. The humble pride he had taken and felt in every created note of it.

The symphony was his real musical love. And it had died.

Stanislaus Joseph answered Hans's financial question. "I want this first check to go entirely to the Fund. I am sure Olga would wish her part of it that way. And I so wish mine. Then, if I receive more money from the song, I will send her half to Wilkes-Barre, and keep the other half.

"I don't know what I will be keeping it for—but I'll keep it."

And he told Hans one other thing.

"One day, when I was very down, Hans, I went to the neighborhood lawyer I know and made a will.

"For me to have a will is probably a joke—but I am alone in the world except for my friendship with you and the kindly electrician at the Night Club. I've made you two what they call the executors. For there were some little matters I wanted to be carried out, if I quit suddenly, as I then felt I might, so discouraged was I. And so lonely for Olga, Hans.

"That will is in a drawer of my desk. I want the pianoforte, the *Renoir* left me by the voice-teacher Albert Rouchard, and Olga's pictures to go to Wilkes-Barre to the Fund. They're going to have a small studio-office soon. Her pictures and the Steinway should surely be there.

"And the symphony on the closet top shelf I left to Father Joe. He also is my friend, but he is not here in New York. Maybe his organist will play a part of the symphony someday. It won't ever be played by an orchestra, unless the Fund organizes one in Wilkes-Barre, as Father Joe is thinking about doing. Then maybe it can get played at least once. I think my Olga will like it, even if no one else does. And maybe Kommodore Hugo Frederick von Steinburg.

"I made electrician Bennie a co-executor so as to save you, my first American friend, from also jumping in front of a subway train—as I sometimes thought of doing! Bennie likes animals. He gets the five cats. And five hundred dollars—if I then have five hundred dollars in the bank, or five hundred dollars more is earned—to feed them. And Olga's clothes. He has a fine, growing daughter who might like the clothes.

"You get five hundred dollars—if there's still any left or earned—to play the races with, and I'll beg the Kommodore, who knows horses, to try to help you pick a couple of winners.

"The rest—if there is any rest—to the Fund.

"Oh yes, I'm going to put in a codicil—that's what they call it—now that there is something more in prospect beyond what I save from my salary—a codicil to pay five hundred dollars to a guard up at the Cloisters. His name is Dennis O'Rourke. But he won't have that entirely clear. He's got to buy a rose once a year, and place it before a statue he well knows on the anniversary of my Olga's death.

"And you and Bennie will have the job of taking me down to Wilkes-Barre—'In The Baggage Coach Ahead,' as one of the songs they sing at the Horse and Buggy expresses it——"

Hans Beuter interrupted this gloomy recital.

"For God's sake, stop!" he said. "You'll have me next taking a day off to look up a reliable undertaker! And picking out a nice, solid oak, satin-lined, bronze-handled coffin!

"Listen. I've got a sweet long-shot coming up in about two weeks. A real sleeper! Can't miss. Will pay the limit. Twenty to one. I'm going to shoot a hundred bucks on it. That will mean a cool two thousand simoleons payoff.

"Then I'll go with you straight to that damn first publisher you interviewed, and I'll say to him: 'Here you are, you damn cheapskate, two thousand smackers; and I want those damn parts or whatever they are called, extracted or broiled or baked—whatever they do to damn symphony orchestra parts! And I want it played by the best damned orchestra in America!' "

Hans gave Stanislaus Joseph no opportunity to comment on this somewhat unorthodox approach to a music publisher.

He jumped to: "Right now, my friend Stanislaus, we're going out to have a drink. Double Scotch! I need one after hearing this obituary of yours! Then we go to lunch at the King of the Sea. Snap out of it, Stanislaus Joseph! You're a big song-writer success now. You'll live to be a hundred. You'll bury Bennie and me and all the cats. Here—read the *Racing Form* while I get dressed. Maybe you'll find a title for a new song. Them race horses have nifty names——"

But Dr. Stanislaus Joseph Halka had a premonition that his work was done. He had no desire to write another song unless the lyric was by Olga Lasenka. And Olga Lasenka would write no more song lyrics.

And why write more symphonies when they would never be played?

He had received a saddening letter from Vienna. His bakeshop-owner patron had died. He and his wife had died within a week of each other. Well—they were together in death, as well as in life.

He wanted to be with Olga, if God so willed it.

Would so will it.

That week he taught Annette Blair the *Olga Song*.

They would do it first in one of the shows that Saturday night. It would be a big night at the Horse and Buggy. Another "football night." Notre Dame and Army at the Polo Grounds. All tables at every night club in town were already reserved.

✣ 6 ✣

It was also a busy week at the York Avenue bakery. Stanislaus Joseph went there every night at three-thirty A.M. Directly after his last show at the Night Club. Many special cakes to decorate with the *dressiersack.*

There was one special cake baked on that Friday night—it was five A.M. Saturday morning when Stanislaus Joseph actually did his task about it. There was to be an anniversary party for the world famous conductor of the New York Philharmonic Symphony, directly after this gentleman's hundredth concert in Carnegie Hall that Sunday afternoon. Hans Beuter's bakery had been commissioned to bake a huge cake for this party.

It measured four feet across its oval top. This top being a great musical note. There was a dedication to be written on the cake—the great conductor's name—and the well wishes of his Board of Directors.

Stanislaus Joseph wrote the requested words in gold icing. Beneath it he was to put some bars of music.

The Board of Directors had ordered their cake from this special bakery because one of its members had once had a birthday cake from this shop, with the first notes of "Happy Birthday To You" written across its top. It was known that this bakery had a *dressiersack* writer who knew music, and could do this.

The request for this special cake was to write thereon the first bars of "something classical." They did not specify what composition should be used, except to suggest that it might fittingly be something "from the works of Beethoven, Mendelssohn, even Strauss. All favorites of this conductor."

Stanislaus Joseph, having made the dark, ruled music lines in dark chocolate icing, was about to set down the opening bars of the overture of *Ruy Blas* by Mendelssohn, which he knew to be a favorite of this maestro.

And then a strange, perverse idea occurred to him.

It seemed to come to him from without. To be at the dictation of someone wiser than himself. Or more daring.

His own *Olga Lasenka Symphony* commenced with a striking musical phrase which expressed the spirit of the New World, as viewed through the eyes of the two Polish immigrants arriving in America. Olga Lasenka's father and mother.

How they felt as they first saw the Statue of Liberty and the towers of lower Manhattan.

He wrote that phrase—four measures of it—on this cake.

Having done so, he was suddenly fearful of what he had done. Suppose someone realized that those notes were not from the works of a great classical composer? Would the friendly bakery be in trouble?

But once written with the flowing icing, which quickly hardened, it was too late to change them. No one would probably notice what they were anyway. Just music notes in sugar icing. The cake would be cut—eaten.

He hoped his notes would not poison the exalted Symphony Society guests.

PART SIXTEEN

THE GREATER DESTINY

✣1✣

ANNETTE BLAIR WAS INDEED the first vocalist to sing the *Olga Song,* when it was introduced that Saturday night, late in November, at the Horse and Buggy Night Club, but she did not sing the entire song. It was finished by piano player Tightpants Halka and one other.

Quickly-forgetting New Yorkers would not soon forget the holocaust that swept through that festive firetrap at about eleven P.M. on that evening.

There were various stories as to how that fire had started. These are the facts.

There were at the time some two hundred patrons in the first floor Harmony Lounge, where was the big circular bar. They stood ten deep around this bar, and five extra bartenders were desperately shaking up alcoholic concoctions to meet the demands of the celebrants. For, as before stated, it was a football night. That, and a week-end holiday.

Hilarity and free spending reigned supreme.

Up the narrow stairs, in the "dine and dance floor" room, eight hundred and fifty patrons were packed at tables from wall to wall. Some were sitting around the base of the performers' small platform, drinks in hand, hopeful of a seat if someone vacated a table. Waiters needed the skill of the line-plunging and broken-field football runners of the afternoon game, to deliver without fumbles food and liquid refreshment.

Viewing this cash-on-the-barrel-head eating and drinking throng, Mr. Levine made a mental note that they had better maybe look into putting out the necessary funds to correct the long overdue code-violating electric wiring, the drapery and decoration fireproofing, at several places in the establishment.

He would speak to Mr. Kennedy about it the following Monday.

Rubber Face Newman and John Alten had finished their act for the second show, and Tightpants and Annette Blair had taken their places.

Annette had finished *Kiss Me Again,* and after her next number *On the Banks of the Wabash,* she and Tightpants were to give the new *Olga Song* its initial try.

In the audience to hear the new number was the professional manager of the Radio City publishing house, several of his newspaper friends including a noted columnist, and the first great recording artist he had already arranged with, to put the song on more or less enduring wax.

We return to the downstairs bar.

This room was ordinarily kept in semi-darkness. It gave a proper atmosphere, on less crowded evenings, for couples who liked to sit on high stools and mingle liquor with endearments.

It also helped in the telling of life-stories to bartenders.

Even this in-the-gloaming lighting was not dark enough that evening to suit an ever-loving pair near the wall, and the gentleman involved reached up and unscrewed a wall light-bulb, so that he and his girl friend could be in near-total darkness.

This act of admirable modesty drew the wrath of the standees beyond them, who were not in a mood for romance, and moreover wanted to see their drinks. Mr. Levine, always mindful of patrons' comfort—and applying the sound, Christian-like ethical principle of "the greatest good to the greatest number"—instructed a bus boy to replace the bulb.

The boy—so he afterwards stated—climbed on a chair to replace the bulb.

He could not locate the light socket, and lit a match to assist his endeavor.

The darkness-loving patron at this point (so the bus boy afterwards told the police), kicked out the chair from under him, and he and the lighted match pitched headlong into an artificial palm tree, placed there to give a romantic, Isle-of-Capri atmosphere to the corner.

So started the Horse and Buggy Night Club fire.

It spread with terrifying swiftness along the walls which were hung with flimsy draperies on which were painted scenes of South Sea Island fancy. Non-fireproofed fancy. More lights went out, as non-insulated wiring collapsed and acted as fuses for dry plaster and lath work. A dense smoke arose from the imitation leather coverings of the wall settees. There were shrill cries of "Fire!" and "Let us out!"

A panic was in the making.

To co-owner Levine's credit, he kept his head. He mounted a bar stool. He ordered two husky waiter-bouncers to smash in the large front window hidden from patrons by a tall screen, thus hiding them from the street. He shouted at the top of a bull-like voice—"Out through the front! Out through the window!"

An equally level headed doorman, sensing the panic within, and seeing the clouds of smoke and flame pouring out, broke the central binding catch on the revolving entrance-doors, flattened them, so that there was, at this means of exit, a clear passage to the sidewalk.

Except for minor injuries by trampling or burns or broken glass, all but a few of the Harmony Bar patrons on that street-floor managed to escape into the night.

Two dozen or so had pushed in the other direction through a swinging door leading into the kitchen, and were trapped there. These perished from smoke and flame and aimless, insane battling in pitch darkness to find a small rear exit door.

The kitchen help had fled at the first smell of smoke and flame.

The real danger of a nation-stunning disaster with headlines "DEAD MAY PASS SIX HUNDRED" and "CHARRED BODIES PILED BEFORE LOCKED DOORS AND IN NARROW EXIT PASSAGES"—the terrible carnage resulting from blind panic—*that* danger was in the upstairs room, overcrowded with its eight hundred and fifty diners and merrymakers, fully half of whom were women.

For flames and smoke did not remain in the Harmony Bar.

Great tongues of flame and acrid fumes shot up the stairwell to break in rudely on the upstairs clink of glasses and the laughter; to spread along draped walls and false, cloth-hung ceilings; to turn a place of merriment into a furnace-like inferno. All this accompanied by the sudden failure of the electric lights, so that the room would be plunged into darkness, except for the balloons of fire that would soon commence to drop on tables; the thrusts of fire that would reach out from tinder-dry wall curtains.

Death-dealing panic would here result at the first alarm—the first hysterical cry of "Fire!"

But even when the regular light-bulbs *were* suddenly extinguished—along with the first smell of smoke and the first tongue of flame—there fortunately remained in that dine-and-dance room a great streamer of bright light.

It was directed at and illuminated the small performers' platform where Tightpants Halka sat at his upright piano and Annette Blair had just finished *On the Banks of the Wabash.*

Those light-streams were the spotlights of show-electrician Bennie. Bennie and his lights were stationed over against the front wall, on a smaller platform.

Because of the extra power that Bennie's "floods" required, they were not a part of the regular Club lighting system. They were fed by a heavy cable, which went through a window aperture out into the adjoining alleyway, and down the side of the building to a special feed plug leading to a heavy-voltage cable under the street below.

Electrician Bennie had, as a very young mechanic, been in the Iroquois Theater fire in Chicago, with the touring company then playing there. He had kept his head then, and he kept his head now, and kept on his flood lights.

He also shouted to a waiter to break open a steel door leading out to a fire escape and down into the alley. This door was completely hidden by draperies, and of course locked and bolted.

Psychologists have often attempted to analyze the reasons for panic; that mental collapse that causes grown men and women to act like frightened children, or what is more terrible, like wild beasts or stampeding cattle.

That kindly, generous, law-abiding citizens should suddenly lose all mental balance, and claw and fight and trample; that sudden dark forces hidden in our natures should suddenly kill all idea of discipline; submerge good sense; destroy all regard for your neighbor; these awful manifestations at times of sudden catastrophe have baffled the most learned.

But it has been discovered that certain forces can help to restore sanity.

Notable among these forces is music.

It is said that this music should be simple, but strongly rhythmic; of a tempo slower than the excited movements of the agitated crowd; that it can then "dissolve the disastrous concentration of will and emotion" on a mere breaking out from a caged area of danger; that it can bring about a realization that there is much more danger in the panic element than in the forces that momentarily seem to "prohibit an escape."

In most disasters of this kind, it has invariably been found that panic claimed many more lives than flames.

✣ 2 ✣

THIS REPORTER does not know of the truth or falsity of this Panic Thesis, but he does know what happened at the Horse and Buggy Night Club, Inc., that fateful night.

He was there. The guest of the music publisher's professional manager.

Stanislaus Joseph was about to announce the debut of the *Olga Song*. He was conscious of the smell of smoke fumes—of the tongue of flame that sprang from the head of the stairs leading to the bar below, and the dine-and-dance room's only regular exit.

He was certainly conscious of the sudden extinguishing of all lights and the shrill cry of "Fire!" in the voice of a woman.

He was conscious of the commotion in the room below, sounds of which came through the ceiling, which in turn was the floor of the dine-and-dance room.

But he was also conscious that electrician Bennie was keeping his lights in a steady, white stream on the entertainers' platform. Rubber Face Newman had left his small megaphone on the piano's top. The megaphone through which he would "put over" his sure-fire, subtle "laugh gags."

Stanislaus Joseph seized that megaphone. He spoke:

"Ladies and gentlemen, Miss Blair and I want you to hear a new song. Its very first public rendition. Please pause and hear just a little of it. There is no danger. Some small trouble in the bar below. There is a fire-escape exit on your right—at the front of the right wall. Please move toward it, as Miss Blair and I sing our new number. Thank you."

Tightpants knew about that fire-escape door. Bennie had shown it to him the first time they had tuned the piano. Bennie now turned one of his two "spots" toward it.

And those calm, every-day words, coming clearly through Rubber Face's megaphone, had their effect. A shrieking admonition to be calm would only have hastened panic.

Stanislaus Joseph had done exactly the right thing.

Why? How? Because the trained performer who had not lost his head when his music was scattered about the Carnegie Hall platform floor; the trained performer who could keep his head when it was announced at the Ziegfeld party that Olga's *Broadway Bungalow* was about to be performed—an emotional shock of no small dimensions to him then; this trained performer did not succumb to a constriction of all common sense—to an insane lust for self-preservation.

He could not have operated a nut and bolt factory; he could not have invented an atom bomb or a new miracle washing powder; he did not even have the ability to arrogantly push himself forward as a composer or a pianoforte artist; but he could keep his head at the Horse and Buggy Night Club, Inc., that fateful night.

Beyond the shadow of doubt he saved the lives of the eight hundred and fifty occupants of the dine-and-dance floor. He and Annette Blair, and a humble theatrical electrician. And one other whom we shall meet.

Despised show people all. Crazy children of the thing called "show business."

For by the time Stanislaus Joseph had made his brief speech, red flames had completely engulfed the narrow exit stairway toward which there had been an impulsive movement at that woman's cry of "Fire!" That was how they had entered. That was the way to leave. Not one of them would have known of the fire-escape door behind the curtains on a side wall.

Two waiters, having ripped down the concealing draperies, now forced it open.

Meantime Tightpants Halka sat at the piano. He had handed Annette Blair the small megaphone.

"For God's sake, sing!" he said to her. He struck the opening chord.

Miss Blair sang. A new flood of light struck them. Bennie had managed to get still another "spot" going, to take the place of the one he had trained over toward the small door leading out onto a fire escape.

Tightpants also sang with Miss Blair, softly, under her really fine soprano. And he played with all the genius he possessed. Those poignant, plaintive, first notes that had thrilled Hans Beuter; that melodic line that had caused the music publisher's professional manager to exclaim "Christ!" had their effect.

The simple sincerity of the rhythmic words also helped.

That seething, jammed-in gathering, on the verge of panic and mob-madness, *did pause*. Their "discriminatory reason" was restored.

They of course realized it would be well to leave a burning building—they moved toward the fire-escape exit—but they moved as rational beings, in reasonably orderly fashion. They did not scream and curse and trample and claw.

If these simple performers on that platform could remain calm, so could they.

And they were hearing unusual music. An inspired song. A song they had never before heard. Even when the flames jumped to the four side walls, they would sometimes seem to pause. An especially beautiful phrase was being played and sung.

So long as Love remembers—

✤ 3 ✤

IT WAS AT THE END of this song-line that Annette Blair collapsed.

Smoke fumes from the now flaming ceiling had choked her. Panic had also seized her. She had suddenly thought of her son in Harvard. What would happen to him and his career, if *she* did not escape? So perhaps she should not be censured.

"For God's sake, Tightpants," she gasped, "let's get out!" And she slumped down onto the platform.

Tightpants did not get out. He did not miss a single note in his playing. Because the moment Annette Blair had stopped singing, a new voice took up the *Olga Song—*

"—I am always near—
Olga—whose eyes were violets—
Olga—whose tears were pearls—"

Two male patrons picked up Miss Blair and dragged her along with them to the exit door.

"Violets and brook-tears cry
That someday—somewhere—you and I
Will meet—and mingle violets with pearls!
Olga!—Olga!—Olga!"

Stanislaus Joseph Halka did not need to look around to see who was now singing his song. *Her* song.

This new voice was glowing and thrilling. The singer was standing where Annette Blair had stood. She did not use the megaphone which by now had been trampled under the moving feet of the throng still slowly leaving.

Electrician Bennie had seen Annette Blair collapse. He had thought: *This is the finish. Now the panic.* For the room was only half emptied, and all the walls and ceilings were in flames. But he remained at his post and kept on his lights, when the new singer suddenly appeared.

She was very beautiful. Bennie said he had never seen any woman so beautiful. Her hair was parted tightly in the middle, and a thick braid drawn across its top and downward to conceal the left ear.

His lights caught this braid and made it appear like a halo.

The young man at the piano and the new girl singer went into a repeat refrain. Many patrons were still to be cleared from that blazing room. Bennie said afterwards he had never heard such playing and such singing. He said it was *as if a great orchestra had suddenly joined in!*

This effect was also noted by others who were among the last to push out of the small side-wall door, and onto the alley fire-escape. They all agreed it prevented any final rush and pile-up, though flames and smoke were almost unbearable.

By now the street outside was filled with fire apparatus, criss-crossed hose, ladders, helmeted and rain-coated firemen, police. The flames had long since reached to the top floor above the dine-and-dance room—completely gutted it, and eaten through the roof. The reflection of these flames against the sky had attracted a huge after-theater crowd.

Back in the shambles of what had been the dine-and-dance room, the *Olga Song* was finished. The final note of the second singing of the refrain. All patrons were safely out. A flood of water was pouring into the room from hoses hoisted by ladders to the small front windows.

And it was then that the side wall and the roof collapsed. They blotted out the small upright piano and its player and the girl who had taken Annette Blair's place there.

Bennie's light was blotted out also. His electric current had been broken off. Two firemen, climbing through a window, seized the almost smoke-suffocated and clothes-burned electrician, and drenching the flame, carried him down a ladder to the street below.

Rescue squads had been bringing out the dead and injured from what had been the kitchen—those hapless Harmony Bar patrons on the lower floor, who had tried to escape in that direction.

It was a tragic picture of what might have happened to all of the eight hundred and fifty revellers in the dine-and-dance room!

Newspaper reporters had arrived on the scene; passed the police lines with their identification cards; and were gathering the facts. The survivors of the dine-and-dance floor—those still there, and marveling at their escape as they watched the entire brownstone in flames and its ultimate collapse, were unanimous in praise of a piano player—one of the entertainers—who had first calmed the diners, and then proceeded with two successive singers to go on with the performance of a new song, which had been so striking and so beautiful it had prevented a panic. Probably saved all their lives.

Who was he? Where was he?

He had apparently remained till the very end—till the room was completely cleared. Had he perished in the final collapse of the fire-gutted building?

An electrician who had remained and kept his flood lights on, had also been a heroic figure.

When this man had recovered sufficiently from smoke suffocation in a nearby drug store, so that he was coherent, he had begged to go back; and when he discovered that he could not walk because of leg burns, had begged others to go back and rescue a piano player named Tightpants Halka and some girl, the girl who had finished out the song with this Tightpants when the regular singer had collapsed.

And when this electrician learned that the entire building had now collapsed, he was frantic. "Maybe I could have saved him!" he cried. "Why did I have to pass out with my damn lights!"

Two interns took Bennie to a hospital.

It was feared this piano player and his substitute singer had indeed perished with the final roof-debacle into the fire-gutted dine-and-dance room.

✣ 4 ✣

AT THE BAKERY ON YORK AVENUE, Hans Beuter had turned on the shop radio for the midnight news, to listen while he and the other workers paused to have their midnight snack.

Almost the first words that came over were:

"There is a five-alarm fire at the well-known Horse and Buggy Night Club on West Fifty-first Street. The building is in complete flames, and it is feared that many lives have been lost, although it is reported that many of the patrons have escaped to the street, due to the calmness of one of the entertainers—a piano player, who is still among the missing——"

Hans Beuter remained at the bakery no longer. He did not stop to change to his street clothes. He seized his top coat and hat, and was on the street and into a passing taxi within the next two minutes.

He had a dreadful premonition. When Stanislaus Joseph had half jokingly spoken of his will a week before, had the young musician *felt that death was imminent?*

So in spite of a benumbing feeling of heart-clutching sadness lest tragedy had descended on his friend, Hans unwillingly realized that at least he could now cope with such a catastrophe.

He knew of this will in the desk at Madison Avenue. He knew Stanislaus Joseph's wishes about his pictures, his piano, the ill-fated symphony.

Hans even had, on his keyring, a key to the top-floor front apartment, given him in case he had to feed the cats during the musician's absence.

But please God, all such unwelcome thoughts were foreign to any need! Stanislaus Joseph was not the only piano player at this Night Club. Still——

Hans Beuter urged the taxi driver to proceed more rapidly. "Jump lights—I'll pay any fines!" he cried.

They could not get beyond Sixth Avenue when they reached the lower Fifties. All traffic was being detoured. The Night Club was west on Seventh Avenue.

Hans paid his taxi and pushed down Fifty-first Street through dense crowds to Seventh Avenue. There, police lines had been set up. Perhaps he had best telephone the Madison Avenue apartment and the bakery, in case Stanislaus Joseph was whole and well, and had proceeded to either place.

Hans went into a tobacco store and did so.

No answer at Madison Avenue.

The men at the bakery had continued to listen to their radio, for they were all fond of this musician who was not too proud to come and decorate their special cakes; and the additional news they reported to Hans was not encouraging.

It was not such a disaster as the Chicago Iroquois Theater fire, but there had been twenty-five or thirty bodies brought out, and among the still missing was the piano player "whom all agreed had prevented panic and almost certain, horrifying disaster in the most crowded part of the Club."

Hans managed to persuade a police officer to let him through the lines, explaining that his closest friend was an entertainer in this establishment. His work clothes, his desperate honesty, got him by.

But there was considerable confusion within the police lines. Many who had escaped had not left the vicinity, held by the fascinating horror of what might-have-been. Others were trying to find friends from whom they had become separated—and in the case of the downstairs circular bar crowd, not always finding them.

Others, like Hans, who had relatives or friends they knew had gone to the popular Horse and Buggy that evening, had managed to pass the lines and were milling about in frantic inquiry.

And there was the usual horde of the simply curious.

There were also doctors and nurses, summoned from the nearest Roosevelt and Polyclinic and St. Claire Hospitals, and several priests from the nearby St. Malachy's parish house.

The Red Cross had set up a roped-off space for the injured.

By the time Hans Beuter could force his way to the front of the actual building, most of the dead and injured had been removed from the kitchen shambles.

Ambulances took the still living to the hospitals. The dead—some burned beyond identification—were carried on stretchers to a neighboring garage, where a temporary morgue was established by police.

The bodies lay in rows on the cement floor.

The flames were by now under control, and the building—what was left of it—was lighted by the powerful flood lights mounted on the fire apparatus.

Three firemen were coming down the still standing skeleton iron fire-escape into the adjoining alley way. They had at last managed to penetrate that second floor, which had not caved in, since in the conversion of the building into a night club, it had been reconstructed with steel girders to support the weight of a capacity crowd of diners and dancers.

These firemen were carrying a body—apparently a lifeless body.

They had pried up an overturned piano which sprawled face downward and almost covered a small platform. Across this piano was also the still smouldering wreckage of the ceiling above, and even roof beams.

A human hand projected from this wreckage. The piano had protected the body attached thereto from flames and wreckage—the projection of the keyboard, and the high upright top at right angles to it, had formed a kind of angular coffin. So these firemen explained afterwards to the newsmen.

But the man—it was a man—was lifeless. Dead of smoke fume suffocation, even if he had survived a great gash across the top of the skull, where an iron girder from the ceiling above had apparently fallen before the piano had been overturned, and thus prevented a complete cremation of the body.

The firemen reached the foot of the fire-escape. The newsmen and the curious pressed forward.

The dead man wore the costume of a Horse and Buggy Night Club, Inc., male entertainer. A suit of loud plaid, an upstanding collar, an old fashioned Ascot cravat with a huge imitation pearl stuck in its center.

The face was not terrorstricken. It was utterly calm, and one might say, joyful. As if the last sight of the now sightless eyes had rested on someone—something—of great endearment.

"It's the piano thumper Tightpants," a waiter said. "The little guy who prevented a panic on the dance floor."

"His name is S. J. Halka," confirmed co-owner Levine, who had been trying to identify, with small success, the charred bodies that had been carried from the kitchen quarters wreckage.

"I don't know anything about him except that he was our most reliable performer. He once told me he had a close friend named Franz Liszt, but that guy was back in Europe somewhere.

"This lad was a foreigner himself, but he had become an American citizen. I will be responsible for his body, if it is not claimed."

But the body of Stanislaus Joseph Halka, Doctor of Music of the University of Vienna, was quickly claimed. Hans Beuter had moved into the scene.

"Stanislaus! Stanislaus Joseph!" he had cried.

He gazed down at his friend as he now lay on a stretcher which two hospital interns had brought. He looked long at the homely, kindly face. He touched the cheek tenderly with his large, bread-kneading hand.

Slow tears were coming from the eyes of the man from the York Avenue bakery.

"You knew this night club entertainer?" asked three newsmen in chorus.

"I knew him—he was my closest friend," said Hans Beuter.

The professional manager of the Radio City music publisher was there also. He had gone to phone his wife that he was alive, and had returned to learn if this ex-Ziegfeld staff composer had escaped.

"I also knew him," he said. "He'd just written the loveliest song we have had in years. That song did its part tonight to save many lives."

The newsmen were super-busy with their note books. Here was a front page story with a vengeance! A cheap night club entertainer. A new song writer. And Hans Beuter was explaining that the dead man was a Doctor of Music—University of Vienna—had once appeared in Carnegie Hall!

Two photographers were snapping pictures of the body as it lay on the stretcher. An Associated Press reporter had already rushed away to find a telephone.

"There was a strange girl who sang the song with him till the last," said the music publisher man. "Where is she? Was her body there also? I was among the last diners out of that room—and she was still singing when I looked back."

No one seemed to know who this girl was. "A beautiful girl and a beautiful voice," another bystander said.

"This man's body was the only one in the floor wreckage," insisted the firemen. "We fine-combed the room with flashlights and crowbars."

Electrician Bennie was not then there to tell his tale. His burns were so painful (as we know) that he had been taken to the St. Claire Hospital.

Bennie's strange story was only pried out of him by an enterprising newsman something like a week later.

✣ 5 ✣

HANS BEUTER and the music publisher's manager met the newsmen at the Madison Avenue apartment the next morning. There were representatives from the radio stations also, and photographers.

The catastrophe had been too late at night to catch the Sunday papers, but it would be the headline lead on the Monday editions, early editions of which came out Sunday night.

Besides the flaring news stories—double columns, or three or four columns each, with three-column-wide photographs of the wreckage of the Horse and Buggy (one enterprising photographer got a picture of the overturned upright piano), there were dignified obituaries on that special page of all papers.

Dr. STANISLAUS JOSEPH HALKA 32
First Came To America As A Concert Pianist
COMPOSER OF SYMPHONIES AND A NEW SONG
His Heroism Saved Many Lives

The newsmen obtained the facts of his life from Hans Beuter. Stage Manager Dixon came to the Madison Avenue apartment and gave more facts—told how this piano player had played *Songs My Mother Taught Me* at the Ziegfeld office when the great producer had died.

They telephoned Father Joe in Wilkes-Barre and obtained more facts. And more facts were obtained from the Wilkes-Barre newspapers—the Olga Lasenka-Father Joe Music Fund founded by "this young composer"—the Sunday recitals Dr. Halka had been giving there—the booklets of *Exercises For The Young*.

Distant Vienna was contacted by trans-Atlantic telephone.

H. Rodman supplied further information—the Carnegie Hall concert—the work with Albert Rouchard—a belated public praise of this young man's skill as a pianoforte artist.

The Winter Garden comedians in Chicago were reached.

Molly Dorcey told of the watch he carried—the gift of the boy's grandfather who had been the Emperor Franz Josef's coachman.

The newspaper boys—the special writers and columnists—had not had such a harvest of "human interest" material in weeks. The radio commentators waded in knee-deep. But it was all sincere.

Hans Beuter, having established his authority, had the body taken from the city morgue to a well-known undertaking parlor on West Seventy-second Street favored by theater folk. There would be a High Mass at eleven Monday morning in the little church on Second Avenue. Then the body's transportation to Wilkes-Barre "in the baggage coach ahead" as Stanislaus Joseph had half jokingly described it.

Father Joe was making arrangements there.

The Messrs. Levine and Kennedy had told Hans Beuter to send them any bills for these sad expenses.

The little Second Avenue church was crowded for the Requiem Mass. The Ziegfeld chorus people who had known Tightpants and Olga Lasenka. The pupils for whom he had played at Albert Rouchard's. The orchestra men with whom he had played in theaters.

A special delegation from the Musical Union—which Union had also told Hans Beuter that if any money were needed it would be immediately provided.

The workers from the York Avenue bakery were there, and its owner. The small shopkeepers of the Madison Avenue neighborhood where he had lived and who knew him.

A colored hotel clerk from the Hotel L'Esplanade-Plaza. Another colored man—a steamship-dock porter. A guard from the museum called the Cloisters.

The proprietor of a restaurant on Third Avenue called the King of the Sea and many of its employees.

A music publisher who lived in Scarborough. The entire staff and the other entertainers of the late Horse and Buggy Night Club,

Inc., which was already announced to open in a new and "absolutely fireproof location."

H. Rodman, who had also told Hans Beuter that if any money were needed: "just telephone."

And again—the scores of the curious.

I think it would have pleased Dr. Stanislaus Joseph Halka to know that, sitting in a back pew, was a page-turner who taught music in Queens, and loved his dog.

There were cables to the Madison Avenue address date-lined Vienna; from Professor Anton Lavar; from his first teacher Herr Professor Gustav Emil Meyerhoff; from Frau Grete Ebenstein, concierge of a tenement in the *Favoriten* District; from an old actor now in his nineties named Otto Woltner; from the workers of a real Vienna bakeshop.

And telegrams from a Philadelphia hotel man who grew roses; from the entire Winter Garden Company playing in Chicago; from an ex-valet named Franz Rodar who owned a small farm in Kansas, and no longer had to lay out clothes and find the right collar button for a certain violinist.

The New York funeral of an obscure night club piano player who thought he had only one or two friends in the world!

6

ONE FURTHER EPISODE SHOULD BE RECORDED in the saga of Tightpants Halka. It was recorded in detail in all the Tuesday news-sheets.

That previous Sunday afternoon, the anniversary party of the famous Philharmonic Symphony conductor had been held as planned. It was held directly after his hundredth concert in Carnegie Hall. On that spacious, cleared stage.

After the speeches and the champagne toasts, four waiters brought on the huge anniversary cake, carrying it high in the air. It was placed on a large center table.

The great conductor expressed his admiration and gratitude, and thought the bars of music across its gleaming top a most clever and thoughtful compliment.

He stood before the cake—about to cut it with a great silver knife—when he gave a more careful glance at the sugar icing notes painted across its top surface. He had taken for granted they were from some well-known piece of music. Or just meaningless notes.

They were neither. He hummed the four written measures. He rushed to the concert grand piano at the back of the stage and played them.

His excitement was quite obvious. He made no attempt to conceal it. Other musicians in that gathering were also startled and intrigued.

"Who wrote those notes? Where did this cake come from?" the conductor demanded. He was apparently laboring under great emotion.

"Why—we ordered it from a bakery up on York Avenue," said the banker committee-member who had attended to the matter. "A Viennese bakery that makes a specialty of such cakes. Some one of their workmen is a sort of musician. He writes bars of well-known operas on such cakes. I knew about it. I thought it would please and amuse you.

"I hope what is there, signor, has not given you any offense. If so, it is entirely unintentional! Not being a musician, I did not attempt to decipher it. We told them to have this workman write something classical—"

Here it perhaps should be explained that in the history of great music there have been certain clusters of notes, certain musical progressions that have been so striking, or so lovely, so altogether original as well as beautiful, that they live forever in the minds of those who hear them.

These note clusters—these musical phrases—have brought immediate success to the compositions of which they are a part—immediate and lasting fame to their originators.

For example: the first four notes of the *Introduction* to the *I Pagliacci Prologue;* the love music of *Tristan and Isolde;* the tragic theme of *Carmen;* the love theme of *Mimi* and *Rudolfo* in *La Boheme;* the beginning of the *2nd Prelude* of Rachmaninov; the first phrase of Chopin's *Polonaise;* and of course the first eleven notes of that composer's *Funeral March* and the first few notes of Mendelssohn's *Wedding March.*

As we know, Stanislaus Joseph Halka had written on this party cake the first few bars of his inspiration for the viewing of the Statue of Liberty and lower New York's magical towers as seen through the eyes of the Polish immigrant father and mother of Olga Lasenka.

These notes were also the very beginning of his *Olga Lasenka Symphony*—the symphony nobody wanted—and he had written bitterly on its containing portfolio:

To Be Played After I Am Dead.

The great conductor said: "Give me the name of that bakery quickly. I must find out the man—or woman—whoever it was—that composed that cluster of notes. They are pure genius! They have absolute originality! What are they a part of? Who composed them?"

The information could not be had till the next morning.

The name of the bakery was at the committee man's office, and his office building was closed on Sundays. He would phone the information to the conductor early the next morning.

Privately he thought the conductor crazy. Such a fuss over a few musical notes! All musical notes looked and sounded the same! Thank God he himself was in a sane business. Banking.

The conductor evinced a further sign of an unbalanced mind by refusing to cut the cake where the notes were written. He served only the lower part of it—a part incidentally signed in icing with this banker gentleman's name as Chairman of the Board.

Well—these musicians! No sense of values. Still, it gave one social prestige to be Chairman of the Board of the Philharmonic.

The conductor could scarcely wait until this Chairman telephoned him the following morning. Gave him the bakery's name. He tore through the telephone book, found the number, rang up the bakery.

"If you will read any paper this morning you will find that man's name on the front page," said the bakery owner. "Wait a moment. His best friend has just come in."

The bakery owner handed the telephone to Hans Beuter.

Hans knew what had been written on that cake. Stanislaus Joseph had been worried, and told his friend, and hoped it would make no trouble for the bakeshop.

Hans had said: "To hell with it. Don't give it another thought."

Two days later, on his return from the final burial in Wilkes-Barre, with Father Joe's permission Hans Beuter took the *Olga Lasenka Symphony* to this conductor. The conductor called Hans the following day.

"The world has lost a genius," he said. "If I can arrange with Dr.

Halka's estate, I should like to play this great symphony at my next concert. It will then go into our permanent repertory."

Hans Beuter told the conductor about the Wilkes-Barre Olga Lasenka-Father Joe Music Fund.

"Tell them I will provide all necessary arrangement material and pay them one thousand dollars for this first use," said this conductor. "And I will try to have other orchestras play it. They will be as excited as I am, to find such a composition. It will be an inspiration to all new composers. It is as great as Sibelius' *Finlandia.*

"You say the man who wrote it was playing piano in a night club? Good God!"

7

IT WAS NEARLY A WEEK LATER that an enterprising reporter for the *Sun* came through with the most startling story in connection with the Horse and Buggy Night Club fire. Came through, that is, to the city desk; but the city desk refused to print it, as being wholly fantastic and unbelievable.

The report persisted that some unknown singer had taken the place of Annette Blair, when that vocalist had been overcome by smoke that tragic night; and that this new singer had stayed till the bitter end, and performed a major part in preventing panic.

Full credit had been given to Miss Blair, as well as to the late Dr. Stanislaus Joseph Halka, and to the waiters who had kept their senses and broken open the fire-escape door on Stanislaus Joseph's instruction, and to the electrician known as Bennie.

But who was this unknown singer?

Bennie was out of the hospital in two days, and working at his trade in the shop of a stage supply company. This *Sun* reporter dug him out. The electrician was the one person who must have looked steadily at this unknown female for at least ten minutes. Also he had been a friend of this piano player. Knew about his personal affairs.

The song had been—according to the news stories—an entirely

new one. Yet this singer had seemed to know it. She, also, must have been a friend of the pianist-composer, but from all reports he had no girl friends! Completely devoted to the memory of his late wife.

The reporter asked Bennie flatly: "Haven't you any idea who the girl was who sang out the song with this Tightpants Halka that night? They did not find any other body.

"If that girl is alive, she ought to be given credit. Furthermore, with all this publicity, she could pick up some real dough at almost any night spot. A thousand bucks a week, I should think.

"I know newspapers that would pay well for her exclusive story."

Bennie was splicing two cables. He was getting a bit weary of reporters. He was an electrician, not an information bureau! He felt very badly about Tightpants Halka's death. And he had other worries.

"Yes, I know who it was," said Bennie. "But, mister, I had been gettin' awful tired of all the questions from police officers, fire inspectors, building inspectors, insurance people, news guys like you. I didn't want to get my bosses into any more trouble. I'm promised my job back with them, as soon as they start again. And I didn't want no trouble for myself. I did not consider I'd done anything in particular."

Bennie wiped his forehead with his sleeve. "Look, fellow," he continued. "I ain't no hero. I stayed and kept my light on because my friend Tightpants stayed. I couldn't let my friend Tightpants down. If he hadn't stayed, I would have beat it the hell out of there fast! What did I care for all them big spenders who never paid any too much attention to the playing of a fine artist like Mr. Tightpants? Why, mister——"

But the reporter did not want a story about Bennie's evident contempt for night club spenders. The electrician had admitted that he knew who this girl was.

The *Sun* man must get that story before this stubborn workman changed his mind.

"The girl?" he repeated. "Who was the girl? You just said you knew her."

Bennie continued splicing his electric cable. He was now winding the joined wires with heavy, black adhesive tape. He looked at the inquiring reporter shrewdly.

"Mister, will you do me a great favor if I tell you what I know?"

"Why—why, yes. Anything within reason," replied the news man. He had not thought this honest-faced workman would ask for money, but you never could tell.

"Mister, do you like cats?" were the surprising next words of the electrician.

"I—I don't know," stammered the reporter. "Never gave the subject any thought." His face brightened. "My wife does. She's been wanting me to get us a cat."

What was this workman driving at?

"It's this way, mister," said Bennie, again wiping his forehead and with a most worried expression on his round face. "I'm one of the executors of Mr. Halka's will. That is a serious matter I guess. And in his will he left me a mother cat and four kittens that I've taken home. I used to feed 'em sometimes, when Mr. Tightpants had to be out of town. Down to Wilkes-Barre where he went two Sundays out of every month.

"I like cats. My missus likes cats. We already had one whose name is Little Fellow—black with long, beautiful white whiskers—but my wife wasn't pleased to get *five more*. And now, *two of the kittens are going to have kittens!* The missus says, 'enough is enough!' but being a duly appointed executor of Mr. Tightpants'—I mean Mr. Halka's will—and he leaving me five hundred dollars to feed the said cats——"

The reporter broke in. "I'll speak to my wife. I think I can promise you I'll take *one* of the kittens that's going to have kittens."

"And maybe your wife has a friend that would take another one?" said Bennie, pushing his advantage to the limit.

"I'll try," said the reporter. His reputation as a news gatherer hung by a thread. *Two* cats was apparently going to be this electrician's price.

"I know another reporter on our paper who likes animals," he added desperately. "He's our Communist specialist."

"O. K.," said Bennie. "I don't care about his politics, so long as he gives the cat a good home. Any cats I give away must have good homes. You can see how I am responsible under the law to Mr. Tightpants—I mean Mr. Halka."

"You were going to tell me who the girl was who sang," interjected the *Sun* reporter. He wanted to get back somehow to the subject of the girl who finished out the final song at the Horse and Buggy holocaust. To get off the subject of cats.

"Oh, that girl singer," said Bennie. "There was no big mystery.

Only it was queer like. The girl who finished out the song was Mr. Halka's wife."

"I didn't know he had a wife," said the reporter. "The papers all said he lived alone at the Madison Avenue flat."

"He did live there alone," said Bennie, "and he invited me there sometimes.

"Also I was there alone, to feed the cats. A saucer of milk with just a little cream, and *Puss in Boots* out of cans. If you saved twenty of the labels you got a cat collar free. There was a sitting room like, and a bedroom, and a kitchen. And quite a lot of pictures. The pictures was mostly of one woman. His wife it were——"

"You mean he was separated from her?" asked the reporter, "and yet she was in the Horse and Buggy that night, and came up and sang when the place was burning, and the regular singer passed out?"

"She came *down* and sang, I reckon," said Bennie. "Listen, Mister, that's the reason I didn't want to say nothing about this to no one. His wife was dead. Has been dead for two years——"

"His wife dead! How do you know she was dead?"

"He would talk about her sometimes. They were very much what you call in love. Then she got cancer and died at some hospital. I saw her grave in this Wilkes-Barre, Pennsylvania, where she came from. Went there one week end with Mr. Tightpants to light an entertainment—took along some special spot lights that had to be alternate current——"

"Did you know his wife?"

"Alternate current them lights were. You have to have a transformer, mister, to connect with alternate current. Makes extra expense and trouble. I remember one time in Detroit—"

The *Sun* man was showing signs of panic. Bennie reverted to answering the reporter's question.

"No. I didn't personally know her," he said. "His wife died before I met Mr. Tightpants. She were a chorus girl—most of them pictures were from shows she was in. She was a singer in the show he'd played in for Mr. Ziegfeld. Then in a Winter Garden show. That was when she took sick and died."

"How do you know it was his wife at the night club, if you never saw her alive?"

"All them pictures, mister. She was very beautiful. Beautiful eyes and mouth. Polish, he told me she was. Didn't look like most American chorus girls.

"And the thing you couldn't ever forget or mistake was her hair. It was done different from any other girl's hair I'd ever seen. Parted in the middle, pulled down tight like, and a heavy braid of it went slanting like, across the top of her head. Always reminded me of a small crown, like prima donnas sometimes wear at the Met, if the prima donnas had worn it slanting like. I worked there one season, Mister. And I guarantee you they didn't have no musician there any finer than this Tightpants Halka were——"

"Wait a minute. Are you telling me *his dead wife came to the night club and sang that night!*"

"I knew you wouldn't believe me, Mister," said Bennie. "That's why I didn't say nothing about it before to no one. Don't want folks to think I'm nuts or something. I have a family and have to hold jobs.

"I'm a good Baptist. Go to church every Sunday. We don't have saints and such things. But you see, this Mr. Tightpants was a Catholic. He believed his wife was a saint.

"I don't know what to believe, since I seen her in that night club, and her dead for two years!

"There was something else happened too," continued electrician Bennie. "I wasn't the only one who heard it. When his wife started to sing, *it sounded like an orchestra were playing along with her!* Like a lot of harps it were. Not just Mr. Halka at his piano.

"I've heard other Catholics talk about Heavenly Choirs. Had an assistant once that was Catholic. We Baptists don't have stuff like that. But I've got to thinking—maybe them Catholics know something we Baptists ain't yet found out——"

The reporter had taken up his hat.

"You'll not go back on the cat deals?" said Bennie anxiously.

"No. I won't go back on them. Give me your home address and I'll bring my wife tomorrow night to pick up our kitten. And I'll speak to my friend about another one. Thanks, Bennie. Thanks."

The news man started to leave, then paused. He said: "I don't think you're crazy, Bennie. You see, I'm a Catholic also. But I guess my news editor will think we've both gone daffy, when I try to turn in this story."

8

THERE IS ANOTHER GRAVE on the sun-bathed hillside cemetery, in the outskirts of a city named Wilkes-Barre, State of Pennsylvania, where sentimental folk go on Sunday afternoons to look at the two side-by-side headstones, on which bars of music have been carved.

On one tombstone are the first notes of *Als die alte Mutter,* composed by Anton Dvořák; and on the other the first notes of a now equally famous composition—the *Olga Lasenka Symphony* by Stanislaus Joseph Halka.

The symphony he wrote for his girl wife by whose side he is buried.

The symphony never played—like many another of its kind—until after its composer's death, and now a part of every great orchestra's repertory, and every music student's study. Because it expresses so dramatically, through the eyes of an immigrant, the unfettered spirit of America.

In the Spring and Summer the bars of music are sometimes difficult to find, for they are carved at the very base of the headstones, where these headstones disappear into the earth; and that earth is blue and green with wild violets.

Legend says these violets suddenly started to grow there, when the second grave was occupied; but the truth is that a very old priest named Father Joe first planted them.

And although it is a burial ground, the grassy slope is a favorite spot for young lovers, especially on clear Autumn evenings when the sunsets are most beautiful. It is said that these two, who are buried there beneath the two headstones, were the perfect lovers, and the words of a song written by the girl and composed by the boy are often quoted.

"Olga—whose eyes were violets—
Olga—whose tears were pearls—"

And there is another favorite phrase of that song which says—

"So long as Love remembers, I am always near—"

It has even been reported that the figures of this boy and girl have sometimes been seen, standing hand in hand, watching the sunset—

the boy recognized because of his quaint, tight-fitting trousers and coat—the girl because of the manner in which her hair is done.

But one must not approach them too closely. For always they are guarded by a third figure who stands some distance at one side.

It is the figure of a very tall and powerful man in full chain armor, like the armor you would see in the great Hall of the Armor Room at the Metropolitan Museum in New York. He leans with one hand—the left—on a great two-handed sword; leans with one hand only, because his right hand is severed at the wrist.

It all has to do with some vague legend going back to the days of the Holy Crusades, and both he and the appearance of the two lovers are without doubt simply the imaginings of romantic-minded souls.

The cemetery is a Catholic one, a Faith that still believes in miracles.

But in the City of New York, up at the buildings called the Cloisters, a branch of the Metropolitan Museum of Art, located on the heights of Fort Tyron Park overlooking the river Hudson, all miracles have ceased regarding a statue of the Queen of Heaven in the Early Gothic Room.

No longer does it seem to truly smile, nor does its breast become blood red except when the weather is very damp and the columns of the outside adjoining Cuxa Cloister are also red.

This reporter, of a hopelessly sentimental and romantic nature, believes that the spirit of that statue, having completed its circle of Earth Destiny, has joined that of a Ziegfeld (and later a Winter Garden) chorus girl, and moved on to the greater life, the greater love, the greater Destiny which we all (God willing) will someday be permitted to know.

But Guard Dennis O'Rourke, of this Early Gothic Room, on a certain date each year still places a red rose before that statue.

He is carrying out the wishes, and indeed the recorded will, of the late Dr. Stanislaus Joseph Halka, known in Broadway circles as Tightpants.

Known in perhaps more cultural circles as a young Doctor of Music, composer of a Symphony; a Song; some Exercises for young pianoforte students; the founder of a Fund with headquarters in Wilkes-Barre, Pennsylvania, to help these students, which Fund has influenced the starting of like Music Funds in many other cities.

He died at the early age of thirty-two. But on the Great Scroll, mere years are perhaps not the measure of the stature of a man.